DENIS O. SMITH's interests range from logic and the history of London to Victorian society and railways, all of which contribute to giving his stories a true flavour of the period. He lives in the heart of Norfolk, England, from where he makes occasional trips to London to explore some of the capital's more obscure corners.

Other titles

The Mammoth Book of New Sherlock Holmes Adventures
The Mammoth Book of the Lost Chronicles of Sherlock Holmes
The Mammoth Book of the Adventures of Moriarty
The Mammoth Book of Historical Crime Fiction
A Brief History of Sherlock Holmes
The Mammoth Book of Sherlock Holmes Abroad
The Ultimate Jack the Ripper Sourcebook
How To Write Crime Fiction

The Lost Chronicles of Sherlock Holmes Volume 2

Denis O. Smith

ROBINSON

ROBINSON

First published in Great Britain in 2016 by Robinson

A CIP catalogue record for this book
is available from the British Library.

ISBN: 978-1-47213-625-1 (paperback)
ISBN: 978-1-47213-626-8 (ebook)

Typeset in Whitman by Hewer Text UK Ltd, Edinburgh
Printed and bound in Great Britain by CPI Group (UK) Ltd, Croydon CR0 4YY

Papers used by Robinson are from well-managed forests and other responsible sources

MIX
Paper from
responsible sources
FSC® C104740

Robinson
is an imprint of
Little, Brown Book Group
Carmelite House
50 Victoria Embankment
London EC4Y 0DZ

An Hachette UK Company
www.hachette.co.uk

www.littlebrown.co.uk

Contents

The Adventure of the Black Owl

Mr Sherlock Holmes was undoubtedly an enthusiast, if a somewhat eccentric one. For some men, the discovery of a rare stamp or a broken fragment of ancient pottery is the occasion for joy approaching almost to ecstasy. For others, such joy comes from the chance discovery of an old, forgotten book, or a rare and dusty bottle of wine. For my friend, Sherlock Holmes, the world's first consulting detective and a man of the most singular tastes, those things which aroused the greatest enthusiasm in his breast were crime and mystery. It should not be supposed, however, that his interest in such matters was at all sordid or sensationalist. Indeed, those crimes which tend to fill the front pages of the more lurid newspapers were generally among the least interesting to him. Whether the crime had been marked by violence, or had involved any celebrated public figures, these facts were perfectly immaterial to Holmes's interest. For what he valued most highly was the mystery with which crimes are so often enveloped, and the more impenetrable the mystery, the more my friend's interest and enthusiasm were aroused.

Fortunately for Holmes's taste in these matters, he had, at the time of which I am writing, achieved a certain celebrity in the solution of mysteries, criminal and otherwise, and it was thus rarely necessary for him to actively seek out the conundrums which would give his brain the exercise it craved, for any mystery worthy of the name would almost inevitably be brought to his attention sooner or later. Thus it was in the case of the Holly Grove Mystery, a crime which, as readers may recall, shocked the whole of London. One or two of the daily papers had carried a brief report of the matter on the morning following the murder, and a day later they were all full of it, but Holmes, who had been closely engaged in other work, had passed no comment. When I tried to interest him in the matter, he rebuffed my efforts, and it was clear that he did not regard it as likely to offer any opportunity for the exercise of those analytical powers for which he was renowned. His opinion was to change, however, following a visit that evening from our old friend, Inspector Gregson of Scotland Yard.

Our supper concluded, the remnants had been cleared away and we had settled to our evening reading, mine a treatise on diseases of the nervous system, Holmes's a report he had received from Dublin on a case which interested him, when there came a sharp tug at the front-door bell. A moment later, Inspector Gregson was shown into the room.

'Ah! Gregson!' said Holmes in an affable tone, as he brought another chair up to the fireside for the policeman. 'What brings you here this evening, I wonder? Surely not more difficulty with the Kensington forgery case?'

'No, that was straightforward enough, after you put me on the right track, Mr Holmes. Yes, I will have a whisky and soda, Dr Watson – that is very civil of you. My problem now,' he continued as I passed him the glass, 'concerns the Highgate murder. No doubt you have read something of it in the paper, Mr Holmes?'

'Dr Watson read me a brief account earlier. A shocking business, no doubt, but it did not strike me as possessing any great features of interest.'

'So I thought, too, when I began my inquiries,' responded the policeman. 'However,' he continued, taking a sip of his drink, 'it has taken one or two turns in the complicated direction, if you know what I mean.'

'Oh?' said Holmes with interest. 'Perhaps you could describe it to us.'

'With pleasure. I am very keen to know what you make of it.'

'Very well, then,' said Holmes, leaning back in his chair and closing his eyes. 'You have my full attention. Begin at the beginning, as if we know nothing of the matter, and omit no detail known to you, however trivial it may seem.'

'In the first place,' said Gregson after a moment, 'you ought to know something of the dead man's household. It is soon described, for it is not a large one. Professor Humphrey Arbuthnot and his wife, who did not have any children, have lived at the house in Holly Grove, Highgate, for more than twenty-five years and are both fairly advanced in age now. Professor Arbuthnot used to be the most famous medical psychologist in London, but retired from practice about ten years ago, since which time he and his wife have lived a quiet, secluded sort of life. Indeed, the professor, who has been in poor health for some time, had scarcely left the house in the past ten years. The wants of this elderly couple have been few, and their domestic staff has accordingly never amounted to more than a cook and two maids at the most. At the moment, since one of the maids left their employment at the end of July, it is not even that, but amounts to just two, a cook, Mary Cartwick, who has been with them for eight years, and, as general housemaid, a young girl by the name of Ruby Parrish, who came to them about six months ago.

'The house itself is a substantial, double-fronted one. A short, straight path, of perhaps twenty yards, connects the garden gate to the front door. On the left of the door is the dining-room, and on the right a drawing-room. The garden, which contains some very big trees, and is thus rather shady, continues round the right-hand side of the house. There, towards the back of the house, there is a pair of French windows to the professor's study. It was in this room that the crime took place, the evening before last.'

'Were the French windows open at the time?' queried Holmes, without opening his eyes.

'Yes, they were, but there was nothing unusual about that. It seems it was the professor's habit to have the windows open whenever he was working in the study, even in the evening. He was a man who liked fresh air, so I am told, and, being round the side of the house, it was, of course, perfectly private. On the day in question, he had, apart from a short break for lunch, been working in the study all day, and had not left the house.'

'I see. Pray, continue!'

'The Arbuthnots did very little entertaining and had not had anyone to dinner for a year or more, but on the evening in question they were expecting two dinner guests. The first of these was an old colleague of Professor Arbuthnot's, Dr Ludwig Zyss. He now makes his home in Vienna, but is at present visiting London, staying at the Belvedere Hotel on Southampton Row. The second was Professor Arbuthnot's sister, Lady Boothby, whose late husband, as you may recall, was under-secretary at the foreign office some years ago. Apparently, Lady Boothby rarely goes out these days and it was only because Dr Zyss was to be there that she had agreed to attend the dinner. The history of these two men, Arbuthnot and Zyss, is an interesting one. Some years ago, they had a joint medical practice in Harley Street, which was renowned throughout Europe, so I am told, but they fell out quite badly about a dozen years ago and subsequently went their separate ways, Dr Zyss returning to his native Austria. This did not, however, end the dispute or ill-feeling between them, for although the two men never met again, nor communicated with each other in any way, they pursued their quarrel for several years in the pages of various learned journals, and neither, so I am informed, ever missed an opportunity to vilify the other. Thus the fact that Dr Zyss had an appointment to call upon Professor Arbuthnot on Wednesday evening is somewhat surprising. One can only presume it was an attempt to bury their differences, let bygones be bygones, and so on. That seems to be the general belief. My information is that Dr Zyss, who is about the same age as Professor Arbuthnot, is also not in the best of health, and may not be long for this world, so it may be that he wished to effect a reconciliation with his old colleague before it was too late for such things.'

'You speak of the information you have concerning Dr Zyss,' interrupted Holmes. 'Have you not interviewed the man himself?'

Inspector Gregson shook his head. 'I shall come to that problem in a moment,' said he.

'Very well. Pray proceed!'

'Dr Zyss was expected to arrive at about quarter to seven. However, a message was received at about half past six, informing them that Dr Zyss would not be able to fulfil the appointment after all. Learning this, Mrs Arbuthnot, who had been sitting reading in the drawing-room for some time, sent a note to her husband's sister telling her that the dinner party was cancelled, and then went to the study to inform her husband. To her horror, she found him lying dead on the study floor, blood everywhere, and a dagger protruding from his breast.'

'What a dreadful business!' I cried.

'It is, Dr Watson; and such a frail and defenceless old man, too!'

'Who brought the note concerning Dr Zyss?' queried Holmes.

'A messenger of some kind. Mrs Arbuthnot saw him walking up the path holding the note in his hand as she was closing the drawing-room curtains, so she went to the front door to see what he wanted, whereupon he handed her the message. He also took her message to Lady Boothby.'

'Was any reason given for Dr Zyss's non-attendance?'

'No. The note was very brief, she said, and simply stated that he couldn't come. Mrs Arbuthnot says she assumed that he must be ill; but of course she couldn't know one way or the other. Anyway, as I say, she went to inform her husband, found him dead, and sent the maid to find the local constable, who is usually somewhere in the vicinity at that time in the evening. It was then about quarter to seven. The maid arrived back with the constable about ten minutes later, and having made a preliminary examination of the scene of the crime, and established that Professor Arbuthnot was definitely dead and that nothing could be done for him, he locked up the room and went to inform the local station of what had happened. They at once communicated with Scotland Yard, and the information was passed to me. I set off as soon as I could, and reached Holly Grove at about half past eight.

'My first impression when I opened the study door was that there had been a considerable struggle in there. The professor was lying on his back on a rug in the middle of the room. He had been stabbed through the heart with a sharp paper-knife, and had bled freely. All about him was chaos and disorder. A chair and a small table had been knocked over. Books and papers which appeared to have been knocked off the desk were scattered about on the floor. It was clear that, advanced in years though he was, Professor Arbuthnot had not given up his life without a fight.'

'Such a struggle can hardly have been noiseless,' observed Holmes, 'and yet it would appear to have passed unheard; for no one came to see what was happening, and Mrs Arbuthnot only discovered that her husband was dead when she took him the note concerning Dr Zyss.'

'Yes, that is surprising,' agreed Gregson; 'but the house is a very solidly built one, with thick walls, and the cook and the maid were in the kitchen with the door closed, preparing the meal, and no doubt making noise of their own. It is perhaps more surprising that the professor's wife did not hear anything, but she says she did not. Anyway, after the body had been removed, I examined the whole room carefully, looking for any clue as to what had occurred there. In the course of this examination, I picked up a few pencils and suchlike that had obviously been knocked off the desk, and it was while I was doing this that I encountered something surprising.'

Gregson put his hand in his jacket pocket and produced a small object which he held out for us to see. It was a small black figure of an owl sitting on a bough, about three inches tall. Holmes took it and examined it for a moment, then passed it to me, and I was at once struck by the surprising weight of the little figure.

'Why,' I said, 'it feels as heavy as cast iron!'

'Lacquered brass, I think,' said Holmes. 'It is evidently a paper-weight. What is it you find so surprising about it, Gregson?'

'Mrs Arbuthnot happened to pass the open doorway of the room just as I was picking it up from the floor,' responded the policeman, 'and she asked me what it was.

'"Does it not belong to your husband?" I returned in surprise. "I assumed it had been knocked off the desk."

'She shook her head. "I have never seen it before in my life," said she.

'I later showed it to the maid and the cook, and both stated that they had never seen it before.'

'That is strange,' said Holmes. 'Why should anyone bring a paper-weight to the house? I take it that it wasn't used as a weapon – to strike the professor on the head for instance?'

'No,' said Gregson. 'Apart from the savage wound in the chest, there were no other marks of violence on the body. I had examined his head very carefully, to see if he had been struck there, but he hadn't.'

'Did you find anything else of interest in the professor's study?' asked Holmes, but the policeman shook his head. 'Very well. Pray proceed with your account. When was the last time Mrs Arbuthnot saw her husband alive?'

'About five o'clock. She went into the study to speak to him on some trivial matter, and was there about five or ten minutes. While she was there, the maid brought him in a cup of tea, and informed Mrs Arbuthnot that she had placed a cup for her in the drawing-room. A few minutes later Mrs Arbuthnot left the study for the drawing-room, and did not see her husband again. She says that when he was at work on something, he had an intense dislike of being disturbed. So we can say for certain that the assault took place between about ten past five and half past six, when the messenger from Dr Zyss arrived.'

'Had anyone else called at the house during that time?' queried Holmes.

Gregson hesitated. 'Just one person – and that a rum one, if the maid is to be believed.'

'Pray be precise,' said Holmes.

'Well, the maid says that at about a quarter past six, there was a ring at the front-door bell. She was in the kitchen at the time, helping the cook, but she quickly wiped her hands and hurried to the front door. When she opened it, she says, she saw to her surprise that there was no one waiting on the doorstep; but at the other end of the path, near the gate, stood a woman dressed all in black, who seemed to be just staring at the house. The maid called to her "Yes, madam? Can I help you?" or something of the sort, but the woman did not reply. For a moment, the girl says, the woman just stared with a fixed gaze at the house, then she slowly raised her arm and pointed at it. After a few moments, she turned away and, without a sound, passed through the gate and out into Holly Grove. The maid was frightened, so she shut the door quickly, and ran back to the kitchen to tell the cook what she had seen.'

'Did the maid recognise the woman?'

The policeman shook his head. 'She was wearing a heavy black veil, which completely concealed her face. The girl described her as looking, she said, "like a great black bird standing on the path", and when she raised her hand and pointed with her finger at the house, the girl said it was "like the claw of a bird".'

'So, leaving aside the poetic description, she has no idea who it was?'

'When I put the point to her later in the evening, in the course of my inquiries, she surprised me by saying that she thought she did know.'

'Oh?'

'"Yes, sir," said she, nodding her head vigorously, "I didn't know then, but I do now. That woman was Death, come to call the master away."'

'I see,' said Holmes in a dry tone. 'That is an example of what I classify as a non-helpful hypothesis. Did anyone else see this apparition?'

'No,' replied Gregson. 'So, of course, we have only the girl's word for it. But both the cook and Mrs Arbuthnot had heard the door-bell.'

'It seems odd that Mrs Arbuthnot saw the man with the note, but not this woman in black,' observed Holmes.

'It might have been odd, had she been in the drawing-room at the time; but in fact she wasn't. After finishing her tea, at about half past five, she had gone upstairs to her bedroom, which is at the back of the house, to change for the evening, and was up there for about forty-five minutes. She says that she heard the door-bell, and supposed that it was Dr Zyss arriving. Of course, when she came downstairs, she saw that there was no one there. She was standing at the drawing-room window, in the act of drawing the curtains – for the light had almost gone, and night was setting in – when the messenger opened the gate and walked up the path, which is why she happened to see him before he rang at the bell.'

'I see,' said Holmes. 'What sort of a lock is on the front door? Is it possible to open it without a key?'

Gregson shook his head. 'It is a modern sprung lock, which engages every time the door is closed. No one could get in that way without a key.'

'So we must assume as a working hypothesis that whoever killed Professor Arbuthnot entered his study by the French windows.'

'So I concluded, Mr Holmes. Unless, of course, he was murdered by his wife, or by one of the two domestic servants. But that is practically unthinkable. Besides, all three of them are small women, and none of them looks powerful enough to have engaged in the struggle which there must have been in the study to disarrange it so much.'

Holmes nodded. 'Very well,' said he. 'Pray proceed with your account!'

'I interviewed Mrs Arbuthnot, and elicited all the facts I have mentioned, as to her whereabouts and those of her husband at the time of the tragedy, and also confirmed with her that nothing appeared to have been stolen. Then, having concluded, as you say, that the murderer must have gained access to the house by way of the French windows in the study, I made a preliminary examination of the ground outside. The night was a dark one, though, and I couldn't really see anything, so I instructed the constable to make sure that the ground remained undisturbed until I had had a chance to examine it properly. I then left the house in the care of the constable, and made my way into town, to the Belvedere Hotel, with the intention of interviewing Dr Zyss. My view, you see, was that it seemed something of an odd coincidence that he should have abruptly cancelled his visit to the Arbuthnots' house on the very day that the professor was murdered. Of course, I realised that there might be nothing in it, but it was a little odd, anyway, so I intended to ask Dr Zyss why exactly he had decided to cancel his visit.

'It was half past ten by the time I reached the hotel, so I was not very surprised to be informed that Dr Zyss had already retired for the night. The night porter who was on duty told me that he had seen Dr Zyss earlier in the evening, and that he hadn't looked at all well. He had apparently left the hotel at some time in the afternoon – the porter could not say when, exactly, as he had not been on duty then – and had returned at about seven in the evening, in the company of a lady who was dressed all in black, and who wore a heavy black veil over her face. On entering the hotel, Dr Zyss immediately sat down heavily on a chair by the door. He was breathing in a laboured manner, and appeared, said the porter, as if he could hardly stand without assistance. His companion approached the porter's desk and asked for the doctor's room-key, saying that the gentleman felt a little ill, and would not be requiring dinner that evening. The porter asked if she wished a medical man to be called, but she declined the offer, saying that Dr Zyss had simply over-taxed himself during the day, and would probably feel adequately restored after a good night's rest. The lady then assisted Dr Zyss to his room and, about twenty minutes later, returned to the porter's desk with the information that Dr Zyss was very tired and did not wish to be disturbed, but that if he had not risen by nine o'clock the following morning, he would appreciate a call then and a cup of tea. After the lady had passed on this message, the porter informed me, she did not leave immediately, but sat for a while near the door, looking out through the glass panel at the street outside, and glancing at the clock from time to time, as if waiting for someone. She was there seven or eight minutes, he says, but then he was called away from his desk for a couple of minutes and when he returned she had gone.

'I thanked him for this information, wrote a note for Dr Zyss, to say that I should call in the morning, and left it at that. I couldn't see that there was much else I could do. The following morning, I called round at the hotel at half past nine, but when I enquired for Dr Zyss the porter on duty gave me an odd look and suggested I speak to the manager. I explained my purpose in being there to that gentleman, at which he shook his head.

'"I'm afraid it will not be possible for you to speak to Dr Zyss," said he.

'"Why?" said I. "Has something happened to him?" In truth I feared, from what I had heard of his condition, that he had died in the night.

'"I can tell you nothing about him," said the manager, "for he has vanished into thin air." He explained to me that as Dr Zyss had not come down for breakfast, a cup of tea had been taken to his room as requested, but the chambermaid who took it had found the room empty and its occupant gone. It appeared, said the manager, that Dr Zyss had risen much earlier than usual and left the hotel before breakfast.

'"Did no one see him go?" I asked.

'The manager shook his head. "We were very busy for a while this morning," he said, "dealing with a large party who had arrived in London on the overnight train from Edinburgh. Dr Zyss did not hand in his room-key at the desk, but simply left it in his room, and nor did he pick up the note you had left him, so I suppose he just stepped out without speaking to anybody."

'I at once ascended to Dr Zyss's room. There were numerous heaps of documents and books on a side table, but, apart from that, and the bed, the covers of which had been thrown back, the room was in fairly good order. I decided to get as much information as I could from the hotel staff, and hoped that while I was doing so Dr Zyss would return. What I learnt was that Dr Zyss had been staying at the Belvedere Hotel for six days, during which time he had generally worked in his room in the mornings, and then gone out shortly after lunch and returned about tea-time – that is to say, between about four o'clock and five o'clock. The porter on duty at the desk was my chief source of information. He had seen Dr Zyss go out every afternoon and, except for the previous day, had never known him not to return by five at the latest. He was able to give me a description of the missing man, which I have since circulated to all the police stations in London, so I am very hopeful of finding him somewhere. He is apparently quite a thin man, of medium height, with a trimmed grey beard and thick spectacles. The porter informed me that his eyesight is very poor, as is his hearing. His customary outdoor garb is a grey woollen overcoat, and soft felt hat, also in grey. This description tallies with that given to me by the night porter the previous evening, and as these garments are not in his room, that is certainly what he was wearing when he left the hotel in the morning.

'The porter had one other interesting thing to tell me and it is this: as well as the previous day being the only one on which Dr Zyss had not returned by the time the day porter went off duty at six o'clock, it was also the only day on which he had received a visitor at the hotel. This struck me as another interesting coincidence and I questioned the porter on the matter.

'"About eleven o'clock in the morning," he said, "a lady entered the hotel and asked me to inform Dr Zyss that Mrs Routledge had arrived. I did so, and a few moments later he descended from his room. After a brief exchange by the desk, he ordered a tray of coffee to be brought to the morning-room, to which he escorted the lady. There they sat in conversation for about an hour and a half. The lady then departed, and Dr Zyss returned to his room. He subsequently took lunch at the hotel as usual, but then returned once more to his room, worked there for a further couple of hours, and did not go out until nearly four o'clock, which was much later than his usual habit. That was the last time I saw him."

'I asked the porter if he had ever seen this Mrs Routledge at any other time, but he said not. He described her to me as a lady of medium height and late middle age. He said she was well dressed in black, with a veil on her hat, but she lifted her veil as she spoke to Dr Zyss by the porter's desk, and he said he was confident he would recognise her again.

"'Did you overhear any of their conversation?" I asked him.

"'No, sir,' said he.

'I then had another look in Dr Zyss's room, to see if I could find a letter from Mrs Routledge. I thought it likely, for it seemed from what the porter had told me that her arrival at the hotel was not unexpected. After ten minutes I found what I was looking for. I have the letter here,' he continued, pulling a bundle of papers from his pocket. He sifted through the bundle for a moment, then selected one and passed it to Holmes, who studied it for a few moments, then handed it on to me.

It was a plain white sheet. The address at the top was 14 Trenchard Villas, Gospel Oak, the date 19 September, and the message ran as follows:

> DEAR DR ZYSS,
>
> News of your visit to England has reached me in the past twenty-four hours, and I should wish to take the opportunity to see you to discuss a matter of mutual interest. Please reply to the above address, stating a day and time which would be convenient to you.
>
> YOURS SINCERELY, J. T. ROUTLEDGE

'As she wrote the letter on Saturday,' said Gregson, 'Dr Zyss no doubt received it on Monday and sent a reply which Mrs Routledge received on Tuesday, naming Wednesday morning as a suitable time for their interview. Of course I had no evidence that this lady had anything to do with Dr Zyss's mysterious disappearance, far less with the tragic events at Highgate; but in the absence of any real clues, I thought I had better interview her and see what she had to say for herself. I therefore took myself up to Gospel Oak yesterday morning. Unfortunately, the lady was not at home, and the maid who answered the door said that her mistress had gone to visit friends in St Albans and would not be returning until Saturday. Of course, I could have taken the train to St

Albans to see her, but I had other things to do, so I decided to postpone the interview until tomorrow.

'I therefore returned to the Arbuthnots' house in Holly Grove, where I examined the lawn very carefully, especially that part of it which extends round the side of the house to the French windows of the study. The earth is somewhat damp there, and overhung with trees, so there were several well-preserved footprints. From these it was apparent that my initial surmise that the murderer had entered the study by the French windows was correct. There were very clear footprints crossing the lawn from the garden gate to the French windows, both coming and going. To make sure that these were indeed the footprints of the murderer, and not those of some innocent party who had called earlier, I asked Mrs Arbuthnot if they had had any visitors in the past couple of days. There had been only one, she informed me, that being the professor's nephew, Lady Boothby's son, Terence Chalfont, who had called early in the afternoon the previous day.

"'Did Mr Chalfont walk round the garden to the professor's study?" I asked, but she shook her head, and said that he had rung the front-door bell and been admitted in the usual way. I asked if Mr Chalfont was a frequent visitor, but again she shook her head.

"'No," said she. "He and my husband did not get on very well, and had a severe falling out a couple of months ago, since which time we have hardly seen him here at all. I was the one he had come to see. He did suggest that he went in to speak to my husband, who was working in the study at the time, but I dissuaded him from that. As I mentioned to you, my husband disliked being disturbed when he was working."

"'Mr Chalfont's visit was a purely social call, I take it."

'Mrs Arbuthnot hesitated. "Of a sort," she said at last. I asked her what she meant. "Mr Chalfont is a playwright," she explained after a moment, "and moves in the world of actors and other such shallow and insubstantial people. He writes plays which are said to be highly artistic, and are put on occasionally at some of the smaller theatres.

They are generally praised highly by the critics – most of whom seem to be personal friends of his – but are utterly unremunerative. His visit yesterday was partly to ask if we would care to contribute to the cost of staging his latest play, but I told him we certainly would not."

'The lady seemed unusually vehement on the matter, and I asked her why.

'"Really," said she in a tone of exasperation. "This is all perfectly irrelevant! If you must know, Inspector, Terence's latest play, in so far as I understand what he has told me, is to be concerned with the subject of mental illness and the treatment of it."

'"Your late husband's profession, in fact."

'"Precisely. Not at all a suitable subject for a theatrical presentation, especially in the hands of a self-indulgent young man like Terence Chalfont."

'"Why so?"

'"Because he is the sort of young man who has always had his own way. Indulged appallingly by his mother – my late husband's sister – especially since his father died, he now presumes to argue and quarrel about subjects of which he knows nothing at all."

'"It was on this subject that he fell out with your husband?"

'"Yes it was," said she with great emphasis. "He felt qualified to argue from a position of complete ignorance with the man acknowledged as the greatest psychologist in Europe. It was this that infuriated my husband so." She paused. "But if you are thinking that Terence Chalfont might have had anything to do with my husband's death, you are utterly mistaken. He called here at about half past two, stayed barely half an hour, then left, and I did not see him again. He may be a worthless and impertinent young fool, who likes the sound of his own voice too much, but he is certainly not violent. He is too feckless and feeble to have any violence in him!"

'"Of course," I said; but I took down Mr Chalfont's address nonetheless, and made a mental note to go and see him. For it seemed to me possible that, despite Mrs Arbuthnot's belief to the contrary, he might have returned to Holly Grove later in the afternoon. Knowing that he was not going to get any money from Mrs Arbuthnot, he might have gone directly round the side of the house to catch the professor in his study, and ended up having a violent row with him. Up until that point, I had presumed that the murder was the work of a chance intruder, but the information concerning Mr Chalfont and his fraught relations with his uncle gave me another line of inquiry.

'Chalfont lives in Hampstead, where he occupies a set of rooms over a baker's shop in Heath Street. I went there directly from Highgate, but found no one at home. At least, no one answered my knock at the door, although I thought I heard some slight sounds from inside the apartment. There was nothing more I could do there, so I took myself down the road to Belsize Park, where Professor Arbuthnot's sister, Lady Boothby, has a house. The poor old lady was in a state of the utmost shock and mourning, as you can imagine, and I got no useful information from her. She was aware, of course, that Dr Zyss was visiting London for the first time in ten years, but said she had not seen or heard from him. Nor could she shed any light on her son's whereabouts, as she had not seen him in the past fortnight.

'I therefore returned to Scotland Yard, to see if we had had any news of Dr Zyss, but I was disappointed in that enquiry, too. We had had several reports concerning possible sightings of him, from Stepney, Walworth, Finchley, Ealing and another half dozen places, but although I spent several hours following them up, they all turned out to be false leads. This brings me to today.

'I had left a note at Chalfont's apartment to say when I should call again, and duly went up there this morning and found him waiting for me. He is about thirty years of age, with a manner which struck me as unduly defensive and argumentative. I questioned him about his recent visit to Holly Grove and he confirmed the account that Mrs Arbuthnot had given me.

'"You did not see Professor Arbuthnot on Wednesday?" I asked.

"'No," said he, "as I'm sure you're already aware."

"'You did not, for instance, walk round the side of the house after you left, to the French windows of the study?"

"'No."

"'Or return to the house later for any reason?"

"'Certainly not."

"'I understand," I said, "that your latest play is to be about the work of a medical psychologist, which one would imagine would have been of interest to your uncle and his wife, but I gather they were somewhat unenthusiastic. Why was that?"

"'How would I know?" said he brusquely.

"'Well, you are the one writing the play, you are the one who has discussed it with them."

"'Oh, all right," said he at last, in a tone of annoyance. "They didn't like the sound of my play, Inspector, because they realised that it would be more than simply a paean of praise to the wonderful, highly esteemed Professor Arbuthnot!" These last words were spoken in a tone of great sarcasm.

"'Am I to take it, then, that it is critical of him or his work?"

"'It just aims to tell the truth, that's all. Look, Inspector, I fail to see the relevance of any of this, and I don't see any point in discussing it further."

"'You didn't like your uncle?" I ventured.

"'Not much, no."

'I didn't get any more of interest from Mr Chalfont, but just as I was leaving, I heard a slight sound from an adjoining room. "Oh, that's just Martin," Chalfont said by way of explanation, "an actor friend of mine. I'm putting him up for a few days. He never rises before lunchtime."

'I returned to Scotland Yard then. There had still been no word of Dr Zyss, so I sent a message to our colleagues in St Albans, asking them to go to the address at which Mrs Routledge was staying and inform her that I should be calling at her house in Gospel Oak on Saturday. I also asked them to make inquiries about Dr Zyss, in case he was staying in St Albans with her, or had been seen anywhere in the vicinity. They later reported that there was no trace of him there. I seemed to have reached a dead end, and could not think what to do next. Then, about five o'clock, a message reached me from Hampstead which sounded more promising, so I took myself back up there. But if it had already been a puzzling case, with no obvious explanation, this latest information took it almost into the realm of absurdity. It is this that has brought me to see you, Mr Holmes, to see if you can see any chink of light in the business where I cannot.'

'You intrigue me,' said Holmes. 'Pray, what is this latest information?'

'An elderly woman by the name of Tuttle had been into Hampstead police station earlier and made a statement. A friend of hers, she said, a Miss Cracknell, who was, she said, too shy to come forward herself, had taken tea with her that afternoon. In the course of their conversation, Miss Cracknell had said, "You will never guess who I saw crossing the high street this morning, Minnie! It was one of those old professors! I thought at first it was Professor Arbuthnot, then I realised it was the other one – Dr Zyss – the one with the thick glasses. I haven't seen either of them for years – I didn't even know if they were still about – and, in any case, I thought Dr Zyss had moved to Austria or Germany or somewhere like that. Anyway, he didn't see me, but just seemed to sort of float across the road like a spirit. He had a far-away look on his face, and was staring straight ahead. I called to him, but he didn't hear me. Then he turned into Church Row and walked on towards the church. Please don't think me fanciful, Minnie, but there seemed something ethereal, unworldly almost, about him. I couldn't help but think that he wasn't long for this world. I was going that way myself, so I followed him along the street. Without pausing, he went into the church, so, on the spur of the moment, I did, too. But I got a terrible shock, I can tell you. Inside the church, there wasn't a living soul, not one! Dr Zyss had just vanished into thin air!"

'As Miss Cracknell was recounting her experience, Miss Tuttle was, she says, in a state of shock. "Susannah, have you not heard?" she said at length. "Professor Arbuthnot was murdered on Wednesday night and Dr Zyss has disappeared!"

'So that was that,' said Gregson. 'Miss Tuttle and her friend decided that we should be informed of this sighting, but apart from confirming that Dr Zyss is still in the area, it doesn't really help us very much. He may have reappeared, but only to vanish once more!'

'Do you know what connection there was between these two elderly ladies and the two psychologists?' Holmes asked after a moment.

'Apparently,' replied Gregson, 'both Professor Arbuthnot and Dr Zyss used to give public lectures on their theories at the Hampstead Educational Institute, which were well attended. Some of those who attended became almost like disciples, I understand, and used to help them with practical work, keeping records and so on. Miss Tuttle and Miss Cracknell had been two such disciples, so I am given to understand.'

Holmes nodded. 'So,' said he after a moment, as Inspector Gregson leaned back in his chair and sipped his whisky, 'to sum the matter up: Professor Arbuthnot, a prominent, retired psychologist, has been murdered in his own home, apparently by an intruder, although no such intruder was seen or heard by anyone. Nothing appears to have been stolen, but an unusual little black owl has appeared in the murdered man's study. An old colleague of Arbuthnot's, Dr Zyss, was due to call that evening, but sent a note to say that, after all, he could not. This gentleman has subsequently disappeared from his hotel and his whereabouts are unknown. A woman who visited him at his hotel on the morning of the same day has also disappeared – temporarily, you hope. The maid at the murdered man's house reports that a veiled woman rang the front-door bell on Wednesday evening, but did not respond when addressed, instead turning and walking away, and today a woman reports seeing Dr Zyss in the middle of Hampstead High Street, but he then proceeded to vanish for a second time, even more mysteriously than the first time.'

'That just about covers the matter,' said Gregson with a rueful chuckle.

'And you would like me to look into it for you?'

'Well, I would very much value your opinion, Mr Holmes – if one can form an opinion about such a confusing business!'

'Very well,' said Holmes after a moment. 'We can do nothing this evening, so what I propose is this: you come round here at nine tomorrow morning and we shall be ready to set forth.'

———

In the morning, however, it happened that Inspector Gregson was detained elsewhere and could not join us as arranged. Shortly before nine we received a message from him containing a signed authority for us to view the body of the murdered man, which was at the police station on Kentish Town Road, and to make any enquiries we saw fit, and also a note of the time he intended to interview Mrs Routledge at her house in Gospel Oak, when he hoped, he said, that we would be able to meet up and share our conclusions. It was a chilly morning and I warmed myself before the fire as I glanced over the morning papers.

'Any fresh news of the matter?' asked Holmes as he stood up from his desk, where he had been studying a map.

I shook my head. 'It remains as puzzling as ever. How do you intend to proceed?' I asked as my friend put on his hat and coat.

'I have been considering the matter from a geographical point of view, Watson,' he replied. He took an envelope from his desk and held it up. 'If we say that this envelope represents roughly the extent of Hampstead Heath, Parliament Hill and so on, then here, at the bottom right-hand corner, is the police station in Kentish Town Road where the professor's body lies; here at the top right-hand corner is Highgate itself, scene of Wednesday's tragedy. The top of the envelope represents the long road across the north side of the Heath, from Highgate to Hampstead, which lies here, at the top left-hand corner. In Hampstead is the home of the Arbuthnots' nephew, Mr Terence Chalfont, who visited their house on Wednesday afternoon. It is also the place where Miss Cracknell saw Dr Zyss, as he floated in a spiritual manner across the street, before disappearing once more. Down here,' he continued, running his finger down the side of the envelope to the bottom left-hand corner, 'is Belsize Park, the home of Lady Boothby, sister of Professor Arbuthnot, and here, in the middle of the bottom edge, is Gospel Oak, home of the mysterious Mrs Routledge. That is, approximately, the route I propose to take. Are you free for a few hours?'

'Certainly. I am at your disposal.'

'Excellent! I have booked a four-wheeler for the day, so we shall not be short of transport. Ah! Here it is now!' he continued, as there came a peal at the bell.

In a minute we were in the cab and rattling through the busy streets of north London. Twenty minutes later, we alighted at the police station, where the duty sergeant conducted us to a back room in which the professor's body was lying. In the left breast was a sharply edged puncture wound, and it was evident from a brief examination that the weapon had penetrated the ribs and entered the heart. For a few moments Holmes examined the body carefully, then he turned his attention to the bundle of clothes on a side table nearby, holding up the jacket and waistcoat of a greenish-brown tweed suit, and examining them closely with the aid of his magnifying lens. Something on the jacket seemed to particularly arrest his attention. In answer to my query he indicated a slit in the lining.

'Made by the knife that killed him, no doubt,' I remarked, but Holmes shook his head.

'No,' said he. 'This little cut was made separately, which is what makes it so interesting.' He replaced the clothes and took up a pair of brown shoes which lay beside them.

'May I borrow these?' he asked the sergeant. 'I wish to compare them with the footprints in the garden of the professor's house.'

'By all means,' replied the other. 'We have no immediate use for them. If you will just sign for them, you may keep them for forty-eight hours.'

We returned to our cab and began the long ascent up the steep hill to Highgate village, perched on top of the ridge overlooking north London. Holmes had said nothing as we left the police station, but there was a thoughtful look upon his features, as if he were turning the matter over in his mind. Although I attempted to discuss the case further, however, my friend would not be drawn. Presently, at the summit of the hill, we alighted in a short, pleasant tree-lined road, which a sign identified as Holly Grove. A police constable stood on duty beside a green-painted wooden gate, but admitted us without demur on being shown Inspector Gregson's letter of authority. On either side of the gate were large trees, the branches of which met overhead, forming a shady arch. Within the garden a straight paved path led to the front door of the house, as Gregson had described. To the left of this lay a narrow strip of grass, a flower-bed and a tall hedge, and to the right, a larger expanse of lawn which passed out of view round the side of the house. Beyond this lawn was another tall, dense hedge.

Our ring at the bell was answered by a young maid, who showed us into a drawing-room. A moment later we were joined by the lady of the house. She was dressed in black, and her features were drawn and showed evidence of the tragedy which had so recently come upon the household. In answer to our questions, she described to us the events of Wednesday evening, much as we had already heard them from Gregson.

'You say you heard the door-bell ring while you were upstairs in your bedroom,' said Holmes. 'Did it surprise you, then, when you descended, to find that there was no one here?'

Mrs Arbuthnot hesitated a moment, as if struggling to remember.

'I suppose it did,' she said at last; 'but then I thought it was perhaps someone collecting for some charitable cause or other and I thought I would ask Ruby about it later.'

'And shortly after that you saw the man approaching the door with a note in his hand?'

'Yes. Just as I was drawing the curtains.'

'Can you describe him?'

'Not really. I mean, he was rather nondescript. About thirty years of age, I suppose, with a black moustache. I really can't remember anything else about him.'

'And then, when you took the note to show your husband in the study, you found him dead, stabbed?'

'That is correct.'

'May we see the study?'

'By all means. But you must excuse me. I do not wish to enter that room. I will wait in here to answer any further questions you may have.'

The study was situated immediately behind the drawing-room. A large desk, covered with papers, stood in the centre of the room and in front of it was a small rug, its pattern obscured by an irregular dark stain, which I needed only the briefest of glances to identify as blood. In the wall opposite the door was a pair of French windows, through which I could see the shady garden.

'So,' said Sherlock Holmes, as he prowled about the room, his keen eyes darting here and there to take in every detail of the scene of the tragedy, 'the professor is seated behind his desk, working at his papers; someone enters through the French windows; the professor stands up, comes round to this side of the desk, either to talk to or to confront the intruder. Hum! Let us take a look outside!'

He opened the French windows and stepped out, and I watched from the study as he began slowly circling round on the lawn. After a few minutes, he dropped to his knees and examined closely some mark upon the lawn.

'Would you be so good as to bring me the shoes, Watson?' he called without looking up. 'Make sure you keep well to the side!'

I unwrapped the parcel and took him the shoes. He turned them over and studied the undersides for a moment, then returned his gaze to the ground. Then he shook his head.

'They do not match,' said he. 'These prints are therefore those of another man.' He took a handkerchief from his pocket and placed it on the ground by the footprint, then continued his examination. After a few moments he dropped to his knees again. 'A very clear print here, in this small muddy patch,' he murmured. 'Same as the first one. It seems – ah, yes! – this person is turning back in, towards the house wall. Here is another – and another! But wait! Here are some other prints, quite different from those! Let us see!' He looked again at the shoes he was carrying, then back again at the ground. 'It is a perfect match!'

'So the professor was out in the garden, as well as the other man,' I observed.

'So it would appear,' returned Holmes. 'Of course, there is nothing remarkable about a man taking a walk round his own garden. And we cannot yet say whether the two men were in the garden at the same time or not. Let us cast our net further afield!'

'Is it of any significance when the professor was in the garden?' I enquired, as Holmes moved slowly away, his keen, hawk-like eyes fixed upon the ground at his feet.

'It might be,' he answered without looking up. 'If the two men walked about together, it would of course suggest that they knew each other and had been strolling about whilst in conversation.'

My companion then fell silent once more as he continued his examination of the lawn. In a few minutes he had covered the whole extent of it, and reached the garden gate. There he stood for a while, his chin in his hand, evidently pondering his findings, before making his way back to where I stood, near the corner of the house.

'If the two of them had been walking together,' he remarked, 'one would expect the two sets of prints to be closely aligned; but they are not. It is true that they come together in one or two places, but that is evidently mere chance, for where they cross, they are going in opposite directions. In every case where the two sets of prints intersect, those of the other shoes are overlaid upon those of the shoes we have here and were therefore made later.'

'It appears, then,' I said, 'that the professor simply took a walk earlier in the day and the other man arrived later. You therefore cannot tell from the prints whether the other man was someone known to the professor or not. From that point of view the prints are of no use to you.'

Holmes chuckled. 'The fact that one set of prints was certainly made later than the other is not the only discovery I have made,' said he. 'Footprints can tell you a great deal, if you read them carefully, Watson! I have, as you know, written a short monograph on the subject. But come!' he continued, as I made to ask him more. 'I shall make a quick sketch of one of the prints made by the other shoes for future identification and we can then return to the house.'

In the study, Holmes resumed his close examination of the room. After a few minutes, he paused before a framed photograph, which was hanging on the wall behind the desk. In it, a group of perhaps fifteen or sixteen people were standing on the steps of what appeared to be a college of some kind. Most of them were men, almost all of whom were bearded and bespectacled, and staring at the camera with such an intensity that they appeared like nothing so much as a row of owls sitting on a perch. After a moment, Holmes unhooked the photograph from the wall and, indicating that I should follow him, led the way through to the drawing-room.

'That photograph was taken about twenty-five years ago,' said Mrs Arbuthnot, in answer to Holmes's query. 'A conference was held in Oxford, at Montgomery College, and people came from all over Europe to contribute to the discussions. It was a great success.'

'Is your late husband in the picture?' asked Holmes.

'Yes. That is he, there,' she answered, indicating the end figure of the front row of intense-looking, bearded men.

'And Dr Zyss?'

'Two to the left of my husband, the man with the spectacles.'

'And this woman, standing at the side?'

'Yes, that is me. Of course, I was much younger then. I dare say I have changed rather a lot. Sometimes it seems to me that women age less well than men.'

'Not at all, madam,' responded Holmes suavely. 'And this other woman: could that be Mrs Routledge?'

'Mrs Routledge?' repeated Mrs Arbuthnot sharply. 'Certainly not! Whatever made you think such a thing? Why should Mrs Routledge be there?'

'I beg your pardon, Mrs Arbuthnot. I have evidently spoken in error. I had heard the name of Mrs Routledge in connection with your husband or Dr Zyss and assumed, perhaps incorrectly, that she was a professional colleague of his. If I have made a mistake, I apologise.'

'You certainly have made a mistake!' said Mrs Arbuthnot with feeling. 'Mrs Routledge was the mother of one of my husband's patients and nothing, if I may say so, but a troublemaker. Her own husband had died, she had brought up her son alone and was devoted to him. I say "devoted", but "over-devoted" would perhaps be more accurate. That, in my husband's opinion, was the source of the young man's troubles, but, of course, the mother would not hear of it. My husband had been treating him for some time, on the recommendation of their own family physician, when unfortunately, and to everyone's great surprise, the young man took his own life. The mother, Mrs Routledge, was naturally terribly distraught, which was understandable; but after a few days she began to lay the blame for what had happened on my husband and Dr Zyss. She accused them of putting strange ideas into his head, which was quite untrue and a wicked thing to say. At first my husband excused these accusations as the reaction of a sorrowful, bereaved mother and did not respond; but after a time her lies began to affect his professional standing and he could no longer simply ignore them. He therefore applied for a court injunction to prevent her from spreading these malicious and unsubstantiated falsehoods. The case was won and Mrs Routledge was thenceforth restrained, but serious damage had already been done to my husband's reputation, and it took some time for the practice to recover. That was about a dozen years ago.'

'Was it not also about that time that Dr Zyss returned to Vienna?'

'Yes, approximately.'

'Was there any connection between the Routledge case and Dr Zyss's decision to leave?'

'No. He had been considering for some time returning to Vienna, to set up his own practice there. He and my husband had had various professional disagreements – I will not bore you with the details – and for that reason, also, decided to go their separate ways.'

Holmes nodded. 'I see,' said he. 'I understand that although retired from active practice, your husband continued to write and publish in the professional journals.'

'That is correct. My husband's work was his life's passion and nothing could have kept him from it.'

'What was the subject of his latest work?'

'I cannot see the relevance of the question, but, as you ask, it concerned the treatment of those suffering from a depressive illness, young people especially.'

We returned to the study then and, after hanging the photograph back up, Holmes continued his general examination of the room. After a while he looked up from where he was examining something by the fireplace, a thoughtful expression on his face.

'I don't think there is much more we can learn from this room,' said he, 'but while I finish off here, Watson, perhaps you could ask Mrs Arbuthnot about Terence Chalfont's visit on Wednesday, if you wouldn't mind?'

'Not at all.'

Mrs Arbuthnot was still seated in the same position as I had last seen her, staring into the hearth. I put the questions to her that Holmes had suggested and she shook her head with a sigh.

'As I have already told Inspector Gregson,' she replied, 'Mr Chalfont called at about half past two in the afternoon, stayed about half an hour and then left. His reason for calling was purely social, a family matter, and can have nothing to do with what has occurred.'

'Was he a frequent visitor to your house?'

'No, he was not. My husband did not encourage visitors.'

'When was the last time he called?

'I'm not sure. About three weeks ago. What does it matter?'

I could not think what else to ask, but at that moment, Holmes put his head in at the door and announced that he had finished in the study. 'Do not trouble to ring for the servant, madam,' said he. 'We shall let ourselves out and bother you no longer. Good day!'

'She did not really add anything to what we had already heard about Chalfont's visit,' I remarked, as our cab set off in the direction of Hampstead.

'That is no more than I had expected,' returned my companion, then fell into a profound silence. 'No doubt you observed, Watson,' he said at last, breaking his silence as we rattled along the road across the north side of the heath, 'that some of Professor Arbuthnot's papers are missing. Most of the sheets are dated, but there are none dated more recently than about three weeks ago, and none which appear to relate to his most recent work, as his wife described it to us. It is evident, however, that some sheets have been burnt in the fire, for there are several charred corners of paper lying in the hearth.'

I shook my head. 'What does it mean?' I asked.

'It means, Watson, that what has not been burnt has been taken.'

'But why? Could that be the motive for the crime?'

'Ah! That is what we must discover!'

We alighted from the cab in the centre of Hampstead and soon found the front door to Chalfont's apartment, at the side of a bakery in Heath Street. Our knock at the door was answered by Chalfont himself, a thin, pale, clean-shaven young man. He appeared none too pleased to see us, but agreed, in a reluctant fashion, to answer our questions.

'I have already told the policeman everything I know about my uncle's death,' he said, as he led the way up a steep flight of stairs to his apartment. 'As I said to him, it amounts to precisely nothing.'

As he was showing us into a small sitting-room at the top of the stairs, there came some slight noise from beyond a closed door at the side of the room.

'That will just be my lodger leaving,' he remarked in an off-hand tone, as we looked in that direction.

'I was not aware there was another way out,' said Holmes.

'Only by the window,' replied Chalfont in a matter of fact voice. 'Martin often leaves in that way. He owes a little money to various people, which is why I'm putting him up here at the moment. He probably heard you coming and thought you were debt collectors. Now, please ask your questions and let's get it over with.'

'You called upon the Arbuthnots on Wednesday afternoon, at about half past two, but did not stay long and did not see the professor,' said Holmes.

'That is correct. If you know all this, why are you asking me?'

'You didn't call again later, for any reason?'

'No.'

'Mrs Arbuthnot says that you are not a very frequent visitor these days.'

'That is true. What of it?'

'I understand that you were hoping that they would make a financial contribution to the production costs of your latest play. Was that your main reason for calling?'

'That came into it,' Chalfont responded after a moment. 'After all, people do sometimes contribute to worthy things that are of interest to them. At least, they used to. It's become harder lately to raise the money you need. People are getting meaner. As for the Arbuthnots: trying to get money out of them was like trying to get blood out of a stone. I'd thought that the new play might be of interest to them, considering that it's all about the professor's line of business. You would have thought they'd have welcomed a little free advertising for his racket. But they weren't interested.'

'You had spoken to them before about it?'

'Yes, two or three weeks ago.'

'Forgive me for pursuing the point, Mr Chalfont,' said Holmes after a moment, 'but I am interested in this play of yours. I have the impression that you intend it to be somewhat critical of what you describe as "the professor's line of business". If that is so, why would you expect Professor Arbuthnot or his wife to contribute to its production?'

Chalfont did not reply at once. He sat down heavily in an armchair and, by a wave of his arm, indicated that we should do the same. 'Because,' he replied at length, 'I was being dishonest. I make a big show of detesting dishonesty in others, but there was I, being just as dishonest as anyone else. When I first told them of the play, I tried to make out that it would simply be about the difficulties involved in that line of work, but as we discussed it, my own opinions inevitably came out, even though I tried to keep them to myself, and the professor and I ended up having a blazing row. That was three weeks ago. My visit on Wednesday was to try and smooth things over a bit, and tell them that they might have gained a misleading impression of the play. But that, too, was dishonest.'

'In reality, then, you had always intended it to be critical of the professor's work?'

'Yes,' he replied after a long moment of reflection.

'You have studied your uncle's work closely?'

'Closely enough. Listen, Mr Holmes, when I was a boy, old Arbuthnot often used to call at our house and make personal remarks about me to my mother, sometimes when he thought I couldn't hear what he was saying, and sometimes even in my presence, as if I was of no account compared to his almighty opinions. Grossly offensive, I call that, and damned impertinent!'

'I see,' said Holmes after a moment. 'Is your new play based on your own experiences, then, or on a specific case?'

'Neither precisely,' replied Chalfont in a cautious tone. 'I didn't want to embarrass anybody or get into trouble by following a real case too closely. So it's a blend of incidents and themes from several different cases I've read about, with some of my own experiences thrown in for good measure.'

'And how, if I may ask, does it end up? Which character in your play comes out better?'

'I really don't see what your interest is, but as it happens, the issue is not so simple as that. The patient deteriorates, but I leave it ambiguous as to whether this is the psychologist's fault, or whether the young man would have got worse anyway. At least, I think I leave it ambiguous; I am at present rewriting the final scenes. I am conscious that I lack some telling incident, some crucial detail which will make the point I wish to make in an unequivocal way.'

'Are you acquainted with Mrs Routledge?'

'No I am not. I've never heard of her. Who is she, anyway?'

'No matter. Do you know anything of a black owl?'

Chalfont's features expressed puzzlement and he shook his head. 'I thought most owls were brown,' he said.

Holmes glanced at his watch as we boarded our cab once more. 'We are running a little late now,' said he. 'I think we should postpone our visit to Professor Arbuthnot's sister and get along to our meeting with Inspector Gregson at Gospel Oak.'

My companion fell silent then, as our cab rattled down Rosslyn Hill and along the south side of the heath towards Gospel Oak. As our cab turned into Trenchard Villas, however, he turned to me with an odd smile on his face.

'That last interview took somewhat longer than I had expected,' said he, 'but I think it was worthwhile. Chalfont was lying, of course. It is inconceivable that he has researched the subject of psychic illness for his proposed new play, a subject upon which his own uncle has been one of the leading writers for many years, and has not encountered the Routledge case, a case which, from what we have heard, caused quite a disturbance in that field ten years ago.'

'The same thought had struck me,' I returned. 'It certainly sounds as if there are similarities between Chalfont's play and the Routledge case. But if he does know Mrs Routledge, why should he deny it?'

Holmes shook his head. 'It is proving a more interesting case than at first seemed likely,' he remarked. 'I hope that Gregson has—ah, yes! There he is!'

A four-wheeler was standing at the side of the road and, as we approached, a man in a bowler hat clambered out.

'Good afternoon, gentlemen!' said Gregson as we alighted on the pavement. 'This is the place,' he continued, indicating a neat gabled villa, set back behind a small front garden. 'I thought I would wait for you, Mr Holmes, so that we could conduct the interview together.'

We were shown by a maid into a tastefully decorated parlour and a moment later Mrs Routledge entered. She was a neatly dressed woman of medium height, with faded sandy hair tied back in a bun. Gregson introduced us and explained the nature of his investigation, at which Mrs Routledge shook her head.

'Of course I have heard what has happened,' said she. 'It is a shocking business that Professor Arbuthnot should be murdered, but I don't see how I can help you in the matter.'

'You called upon Dr Zyss at the Belvedere Hotel on Wednesday morning?'

'I did, but I fail to see what that has to do with anything.'

'Dr Zyss and Professor Arbuthnot were old colleagues.'

'Yes, of course I am aware of that.'

'Dr Zyss has disappeared. He is nowhere to be found.'

I observed her face closely, but she remained composed and it was difficult to tell whether this information was news to her or not.

'How very strange,' she remarked after a moment in a quiet voice.

'You will appreciate, then, madam,' said Gregson, 'that your visit to Dr Zyss is not quite so unimportant as you suggest.'

'I don't see how my visit has any bearing on the matter,' Mrs Routledge responded in a dismissive tone. 'I can understand that you would wish to interview everyone who has seen Dr Zyss recently, if he has, as you say, disappeared. But I only saw him for an hour or so, quite early in the day, and he seemed perfectly normal then, I can assure you.'

'You have not seen him since that meeting – on Wednesday evening, for instance?'

'No.'

'Did you also see Professor Arbuthnot on Wednesday?'

'No.'

'You did not go up to his house?'

'Certainly not.'

'But you know where it is?'

'Yes, it is in Highgate. I have been there once or twice, but not for many years.'

'What did you do when you left the Belvedere Hotel?'

'I took lunch at a restaurant in Holborn, did a little shopping there, then walked over to the British Museum where I spent a pleasant couple of hours in the company of the Egyptian antiquities. I then took a cab to St Pancras station, from where I caught a train to St Albans, to visit my friend, as I had previously arranged.'

'What time did you arrive at St Albans?'

'Just before six o'clock, which was the time my friend was expecting me. She lives only a short walk from the railway station.'

'What was your purpose in visiting Dr Zyss?' interjected Holmes.

'A purely private matter.'

'Concerned with your son?'

For a moment, Mrs Routledge appeared surprised and discomfited, but in a moment she had recovered her composure. 'I repeat,' she said, 'that my conversation with Dr Zyss was private. I am not prepared to discuss it further.'

'Come, come, Mrs Routledge,' said Holmes in a voice that was quiet but firm. 'Your refusal to speak serves no purpose. We are aware of the tragic history of your son, and aware that you blamed Dr Zyss and Professor Arbuthnot for what happened.'

'If you know so much, then why ask me about it?' responded Mrs Routledge sharply.

'We simply wish to confirm the details of your visit to Dr Zyss on Wednesday.'

'Very well. Yes, I discussed the case of Nicholas with him.'

'Could anything in the conversation have caused Dr Zyss to alter or cancel his own arrangements for later in the day?'

'I should not have thought so. We were largely discussing the past.'

It was evident that we should get little further information from Mrs Routledge and a few moments later we rose to take our leave. At the doorway, however, Holmes spoke a few words to Gregson, who turned once more to Mrs Routledge, taking from his pocket as he did so the little black owl.

'Have you seen this object before?' the policeman asked her.

For a moment she hesitated and a variety of emotions passed in rapid succession across her face. 'No,' said she at last. 'I have never seen it before.'

Outside, on the pavement, Inspector Gregson shook his head, as he pushed the little brass owl back in his pocket.

'She's lying,' he said. 'Your guess was right, Mr Holmes. She certainly has seen this owl before, or my name is not Tobias Gregson! What it means, I don't know, but she is definitely implicated in the murder!'

'Not necessarily,' returned Holmes, as the three of us climbed into our cab. 'The fact that she has seen the owl before scarcely proves she is a party to murder.'

'But why, then, does she lie about it? You could see the guilt written all over her face. And I'll tell you another thing: her account of her afternoon is not satisfactory. Two hours at the British Museum! I don't believe it!'

'Such recreation is not unknown,' remarked Holmes with a chuckle.

'Perhaps not,' Gregson conceded, although he still sounded unconvinced; 'but that's not all that is suspicious about her afternoon. The railway line from St Pancras to St Albans passes right through this part of north London, not far from Gospel Oak, and, more significantly, not far from Highgate. She could easily have left the train at an intermediate station and walked up to the Arbuthnots' house at Highgate, afterwards returning the same way and continuing her journey to St Albans.'

Holmes nodded his head. 'Yes,' said he; 'the geographical

possibilities were not lost upon me, Gregson. What you suggest would certainly have been possible.'

'Aha!' cried the policeman. 'So you, too, suspect Mrs Routledge of having a hand in this affair?'

Holmes shook his head. 'I did not say that,' he returned, and would not be drawn further on the matter.

'It's a rum business, all right!' said Gregson to me as our cab rattled its way westwards, towards Belsize Park. 'I've seen plenty of men knifed – more than I'd care to count – but, between you and me, Dr Watson, the victims were very often no better than the villains that did for them. This, though, is the sort of case that just makes you scratch your head,' he continued, taking off his hat and suiting the action to the word. 'Why would anyone want to murder a harmless old retired professor? Have you formed any opinion?'

I shook my head. 'I feel as much in the dark as you,' I said. 'It seems like nothing more than insane brutality.'

Our cab set us down before a large stucco-fronted house, in a side-road off Haverstock Hill. Our ring at the bell produced no immediate response and Gregson turned to us as he gave it a second sharp tug.

'Lady Boothby's servants are a little hard of hearing,' he said in a low voice. 'Between you and me, they are somewhat on the aged side. Most of them have been with her for around thirty years.'

The front door was eventually opened by an elderly maidservant, who showed us into a drawing-room on the left of the hall. There came the sound of footsteps overhead, then, after a few moments, the maid returned and conducted us to a room at the rear of the house. There, in a high-backed armchair drawn close to the fire, Lady Boothby was seated. She apologised for receiving us in the dining-room.

'The fire is better in here,' she explained, 'and at my age I feel the cold rather badly. Do take a seat,' she continued, indicating the chairs at the table. 'Now, Inspector, what can I do for you? I was under the impression that I had answered all possible questions on your previous visit.'

'There are one or two points we wished to clear up,' Holmes

interjected. 'In the first place,' he continued, as she turned to him with a look of curiosity on her face, 'I should be obliged if you could tell us what you know of Mrs Routledge, the mother of a former patient of your brother's.'

Lady Boothby's features assumed an expression of distaste.

'A wretched woman!' she responded after a moment. 'Her son was the subject of odd delusions and was being treated by my brother – quite brilliantly, I might add – when he unfortunately took his own life. His mother instantly put it about that my brother was to blame, quite overlooking the fact that the treatment he had been giving the boy had been his only hope of leading a normal life. When that woman's slanderous lies began to reach a wider audience, my brother was obliged to take legal action to restrain her. She was duly bound over to keep the peace and we heard no more of her lies.'

'You followed your brother's work very closely, I take it,' remarked Holmes.

'Indeed, and always admired it greatly. It was work of genius, from a man of genius. One day my brother's name will be honoured as one of the greatest figures – perhaps the very greatest – in the history of this unappreciative country!'

'And Dr Zyss? Is he also a man of genius?'

'Certainly not! Ludwig Zyss was always a mere follower of the insights of others. He achieved a certain celebrity by his association with my brother; but since their partnership was dissolved he has quite faded into obscurity.'

'Does he not practise in Vienna?'

'I believe he does – in an obscure sort of way and with many wrong-headed ideas.'

'His ideas were not quite the same as those of your brother, then? Did the breach in their partnership come about because of these differences of opinion?'

'Partly, yes – and in every case Dr Zyss was wrong, and Humphrey was right.'

'Did they disagree in the case of Nicholas Routledge?'

'I cannot discuss individual cases with you. It would not be proper to do so.'

'But you could perhaps tell us whether they disagreed on the matter.'

'Very well. Yes, they did disagree on the matter, very strongly. It was this disagreement which precipitated the rift between them; but the rift would have occurred eventually in any case, as the disparity between their respective talents became more apparent.'

'What will become of Professor Arbuthnot's papers now?'

'They will be collected and edited by his wife and myself, and published as soon as possible. The world must not be denied the opportunity to behold the fruits of my brother's genius.'

'Had your brother been working on anything in particular recently?'

'Yes. He has never ceased to push back the boundaries of human knowledge. His most recent work had been on certain species of mental illness to which young men in particular are prone, and the best treatment thereof.'

Holmes asked Gregson for the little black owl, which he held out for Lady Boothby's inspection. 'Have you ever seen this before?' he asked, at which she shook her head. 'It did not belong to your brother, perhaps?'

'Certainly not. Is it brass? It looks to me like a paper-weight. I seem to remember reading somewhere that Charles Dickens had something of the sort on his desk, whilst writing his novels.'

A few minutes later, our interview concluded, Holmes, Gregson and I stood by the cab at the pavement edge.

'The old professor certainly seems to have inspired an uncommon degree of loyalty and admiration in his womenfolk,' remarked Gregson in a low tone. 'I would like to think that Mrs G would speak in similar tones of me, if I was no longer here, but somehow I doubt it. Still, that's neither here nor there – which is pretty much where we are in this case, it seems to me: neither here nor there! Between us we've spent several days plodding round the place, but have blessed little to show for it!'

'Come, come!' said Holmes. 'We have learnt a great deal!'

'Have we?' asked Gregson in a dubious tone. 'I can't say that I have, Mr Holmes. We have an elderly, retired professor murdered in his study; a wife and sister who both think he was wonderful; an old colleague of the professor's who seems to have disappeared; a woman – the mother of a former patient of the professor's – who probably holds a grudge against him; a nephew who is writing a play which may or may not be based on one of the professor's cases. It doesn't seem to amount to much to me! What do we actually know? The only thing I feel really confident about is that Mrs Routledge lied to me about that blessed owl – and what the devil that might mean, I have no idea!'

'Being lied to is an inherent hazard of our profession,' returned Holmes with a dry chuckle. 'If it is any consolation to you, Gregson, I can tell you that every single person I have interviewed today has lied to me about something. Of that I am certain!'

'I'm sure you're right,' said Gregson, shaking his head, 'but that doesn't help me much. What can I put in my report, to show to my superiors? Who murdered Professor Arbuthnot and why? Where is Dr Zyss? And what the blazes is the significance of that brass owl?'

Holmes chuckled. 'I think I can answer some of your questions,' he said. 'As for what you can tell your superiors,' he continued; 'would the address at which the murderer is to be found be of any use?' He took out a little note-book from his pocket and scribbled a few words on a sheet, which he tore off and passed to the policeman. 'In my opinion, that is where you will find the murderer,' he remarked as he put the note-book back in his pocket.

'What!' cried the policeman, as he read the note. 'Eight, Belsize Park Crescent! But that is Lady Boothby's house, where we have just been! This is not the time for jokes, Mr Holmes!'

'I quite agree, Gregson. Look,' he added, as a uniformed policeman appeared round the corner from Haverstock Hill, 'here is the local constable! I suggest you enlist his aid, re-enter Lady Boothby's house and make your arrest!'

'But this is madness!' persisted Gregson. 'I cannot possibly do as you say! I should make myself a figure of ridicule and lay myself open to legal action!'

'Very well, then,' said Holmes, in a measured tone. 'I shall accompany you and take upon myself all responsibility for the business. If I do anything legally improper, you have my permission to arrest me instead!'

After a moment, Gregson agreed to this, but his features expressed the doubts he evidently still entertained about the proposal. He crossed the road and intercepted the constable, who was passing by on the other side.

'You do not object to forming the audience for our expedition, Watson, do you?' Holmes asked me, as I watched Inspector Gregson speaking to the constable.

'Not at all,' I returned. 'I am curious to see what you have in mind. I confess I have no idea at the moment what it is.'

Gregson returned with the constable, introduced to us as PC Harper of the Hampstead Division, and a moment later we were ringing the bell once more at the front door of Lady Boothby's house.

We were conducted by the elderly maidservant directly to the dining-room at the back of the house, where Lady Boothby still sat in the armchair by the fire.

'Well?' she asked, in a voice full of irritation. 'What is it now?'

'We should be obliged,' said Holmes, 'if you would ask him to come down.'

Lady Boothby's mouth fell open in surprise. 'Who?' cried she. 'Who should I ask to come down? What *are* you talking about?'

'Your brother, Humphrey,' said Holmes in a calm tone. 'He has been staying here since Wednesday night, has he not?'

The lady's cheeks burnt bright red. 'How dare you!' cried she. 'How dare you speak in this way, when my brother has been struck down in his prime, less than three days ago, and his body is scarcely cold yet!'

'The body which is scarcely cold is that of the unfortunate Dr Zyss,' interjected Holmes in a firm voice, 'who was killed by your brother in the course of a quarrel. The body was deliberately misidentified by your sister-in-law, Mrs Arbuthnot, so that her husband could complete his latest work, which is why he took the papers relating to it away with him.'

'What nonsense!'

'You had called at the house, to be present at the meeting which your brother had informed you was to take place between Dr Zyss and himself. But Dr Zyss had arrived before you, and the two men had already had a violent quarrel, which had ended with Professor Arbuthnot seizing the paper-knife from his desk, and plunging it into the breast of his opponent, killing him instantly. His wife heard the disturbance, entered the study and saw what had happened. Professor Arbuthnot and his wife thereupon concocted the idea of letting it be thought that it was the professor who had been struck down by an unknown assailant. No doubt they had been impressed by the great similarity in appearance of the two men, for if Dr Zyss's spectacles were removed, only those who knew them well could have told them apart; and as your brother had scarcely left the house in ten years, and received no visitors save yourself, they must have been confident that this deception would not be uncovered. It remained only to prevent the domestic staff from learning the truth of what had occurred, and for the professor to make his escape from the house. To this end, having gathered up the papers he required, he left the study by the French windows, intending to meet you when you arrived and leave with you in your carriage. Unfortunately for his plan, he saw as he reached the corner of the house that you had already arrived, and had just rung the front-door bell. He signalled to you to go back down the path to the gate. Before you reached it, however, the maid opened the front door of the house and spoke to you. Unsure what to do, you hesitated for a moment, then turned away again and walked to the gate. A moment later, the maid had shut the door, whereupon your brother quickly joined you and left with you in your carriage. Is my description of the events correct, madam?'

Lady Boothby did not reply. All colour had drained from her face, and she sat rigid and unmoving.

'Yesterday morning,' Holmes continued, 'your brother decided to take a walk up to Hampstead. No doubt he was confident that he would not be recognised, as he had seen no one he knew for the best part of ten years. Unfortunately for him, he was seen by a lady who had attended lectures he gave many years ago, who mistook him for Dr Zyss. He pretended he had not seen or heard her and walked quickly on, making for the church. She followed him there, however, and he was obliged to hide somewhere in the church until she left. She later reported this incident to the police, but they made nothing of it.'

Without speaking, Lady Boothby reached out her hand and gave the bell-rope a tug. A moment later, when the maid entered, Lady Boothby instructed her to ask Professor Arbuthnot to come to the dining-room.

For a minute we sat in silence, then the door opened again, and a thin, elderly man with a grizzled beard entered the room.

'What is it?' he began in an irritable tone, but stopped when he saw us. 'Who are these men?' he asked his sister.

'It's no good, Humphrey,' she replied. 'These men are from the police. They know the truth.'

With a cry of anger, he advanced upon her. 'You have betrayed me!' he cried. 'Have you no thought for my work?'

'Professor Arbuthnot,' said Gregson, rising to his feet, and placing his hand on the other man's shoulder, 'I am arresting you for the murder of Dr Ludwig Zyss.'

'No!' cried Arbuthnot in a wild voice. 'No, you are not!' In one swift move, he had stooped and snatched up the poker from the hearth. 'You will never take me!' he cried, swinging it violently at the police-man's head.

As one, Holmes and I sprang up and seized the professor's arms, as Gregson ducked to avoid the blow. For several moments we struggled violently to hold him, for the old professor seemed possessed of amazing strength for such an elderly man. Eventually he was subdued, the poker was wrenched from his grasp, and Inspector Gregson clapped a pair of handcuffs on him. Lady Boothby had shrunk into her chair while this violent conflict had been in progress. Now, she turned away, and made only a silent, dismissive gesture as we led her brother from the room.

We accompanied Gregson and his prisoner to the Hampstead Police Station, where he was formally charged with his crime and taken to the cells. A few minutes later, Gregson rejoined us in the front office.

'Well, that's that!' he declared, rubbing his hands together. 'Mad as a hatter! What do you think, Dr Watson?'

'I'm inclined to agree,' I replied. 'I shouldn't think he will be judged fit to stand trial.'

Gregson nodded. 'Still, we've caught him! That's the main thing! Now, Mr Holmes,' he continued, turning to my friend, who was sitting on a bench, smoking his pipe in a contemplative fashion, 'you must tell me how you worked it all out. How did you guess that it wasn't the professor but Dr Zyss who had been done to death, what made you think he was at his sister's house and where, precisely, does that blessed black owl fit into the matter?'

'Guessing doesn't come into it,' rejoined Holmes sharply. 'I never guess: there is no surer way of destroying the logical faculty. As to the little owl, it appeared earlier that Mrs Routledge knew more about it than she was prepared to admit, so what I propose is that we call on her again now and repeat our questions. I rather suspect that the news of Professor Arbuthnot's arrest will free her tongue. As to the other points of interest in the case, I will gladly enlighten you on those, such as they are, on our way there.'

Thus it was that, five minutes later, we were once more in a cab, bound for Gospel Oak.

'One of the first things that caught my attention,' said Holmes, as we rattled along in the fading daylight, 'was a curious little cut in the lining of the dead man's jacket, which I examined at the police station. It was not caused by the knife that struck its wearer down, for although the knife blade had passed through the waistcoat, there was no corresponding cut in the fabric of the jacket, which must therefore have been unfastened and open at the time of the assault. Yet it was evident that the cut in the lining had been made very recently, for the fabric, a shiny, satin-like material, had scarcely frayed at all along the edge of the slit. I examined the lining more closely with the aid of a lens, and two things at once became clear. The cut had been made with a small pair of nail-scissors – the irregular line of the slit made that apparent – and a series of small holes, in line with the direction of the cut, indicated that something had previously been sewn to the lining of the jacket. I followed this line of thread-holes, and found that they enclosed an area two inches by three. The solution of this little mystery then seemed obvious: a label of some kind – probably the tailor's own label – had been sewn inside the jacket, but had been recently removed, in the course of which the scissors had accidentally pierced the lining and cut a small section of it.

'Of course, I realised that this trivial matter might be of no relevance to the case, but it was at least possible that there was a relevance there, if I could see it. Why should anyone wish to remove the label? Presuming that the jacket belonged to Professor Arbuthnot, I could see no point to it. What would it matter to anyone where the professor had had his suit made? But, applying the law of contraries, it followed that if there *were* some significance to the act of removing the label, then the jacket did not belong to the professor at all. This made great sense; for the obvious hypothesis was that the label had been removed to prevent the discovery of this fact. The label might, for instance, be that of a tailor working far away from London, whom the professor could not have visited. But the dead man had certainly been wearing that tweed suit when stabbed, for the fatal blow of the knife had, as I mentioned, passed straight through the waistcoat, which was of the same material as the jacket, and therefore part of the suit. Why, then, should Professor Arbuthnot have been wearing someone else's suit when he was murdered and why was someone else concerned to conceal this fact? Of course, this is an absurd question, and the absurdity of it at once suggested the correct solution: the murdered man was not in fact Professor Arbuthnot at all, but someone else.

'I reconsidered then what you had told me of the case, Gregson. As far as I could recall from your account, after Mrs Arbuthnot had discovered the body and had sent the maid to find a policeman, no other family member had seen the body, nor any of the domestic staff. The identification of the body had therefore been made by Mrs Arbuthnot alone and it was possible that she had lied. The obvious explanation for this course of action was that it was Professor Arbuthnot himself who had committed the murder and his wife was seeking to protect him.

'You see, then, that even before we reached the scene of the crime at Highgate, I had formed a preliminary hypothesis which explained the matter satisfactorily and was completely at variance with the officially accepted course of events.'

'You say your hypothesis explained the matter,' I interrupted, 'but it left unanswered the identity of the victim.'

'That is true, Watson, but there was of course one outstanding candidate for that unfortunate role, namely Professor Arbuthnot's old colleague, Dr Zyss. Except for the spectacles he wore all the time, his description was not so different from that of Professor Arbuthnot himself – medium height, spare build, grey hair and beard. I could not really doubt, then, that the dead man was Dr Zyss. Of course, Mrs Arbuthnot stated that Dr Zyss had sent a note to say that he could not keep his appointment that evening; but if she had lied in her identification of the dead man, how much more easily might she have lied about the note.

'I had taken the dead man's shoes with me to Holly Grove and, with the aid of these, I examined the footprints in the garden. I very quickly found that there were just two significant sets of footprints upon the lawn. The first, which exactly matched the shoes I had brought with me, passed in a regular and even manner from the garden gate towards the corner of the house, and on towards the French windows. I examined the whole of the garden very closely, but could find no further traces of these prints. Had the shoes from the police station really been those of Professor Arbuthnot, as was supposed, this discovery would have been most mysterious. The only rational explanation would have been that the professor had left the house by the front door, walked down the path to the gate, and then returned to the house by way of the lawn and the French windows to the study. This would have been possible but unlikely, especially as the other evidence – the testimony of the servants and so on – was that he had not left the house all day. However, as I believed the shoes to be those of Dr Zyss, the track across the lawn made perfect sense. Clearly, when Dr Zyss had arrived – being no doubt familiar with his old colleague's habits – he had decided not to bother ringing the front-door bell, but to walk round to the study window, where he would have been confident of finding the professor at work.

'The second set of prints, made by shoes which were of a similar size to the first but of a slightly different shape, began just outside the study window. From there they followed the side of the house to the corner of the building, where their owner appeared to have remained standing for a moment – to judge from the large number of prints close together there – and then proceeded to the gate. Between the corner of the house and the gate, the impressions of this second pair of shoes were very much lighter, and hardly ever showed the heel distinctly, from which I inferred that the owner of these shoes had been moving with great haste. These footprints I could only regard as those of Professor Arbuthnot himself. Evidently, he had left the study – taking with him, incidentally, all the papers relating to his current work – just as his sister arrived and rang the bell at the front door. From the corner he must have signalled to her to return to her carriage, which was waiting in the street. No doubt puzzled by this strange behaviour, she nevertheless complied with his request and had almost reached the gate when the front door was opened by the parlour-maid, Ruby. Lady Boothby turned, but as she could see – which the maid could not – that her brother was urging her to leave at once, she did not respond when the girl spoke to her. When she raised her arm and pointed at the house, in the way that the maid found so menacing and frightening, she was no doubt simply trying to indicate to her brother that the front door had been opened and someone was standing there. Then she turned away and went out at the gate. Thereupon, the maid hurriedly shut the front door, Professor Arbuthnot no doubt left his hiding-place round the corner of the house, and ran across the lawn to join his sister in her carriage and furnish her with an explanation of this strange behaviour.

'To sum up the matter, then,' Holmes continued after a moment: 'Dr Zyss probably arrived shortly before six, saw Arbuthnot in his study, had a quarrel with him and was stabbed. Although Mrs Arbuthnot stated that she had heard nothing of what had taken place in the study, that was an obvious lie. When I was in the study, I asked Dr Watson to put some questions to her in the drawing-room and I listened as he did so. Although I could make out few individual words, I could hear both their voices quite clearly, as Mrs Arbuthnot must have heard the voices of her husband and Dr Zyss. Knowing that Lady Boothby would probably be arriving shortly, the Arbuthnots made the plan to smuggle the professor away in his sister's carriage, pretend that a note had been received from Dr Zyss to say that he could not come and make out that it was Arbuthnot himself that had been murdered. Of course, there was in reality no message from Zyss, no message from Mrs Arbuthnot to Lady Boothby and the messenger himself did not exist.'

Inspector Gregson nodded his head. 'Yes,' he said. 'You must be right, Mr Holmes. That must be how it happened. But what made you so sure that Arbuthnot was at his sister's house?'

'That seemed to me practically certain,' replied Holmes. 'In the first place, according to my theory he had left Holly Grove in her carriage with her on Wednesday evening. In the second place, our information was that he had had little social contact with anyone else in the past ten years, so where else could he be? In the third place, when one of those elderly ladies thought she had seen Dr Zyss in Hampstead, I considered that it must in fact have been Arbuthnot she had seen and this indicated that he was in the vicinity of his sister's house, for Hampstead High Street is, of course, only a short walk from Belsize Park. In the fourth place, Lady Boothby's servants were, as you informed us, all elderly and long-serving, which made it less likely that they would question Arbuthnot's presence there, or betray him to the authorities. In the fifth place, on our first visit, I heard someone pacing backwards and forwards on the floor immediately above the drawing-room. They were certainly not, I judged, the footsteps of a servant. I believe that Lady Boothby realised that we might hear her brother moving about in the room above the drawing-room and that was the true reason she elected to receive us in the dining-room; the fire had nothing to do with it. In the sixth place, when we first saw Lady Boothby, she did not ask you, Gregson, if you had any news, or if you had caught the murderer, which, it seems to me, would have been very natural questions, but instead presumed that you simply wished to interview her again. The reason, of course, that it did not occur to her to ask you if you had caught the murderer was because she already knew you had not, as the murderer was at that moment upstairs in her own house.'

Gregson shook his head ruefully. 'You have me there with that last point, Mr Holmes,' he said. 'I should have noticed that. People often give themselves away not by what they say, but by what they don't say because of what is in the back of their minds.'

'But what of the evidence of the porter at the Belvedere Hotel?' I asked. 'He stated quite clearly that Dr Zyss had returned to the hotel in the evening, before subsequently disappearing again.'

'It seems a certainty that the callers at the Belvedere Hotel on Wednesday evening were in fact Professor Arbuthnot and his sister.'

'But surely the porter would have realised that the man before him was not Dr Zyss?'

'Not necessarily, Watson. You must remember that the porter in question was the night porter, and as Dr Zyss had previously left and returned to the hotel only during the daytime, this particular porter had probably never seen him before at close quarters. Professor Arbuthnot would have been wearing Dr Zyss's spectacles, hat and overcoat, to improve the likeness. You will recall also from the porter's account that the man did not approach the desk, but sent his companion to ask for his room-key. After the two of them had ascended to Dr Zyss's room, if you remember, the lady returned to the entrance hall of the hotel, where she remained seated for some time, as if waiting for someone. After a while, the porter was called away from his desk for a few moments and when he returned the lady had gone. What I suggest is that all she was in fact waiting for was the porter's absence, so that Professor Arbuthnot, who was no doubt loitering on the stairs, could take the opportunity to pass through the hall unseen, and thus leave the hotel without being observed to do so.'

'But why did they go there at all?' I asked in puzzlement. 'Why risk discovery in that way?'

'Evidently there was something in Dr Zyss's room that the professor wished to get his hands on, no doubt papers of some kind, and probably something that Dr Zyss had mentioned in the course of their quarrel. If that is so, then that brief period of the evening, between the death of Dr Zyss and the murder becoming general knowledge, was the only opportunity there would be. But, yes, it was a dangerous course of action and we can only assume that the professor's desire to acquire whatever it was he sought was a strong one. More than that we cannot say at present. It may be that Mrs Routledge will be able to cast some light on that aspect of the case, as she had spoken to Dr Zyss at some length earlier in the day.'

Holmes's supposition proved correct. Mrs Routledge was startled to see us back so soon after our previous visit, and there was a look of fear in her eye; but once my friend had told her of the arrest of Professor Arbuthnot, and had explained what we had learnt, she recovered her composure.

'Although I cannot say that I expected such an outcome,' said she in a sombre tone, 'I am not altogether surprised. Professor Arbuthnot was always such a dogmatic, fanatical man. Indeed, I have often thought recently that that was the fundamental cause of the trouble between us. There was something in his nature which prevented him from ever admitting that he might be wrong about anything, or that he had ever made a mistake in his life. You are certain that your account of this dreadful crime is the true one?' she asked abruptly.

'We are,' replied Gregson. 'Professor Arbuthnot has been arrested and charged with the crime. All that remains for us now is to secure a positive identification of the deceased, in which melancholy task I shall have to ask for your assistance, madam. Of course,' he continued, as Mrs Routledge nodded her head, 'we did not seek any corroboration of the identification before. As Mrs Arbuthnot had stated that it was her husband that had been murdered, we naturally assumed that that was true and no further thought was given to the question of his identity.'

'We should be obliged now, madam,' said Holmes, 'if you could provide us with a little more detail as to your discussion with Dr Zyss on Wednesday morning and also tell us what you know concerning the black owl we showed you earlier.'

'The two things are intimately connected,' responded Mrs Routledge after a moment. 'I had read in the newspaper that Dr Zyss was visiting England and staying at the Belvedere Hotel, and I ventured to write to him there, in the hope that I might be able to discuss with him for a few minutes the case of my son, Nicholas. My attempts to discuss the matter with Professor Arbuthnot had ended only in failure, as he had simply rebuffed all my overtures, sometimes in the rudest, most insulting terms imaginable; but I thought that I might get a little further with Dr Zyss, who had always been the more reasonable and pleasant of the two men.

'To my great delight, Dr Zyss replied by return, inviting me to come to the hotel on Wednesday morning. And nor was his courtesy merely a superficial one. He listened patiently to everything I had to say, never interrupting, save only to clarify some point or other. When I had finished, he shook his head.

"'I wish we had had this talk ten years ago," said he, in a voice tinged with regret.

"'What do you mean?" I asked.

"'The view of your poor son's case that you have just expounded is very close to my own view," he explained. "Indeed, this meeting seems to me a remarkable chance. I am delivering a paper to the British Psychiatric Association at the end of the week on the diagnosis and treatment of certain unusual mental conditions, including that from which, I believe, your son suffered. I may tell you, my dear madam, that your son's case was an epoch-making event in my own professional career."

"'Whatever do you mean?"

"'It was over your son's case that Professor Arbuthnot and I first fell out very seriously. Our views had been diverging for some considerable time, but we had continued to work together. Looking back on that period now, it seems to me that I was the one who compromised his beliefs and intuitions; Arbuthnot never once admitted the slightest doubt or reservation concerning his own views. In the case of your son, Arbuthnot's opinion was that Nicholas was motivated in his irrational moods by a deep-seated resentment of you and his father."

'I nodded my agreement, for Professor Arbuthnot had often expressed this opinion to me very forcibly.

"'I, however, was of quite a different opinion," Dr Zyss continued. "My interviews with your son had convinced me that, on the whole, he had nothing but a normal affection for his parents. His problems, as I saw it, stemmed from certain irrational urges to which he was subject, and which, in his more rational moments, he regretted bitterly. The most notable of these was what has been termed 'kleptomania' – an urge to steal things. I cannot pretend to fully understand or explain this, but in the course of my conversations with Nicholas, I became convinced that this strange, aberrant urge arose from some innate cause within him, and bore no relation whatever to anything you or your husband had ever said or done. The bouts of kleptomania would always be followed, sooner or later, by periods of the very deepest remorse, when, as I knew from what Nicholas had told me, he would become bitterly unhappy and frequently almost suicidal. On one occasion that I recall, he confessed to me that he had attempted to steal some trifling bauble from a shop in Holborn. He had been discovered in the act, the manager had been called and there might well have been an unpleasant scene. But fortunately, Nicholas apologised, the manager took a lenient view – I dare say he saw that your son was not well – and the matter blew over. When Nicholas recounted this to me, he was deeply ashamed and begged me not to mention it to you."

"'It is a strange thing,' I said, "that you should have spoken of these things, Dr Zyss, for I had two reasons for wishing to see you today. The first was to discus my son's case with you. The second was to return this." I took from my bag the little black-painted brass owl you showed me earlier. "I believe," I said, "that Nicholas took it from your consulting-room. I found it among his belongings some time after his death. By then, you had left the country, so I was unable to return it to you, but it was the first thing I thought of when I read that you were visiting England once more."

'At this, Dr Zyss sprang from his chair and paced the floor in an agitated manner.

"'But this is remarkable!" he cried at length. "Astounding! You may not be aware, Mrs Routledge, how rare it is in my profession to receive good solid verification of one's theories. But your production of this paper-weight confirms my diagnosis almost beyond doubt! I remember missing it at the time and wondering where it had got to. I assumed in the end that the maid had accidentally knocked it off my desk and that it had fallen into a waste-paper basket and been inadvertently thrown away. But it is evident now what really occurred: your son must have taken it from my desk while my back was turned and put it in his pocket. Why he should want such a dull-looking little thing, I cannot imagine. He had never expressed any interest in it before. But, of course, to ask the reason 'why' in such cases is perfectly pointless. For sufferers from kleptomania, there *is* no reason, other than a momentary, irresistible urge. It saddens me to say it," Dr Zyss continued after a moment, "but I consider it quite possible that it was shame at having stolen this trifle from me – his friend – that led your son to take his own life. When I go to see Arbuthnot, I shall take this little owl with me and explain to him how it vindicates my theory. Bah! That dogmatic old fool! I shall teach him a lesson in humility! I shall rewrite my notes this afternoon, and when I deliver my lecture on Saturday evening, I shall incorporate the story of this little black owl into it to emphasise my point!"

'I left soon after that and that was the last I saw of Dr Zyss,' concluded Mrs Routledge.

'So presumably,' said Inspector Gregson, 'he called on Professor Arbuthnot, as Mr Holmes suggests, showed him the paper-weight, and no doubt crowed a little about what he felt it proved. They had a quarrel, exchanged insults, and then the professor grabbed his paper-knife and stabbed his rival through the heart.'

'It must be so,' said Holmes. 'Arbuthnot seems to have been a very arrogant man, who could not bear to be disagreed with. No doubt it was Dr Zyss's rewritten lecture notes that he wished to get his hands on at the Belvedere Hotel. I believe,' he continued, turning to Mrs Routledge, 'that you are acquainted with Professor Arbuthnot's nephew, Mr Terence Chalfont.'

'Yes. He came to see me some time ago. He was doing research for a play he was writing and we met on several occasions. We discussed Nicholas's case and related matters at some length, and I always found him very thoughtful and understanding. One day, he introduced me to a friend of his, Martin Ferris, who he said would be playing the leading part of the young man in the play and I must say I found him a very pleasant young man, who reminded me a little of my own son. When our discussions were eventually concluded, Mr Chalfont promised me solemnly that he would never tell anyone that he had spoken to me, to avoid bringing the glare of unwelcome publicity upon me again.'

'I don't imagine you mentioned the black owl to him.'

'No. It never occurred to me to do so. I was not aware then of its significance.'

Holmes nodded. 'I think, Mrs Routledge, that you should now tell Mr Chalfont about the black owl, and suggest that he incorporates the incident into his play. He may find it is the one telling moment which, he informed us, the play currently lacks. Then, when the play at last opens, you and your son will finally receive a kind of justice, and this whole unfortunate business will have reached its conclusion.'

The Adventure of the XYZ Club

'It is a singular fact,' said Sherlock Holmes to me one morning, as we sat either side of the fire after breakfast, 'that although mankind advances in the sphere of material accomplishments with almost every day that passes, his progress in the moral sphere is somewhat less marked.'

'At least we are less likely nowadays to be attacked in the street by someone wielding a battle-axe,' I responded in some amusement.

'No doubt,' said my friend, 'but I often suspect that that is only because of the increased likelihood of apprehension and punishment. If it were not for the forces of law and order, we should probably have battle-axe-wielding villains bursting in upon us two or three times a week. Our modern life may seem one of civility and relative peace, but it often strikes me as but a fragile shell, beneath which the urge to evil-doing is as strong as ever.'

'But, as you yourself have frequently observed, Holmes, human nature is much the same from one age to another and there is nothing any of us can do about that. Besides, the material advancement to which you refer, while it would no doubt have seemed like magic to our distant ancestors, often consists, when one examines it closely, of simply putting substance "A" on top of substance "B", rather than the other way about, and discovering to our very great surprise that the result is more effective or agreeable in some way.'

Holmes chuckled. 'That is certainly true,' said he. 'Nothing changes in its essential nature. We simply arrange things in different patterns and produce different results. These patterns are then recorded and the details passed on to our successors. No one trained in a scientific discipline can fail to see the worth of such records. On moral questions, however, there is no such agreement.'

'You are too pessimistic,' I returned. 'The vast majority of our fellow citizens would, I am sure, agree upon most moral questions and that in itself is progress. The fact that your profession brings you into frequent contact with those who do not share the moral beliefs of the majority has surely influenced your opinion adversely.'

'Perhaps you are right, Watson, and I am becoming a little cynical. Still, the true cynics are those – however small their number – who seek to take advantage of the moral behaviour of the majority to achieve their own selfish and immoral ends.'

It was a bright Saturday in the early spring of 1886, the sort of day that can feel as warm as summer when the sun is out, and as cold as winter when it is hidden by clouds. Our discussion was interrupted by a sharp peal at the front-door bell, and a moment later a young man in a blazer with a bright striped muffler wrapped round his neck was shown into the room, and introduced himself as Julian Ashby.

'Excuse my bursting in upon you without prior warning,' said he in a breathless voice. 'You must think me very rude, but I have little time. My train only arrived about eight minutes ago, and I have run like the wind to get here!'

'Not at all,' said Holmes in an affable tone, pulling forward a chair for the young man. 'Pray let us know how we can be of assistance. You have, I perceive, just arrived from somewhere up the Thames valley, but not, I think, from Oxford on this occasion, although you are of course an undergraduate there, where you spend a fair amount of time on the water. How are the daffodils by the river this year?'

Our visitor looked surprised. 'You appear to know half of what I was going to tell you before I have even opened my mouth,' said he.

'It is not so amazing,' said Holmes. 'The only railway station from which you could reach here in less than ten minutes, however wind-like your progress, is the Great Western terminus at Paddington. All the trains arriving at Paddington have come down the Thames valley, but those from Oxford are run to a fairly regular timetable and do not reach London at the time your train must have arrived, hence you have come from elsewhere. Your blazer and muffler give you the cut of an undergraduate and that you spend some time on the river is suggested by the little enamel badge on your lapel, which displays the crossed oars of a college rowing club.'

'Oh, I see!' said Ashby. 'How very observant of you! Although I suppose it is all fairly obvious!'

'Everything is obvious when someone has explained it to you,' returned Holmes with some asperity. 'But, come! What has brought you to consult us on this bright Saturday morning?'

'I am, as you say, a member of the rowing club at my college,' replied Ashby after a moment. 'The college is All Saints and the rowing club is Pegasus. I am also a member of several other clubs and societies. There are, of course, innumerable societies at Oxford, catering for every possible interest. One of these at All Saints is a rather stuffy organisation, the Independent Language Society, the members of which seem to place an inordinate amount of emphasis on punctuation and the minutiae of grammar, and which has thus come to be known to outsiders, somewhat disparagingly, as "The ABC Club". Inspired by that, some of my fellow undergraduates at All Saints proposed setting up a new society, devoid of all pretensions to learning and scholarship, and devoted only to trivial enjoyment, to be known as "The XYZ Club". I joined last autumn, largely because the other fellows on my stair did. Altogether there were about a dozen of us, and at first it was very democratic, but it has since come to be dominated by one particular member.'

'Who is that?'

'Charles Churchfield. His family are very wealthy, I understand.'

'The bankers?'

'Yes, that is it. As far as I can make out, his whole life has been one of hedonistic pleasure, so why he should wish to institutionalise it by creating the XYZ Club, I'm sure I don't know. It was because of his domination of the group, I think, that several members left. There are now just five of us: Churchfield, myself, Stavros Xantopoulos, Archibald

Loxton and Philip Warnock. I, too, had had enough of it and intended to resign some time ago, but was dissuaded from doing so by some of the others. The trouble is that although I certainly have no objections to enjoying myself, Churchfield's idea of pleasure strikes me as fairly unpleasant at the best of times and downright malicious at others. Sometimes it just seems like old-fashioned debauchery, and at other times he seems to derive his greatest pleasure from being offensive to perfectly ordinary and unexceptionable people, and going out of his way to humiliate those less wealthy or less well-connected than himself. Just recently we had an elaborate supper at a restaurant. By the end of the evening, Churchfield had managed to insult all the waiters, break several dishes, two wine bottles and a chair, and then complained to the manager about the service we had received. The others were drunk and did not care, but I felt so ashamed I did not know where to look.'

'I think we understand the situation,' said Holmes. 'But what has brought you to consult us on this matter? My only advice would be for you to relinquish all connection with this unsavoury group of people and their immature and unpleasant activities.'

'I quite agree,' I said. 'Do not let them persuade you to do anything you do not wish to do. People of that sort always need weak cronies about them, without whom they are nothing. Plough your own furrow, not someone else's, and you will gain the respect of all decent-minded people, and, more importantly, you will retain your own self-respect.'

'Yes, of course, you are right,' said our visitor. 'I had already practically decided to do as you suggest. But the difficulty is that I am rather stuck with them for the next day or two and I fear there is something odd afoot, something that I don't understand.'

'Pray, let us have the details,' said Holmes.

'It was decided that we would spend the end of this week at Churchfield's family home, Challington House, which we have visited once before and which lies beside the Thames, not far from Bourne End. Don't ask me how this was decided, or by whom, as I wasn't present when the others were discussing it. The house is apparently closed up at the moment, as Churchfield's family are travelling on the Continent, and Churchfield said we could have an entertaining time there, "untrammelled by social conventions and artificial restrictions" as he put it. The others all travelled down there yesterday afternoon, but I pleaded a prior engagement of having to visit a cousin of mine at Maidenhead and said I would join them later. In fact, this "engagement" was not such a definite one as I pretended. It was true enough that I had been meaning to visit my cousin for some time, but my main reason for absenting myself from Churchfield's house for a few hours was to avoid the excessive drinking and gambling that I knew would be a prominent feature of Friday afternoon.

'I paid a pleasant visit to my cousin and then, the day being a breezy one, had an idea. He is a keen rower and sailor, as I am, and has a small sailing dinghy in which we have passed many a pleasant hour on the river. I asked if I might borrow the dinghy, my idea being that I would sail it upriver and arrive at Churchfield's house by water. Just before I was about to set off, however, there was a heavy and prolonged shower of rain which set me back about an hour, and by the time I left the day had become grey and overcast.

'I had been making reasonable progress for some time when there came another heavy rain shower and I was drenched. I didn't mind that too much, but as the rain cleared, the wind dropped and I found myself becalmed in the middle of the river. I unshipped the oars and rowed for a while, but the current was running strongly against me and my progress was very slow. Presently the wind got up again, but it was very uneven and gusting from almost every quarter but the south, which, of course, is where I would have liked it to be. I was thus obliged to tack back and forth across the stream, and progress was again very slow. All this time, the light was fading. However bright the day may be at this time of the year, it never lasts very long. Soon the light had gone altogether, when I was still some distance from Churchfield's boathouse.

'The moon was up, which was a help, but whenever it went behind a cloud, I couldn't see a thing. Eventually, one brief burst of moonlight revealed that I was at last approaching the boathouse. It was fortunate that I knew where to find it, as it appeared now as little more than a vague, grey shape. I dropped the sail and took up the oars again. Next moment I ran slap-bang into a very large houseboat which was riding at anchor in midstream with no lights displayed. The collision almost threw me into the water and I very nearly lost my oars in the darkness. At least I was only rowing; had I been sailing I think the dinghy would probably have capsized. I was a bit shaken up by this, but recovered and rowed my way into the boathouse without further mishap. Of course, it was pitch black in there, and I couldn't see a thing, but I knew there was a wooden walkway by the side wall and I felt my way along this with my hands, until, with a jolt, the dinghy hit something. I leaned over the prow and my hands touched what was clearly another small skiff. Returning my hands to the footway at the side, I located a mooring-ring, tied the boat up, picked up my bag and stepped out.

'It was at that point that I felt I could do with a spot of light. I didn't want to trip over something and break my neck, or fall into the water. I took out a box of matches and struck one. For half a second I was dazzled by the sudden light, then, with a shock so unexpected and alarming that I can scarcely describe it, I saw that there was someone else there in the boathouse, someone who was standing perfectly still and watching me. It was the face of a young lady, quite beautiful, staring rigidly at me in perfect silence. I think I cried out in surprise and took a step backwards. The match burnt my finger and I tossed it away as it went out. Then – I don't quite know what happened – I think I struck my head on something hard behind me and can remember no more.

'When I came to, I was lying on the lawn in the dark, with Churchfield leaning over me, holding a lantern, a look of concern on his face.

'"Thank goodness!" said he as I stirred. "I thought you were never going to wake up!"

'He turned and called out, and the others – Loxton, Xantopoulos and Warnock – appeared out of the darkness from somewhere behind him. They asked me what had happened to me and I said I didn't know. "I must have banged my head on something," I said.

"'I was in the garden," said Churchfield as he helped me to my feet, "when I heard a noise – a cry, I think – from the boathouse. I went in to have a look and found you laid out, unconscious, on the walkway. I carried you out here and went to tell the others. What on earth were you doing in there?"

"'I came by sailing-boat," I replied, gingerly feeling the back of my head, which was throbbing with pain.

"'Yes, I could see that," said Churchfield. "Your boat is in there."

"'Wait a moment," I interrupted as the recent events came back to me. "There was someone else in there."

"'What!" cried Churchfield. "Burglars?"

'I shook my head. "I don't know who it was. I saw a girl – a young lady, I mean. She was just staring at me."

'Churchfield looked puzzled. "Did she say anything? No? Oh, wait a minute!" he cried all at once. "I think I know what it is."

'He led the way to the boathouse, and pushed open the back door. "My sister, Lavinia, had her portrait painted a few months ago, but when she saw the result, she hated it. She refused to have it in the house, and it ended up down here. That must be what you saw, Ashby."

'He held his lantern up to show me. Leaning against the wall on a broad work-bench at the back of the boathouse was a life-sized portrait of a handsome young lady. "There," said he. "Isn't that the face you saw?"

'I frowned, trying to remember. "I suppose it must be," I said, "although it doesn't seem exactly the same."

"'But you saw it for only a moment," said Churchfield. "It must be the same. I don't blame you for being startled, Ashby. It's enough to unnerve anyone, having that face staring at you out of the darkness!"

"'Oh, I don't know," said Loxton, laughing. "I can think of worse faces to see! Come along, Ashby! Let's get back to the house and I'll mix you a restorative drink!"

'Later that evening, when the others were playing cards, I went to get myself some bread and cheese from the kitchen, but mistakenly went through the wrong doorway and found myself in what appeared to be a dining-room. As I glanced about, holding up a lamp, my eye was drawn to a blank space on the wall at one end of the room. A large rectangular shape on the wallpaper was a slightly lighter shade than the rest of the wall, as if a picture that had hung there for some considerable time had recently been removed. I could not help wondering if the picture in question was the portrait of Churchfield's sister, Lavinia.

'I used my sore head as an excuse to retire early and, as I lay in bed, reconsidered the events of the evening. I had a strong suspicion that the picture that was now in the boathouse had only been placed there that evening, while I lay unconscious. There was something about the girl's hair in the picture and the angle of her gaze that were not quite as I remembered them. Of course, I might have been mistaken, but I did not think I was. What it might mean, though, I could not imagine.

'This morning I rose earlier than the others and told Churchfield, who was still in bed, that I had previously promised to visit my great-aunt today. She lives in Bayswater, just a stone's throw from Paddington Station.

'"Are you not coming with us to poke fun at the hopeless local football team?" asked Churchfield in a tone of disappointment. "You are becoming something of a part-time member of the XYZ Club, Ashby!"

'I apologised for not telling him of my plans earlier, but insisted that I could not let my aged great-aunt down. "Don't worry, Churchfield," I said. "I shall be back this afternoon without fail."

'"If you get back before four," he said, "don't come here, but go directly to the football field. We'll all be there." With that, he closed his eyes, as if to go back to sleep. As I was leaving his bedroom, however, I happened to glance back and saw that his eyes were open and he was watching me. He closed his eyes quickly as I turned, but he had not been quite quick enough. This little incident left me with an unpleasant feeling, as I hurried off to the railway station.'

'It is an entertaining story,' said Holmes, when we had sat for some time in silence, 'but I am not clear what it is you wish us to do.'

'Possibly, nothing,' replied Ashby. 'It may be that my misgivings are groundless, and that today and tomorrow will pass off with nothing untoward occurring. But I cannot shake off the feeling that something odd is afoot, something of which I know nothing, and if so it will be a great support to me to know that I have related the matter to you. Would you be able to come, if I were to send for you?'

'Certainly, if you considered the circumstances warranted our presence. Is there anything else you can think of that has increased your misgivings?'

'It is difficult to put my finger on anything definite, but there seems something at Challington House that is not quite right. More than once yesterday evening, I had the impression that one or more of the others was watching me and, in the case of Churchfield, it was always with a calculating expression in his eyes.'

'Very well,' said Holmes, taking out his note-book. 'If you could give me a little more detail about your fellow-members of the XYZ Club, it would be helpful.'

'There's not much I can tell you, I'm afraid. These men are friends of mine in college, but I don't know a great deal about them outside of that. Loxton's family come from Warwickshire, their claim to fame being that some forebear invented the Loxton Steam Regulator, which, I understand, had a great vogue in the early days of steam locomotion, although it has now been superseded. Xantopoulos is from Greece, as you would guess from his name, where his father apparently owns a great number of olive-groves and fishing-boats. Warnock's father is vicar of some rural parish near Ashbourne, in Derbyshire. Churchfield, as I mentioned earlier, is from the banking family of that name. Churchfield's Bank is, I believe, one of the very oldest in the City of London.'

'Thank you,' said Holmes. 'That will do for the moment. I shall see if I can discover anything today which might be relevant, but I shall do nothing more unless I hear from you. If you do wish us to come, a telegram any hour of the day or night will bring us. If the situation meets your worst fears, do not attempt to explain it in your telegram. Simply use a code-word.'

Ashby nodded. 'I understand. In that case I shall use the name of my rowing-club – "Pegasus" – but hope I shall not have to do so. Now I shall leave the matter in your hands, Mr Holmes, and pay my belated respects to Great-Aunt Caroline!'

Holmes went out shortly after Ashby had left us and did not return until late in the afternoon. He had, I knew, numerous sources of information scattered about London and I looked forward to hearing the results of his enquiries. When he returned, however, he was unforthcoming. I asked him if he had learnt anything of significance, but he shook his head.

'There are several possibilities,' he replied, and no more than that would he say.

As I retired to my bed that night, I wondered when – if ever – we should hear from Julian Ashby again. I could not have imagined then quite how soon it would be.

I was awakened abruptly the following morning to find Holmes drawing back my bedroom curtains.

'What is it?' I asked in momentary confusion. 'What is the time?'

'Just before eight. We have had a message from young Ashby.' He held up a telegram. 'It's "Pegasus", Watson. Mrs Hudson was woken up earlier by the messenger and was none too pleased, but her temper is now soothed and she is making us a pot of coffee. You will have to hurry, though, old fellow. The train to Bourne End leaves Paddington at eight-forty.'

The streets were still almost deserted and very quiet when we left the house, a lone church bell ringing somewhere in the distance. At Paddington station, however, which we reached with just a few minutes to spare, there was already quite a crowd, and a general air of bustle. We had bought our tickets and were looking for our train when I observed a familiar figure hurrying on to the platform ahead of us.

'Surely that is Inspector Lestrade,' I said.

'It certainly is,' said Holmes. 'Lestrade!' he called, and the policeman turned in surprise.

'Why, Mr Holmes and Dr Watson!' he said. 'I can't stop to talk, I'm afraid. My train leaves in less than a minute.'

'Where are you bound?' asked Holmes.

'Somewhere called Bourne End,' replied Lestrade, resuming his hurried progress along the platform. 'And you?'

'Bourne End,' said Holmes. 'We can travel down together and see if our business bears any relation to yours. Here is a suitable compartment!'

In a moment we had climbed aboard. A few seconds later the guard blew his whistle and, with a hiss of steam, the train pulled slowly out of the station.

'Now,' said Holmes, as we picked up speed and were rattling along through the western suburbs, 'this train doesn't stop until Maidenhead, so we have plenty of time in which to compare notes.' He gave Lestrade a sketch of what Julian Ashby had told us the previous day. 'Are your inquiries related to any of that?' he asked the policeman as he finished.

'I'm not sure if they are or not,' replied Lestrade with a frown. 'What you've told me all seems fairly inconsequential, if I may say so. My own business is considerably more substantial. It's a suspicious death,' he continued, in answer to Holmes's query, 'probably murder.'

'Murder?'

Lestrade nodded. 'I don't know the name of the victim, but it's evidently not your client if he's been able to send you a telegram. I was on early duty at Scotland Yard this morning when a message came through from the Buckinghamshire Constabulary, asking us to send a detective inspector as soon as possible to this Bourne End place. Apparently there's been a bad fire there, but whether that's connected to the murder or not, I have no idea. And that, I'm afraid, is all I know.'

I could see that Holmes was disappointed at this lack of information, but as there was nothing we could do about it, the conversation passed on to other subjects. The day had started brightly, but by the time we reached Maidenhead, heavy clouds were rolling in from the south-west and, as we alighted at our destination, the sky was overcast and grey. We were met outside the station by a uniformed police officer who introduced himself as Inspector Welch. Lestrade explained the reason for our presence, and Welch nodded his head.

'Yes,' said he. 'It's Challington House where it's all happened. There were five young men staying there alone. They had been drinking, and we think that one of them must have left a candle burning downstairs, for a fire broke out after they'd all retired to bed. By a stroke of good fortune, the local constable was passing on his beat at that time, saw smoke pouring out of a window and at once took charge of the situation. After making sure that everyone was out of the house, he summoned the fire-brigade, but by the time they got there the house was a raging inferno and they haven't been able to save it. It's little more than a burnt-out shell now.'

'How does the suspicious death fit into all this?' asked Lestrade.

'It's not clear,' said Welch. 'The facts of the matter are a bit muddled at the moment. I think it best if you hear an account of it from the young men themselves. They're all in the Black Bull at present.'

He led the way along the road to a large old inn. As we entered, a group of young men sitting round a table turned to look, their features expressing tiredness and anxiety. One stood up as he saw us, whom I recognised as Julian Ashby.

'Mr Holmes,' he cried, coming forward to meet us. 'Thank the Lord you have come! The past twelve hours have been like a nightmare!'

At Holmes's request he introduced us to his companions, Warnock, Xantopoulos and Loxton.

'And Churchfield?' queried Holmes. 'Is he not here?'

'I very much fear that he may have perished in the blaze,' replied Ashby in a distraught tone. 'He was going to rouse the fire-brigade, but said that there was something he wanted to save from the house first and that was the last time I saw him. He never reached the fire-station, and the constable, who arrived only a few minutes after Churchfield had spoken to me, said he had seen no one on the road.'

Holmes nodded. 'Perhaps you had best start at the beginning. Tell us, as briefly as you can, all that has happened since you left us yesterday morning. I have given Inspector Lestrade a sketch of what you told us then, and I am sure he is as keen as we are to know what has happened.'

'After leaving your chambers,' said Ashby, 'I went straight to my great-aunt's house and was there nearly two hours. I then caught the next train from Paddington and got back here in the middle of the afternoon. I went directly to the football field, as Churchfield had suggested, where my friends were watching the local team play. When that finished, we returned to the house, lit a fire and made something to eat. Our evening passed pleasantly enough, in drinking, eating, playing skittles and cards and so on. We were all so tired in the end that we were not particularly late in retiring and were all in bed before midnight.

'I suppose I had been in bed about an hour, but had probably only been asleep for half an hour, when I was awakened by the sudden opening of the door. Churchfield was standing in the doorway fully dressed, with a candle in his hand.

'"Ashby!" he cried. "Get up, man! Quickly! There's a fire! Throw your clothes on and wake the others, then get out of the house! Quickly now!" he repeated. "I'm going for the fire-brigade, but first there's something I must try to save!"

'With that he was gone. I sprang from my bed, flung on my dressing-gown and slippers, and went to wake the others. I remembered that the door to Warnock's room was opposite mine, but was not sure where anyone else was sleeping. It's a very big house, with an enormous lot of bedrooms, some of them off odd branches of the upstairs corridor, and I really wasn't familiar with it. I woke Warnock first and gave him the alarm, then, after looking into an empty room next to his, found Xantopoulos's room and shook him awake. I looked into another empty room and then tried the door of the room next to mine. The door was locked, so I felt sure it was Loxton's room, although why he should have bothered to lock it, I couldn't imagine. I banged on the door several times, but got no answer.

"'Loxton!" I called. "Loxton! Wake up, you idiot!" Again I banged on the door without eliciting any response.

"'Break the door down,' called Warnock from his bedroom. "You'll never wake him otherwise!"

'I threw all my weight against the door, but it did no good. I then kicked violently at the lock and, on the third attempt, with a splintering of wood, the door burst open. I dashed into the room, shouting as I did so. I could feel heat rising from the bare wooden floor.

"'Loxton!" I cried. "Loxton! Wake up!"

'I had bent to the figure on the bed and started to shake him by the shoulder when there came a loud voice from behind me.

"'What the devil is all this racket, Ashby? And why are you bellowing my name over and over?"

'I turned in astonishment. Loxton was standing in the doorway. "What is all this?" he asked. "What's going on?"

"'But if you're there," I said, "who on earth is this?" I pulled back the bed-cover and stepped back in horror at what was revealed: an older man, his mouth agape, his sightless eyes staring at the wall. "This man is dead," I cried.

"'Who is it?" cried the others, crowding into the room.

"'I've no idea. I've never seen him before. We've got to get him out of here. This floor is hot. The fire must be directly beneath it."

'I flung on my clothes in a trice, as did the others, and between us we carried the dead man out on to the lawn behind the house. Warnock took a look into a couple of the downstairs rooms and told us it was hopeless; the fire was blazing like a furnace. I told them that Churchfield had gone to rouse the fire-brigade, and as we were standing there on the lawn, wondering what on earth we should do, the local constable arrived in a great hurry and took charge of the situation. The rest I imagine you know.'

'Has anyone identified the dead man yet?' Holmes asked Inspector Welch, who shook his head. 'Any sign of Churchfield – dead or alive?'

Again the policeman shook his head. 'No one knows what it was that Churchfield wanted to get out of the house, but I think, as Mr Ashby says, that the poor devil may have been overcome by the smoke and heat. Once fires like that catch hold they can spread like lightning, and the constable says that it was already a raging inferno when he got here.'

Welch then suggested that Lestrade view the body of the dead man, which was at the police station, just a short walk away. Holmes went with them while I stayed with the young men in the Black Bull. They returned about five minutes later and I asked Holmes if he had learnt anything.

'Death was undoubtedly caused by a severe blow to the back of the head, some time in the past twenty-four hours,' said he, 'but of course it's impossible to say if the blow was the result of an accident or a deliberate attack. There's nothing in his pockets which might serve to identify him, but I found a small name-tag just below the collar inside his shirt, which bears the name "T. Wilkinson". There is also the return half of a ticket from Paddington to Bourne End in a pocket of his waistcoat. Inspector Lestrade has therefore sent a message to all London divisions, enquiring if anyone by the name of Wilkinson has been reported as missing there. And now,' he continued, addressing the policemen, 'I should like to examine the scene of this drama, at Challington House.'

'You'll not learn anything there,' said Inspector Welch in a dismissive tone, 'except how quickly a large house can be utterly destroyed by fire.'

'Well, well. Let us not prejudge the matter,' returned Holmes, as we left the inn, accompanied by young Ashby.

A walk of seven or eight minutes brought us to the gateway of Challington House. A broad drive swept up to the front door of what must have been a very large house, but was now just a blackened shell. Smoke still drifted up from somewhere within this ruin, but it appeared that the fire had all but burnt itself out.

'You see?' said Welch. 'The house is completely destroyed. There is nothing to be seen here.'

'It was not the house I wished to inspect,' returned Holmes, leading the way along the side of the smouldering ruin and into the large rear gardens, which sloped down gently towards the river. There, after a swift glance round, he made his way down to the boathouse at the end of the garden, pushed open the door and we followed him inside. It was a gloomy, shaded building. Most of it was taken up with space for mooring boats, but there was a broad flagged area at the back, upon which ropes, spars and general clutter were heaped. Against the rear wall was a work-bench on which a painting of a young lady stood, as Ashby had described. Along the side-wall was a footway made of wooden boards which extended to the front of the building.

'This, I take it, is your cousin's boat,' said Holmes to Ashby, indicating a small sailing-dinghy, moored to a ring on the footway. 'When you arrived on Friday evening, there was, you said, another small boat here, but now there is not.'

'Yes, that is strange,' remarked Ashby. 'Where can it have gone?'

Holmes did not reply, but walked to the very end of the footway and looked out on to the river. 'You also mentioned that there was a very large houseboat anchored in midstream with which you collided in the dark. That, too, is no longer present. Do you know if it was here on Saturday morning?'

'Yes, it was. I put my head in here briefly before setting off to catch the train to London, to make sure that my boat was tied up properly, and I remember noticing then that the houseboat was still there.'

'That is as I suspected. You know something of boats?'

'Yes.'

'Do you believe that such a vessel as the houseboat might be able to venture out on to the high seas?'

'I cannot be certain, but I think it might well be possible. It would depend on what sort of keel the boat has, and how rough the sea was, of course.'

'When you clambered from your boat on Friday evening, you must have been standing about here,' Holmes continued, 'but there is nothing hanging up here on which you might have struck your head. What I believe happened is this: they probably heard you collide with the houseboat and the sound of your oars in the water. One of them walked to the end of this footway, to see what was happening. You would have passed him in the dark and had no idea he was there, so that when you tied up your boat and climbed out, he would have been standing behind you. When you struck the match and saw the young woman over there, near the back wall, the person behind you struck you on the head with something. It was probably this!' Holmes added, as he bent down and picked up a short length of wood which was lying on the footway, by the wall.

'But who were these people?' asked Ashby in puzzlement.

'The Churchfields. Surely that is apparent.'

'The Churchfields? But they are travelling on the Continent.'

'I very much doubt that they were doing so before, but I believe that that is their aim now. Do you know if they have any property abroad?'

'Yes. I believe they have a house in the south of France.'

'Then that is where they are probably making for. Their intention is no doubt to cross the channel in the houseboat and enter the French canal system, getting as far south as they can that way and completing their journey by train if necessary.'

'This is absurd!' cried Inspector Welch. 'You make it sound as if they are running away!'

'That, I believe, is precisely what they are doing.'

'But the Churchfield family is one of the most respected in the district, one of the pillars of South Buckinghamshire society. Sir Lionel Churchfield is a local Justice of the Peace, and has been spoken of as a future Lord Mayor of London!'

'I cannot comment on the family's reputation here or anywhere else,' said Holmes, 'but only on what I learn with my own eyes and ears.'

'And what, precisely, have you learnt?' asked Lestrade.

Holmes hesitated a moment. 'Do any of you gentlemen have an account at Churchfield's Bank?' he asked at length. 'No? That is fortunate. What I am going to tell you is in the very strictest confidence. You must not breathe a word of it until these people have been apprehended. I have one or two very good sources of information in the City of London, and yesterday, after Mr Ashby had consulted me, I made some very detailed enquiries. It is common knowledge there that Churchfield's bank has been in difficulty in recent months over some very large loans they made last year in Brazil and Uruguay. They themselves have stated that there is no problem and have taken out loans from other financial institutions to cover any possible defaults. My source informs me, however, that these latter loans are all specifically short-term and the time for their repayment or renewal is this coming week, which is also the time that Churchfield's are due to announce their annual financial results. What will happen then, no one knows, but there are strong rumours circulating in the City that the bank will not be able to honour these loans and may collapse altogether. This, I believe, is the background to the little drama that has been played out here in the past two days.'

'I do not understand,' said Inspector Welch in a tone of perplexity. 'What can these financial rumours have to do with the fire here, or the dead man?'

'They must be related,' returned Holmes with emphasis. 'Mr Ashby saw Churchfield's sister in this boathouse on Friday evening – I don't believe for a moment that he could really have mistaken an oil-painting for a live woman – which means that the story of the family's travels on the Continent is a lie. But if they are not on the Continent, where are they? The fact that there has been a large houseboat moored here, which has vanished in the past twenty-four hours surely suggests the answer to that question.'

'But why on earth should they hide in the houseboat?' cried Lestrade in disbelief.

'Because, I should say, they know the bank will collapse on Monday and thousands will lose every penny they possess. It is Sunday today, when every bank and business in the country is closed, which of course gives them their best chance of escape. I think that everything that has happened here has been planned with precision. Had it not been for Mr Ashby's blundering into their meeting here on Friday evening, we should have had no idea what was afoot and they would probably have got clean away.'

'What can they hope to achieve by running away?' I asked.

'A life of ease and luxury, in all probability, Watson. I imagine their intention is to drop completely out of sight, perhaps even change their names, and to be never heard of again.'

'This all seems wild speculation,' said Welch. 'How does the dead man fit into your view of things? And what became of the Churchfield boy? Is he dead, too?'

'I imagine he is on the boat with the rest of his family,' said Holmes, shaking his head. 'Something that struck me in my client's account was that when Churchfield came to his room last night and asked him to give the alarm, Mr Ashby threw on his dressing-gown and hurried off to rouse the others, only returning to dress when he was sure they were all awake. He recognised instinctively, you see, that the preservation of life is far more important than being correctly dressed. But Mr Ashby said that when Churchfield appeared in his room he was fully dressed. This strongly suggests to me that Churchfield's apparent air of alarm and urgency was completely false. If he had just discovered the fire as he said, would he really have stopped to get dressed and do up all his buttons before warning his friends? Of course not. In fact, I doubt if he ever got undressed at all last night. More likely, he just waited until he judged the others were all asleep, then set about making the fire, no doubt watching it carefully to make sure it had taken hold and was blazing strongly before going to wake Mr Ashby. Also, his talk of trying to save something from the house, and then going to fetch the fire-brigade, was, I'm sure, nothing but a tissue of lies. I strongly suspect that after he had spoken to Mr Ashby, he came straight down here to join his family. He would have expected the house to burn down and for the remains of the dead man – if they were ever found – to be taken for his own. It is significant that the centre of the fire seems to have been directly beneath the room in which the body of the dead man lay. Of course, Churchfield did not expect that anyone would break down the locked bedroom door. That was the second thing that went wrong with their plan, the first, of course, being my client's surprise arrival in this boathouse on Friday evening. As to this poor fellow, Wilkinson, we cannot yet say who he is, but it would not surprise me if we learnt that he was an employee at Churchfield's Bank – and probably a fairly senior one, too.'

'What makes you think that?' I asked.

'If the Churchfields were loitering here when they were supposed to be abroad – which seems to me a certainty – then there must have been some good reason for it. The likeliest explanation is that they were waiting here for something and the fact that they have now gone suggests that that something arrived yesterday. If so, who could have brought it but the unfortunate Mr Wilkinson? What I suspect is that at close of business at the bank – which is early, of course, on a Saturday – he brought sufficient funds here to keep the Churchfield family in comfort for the rest of their lives. That, of course, is why Mr Ashby was told to go directly to the football ground when he returned from London. Churchfield did not want to risk Ashby running across his family or Wilkinson.'

'What exactly are you suggesting?' queried Lestrade. 'Do you think that Wilkinson came here with a satchel full of banknotes?'

'I doubt it, especially considering the family's probable destination. More likely it was internationally negotiable bonds, which the family could sell anywhere on the Continent, whenever they wished. If so, it is theft on a very grand scale: the money is not theirs, but belongs to their customers.'

'I can scarcely credit what you are saying!' said Inspector Welch in a tone of amazement. 'Such upright and correct people! Such esteemed figures in the district! What about Wilkinson, though? He must have been in it with them, so why is he dead?'

Sherlock Holmes shook his head. 'That we cannot say. Perhaps he had scruples about the whole business, or had only just realised what they were up to and threatened to make the matter public, or perhaps he had no scruples but demanded money from them to buy his silence. In any event, I imagine a quarrel blew up, blows were exchanged and one blow cost Wilkinson his life. Alternatively, they may have intended to murder him all along when he had served his purpose. They certainly intended to burn the house down. I can think of no other good reason why the members of the XYZ Club should have been invited here on this particular weekend, except to act as scapegoats and take the blame for the fire. Presumably there were things in the house – documents and so on – that the Churchfields wished to destroy. Wait a moment!' said Holmes, abruptly breaking off.

He slipped past the policemen, bent down and pulled something out from the dusty jumble of litter beneath the work-bench by the back wall. As he stood up, I saw that it was a black silk hat, bent and crushed out of shape. 'The name on the inside is "T. Wilkinson",' said Holmes. 'He was right-handed and spent much of his time using a pen,' he added, indicating a small inky stain on the front right edge of the rim. 'There is also a trace of blood inside the hat, at the back. It was here in this boathouse that Wilkinson was probably murdered.'

'That's good enough for me!' said Lestrade. 'Let's get back to the police station and see if we can't find where that boat has gone!'

'I can send a wire to Teddington Lock, to see if they've seen anything of it,' said Welch as we left the grounds of Challington House and hurried down the road.

When we reached the police station, the sergeant on duty informed Lestrade that a reply had already been received to his earlier enquiry concerning Wilkinson. The police station at Norwood stated that a Mr

Thomas Wilkinson had been reported missing the previous evening. He was, they said, deputy chief cashier at Churchfield's Bank in the City, but had failed to return from work that afternoon as usual. A few moments later, Inspector Welch received a reply from Teddington Lock, stating that such a houseboat as he described had passed through the lock earlier in the morning.

'Notify Scotland Yard, Deptford and all points east,' said Lestrade. 'Tell them that this boat must be stopped at all costs! I'm going back to town at once, Welch. You'd better come with me, Mr Ashby. You can help identify the boat and the Churchfield boy. Will you come, Mr Holmes?'

'We'll come with you as far as Paddington, at any rate,' returned Holmes. 'Then, I think, we'll leave the matter in your capable hands, Lestrade!'

Everything that my friend had predicted came to pass exactly as he had foretold, as I learnt from the newspapers the following evening. According to the *Echo*, the Churchfields' houseboat had eventually been stopped just off Greenwich Point, the whole family being taken into custody for questioning. They were subsequently charged with fraud, theft, arson and murder, although the last charge was later reduced to culpable homicide as it could not be proved that they had intended to murder Wilkinson when they struck him. Meanwhile, it was reported in the *Pall Mall Gazette* that Churchfield's Bank had been in chaos, and had not opened its doors to the public all day, eventually announcing at three o'clock in the afternoon that it could no longer continue trading. The *Globe*, taking a different perspective on the affair, heaped praise on Inspector Lestrade, 'without whose smart work and initiative', it remarked, 'a great crime might have gone undetected'.

'They do not mention you at all,' I said to my friend, as I finished reading these accounts of the case. 'They seem to believe that Lestrade solved the whole business by himself!'

'Thank goodness for that!' returned Holmes with a chuckle. 'I can assure you I had no desire to see my name linked with such a simple affair. Let Lestrade enjoy his moment of glory, Watson. One day we may need a favour from him. Meanwhile, let us hope that something a little more challenging turns up soon to exercise our intellects!'

The Adventure of the Velvet Mask

The cold winter of 1886 was made memorable for me by the remarkable series of cases handled by my friend, Sherlock Holmes, in which it was my privilege to observe his methods of work and make a record of the details. Especially notable among these cases were the mysterious death of the eminent archaeologist, Sir Montague Knelling, the scandal concerning the Liverpool and Malabar Shipping Company, and the outrageous theft of one of the most precious possessions of the Empire. Yet, sensational though these cases were, none was perhaps so interesting as that which concerned the old Albion Theatre and the peculiar persecution to which those employed there were subject. Indeed, of all the cases in which I was able to assist Sherlock Holmes, during the time we lodged together in Baker Street, there are few which are impressed more vividly upon my memory.

I had returned to our chambers early in the afternoon of a chilly January day, to find that Sherlock Holmes was entertaining a visitor. Beside the blazing fire sat a graceful, handsome woman, elegantly attired in a maroon costume with salmon-pink trimmings and overskirt. Upon her head was a small turban-like bonnet, adorned with feathers of the same colours.

I had pushed open the door of our sitting-room with my thoughts elsewhere, hardly aware of my surroundings. But now, as I mumbled an apology for intruding, and made to withdraw, I hesitated. Something in the visitor's features plucked a cord in my memory, as she turned her head in my direction and raised an inquiring eyebrow. We had met before, I was convinced. If so, I ought, from politeness, to acknowledge the fact. But I could not think where this meeting might have taken place and, thus, for a long moment, stood in what no doubt appeared perfectly idiotic silence. Sherlock Holmes evidently perceived my difficulty, for, in an instant, he had sprung from his chair and come to my rescue.

'My esteemed friend and colleague, Dr Watson,' cried he with a chuckle, as he took my arm and drew me into the room; 'Miss Isabel Ballantyne, with whose celebrity you are doubtless already familiar.'

I took the hand which the lady extended, thinking what an idiot I was not to have recognised at once one of the most celebrated actresses of the day. Scarcely three months previously I had sat in the stalls and applauded at Isabel Ballantyne's performance in a musical comedy entitled *The Pirate Queen*, in which her distinguished presence had served to elevate what was really only mediocre fare into a most enjoyable evening. I had also seen her be both captivating and amusing as Beatrice in *Much Ado About Nothing*, a portrayal which most critics thought unlikely to be bettered.

I recalled, also, in that instant of recognition, other things I had read of Miss Ballantyne over the years, of how her glittering success upon the London stage had not been accompanied by equal felicity in her private life. Those in the society papers who claimed to know about such things had spoken frequently of her many friends and admirers, but had hinted, also, at a private loneliness or melancholy at the centre of this giddy whirl of public life. Until, that is, the arrival upon the scene of Captain William Trent, the dashing former cavalry officer and big-game hunter, who had, against general expectation, wooed and won Miss Ballantyne's heart. Hitherto little known in London society, he had at once assumed the heroic status of a modern-day Lochinvar, riding in from afar to rescue Miss Ballantyne from her melancholy. Anyone who could achieve what so many had aspired to in vain was clearly worthy of the very highest respect. The attitude of other men towards Captain Trent was, in consequence, therefore, largely one of genuine admiration, but tinged just a little, perhaps, with envy. Since Miss Ballantyne's marriage to Captain Trent, eighteen months previously, her name had appeared less frequently in the society press, and it was supposed that she had at last found that private peace with which to balance her public glamour.

I stole another swift glance at our visitor's face as I took her hand. Although no longer in the first flush of youth, she was, if anything, more attractive than ever. Those soft, dark, expressive eyes, that gentle, warm smile upon her lips – in an experience of female beauty which extended over many nations and races, I had never, I felt, descried a more winning or charming face.

'I am very pleased to make your acquaintance,' said I, sounding somewhat more formal than I had intended.

'Delighted,' returned she.

'Miss Ballantyne was about to describe to me a curious series of incidents which have occurred lately at Hardy's Theatre,' said Holmes. 'Richard Hudson Hardy's company is in rehearsal there for a new production which is to open in three days' time. I wonder, madam, if I could trouble you to repeat the gist of what you have already told me, so that my friend may understand the situation?'

'Certainly,' replied Miss Ballantyne, in that light, musical voice which had so captivated and bewitched London theatre-goers in recent years. 'You should first understand, then, Dr Watson, that I was invited by Mr Hardy to join his company last autumn. He wished me to take the principal female role in a new production he was mounting, of a play entitled *The Lavender Girl.*'

'I don't believe I've heard of it,' I remarked.

'It is newly written, by Mr Hardy himself. His intention is to offer the theatre-going public something a little different. At this time of year, as you will know, theatres present pantomimes in such abundance that even the most avid enthusiast must at last become sated, and long for something different. It is Mr Hardy's belief that *The Lavender Girl* might be just the thing to tempt the public's jaded palate. It is something of a tragicomedy, and has a great number of songs, both old and new. From the first moment I saw the script I was convinced it would be a success, and at once agreed to take part. The other principal actors are Ludovic Xavier, who is always popular, and is returning to the London stage for the first time in over a year; Jimmy Webster, who can generally be relied upon to amuse an audience; and a young girl, Lydia Summers. She is a newcomer. She is a little unpolished at the moment and I'm not certain that she has much talent, but she seems keen to learn, anyway.

'We began rehearsals at Hardy's Theatre a few weeks before Christmas. I don't know if you are aware, Dr Watson, but Hardy's Theatre is the old Albion. It had been closed down for some years when Mr Hardy bought it, about three years ago, and he thought that by renaming it he might give it a fresh start. He also considered that by attaching his name to it, the reputation he had acquired for providing entertaining fare would help to stimulate interest. Do you know the Albion Theatre, Dr Watson?'

'Is that not the theatre down the Waterloo Road, where the comedian Solomon Tanner used to reign supreme, a decade and more ago?'

'That is correct. If you recall Solomon Tanner, you may recall, too, that his popularity was such that he also took the theatre next door to the Albion, the Southwark Palace, and at the height of his fame used to perform in both theatres in the course of a single evening, in two different plays. This *tour de force* of the Thespian arts – or financial greed, as some termed it – was not destined to last very long, however. As you may remember, he lost his life in the terrible fire that consumed the Southwark Palace late one night, following a performance there. Since then, the Palace has remained boarded up and unused, a blackened shell beside the Albion. I mention this matter because there have been persistent stories since that time that the Albion is haunted by the ghost of Solomon Tanner, who returns to appraise what is being offered to the public there. It is said that if he does not care for what he sees, he causes disruption to the production.'

My features must have betrayed my surprise at this digression into the supernatural, for Miss Ballantyne paused.

'You are wondering, no doubt,' said she after a moment, 'why I should be speaking to you of such things. After all, there are many theatres which are popularly supposed to be haunted in some way and, of course, the very idea sounds absurd when one speaks of it in broad daylight. But when one finds oneself alone late at night, backstage in a dark, silent theatre, then it is not so easy to rid oneself of these thoughts. I would offer ten guineas to anyone who undertook to remain all night alone in the Empire Theatre in Birmingham, for instance, or the old Playhouse in Bristol, confident that I should not be a penny poorer when the next day dawned. But, still, as it is unlikely that you are acquainted with these theatres, and I certainly have no intention of renewing my own acquaintance with them, this is not to the point. I mention the matter only so that you will understand that such traditions are not uncommon in old theatres. Any odd or unexplained occurrences are likely to provoke such beliefs, especially in the younger or more timid members of the company. That is precisely what has occurred at the Albion, where several members of the chorus have become very nervous at what has been happening there. Already, one young lady has left the company altogether, as a result of an incident.'

'But,' interrupted Sherlock Holmes, who had all this time been leaning back in his chair, with his eyes closed, as he listened to his visitor's account, 'as I have no reputation for laying troublesome ghosts by the heels, but only their earthbound counterparts, you consider, I take it, that the mysterious occurrences at the Albion have a more mundane cause.'

'That is correct,' returned Miss Ballantyne. 'I am convinced that some malicious person is deliberately creating mischief and I should very much like to know who that person is. It may be that it began as a series of practical jokes, by someone with an unpleasant sense of humour; but it has now gone beyond that. The more recent incidents have been very dangerous and I am concerned that if it continues one of the company will be seriously hurt.'

'The details, if you please!'

'Some of the things that have happened are so trivial that I am almost embarrassed to mention them,' began Miss Ballantyne.

'Nevertheless,' returned Holmes, 'omit no incident, however trivial, and permit me to judge as to the importance or otherwise of each of them.'

'Very well. In the very first week of rehearsals, Jimmy Webster arrived at the theatre one day to find that someone had emptied a tin of paint on to the floor of his dressing-room.'

'Was the paint of a type which was being used in the theatre?'

'Yes. It had been taken from the decorators' store. That same day, a small set of steps upon which I was standing collapsed and I twisted my ankle badly. Of course, it may have been an accident. One cannot know for certain. Under other circumstances I should probably have thought so and forgotten it by now; but in this case I am not so sure. At the beginning of the second week, we were rehearsing a scene in which Ludovic – Mr Xavier – is required to yank open a door fiercely. He accordingly seized the door-knob, as he had done on previous occasions, and gave it a sharp pull. This time, however, he at once let out a cry of pain. Even as he did so, the flat – that is, the piece of scenery – in which the door was set tumbled forwards and fell upon him. He was not seriously hurt, for the scenery was not heavy, but he was, as you will imagine, extremely upset. When the flat was lifted off him, there was blood on his clothes and it was feared at first that he was badly injured. But the blood had all come from a cut on his hand and it was discovered that protruding from the door-handle was a sharp nail. Ludovic was shouting and crying out that someone was trying to murder him, and it took some time to soothe his agitated nerves.

'The carpenters who were responsible for the scenery were summoned, but expressed puzzlement at what had happened. The scenery, they said, had been adequately fixed when last they had inspected it, the door had opened easily and the door-knob had not had any nails sticking out of it. At length, the incident was ascribed to that species of ill-fortune which does sometimes bedevil the preparation of a large and complex theatrical production. A few days later, however, a young girl in the female chorus hurt her arm when she fell heavily as she came on to the stage. It was found that a length of cord had been fastened across an opening on to the stage, a few inches above the ground, and this is what had tripped her up. No one knew why it was there and the matter remained a mystery. The girl was badly shaken by the incident, however, and within two days had withdrawn from the production altogether. This was a great shame, for she was a very nice young lady. Physically, she was not badly injured, but her heart was sorely wounded to think that someone should dislike her so much as to play such a nasty trick upon her. Personally, I wondered if the trick had really been intended for someone else, for it seemed likely that the cord over which she had tripped had been in position since the morning, and the schedule of rehearsals had been altered during the day.'

'Do you know who might have fallen foul of the cord if the order of rehearsals had not been changed?' interrupted Holmes.

'I think it might have been Lydia Summers. I cannot be certain on the point, however, and I did not mention my thoughts on the matter to anyone else. At any event, Miss Summers was not spared for long. A day or two after this incident, she came to my dressing-room. She was pale and appeared upset, and when she spoke she was very agitated. She told me that she had been passing along the basement corridor, near the wardrobe rooms, when someone had come up behind her and pushed her violently to the floor. When she looked round, there was no one to be seen. She was not badly hurt, but the incident had left her feeling shaken and nervous.

'The following week, I was rehearsing on stage with the chorus, under the direction of Mr Hardy, when all the lights in the house abruptly went out and we were plunged into pitch blackness. It was evident that the gas supply had failed. It was very dangerous, as we could not see where we were treading, and parts of the stage were littered with pieces of half-made scenery, lumps of wood, tools and so on. Not only that, but of course if the gas supply had then been restored, the theatre would soon have been full of it, escaping unburnt from the unlit lamps. There could have been a dreadful explosion, and we might all have been killed. Fortunately, Mr Hardy had a lantern with him. He quickly lit this and hurried down to the basement, to examine the main stop-tap. It was turned fully on and it seemed the gas supply had been restored, for there was a dreadful smell of gas everywhere. He at once turned the stop-tap off, and sent everyone round the theatre to turn off all the individual taps by the lamps and open all the windows. It was some time before the gas cleared and we were able to light the lamps once more and continue with our rehearsal. Mr Hardy reported the matter to the gas company and they sent an inspector round to investigate, but he could find nothing wrong. He said that there had certainly been no interruption to the main gas supply and could only suggest that someone had turned off the main tap in the theatre basement, waited for a few minutes and then turned it back on again.

'Mr Hardy, understandably, declared that a preposterous suggestion. "Why should anyone do such a thing?" he demanded.

'At this, the gas inspector shook his head and said he was sure he didn't know. Then he swore again that the gas supply had been perfectly in order until it reached the theatre. There was nothing to be done, so Mr Hardy let the matter drop. But although he has not referred to it since, it has caused him, I believe, some anxiety.'

'You say you were rehearsing with the chorus, when the gas went out,' interrupted Holmes. 'Where were the other principal players at that time?'

'In their dressing-rooms, I believe,' replied Miss Ballantyne. 'Each of us – Mr Xavier, Mr Webster, Miss Summers and myself – has a private dressing-room, in the basement. I believe I heard some of them calling out in the dark when I followed Mr Hardy down into the basement after the lights had gone out.'

'Was there anyone else in the basement at the time?'

'Only the seamstresses. There are four of them. The sewing-room in which they work is next to the large rooms in which the company's costumes are stored. They have been working hard for several weeks on getting the costumes ready for *The Lavender Girl*. It is a sizeable task, for some of the costumes are very elaborate, and there are a lot of them.'

'I see,' said Holmes. 'Did any of the seamstresses report hearing or seeing anyone in the basement at the time of the incident?'

Miss Ballantyne shook her head. 'The door to their room is a stout one and it was closed at the time. Besides, they prattle so much while they are working that they probably would not have heard anything, anyway.'

'Very well,' said Holmes. 'Pray continue with your account!'

'One afternoon last week, I was in my dressing-room when there came all at once a terrific racket of shouting and banging. I left my room and hurried along the corridor in the direction of the noise. As I did so, it abruptly ceased, but when I turned a corner of the corridor, I ran into a crowd of people surrounding Jimmy Webster, just outside his dressing-room, which is some distance from mine, near the costume department. I gathered that someone had locked his door and turned his light off, leaving him in the dark.

'"How did you get out, then?" I asked him. "Did someone unlock the door from the outside?"

'He shook his head. "That's the strange thing: when the girls from the sewing-room tried my door, they say it opened easily and wasn't locked at all!"

'"How do you explain it?" I asked.

'"The door was certainly locked when I tried to open it," said he. "There is always a key in the outside of the lock, although I never use it. Someone must have turned the key and locked it. Then, just before these ladies arrived, when I had given up trying to open the door and was reduced to simply banging on it for all I was worth, he must have unlocked the door again and run off."

'"Did you see anyone?" I asked the seamstresses, but they shook their heads.

'"How was your light turned off?" I asked Jimmy.

'He pointed to a gas-tap on a pipe which runs along the corridor outside his room. "It must have been turned off there," said he.

"'It's not turned off now," observed Ludovic Xavier, who had joined us as Jimmy had been speaking.

"'I don't need you to tell me that, Xavier," returned Jimmy. "Clearly, whoever had turned it off also turned it back on again when my light had gone out."

"'It's turned off inside your room," said Xavier, putting his head into Jimmy's dressing-room. "There's no smell of gas in here."

"'Well, of course there isn't," retorted Webster. "I turned it off myself after the light went out! I wasn't inclined to sit there patiently waiting to be asphyxiated!"

"'It all seems a little odd to me," remarked Xavier with a shake of the head.

"'How very perceptive of you!" cried Webster in an ironic tone. "'Odd' is certainly the word, Xavier; and it ain't so little, either!" With that, he pushed his way past us into his room, relit the gas, and shut the door.

'I did not know what to make of this incident. By itself, it might have appeared merely a silly prank, but following all the other incidents as it did, I could not but think that it was connected with them in some way. Some of the things that have happened may have been simply accidents, some appear to be spiteful little tricks, unpleasant but not serious; but the recent incidents with the gas are more serious. If interfering with the gas supply is someone's idea of a joke, then that person must have a very warped and unpleasant sense of humour.'

There was a note of great agitation in Miss Ballantyne's voice as she spoke these last words, and she clasped and unclasped her hands in a tense, nervous manner. Sherlock Holmes opened his eyes, leaned forward in his chair and placed the tips of his fingers upon the back of her hand.

'Madam, you are frightened,' said he in a soothing tone.

'I would not deny it,' returned his visitor, in a voice which trembled with emotion. 'You may dismiss it as a mere fancy, but I have had an apprehension of danger since the first moment I entered the Albion to begin rehearsals. It is a place of strange noises and echoes, especially in the basement. Once or twice I have been down there alone – or so I thought – and have heard footsteps in the corridor outside my room, but when I looked, there was no one there. Whether what I heard could have been caused by the odd draughts that blow down there, or by the dripping of rainwater, I don't know. On another occasion, when I was really sure there was no one about, I had come down the stairs from the auditorium and turned into the basement corridor, when, out of the corner of my eye, I thought I saw someone at the other end of the corridor, who vanished round a corner at that precise moment.'

'Could you see who it was?'

Miss Ballantyne shook her head. 'The lighting down there is very dim. I had the merest impression of a dark figure, that is all. I do not know what will happen next, Mr Holmes, but I fear that it may be something dreadful.'

'Perhaps, also, you fear that you may be the next victim selected by this unseen malefactor?'

'That is so. I have seen others fall foul of his tricks. Perhaps next time it will be me.'

'What does anyone else think of it all?' enquired Holmes after a moment. 'What, for instance, is your husband's opinion?'

Miss Ballantyne hesitated, and her hands began again their restless twining.

'There is a difficulty there,' she responded at last. 'My husband is not greatly interested in theatrical matters generally, except in so far as they affect my own career, and until this week I had spoken little of these things to him. I had mentioned one or two of the incidents, but in a light-hearted way only. I have been afraid to unburden myself of my true feelings.'

'Afraid? Why?'

'I know his character only too well. I knew that if he understood my anxieties he would consider nothing but my safety and insist that I withdraw from the production at once. When I did at last speak freely to him on the subject, two nights ago, his response was precisely as I had expected. "Leave the production," said he. "I will square it financially with Hardy." But I told him I could not do it. Such a course would be disastrous. It would let down badly everyone who has worked so hard to get *The Lavender Girl* ready and to ensure that it is a success. He himself would lose a considerable amount of money if the play did not open, for he has provided a third of the finance for the production. But I know he would dismiss that as unimportant in comparison with my well-being.'

'If so,' interrupted Holmes, 'he would be correct. You must not place yourself in danger merely on account of financial considerations, Miss Ballantyne. You no doubt consider you owe some loyalty to your theatrical colleagues, but this loyalty must be tempered by regard for your own safety. The difficulty, of course, lies in estimating the degree of danger which you and your colleagues face.'

'My husband said much the same, Mr Holmes. I did eventually succeed in persuading him that I must continue with *The Lavender Girl*; but he has proposed that in future he be present in the theatre as often as possible, whenever I am working there. I readily accepted this suggestion, as you will imagine. It will be heartening for me, to know that he is close at hand. And yet,' Miss Ballantyne added after a moment's pause, 'so secretly and cunningly has the persecutor wrought his work, that I wonder whether the presence of even a regiment of soldiers could prevail against him.'

Holmes nodded. 'How does Mr Hudson Hardy view the matter?' said he.

'He dismisses my fears as groundless,' returned Miss Ballantyne, 'and tries to laugh them away. "Why," said he, yesterday evening, when we were discussing the matter, "I have never known a production yet in which there were not unexplained accidents, malicious pranks, heated quarrels, injuries and last-minute resignations! It is simply the way of the theatrical world, Isabel, as you must surely have observed over the years!"

'I acknowledged that there was some truth in what he said, although he exaggerated a little. But I insisted that on this occasion there was something more malicious and sinister in the circumstances. He was still inclined to dismiss the matter, however, and I could not think how to convince him otherwise. Then I thought of you, Mr Holmes. I was in Oxford for a time last summer, appearing in *As You Like It* at the theatre there, and I recalled reading a report in the *Oxford Mail* of the part you had played in what sounded a very strange affair, at somewhere called Fox House, I believe.'

'Foxwood Grange?'

'Yes, that is the place.'

'A most interesting case! I was not aware that the *Oxford Mail* had reported it.'

'It was a very full report. It made it clear that you had been chiefly responsible for uncovering the truth and bringing the whole affair to a successful conclusion. As I remembered it, I wondered if you could perhaps achieve the same with our little problem, and suggested as much to Mr Hardy.'

'What was his response?'

'He said that he would bear the suggestion in mind, should anything further occur, but thought it unnecessary to consult you at present. I considered the matter further last night, however, and decided at length that I would ignore Mr Hardy's opinion, and engage you upon my own account.'

'I should be pleased to look into the matter for you,' began Holmes, but he paused as there came an interruption. The door-bell had sounded as Miss Ballantyne had been speaking, and now the sitting-room door opened and our landlady put her head in, and apologised for the intrusion.

'I did not know you were still engaged, Mr Holmes,' said she. 'There's a gentleman called to see you. I can ask him to wait downstairs.'

'What is the gentleman's name?' asked Holmes.

'Mr Richard Hudson Hardy,' said she.

II

Holmes glanced at his visitor, who had raised her eyebrows in surprise.

'What is your wish?' asked he. 'Should I invite Mr Hudson Hardy to join our little discussion?'

'By all means,' returned Miss Ballantyne. 'I am pleased he has had a change of heart.'

'Kindly ask Mr Hudson Hardy to step up,' said Holmes to the landlady, and a moment later we were joined by the well-known actor, manager and theatrical producer. He was a portly, middle-aged man, with a broad, clean-shaven face and close-cropped greying hair. He paused for a moment in surprise as his eyes lit upon Miss Ballantyne; then he reached forward to her, his hands outstretched.

'My dear!' cried he, smiling broadly. 'So you find me out!'

'I do not know what you mean,' she returned, a frown of puzzlement upon her face; 'but I am glad that you have altered your opinion as to the worth of consulting Mr Holmes.'

'My meaning, Isabel, is that I was not, I regret to say, entirely honest with you,' said Hardy, looking a little shamefaced, as he took the chair I offered him. 'The fact is, my dear, that I thought your suggestion a good one. But I was apprehensive that if I appeared too eager to accept it I should confirm in you those very fears which I was most anxious to alleviate. I therefore said nothing, but resolved there and then that I would consult Mr Holmes at the very first opportunity. So here I am!' he concluded, looking from one to the other of us with a beaming smile.

'In that case,' said Miss Ballantyne after a moment, rising to her feet. 'As you are here, Mr Hardy, and as I have told Mr Holmes all I can recall at present in connection with the matter, I think that I shall take my leave of you. There are one or two things I wished to do before attending today's rehearsal. I had thought that I should have to cancel them, but if I leave now, I might be able to fit them in.'

A moment later, with a brief nod to us, and a swish of her maroon and salmon skirts, the celebrated actress took her exit from our humble rooms.

'Now,' said Holmes to the newcomer, 'Miss Ballantyne has described to us certain recent occurrences at your theatre which have caused her anxiety. I take it from what you say that you share her concern.'

'Broadly speaking, that is correct,' returned Hardy, 'although I am still hopeful that it will blow over. Perhaps the mean-spirited individual who has delighted in playing malicious pranks on his fellow-actors has now satisfied his depraved urges. In which case, we may already have seen the last of it. One cannot know for certain, however, and I have sometimes wondered if there is not someone in the company who has a profound determination to wreck the production, and who will not stop until he has done so. In any case, whether there is yet more of this unpleasantness to come or not, I should certainly like to know who is behind it all and expel him from the company. I thus place the case in your hands, Mr Holmes.'

'Very well,' said Holmes. 'First, then, Mr Hardy, I should be obliged if you could furnish me with a little general information as to the company. Leaving aside for a moment the malicious incidents, would you say that it has, generally speaking, been a happy and contented company?'

'So I believe. Of course, there has been the occasional disagreement, and no doubt one or two of the company have sometimes wished themselves elsewhere.'

'Did you have anything specific in mind?'

'It is no secret that some of the actors could very easily find themselves alternative employment, and some of that alternative employment might possibly be better than that which they have at present. I was thinking only the other night what the consequences might be for Miss Ballantyne, for instance, should *The Lavender Girl* fail to open on time, or be cancelled altogether. Neither of these possibilities is very likely, but one has to have regard for every eventuality. Anyway, my conclusion was that she would not be particularly inconvenienced.'

'What do you mean?' asked Holmes, a note of curiosity in his voice.

'To speak frankly, we were very fortunate to secure the services of Miss Ballantyne for *The Lavender Girl*. At the time I approached her with the offer, she happened to be between engagements. Since then, however, as I am only too aware, several other offers have been made to her and she could probably increase her earnings, and appear in a somewhat more fashionable class of theatre, by accepting one of these other offers. I know for a fact, for instance, that my great rival, Kempston Vernon, would dearly love to have Miss Ballantyne as his leading lady in his forthcoming production at the Agora. This offer, of course, she would be free to accept if *The Lavender Girl* were cancelled.'

'But that is surely not a circumstance she would welcome,' interrupted Holmes. 'As one of the financial sponsors of the production, her husband would, I take it, be considerably out of pocket if your production were cancelled.'

'That is certainly true – and the sum would not be a small one. A great deal of money has already been invested in *The Lavender Girl*.'

'The financing of the production is divided between the two of you?'

Hardy shook his head. 'It is divided three ways. Count Laszlo of Sipolia is also standing for a third of it. You may be familiar with his name. He is a great patron of the London stage, renowned, among other things, for the lavish receptions he holds at the Langham Hotel, and a man I have known for many years. It was largely as a result of his encouragement – and financial support, too, I must admit – that I made the decision to purchase the Albion and the Southwark Palace three years ago. Of course the Palace is a ruin and was consequently thrown into the bargain for practically nothing. Count Laszlo's idea was that we would use the profits from successful productions at the Albion to finance the rebuilding of the Palace, which we could then let out to others. Count Laszlo is also, I might add, a long-time admirer of Miss

Ballantyne. I believe he once even entertained thoughts of seeking her hand in matrimony. Whether he asked her and she turned him down, or whether he never quite reached the point of asking the question, I cannot say. Either way, it doesn't matter now, as his opportunity has gone; but I know that he still follows her career with great interest. When he heard that she had agreed to appear in *The Lavender Girl*, he approached me and offered to provide some, at least, of the finance for the play. I say that he "offered" the money, but to say that he insisted on my taking it would be nearer the mark. "With Isabel Ballantyne in the leading role," said he, "the play cannot fail to be an unparalleled success!" I hope he is right.'

'If Miss Ballantyne were to withdraw from the production for any reason, could it continue without her?' asked Holmes.

'In theory it could; but our chances of having a success with it would be very greatly reduced. If it were to happen, Lydia Summers would take over Miss Ballantyne's role and one of the girls from the chorus would take over that of Miss Summers. I am sure they would all do their best to make it a success, but it would not be the same, either for us, or, more importantly, for the public. Isabel Ballantyne is like one of the stars in the firmament at the moment: in respect of her gifts and her accomplishments, she is an immeasurable distance above all her rivals; her radiance is steady and unblinking, and the public's desire to gaze upon it appears to be insatiable. For Miss Summers to take over Miss Ballantyne's role would be a difficult and unenviable task. Miss Summers is an enthusiastic enough young lady, and has a reasonably pleasant singing voice, but she is very inexperienced and her acting perhaps leaves something to be desired.'

'What, if I may ask, made you choose Miss Summers for the present production, considering that you appear unsure as to her accomplishments?' asked Holmes.

A look of discomfort came over our visitor's features. 'It is one of those compromises which life is constantly demanding of one,' he replied at length. 'Her father is Sir Cecil Summers, the wealthy ship owner. I met him socially some eight or nine months ago, and in the course of our conversation he implied that he was interested in becoming a patron of the theatre and perhaps investing money in our future productions. He even offered to purchase the Palace from me, although what he intended to do with it, I don't know. Anyway, you will understand that when his daughter applied for the second female role in *The Lavender Girl*, I felt obliged to give her application greater consideration than I might otherwise have done. I discussed the matter extensively with Count Laszlo and Captain Trent, who both thought she should be given a chance, and it was decided in the end that we would offer her the part. She would not, in all honesty, have been my first choice, but she is acceptable and will not, I think, let us down. Whether, in the long run, she will make much of a career upon the stage, I do not know. She is not the most gifted young performer I have had under my wing; but on the other hand, I have observed in her a certain streak of ruthlessness, which can be useful in this business. No doubt she takes after her father. They do say that it was his ruthlessness which brought Sir Cecil Summers his great wealth.'

'And your leading men, Ludovic Xavier and Jimmy Webster?' queried Holmes, as his visitor paused.

'The first thing to say is that they are like chalk and cheese, and do not get on very well together.'

'I rather fancied as much from an incident Miss Ballantyne recounted.'

'And yet they play well together on the stage, and the public seems to like both of them; so the fact that they scarcely speak to each other when off the stage does not appear to matter. I dare say you are familiar with their names, for both have enjoyed considerable success and popularity in recent years, and have had their names blazoned across theatrical posters throughout London.

'The case with Ludovic Xavier, however, is an unusual one. A year ago, I should have said, as in the case of Miss Ballantyne, that we were fortunate to secure his services for the present production. He has always been a useful sort of actor, known for his fine speaking voice and a certain "presence" on stage. He is also very experienced, having played in many different types of theatrical production. Indeed, many years ago, as a young man, he worked with Solomon Tanner himself, at the Albion. This last year, however, has been something of a singular one for him, as a result of which I am inclined to think that he benefits from our present agreement quite as much as I do.

'Somewhat over a year ago he became bored with the London stage and determined to display his talents to the country at large. He therefore booked theatrical halls here, there and everywhere, and set forth on a tour of the provinces in a special entertainment devised and performed entirely by himself. This seems to have consisted largely of brief extracts from *Hamlet*, *Macbeth* and others of Shakespeare's plays, blended together with selections from *Gulliver's Travels* and *Robinson Crusoe*, with numerous connecting passages written by Xavier himself, which were, according to his brochure, both humorous and pathetic. This bizarre concoction was described by one critic, with what I must admit seemed like justice, as a "monstrous farrago". The title Xavier gave to it, incidentally, was "Ludovic Xavier in Strange Times and Places", and I gather that this title rather summed up his tour of the country. In many places, I understand, the patience of the audience proved less enduring than the performance. In Newcastle-upon-Tyne, I am told, half the audience took advantage of the first interval to escape from the theatre altogether and, in Carlisle, Xavier was heckled from the stage. It was therefore in a somewhat chastened humour that he returned to London. In some quarters he had by then been re-christened "Ludicrous Failure", although I don't think he was ever aware of it. No one would dare say such a thing to his face. He is a dangerous man to cross and he never forgets a slight. Anyhow, at the time I met him he was feeling somewhat lowered, and eager to accept any part which promised to restore in some measure his professional pride and his fortune, both of which had taken something of a battering in the previous months. Since our rehearsals began, however, his old pride being evidently rapidly restored by his new employment, he has scarcely ceased to complain about the limitations of his role in *The Lavender Girl*, the inadequacy of the dialogue I have written for him and goodness knows what else. If he were able to cancel his contract tomorrow and seek another production, I suspect that he might do so. Much to my surprise, however, in the midst of his dissatisfaction, as it were, he has taken a professional interest in Lydia Summers. Perhaps he sees something in the girl which reminds him of himself when he was first starting out in the profession, many years ago. Who can say? Anyway, whatever the reason, he has been helping her a little, coaching her with her performance and so on, which I have been pleased to see.

'Jimmy Webster, the comic actor, is, on the surface at least, as different from Xavier as it is possible to be. He is generally an agreeable sort of person and is fairly amenable to most suggestions put to him. He has been very popular with the public in recent years and, as with Miss Ballantyne, I considered myself fortunate to secure his services. I know, from previous experience, that there is an odd, dark side to his character, but he keeps it well hidden in public. He can also be extremely bad tempered sometimes; but at least he is usually sober, unlike many other comic actors I have known. His chief vice, at least as far as his fellow-actors are concerned, seems to be to deliberately provoke irritation in others for no reason other than his own satisfaction. He also has a habit which some people find tedious, of couching much of what he says in mock-Shakespearean language. This irritates Xavier intensely, for some reason, but most other people simply ignore it.'

'Is Webster content to be in *The Lavender Girl*?' asked Holmes.

'So I believe. He has certainly given me no indication otherwise.'

'And the remainder of the cast?'

'They are in the main fairly young and inexperienced. As far as I am aware, they are all keen to play their parts in the production.'

Holmes sat for some time in silent thought, his brow furrowed in concentration, as he considered the matter. Presently, with a shake of the head, he took up his pipe from the hearth, knocked out the old tobacco and began to refill it with fresh. As he did so, he recounted briefly to his visitor the incidents which Isabel Ballantyne had described to us earlier. 'Is there anything else you can recall which Miss Ballantyne has overlooked?' he asked at length, as he lit a spill in the fire and applied it to the bowl of his pipe.

'As a matter of fact,' responded Hardy, 'there is an incident of which she is quite unaware, as it occurred only yesterday evening, after she had left the theatre. To speak plainly, it was this incident which finally made up my mind that I would seek your advice. I did not wish to mention it earlier, whilst Miss Ballantyne was present, as I feared it would only increase her anxieties.'

'The details, please!'

'I cannot vouch for the reliability of my informant, who is one of my seamstresses, but I will describe it to you as it was described to me. I must first, however, tell you something of our costuming arrangements. You may not be aware of it, but many theatrical companies nowadays have only very small wardrobes of their own and hire in most of what they need from a few large specialist costumiers. The inevitable consequence of this, of course, is that whichever productions theatre-goers choose to attend, they are likely to see exactly the same costumes over and over again at different theatres. I made the decision, when we took over the Albion, that we would make as many of our own costumes as possible, and thus present the public with something fresh to look at on almost every occasion they could be lured into the theatre. I have, I believe, a certain flair in the costume line myself. I may be no Charles Worth, but, between us, my needlewomen and I have produced many memorable stage costumes. After all, you don't need the services of a master tailor to produce outfits for pirates, brigands and the like, and my ladies have a real eye for pretty outfits to costume their own sex. Already, my decision to be independent of the large costumiers has reaped its own rewards: we now hire out our costumes to other companies and, I might say, make a handsome profit from doing so! I dare say the public is of the opinion that the actors are the most important part of a theatrical company, but their contribution to a production is frequently exaggerated – and I speak as one who was an actor for more years than I care to remember! Apart from exceptional talents, such as Isabel Ballantyne, most actors could in fact be replaced by others without any difference in the performance being apparent. This, however, is certainly not the case with seamstresses. A gifted needlewoman, Mr Holmes, is truly worth her weight in gold! It is for this reason that I am especially anxious at yesterday evening's incident, which concerned these ladies. There are four of them and each one is a treasure! They have all been with me for almost as long as I have had the Albion and have played a large part in making our company the success it is. I cannot have them upset in this way! Were they to leave, I really don't know how I should carry on!

'Now, as to the incident in question. It occurred early yesterday evening, not long before the ladies were due to set down their needles for the day. One of them had left the sewing-room and entered the costume store-rooms, which are immediately adjacent, in order to select a dress, which was to be altered slightly and adapted for Miss Summers. These store-rooms, I should explain, consist of several interconnecting chambers. The two which are nearest to the corridor contain our ladies' wardrobe. As the girl entered the first of these rooms, she had a lantern in her hand, for there is no gas laid on in there. She hung the lantern on a hook by the door and proceeded to sort through a rack of dresses. Whilst she was so engaged, she became conscious of a slight noise somewhere in the room. Next moment, something touched her upon the shoulder. She turned, and was startled to see someone standing immediately behind her.'

'Who?'

'She could not make it out. All she can say is that it was a dark figure, wearing some sort of hood, which hid his face. Then he blew out the lantern, leaving her in the dark, and ran off. Of course, she screamed and carried on screaming until the other seamstresses, hearing her cries through the adjoining wall, hurried to see what had happened.

It took them some time to calm her down, as you will imagine, and then they all came together to report the matter to me. I have promised them that I will take steps to improve the lighting in the basement and have given them strict instructions not to mention the incident to anyone else. If it were to become public knowledge, I have little doubt that the result would be absolutely disastrous. My staff would resign in such numbers that it might prove impossible to keep the theatre open at all. It is bad enough having the needlewomen upset. It would be even worse if everyone else was in the same state! As it is, one of the other needlewomen told me that she, too, had heard odd noises in the costume store a week or so ago, but had kept the matter to herself. Whether that is true or not, I don't know; but in any case they have all vowed not to enter the costume store alone in future.'

'When this dark figure ran off,' Holmes interrupted, 'did the girl see in which direction he went?'

'Unfortunately not. The light had, as I say, been extinguished, and in any case, she was too frightened to look. She heard his footsteps in the corridor, that is all.'

'Very well,' said Holmes. 'You are returning to the theatre now, I take it? Will your seamstresses still be there?'

'Certainly.'

'Then I shall come with you, take a look about, and interview these ladies of yours. Would you care to accompany us, Watson? It may prove an interesting experience!'

I readily agreed, and three minutes later, heavily muffled against the bitter cold, we were in a cab and rattling through the West End towards the river. As we passed along the Strand, a heavy shower of hail beat upon the roof of the cab like lead shot. This was followed, just moments later, as we turned on to Waterloo Bridge, by sheets of icy, driving rain.

'Thank the Lord for civilisation!' cried Hardy in a humorous tone, as he surveyed the dismal scene outside. 'Thank goodness for coal fires and warm sitting-rooms! Let us just hope the weather is not so bad on

Saturday, when *The Lavender Girl* opens, or no one will turn up! I don't suppose,' he continued, turning to Holmes, 'that you have been able to form any theory as to why we have been suffering such persecution lately, at the Albion?'

Holmes shook his head.

'The data are very meagre,' he replied, 'and one cannot make bricks without clay. There are too many possibilities for it to be worth our while even enumerating them.'

'Oh, quite,' said Hardy, sounding a little disappointed at the response.

'Nevertheless,' continued Holmes with a chuckle, 'I am confident of turning something up. I appreciate how highly you esteem your needlewomen, Mr Hardy, and shall devote all my energies to bringing peace and tranquillity to your sewing-room once more!'

III

The rain had stopped by the time we reached the theatre, but the pavements were wet and greasy, and the front of the theatre, its brickwork darkened by years of exposure to London soot and smoke, had a damp and dilapidated appearance after the recent showers. A grimy glass canopy stood out from the wall all along the front of the building and protected the lower part, which was adorned with bright posters announcing the forthcoming play, upon which the name of Isabel Ballantyne was prominent.

'This way, if you please,' called Hardy over his shoulder, as he led us in through the front entrance of the theatre. Off to one side, just inside the doors, was a small room, with little windows which overlooked the entrance lobby, and here we left our coats before following our guide through into the auditorium. There, a group of cleaners was at work in the stalls, and from the rear of the stage came busy sounds of sawing and hammering. We passed through a door on the right, near the front of the auditorium, then through a second door, and down a stone staircase to the basement, where corridors went off to right and left.

'That way leads only to the stage door and the caretaker's office,' said Hardy, pointing to the right, as he turned left, into a long and dimly lit corridor, the walls of which were covered with grimy, whitewashed plaster, which was flaking off in many places. Near the top of the walls ran numerous water-pipes and gas-pipes. On the left side of the corridor was a pair of doors, which, our guide informed us, gave access to the chamber beneath the stage and, on the right a whole series of doors, closely spaced. 'Miss Ballantyne's dressing-room,' remarked Hardy, as we passed the first of these; 'Mr Xavier's; Miss Summers's; female chorus; male chorus; store-room for swords and umbrellas – equally dangerous objects, in my experience; store-room for hats and bonnets.' The corridor then took a sharp turn to the right and, a few yards further on, a turn to the left.

'Mr Webster's dressing-room,' said Hardy, as we passed another door on the right. A little further on was an open doorway. It was dark in the chamber beyond, but I had an impression of rows and rows of dresses. 'One of the costume stores, as you can see,' remarked Hardy, 'for ladies' day-dresses and historical costumes. The doors are always open, for it is important for the clothes to have air circulating about them all the time.'

As he spoke, we passed another open doorway. The room within was, like the previous one, full of ladies' costumes.

'Ladies' evening-dresses,' explained Hardy. 'This room has an interconnecting doorway with the other one, and to the rear of both of them are further rooms, containing the gentlemen's costumes. And this,' he continued, stopping before a closed door, 'is the sewing-room. Further along the corridor is the boiler-room and another stair up to the main part of the theatre.'

He pushed open the sewing-room door and we followed him in. It was a crowded room, with a very large table in the centre, several large rolls of material leaning against the walls, and three or four tailors' dummies dressed in a variety of colourful costumes. A stove in the corner was blazing away and made the room seem very warm after the chill air of the corridor. An animated conversation appeared to be in progress, but it stopped as we entered.

'Good afternoon, ladies!' cried Hardy, in a cheery voice. There were four women there, engaged in various tasks. One was standing at the large table, cutting out a piece of material with the help of a paper pattern. Another was working a sewing machine, a third was by the stove, pressing some garment with a heavy iron, and the fourth woman was seated on a chair in the corner, with a highly decorated costume draped across her lap, and a needle and thread in her hand.

'These are the ladies who make the costumes which are the envy of all other companies!' cried Hardy in a tone of great pleasure. 'I am sure there are no finer seamstresses anywhere in London! From near and far they have come, to help make our company the success it is! Isn't that so, Kathleen?'

'From the four corners of the Earth, as you might say, Mr Hardy,' responded the small sandy-haired woman he had addressed. 'Greenwich, Hackney, the wilds of Norfolk and—' she paused and glanced in the direction of the small, dark-haired girl, who was frowning with concentration at the ornate dress on her lap '—the North,' she concluded at length.

'Excuse me,' responded the dark-haired girl, without lifting her eyes from her needlework, 'but Dudley is in the Midlands.'

'Well, it's north of here, anyway,' returned the sandy-haired woman with an air of finality.

Mr Hardy chuckled and rubbed his hands together. 'And how are you today, Jeanie?' he asked, addressing the slim, auburn-haired woman, who was wielding the iron. 'Jeanie is a woman of many talents,' he remarked to us, 'and has herself known the glamour of the footlights' glare.'

'That's right,' agreed the blonde-haired girl at the sewing-machine, in a quiet voice. 'She played a duck in last year's pantomime!'

'Actually, it was the goose,' returned Jeanie in an indignant tone.

'And I am sure the goose was never played better!' cried Hardy. 'Now,' said he, 'to complete our introductions: over in the corner there is Katharine; and this very quiet young lady is Michéle.' He indicated the blonde-haired girl, who nodded her head and mouthed some response, but so softly as to be almost inaudible. 'Michéle has somewhat exotic antecedents,' murmured Hardy to us.

'She certainly has,' said Kathleen. 'Her father used to keep a pub out Hackney way.'

Hardy chuckled again. 'Now, ladies,' said he, 'this is Mr Holmes and Dr Watson, who have kindly agreed to help me get to the bottom of our recent troubles. Was it you, Katharine, that had the – hum! – unpleasant experience yesterday?'

The small, dark-haired girl nodded her head.

'I wonder then, Katharine, if you would be good enough to show these gentlemen where the unfortunate incident took place?'

The girl put down her sewing with an air of reluctance, and led the way out of the room and along the corridor to the open doorway of the costume store. Hardy lit a lantern which hung on a hook beside the door and we followed him inside.

'I was standing by this rail, sir,' said the girl, indicating a long row of elaborate evening-dresses which hung from hooks on a rail by the left-hand wall. 'I heard a noise behind me.'

'What sort of noise?' asked Holmes.

'It's hard to say, sir,' she replied after a moment. 'A little noise. I thought it might be mice – that sort of noise. There are lots of mice down here.'

'But not so many as there used to be, I trust,' interrupted Hardy quickly. 'We took steps to deal with them,' he explained to us.

'Not so many, but still a few,' the girl responded. 'Anyway, I stopped what I was doing and listened, but the noise had stopped, too, so I thought perhaps I had imagined it. I went back to looking through the dresses and the noise came again. It sounded as if somebody was pushing through a rail of clothes and seemed to be right behind me. I stood very still and the noise stopped again. Then something touched me on the shoulder, like this.' She raised her right arm and touched her right shoulder lightly with the tips of her fingers. 'I thought it was a spider and tried to brush it off, but there was nothing there. Then I turned. Just here, where you are standing, sir, was a horrible dark figure, all in black, with a black hood on, just standing, looking at me.'

The girl shut her eyes tightly and put her hand up to her face, as if to ward off the memory of the evil figure.

'It must have been a horrible shock for you,' said Holmes in a sympathetic voice. 'I regret the necessity of asking you these questions, and thus rekindling the unpleasantness in your mind, but we must have all the facts. You say this figure was looking at you. You saw his face, then?'

'No, sir,' the girl replied, her breath short and sharp. 'For he had no face.'

'No face?'

'There was nothing there, sir. Inside the big hood it was all blackness, just as if it was empty. Only the eyes showed, sharp and glittering.'

'He was wearing a mask, perhaps?'

'Perhaps, sir. I don't know.'

'What happened next?' asked Holmes.

'He lifted his hand up. It was all white and bony. He was holding one of these hooks.' She pointed to the large 'S'-shaped metal hooks, like pothooks, which hung on the rail, and from which the dresses behind her were suspended. 'He held it up, then brought it down at me. I screamed and turned away, and covered my face with my hands. Everything went black and I heard him run off into the corridor. I don't know what happened after that, sir. The next thing I remember, Kathleen and the others were here, telling me to stop screaming.'

'And there's no possibility, I suppose,' asked Hardy, in a vaguely hopeful voice, 'that you imagined it all?'

'Certainly not, Mr Hardy!' replied the girl indignantly.

'You say the figure was all in black,' said Holmes. 'Were you able to see what sort of clothes he was wearing?'

'It was like a monk's robe, sir, with a hood attached.'

'Do you have any costumes of that sort in your wardrobe?' Holmes asked Hardy.

'We do indeed. I'll get Kathleen to show you. Among her other duties, she acts as wardrobe mistress and knows where all the costumes are hung.'

The sandy-haired woman was sent for and took us through to the chambers at the rear, which contained the men's costumes.

'These are the monks' robes, sir,' said she, stopping before a long rail of assorted clerical garments and holding up a lantern. 'These are the white friars, these are the black friars and these are some brown 'uns.'

'Could your assailant have been wearing one of these?' Holmes asked the dark-haired girl. She nodded, averting her eyes as she did so. 'Are all the black robes here?' he continued, addressing the other woman.

'I think so,' she replied, as she counted them. 'No, wait a minute, there's only five of the black ones here now and I think there should be six. Isn't that right, Mr Hardy?'

'It certainly is,' said Hardy, nodding his head. 'We definitely made six of them, eighteen months ago, for *The Gipsies of Bohemia*.'

'So it appears that your mystery intruder is indeed wearing one of these robes,' said Holmes, 'which he has still got with him, wherever he is. They are certainly commodious garments, perfectly suited to anyone wishing to conceal his identity. Now,' he continued after a moment, addressing the sandy-haired woman again, 'when you had calmed Katharine down, did you search these rooms to see if there was anyone still about?'

'No, sir, we did not. We didn't know what we might find! We went straight to Mr Hardy to tell him what had happened.'

'I understand,' said Holmes. 'Thank you, ladies. That is all, for the present.'

'What do you make of it?' asked Hardy, when the women had left us.

Holmes shook his head. 'It is a puzzling little problem,' he replied. 'The point of all this mysterious activity is not yet clear to me. In this latest incident – the first, it seems, in which your mysterious persecutor has been seen – his appearance was threatening and he no doubt frightened the girl out of her wits; but in the end he did not harm her.'

'Perhaps he was deterred by her screaming,' I suggested. 'He would have realised that that would bring others here.'

'Possibly,' said Holmes. 'But he had raised his arm as if to strike her, yet did not do so, even though it would have taken him but a moment. The inference is surely that he never really had any intention of harming her.'

'What, then?'

'He has never previously shown any inclination to reveal himself. It is possible, then, that the girl's encounter with him in here was the merest chance and that he simply took the opportunity to frighten her which that chance had presented to him.'

'Whatever the explanation, it certainly must have been unnerving for her,' I remarked. 'What do you make of the white, bony hands she described?'

'Perhaps he was simply wearing a pair of these,' replied Holmes, indicating a wooden box which stood on the floor by the wall. Inside the box were several dozen pairs of white evening-dress gloves. He took a pair and slipped them on to his long, thin hands. 'Observe,' said he, 'how, if one clenches one's fist, one's hands appear more bony in these than if one were not wearing gloves at all.'

'But if, as you suggest, this villain did not deliberately set out to frighten anyone, but encountered the girl by chance, why should he have been wearing these white gloves at all?' asked Hardy.

'Perhaps simply to conceal his hands from anyone who did happen to see him,' replied Holmes. 'The human hand is a very individual thing and a man's hand can sometimes identify him every bit as precisely as his face. Now, let us proceed: the women did not search these rooms when they found their colleague in distress. It is possible, then, that the girl's assailant remained hidden in some dark corner here until they had gone.'

'She says she heard his footsteps in the corridor,' I interjected.

'That is true, but it is possible that he ran only a few yards along the corridor, then turned in at the next doorway, the other entrance to these rooms. He would certainly not wish to encounter anyone else who might be drawn into the corridor by the girl's screams, and these dark rooms would probably offer the best hiding place. He could lie low in here for a while, wait until the hue and cry had died down, and then make good his escape. Can you recall the whereabouts of the various members of the company yesterday evening, Mr Hardy, at the time of this incident?'

'All members of the chorus, both male and female, were on stage at the time,' replied Hardy. 'We had the orchestra in and were rehearsing some of the musical ensemble pieces. I know that Miss Ballantyne had left for home by then, but I am afraid I cannot tell you offhand where anyone else was. I have been so preoccupied lately that the days have passed as if in a blur. Except for those members of the company with whom I am rehearsing at any given moment, I am generally unable to say who is present and who is not. I have all the rehearsal details in my office upstairs, however, if you would care to consult the book.'

'In a moment. First, let us take a look round these chambers. I see that there are yet more rooms behind these. What are they used for?'

'Nothing in particular. This theatre is full of dusty old store-rooms and cupboards, a good half of which we do not use at all. Come, I will show you!'

We passed through an open doorway at the back of the men's costume store, into another large, low-ceilinged chamber, stacked high with wooden crates of various sizes, most of which appeared to be empty. Hardy held up his lantern and we followed the spread of its light about the room. It was a grimy chamber, with a dank, earthy smell about it. At the top of each of the damp-stained, whitewashed walls was a small grating, through which cold air brought the sound of dripping rain into the room. In the far wall were three dirty and mildewed doors.

'As you can see,' remarked our guide, 'this room is little used. There are a few odd stage properties in these boxes, but most of them are empty. I doubt if this room has been used for anything much since Solomon Tanner's day.'

Holmes took the lantern and prowled slowly about this gloomy chamber for several minutes, examining the walls and the flagstone floor very closely, until at last he paused before the rotten-looking old doors and tried the handle of each in turn.

'These doors all appear to be locked,' he remarked.

'They are only dirty old cupboards,' returned Hardy dismissively. 'I don't think they've ever been opened since we've had the theatre.'

'Do you know where the keys are?' enquired Holmes, peering closely at the lock of the middle door of the three.

'There are two large bunches of keys somewhere in the office upstairs,' replied Hardy. 'The keys to these cupboards may be among them, but none of the keys is labelled, so you would have to try them all. I don't know why you are so interested in them, Mr Holmes!'

'Professional thoroughness,' returned Holmes with a chuckle.

'If you would care to accompany me to my office, then, I'll find the keys for you – and while you are there you can look over the records of recent rehearsals.'

'I shall follow you upstairs in a moment,' said Holmes. 'Do you also have in your office any information on the history of this theatre?' he asked, as Hardy turned to leave.

'Indeed I do. We have a scrapbook of newspaper cuttings, dating back many years, to the heyday of Solomon Tanner and even beyond. It belonged to the old doorman of the Albion, who had compiled it over many years' service here. He is retired now, living with his daughter down Walworth way. About three years ago, however, when he heard that we had bought the theatre and were planning to reopen it, he arrived here one morning and presented the scrapbook to me, which was very kind of him. It forms a detailed historical record, of both the Albion and the Southwark Palace, next door. As a matter of fact, Miss Ballantyne was asking me about the scrapbook only the other day and I found it for her. It will be in her dressing-room still, I should think. She won't mind your having a look at it in there. I'll light the gas for you as I pass.'

The moment that Hardy had left us, and we heard his footsteps in the corridor, Holmes handed the lantern to me.

'Hold it down here,' said he, as he bent to inspect a patch of floor which lay immediately in front of the middle cupboard door.

I did as he asked, and watched as he subjected the flagstones to the most minute examination. Down on all fours, and with his nose scarcely an inch from the floor, he resembled nothing so much as a bloodhound following a trail. Then he pulled from his pocket his powerful lens and a tape-measure, with which he made several measurements.

'I cannot see what you are measuring,' said I.

'Footprints,' replied he, jotting down some figures in a note-book.

'I cannot see them.'

'The marks are not very clear, but they are clear enough for my purposes. I observed them earlier. You no doubt remarked that I avoided stepping on this damp patch of floor. I did not mention the matter in front of Mr Hardy, for I wished to avoid putting anything into his head which he might inadvertently let slip to someone else. The fewer people who know what we have discovered, the more likely we are to bring the matter to a successful conclusion.'

After a while, he stood up and began to examine the frame around the middle door, making further notes in his book and muttering to himself as he did so. Some mark on the door-frame, at about shoulder height, seemed particularly to interest him and he studied it for some time through his lens. Then, very carefully, he removed something from the woodwork at that spot. 'A thread, caught on a sharp splinter of wood,' said he, as he placed it in a small envelope he had taken from his pocket. Presently, he stood back, with an expression of satisfaction upon his features.

'Well, well,' said he, as he put his note-book away; 'that is all clear enough. No doubt you observed that the hinges of this middle door have had some kind of grease smeared on to them. No? Look, then, Watson: the edges of the hinges are just visible in the gap between the door and the frame. It is evident that this door has been opened very recently.'

I held the lantern close to the edge of the door and saw it was as he said. The edge of the hinge glistened with grease.

'Another discovery I thought I would not mention in front of Mr Hardy,' remarked my companion. 'Let us now re-examine the monks' robes.'

We returned to the men's costume store, where Holmes took from his pocket the little envelope and compared the thread within it to the material of which the monks' robes were made. 'It is undoubtedly the same,' said he.

'What does it mean?' I asked.

'I have an idea about that,' replied my companion. 'But first, let us get along to Miss Ballantyne's dressing-room and take a look at Mr Hardy's historical scrapbook.'

We made our way to the other end of the corridor, our footsteps ringing hollowly in the silent basement. The gas was lit in Miss Ballantyne's room and on a table near the door lay the scrapbook. Holmes lifted it up and turned the pages over for a moment, and I saw that the yellowing cuttings touched on every conceivable topic of relevance to the theatre: Solomon Tanner's nights of triumph, occasions when the performances had been less well received, an occasion when a gas leak had obliged the audience to be quickly ushered from the theatre in the middle of a play, records of when parts of the building had been freshly painted and many other such matters.

'What a fascinating record!' I remarked.

'If you would be so good as to take a look through it, Watson,' said

Holmes, handing it to me, 'I shall attend to the other matters in Hardy's office, and return shortly.'

I sat down at the table and began to study the history of the Albion Theatre. The door had swung shut as Holmes had left and, once the sound of his footsteps on the stair had faded away, the basement had fallen utterly silent and still. As far as I was aware, there was no one else there save the four seamstresses and they were far out of my hearing, at the other end of the corridor. For some considerable time I turned the pages over, absorbed in what I was reading. Once, some slight noise came to my ears and I looked up and listened, expecting to hear my friend's footsteps approaching. But all was silence, and I returned after a moment to my perusal of the scrapbook. Clearly something had delayed Holmes upstairs.

I had just finished reading of a gala night at the old theatre, attended by the Duke of Balmoral, when a faint sound, as of the soft closing of a door, made me pause and look up. For a moment I remained motionless, but could hear nothing. As I sat there listening, it seemed to me that the air in the basement had become colder in the past twenty minutes and I shivered. At that moment, I heard a footstep, soft and furtive, in the corridor outside. I turned down the gas, opened the door cautiously and peered out.

The light in the corridor was poor, for only one gas-jet was lit and that appeared to have been turned lower than before. But even by this dim light I could see quite clearly that there was someone in the corridor. Not more than thirty feet away, a dark figure in a long black robe and hood was moving silently away from me. For a moment, it was as if an icy hand had touched the back of my neck and I was frozen into immobility. Then, gathering my senses together, I licked my dry lips and called out, my own voice sounding strange and almost startling to me after the silence in which I had been sitting for so long. The dark figure stopped abruptly as I called, then, very slowly, turned round. Within the shadowed cowl, no face was visible; nothing but a dense blackness.

'What are you doing?' I called out.

No reply came, but next moment, the figure began to advance, slowly and in complete silence, towards me. Every muscle in my body seemed to have become paralysed and unresponsive, and the blood seemed frozen in my veins. Then, with an effort of will, I took a step forward. I gave no credence to apparitions, I told myself, and wanted to know who this hidden villain was, and what he was up to. But I confess that it is easier to write these words now than it was to speak them to myself at the time, as I stood facing this dark menacing figure in that cold and dimly lit underground passage.

For what seemed an age, but was probably, in reality, but a second or two, the figure continued his slow, silent approach.

'What do you want?' I called out loudly, my voice ringing round the hard walls of the corridor, and sounding forced and unnatural.

As the echo of my words faded, and silence returned, the dark figure halted and remained for a moment motionless. He had drawn level with the one gas-jet in the corridor. Now, in one swift movement, and before I realised what was happening, he had raised his hand, the gas-tap was turned off, and the corridor was plunged into utter blackness.

IV

For a moment, it was as if a heavy shutter had descended before my eyes. I could see nothing whatever and held myself absolutely still, so that I might hear if the dark figure approached any closer. But a faint glimmer of light came from beneath the door of Miss Ballantyne's dressing-room and, as my eyes adjusted to this dim illumination, I could just make out that the dark figure had not moved. Even as I screwed up my eyes, however, struggling to see more clearly through the darkness, I had an impression that the figure was stooping. There then came a swifter movement, of his arm, and I knew at once that he had flung something at me. Instinctively, I put up my arm to shield my face, but I was not quick enough, and something – a small lump of wood, perhaps – struck me on the side of the head. At the same instant, I heard rapid footsteps and when I looked again, as the footsteps faded into the distance, the corridor was empty. Without pausing for thought, I at once gave chase. But in advancing along the corridor, I was moving further away from the faint illumination from the dressing-room, so that in a matter of seconds, utter blackness had closed in about me. I cursed myself for my stupidity in not re-lighting the gas as I passed it. But I was reluctant now to stop and even more reluctant to retrace my steps, and thus turn my back upon what might lie ahead of me. I therefore pressed forward, but very slowly and with great caution. I knew that I must be approaching the point at which the corridor took a right-angled bend, so I held my hands out in front of me until they touched the cold corridor wall. Then, slowly feeling my way along the wall, I followed the passage round to the right and, a few yards further on, round to the left. For a few seconds, then, I stood perfectly still in that impenetrable darkness and listened. The whole basement was in utter and complete silence. For all I could tell, my assailant might be far away by now, or might be within a few feet of where I stood, waiting to spring at me. After a moment, I took a step forward, with no great enthusiasm, I must admit, and advanced very slowly along the corridor, ready at any moment to defend myself if attacked. A sensation of colder air upon my face told me that I was passing the first open doorway of the costume store, and it occurred to me that the mystery figure might have gone to ground there. But it was pointless attempting to look in there without a lamp of some kind, so, tense and breathing heavily, I continued along the corridor.

A little further on, I again felt a draught of cold air and knew I must be passing the second doorway of the costume store. Then I caught the faint murmur of voices and saw a thin line of light upon the floor to my right, which I knew must come from the narrow gap at the bottom of the door to the seamstresses' room. For some time, I felt for the door-knob, then, just as I had my hand upon it, the door was abruptly opened from the other side. Light from the room within seemed to burst about me and I put my hand up to my eyes to shield them. The woman who had opened the door stepped back with a sharp cry of alarm as she saw me.

'Oh, sir!' cried she, as I stepped forward into the room. 'I thought you was the ghost!'

'He looks as if he's seen one, Kathleen,' remarked the woman holding the iron.

'Did you hear anyone pass this way in the past few minutes?' I asked.

'No, sir,' replied Kathleen. 'Sir, your head is bleeding,' she added, picking up a scrap of cloth from the table and handing it to me.

'It's nothing,' I responded, dabbing the cloth on my left temple, where the block of wood had struck it. 'There was somebody out there just now.'

'Who?'

'I don't know. The same person as your friend saw yesterday, I believe.'

'Why aren't there any lamps lit in the corridor?' asked the woman, peering out of the doorway.

'He must have turned them all off,' I replied. 'I'll re-light them now. I should stay in here for the moment if I were you. I'll probably be back in a few minutes.'

I re-lit the gas-jet on the wall outside their room, then made my way back along the length of the corridor. There was no sign of anyone there and, after re-lighting the gas-jet which I had seen the mystery figure extinguish, I made my way up the stairs to the auditorium and through to the front of the theatre. There, I found Holmes in the small office by the entrance lobby, in which we had earlier left our coats. He was busily rooting through a deep drawer in a desk, but looked up as I entered.

'I do apologise for keeping you waiting for so long, Watson,' he began, rising to his feet. 'Mr Hardy has misplaced the keys. And now he has been drawn away by the arrival of a reporter from the *Globe*, who wishes to interview him about the forthcoming production. But, you are injured, old fellow!' cried my friend all at once. 'You have a cut on the side of your head! What ever have you been doing with yourself?'

'I have had an encounter with the mystery persecutor,' I replied.

'What!' cried Holmes. 'Where?'

'In the basement corridor.'

'Is he still there?'

'No. He got away.'

'Sit down here,' said Holmes, pushing a chair towards me, and seating himself on the edge of the desk. 'Tell me precisely what happened, Watson.'

I quickly recounted my recent experiences.

'How very interesting!' said he as I finished, a thoughtful expression upon his face. 'I shall just complete my search for the keys while you sit there, Watson, and then, if you are up to it, we can take another look in the basement and see if we can find any fresh traces of this mysterious visitor.'

'I am up to it,' I returned vehemently. 'Nothing would give me greater pleasure than to get my hands on that villain!'

I watched as Holmes turned out the contents of the drawer. In truth, I was glad to sit there and do nothing for a few minutes. My adventure in the basement had left me somewhat shaken and my nerves felt a little raw. The cut on the side of my head had stopped bleeding, but my head had begun to throb painfully. As I watched my friend's efforts to find the keys, I could see, also, through the little windows which overlooked the entrance lobby, the comings and goings of various of the theatre staff, as they bustled about their work. I wondered what they would say if they knew of my recent strange and unpleasant encounter in the basement. It was certainly difficult to imagine, in broad daylight and in the midst of all this determined activity aimed at getting everything ready for the opening of *The Lavender Girl* on Saturday night, that, moving stealthily and secretly in the darkness beneath the theatre, was someone who was equally determined to thwart that aim.

I was recalled from my reverie by a groan of disappointment from my friend. It was evident he could find no sign of the keys and, with a sigh, he stuffed everything back into the drawers again. 'Mr Hardy assures me,' said he, 'that there are – or were, at any rate – two identical bunches of keys, the one being the duplicate of the other. But one of these bunches seems to have disappeared completely and the other has been recently mislaid somewhere in one of these offices. He says he saw it only the other day, but he cannot recall where. I may as well abandon logic and look anywhere,' he continued in a dry tone, as he pulled open the door of a tall broom-cupboard. At the back of the cupboard was a row of hooks, upon which several coats were hanging, including our own, but otherwise the cupboard was empty. One by one, Holmes lifted the coats from the hooks and looked beneath them, until, with a sudden cry of triumph, he stood aside, a coat in his hand, and I saw that on one of the hooks hung a large rusty iron ring, upon which were two dozen or more large keys. 'Success at last!' cried he. 'Of course, even when acting in an apparently illogical manner, one never really abandons logic. It is merely a question of casting one's logical net a little wider. I remembered hearing a little metallic noise as we hung our coats up here earlier and I was not mistaken! Are you prepared to re-enter the fray, Watson?'

'Perfectly so!'

'Good man!' cried my friend, as I rose to my feet. 'Let us make haste, then, before the trail goes cold!'

We were destined to be delayed a little longer, however. We were about to leave the office, when Holmes put his hand on my arm and indicated that we should wait a moment. Hardy was approaching, across the lobby, shaking hands with a thin, middle-aged man, as they made their way towards the front doors. 'It will be in the paper tomorrow evening, Mr Hardy!' said this latter. 'Have no doubt! A good paragraph from me will add two hundred to the audience!'

'I am more anxious at present as to whether you will be washed away, Mr Edgecumbe!' returned the theatre manager, opening the door for his visitor. Outside, as I could see, the rain was teeming down again.

'Don't you worry, Mr Hardy!' returned the newspaperman, holding aloft an umbrella. 'I am equipped for all eventualities, as you see!' With a final farewell, he slipped out of the front door, put up his umbrella and disappeared into the pouring rain.

For a moment Hardy watched the heavy downpour, splashing up in fountains from the surface of the street, and had only just turned away from the doors when they were flung violently open again and a thin, wiry man, clad only in a light suit, burst in with a loud groan. He pulled off the bowler hat he was wearing and cast it to the floor.

'What a day!' cried he, shaking himself like a dog, to fling off the rain. 'Ho, my liege!' he continued in a jocular tone, as he caught sight of Hardy. 'What news from Ghent? How fares our cousin's quest to smite the sledded Polak?'

'I don't know about any of that, Jimmy,' returned Hardy with a chuckle; 'but there's no news to speak of here. You're the first to arrive, I believe.'

'More fool me! I was in a coffee-shop down the road and thought I'd make a dash for it as the rain seemed to have let up. Of course, I'd got precisely halfway here when it came down again heavier than ever! My own quest had better be for a towel to apply to this idiotic head of mine.' So saying, he picked up his hat and hurried on into the theatre.

Hardy turned away, but even as he did so the front doors were pushed open once again, this time by a large, well-built man with an upright military bearing. He was dressed in a heavy overcoat and top hat, and had a cape about his shoulders, from which water was streaming.

'Wretched weather!' said he, as he unfastened his cape and shook the water from it.

'Good afternoon, Captain Trent,' said Hardy. 'Yes, it is certainly dismal. I am hoping it does not affect the turnout on Saturday evening. I have just had Edgecumbe of the *Globe* here. He is going to give us a paragraph in the paper tomorrow.'

'Really? That is excellent news!' cried the newcomer, as he took off his hat and tipped a rivulet of water from the brim. 'I've just come from my club and I've been doing my best to drum up a bit of interest there, telling all the fellows that if they don't get along to *The Lavender Girl* they'll miss the best thing in London.'

Hardy chuckled. 'That is good of you, Captain Trent, but I am not expecting a very large proportion of our audience to come from the clubs of Pall Mall!'

'Perhaps not, but every little helps, y'know, Hardy. Is my wife anywhere about?'

'No. She has not yet arrived. No doubt she will be here shortly.'

'In that case I shall find myself a cup of tea. Is there a pot on the go anywhere?'

'Mrs Abbott was boiling the kettle, the last time I saw her,' returned Hardy. 'If you look into the kitchen, I think you will find a fresh pot there.'

'Excellent!' cried Trent with feeling. 'Perhaps I will find Count Laszlo there, too!'

'No, he is not here yet. You will have the teapot to yourself!'

'Really? I thought I saw his carriage outside. Well, I'll see you in a minute, Hardy!'

The theatre manager turned in our direction as the other man disappeared through a doorway on the other side of the lobby. 'Please excuse me for neglecting you, gentlemen,' said he, as he entered the room. 'There are always people coming and going in a place like this, I'm afraid, and every one of them invariably wants to speak to me. Ah! Good! I see you have found the keys!'

'Indeed,' said Holmes, 'and we are now going to take another look in the basement.'

'Very well. You will find me here, should you want me for any reason. And don't forget,' he added, putting his finger to his lips: 'not a word to anyone!'

We descended to the basement corridor once more, and made our way along towards the other end. Holmes lit a lantern he had with him, and at the place where the corridor turned sharp right, he paused, and peered closely at the wall.

'This is where you held your hands out in front of you until you felt the wall, I take it,' said he, producing his lens from his pocket and squinting through it at a faint mark. 'It is more than likely that our mystery man did the same, as he was fleeing ahead of you in the dark. Yes! See, Watson! Here are the two smudges you made on this dusty wall, and here is another, a little to the side. Hum! Let us proceed, then!'

We followed the corridor round the first corner and the second, and past the closed door of Webster's dressing-room. A little further along, at the first of the two entrances to the costume-rooms, Holmes stopped and held up his hand. Within the dark chamber, a faint light was moving silently behind the rows of clothes. As we watched, a slim young woman emerged all at once from behind a row of dresses, a lantern in her hand. She stopped abruptly when she saw us and cried out, an expression of apprehension on her features.

'Who are you?' she asked, breathing heavily. 'You made me jump!'

'Miss Summers?' enquired Holmes, at which the girl nodded her head. 'I'm sorry if we startled you. We are friends of Mr Hardy's. He said we might have a look round. It is fascinating to see all these different costumes, I must say.'

'It might be fascinating, if you could find one to fit you,' she returned in an ill-natured tone, as she pushed past us and made her way down the corridor. Holmes waited until her footsteps had quite faded away, then turned his lantern up and led the way into the costume store. We had gone scarcely three paces, however, when he stopped again. He handed the lantern to me, stooped down and picked up a scrap of black cloth, about a foot square, which lay at his feet. As he held it up, I saw with a thrill that it had had two small eye-holes cut into it, and short pieces of tape tied through holes at either side.

'It is a mask!' I cried.

'It must be the mask of your assailant,' said Holmes. 'It confirms that this was the way he came. It is probable that in his headlong flight in the dark, the mask slipped and he could not see where he was going. He would therefore have pulled it off as he ran in here. No doubt it was knocked from his grasp as he pushed his way between these rows of costumes and, in the dark, he could not see where it had gone. Before we proceed any further, let us see if Hardy's seamstresses can shed any light upon it.'

In the sewing-room, Holmes spread out our prize upon the cutting-table.

'Have you ever seen this mask before?' he asked.

The women gathered round to look, but they all shook their heads.

'I should like to know who was behind that mask,' said the small, dark-haired girl, Katharine, dabbing at the eye-holes with her needle.

'It's a very wide mask,' observed Kathleen. 'Even with a head as big as Jeanie's, which is as big as you could want, you'd find it a bit on the large side.'

'Yes,' agreed Holmes with a chuckle; 'but the spacing of the eye-holes is quite normal, as you see. Evidently, the mask has been made as wide as it has so that it will cover not merely the front of the face, but the sides, too.'

'Well, you can see it's nothing we've made, sir, anyway. It's not been finished off properly. The edges are all fraying!'

'Never mind "finished off", Kathy,' interjected the blonde-haired girl in a soft voice; 'it's not even been started properly. See how badly it's been cut out! It's all crooked and the eye-holes aren't even level!'

'It was made, then, I take it, by someone with little sewing skill,' said Holmes.

'None at all, sir, I should say.'

'Do you recognise the material? It is some kind of velvet fabric, is it not?'

Kathleen stooped and looked under the table, where numerous rolls of cloth were stacked. After a moment, she pulled one out and unrolled it on the table-top.

'It is this sort of thing,' said she. 'Yes, see!' she cried, pointing to the uneven edge of the material. 'Someone has cut the end off crookedly with a pair of scissors!'

'I suppose it would have been a simple enough task for someone to come in here when you had all gone home and take a piece of this material?' queried Holmes.

'It would, sir. We might have noticed, if it was material we were using; but we haven't used this black velvet for a little while now.'

Holmes thanked the needlewomen for their assistance, folded up the mask and put it in his pocket, and we returned to the costume store. 'Still only five black robes here,' he remarked, as we paused at the rail on which the monks' robes were hanging. 'The width of that roll of velvet, incidentally, was a yard, only about a third of which has been used to make the mask. Your assailant therefore retains his robe, and has ample material left to make a replacement mask. Somehow, I do not think we have yet seen the last of him!'

'But where has he gone to?'

'We may be able to shed some light on that question if we take another look at the disused cupboards at the back of the next room,' returned my companion.

As he had done earlier, he subjected the floor in front of the middle cupboard to a close examination. When he rose to his feet again, there was a glint of excitement in his eye.

'There are fresh marks here,' said he, 'marks which were certainly not here earlier. They were therefore made in the past hour and indubitably by your assailant. Now,' he continued, taking out the large rusty-looking bunch of keys from his pocket, 'let us try these, and hope for success!'

I held the lamp up by the door, as, for several minutes, my companion tried each of his keys in turn in the keyhole of the middle door.

'It is possible, of course, that none of these keys will fit,' said he as he paused for a moment. 'The correct key may already have been removed. But, wait! Ah! There it is!' There was a note of triumph in his voice, as one of the last remaining keys turned without difficulty in the lock. 'Now to see what lies behind this old door!'

He took the lamp from my hand, and pulled at the door, which opened easily. There before us, rather than the shallow dusty cupboard I had expected to see, stretched a narrow corridor, which vanished into darkness. As my companion stepped forward with the lamp, however, and the darkness retreated before its light, I saw that at about a dozen feet from the door the corridor ended at a steep flight of stone steps which descended to a lower level. What might lie down these steps I could not imagine and I certainly could not see, for the foot of the stair was in utter blackness. In silence, and with every sense alert, I followed my companion down these steps to the bottom, which lay about fifteen feet below the level of the costume store. There, a passage went off to the left. This ran dead straight for nearly thirty feet and ended at the foot of another stone staircase, an exact duplicate of the one we had descended. Slowly, we mounted these steps, until, at the top, we found ourselves before an old and crumbling wooden door. For a moment, we stood and listened, but all about us was utter silence; then Holmes pushed open the door and we entered a bare chamber, festooned with dusty cobwebs. Directly opposite, another door stood ajar and, passing through it, we found ourselves in a long, narrow corridor, which stretched away into darkness in either direction.

'We are now in the basement of the Southwark Palace,' said my companion in a low voice. 'The tunnel we have followed evidently passes deep beneath the narrow street which lies between the two theatres. It must have been constructed in Solomon Tanner's day, to enable him to get quickly from the one theatre to the other, without having to go out into the street. Did you find any mention of it in that collection of historical cuttings you were reading?'

'Not specifically. There were several references to the fact that Tanner was often on the stage of the Palace at the close of the programme there and on the stage of the Albion less than five minutes later, but no specific mention of the existence of a tunnel between the two theatres. But I had not finished reading through the scrapbook when I was interrupted. Perhaps it is mentioned on a page I have not yet read.'

'Perhaps. But I observed that a leaf near the beginning of the scrapbook had been torn out. It is therefore possible that the tunnel was mentioned on that page, and that it was deliberately removed by our mystery villain to prevent anyone else learning the secret. He himself has evidently discovered it somehow, anyway. I think it is clear that he has used this tunnel to come and go whenever he wished, without being seen. You have done some fishing in your time, I believe, Watson?'

'Fishing?' I repeated, surprised at the question. 'Certainly. When I was stationed with the Medical Department in Hampshire, some of my companions were keen anglers and we made many expeditions to the rivers there.'

'And sometimes, perhaps, as you waded out into what appeared a shallow, rocky stream, you would find that the bottom was not as even as you had supposed and that the water was running over the top of your boots?'

'What fisherman has not had that experience!' I replied. 'But why do you ask?'

'Because that is the sensation I have with this case, Watson. I was asked to investigate a series of spiteful, but largely trivial, incidents. But as we have stepped into these muddy waters, they have revealed themselves to be considerably deeper than was at first apparent. Come! Let us return now to the Albion and see if we can determine what this villain was up to on his last visit there. Careful where you step! We must not leave any indication that we have been here, to warn him that we are on his trail!'

We retraced our steps, taking care to leave everything as we had found it, until we were once more in the basement corridor of the Albion, just outside the costume store.

'You say that when you first saw the dark figure, he was twenty-odd feet this side of the room in which you were sitting?' asked Holmes.

'That's right; making his way along in this direction, away from the room I was in.'

'Could he have passed your door without your hearing?'

'I doubt it. It was very quiet at the time and the door was not tightly closed.'

'So, he was walking away from where you were, but had not passed your door. He must therefore have come from some point this side of Miss Ballantyne's room.'

'That must be so. Perhaps he had been in one of the other rooms. I had heard a door close, just before I looked out and saw him. It was that which first attracted my attention.'

We made our way along to Isabel Ballantyne's dressing-room, then turned and surveyed the corridor from that standpoint, as I had done when I had first caught sight of the masked figure.

'The place from which he had come must have been quite close to here,' remarked Holmes. 'But if he had been in the next dressing-room, that of Ludovic Xavier, I think you would have heard him in there. Perhaps the door he closed was one of the pair on the other side of the corridor, which, as Mr Hardy informed us, give access to the under-stage area.'

These doors were a dozen feet or so along the corridor from Miss Ballantyne's room. Holmes opened one of them, then softly closed it again and looked at me enquiringly.

'That certainly could have been what I heard,' I remarked.

'Then let us take a look inside!'

Behind the doors, a short flight of stone steps led downwards, for the floor of this chamber was at a lower level than the corridor. We descended the steps, lit a gas-jet on the wall, and looked about us. It was a very large chamber, which evidently extended the whole width of the stage above. The ceiling was much higher than those of the other rooms in the basement, and was composed of thick planks and sturdy crossbeams, which were supported upon stout wooden pillars, as broad as tree-trunks. Stacked about the flagstones of the floor, in between these pillars, were a great number of boxes, crates and wicker hampers.

'We are now immediately beneath the stage,' remarked my friend and, as if to confirm his words, the orchestra at that moment struck up a lively tune and dancing footsteps began tripping across the boards above us. 'There is only one person dancing and it is evidently a woman,' observed Holmes, 'so it is probably Miss Ballantyne. The intention this afternoon, as I understand it, is to begin the rehearsals with the closing scene of the first act, during which Miss Ballantyne is alone on the stage.' As he spoke, there came a pause in the tap-tap of the feet and we heard Miss Ballantyne's voice, slightly muffled, but still distinct enough for us to make out the words of her song:

> On the street at seven,
> Not home until eleven,
> On the corner with my flowers,
> Whether in sunshine or in showers

As she sang, Holmes walked quietly about, his keen eyes darting hither and thither, as he sought for some indication as to why the mystery figure might have been in this room. Presently, he stopped and examined some dust on the floor. Then, after a moment, he turned his gaze to the ceiling. It was dark, especially in the shadows of the crossbeams, but it appeared that directly above his head was a trap-door.

'This is presumably how the genie is produced on stage, in *Aladdin* and similar exotic productions,' said he to me in a low voice, as I joined him beneath the trap-door. 'That equipment,' he continued, indicating a disordered heap of pulleys and poles and ropes, some of which were attached to a wooden platform, 'must be how the actor playing the genie is raised to the level of the stage, above. The actor stands on that platform, the pulleys are attached to those large hooks in the ceiling above us and the stage-hands pull him up, the ascent of the platform perhaps being guided by some structure made out of those poles. For that purpose, of course, the equipment would be positioned immediately beneath the trap-door, but at the moment it is dismantled and pushed to one side. Does anything strike you about the trap-door itself, Watson?'

I looked up. Above our heads, there came a pause in the singing and Miss Ballantyne resumed her skipping dance.

'It is difficult to make it out,' I said, 'but there appear to be four bolts, two on each of the doors, which are placed sideways, so that the doors are secured to the underside of the stage. There is also a stout wooden bar, passing across both doors and presumably secured to the ceiling at either end. At one end of this wooden bar, a length of cord is attached, which passes along the ceiling, through a metal ring and down this pillar. What the point of that is, I cannot imagine.'

Holmes nodded his head, a thoughtful expression upon his face. 'There is a little sawdust on the floor here,' he remarked after a moment, indicating the flagstone at our feet. 'It was that which caught my attention. The inference is that some work has recently been done on the trap-door, or its fixings; but it is difficult to see from here what that work might be. Ah!' he cried all at once, as he glanced rapidly about the room. 'I see there is a long ladder lying by the wall over there. If you would help me bring it here, Watson, I shall climb up and take a closer look!'

We put up the ladder directly beneath the trap-door, its top resting against one of the large crossbeams which supported the ceiling. Then, as I held it steady, Holmes climbed to the top. For several minutes, he examined the trap-door and the surrounding woodwork very closely. As he descended, his face was grave.

'What is it?' I asked.

'It is as I suspected,' said he. 'None of the bolts is fastened, so that the only thing which is now preventing the trap-doors from falling open is that stout wooden bar which runs across beneath them. Under normal circumstances, that would be perfectly adequate, but the fixings of the wooden bar have been recently altered in a subtle and ingenious way. It is evident that it was originally screwed into the ceiling, but the screws which held it have been removed. The wood in the empty screw-holes – two at either end of the bar – is very clean and fresh-looking, indicating that the screws have only recently been removed. The bar is now held in place by two metal brackets, which are screwed into the boards of the ceiling at either side of the trap-door. The brackets are fixed and secure, but the bar itself is not. It can slide along within the brackets, or be pulled out of them altogether, in which case nothing would then be supporting the trap-doors and they would at once fall open. At one end of the wooden bar is a metal ring, to which a length of cord has been attached, as you observed. This cord, as you remarked, passes along the ceiling, through another metal ring and so down to a hook on this wooden pillar, around which the end of it is wound.'

'What does it mean?' I asked, as there came a pause in Miss Ballantyne's dancing and she returned to the song, very loud and clear, immediately overhead.

'I'm very much afraid it means murder, Watson,' returned Holmes in a quiet voice.

'Murder!' I cried in horror. 'Surely you are mistaken! If some malevolent person wishes to delay the production of this play, or even to destroy it altogether, there must be a thousand subtle ways he could achieve his end without resorting to such violence. I simply cannot believe that in these circumstances anyone would contemplate such a dreadful crime!'

'Nevertheless, that is what the evidence indicates, Watson. If that trap-door falls open, anyone standing upon it will plunge on to these flagstones and I cannot think that anyone could survive such a fall. I agree that it would mark a considerable increase in violence compared with what has gone before, but that does not make it impossible. The matter is not so straightforward as you perhaps suppose. But, come! Let us put the ladder away, leave everything down here as we found it and see what is happening upstairs!'

When we returned to the auditorium, Isabel Ballantyne had

completed her rehearsal, and the stage was occupied by the dozen or so young men and women of the chorus, singing and dancing with energy and enthusiasm. Richard Hudson Hardy was personally directing the proceedings from the front of the stalls, standing with the script in his hand and shouting out instructions from time to time. A couple of rows further back, Miss Ballantyne was now sitting with her husband and Jimmy Webster, watching the progress of the rehearsal. Half a dozen rows behind them, a powerful-looking man, with dark hair and moustache, and a dark, sallow face, was sitting, smoking a cigar. For some time we stood at the side of the auditorium, watching the rehearsal, then Holmes plucked my sleeve.

'We have seen all that is necessary for the moment,' said he. 'I doubt that Mr Hardy would welcome an interruption now, so I shall leave him a note in his office.'

As we approached the doors at the back of the auditorium, they were pushed open and a middle-aged man entered, who stared at us for a moment. He was what some might describe as 'well-groomed', but there was an affectation about both his appearance and his manner which I did not much care for.

'Hello!' said he in an arch tone, staring at us as he spoke. 'Gentlemen of the press!'

Holmes shook his head. 'Friends of Mr Hudson Hardy's,' said he.

'Really?' returned the other man. 'I was not aware that he had any!' Then he turned away from us and passed on into the auditorium without another word.

'What a rude, offensive man!' I remarked, as we made our way along to Hardy's office.

Holmes laughed, in that odd noiseless way which was peculiar to him. 'I think we may assume that that was Ludovic Xavier,' said he.

In the office, Holmes wrote a brief note for Hardy, and picked up a large manila envelope from the desk, which contained, he informed me, a copy of the script of *The Lavender Girl* and notes he had made earlier from the record of rehearsals.

Outside, the daylight had now gone and the street lamps were lit, casting their weak, gloomy light upon the many puddles on the surface of the road. The rain had stopped falling, but the night was a bitterly cold one and I shivered as I stood for a moment on the pavement outside the theatre, while my companion paced up and down, looking about him. It was a dismal enough prospect. The road was still busy, with a constant stream of carts and wagons passing by, throwing up cascades of water and mud from the road as they did so. After a moment, I followed Holmes to the corner of the theatre, where he was looking into the little street which lay between the Albion and the blackened ruin of the Palace. It was a short cul-de-sac in which there was nothing to be seen but the sides of the two theatres and, at the end, a tall, blank wall, which was evidently the back of some other building.

'The underground corridor we followed must pass beneath this little street,' remarked my companion in a thoughtful tone. Then, instructing me to wait for him, he crossed to the other side of the cul-de-sac and set off along the main road, passing by the front of the Palace. Presently, when he had gone perhaps fifty or sixty yards, he abruptly stopped, turned on his heel and returned to where I was standing. As he passed, he gestured for me to follow him, and we walked the same distance in the opposite direction. I observed as we did so that he kept glancing at the other side of the road.

'Are you looking for anything in particular?' I asked at length.

'A post office or tobacconist's shop,' he replied.

'You should have told me,' said I in surprise. 'I have both tobacco and stamps in my pocket. You are welcome to help yourself, Holmes.'

'I do not require either tobacco or stamps, Watson,' returned my companion. 'I have some of my own. Thank you for the offer all the same.'

Then, without further explanation, he whistled for a cab and within a minute we were rattling along towards Waterloo Bridge, just as the rain began to fall heavily once more.

V

For a long time that evening, my companion sat silently curled up in his chair by the fire, puffing away at his pipe, and poring over the script of *The Lavender Girl* and the notes he had made earlier. I did not question him on the matter. I knew that he disliked being questioned about a case upon which he was still working and that he would enlighten me of his own accord when he was ready to do so. I occupied myself, therefore, in writing up my own journal and in attempting to bring a little order to my somewhat chaotic records of the previous year's experiences. But my thoughts kept wandering from the old cases on the table before me, to ponder the present singular business at the Albion Theatre. My association with Sherlock Holmes had led me over the years into some very strange affairs, in unlikely places, but none, surely, was more bizarre than our present investigation, and I returned again and again in perplexity to the question of what it all might mean. Outside our chambers, the wind had risen, hurling rain and hail against our windows with ferocious violence, and moaning like an angry beast in the chimney. As I reflected upon Hardy's fear that the weather might affect the attendance at the opening night of *The Lavender Girl*, I wondered again who the mysterious enemy might be who appeared so determined to wreck the production and to what lengths such a person might go. Holmes's suggestion that murder was planned struck me again as utterly beyond belief, and yet it could not be denied that the way the fixings of the trap-door had been interfered with could mean nothing else. At about nine o'clock, my meandering thoughts were abruptly interrupted, when, scarcely audible above the howl of the elements, there came a sudden sharp peal at the bell.

'You are not expecting anyone?' asked Holmes, looking up from his papers.

'Not I.'

'No doubt it is some friend of Mrs Hudson's, then,' said he, and returned to his study.

A moment later, however, the door of our sitting-room was opened and I looked up in surprise as our landlady ushered in a broad-chested, powerful-looking man, with dark, sallow features and a large dark moustache. I recognised him at once as the man I had observed watching the rehearsal in Hardy's Theatre, earlier that day.

'Count Laszlo of Sipolia,' read Mrs Hudson from the card in her hand.

'It is a wild night to be abroad, Count Laszlo!' said Holmes, putting down his papers and rising to his feet. 'Pray, take a seat!'

Our visitor shook his head. 'If it is all the same to you, I will remain standing,' he returned. 'I do not expect to be here very long. I regret the lateness of this visit, but I was unable to cancel my earlier engagements and I was determined to see you this evening. I understand,' he continued after a moment, 'that Mr Richard Hudson Hardy has asked you to look into certain matters for him. That is so, is it not?' he queried, as Holmes did not reply.

'May I enquire who gave you this information?' asked Holmes.

'Hardy himself did. I observed you in the theatre this afternoon and later asked him who you were. He told me that he had engaged you this morning.'

'If Mr Hardy has elected to give you that information, you must suppose that it is true,' said Holmes. 'I cannot see that there is anything I can add to the matter. I do not understand what it is you expect me to say.'

'I have come here to ask you what you have learnt – if anything – since you have been looking into the matter.'

Holmes raised an eyebrow. 'You must surely realise, Count Laszlo,' he replied, 'that I am not at liberty to answer that question, even supposing for a moment that I wished to do so. Anything I learn in the course of my professional work is a matter of the strictest confidence between my client and myself. Your question is therefore a most improper one and I am surprised at your even thinking to ask it. It is an offence at law in this country, Count Laszlo, to seek to learn confidential matters with which one has no business.'

A look of impatience and annoyance crossed the nobleman's face. 'Not my business?' cried he. 'How dare you speak so! Quite apart from any other consideration, I have invested a large amount of money in Mr Hardy's present production. Anything which might affect that production, and my investment in it, is therefore certainly my business.'

'What your interest in the matter may be is for you to judge, Count Laszlo. For myself, my duty is clear. If I am indeed retained by Mr Hardy, it is to look into certain matters and report back to him. I am not retained to retail his private business to anyone who happens to drop by of an evening.'

'Bah! You are making a mistake, Mr Holmes, to trifle with me in this way!'

'I assure you it is no trifling matter to me,' returned Holmes.

'And nor to me, sir! I must insist upon your answering my questions!'

'And I must insist upon declining. May I make a suggestion?'

'What is it?'

'That if there is anything you wish to know, you put your questions to Mr Hardy.'

'But he tells me he knows nothing! He says that you have not yet reported to him!'

'Well, well. No doubt I shall do so within the next few days, if I have anything to report. You can ask him again then.'

'You refuse to tell me anything?'

'It is not a matter of refusal, Count Laszlo; the questions you are asking are quite improper and as such are not questions which it is in my power either to refuse or allow. Indeed, it may be that I am guilty of a professional lapse by even standing here, speaking to you at all.'

'Bah!' cried our visitor again. 'You have not heard the last of me, Mr Holmes! This matter is not closed!'

'But I regret, Count Laszlo, that this interview must be.'

With a look of anger in his eye, our visitor thereupon clapped his hat on his head and left the room without another word. A moment later, I heard the front door slam.

'What a modest, unassuming gentleman Count Laszlo is!' remarked Holmes with a chuckle, as he resumed his seat by the fire. 'If he would but exercise a little patience, he will discover soon enough what I have learnt! As I remarked earlier, Watson, we are wading in deeper waters than was at first apparent!'

VI

Holmes was out all the following morning, but returned at lunch-time. He appeared in good spirits and, as he helped himself to bread and cheese, he described his morning to me.

'I have been endeavouring to interest the authorities at Scotland Yard in our little investigation,' said he. 'It has been a decidedly uphill task, somewhat, I imagine, like trying to interest a costermonger in the subtleties of medieval Latin. I was passed in turn from one official to another, until I ended up at length with Inspector Athelney Jones. I don't believe you have met Jones, Watson. It is a pleasure you will have this afternoon, should you care to accompany us. He is a large, burly man. Indeed, so stout is he that I have wondered sometimes if his corpulence was not perhaps designed by a benevolent Nature to compensate for his intellect, which tends in the opposite direction. Still, on this occasion he did eventually manage to grasp the relevant fact, that in my opinion an attempt at murder is in prospect, which may well succeed unless we act to prevent it. In short, he has agreed to accompany me to Hardy's Theatre this afternoon and observe things for himself. I rather fancy that the drama off stage will prove every bit as compelling as that on stage. Will you come?'

'Nothing could prevent it!'

'Excellent! I may require you to hold Inspector Jones in check. He has a tendency to approach matters like a bull at a gate, and if by his lack of subtlety he reveals our intentions too soon it could be fatal to our plans. If our murderer is frightened off, we may lose the chance of making an arrest.'

'You are confident that he will make his attempt today?'

'It must be so. The full dress-rehearsal takes place this evening. Provided it goes acceptably well, many of the company will not come to the theatre at all tomorrow and the day after that will be opening night. Tonight, then, we may be certain, is the moment that hooded villain has planned for his diabolical scheme.'

'We must prevent this monstrous crime at all costs!' I cried.

'Certainly we must,' agreed my friend. 'That is, of course, the paramount consideration. Nevertheless, there are others.'

'I cannot think of any.'

'There is the consideration, for a start, of apprehending the villain.'

'Surely, if we prevent the crime, it will be by apprehending the villain.'

'Not necessarily. If he realises we have discovered the truth, he will not act. Thus, although we should have prevented the crime, we would have no grounds for an arrest. The villain might be able to provide some perfectly plausible explanation of his actions and deny all knowledge of the deadly trap-door. If so, it would probably be impossible to prove that he was not telling the truth.'

'We should have prevented his mischief, anyway.'

'That is true, but he may find some other way to achieve his end. In my experience, those with murder in their heart rarely abandon their plans after the first setback. We must, therefore, seize the villain in the very act of carrying out his monstrous design, at the point when it will be utterly impossible for him to protest his innocence. It is for this reason that we must be in position in good time. I am afraid, therefore, that our vigil is likely to be a long and tedious one. There will be no light by which we might read and we shall have to remain in complete silence. Taken all in all, it may be that our chief occupation will be in preventing Inspector Jones from falling asleep.'

We took a cab to Scotland Yard shortly after lunch, from where Inspector Jones accompanied us to the theatre. He was, as Holmes had described, a large, burly and plethoric man, but with a pair of very keen and twinkling eyes, which had the appearance of spying furtively upon the world from behind his puffy red cheeks. As we travelled to Hardy's Theatre, he asked numerous questions concerning the business that was taking us there, to all of which Sherlock Holmes gave patient and detailed answers.

'So,' said the policeman at length, in a husky, wheezy voice, 'let us sum the matter up. Some person has, it seems, been making a nuisance of himself and now, if your theory is to be believed, Mr Holmes, this same person intends to commit murder.'

'That is correct.'

'If you don't mind my pointing it out,' remarked Jones after a moment, in a portentous tone, 'it seems something of an increase in violence, I must say, to pass from pushing people over and turning gas-taps off, to plotting a murder.'

'I quite agree, but it is the only conclusion possible from the care with which the trap-door in the stage has been prepared.'

'Well, I shall have a look at it when we get there and give you my opinion.'

'By all means.'

At the theatre, we found Hardy in his office, sorting through piles of papers on his desk. He had the air of one with much work to do and little time to do it in, and hardly seemed to be listening when Holmes explained that we wished to take another look in the basement, but would probably not stay long. I had the impression that Inspector Jones was about to hold forth on some topic or other to the theatre manager, but Holmes ushered him along the corridor.

'I do not want to tell Hardy our true purpose in being here,' said he, as we descended the stairs to the basement. 'I am not confident that his discretion can be relied upon, especially in his present distracted state of mind.'

In the chamber beneath the stage, we lit the gas and made a careful examination of every alcove and corner, until we were satisfied that there could be no one hiding there. Then Holmes put up the ladder immediately beneath the trap-door, and invited Jones to clamber up and take a look for himself.

'As you can see,' said Holmes, when the policeman had taken his burly frame to the very top of the ladder, 'the safety-bolts are all unfastened. If you now examine the wooden bar, to which the cord is attached, you will observe that the four screws which secured it to the ceiling have been removed. It is now held in place only by the two brackets, which have been recently added. Careful, Inspector! If it slips from the brackets, it will fall and the trap-door will at once drop open!'

'I don't need you to tell me about screws and brackets, Mr Holmes,' returned Jones in a husky voice. 'I've seen one or two screws in my time, I can tell you. What we have to establish is *why* these changes have been made.'

'Surely it is clear,' returned Holmes in an impatient tone. 'Dr Watson saw the mystery figure in this part of the basement. It is evident that he intends to pull out the wooden bar by tugging on this cord, in which case anyone standing up there would undoubtedly fall on to these flags and would almost certainly be killed.'

'Well,' said Jones as he slowly descended the ladder; 'that is *your* theory, anyway, Mr Holmes.'

'What else do you suggest?'

'I am not much of a one for theories,' replied the policeman, in an annoyingly complacent tone, 'but I can see flaws in other people's. How, for a start, can the murderer know that anyone will obligingly stand on the trap-door just when he wishes them to?'

'Because he has observed where the various actors stood at the rehearsals.'

Jones snorted. 'Just because an actor stands in a place once doesn't mean he will stand there again,' said he dismissively.

'But it does,' Holmes persisted. 'There are marks painted on the stage, to guide the actors, so that they will be in approximately the same position at each performance.'

'I didn't know that.'

'Well, it is the case, I assure you.'

'Mind you,' said the policeman, 'I have never seen any play more than once, so I wouldn't know if the actors occupied the same positions on different nights or not. Once is quite enough for me, I always say.'

'I am sure you do; but may we return to the matter in hand?'

'The matter in hand, as I see it,' returned Jones, looking up at the ceiling, 'is that trap-door. In my opinion, there is something decidedly suspect about it. But what makes you so sure that murder is intended?'

'Simply because I think it more than likely that anyone falling through the trap on to this hard floor would break his neck. Would you not agree?'

'Possibly,' replied the policeman in a cautious tone. 'Rather than rushing into theories, I prefer to wait and see what happens.'

'We are not likely to see anything if we don't conceal ourselves soon,' said Holmes with a glance at his watch. 'Let us put the ladder away, dowse the light, and make ourselves somewhat less visible!'

In a few moments, we had taken up our position behind a large stack of crates, packed with boots and shoes of all shapes and sizes. Above our heads, someone was sweeping the stage, but, save that soft, rhythmic sound, the whole theatre was in perfect silence. Crouching on the floor in that dark room, I found myself reflecting on the events that had brought us there. If Holmes was correct – and I could not doubt that he was – a most devilish plot was about to reach its climax. This thought appalled me beyond measure. How could anyone plan such a cruel and heartless crime? I had seen vicious fighting during my army service in India; I had witnessed death, both of friend and foe; but this cold, calculated plotting of murder, by someone probably known to the intended victim, was surely of another order of cruelty altogether. Merely to contemplate it made the hairs rise on the back of my neck and my blood run cold. And what, besides, could be the purpose of so horrible a crime? For some time, I considered the matter from every angle, but could reach no definite conclusion.

After a while – perhaps forty-five minutes, although it was difficult to judge the passage of time with any accuracy – there came the sound of footsteps, and several distinct voices, from the stage above us. Shortly afterwards, I heard someone playing what sounded like an oboe and the sound of other instruments being tuned up. The general hubbub gradually increased, over the course of half an hour or so, and many footsteps and gay voices passed by in the basement corridor outside our room. Then, at length, the noise in the basement died away, as that on the stage above us increased, and it was evident that the rehearsal was about to begin.

A few minutes later, there came a moment or two of relative silence, during which I heard what was probably Hardy's voice, then the orchestra struck up what I took to be the overture and soon the rehearsal was in full flow. The music, the singing and the dancing seemed very loud in our chamber, but they were punctuated at regular intervals by quieter passages, when the characters in the play were speaking. During these interludes, although the voices of the actors came to my ears clear enough, I found it impossible to pick out their words. For perhaps another forty-five minutes, I followed the progress of the first act of the play, then, after a particularly rousing song, there came the sound of a general exodus from the stage. I also heard odd, isolated footsteps in the passage outside our room, but most of those who had left the stage appeared to have remained upstairs, no doubt watching the progress of the rehearsal from the wings. All at once, I realised that I was holding myself very tense. Intuitively, I think I knew that if the mystery figure were going to put in an appearance at all, it would probably be in the next few minutes.

Scarcely had this thought crossed my mind when I heard the door of our chamber open softly. For a brief moment, a flash of dim light from the lamp in the corridor lit up the ceiling, then vanished, as the door was closed again. Every nerve in my body tensed and I longed to see who had entered, but I dared not make any sudden movement, lest I give away our presence. Above our heads, the first act of *The Lavender Girl* was continuing with a quiet scene. A moment later, I heard a match being struck, somewhere on the other side of the crates of boots, then a hiss, as the gas-jet by the door was lit. For a moment, the light flared up, casting strange black shadows on to the walls of the room, then the gas-tap was evidently turned right down, for the illumination subsided to a dull glow.

I had positioned myself so that by leaning out sideways I should be able to see round the side of a large crate. Slowly now, and with infinite care, I inched my head and shoulders to the side in that direction. Near the centre of the room, beneath the trap-door and facing away from me, stood the figure I had encountered in the corridor the previous day. Though I could make out little more than a silhouette against the dim light of the lamp beyond, there could be no mistaking that long robe and large, enveloping hood. Beside me, Inspector Jones was peering intently through the narrow gap between two boxes and, beyond him, Holmes was craning over the top of a wicker hamper.

From above us now came an increase in the noise and I judged that the whole of the chorus had returned to the stage. This passage was brief, however, ending with a rousing flourish from the orchestra. Then came softer music, which I recognised from the day before, and I realised that the rehearsal had almost reached the end of the first act. A moment later, Isabel Ballantyne began her song and her dance across the stage to the fatal trap-door. The hooded figure looked up, clearly following the tap-tap of her footsteps, and reached out a white hand to where the end of the cord was coiled round the hook on the wooden pillar. Slowly, without a sound, he uncoiled it and held it looped in his hand. Miss Ballantyne had paused in her dance now and was, I reckoned, standing upon the trap-door itself.

All at once, with a suddenness that startled me, there came an abrupt scraping noise from beside me. Inspector Jones, in craning forward, had evidently leaned too heavily upon the box in front of him, which had abruptly given way and had slipped forward across the floor. The hooded figure looked round sharply in our direction. Within the hood, nothing was visible but unfathomable blackness. At that instant, Sherlock Holmes stood up and stepped forward.

'I should not pull that rope if I were you,' said he in a clear firm voice.

The figure started visibly. Then, as Jones and I also stood up, he took a quick pace backwards and surveyed us all. An instant later, he had thrust his free hand into a pocket in the robe and brought out a large revolver.

'You!' said he to me in a deep, growling voice, directing the pistol in my direction. 'Get over there with the others!' Then, as I took a pace sideways, he glanced up at the trap-door above him. Isabel Ballantyne had almost reached the end of the verse and would at any moment dance away from where she stood.

'Don't be a fool!' cried Jones. 'If you pull that rope, and she falls, you'll hang for it.'

'Quiet!' cried the dark figure in a loud, angry tone, raising his pistol and pointing it at the policeman's face. Then, as the music above us reached a crescendo, his grip on the cord tightened and, stepping backwards, he gave it a firm tug. The cord went taut, Inspector Jones cried out and I looked up at the trap-door with a hollow feeling in my stomach. But nothing happened. The dark figure grunted with surprise and anger, looked up and pulled hard on the cord again. In the split second that his attention was concentrated upon the trap-door, Sherlock Holmes sprang forward, like a tiger upon its prey, and seized the hand holding the revolver in both of his, forcing it up and back.

His adversary at once released his hold on the cord and brought his free hand down upon Holmes's throat, his fingers closing in a powerful grip. But Jones and I sprang forward and threw our weight into the struggle. Our enemy was a very powerful man, of that there could be no doubt, but between the three of us we forced him off his feet and down to the floor. In another moment, Holmes had wrestled the gun from his grasp and Jones had managed to clap a pair of handcuffs upon his wrists. At that very moment, as we struggled to regain our breath, the door from the corridor was flung back with a crash. In the open doorway at the top of the steps stood Count Laszlo of Sipolia, a pistol held rock-steady in his hand.

'What is happening here?' he demanded in a fierce voice. 'Hah!' he cried, as he caught sight of our prisoner on the floor. 'I thought as much! Stand aside, and I will put a bullet in that blackguard's heart!'

Inspector Jones rose quickly to his feet.

'I am a police officer,' said he in a voice of authority, 'and I must ask you, sir, to put that firearm away. The situation is under control, and no assistance from the public is required.'

'More's the pity!' said the Count. 'I had hoped to catch the villain alone and to deal with him myself.' With an air of reluctance, he thrust his revolver deep into his overcoat pocket. 'If any harm had come to Isabel Ballantyne, I can assure you that this man would never have left the theatre alive!'

He was interrupted as a stream of the most foul oaths and vicious abuse poured from the lips of our prisoner, who lay, breathing heavily, upon the floor. 'You infernal, interfering busybody!' he cried at last at Sherlock Holmes, in a voice which was wild with anger. 'Damn you!'

'Now, now,' returned Holmes in a calm voice, as he adjusted his collar. 'You know it is every man's solemn duty to interfere and be a busybody if he knows that murder is planned!' Then he leaned down and, in one swift movement, pulled away the velvet mask, to reveal the features of Captain William Trent, so twisted with rage as to be almost unrecognisable.

VII

'It is evident,' said Sherlock Holmes, as we sat either side of a blazing fire in our rooms in Baker Street, later that evening, 'that for some time Trent had been determined to rid himself of his wife. He would have realised, however, that should she meet her death in sudden and suspicious circumstances, he would inevitably be a chief suspect in the eyes of the authorities. He therefore conceived a scheme in which a series of malevolent actions would appear to be directed at Richard Hudson Hardy's theatre company in general – for which no suspicion could possibly attach to him, he being one of the financial sponsors of the company – which would culminate, however, with the murder of his wife.'

'But if *The Lavender Girl* had been cancelled, Trent stood to lose a large amount of money,' I protested.

'Perhaps so; but that was evidently of less importance to him than being rid of his wife. In any case, it is not certain that Miss Ballantyne's death would necessarily have entailed the cancellation of *The Lavender Girl*. It would, of course, have been postponed, but it might have opened later, with Lydia Summers, or someone else, in the leading role.'

'I suppose it might,' I conceded; 'although I doubt if anyone else could have adequately replaced Isabel Ballantyne. Why on earth,' I cried, as I reflected upon this possibility, 'would anyone wish to be rid of a woman of such charm and such gifts?'

Holmes chuckled. 'As I have had occasion to mention to you once or twice before, my dear fellow,' replied he in a tone of amusement, 'you must never let your admiration for the fair sex affect your assessment of a case! You perceive Isabel Ballantyne only from a distance, as it were, in the form in which she presents herself to the public. Perhaps upon closer acquaintance she appears somewhat less charming and gifted. Who knows? Perhaps she had an annoying habit of singing whenever her husband wished to discuss the movement of prices on the Stock Exchange, or perhaps she fell asleep and snored each time he began to describe the hunting of tigers in India. We cannot say. I am hopeful that Count Laszlo might be able to enlighten us on that side of things. He promised he would call by this evening on his way home.'

'Did you ever suspect that Trent was behind all that had happened?'

'I was certain of it.'

'What! How on earth could you know? After all, Miss Ballantyne herself had described to us how her husband had tried to persuade her to leave the production.'

'Yes, the cunning devil! It is evident he made the suggestion in the full and certain knowledge that his wife would never agree to it. But, to describe to you how I came to perceive the truth: when first we went down to the Albion yesterday, I suspected no one. The data with which I had been supplied were too meagre for me to form any meaningful suspicions, and it would have been a capital mistake to attempt to do so. Whilst we were there, however, an incident occurred which led me to know, with almost complete certainty, that Captain Trent was responsible for what had been happening at the theatre. This incident occurred after we had come up from the basement for the first time. Whilst down there, I had made a few measurements, of footprints, marks on the door-frame and so on, as you will no doubt recall.'

'Certainly.'

'A few simple calculations from those measurements enabled me to form a mental image of the man who had left those traces, an image which was subsequently confirmed, as to height at least, by the mark your assailant left upon the corridor wall as he fled, which was slightly higher than the marks you had made. This image, Watson, was exactly matched by a man who walked in at the front door of the theatre just a short time later. That man was Captain William Trent.'

'But there must be thousands of men in London who are approximately of the same height and build as Trent.'

'There may well be; but just how many of those thousands are intimately connected with Hardy's Theatre? Besides, Trent would have been drawn to my attention in any case because of the incident to which I alluded.'

'What was that?'

'He entered the theatre soaking wet.'

'I may be obtuse,' I remarked, 'but I can see no significance whatever in that observation, Holmes. Why, it was pouring with rain at the time! Anyone would have been wet! If you recall, Jimmy Webster arrived at the theatre in precisely the same condition.'

'That is so; but Webster had come on foot, he informed us, from a coffee-shop some distance away. Whether true or not, his account was at least plausible. Captain Trent offered no such explanation. He had, he said, come directly from his club. He must, then, have come in a cab. But if so, why was he so wet? At the front of Hardy's Theatre is a large glass canopy, which extends across the width of the pavement. Anyone alighting from a cab there could step almost directly under the canopy and thus practically avoid the rain altogether. Clearly, then, Trent had not alighted from his cab outside the front of the theatre just before we saw him, despite the impression that he tried to give. It was evident he had walked from further afield, but there was no clue at that time as to where he might have come from. The only innocent explanation which seemed likely was that he had alighted early from his cab in order to call at a tobacconist's shop or a post office, or somewhere similar. When I surveyed the area later, however, I established that there was no shop of that sort nearby. In the meantime, you and I had discovered the old tunnel which runs between the Albion and the Palace, and it was clear that anyone using it – specifically, the mystery persecutor of Hardy's company – would have emerged into the daylight from the ruined Palace. At the side of the Palace, in the short cul-de-sac between the two theatres, is a little side-door which seemed to me the most likely exit from the building, and the distance from that door to the front of the Albion would be just sufficient for a man to get caught in a sudden downpour and arrive at the Albion soaking wet. I have little doubt that Hardy's missing bunch of keys will be found in Captain Trent's possession and little doubt, either, that one of the keys upon it will fit the side-door of the Palace.

'Of course, if Trent were behind the recent incidents, as I was compelled to believe, then the whole matter was cast in a somewhat different light. Hardy had assumed that the actions of the anonymous miscreant were designed to wreck his production, so that it would not be a success and would not run for long, or might possibly not even open at all. But this motive could not apply to Trent, one of three men who stood to lose money if *The Lavender Girl* were not a success and whose own wife was the leading lady in the production. It seemed to me possible, then, that the whole series of fairly trivial incidents might be nothing more nor less than an elaborate blind, to distract attention from Trent's true aim. What this might be, I could not at first conceive; but when – thanks to your alertness, old fellow! – we learnt that he had been in the chamber under the stage and discovered that the trap-door there had been tampered with in an elaborate and highly ingenious manner, I felt sure we had discovered the kernel of his evil scheme. Anyone falling through that trap-door to the flagstones below would surely break his neck. This little piece of malice was therefore on an altogether higher plane of devilry than the spiteful tricks which had gone before. Here, surely, then, was the goal towards which that callous villain had been working.

'But if it was Trent's intention to murder someone, who might that someone be? In the absence of any other obvious motive, his wife – despite all those charms and gifts which have impressed you so greatly – seemed to me the likeliest candidate. Why else would Trent have gone to such lengths to disguise his true intentions? By an examination of the script, I was able to establish that Isabel Ballantyne spent some parts of the play alone on the stage, which was not the case for any of the other characters. Moreover, as you and I observed yesterday afternoon, for some time at the end of the first act she passed over, or stood upon, the trap-door itself. I was convinced, then, that this was when the attempt would be made upon her life. But there is the bell! This may well be our visitor!'

A moment later, our landlady announced Count Laszlo of Sipolia and that broad, powerful-looking figure was shown into the room. I pulled a chair up to the fire for him and, having rubbed his hands together in the warmth for a few moments, he got quickly down to business.

'First of all,' said he, 'I must apologise most profoundly for my conduct at our interview yesterday. You were quite correct. I had no right to ask the questions I did, and you had every right not to answer them. But you must understand, gentlemen, that my position was an extremely difficult one. I have had very grave suspicions for some time as to what might be afoot, but have had no proof of these suspicions. Naturally, I was keen to know if you had discovered anything which might have tended to confirm or refute my suspicions. But, just as you, who had been retained by Miss Ballantyne and Mr Hardy, could not speak freely to me of what you had learnt, so I, who had the most terrible suspicions but no proof, could scarcely speak freely of the matter to you, a perfect stranger to me. I did not doubt your integrity; but I had no way of judging your competence. For all I could tell to the contrary, you might have discovered nothing at all, or you might have discovered some vital fact and, not suspecting Trent's involvement, have spoken of it in front of him. All of this left me in a perfect agony of indecision.'

'Did you reach any conclusion, as a result of our interview?'

'I judged – forgive me – that you had discovered nothing of significance, but were reluctant to admit it. I therefore determined that I should have to act alone. As it turned out, it appears I would have been too late to prevent that devil murdering Miss Ballantyne. In which case, I would have shot him dead.'

'You would have hanged for it,' remarked Holmes, in a matter-of-fact voice.

'If so, then your intervention in this business has saved not one life, but three.'

'How came you to be so intimately involved in the matter?' asked Holmes; 'and what caused the suspicions you have spoken of?'

'I will tell you,' said Count Laszlo. 'As you may be aware, I have followed Isabel Ballantyne's career with very great interest and appreciation, and have known her personally for many years. Indeed, I will admit to you, gentlemen, what it might embarrass me to admit before a larger audience, that I harboured hopes in the past that she would one day do me the honour of consenting to be my wife. You may consider such a hope absurd, or impertinent, but nevertheless, that was the case. When, however, Captain Trent appeared upon the scene, and conducted his courtship of Miss Ballantyne with the ruthlessness and dispatch with which he no doubt conducted his tiger-hunts, I bore him no ill-will. Indeed, I wished him well, for it appeared, for a time at least, that he had achieved what no one else had managed, including, I regret to say, myself, which is that he seemed to have made Miss Ballantyne happy. After a while, however – for I still saw them from time to time, although not so frequently as before their marriage – it seemed to me that this was no longer so. Indeed, to one who knew her of old, it was apparent that Isabel was profoundly unhappy. This, as you will imagine, caused me great concern. Then, quite by chance, information came my way which suggested that Trent was being despicably cruel to his wife, both mentally and physically. At first I was shocked at this and could not believe it was really true; but further information which reached me confirmed the suggestion beyond doubt.

'I suppose the fact that I had become anxious about the situation opened my ears a little and gossip which would have previously quite passed me by began now to catch my attention, and contribute to the ugly picture which was forming in my mind. It must have been something of the sort, for I assure you that I did not go out of my way to discover things, or to interfere in what was not my business; but, little by little, further intelligence relating to Trent came my way: that he had been engaged to be married once before, whilst in India, and that the engagement had been broken off by his fiancée when certain facts about his conduct had come to light; that he had come very close to being charged with murder over the death of another man during a tiger-hunt; that he was not quite so wealthy as he liked people to believe; and that shortly before his whirlwind courtship of Miss Ballantyne he had spoken to acquaintances of how great he believed her own wealth to be.

'I imagine you can see now the picture that formed in my mind: of a ruthless, reckless man, who had pursued Miss Ballantyne chiefly on account of the wealth he imagined she possessed. But I have, as I remarked, been intimate with Miss Ballantyne for many years, and I know that she is not nearly so wealthy as is popularly supposed.

Her antecedents were very humble ones. Her father was a railway employee, at a place called Laisterdyke, near Bradford in Yorkshire, and when he died, some years ago, her mother was left in very difficult circumstances. Throughout her professional life, Miss Ballantyne has been sending money regularly to her mother and to her two younger sisters. She has also, although she does not wish this to be generally known, contributed a great deal of money to various charitable and philanthropic causes. Thus, although she has earned considerable sums of money in recent years, she has given much of it away and has amassed very little for herself. How disappointing it must have been for the grasping Captain Trent to discover this after they were married!

'Recently, I engaged a private detective to report to me on Trent's activities. It may not seem a very honourable thing, to spy upon another man's private life; but the conduct upon which I was spying was itself not honourable. The very first report I received informed me that Trent had dined privately, on several occasions, with Lydia Summers. At once I recalled how keen Trent had been to recommend Miss Summers to Mr Hardy when the latter was first beginning work on *The Lavender Girl*, and how he had laid great stress upon her father's wealth, and how useful it might therefore be to have Sir Cecil Summers connected with the theatre company. Again, that villain was thinking of wealth and, I was convinced, of how he might acquire it. It was then that I began to seriously fear for Miss Ballantyne's safety. When a man is as reckless and unprincipled as Trent, there is no knowing what he might do.

'The part played by Miss Summers in all this, incidentally, is, in the main, I believe, an innocent one. She is a somewhat dull-witted girl, and her chief points of attraction definitely lie in her purse – or in that of her father, at least. Whether it struck her as at all unusual or improper to dine alone in an obscure restaurant with another woman's husband, I cannot say. No doubt Trent convinced her that it was the most natural thing in the world. He talks well to women. But she is not essentially dishonourable. Had she guessed the fiendish scheme that was in his mind, I strongly suspect that she would have declined to have anything more to do with him.

'This scheme, I am convinced, was first to rid himself of his wife, and then to woo and wed Miss Summers. And had it not been for your timely intervention, gentlemen, the despicable villain might well have succeeded!'

'It cannot have been very pleasant for Miss Ballantyne to learn that her husband has been plotting to murder her,' remarked Holmes. 'It is scarcely a morale-boosting discovery, two days before opening night. What will happen to *The Lavender Girl* now, Count Laszlo? Will it be postponed?'

Our visitor shook his head. 'Isabel Ballantyne is very brave,' said he, 'and if anyone can survive such a blow, she can. She is staying with friends now, who will, I know, treat her with a kindness she has never received from her husband. Besides, terrible though the revelation is, I suspect that in her heart Isabel has known for some time that something was seriously amiss. I believe that intuitively she suspected that Trent was behind the recent events at the Albion, but could not bring herself to acknowledge that suspicion. Now, her chief consideration is not to let her friends down. She insists that *The Lavender Girl* will open as advertised, on Saturday evening. Miss Summers, I might add, has withdrawn from the production. She could scarcely do otherwise. Her name will inevitably figure in any future court case involving Trent, either criminal or civil. Her role in the play has been taken by a delightful girl from the chorus, who has a sweet voice and will, I believe, do very well. Hardy is already reconciled to the likelihood of managing without Sir Cecil Summers's bounty, but as he has not yet seen a penny of that fabled wealth, that will be no loss. In any case, I have informed him that I shall in future take a more active part in the business, especially upon the financial side. I look forward to a prosperous future for the company.'

'How came you to appear in the room beneath the stage when you did?' asked Holmes.

'As I have described, I had suspected for some time that Trent was planning something, but had no idea what form his evil plans might take. Yesterday afternoon, however, a curious thing happened. It was raining very heavily when I arrived at the theatre, so I sat in my carriage for a few moments, waiting for it to let up. I was thinking about Isabel and her husband, when, to my very great surprise, Captain Trent himself appeared from round the side of the theatre. I leaned back in my seat so that he would not see me, and reflected on the matter. What, I wondered, had he been doing round there? I instructed my coachman to turn into the little street by the side of the theatre. There was only one place there from which Trent could possibly have come, the locked side-door of the old Palace Theatre. But what possible business could he have in there? And then it was as if the scales fell from my eyes! Trent had discovered the old tunnel between the two theatres which I remembered having read about two or three years ago. It was he that was responsible for all the nasty little tricks which had been played upon the company recently and on each occasion he had used the tunnel to make good his escape! I saw it all now and feared that some serious harm might be intended for Miss Ballantyne. I therefore resolved that I would keep guard in the basement corridor today, during the dress-rehearsal. It seems, however, that I would, nevertheless, have been too late. Somehow, that devil slipped by me and I heard nothing until the sounds of your struggle came to my ears. How fortunate it was for Miss Ballantyne that you were more alert than I and cleverer than that serpent, Trent, to foil his devilish plot!'

'And how fortunate it was for Miss Ballantyne,' I interjected, 'that the wooden bar which held the trap-door had jammed and did not slide free!'

Holmes chuckled. 'I am always ready to acknowledge the part played by chance in the affairs of men,' said he; 'but in this case, with regard to the trap-door, at least, I must insist that chance had very little to do with it. The wooden bar did not slide free because I had called in at the theatre in the morning, borrowed a hammer from one of the stage-hands and banged two large nails into the back edge of it, where they could not be seen by anyone looking up from the floor.'

'What!' I cried. 'You might have told me, Holmes! I had no idea that you had been there earlier in the day!'

'My dear fellow! You can hardly suppose that I would leave my client at risk of plummeting to her death. I had been pondering overnight how best to secure the trap-door without making it apparent to Trent that I had done so. In the end I decided that the simplest method was the best. I really could not leave it as we had found it, Watson. The risk was simply too great. Consider, for instance, the number of brewers' drays in London on an average day! Any one of them might have run us down on our way to the theatre and thus prevented our reaching there in time to save Miss Ballantyne!'

'And even though we were there in good time,' I remarked, 'Trent still succeeded in holding us all at bay until he had pulled on the rope.'

Again my friend chuckled. 'I had a pistol of my own in my pocket,' said he. 'When Inspector Jones's slip gave away our position, I could have whipped it out and had Trent at my mercy at once. But I wished him to think himself secure and thus proceed with his plan, so that his guilt could be proved beyond doubt before three reliable witnesses! I am sorry that I had to keep you in the dark about the trap-door, old man! But I was concerned that if you knew that I had secured it, you might inadvertently reveal the fact to Jones; and if Jones knew about it, he might inadvertently reveal it to Trent. I am sure that under the circumstances you will forgive my reticence on the point!'

'I am more than familiar with your tendency to reticence,' said I, laughing. 'Frankly, I doubt that my granting or withholding forgiveness will make the slightest difference to it! But if you would value my forgiveness, I hereby grant it!'

'For what you have done,' said Count Laszlo in a serious tone, 'I can never repay you and any gesture I might make would be but a trifle. Nevertheless, I should be greatly honoured if you would be my guests on Saturday evening. I have a private box for the opening of *The*

Lavender Girl, and am entertaining the entire company afterwards in my rooms at the Langham Hotel.'

'I am honoured by your invitation,' replied Holmes, 'but regret that I shall be otherwise engaged on Saturday evening.'

My face must have betrayed the disappointment I felt at this response; for after a glance in my direction, and a moment's pause, my friend's features broke into a smile and he chuckled.

'But, perhaps, on this occasion, I could cancel my other engagements!' said he with a merry laugh. 'After all, both Dr Watson and I have certainly made a contribution, however indirect, to the eventual success of *The Lavender Girl*; so it is perhaps no more than fitting if we are in attendance when she is at last presented to the world!'

The Adventure of the Old School Friend

It has been justly observed of medicine that it can never be wholly a science, but must also be at least partly an art. For unlike the other scientific subjects, its field of study is not that of inanimate substances and forces, but living and breathing human beings, who are not always amenable to being treated in a purely scientific manner, and who are, generally speaking, less interested in hearing one's opinion of what is wrong with them than in achieving full health once more. This fact serves not only to distinguish medicine from the other sciences, but also to mark a division in the ranks of medical practitioners themselves. All medical men serve the same deity, but an individual's temperament will determine the character of his service.

There are medicos of my acquaintance, for instance, to whom the presence of other human beings seems nothing but an irksome distraction, except when it is a downright nuisance, especially if the human beings in question should actually have the effrontery to be ill. Such men find their most useful employment in medical research. For others, the study of one particular aspect of the complex that is a man becomes so absorbing that it is only as specialists that they can achieve professional satisfaction. But for many – and among these I would number myself – the chief interest lies not in any one illness or condition to which a person may fall victim, but in that person as a whole, whatever may ail him. For such medical men, who derive their satisfaction from diagnosing and treating the quite unpredictable variety of complaints with which their patients present them, there is nothing so good as general practice.

The choice of general practice – the specialisation in generality, as it has been termed – has the added advantage, also, that in following it, one comes into contact to a quite singular degree with the multifarious panorama of life; for one's patients have a habit of adulterating their descriptions of what ails them with large measures of personal history and local anecdote. The years I had shared chambers with Sherlock Holmes had sharpened my taste for all that was *outré* and out of the common, and I enjoyed hearing the unusual experiences of my patients. Only when it was apparent that some unusually garrulous patient regarded his physician as a captive audience for as long as he chose to hold forth have I been tempted on occasion to regret my choice of medical career.

When I took over the Paddington practice of old Dr Farquhar, shortly after my marriage, I was at once involved in a more strenuous round of work than I had known since my days in the Army Medical Department. No longer in his prime, Farquhar had had neither the energy nor the inclination to put any great amount of effort into the practice, with the inevitable result that a decline had set in, and many of his patients had transferred to the rival practice of the young and vigorous Dr Jackson. The temptation to effect such a change must indeed have been a great one, for the temptation most difficult to resist is that which calls for the least expenditure of effort; and in this respect the circumstances could scarcely have been more agreeable, the premises of the two doctors standing side by side in the same street. Still, the physical proximity of our consulting-rooms could just as well work to my advantage as to that of my rival, I reasoned, and I was confident that by dint of hard work I could more than recoup the losses that my predecessor had suffered.

Thus it was that I found myself busily making acquaintance with all manner of folk, and if I had hoped to learn something of the eccentricities of the human race as I learnt something of their bodily infirmities, I was not disappointed. For although it was not a large practice that I had inherited from Dr Farquhar, it was certainly a varied one. Scarcely a day passed but I encountered some surprising novelty of human behaviour or experience.

One frail old lady, whose delicate and refined appearance had led me to suppose that she had never in her life travelled beyond the bounds of London, surprised me greatly one day, when she began to speak of the twenty-five years she had spent in the jungles of Borneo. Another of my patients, an unexceptional-looking, middle-aged man, a railway employee at Paddington station, turned out to have the most profound and erudite knowledge of Anglo-Saxon coins and medallions, upon which subject he had written numerous monographs. There was also, I regret to recall, Mr Septimus Witherington. He was a softly spoken, learned-looking man and I had mentally marked him down as something of a scholar. Unfortunately, scholar though he may have been, he was also a monomaniac.

Upon my expressing enthusiasm for English literature, in response to some casual remark of his, he at once launched into the most rambling and long-winded disquisition that it has ever been my misfortune to hear, the chief theme of which was that the works generally ascribed to William Shakespeare were in fact written by someone else altogether. I had no especial objection to this thesis; indeed, the detective-work which was involved in it appealed to my inquisitive nature; but his mode of argument was quite intolerable; for, like all true fanatics, he was unable to present his views except in the most violently abusive of terms.

In vain I attempted to interrupt him; in vain I shuffled the papers upon my desk and rearranged my medical instruments; in vain I consulted my watch ostentatiously, stood up from my desk and wound the clock upon the mantelpiece. Nothing, it seemed, could stem his flow. At length I was obliged to be a little brusque with him, whereupon he at once took great offence, informed me that I was as big a fool as I looked, and stamped out of the room in high dudgeon. Of Mr Witherington and his theories I have since heard no more, but I cannot say in all honesty that this state of affairs has ever caused me any great regret.

Not all my patients turned out so eccentric as this, however –

perhaps fortunately, from the point of view of their physician's good humour – and I was privileged to be the recipient of many interesting – and some most surprising – anecdotes. Perhaps most memorable of all is the story I now propose to relate, which concerns the curious adventure of Mr Alfred Herbert and the oriental idol. This was remarkable not only for its surprising turns of events and unforeseen outcome, but also because chance decreed that I was myself to play an active part in the matter – and because, also, it provided an opportunity for me to observe once more the singular talents of my remarkable friend, Mr Sherlock Holmes.

———

It was a bright, sunny period in August, the very type of the perfect English summer, with blue skies from dawn to dusk and a gentle breeze to moderate the heat. The weather being so good, there were few calls upon my professional services and I was taking the opportunity to catch up on my reading of the medical journals when Mr Herbert was shown into my consulting-room, early one evening. He was a short and stockily-built man of about my own age, with a large, round, clean-shaven face and slightly protruding eyes. His ailment was mild but chronic bronchitis, which, surprisingly, had not improved at all during the fine weather. I applied my stethoscope to his chest and listened for a moment to the tell-tale rattle from within.

'Well, well; it is not too bad,' said I. 'A little squill in syrup should help.'

'I dare say you have seen more interesting cases, Doctor,' he remarked with a smile, as he pulled on his jacket. 'My illness must be a fairly dull one from your point of view, I imagine.'

'Not at all,' said I, amused by his tone. 'Of course, it is true that yours is hardly the first instance of bronchitis to come my way, but it is none the less interesting for that. It is rare to find two cases exactly the same, even during an epidemic. That is what makes the study of medicine so interesting. The general symptoms of every common complaint are, of course, well known to the newly qualified man, fresh from medical school, but it is only from personal experience that he can gain an appreciation of the amazing variety of forms that each complaint can take. To the man with an enquiring mind, these oddities of variety are endlessly fascinating.'

'Ah!' said Mr Herbert, nodding his head. 'A fellow spirit, I see! I, too, have a taste for oddities, Doctor, although not generally of the medical variety. If you are interested, I can give you a real oddity for your collection! You will never imagine what happened to me the other day!'

'Oh?' said I after a moment, for he stared at me in silence, his eyebrows raised in encouragement, and showed no inclination to proceed until I had responded in some way. It was clear from the look in his eye that he was keen to tell me something, and I confess that I was filled with apprehension as the memory of my interview with Mr Septimus Witherington came back to me.

'I met an old school friend,' he continued at length.

'Really?' said I, as he fell into silence once more, his protruding eyes beckoning me to respond. My experience with Mr Witherington had served as a salutary lesson to me and I was wary of appearing too enthusiastic in my interest.

'I'll wager you don't think that a very odd incident, Doctor!'

'It does not sound especially remarkable,' I conceded.

'But wait until you hear the rest of it! Then I'm sure you'll agree that it is quite the oddity of the year!'

'Excuse me one moment, Mr Herbert, but were there any other patients in the waiting-room?'

'No, sir; I am your last nuisance for today! That gives me an idea, Doctor: what would you say to a bench in a sunny garden, with a glass of the most excellent beer in your hand? I know a splendid place where we can sit and discuss my odd experience.'

I hesitated. In my position it was not desirable for me to be seen frequenting the local public-houses, especially as several of them enjoyed somewhat dubious reputations.

'It is a very quiet and respectable house,' added Herbert, evidently reading the expression upon my face; 'I know the landlord, a smart man by the name of Henderson.'

'What, Tobias Henderson of the Star and Garter?'

'The very same. You know him, then?'

'Only professionally. He got his toe crushed under a hogshead of beer a few weeks ago. He seemed a pleasant enough fellow, considering the somewhat trying circumstances of our meeting.'

'You will come, then?' urged my companion. 'It is a matter upon which I should very much value your opinion, Doctor.'

At that moment I heard the sound of my wife's footsteps as she bustled about upstairs, and this gave me an idea.

'Very well, then,' I agreed with a smile. 'But I cannot stay long. My supper will be on the table shortly.'

In a few moments I had explained matters to my wife and was strolling along the sunny street with Mr Herbert. At least I now had a ready-made excuse to take my leave of him should he reveal himself to be some sort of fanatical bore in the mould of Septimus Witherington. He could scarcely follow me home from the pub, after all, I reasoned. Had we pursued the conversation in my consulting-room, on the other hand, it might have proved difficult to dislodge him had he chosen to ignore my hints.

A walk of ten minutes brought us to the Star and Garter. A garden at the rear was set out with tables and chairs, and dotted about with pots of geraniums and petunias. It was indeed a pleasant spot. The mellow evening sun cast its warm light upon us and I was glad to be out of doors on such a lovely evening. As for my misgivings, they proved quite unfounded, for my companion soon showed himself an engaging narrator and his story was indeed one of the very oddest to come my way.

'Before I tell you of my recent experience,' he began, 'I must first tell you something of my early life, for it has a decided bearing on the matter.' He opened his eyes wide and raised his eyebrows quizzically, I murmured some encouragement and he continued.

'I am not a Londoner by birth, although I dare say you would not guess it to hear me speak now. I was born and raised in Preston, in Lancashire, the county of the red rose. However, this is not especially important. What is important is that I received my preparatory education at Whalley Abbey School, not far from my birthplace. Have you ever heard of the Bowland Forest, Dr Watson, or of Pendle Hill? They are high, wild and exposed regions, such as one can hardly imagine when seated here in the soft lowlands of the Thames.'

'That is where your school was situated, then?'

'Indeed it was, and a more remote and inhospitable situation you could not conceive! I was never very happy at the school – I cannot think that anyone was – and was not sorry when I left, at the age of thirteen. That was twenty-two years ago. I went on to a school at Clitheroe, the only one of my form to do so. My classmates proceeded to various other schools, in different parts of the country, and I did not keep up with any of them, although one or two had been my friends.

'The intervening years of my life, up until the recent events, are not especially relevant: I grew up, received an education which consisted largely of learning how to conjugate Latin verbs and decline Latin nouns, and came to work in London. I had always had something of a talent for figures and this enabled me to find myself a suitable berth in the City, with the stockbroking firm of Persquith and Moran, where a talent for adding and subtracting is of somewhat greater value than an ability to entertain those around you with hilarious remarks in Latin. The few friends I have in London are fellow members of my club, where I generally dine in the evenings, the Lancashire and Yorkshire in St James's Square. It has nothing to do with the railway of the same name,' added my companion quickly with a broad smile, as if he were used to correcting the misapprehension, or were glad, at least, of the opportunity to unburden himself of a long-cherished witticism for which he had not previously been able to find an audience. 'It is, rather, a haven for those from the north of England, where we can meet and discuss the things which are of interest to us. London can be a very lonely place for those who are strangers here, Doctor.'

'I am well aware of it, from personal experience,' I responded. 'I am no more from these parts than you are.'

'Indeed? Then that is something else we have in common. Now, to come to the crux of the matter: about a week ago I was obliged to travel down to Kent to see old Mr Persquith, the head of our firm. He has practically retired, and no longer takes an active part in the business, but wishes still to be advised of any important developments which might affect our standing. With this trouble over the Argentine Southern Railway about to reach a crisis – as I'm sure you've read – I was sent down to inform him of the firm's present position in the matter. As is his wont, he kept me talking for hours, and then, just as his servant sounded the dinner-gong, declared that he was satisfied with my information and that I could go. I thus found myself, after a fair walk down a dark road, tired and hungry, in an ill-lit waiting-room upon the platform of Little Wickling Halt, which is on the line between Maidstone and Ashford.

'It is a lonely spot, for the station is remote from any houses and is little frequented. It lies down in a cutting, so that there is nothing to be seen from the waiting-room window but the railway track, the empty platforms and the bare embankments which rise up on either side of the line. There was no one else about and I had fallen into a brown study, the essential subject of which was my own sad plight and empty stomach, when out of the corner of my eye I saw a pale blur appear at the window. I looked up sharply and there behind the dirt-smeared pane was a man's face, staring in at me, with a look as rigid as a basilisk. My scalp prickled, and for several seconds this apparition and I stared at each other without moving. So still was it that I began to think I was suffering an hallucination. I therefore shut my eyes for a moment, to see if this would drive away the vision. When I opened them again, the face had indeed gone and the window framed nothing but blackness.

"'Well, I never did!" I cried aloud. "Whoever would have thought it!" I began to speculate as to what could have caused the hallucination and had just concluded that the responsibility lay with the toasted cheese I had had for lunch, when the door abruptly opened and a man walked briskly into the room.

"'Hallo!" said I in surprise, rising quickly to my feet.

"'Good evening," returned the newcomer, sitting himself down without further ceremony. He was a gentleman of about my own age, tall, slim and well-groomed, with dark hair and moustache

'We sat in silence for some time. To speak frankly, I felt rather foolish at having spoken aloud to myself and deemed it best to preserve silent dignity. Abruptly, however, my companion broke the silence in the most startling manner.

"'Whalley boys forever!" cried he suddenly in a loud voice, and I nearly jumped out of my skin. "I thought as much," he continued, eyeing me with a smile. "Unless I am very much mistaken, you are Herbert, the boy with the broken desk. You were in Dr Jessop's class when I was in old Newsome's. Do you remember Dr Jessop? –'Stop squirming in your seat, boy! Or I'll give you something to squirm about!'"'

"'My goodness!" I cried in surprise, laughing at his imitation of the old schoolmaster. "You have an excellent memory! My own, I am afraid, is not so good. Your face, now I look at it, is vaguely familiar, but I fear I cannot recall a name to go with it."

'He regarded me with an inscrutable expression for a moment, and then smiled.

"'I very much regret," said he, "that I made less of an impression upon your memory than you did upon mine. You do not recall Stephen Hollingworth?"

"'Why, bless my soul!" said I. "Stephen Hollingworth! I recall the name, of course, now that you mention it. Well, well, well! Who would have thought it!"

'We shook hands warmly, and entered at once into a deep conversation. As might be expected, this largely consisted of reminiscences of our days at Whalley Abbey School, which would be of no interest whatever to anyone else, but at that moment constituted the most interesting subject on earth to us. He asked me how I came to be in the middle of Kent at such an hour and I described the business which had taken me down there.

'"What rotten luck!" cried he, when I told him of the lack of sustenance from which I was suffering. "There I have the advantage of you, Herbert! My family live at Wickling Place, which you probably passed if you walked down the road, and I dined before I left." He rummaged in his pocket for a moment. "I am afraid I can offer you nothing better than a mint humbug," said he at last.

'"I usually dine at the Lancashire and Yorkshire Club," I remarked, taking the proffered sweetmeat. "You are not a member, by any chance?"

'He shook his head. "My sojourn at Whalley Abbey was the only time I spent in the north of England," he returned with a smile. "Other than that, my life has been passed here in the south. But perhaps I could look you up at your club some day. I have heard that it is a splendid place!"

'"Indeed it is," said I with enthusiasm. I invited him to dine with me there the following evening, but he declined, pleading a prior engagement. We promised each other, however, that we should certainly dine together in the near future.

'"After all," said he; "it is not every day that two old school friends meet and in such an oddly out-of-the-way spot, too!"

'We travelled back to town together, chatting animatedly the whole way, and shared a cab from Victoria station. When we reached his house, which lies just north of Oxford Street, he invited me in for a little cold beef and wine, an offer I readily accepted. His house appeared in a state of some disorder, I must say, but he explained to me that he had recently been obliged to dismiss his servants for dishonesty, and had not yet succeeded in finding suitable replacements. I enjoyed his comestibles and his conversation, and returned home with my spirits considerably raised from the depths into which they had sunk earlier in the evening.

'Three days later, I was reading the *Standard* at breakfast-time when the name "Wickling Place" – my old school friend's family home – caught my eye.'

Mr Herbert paused and took out his pocket-book. 'I have the paragraph here, Doctor,' said he, extracting a small oblong cut from a newspaper. He passed it to me, and I read the following account:

SENSATIONAL BURGLARY AT ANCIENT HOUSE

Wickling Place, the home of Colonel Sir Reginald and Lady Hollingworth was burgled on Tuesday night, several valuable works of art, including an early painting by Titian, being stolen. The thieves apparently entered by a French window, at some time between midnight and 6 a.m, without disturbing the household. They appear to have selected for theft the most precious works of art in the house, leaving untouched the less valuable pieces. How they arrived in and left the district is not known, although it is reported that three strangers were seen by several witnesses earlier in the day, upon the Maidstone road. Sir Reginald Hollingworth, a local Justice of the Peace, is well known and respected in the area. This incident is a further blow to the family, coming so soon after the tragic death of his son, Stephen, who was drowned off the coast of Ireland in May.

'Why!' I cried in astonishment. 'It says here that the man you met is dead!'

'One moment,' returned Herbert. 'I will tell you what happened next. All that day I turned the matter over and over in my head, such that I could hardly concentrate upon my work, but I could make nothing of it.

'That evening, I arrived at my club as usual, at about six o'clock, and had my foot upon the doorstep, when the door in front of me was flung open and out stepped Hollingworth. In his hand he carried a small black valise.

'"Thank goodness I have found you!" he cried, his voice throbbing with emotion. "I have been waiting some time, in the hope that you would come." He glanced quickly up and down the street, with an air of great caution, then stepped back inside the doorway. I followed him, and we sat on a settle in the entrance hall. He seemed terrifically agitated.

'"What is the matter?" I asked. "I read this morning of the burglary at your father's house."

'"It is in connection with that business that I wish to speak to you," he responded, nodding his head.

'"It said in the report I read that you had died some time ago."

'Again he nodded, the trace of a grim smile upon his face.

'"That," said he, "was the usual culpable carelessness of the press. They have confused the names: it was my younger brother, Philip – sadly – who drowned. But their carelessness has certainly cost me some trouble – I spent half the morning sending telegrams here, there and everywhere to assure everyone that I am still very much alive. However—" He broke off, and his eyes assumed a faraway look, as if some novel train of thought had occurred to him. "Do you know," cried he at last; "we may yet be able to use the press's blundering to our advantage! Yes, by God, we'll win through yet!"

'"I do not understand," said I, alarmed at the wild tone of his voice.

'"No, no, of course not. I'm sorry, Herbert. It's a rather complicated matter. We had to give the newspapermen something to print; but there's more to this so-called burglary than meets the eye!"

'"Oh?"

'"Yes. The burglars were looking for something, but they didn't find it – the pieces they got away with are of no consequence in comparison – and they never will, so long as I have anything to do with it!"

'"It all sounds very mysterious, Hollingworth!"

'"I suppose it must, to you, Herbert. Look, old man, I'd love to explain it all to you; indeed, I most certainly will do; but I cannot do so at the moment; the matter is too pressing. It touches upon the honour of the family – nay, upon the very existence of the family! – and concerns particularly my mother, God bless her! Our backs may be against the wall at the present moment, but, by Heavens, they won't be for long!"

'I knew not what to make of all this and was about to express my bewilderment to him, when he abruptly turned and gripped my arm.

'"Herbert," said he in a grave tone; "I have come to you because I can think of no one else who can aid me in this dark hour. I regard it as an uncanny piece of good fortune that we should have run across each other in the way we did the other day. It is as if fate had stepped in, to throw a lifeline into my sea of troubles! I have two favours to beg of you, Herbert, both as a man and as an old school friend. Will you help me?"

'"Certainly, if it is in my power," I returned. "What is it that you wish me to do?"

'For answer he held out his black leather bag, and I took it from his hand.

'"Guard that with your life," said he in a low tone. "There is no one else in London I can trust, and I believe I am being followed."

'"What is it?" I enquired, feeling the weight of the bag in my hand. It was heavier than I had expected and clearly contained more than just documents.

'He shook his head.

'"You will see that it is locked," said he. "It is not that I wish to keep the matter a secret from you, Herbert. Indeed, one day you will know the whole story. But it is better for the present – for your own safety – that you do not know any more than is absolutely necessary."

"'Very well, Hollingworth. What do you wish me to do with it?'"

'He glanced cautiously about him, but there was no one there save the hall-porter behind his desk. "I shall send you a message in a few days' time," said he at length, "giving you specific directions. Do you understand?"

"'Perfectly." said I. "You can trust me. What is the other favour you wished to ask of me?"

'His voice sank to a whisper. "Can you lend me a little money, Herbert, just for a few days? They are keeping a watch on my bank. This afternoon, as I arrived there, I recognised one of their men in the street outside, so I told the cabbie not to stop but to drive on. I don't think I was seen, but it meant, of course, that I was unable to withdraw any money."

"'I should be pleased to help you, Hollingworth," I responded. "How much do you require?"

"'Good man!" he cried, squeezing my arm. "I knew I could rely on you! I think that fifty pounds should suffice for the moment."

'I was a little taken aback at this. I had not expected him to ask for so large a sum.

"'I do not carry such an amount on me," I said, "and my bank will be closed now. I could get it for you tomorrow. Come to that, if you write me out a cheque, I could get money from your own bank for you tomorrow."

'His face clouded over and he gripped his chin with his hand. "I must have it tonight," said he in a tone of desperation. "Tomorrow may be too late. I don't know what I shall do." He stood up and began to pace to and fro across the hallway, his chin sunk on his breast.

"'I have it!" said I. "I can probably obtain that amount from the club secretary. I am well known here, and there should be no difficulty."

"'Are you sure?" said he, ceasing his pacing. "I should not want to cause you any inconvenience, Herbert. Lord knows! You're doing enough for me as it is!"

'"It will be no trouble," I assured him. "If you will wait here a moment, I will see the secretary now."

'In a few minutes I was back with the money, in a mixture of gold and notes. He took it from me and clutched my hand as he did so. "You are a true friend," said he with great feeling. "I will write you out an IOU at once." I told him that that would not be necessary, that his word was a good enough bond for me, but he insisted on the correct form, as he put it. "Is there a back door to this building?" he enquired as he finished writing the note; "I may have been seen as I entered."

'I took him down to the basement and along the passage by the kitchens, to a door which gives on to a small courtyard at the rear of the building.

'"I have been a member here for many years," I remarked, "and know the place like the back of my hand."

'"A lucky thing for me that you do!" returned my friend with a smile. "I don't know what I ever should have done without you, Herbert!"

'We shook hands warmly in the yard, then he slipped out through the back gate and was gone, his footsteps hurrying away on the cobbles. That night I took his valise home with me when I left the club and hid it in a box beneath my bed. That was exactly a week ago. For the first few days I could scarcely sleep, such was my state of excitement. Every hour I have expected to hear something fresh on the matter. Each time I have left the house I have looked carefully this way and that, to see if any stranger were loitering about and I have taken particular care to see that I was not followed. So far, however, nothing untoward has happened.'

'It is a curious tale,' I remarked as my companion paused. 'You asked for my opinion, Mr Herbert, but I am afraid I have no sensible observation to offer on the matter! I can certainly understand why you described it as an oddity!'

'Ah! But the oddest part is still to be told!'

'I understood you to say that nothing further had occurred since this day last week.'

'That is true. Nothing has occurred, exactly; but, still, something has changed.'

'I do not follow you.'

'Two nights ago, I woke suddenly from a deep sleep. What I had been dreaming of, I do not know, but it may have been my early school-days, for that is what I found myself thinking of, as I lay there in the darkness. I let the train of thought lead me where it would, and scenes from my days at Whalley Abbey School sprang vividly to my mind. I seemed to see them re-enacted before me, as it were. There were the companions of my youth, acting and speaking as they had acted and spoken a quarter of a century ago, boys whose names and faces had scarcely crossed my mind in all the intervening years. There was that fat boy from Manchester, Albert Ormadone; there was that thin, feeble lad, Wellington Worsley, the class sneak, as I recall; then a dark-haired Scottish boy was speaking, with an accent as thick as your arm, and I recognised Hector Greig. He came from a village by the name of Tillytoghills, I recall, and was teased unmercifully in consequence, although it was scarcely his fault that it sounded such a silly name to our schoolboy ears. And then, into the classroom came Stephen Hollingworth. I recognised at once his wavy, light-brown hair. In a trice I was fully awake, as if a bolt of electricity had shot right through me. For it was at once obvious to me that the schoolboy I remembered and the man I had met at Little Wickling station were not one and the same person. The latter's hair is of a darker brown and not so wavy.'

'Perhaps he uses hair-oil, which might give his hair a darker appearance,' I suggested, but Mr Herbert shook his head emphatically.

'No, no; he is quite different, in all those thousand little ways which one can see easily enough, but cannot quite put one's finger on. Whoever my recent acquaintance is, he is certainly not Stephen Hollingworth.'

'Are you certain?' I cried in amazement.

'As certain as I am that I am sitting here with you in the Star and Garter.'

'Then who is he and why on earth should he pretend to be someone else?'

'That is what I should like to know. It is something of a puzzle, isn't it!'

'All that rigmarole about his family's honour, and all the rest of it, must be just so much humbug, then,' I remarked after a moment, 'if it is not even really his family at all!'

'So it would appear. Of course, as he recognised me, and recalled the boys I was at school with, he himself must have been at Whalley Abbey School; but who he is, I have no idea. I await with interest his message, for I have heard nothing from him since I saw him at the Lancashire and Yorkshire last week, and I cannot imagine what it all means. Yesterday I walked past his house, but I decided against ringing his bell. I thought I would not force the matter, but would give him a few more days' grace, before I insist on knowing what is afoot. I am somewhat uneasy about my fifty pounds.'

'That is very understandable. So should I be, in your position. I wonder what is in the leather bag?'

Herbert shook his head. 'I have not the faintest notion,' said he. 'It is securely locked.'

Still discussing the matter, we left the Star and Garter then, and began to make our way back towards Paddington. The sun was lower now and cast long shadows across the street, but the air was still warm. In and out of the trees in front of the houses flew little sparrows and finches, chirruping their lively songs, while high above us swallows and martins swooped and soared. It was indeed a lovely evening to be abroad and strolling in the street. But the very commonplace and pleasant appearance of our surroundings made Mr Herbert's puzzling experiences seem all the more incredible. In truth, I should probably have been inclined to dismiss the whole story as fantasy, had he not impressed me as completely honest and trustworthy.

'I could, of course, force the lock on his bag,' said he as we walked along. 'But I have given my word of honour that I shall guard it securely; and this I shall do until it is proved to me beyond doubt that my trust has been misplaced.'

'Your story has certainly intrigued me,' I remarked as we parted. 'Do let me know if there are any fresh developments in the matter. It is a fascinating little mystery, Mr Herbert, and I look forward to hearing the outcome!'

––––––––

Over dinner that evening I retailed Mr Herbert's story to my wife, and she was as fascinated by it as I was.

'It is very curious,' she observed, 'that the man Mr Herbert met at Little Wickling should have taken the name – if it is, indeed, not his own – of Stephen Hollingworth, for the Hollingworths do, of course, live near there, according to that newspaper report, at Wickling Place.'

'That is true. I suppose the likeliest explanation is that he had just come from visiting the Hollingworths when Herbert first met him. I wonder what his connection with them might be, if he is not a member of the family?'

Thus we chatted for some time, turning the matter over and over, and looking at it from this way and that, without arriving at any notion of what might lie behind it.

'It almost sounds like one of the cases of your friend, Mr Holmes!' said Mary at length, laughing.

'Indeed,' I concurred. 'I am sure he would enjoy it. He is a connoisseur of such *outré* passages of life!'

––––––––

The dinner-table had long been cleared, and I was sitting smoking my pipe and reading, when there came a ring at the bell. Moments later, the maid informed me that she had shown a bleeding patient into the consulting-room. I dropped my book at once and hurried downstairs.

The door of the consulting-room stood open and I had my foot upon the threshold, when I stopped in amazement. For there, his face cut and bruised, was my companion from earlier in the evening. Upon his forehead, just above the eyebrow, was a raised, discoloured lump, and upon his cheek was a gash from which blood had flowed down his face and neck. In his hand he held a black leather bag.

'My dear fellow!' I cried. 'What on earth has happened to you!'

'You asked me to keep you informed of developments, Doctor,' said he, attempting a grim smile, which clearly caused him great pain, 'so here I am!'

He put down the bag and held out the palms of his hands to me, and I saw that they were grazed and filthy.

'Sit yourself down,' said I, 'and I will set you to rights, while you tell me what has happened.'

'I have been viciously assaulted,' said he.

'Assaulted! Where?'

'Fleet Street.'

'Fleet Street! What on earth were you doing down there?'

'My story has advanced a little,' said he, wincing as I dabbed the cut on his cheek.

'And have the latest developments shed any light on the mystery?'

'On the contrary. It seems yet darker than it did before.'

I glanced at the clock.

'I recommend,' said I, 'that when I have patched you up, you accompany me at once to the chambers of my friend, Sherlock Holmes. He has a vast understanding of these sorts of matters, and it may be that what is dark to us will not be so to him.'

So it was, that, ten minutes later, my companion clutching his black bag tightly, we were in a cab and rattling through the darkness to my friend's rooms. We found Holmes sitting cross-legged upon the floor, sorting through mounds of documents, but he sprang up as we entered.

'Watson!' cried he in a gay tone. 'What a very pleasant surprise! But who is your friend? He appears a little the worse for wear!'

'This is Mr Alfred Herbert, a patient of mine. He has had need of my services this evening, and I fancy he may have need of yours, too.'

The two of them shook hands, and as they did so Herbert broke into a paroxysm of coughing.

'That sounds suspiciously like bronchitis,' remarked Holmes.

'Indeed. That is what first led me to consult Dr Watson.'

'Your work is partly to blame, of course.'

'My work?' echoed Herbert in surprise. 'My work is largely clerical, Mr Holmes. It is neither heavy nor dusty and can have no bearing on the matter.'

'Not the nature of your work, Mr Herbert, but the fact that it obliges you to travel twice a day on the subterranean section of the Metropolitan Railway. You have a season ticket, no doubt, from Paddington or Bayswater to the City. Some people, you know, with more delicate constitutions than their fellows, find that the smoke and fumes on the underground railways are more than their lungs can tolerate, and it may be that you are one of them.'

'How can you speak so confidently of my daily habits when we have only just met?' cried Herbert in surprise.

'It is perfectly obvious. You might as well ask me how I know that you are a stockbroker, that you are right-handed, come from near Preston in Lancashire, but have lived in London for somewhat over a dozen years, and that you take snuff.'

Mr Herbert took a step backwards, and his features assumed a look of the utmost astonishment.

'How on earth—?' he began, but Holmes interrupted him, a trace of impatience on his face.

'You evidently live in Paddington or Bayswater,' said he briskly;

'otherwise you would not have elected to seek the services of my friend here.'

'Twenty-three, Leinster Gardens.'

'Quite so. I observed as we shook hands that there are a large number of figures upon the left cuff of your shirt. You are therefore right-handed, and undoubtedly a dealer in stocks and shares, for the figures can only be stock-prices. You must therefore travel each day from the Paddington area to the City in order to undertake your duties and it seems overwhelmingly likely that you would do so on the Metropolitan Railway, which connects the two areas directly. A man of your common sense would hardly undertake this journey every day of the week without taking advantage of the savings to be had from the purchase of a season ticket.

'As to your birthplace, my dear sir: your accent, although much modified, yet retains traces of central Lancashire. I cannot pretend to an intimate knowledge of every accent in England, but I have a tolerable acquaintance with some four or five dozen and have given special attention to the accents of Lancashire, which perhaps exhibit more variety and extreme development than those of any other area of comparable size. The profession you follow is not one into which a stranger can slip at a moment's notice, in the middle of his life, and nor can one gain much experience of it outside of London. It seems likely, therefore, that you have been in the stock-exchange line for most of your adult life, and as you appear to be about five-and-thirty, that indicates that your employment – and hence your period of residence in London – has been for over a dozen years. The snuff-taking is a trivial matter: a small snuff-box is distending your waistcoat pocket at this moment.'

'Amazing!' cried Herbert.

'Elementary,' said Holmes. 'Let us leave your bronchitis behind and come to the more essential matter. Your appearance suggests that it may be urgent, unless Dr Watson has simply been using you for bandaging practice. Pray, take a seat.'

Mr Herbert thereupon told his story, exactly as he had told it to me. He described his first meeting with his old school-fellow and the subsequent meeting at the Lancashire and Yorkshire Club, and also the sudden realisation that his new acquaintance could not possibly be the man he claimed to be.

'When I returned home this evening after telling my tale to Dr Watson,' he continued, 'I found a letter awaiting me. It may have been there all day, for all I know, for I had not returned to Leinster Gardens since leaving Persquith and Moran's this afternoon. It was from my recent acquaintance – of course, he still signed himself "Stephen Hollingworth" – asking me to bring the bag which he had entrusted to me down to Carstone Court, near Fleet Street. He said it was vital that I was there by eight o'clock and was confident I would not let him down. I paid the cabbie extra to whip his horse up a bit and was in Fleet Street by three minutes past the hour.

'It took me a few minutes to discover Carstone Court and I had to ask directions in a pub, but eventually I found it, on the north side of Fleet Street. It lies at the end of a long, ill-lit passage, a by-way off a by-way, so to speak, and it was not without some apprehension that I entered it. The courtyard was narrow and dark, with tall, unlit buildings on either hand, and was as silent as the grave. It was certainly an odd place to choose to meet anyone, but I supposed that "Hollingworth" had selected it in order to keep the business private. I stood there a moment, but there seemed to be no one about. Once or twice, the sound of distant footsteps came to my ears up the long, narrow alley from Fleet Street, but they were remote and muffled, and, when they had passed, the courtyard returned to utter silence once more.

'"Hallo?" I said tentatively, after a moment. "Is there anyone here?"

'The response made my hair stand on end, for there was a movement in the blackness to the side of me, and a dark figure stepped forward from a shadowed doorway. He opened the shutter of a lantern and held it up to my face.

'"You are A. Herbert, I take it?" said he in a rough, coarse voice. It was certainly not my old school-fellow, but, as he knew my name, I assumed it must be some agent of his.

'"I am," said I.

'Two more figures materialised out of the blackness behind the first and approached. There was menace in the way they loomed up about me, and I began to fear for my safety. I took a step backward, but found myself with my back to a brick wall.

'"Have you the bag?" said the first man.

'"It is here," I replied, holding it out to him.

'He took it from me and cursed when he found that it was locked. He asked me if I had the key, I told him I had not and he cursed again. The thought passed through my mind that the honour of the Hollingworth family would have stood on shaky ground indeed had it depended in any way on such a man as this.

'"Give us your knife, Harrison," said he sharply to one of the other men, who passed him a long-bladed, evil-looking knife, and took the lantern. Then, with more oaths and curses, he bent down and began forcing the clasp of the bag. Presently he grunted with satisfaction, pulled the bag open and lifted from it a large, heavy-looking bundle, wrapped in what appeared to be a length of striped curtain material. The other men held the lantern closer as he unfolded the bundle on the ground, and I must confess that, for the moment, my feelings of fear were forgotten, so consumed was I with curiosity as to what might be contained within the cloth.

'Carefully, he pulled back the last fold of material. There, lying upon the old curtain, was a strange, shining black statue, about nine or ten inches in height. It was clearly from the Orient and quite grotesque, having four arms, and with a ferocious and horrible expression upon its face.

'"What is the meaning of this?" said the first man sharply, looking up at me.

'"I do not know," I returned. "I had no idea what was inside the bag."

'"You liar!" he cried, and sprang at me like a wild beast. I turned away, but he grabbed me by the shoulder and my head struck the wall, with the result which you see. Then he flung me to the ground, which was rough and dirty, and, seizing me by the neck, held the long blade of the knife up to my face.

'"Unless you act cooperative," said he in an evil tone, "I'm going to slit your throat from ear to ear."

'"I don't know anything," I cried, although I could hardly get the words out, so tight was his grip upon my windpipe.

'"Leave him, Strong," said one of the others. For a moment, my assailant was perfectly still and I thought my end had come; but then he relaxed his grip and took the knife away, although he deliberately cut my cheek as he did so.'

Mr Herbert put his hand up to his face and gingerly touched his wound, before continuing: 'The three men spoke quietly together for a minute, then turned to me.

'"Tell your master," said the one called Strong, "that he has had his chance to settle matters his way; now we will settle matters our way." With that they turned and disappeared into the darkness once more. For several minutes, I lay on the ground, not daring to move, until the sound of their footsteps had passed beyond my hearing, then I quickly stood up, gathered together the bag and its contents, and hurried back down the alley to Fleet Street. From there I took the first cab I could find to Dr Watson's house.'

'What a terrible experience!' I cried.

'You have been wading in deeper waters than you realised, Mr Herbert!' observed Holmes after a moment's reflection. 'May I see the bag, and its contents?'

He took the oriental figure from the bag and held it up for a moment, examining it closely. It was jet black and highly polished, and gleamed in the light of the lamp. About its neck was depicted a necklace of human skulls and upon its features was an expression of the most intense evil.

'It is Kali,' said Holmes; 'the fearsome, destructive aspect of an otherwise thoroughly good-natured Hindu deity. What devilry has been done in her name over the centuries! You may regard yourself as fortunate, Mr Herbert, that your assailants did not take their inspiration from this particular goddess, or you might not have emerged from Carstone Court alive! However,' he continued, 'they were evidently uninterested in her history and regarded the figure as of little value.' He turned the heavy statue over and over, and examined it from every angle. 'From a purely practical point of view, their judgement was correct. By its weight, it is solid brass; a heavy piece, but of no great worth, except to a collector of such exotic curios. It was made in Calcutta, where they manufacture these things by the thousand.' He put it down on the floor beside his chair and took up the bag which had contained it, from which he pulled out a piece of striped cloth. 'There is something else here,' said he, reaching into the bag again and withdrawing a small, crumpled slip of paper, which he flattened out and studied for a moment, a frown upon his face. 'What a very singular epistle!' he remarked at length in a thoughtful tone, as he passed the paper to Mr Herbert.

'Good Lord!' cried the latter, looking up from reading the note. 'What on earth can it mean? What shocking business is afoot!'

Herbert passed the note to me and I read the following enigmatic message:

DO NOT FORGET: Windsor – The Monarch – Dynamite

'I rather fancy,' said Holmes, 'that Dr Watson may be able to enlighten us!'

'Why, whatever do you mean?' I cried in amazement.

'Was there not a race meeting at Windsor a week or two ago?'

'Oh, of course!' I cried, clapping my hand upon my knee, as I realised the meaning of the note's terse phrases. 'The Monarch and Dynamite are both horses that ran there. Dynamite is from Lord Thuxton's stables.

He was heavily backed for the big race of the day, but came second, by a length, to Trayles. The Monarch finished last in his race, as far as I remember.'

'So,' said Holmes, 'the owner of this bag moves in the world of the Turf and gambling, the most rapid mode of financial transfer from one man to another that mankind has yet devised. You still cannot recall what his name might be, Mr Herbert? For it is certain, of course, that he is one of your old school-fellows.'

Herbert shook his head. 'Hard as I have tried to remember them all, I cannot place this man's face. If, as he says, he was in Mr Newsome's form when I was in that of Dr Jessop, he must be a year younger than me, but more than that I cannot say.'

'No matter,' said Holmes. 'We may be able to reach our destination by another route. You say you have his present address?'

'Yes, Quebec Street, not far from here.'

'Then I suggest that, if you feel up to it, you confront your old school-mate at once,' said Homes, rising to his feet. 'We shall, of course, accompany you.'

'Then I am more than ready.'

A short walk down Baker Street and around Portman Square brought us to Quebec Street. It was a fine starlit night and the air was mild. Mr Herbert directed us to a narrow-fronted house near the corner with Seymour Street, but before we reached it, we could see that something was amiss. The front door stood wide open to the street, casting a yellow oblong of light across the pavement outside.

Holmes's ring at the bell was answered after a few moments by a stout, red-faced and irascible-looking gentleman in a frock-coat.

'Yes?' said he irritably.

'We are looking for Mr Stephen Hollingworth,' said Holmes.

'Hollingworth? Never heard of him! Good night!'

'One moment,' said Holmes, as the stout man turned away. 'Might I enquire the name of the occupant of this house?'

'You can enquire all you want,' returned the other in a rude tone.

'The house hasn't got an occupant. The occupant has taken himself off, bag and baggage, owing me a quarter's rent.'

'And that gentleman was?'

'George Robinson. What is it to you?'

'A slimly built man, with dark brown hair and moustache?'

'Yes, as it happens. What of it?'

'Ah!' said Holmes, turning to us. 'You are not familiar with the name "George Robinson", Mr Herbert? No? Nevertheless. It must be he.' He turned back to the man in the doorway, who stood with his hands on his hips. 'You are the landlord, sir?' he enquired.

'Yes I am. He told me to come round this evening and everything would be squared up, but when I got here there wasn't a sign of him and most of the rooms look as if someone has thrown a grenade into them.'

'The house was let furnished?'

'Yes; for six months: one quarter in advance and not a farthing seen since.'

'As it happens, my colleague here is also owed a considerable sum of money by this man who calls himself Robinson,' said Holmes, 'and he, too, was sent a message concerning this evening.'

'To come here?'

'No, somewhere else; but Robinson wasn't there either. May we come in?'

With a sigh, the stout man, who introduced himself as Elijah Hassocks, led us through into a room at the back of the house, which appeared to have been used as a study. There were signs everywhere of a hurried departure: cupboard doors standing wide open, and drawers pulled out and hanging at odd, drunken angles. Scattered about, on every available surface, were newspapers and magazines, among which I observed many copies of the *Sporting Times*, *Sporting Life* and other racing papers.

'You see?' said Hassocks angrily. 'He presented himself as a first-rate tenant, but it seems he was a first-rate mountebank! Look!' he continued, pointing his finger at the window, where one of the striped curtains had been cut off halfway down: 'not content with defrauding me out of my rent, the blackguard has been amusing himself by destroying the furnishings! If you can shed any light on his whereabouts I'll be very obliged to you.'

'I fear that something has happened to him,' said Mr Herbert.

'Something will happen to him if I catch hold of him,' retorted Hassocks.

'I mean, he may have been abducted,' persisted Herbert.

'Well if so, his abductors have very considerately taken all his clothes and personal belongings, too.'

'A large number of documents have been burnt earlier today,' remarked Holmes, indicating a mound of blackened ashes in the fireplace, as he bent down and began to sift through papers which were strewn in disordered heaps upon the floor. Presently, he held up a large, battered old album, which had the initials 'G.R.' embossed upon the cover. 'Other than this,' said he, 'which is perfectly empty, there is nothing remaining which bears a name or any indication of ownership. He appears to have gone to considerable lengths to hide his trail. Let us have a look in here,' he continued, squatting down and examining the contents of a waste-paper basket, which had been hidden from view beneath a little side-table. 'The humble waste-paper basket can occasionally be a singularly helpful source of information! Ah! This may be something!'

He had extracted a crumpled slip of paper from the basket, which he smoothed out upon his knee and studied for a moment. I leaned over his shoulder and read the following: 'O. L. Friday morning,' which had been underlined three times, and, below that, '£42–10s– 6d'.

'What a very precise amount,' I remarked.

'Have you the IOU he gave you, Mr Herbert?' said Holmes, looking up.

Herbert produced his pocket-book and pulled from it a small piece of paper which he handed to Holmes.

'It is in the same hand,' said the latter, in a thoughtful tone.

'He has made a note of some debt and the day it was to be paid,' I suggested.

'Possibly,' said Holmes, 'although I fancy it has some other meaning. I think we have seen all we need to see here. Our next port of call must be Scotland Yard.' He glanced at his watch. 'I spoke to Inspector Lanner two nights ago and he informed me that he is on evening duty all this week, which is fortunate, for he is the very man we need to see. My card, Sir,' he continued, turning to Mr Hassocks. 'If I can be of any service to you, pray let me know!'

We walked briskly down to Oxford Street where we hailed a four-wheeler and were at Scotland Yard within five minutes. Herbert and I waited downstairs while Holmes went up to see Lanner. The officer at the desk, no doubt moved to sympathy by my companion's sorry appearance, brought us a cup of tea, and Mr Herbert's spirits, which had begun to flag, picked up again.

'Do you have any idea what is afoot, Doctor?' he asked me.

'None whatever. If I were to guess, I should say that your old school-fellow, so far from being subject to any menace himself, has perhaps subjected everyone else to what one might term financial menace.'

Herbert nodded his head.

'That is how it strikes me, too,' he concurred. 'He owes money to his landlord, he owes money to me, he probably owes money to the men who assaulted me in Carstone Court.'

'Gambling debts, no doubt.'

'No doubt. And I cannot think that there is much hope of ever finding him. If he has left his house of his own accord, as appears likely, he might be anywhere. He might have taken a train to Land's End or John O'Groats, for all we know!'

'My thoughts precisely.'

Our discussion was interrupted by the reappearance of Holmes, accompanied by a smart-looking police inspector, with a neatly trimmed beard and sharp, intelligent eyes, whom I recognised as

Inspector Lanner. They appeared to be in a hurry. Lanner nodded to us, then disappeared through a doorway.

'The man you met at Little Wickling station,' said Holmes, addressing Mr Herbert: 'Might his name by any chance have been Gabriel Tooth?'

Herbert shook his head, but appeared in a state of surprise and confusion. 'I did once know someone of that name,' said he at length, 'a boy in the form below mine at Whalley Abbey School. I had forgotten all about him until you mentioned his name. It could not have been he I met at Little Wickling, however, for I recall now that Tooth had ginger hair and a wide, freckled face. How did *you* hear of him, Mr Holmes?'

'Inspector Lanner informs me that Tooth is the name your mysterious friend called himself when he visited the Hollingworths at Wickling Place; but I doubted that it would be his true name. I rather fancy,' he continued after a moment, 'that the man we are after is one Gilbert Rowsley.'

There was a tension in my friend's voice as he spoke those words, and he regarded Herbert keenly. It was evident that he hoped to see a spark of recognition upon his client's features at the mention of this name. If so, he was not disappointed. Herbert's mouth fell open, he gasped audibly and his eyebrows shot up; then he clapped his hand to his head and remained immobile for several minutes.

'Of course!' he cried at length, rising to his feet in his excitement. 'Gilbert Rowsley! Of course! It is he!'

'Gilbert Rowsley is another of your old school-fellows, then?' asked Holmes, barely able to contain the excitement in his own voice.

'Indeed he is!' cried Herbert. 'He was in the year below mine. But I believe he was only at Whalley Abbey for two or three terms. Though I occasionally saw him about the place, I scarcely knew him at all, which is why I did not remember him before.'

'And now?'

'Now that you have recalled him to my mind,' said Herbert slowly, his eyes closed in concentration, 'I remember that he was one of those boys who seemed always to be loitering round corners – a dark, sly-looking youth, as I remember, with calculating eyes. Wait a moment! I remember now that there had been a spate of petty pilfering one autumn term, and the next term, when nothing of the sort occurred, someone – Greig, I think – remarked in jest that Rowsley must have been responsible, as he had left at the end of the previous term. I remember laughing, without really thinking it to be true; but now that I consider it afresh, from twenty-odd years' distance, I wonder if it wasn't in fact the very truth of the matter! But how on earth have you managed to discover Rowsley's name, Mr Holmes?'

'We shall have to postpone the explanations for a little while,' returned Holmes in a brisk tone. He glanced at his watch. 'We must be off now. It is ten-forty, and there is no time to lose.'

'To where?' I enquired in surprise.

'The Albert Dock.'

'Am I to accompany you?' asked Herbert.

'Most certainly, Mr Herbert. You are one of the very few men in London who can identify this scoundrel. We should, I think, be able to catch the eleven twenty-five from Fenchurch Street.'

'We can do better than that, Mr Holmes,' said Lanner, who had re-emerged as Holmes had been speaking, followed closely by two uniformed officers, hastily fastening up their tunics. 'I have made inquiries. There is a launch available at Hungerford Pier. I've sent a message to tell them to get steam up for an immediate departure.'

'Capital!' cried Holmes, clapping the policeman on the shoulder. 'Nothing could be better! And these men will accompany us?' he queried, indicating the uniformed officers.

Lanner nodded. 'Constables Jefferson and Cook. I think between us we should be able to manage the matter.'

In a minute we were in the street and hurrying to the pier, in five we were in the police-launch, *Ariel*, and on our way down the great heaving river.

It was a perfect night, a night to delight astronomers, cloudless and crystal clear. Above us the great arc of the Heavens was bright with stars, among which the moon floated in milky white splendour, casting its silvery light across the sleeping city.

Our vessel was a swift one, and soon we were flashing past lines of moored boats and lighters, setting them bobbing in our wake. Beneath the bridges we flew, past lines of dark warehouses on our right hand and the spires of the City on our left, above all of which rose the great dome of St Paul's, eerily magnificent in the moonlight.

'This is the adventure of my life,' whispered Herbert to me as we sat side by side in the stern of the boat. For myself, I could not but recall the previous occasion I had made such an expedition in a police-launch, when we had pursued the *Aurora* down the Thames, at the conclusion of the case I have chronicled elsewhere as 'The Sign of Four'.

'The last time you were here, Watson,' remarked Holmes with a smile, sitting himself down beside us and apparently reading my thoughts as he did so, 'we were after the great Agra Treasure. Mr Herbert's fifty pounds may not appear to have quite the same *recherché* quality, but it is a good cause nonetheless, and there is an added piquancy to the enterprise in that we cannot be certain until we arrive at our destination whether the scoundrel who took it is there or not.'

We had passed the Tower as he had been speaking, gaunt and forbidding in the moonlight, and had come to the vast region of the docks. The cranes and hoists and pulleys, so busy and noisy in the day-time, now stood still and silent, as our little vessel shot swiftly past, the smooth, rhythmic beat of its engine almost the only sound to be heard on the river.

At Wapping, we slowed and drew up alongside the jetty. Lanner sprang ashore and raced up the stairs to the police station which overhung the bank above us, but was back again in a matter of minutes.

'It is all arranged,' he called out as we cast off, and, with a roar from the engine and a plume of smoke from the funnel, we resumed our surge down the river once more.

'You are probably wondering what is afoot,' said Holmes, as we flew along, 'and why Inspector Lanner has taken up the matter with such commendable dispatch. The fact is, that, important though Mr Herbert's fifty pounds is, there are yet bigger stakes upon the table tonight.' He glanced at his watch. 'The enterprise is finely balanced,' he continued with a shake of the head, 'and it will be a close-run race. However, to explain to you how matters stand: you may have read in your newspaper of the recent burglaries which have occurred, at some of the finest houses in town. In each case the value of the goods stolen ran into many thousands of pounds. Geographically speaking, the burglaries were fairly widely separated – the first was in Mayfair, the second in Belgravia, the third in Chelsea, and so on – but in other respects they were remarkably similar, so that it is almost a certainty that they are the work of the same gang. In every case, access to the house was gained by what proved on subsequent examination to be the weakest point in the house's defences, but which would not normally have been known to an outsider: in one instance, for example, a landing window which was warped and would not fasten properly, in another, a loose-fitting French window which a child of six could have opened from the outside. In each case, too, the items stolen were very coolly selected from what was available: only the very best things were taken, the less valuable remaining almost completely untouched.

'Inspector Lanner had charge of the first case – in Charles Street, in the West End – and soon formed the hypothesis that the burglars had had assistance from within the household, at least to the extent of helpful information. His suspicions naturally fell upon the domestic staff, and in particular on the butler and the lady's maid, for it was clear that whoever had supplied the information had had more knowledge of the worth of the household contents than is customary among domestic staff. He therefore arranged for these two to be watched closely and followed by disguised police agents whenever they went out. A setback for his theory arrived fairly quickly, however. For as his suspects were being followed about the place, a second, very similar burglary occurred in Cadogan Place, Belgravia, and shortly afterwards there was a third. Clearly the butler and lady's maid from Charles Street could not have had anything to do with these, and Lanner was therefore obliged to modify his theory somewhat. He wondered then if there were a gang undertaking wholesale corruption of trusted domestic staff, although such a proposition seemed distinctly unlikely. Many of the senior domestic staff at the houses in question had been in their employment for upwards of twenty years and had unimpeachable records. It was almost unthinkable that such loyal and valued servants could have been persuaded by a cash bribe, however large, to have betrayed their trust.

'But what, then, was the alternative? Lanner remained convinced that in each case the thieves had acted upon information received from within the household; but if the information had not come from the servants, then it must have come from guests who had visited the houses, of whom there had been a great number in the course of the London season. This suggestion seemed, on the face of it, even more fantastic, but it did have the merit of perhaps explaining more convincingly how the stolen goods had been disposed of. For many of the items stolen were of very great value, and their disposal would have required a greater knowledge and better connections than are possessed by the average London burglar. With considerable difficulty, Lanner eventually managed to compile a list of all those who had recently visited the burgled houses and found that it included two bishops, several of the most senior judges in the country, including the Lord Chief Justice himself, together with half the membership of the House of Lords, and a fair sprinkling of scions of some of the oldest and most distinguished families in the kingdom. Somewhere in the list, there might have been a villain, the criminal brain responsible for the planning of these robberies, but, if so, it was not apparent. The matter was thus a complete enigma. Unable to see how he might make progress, Lanner decided to place his researches in abeyance for the moment and hope that any further activity by the same gang might yield a fresh clue.

'Now, at last, that clue has appeared. He had a wire the other day from one Inspector Clarke of the Kent force, concerning the burglary last week at the Hollingworths' house, Wickling Place. It had struck Clarke – evidently an officer who has his finger on the pulse of things – that the Wickling Place burglary appeared remarkably similar to those in London, of which he had read. The thieves had slipped in quietly, when everyone was asleep and, from all that they might have taken, had selected only the most valuable items. Lanner went down to Kent and the two men went over the case together. Clarke and his officers had of course made extensive inquiries in the district, in case any strangers had been seen at the time of the robbery. In the course of these inquiries they had learnt from the Hollingworths themselves that they had recently been paid a visit by an old school-companion of their late son, Stephen, who had come, he said, to offer his sympathies upon their sad loss.'

'Gilbert Rowsley!' said Herbert.

'So I now believe, although he introduced himself to the Hollingworths as Gabriel Tooth. Now, although this name was not upon Lanner's list of recent visitors to the burgled houses in London, he was convinced that there must be a connection between this man's visit to Wickling Place and the burglary which took place there the following night. He has therefore spent the past week endeavouring to discover the whereabouts of this man, Tooth, but without success. Now, if the identification of him as Gilbert Rowsley is correct, as I am sure it is, Lanner may at last be able to lay his hands on the guiding brain behind these perplexing burglaries.'

'Was Rowsley's name on Lanner's London list?' I asked.

Holmes nodded. 'Gilbert Rowsley had been a recent guest, at some function or other, at every one of the burgled houses. But his name was but one among a great number and until this evening there was no reason to suspect him any more than anyone else.'

'What drew you to that name, then, rather than to any of the others on the list?'

'The old album he had left behind in the house in Quebec Street. The initials upon the front were "G.R.", and although they were correct for "George Robinson", the name he was going under there, it appeared to me that the album was several years old and that "G.R." might thus perhaps be his real initials, too. You can imagine how keen I was to cast my eye over Lanner's list, at Scotland Yard. When I did so, I quickly discovered that one of the names on it matched the initials "G.R.". Still, I could not be certain and I must admit I was very relieved when Mr Herbert was able to confirm my speculation, by recalling that Gilbert Rowsley had indeed been one of his old school companions.'

'It seems to me,' I observed after a moment, 'that Rowsley took a great risk in exposing himself at Wickling Place, even if he was using an assumed name. At the functions he attended in London he was but one guest among many; down in Kent he arrived alone, and his visit was bound to be recalled and speculated upon.'

Holmes nodded. 'That is so; but the season in London was ending, and his opportunities diminishing. No doubt when the possibility of robbing the Hollingworths occurred to him, he thought it too good a chance to pass up and worth the risk. No doubt, also, he considered, as do most criminals who have enjoyed a run of success, that he was much too clever to be caught.'

'What a vile, unspeakable snake he must be, to take advantage of a family's grief and use them so meanly!' cried Herbert with feeling.

'If the little we have heard of him is a fair sample,' I remarked, 'I imagine his debts are many and his creditors pressing. No doubt he was desperate to pay off some of those who were threatening him.'

'I rather fancy he intended to end their persecution in an altogether more decisive manner,' Holmes responded with a shake of the head, 'by showing them a clean pair of heels. I think it likely that he has had his escape planned for some time. It seems evident that he used Mr

Herbert as a decoy this evening, to give himself a clear run as he left his lodgings. The men that Mr Herbert encountered near Fleet Street are almost certainly the other members of Rowsley's gang – the three men who were seen near Wickling Place at the time of the burglary there. Thanks to Mr Herbert, we have two of their names, and Lanner tells me that they are well known at Scotland Yard, so it should not be too difficult to lay hands on them first thing in the morning. No doubt Rowsley had promised to pay them their share of the proceeds of the robbery, once he had disposed of the stolen goods. Indeed, judging by the degree of their anger on being presented with a worthless brass figure, it may well be that Rowsley had not yet settled with them for the earlier robberies. But his great confidence in being able to escape his pursuers has led him into an error, for the use of the Indian figure incriminates him unequivocally in the burglaries. It was one of the items taken from General Appleton's house in Chelsea a few weeks ago, no doubt in error and against Rowsley's instructions, for it is of very little value and he evidently thought it not worth his while to dispose of it.'

Herbert let out a long groan and clutched his head. 'I see it all now!' cried he in a mournful voice. 'I have been played for a fool!'

'Do not judge yourself too harshly, Mr Herbert,' returned Holmes in a sympathetic tone. 'From the very first, he has calculated and sought to deceive you, in case you might ever prove useful to him. Among the very first words he spoke to you, he gave you the false name of "Stephen Hollingworth", which he evidently judged might be more advantageous to him than revealing to you his true identity. I am afraid he is a man who uses people as other men use tools, to procure that which he wants.'

'And now?' I enquired.

'Now,' returned Holmes in a grave voice, 'we approach what should be the last act of this little drama. Despite all his efforts to cover his tracks, Mr Rowsley has made a little slip. You recall the scrap of paper we found in his study?'

'The one with the very precise amount of money recorded upon it?'

'Exactly, Watson. It was in his own hand. I could see no reason why he should record his debt to another, especially as, from what we know of him, he would be unlikely to repay it. Perhaps, then, I conjectured, it was the cost of something. But what?'

'We have no way of knowing.'

'Well, it is a moderately large sum, marked specifically for Friday morning; we may surmise from his actions that Rowsley intends to vanish completely on Friday and leave all his creditors with nothing; and the note is endorsed "O.L.".'

'I cannot see that there is any clue there,' Mr Herbert remarked with a shake of the head.

'No? But what if "O.L." stands for "Orient Line"? They carry the mails to Australia, their boats leaving from the Albert Dock every second Friday and the price of a second-class passage from London to Australia is somewhere in the region of the sum noted on the paper.'

'Of course!' I cried. 'That must be it!'

'They are leaving early in the morning,' Holmes continued, 'so all the passengers will already be on board.'

'Do you know if Rowsley is among them?'

'There has been no time to verify the matter; but we shall soon find out, for we are almost there.'

We had passed Greenwich and were racing down the long broad expanse of Blackwall Reach. Now, as we reached Blackwall Point, a wide, dark opening came into view on the north bank of the river.

'Bow Creek,' said the helmsman, following our gaze. 'And there,' he added, 'is the Victoria Dock Pier.'

He swung the boat round in a broad arc towards the Essex shore, the change of direction pressing our backs against the gunwale and flinging a fountain of white spray into the dark sky. Ahead of us now, I could see a small group of men upon the pier, clearly awaiting our arrival, and two police vans. In a matter of moments we were at the pier and the launch was secured. Holmes sprang on to the steps at the side of the pier and we followed him up.

'It is as we thought,' said he, as we reached the top of the steps. 'Inspector Poynter of the Docks Division has been able to confirm all our suspicions. The Orient Line's *Cuzco* waits to leave on the morning tide and the passenger list contains the name of one Gilbert Rowsley.'

In a moment we were in a carriage and rattling through the deserted dockyards, past dark, shadowed warehouses, and beneath silent cranes and gantries, until we drew up on the dock-side, where a large and handsome ship was moored, its funnels smoking gently, its rigging silhouetted against the night sky.

The matter was soon explained to the officer of the watch, who conducted us without delay in the direction of the passenger accommodation. Although the ship was quiet, essential work still continued, I observed, for several sailors were busy on the lighted deck, absorbed in various tasks, and a bearded crewman passed us, his back bent under a heavy-looking sack, just before we turned into the passengers' quarters. The ship's officer led us quickly to Rowsley's cabin, where he knocked sharply on the door, then pushed it open. The room within was in darkness, and when Lanner took a lantern from one of his officers and held it up, we saw that there was no one there. The little cabin was in perfect order and the cover upon the bed had been turned down, but the bed had not been slept in.

'He is not here!' cried Lanner. 'He has tricked us and escaped again!'

'No,' said Sherlock Holmes, shaking his head, 'Rowsley is here somewhere.' He pointed to the little shelf beside the bed, upon which lay a slim volume entitled *A History of the Melbourne Racetrack*. 'One moment!' he cried abruptly, clapping his hand to his head. 'The last man that passed us on the deck, the bearded man with the heavy sack – blind fool that I am not to heed my own eyes! – he was wearing patent shoes!'

'What!' cried the ship's officer.

'It must be Rowsley! He has managed to acquire a sailor's uniform from somewhere, but could not get shoes to fit him. He has evidently been on his guard, lest his escape be thwarted at the last, and has observed our approach!'

We quickly retraced our steps. Upon the deck, some distance ahead of us, we could see the sailor with the sack, walking briskly towards the gang-plank.

'It is he!' cried Herbert. 'I recognise his figure, even in that disguise!'

In a moment, he had reached the gang-plank. His hand was upon the rail at the top of it when he abruptly stopped.

'He has seen the police vans on the dock-side,' said Holmes.

Our quarry glanced quickly round, as if in a state of indecision. Then his eyes met ours as we approached and he let out a strangled cry, dropped his sack and sprinted across to the rail on the far side of the deck. We raced after him as fast as we were able, but before we could reach him he had climbed the rail. For a long moment, he stood precariously balanced upon the top, as if nerving himself to plunge into the waters of the dock far below. Then, with a gesture of resignation, he sprang down instead on to the deck of the ship and, leaning his back on the rail in a leisurely manner, awaited our arrival.

'It is perhaps a little too dark and cold down there for a man of my sensitive breeding,' he remarked in a casual tone as we reached the rail. 'I see I do not require this tasteless encumbrance any longer, anyway,' he continued, pulling at his bushy beard, which came away in his hand and which he tossed casually over the ship's side.

It was strange at last to be face to face with this man who had been so long sought in vain, and who had proved so elusive that it seemed possible that he would never be apprehended. He was a tall, slim man and his face was a handsome one, if a little thin and fleshless; but there was something weak and deceitful about his mouth which his dark moustache could not entirely conceal.

'Gilbert Rowsley—' Inspector Lanner began, as the two constables seized hold of the fugitive, but Holmes interrupted him.

'One moment, Lanner,' said he, drawing the police inspector aside. 'If you arrest him now,' he continued in a low tone, out of earshot of the prisoner, 'the full weight of the law falls at once upon the matter with unstoppable momentum and Mr Herbert stands little chance, if any, of recovering his fifty pounds. He certainly will not do so until all due processes have been observed, which may take several months. On the other hand, as I see it, there is nothing to prevent his recovering now what he is owed, provided the transaction takes place before the arrest is formally made.'

Inspector Lanner nodded his head. 'I quite agree, Mr Holmes. Considering the service which Mr Herbert has rendered us today, it seems the very least we can do for him.'

Holmes then stepped forward once again and requested that his client's loan be returned.

'Oh, certainly, certainly,' returned Rowsley, in a careless tone. 'I assume a cheque would be acceptable, Herbert?'

'Under the circumstances, my client would prefer to take it in cash,' Holmes interjected.

'Oh, very well,' said the other, a trace of annoyance in his voice, as if he were being put to a very great inconvenience. He took from his pocket a thick leather purse, which he opened to reveal the largest wad of bank-notes which I think I have ever seen in my life. From these he extracted notes to the value of fifty pounds, which he exchanged with Herbert for his IOU.

'Thank you,' said Herbert.

'Pray, don't mention it,' said the other, screwing up the paper and tossing it over the ship's rail.

Lanner made his arrest then, to which Rowsley offered no resistance, other than to remark that the whole business was 'deuced inconvenient', and he and his possessions were removed from the *Cuzco*.

The Friday evening papers were full of news of the arrest, although they gave all the credit to the official police force and made no mention of either Sherlock Holmes or his client. After a brief hearing at the Stepney Police Court the case was referred to the autumn sessions of the Central Criminal Court. Before the case came to trial, however, in an attempt to secure a reduction in his own sentence, Rowsley had implicated the rest of the gang, an action which no doubt rendered him as popular among his criminal associates as he was among the honest citizens of London. His efforts in this regard were not entirely successful, however, and the last I heard of him was that he had been committed for a term of penal servitude at Portland Prison, where, as the judge in the case remarked, he might spend such leisure moments as he had in contemplation of his past misdeeds and perhaps come to see the error of his ways.

Mr Herbert dined at our house in Paddington later that summer and attempted – with indifferent success, I must admit – to educate me in the finer subtleties of the game of chess. Later in the year, acting on Holmes's diagnosis as to the cause of his bronchitis, he moved to Greenwich, where my wife and I visited him the following Easter, and he was pleased to show us the view from his upstairs windows, which commanded a splendid panorama of the river, with its ever-changing kaleidoscope of shipping. This, he said, would always remind him of what he described as the greatest adventure of his life.

As to Sherlock Holmes, when next I saw him he was absorbed in a fresh problem, the consequences of which, he confided to me, might well bring down every government on the Continent. The details of Mr Herbert's strange adventures had quite passed from his mind and he appeared genuinely surprised when I suggested to him that the citizens of London owed him a debt of gratitude.

'They may all sleep a little easier in their beds, as a result of your achievements in the Rowsley case,' I remarked.

'Perhaps you are right,' he responded with little interest. 'I really have no time to consider matters from such a perspective. My work itself is the sole focus of my attention and must be its own reward. Do you know that line of Chaucer's, Watson: "The life so short, the craft so long to learn"? It is an observation that applies with peculiar accuracy to my own line of work. That being so, you will perhaps appreciate that it is the pursuit of professional mastery rather than ephemeral praise to which my energies must always be directed.'

The Adventure of the Brown Box

'Is it really possible, do you suppose,' said Sherlock Holmes to me one morning, as we took breakfast together, 'that a healthy and robust man may be so stricken with terror that he drops down dead?'

'Certainly it is,' I responded. 'There are numerous recorded instances. Of course, in many of them there were also other factors. If a man's heart is weak or diseased, for instance, the likelihood of such an event is increased. And if the fear arises suddenly, and comes as a terrific shock, that also increases the likelihood. Do you have a specific case in mind?'

'Indeed: that of Victor Furnival, of Wharncliffe Crescent, Norwood, who died suddenly on Tuesday. There was a brief mention of it in yesterday's papers.'

'I did not see the report,' I said. 'Was he in a situation of menace?'

'On the contrary, when the blow fell, he was seated at the breakfast table, as you and I are now, no doubt drinking tea and contemplating a boiled egg.'

'What, then? Why should the papers have reported that he died from fear?'

'It is not the papers that mention it. They give the cause of death as heart failure and otherwise confine themselves to listing Mr Furnival's accomplishments – he was, it seems, a local councillor, a magistrate and altogether a notable figure in the district; but I have this morning received a letter from the dead man's niece, Miss Agnes Montague, who has been acting as his housekeeper for the past eighteen months. She informs me that Mr Furnival was seated at the breakfast table, opening his post, when he uttered what she describes as the most dreadful cry of terror she has ever heard. A moment later he was dead.'

'Then the shock he received must have come in the morning post.'

'That is, I agree, the logical inference. And something more than simply a steep bill from the gas company, to judge from the severity of it. Miss Montague proposes to consult me this morning, so perhaps we shall learn a little more then. If she is as punctual as the urgency of her note suggests,' he added, glancing at his watch, 'she will be here in precisely seventeen minutes, Watson; so if you would ring for the maid to clear away the relics of our breakfast, I should be obliged.'

It was a dull morning in September, chilly and damp, and as I stood by the window for a moment, surveying the ceaseless flow of traffic in Baker Street, I was struck by the banality of the scene. It was certainly difficult to imagine anyone dying of terror in modern London and I confess I rather doubted that Miss Montague's problem would be of much interest to Holmes, or would possess any of those *recherché* features which so delighted his eccentric taste.

His client arrived at the appointed time. She was a slim, dark-haired young lady of about five and twenty, a little below the medium size. She had a soft West Country accent and a quiet reserve in her manner which I had learnt to associate with those raised far from the brash clamour of London.

'I understand,' said Holmes, when his visitor was seated in the chair by the fire, 'that you wish to consult me in connection with the death of your uncle.'

'That is correct.'

'And yet I am not clear what it is you wish me to do. As I understand it, the cause of death was given as heart failure. In your letter you suggest that Mr Furnival's heart failed him as a result of fear. Do you have any reason for this supposition?'

'Mr Holmes, there can be no doubt. Mr Furnival cried out in the most terrible fear only moments before he died.'

'I do not doubt your conviction on the point, madam; but is it not possible that his cry was one of pain, occasioned by the heart seizure?'

Miss Montague shook her head. 'No, Mr Holmes,' said she in a firm tone. 'His cry was not one of pain, but of terror. There is a difference, which anyone hearing it would recognise at once. Even as I speak to you now, I can hear his last cry ringing in my ears and it chills my very bones.'

'Very well,' said Holmes. 'Perhaps you could describe to us the circumstances and what you suppose might have caused such fear in your uncle.' So saying, he leaned back in his chair, with his eyes closed and his fingertips together, the very picture of motionless concentration.

'I will tell you what I can,' began his visitor. 'The difficulty is that I have known my uncle and his household for less than two years. I was born and raised at Swanage, in Dorset, where my parents ran a small hotel. Two years ago my father died and when the business was sold, I was obliged to look elsewhere to make my way in the world. Some three years previously, Mr Furnival had paid us a brief visit. He was a distant cousin of my father's and thus not, strictly speaking, my uncle; but I have always addressed him as such. His visit to Swanage was the only previous occasion upon which we had met, for he lived in Norwood, in the suburbs of London, where he was, so I understood, an important and wealthy man. Now, despairing of finding a suitable occupation in Dorset, I wrote to him and asked if he would put me up while I sought employment in London. This he agreed to do and I came up to London about twenty months ago.

'The household then included also Mr Furnival's widowed sister, Mrs Eardley. Her husband had died some years previously, upon which, having no children, she had gone to live with her brother in the West Indies, where he was resident at the time, and had subsequently returned with him to England. The household was a very regular and orderly one, and I soon learnt that I should be required to fit in with its strict routines. Both brother and sister admired order and cleanliness above all else, and had a deep abhorrence of anything which fell short of this ideal. This inclination even extended to the garden of the property, for I subsequently learnt from a neighbour that when Mr Furnival moved into the house, he had most of the flowering plants cut back severely, so that little remains now but a strip of lawn and a row of small rose-bushes, and he had the climbing plants – wisteria and so on – completely removed from the walls of the house, which are now perfectly bare of any such ornament.

'A few months after I took up residence in Norwood, Mr Furnival and his sister fell out. They were both very quarrelsome by nature and had often exchanged sharp words, but on this occasion the rift was more severe, and shortly afterwards Mrs Eardley moved out and went to live by herself in Peckham. Mr Furnival then asked me if I would act as housekeeper for him, which, having no other immediate prospects, I agreed to do. Since that time, Mrs Eardley has called round occasionally, but her visits have almost always concluded with the two of them quarrelling.

'It was not what I had intended when I came up to London,' Miss Montague continued after a moment of reflection, 'and I cannot pretend that the situation has been entirely congenial to me; for, even without his sister's provocation, my uncle was a severe and ill-tempered man. Our conversations were perfunctory and brief and concerned only with household matters, for he had little interest in anything which was not of immediate personal relevance to him. Nor did he read much, except for newspapers, parliamentary reports and the like, which he would pore over for hours, in the hope, it seemed to me, of finding something with which he could quarrel. Save for this consuming passion for politics – Mr Furnival was of some celebrity locally in this field and we often had his political colleagues for dinner, when they would squabble noisily all evening – my uncle had only one interest, and that an unusual one. He had developed a taste for exotic carvings and other curios from the most remote corners of the world and had amassed quite a collection. No doubt his interest had begun during his time in the West Indies, where he spent over twenty years, but his collection had since grown to include objects from many different lands. One evening he showed me some of them.

'"To you, this may be simply a carved piece of wood," he said to me, as he held up some kind of oriental idol, which I must say struck me as perfectly hideous; "but the man that carved it has not simply shaped the wood, he has striven to impress part of his own soul into this object, in the hope of living on in it after his death and gaining revenge on those that have done him down in life. In many parts of the world, you know, such an object is regarded as definitely holding a part of the man that made it – for good or evil." He laughed as he said this, in a hard, callous manner, which I found very unpleasant. "And this is an interesting little pot," he continued, holding up a small earthenware vessel, the size of a small coffee cup, on the lid of which was a hideous figure with its tongue out. "It is a death pot, from Central America. You put something in it belonging to your enemy – a lock of his hair, say – then bury it in the ground. Within one month, so they say, your enemy will die."

"How horrible!" I cried; but Mr Furnival only laughed.

"You are young and high-minded," said he, in a bitter, cynical tone. "When you are older, you will learn that a man has many enemies in the world, and must use what means he has to destroy them and crush them beneath his feet."

'This conversation made a deep and disagreeable impression upon me. After it, I could not look upon my uncle's collection of curios without a shudder and I began to long for the day when I might move away from this household.

'I come now to the events of Tuesday morning,' Miss Montague continued after a moment. 'It was in every respect an ordinary morning. The maid is away at the moment, so I took in my uncle's breakfast myself, then returned to the kitchen, leaving him opening the post, which had just been delivered.'

'Of what did the post consist that morning?' asked Holmes.

'Two letters, which I could see were simply tradesmen's bills, and a brown-paper parcel. I had been in the kitchen scarcely a minute, when I heard my uncle cry out – such a cry as I hope I shall never hear again in my life. I dropped what I was doing and hurried back to the dining-room, to find him sitting rigid with fear at the breakfast table, his eyes very wide and his mouth hanging open, as if in terror.

'"What is it, Uncle?" I cried out, and hurried to his side; but even as I did so, he pitched forward on to the table and breathed his last.'

The young lady bit her lip and shuddered at the memory.

'What was in the parcel?' asked Holmes after a moment.

'A dark-brown wooden box,' replied Miss Montague, 'such as I have never seen before. In shape it is like a cube, about five inches on each side, and very ornately carved all over, in a pattern of twining leaves and vines. The lid, which is attached by brass hinges and fastened with a little brass clasp at the front, is pierced in several places, forming a sort of open lattice-work within the carving. Here and there, among the carved leaves, are little pieces of crystal, in pairs, like horrid and sinister eyes, watching you from among the foliage.' Miss Montague shuddered again and shut her eyes tightly.

'Was there anything in the box?' asked Holmes after a moment.

'No,' returned his visitor; 'nothing whatever. When I re-entered the dining-room and found my uncle on the point of death, I saw at once that the lid of the box was open and I could see that the interior was covered with some kind of thick black lacquer, so dense in its blackness, that as one looked into it, it was like looking into the very depths of evil; but it was perfectly empty. Mr Holmes, there is something sinister and unpleasant about that box and I believe it was sent to my uncle deliberately to bring about his death. You may consider the suggestion ridiculous; but I am convinced it is the literal truth!'

I was surprised at Miss Montague's somewhat fanciful description of the old box her uncle had received and expected Sherlock Holmes to display a certain impatience at her account. But when he spoke, it was in his usual placid tones.

'My dear Miss Montague,' said he; 'you need not fear ridicule for your convictions. I have frequently observed that the intuitions of those most closely involved in a case are generally nearer to the truth than the impersonal reports of the police or newspapers. However, a few more facts would be helpful. Do you have any reasons, other than your own intuition, to believe that there is something sinister about the box your uncle received?'

I was expecting our visitor to admit that she had not and was therefore surprised when she nodded her head vigorously. 'Indeed I do,' cried she. 'My uncle's death is not the only misfortune which that evil box has caused. Yesterday – just one day after his death – it came very close to claiming a second victim!'

'Really?' said Holmes in surprise. 'How very interesting!'

'Yes, Mr Holmes! It was this second dreadful incident which led me to write to you yesterday afternoon. You have a reputation for divining the truth where others see only mystery. Mr Holmes, I pray that you can do so now and destroy this evil!'

'Pray, let us have the facts of the second incident, then,' said Holmes.

'It was yesterday morning. I was making sure the house was in good order, for Mr Furnival's sister is coming today, when there came a knock at the door. I opened it to find a nautical-looking man standing there, a tall, middle-aged man with a grizzled beard and a lined, weather-beaten face, clad in a black pea jacket and cap. He introduced himself as Captain Jex and said he was an old friend of Mr Furnival's from the West Indies. He had been back in England only a few weeks and had been hoping to see his old friend, but had not known his address, when he had chanced upon the notice of his death in that morning's paper. I conducted him upstairs, to see Mr Furnival's body and pay his last respects, and as we left my uncle's room, he appeared very much affected by the experience, so I offered him a cup of tea. He said that, while I made the tea, he would sit in silent contemplation in the room where my uncle had died, so I left him in the dining-room and went to put the kettle on.

'It was scarcely five minutes later that I carried in a tray of tea things. Imagine my horror when I entered the room, to find my visitor lying stretched out, face down on the floor, unconscious. Quickly, I put down the tray and bent down to him.

'"Captain Jex! Captain Jex!" I cried. As I did so, he stirred slightly, lifted his head from the floor and opened his eyes, but his features expressed confusion. "What has happened?" I asked.

"'I don't know,' said he, rubbing his eyes. "I can't seem to remember. I must have come over faint, I suppose, but it's never happened to me before.'

'Even as he spoke, I saw that that horrid box was lying open on the floor beside him.

"'The box!" I cried. "Did you open it?"

"'Why, yes,' said he, looking in puzzlement from me to the box and back again, as he stood up. "It happened to catch my eye and I picked it up to have a closer look at it. I opened the lid and then I can't remember any more. Why do you ask?"

"'My uncle had just opened that box when he had some kind of seizure and died,' I said.

"'Good God!" cried Captain Jex in alarm. "Let's get the thing closed straight away, then!" With a quick stoop, he picked up the box from the floor, clapped the lid shut and replaced it on the sideboard. You will understand, then, Mr Holmes, why I regard that box with such horror, Since that moment, I have not touched it. But if the box does have some evil power, it is but the means by which someone has attacked my uncle. Someone deliberately sent it to him, with malice in his heart. It is that person that is the source of the evil!'

'Does your uncle have any enemies?' asked Holmes.

Miss Montague shook her head. 'He has many political opponents, but I doubt that any of them would do anything so wicked as this,' said she. 'I do recall an odd incident about three weeks ago, however,' she added after a moment, 'which I had quite forgotten until now. My uncle had returned home in a state of great anxiety. He asked me if there had been any callers at the house that day and I said that there had not.

"'What is it, Uncle?" said I. "Why do you ask?"

"'It is nothing," returned he, in an angry voice. "I thought I saw someone I knew, at the railway station, that is all. Forget that I asked.""

Sherlock Holmes sat for a moment in silence. 'I take it there was no letter in the parcel that contained the box,' said he at length.

'No, nor any label on the outside to indicate who or where it had come from.'

'Did you observe where the parcel had been posted?'

'Charing Cross Post Office.'

'Unfortunately, that is not very helpful,' said Holmes. 'So many parcels are received there that our chances of tracing any one of them are practically nil. Tell me, Miss Montague,' he added after a moment, 'did it seem to you that the parcel was damaged in any way when you received it?'

'Why, yes, it was,' returned his visitor in surprise. 'The brown paper it was wrapped in was torn in several places. I pointed this out to the postman, and he said that it had been in that condition when he had received it and must therefore have been mishandled at one of the central sorting offices. As no real damage appeared to have been done to it, however, I gave it no further thought.'

Holmes nodded and I could see from the little smile of satisfaction upon his face that he had already begun to formulate a theory. 'Did Captain Jex say where he was staying at present?' he asked his visitor.

'He mentioned that I might reach him at the Old Ship Inn at Greenwich,' replied she.

'Very well,' said Holmes. 'I shall look into the matter for you. Are you returning to Wharncliffe Crescent now?'

'Yes. Mrs Eardley is coming today, as I mentioned, and I wish to be there when she arrives.'

Holmes nodded. 'I shall call at the house this afternoon, Miss Montague. Until then, you must put all thoughts of that wooden box out of your mind. Do not attempt to do anything with it. Indeed, it is probably best if you do not even enter the room which contains the box and you must keep the door firmly closed. Do you understand?'

When his visitor had left us, I asked my friend why he was delaying his visit to Norwood until the afternoon.

'Because,' said he, 'I wish to go somewhere else first.'

'Where?'

'Greenwich. Do you wish to come?'

'Certainly. You think, then, that Captain Jex may be able to shed some light on the matter?'

'"Shedding light" scarcely does his position justice, Watson. Captain Jex is almost certainly the pivot around which the whole of the case revolves. Surely that is apparent, if anything is! I doubt we shall get to the bottom of it unless we can lay our hands on him.'

I was surprised at Holmes's remark and confess I could not understand his great interest in this man, Jex. But my friend would say no more and I was left to ponder what might be in his mind. Forty minutes later, we boarded the Greenwich train at Charing Cross, and forty minutes after that we were speaking to the landlord of the Old Ship Inn. Our enquiries, however, were met with disappointment. The landlord remembered Captain Jex very well, but informed us that he had paid his bill on Monday, the twentieth, and left that day.

'Did he leave a forwarding address?' asked Holmes, but the manager shook his head.

'He told me that if anyone came looking for him, I was to say that he had gone to stay with Captain McNeill; but he gave no address.'

'Well, well,' said Holmes in a philosophical tone, as we walked to the railway station, 'Captain Jex's disappearance is no more than I had expected; but we could not neglect the possibility of finding him still here, however slight the chance. Now we had best get down to Norwood without further delay. You will come?'

'Most certainly,' I said. I was keen to see what my friend might learn at Norwood. He appeared to have some very definite theory as to what lay behind the facts we had heard from Miss Montague. What this theory might be, I could not imagine, but knowing my friend's remarkable abilities as I did, I could not doubt that, like a ship following the Pole Star, his course was set unerringly for the solution of the mystery.

A ten-minute walk from Norwood Junction brought us to Wharncliffe Crescent, a pleasant tree-lined road of attractive modern villas, set back a little behind neat front gardens. As we turned the corner, however, my friend stopped. Some way ahead of us, a small knot of people was assembled on the pavement and a uniformed policeman stood on duty.

'Halloa!' cried Holmes. 'This looks a bad business, Watson! Surely Miss Montague has not ignored the instructions I gave her?'

We hurried forward and, as we did so, a tall, burly man in a light raincoat and soft-brimmed hat emerged from the house in front of which the crowd was gathered, and I recognised Inspector Athelney Jones of Scotland Yard.

'Mr Holmes!' cried he in surprise, as we met him at the gate. 'I don't know how you got here so quickly, but, take it from me, you've wasted your time.'

'What has happened?' asked Holmes.

'Another death. Heart failure again, by the look of it. There's no reason for me to be here, really, but two deaths in three days sounded a little suspicious, so, as I happened to be at Norwood Police Station, I thought I'd best take a look. However, there's nothing in it. It's obviously just some sort of family weakness, because, of course, the dead man and woman were related.'

I saw Holmes's face fall. 'Is it Miss Montague?' he asked.

'Oh, no, she's all right. She's just been telling me what she told you earlier. It's Furnival's sister that's died. Come inside and I'll show you. Ask these people to move along, will you, Constable,' he said to the policeman at the gate. 'There's nothing to see here.'

We followed the inspector into the house and found Miss Montague in the drawing-room with a middle-aged woman, introduced to us as Mrs Loveday, a neighbour. In a few words, Holmes's client described to us what had occurred.

'Mrs Eardley arrived soon after I returned home,' she began. 'She seemed in an irritable mood, and declared that the house looked untidy and could do with a good dusting, which was not true. "There's no point letting the house go to rack and ruin just because your uncle has died," she said, and began brushing and dusting noisily. Shortly afterwards, Mrs Loveday called and, a little later, when she and I were talking in here, I heard Mrs Eardley open the dining-room door. I went out to speak to her. "That is the room in which Uncle died," I said. "I wish the door to remain closed." "Nonsense!" said she, and would not be contradicted, so I left her to do what she wished. For a few minutes, we heard her clattering about in there, then there came the most dreadful scream, like that of a soul in torment, followed by complete silence. We ran in there and found Mrs Eardley stone dead on the floor, laid out full length, as Captain Jex had been. I at once looked for that horrible box and saw that she had been doing something with it; for I had left it on the sideboard, firmly closed, and now it stood on the dining-table, with its lid flung back. I immediately sent for the doctor, and when he had examined Mrs Eardley's body we carried it upstairs to the spare bedroom. I have not touched the box, Mr Holmes, and the dining-room door has remained firmly closed again since Mrs Eardley's death.'

'You have acted correctly, Miss Montague. Now, I hope, we can bring this unfortunate business to a close. Have you a cardboard box in the house, big enough, say, to contain the wooden box?'

'I have a shoe-box, if that would suffice.'

'That would be ideal. If you could also provide me with a ball of twine, a pair of scissors and a long-handled broom, I should be obliged.'

Holmes and Miss Montague left the room, but were back again in a couple of minutes, with the items Holmes had mentioned; then he, Athelney Jones and I opened the dining-room door and entered that fatal room. It was a square room of modest size, with a window which overlooked the back garden. In the centre of the room was a table, to the left a sideboard and, in an alcove by the fireplace, a large, heavy piece of furniture, consisting of a cupboard above and drawers below. Upon the table stood the carved box, the arrival of which at this ordinary suburban house had begun the series of mysterious and dreadful events.

'I'm a busy man, Mr Holmes,' said Jones in a self-important tone, 'and I can't afford to waste any more time on this business. So, unless you can show me in the next two minutes that there is something of a criminal nature involved in it, I shall be off, and leave you and Miss Montague to deal with her precious box!'

'Very well,' returned Holmes in an affable tone. 'If you would stand over there with Dr Watson, I shall demonstrate the matter for you.' He placed the items Miss Montague had given him on the table, then, taking the shoe-box, from which he had removed the lid, and the broom, which he held by the brush end, he crouched on the floor, in front of the large cupboard.

For a moment, he peered into the dark recess beneath the cupboard, then, with a sudden movement, thrust the handle of the broom into the darkness. Jones glanced at me with a frown on his face and it was clear that he thought that Holmes had taken leave of his senses. Next moment, his expression changed to one of horror, as, at a fearsome speed, there emerged from beneath the cupboard the most monstrous, repulsive spider I have ever seen in my life. It was at least the size of a man's hand, its black, hairy legs as thick as a man's fingers and it ran at a terrifying speed along by the broom handle towards Holmes's hand. But, quick as it was, Holmes was quicker and he clapped the shoe-box over the top of it just before it reached him.

'For the love of Heaven!' cried Jones in a dry, cracked voice. 'What in God's name is *that?*'

'*Tarantula Nigra,*' returned Holmes: 'the black tarantula, the only one of the family whose bite is fatal to man – and a very striking specimen it is, too!' He spoke in the detached tones of the enthusiastic naturalist, but there was a suppressed tension and excitement in his manner which told me that even Holmes was not entirely immune from the horror which the sudden appearance of that fearsome beast had provoked in my own breast. 'Pass me the lid, Watson,' he continued, 'and let us see if we can slip it underneath the box.' In a moment, he had done as he said, then, in one swift movement, had turned the box right-side up. 'Hold the lid down, Watson, while I wrap the twine round it. Hold it down firmly, old man,' he added quickly. '*Tarantula Nigra* is quite capable of pushing the lid off!'

His warning came not an instant too soon, for even as I put my hand to the top of the box, I felt it lift against my touch. With a thrill of horror, I pressed down hard and in a minute Holmes had bound the box up securely with the twine. 'We'd better give the creature some air,' he remarked, as he poked half a dozen small holes in the top with the scissors. 'We don't want it to suffocate! Here you are, Jones!' he continued, handing the box to the policeman. 'Here is your evidence of criminality! This deadly spider was, with deliberate intent, sent to Furnival in that wooden box. Its sudden frightening appearance at his breakfast table undoubtedly brought about his death. Whether it also bit him, we cannot say until his body is examined afresh, but it certainly bit his sister, Mrs Eardley, for I took the opportunity of examining her wrist a moment ago and the mark is quite clear there.'

'The doctor didn't say anything about that,' said Jones.

'He didn't know what he was looking for and the mark of the bite was under the cuff of her blouse.'

'How did you know that you would find this horrible thing here?' asked Jones. As he spoke, the spider evidently made some sudden movement inside the box, for he put it down hurriedly on the table, his face pale.

'It seemed more than likely,' returned Holmes. 'Miss Montague had stated that the box her uncle received had been empty, but as she was not in the room at the moment he opened it, it was always possible that it had contained something able to move of its own volition, which had made itself scarce as she entered the room following her uncle's cry of terror. If this were so, what could it be? The size of the box suggested a spider – although there were other possibilities – and this suggestion received some support from the fact that Furnival himself had spent over twenty years in the West Indies, where large spiders are not uncommon.

'I asked Miss Montague if the parcel containing the box had appeared damaged when it arrived. As a conjecture, this was something of a long shot, I admit; but I was gratified to find that it was correct. The paper on the top of the parcel had been ripped when it arrived at the house. This confirmed the theory yet further: for it seemed to me likely that the sender of the parcel had deliberately ripped the paper, in a way which would appear like accidental damage, in order to ensure that air reached the parcel's occupant during its transit through the post. The lid of the box itself, of course, was pierced in several places, as Miss Montague had mentioned and I had noted. Something else which was suggestive was that Miss Montague's uncle had had all the climbing plants removed from the walls of the house; for it is a fact that one of the reasons that some people do not like such plants is because their stems provide an avenue for spiders to enter the house via the bedroom windows. Taking all these points together, it seemed very likely that Furnival was one of those who have a pathological dread of spiders and that someone, aware of this fact, had deliberately sent him a particularly terrifying specimen. Whether Mrs Eardley suffered from the same aversion to spiders as her brother, we cannot say. She was certainly bitten by the creature, as the police surgeon will doubtless confirm in due course, and may have died from that cause, as the venom of *Tarantula Nigra* is very potent and acts very quickly. In her case, it seems to have been her zeal to clean her brother's house which led to her death. She must have been poking with a brush beneath that cupboard, much as I was, and the spider, considering itself to be under attack, would have sallied forth to repulse the attack, as you saw it do just now. Fortunately for me, I was expecting it; but Mrs Eardley was not.'

'You have certainly confirmed your theory, anyhow,' said Inspector Jones after a moment, eyeing the box on the table warily. 'But who the dickens could have done it?'

'I strongly suspect that Captain Jex, who called here yesterday, was the agent of these deaths.'

'What – the gentleman who had the fainting fit?'

'I think we may safely dismiss the fainting fit, Jones,' replied Holmes in a dry tone. 'It made sense to Miss Montague only because she was convinced that the box possessed some evil power, natural or supernatural. But if that is discounted as a possibility, as I had discounted it, then Jex's actions appear in a somewhat different light. Clearly he had been down on the floor for some purpose, and only pretended to have fainted when Miss Montague entered and found him there. What could that purpose have been, but to find the spider? No doubt he had reasoned as I had done that the likeliest hiding place for the creature was in that dark recess under the cupboard. Spiders have their own fears and anxieties, you know, Jones, and finding itself in unfamiliar surroundings, it would naturally seek the darkest corner it could find. But if Jex was looking for the spider, then he must have known it was there; and how could he know of the spider's existence except if he himself had sent it?'

'He must be a cool customer,' remarked Jones, 'to return to the scene of his crime so soon. Why should he do so?'

'It may be,' replied Holmes, 'that he had intended only to frighten Furnival with the spider and when he heard that Furnival had died, saw at once that if the spider were found it would put a noose round his neck. If, however, he could remove the spider, then that danger would be averted.'

'You may be right,' said Jones. 'Anyhow, we must get after the villain as quickly as possible.'

'Dr Watson and I have already made inquiries at the place he was staying last week,' said Holmes, and described our visit to Greenwich. 'He evidently left there on Monday, took the direct train to Charing Cross, where he posted his parcel and then took himself off elsewhere. You may be able to trace him through his purchase of the box at a curio shop, or through Captain McNeill, the man whose name he mentioned at Greenwich; but I rather fancy that Captain Jex is a resourceful character and not likely to sit about, waiting to be apprehended.'

'We shall see about that,' said Jones in a determined tone. 'If we haven't collared him by this time next week, then you may call me an idiot!'

––––––––

This extravagant offer was politely overlooked, however, the next time Jones called in to see us at Baker Street. Three weeks had passed without any news and I had concluded that Captain Jex had slipped through the net. But Jones began by stating that he had some new information about the fugitive.

'That is good news,' said Holmes.

'It's not so good as you suppose, Mr Holmes,' responded Jones in a gloomy tone. 'We have managed to trace him, but he is dead.'

'Ah! I see. When did it happen?'

'Twelve years ago.'

'What!' cried Holmes and I in astonishment.

Jones nodded his head. 'We are certain we have the right man. Captain Abel Jex was murdered in 1874, on the island of St Anthony, in the West Indies, by a man called David McNeill.'

'What became of McNeill?' asked Holmes.

'There were evidently mitigating circumstances in the case, for he escaped the gallows; but he did ten years in a penal colony and died shortly after his release.'

For some time we sat in silence, too dumbfounded by this information to speak.

'What on earth is the meaning of it all?' I asked at length.

'That is the question, Dr Watson,' said Athelney Jones in a tone of puzzlement. 'As to the answer, your guess is as good as mine.'

––––––––

No further progress was made with the case and it at length passed entirely from our thoughts, as new work took the place of old. In my own mind, I had long since consigned it to that list of cases which were unlikely ever to be cleared up satisfactorily, when, one morning, two years later, Holmes received a communication from Grindley and Leggatt, solicitors, of Gray's Inn. This consisted of a sealed foolscap document, with an accompanying letter explaining that the document had been deposited with them two years previously by a Mr David McNeill, with the instruction that in the event of his death, it was to be forwarded to Sherlock Holmes. McNeill's death, they informed us, had been reported within the past week. The enclosed document ran as follows:

MY DEAR MR SHERLOCK HOLMES,

I know of your reputation and am aware that you have taken an interest in the deaths of Victor Furnival and his sister, Mrs Eardley. I therefore venture to give you the following account, confident that you will recognise it for the truth that it is:

When first I met Victor Furnival, he was the manager of a large sugar-cane plantation on the island of St Anthony in the West Indies, and had a reputation as a brutal and merciless overseer. I was master of a small tramp vessel at the time, sailing about the Caribbean and happy enough with my lot. Sometimes, when we put in at Trianna Bay, which was the largest town on St Anthony, I would meet up with Furnival, and other Englishmen that were there, and we would drink and play cards, as men tend to do when they are far from home. It was a rough place, full of rough people and with no pretensions to gentility; but even there, among such people, Furnival was known for his vicious tongue and his bullying, blustering manner.

Among those with whom we sometimes played cards and passed the time was Captain Abel Jex, who owned a small boat and traded among the nearby islands. Occasionally, he picked up pearls from the local fishermen, which he sold to a dealer in Trianna Bay; but there was a persistent rumour that those he sold were the poorer ones and that he was building up a secret cache of really fine pearls to pay for a life of ease when he finally gave up the sea. I had always doubted this rumour, but it was confirmed to me one day by the man himself. I was in Trianna Bay and ran across Captain Jex down by the harbour. He told me that he had come to town to have his pearls valued by an expert from Jamaica who was staying there for a few days and that the appraisal had been very favourable. Evidently pleased with himself, he showed me the pearls, as we sat in a bar by the harbour. From a small velvet pouch, he tipped on to his hand a dozen of the most perfect and lustrous pearls I had ever seen. What they might be worth, I could not say, but I would guess that they might set a man up for life. I motioned to him to put them away, for I saw that we were being observed by other men in the bar, men of the vilest antecedents, who would think nothing of slitting Jex's throat to get hold of his treasure.

Later that day, I was obliged to see Furnival on business, so I walked out to his house, which lay in an isolated spot, ten minutes from the town. As I approached the front door, I heard raised voices from within the house, which I recognised as those of Furnival and his sister, Mrs Eardley. She had come out from England to live with her brother the previous year, after her husband had died and, to speak plainly, was generally disliked. She was a mean, grasping, shrewish woman, whose presence seemed to have made Furnival even more ill-tempered and disagreeable than before.

'You fool!' I heard her cry in a harsh tone. 'You must seize your chances! Or do you want to rot forever in this stinking place?'

I did not know what they were discussing, nor had any wish to know. I knocked on the door, was admitted by the servant and heard no more. That evening, I attended Furnival's house again, for dinner. I had thought, from what he told me earlier, that there would be half a dozen of us there, but in the event the only other visitor was Captain Jex. The four of us played cards for a while after dinner; but I found Mrs Eardley's company so intolerable that I presently made some excuse and left, returning to my ship in the harbour.

In the middle of the night, I was roughly awakened by a party of soldiers from the nearby military garrison and informed that I was being arrested for the murder of Captain Jex, who had been found beside the road with his head crushed in. I protested my innocence, but it did me no good and I was sent to trial in Jamaica. I will not detail the court proceedings, a full account of which can be found in the Caribbean Law Reports, but note merely that the entire case against me was built on a series of lies by Furnival and his sister. In particular, they both stated that Captain Jex and I had quarrelled on the evening of his death, which was completely untrue, and that they had heard Jex cry out, a short time after he had left their house and, upon going to investigate, had seen me running away, which was also completely untrue.

Of course, what had happened was clear to me, as was the meaning of the words I had overheard Mrs Eardley speak to her brother. Furnival and his sister had learnt of the pearls Jex was carrying, had plotted together to murder him to get their hands on them, and had planned to divert suspicion by putting the blame on to me. Had it been only the two of them testifying against me, I might yet have avoided a guilty verdict; but they had evidently bribed or threatened others, for a number of people I had never even seen before came forward to testify enthusiastically against me. The only thing that saved me from the hangman's noose was the question of the pearls. I, of course, did not have them and nor could they be found anywhere else, as a result of which the prosecution scarcely mentioned them at all, even though they were the obvious motive for the crime. Instead, it was alleged that Jex and I had quarrelled over some other matter and, inflamed by drink, had come to blows. This allowed the defence counsel to argue, from various incidental considerations, that, whatever had occurred, Jex had probably struck the first blow. This argument was accepted by the jury and, thus, although found guilty of causing Jex's death, I was spared the gallows and sentenced instead to ten years' hard labour in the penal colony on Halifax Island.

There I passed a decade of my life, suffering for a crime I did not commit, and sustained only by a burning hatred of those whose lies had condemned me. Thus, when I was at last released to the world once more, a sick, broken man, I resolved that I would devote my last breath to hunting down Furnival and his sister. Shortly after my release, a clerk's error led to an incorrect report that I had died, but I did not trouble to correct the error. What did I care? I had no life, other than to seek justice for Jex and revenge for myself. I learnt that Furnival and his sister had returned to England several years earlier, and it was not long before I followed them there, assuming for my own satisfaction the name of Captain Jex, the man they had murdered. The meagre savings I had from before my imprisonment were just sufficient to pay for my passage and keep me for a little while, and that, for me, was enough.

Once in England, it took me little time to track Furnival down and I discovered that he was living as a respectable, highly regarded man of substance in south London. For some time I followed him about, until I knew his habits almost as well as my own. One day, at Norwood station, our eyes met for a moment, but then the train I was on pulled away and I do not think he recognised me. One thing I had remembered about Furnival was his deep loathing of spiders. I had therefore brought with me a large specimen of the black tarantula. At first, I was unsure how I might use it; but when I learnt of his interest in native curios, I at once thought of putting the spider in a carved box and sending it to him through the post.

The rest you know. I had not expected that the mere sight of the creature would bring about the death of my enemy, although I cannot say in all honesty that that outcome causes me any regret. When I learnt what had occurred, I tried to recover the spider, but without success. I was immensely relieved when I read that you had captured it, for my greatest fear was that Furnival's niece, or some other innocent, would be harmed by it.

Now I am dying and by the time you read these lines my tongue

will be stilled forever, but I rejoice that some degree of justice has
at last been meted out to the true murderers of Captain Jex. For the
peace of your soul, pray that you never fall foul of anyone so vicious
and callous as Victor Furnival and his sister.

    CAPTAIN DAVID McNEILL

'What a dreadful business,' I remarked as we finished reading. 'But it illustrates, I suppose, that even the most banal suburban existence may conceal the strangest of secrets.'

'Indeed,' said Holmes. 'And it illustrates, also, Watson, the truth of the old adage, that the darkest deeds cast the longest shadows.'

The Adventure of *The Tomb on the Hill*

My note-book records that it was in the third week of February, 1883, that the singular business of Mr Dryson's strange oil painting was brought to the attention of my friend, Sherlock Holmes. It was a cold, wet period and I was reading in the morning paper of the flooding that had afflicted many low-lying parts of the country, when there came a ring at the front-door bell. A moment later, a smartly dressed, middle-aged gentleman was shown into our sitting-room and introduced himself as Everard Dryson.

'What can we do for you, Mr Dryson?' said Holmes, taking his visitor's hat and coat and ushering him into a chair by the fireside.

'The fact is,' returned Dryson, 'I have had the strangest experience. I really can't think what to make of it and I was hoping you might be able to look into it for me.'

'Certainly,' said Holmes, rubbing his hands together in delight at the prospect of an interesting commission. A new case of any sort was welcome to him, for he had had little to do for two or three days and had begun to chafe at this enforced idleness. 'Pray, let us have the details.'

'It is soon told,' said the other. 'I am a bachelor and have a house just round the corner from here, in Gloucester Place. One of my interests is in oil paintings, of which I now have a fair number. There is no particular theme to my collection – I simply buy what takes my fancy – although I do have a taste for landscapes and rural scenes. About three months ago, I bought a painting entitled *The Tomb on the Hill* from the Marchmont Gallery in Bond Street. It depicts a raised stone tomb in a rural setting, with trees about it, fields in the background and so on. I thought when I first saw it that it had perhaps been inspired by that well-known painting of Poussin's, but in fact I understand that the scene depicted is not an imaginary one, but a real one, in the north of England. Apparently, some member of the Eldersly family who had soldiered abroad for many years willed that when he died his tomb should be placed on a hill overlooking his estates in Yorkshire. Anyhow, in the foreground a rustic figure is inspecting the tomb and wandering about are a number of small animals. Visible on the side of the tomb are several lines of carved lettering. You will understand in a moment why I am mentioning these details.

'Yesterday, I was out for most of the afternoon. When I returned I was informed by my housekeeper, Mrs Larchfield, that two workmen had called in my absence to deliver a flat wooden crate, such as might have contained a large painting. She told them that we were not expecting such a delivery, but they showed her a handwritten note with my name and address on it, so she let them in and they carried their crate into the drawing-room. While one of them was unfastening the crate, the other had a sort of coughing fit and asked her if he could trouble her for a glass of water. She was a little dubious about leaving them alone in the drawing-room, but as the man was still coughing, she could hardly refuse his request. When she returned with the water, she was surprised to see that they had not proceeded to open their crate.

'"The fact is, madam," said the one who seemed to be in charge, "that I have realised that you are right and we are wrong. This sheet of paper with Mr Dryson's name and address on it is an old one which we have been given in error. We shall have to go back to the shop and get the matter sorted out. I am very sorry that we have troubled you."

'With that, the men picked up their wooden crate again and left the house with it. This all struck Mrs Larchfield as rather odd, and after the men had gone she had a good look round the drawing-room to make sure that they had not stolen anything. When I came home she told me all about it and I, too, made a careful examination of the room but found nothing amiss. It was only later, after supper, that I noticed a very strange thing.

'I had been thinking about the Marchmont Gallery and wondering if the delivery men had come from there, and I suppose it was this train of thought that made me look at the last painting I had bought from them, *The Tomb on the Hill*, to which I referred. No doubt when I had had a look round the room earlier, I had merely glanced at this painting and had not really looked closely at it. Now I saw to my utter astonishment that although the picture and frame appeared exactly as before in almost every way, there was one small but crucial change. The words carved on the tomb were now quite different from what they had been.'

'How very curious,' remarked Holmes. His tone was one of puzzlement, but there was an unmistakable look of delight upon his face, as of a wine connoisseur who has just taken his first sip of a particularly fine vintage. 'Were there any obvious signs that the painting had been altered by hand?'

'Not at all.'

'Then we must assume that while your housekeeper was out of the room, the men substituted a painting that was in their packing-case for the one hanging on the wall.'

'I suppose you must be right.'

'Is the new painting an inferior copy of the original?'

Dryson shook his head. 'It is signed by the same artist, A.R. Philips. Of course, I realise that the signature in itself would prove nothing, but the picture does appear to be by the same hand. Besides, my painting is not particularly valuable. It is not by an "Old Master", or anything like that, but by a young artist who is currently active.'

'Do you know anything of the artist?'

'Not really. I seem to remember hearing that he has a studio out Putney way and has exhibited at the Royal Academy. I believe he is moderately popular without being very well known, if you know what I mean. If you are right, he must have painted two or more versions of the same scene, I suppose, although why he should do so and why someone should wish to steal mine and leave another in its place, I cannot imagine.'

'Hum! I think I should like to see this painting, Mr Dryson,' said Holmes, rising to his feet. 'Would that be possible?'

'Certainly. We can walk round to my house in just a few minutes.'

Entering Mr Dryson's drawing-room was somewhat like entering an Aladdin's cave, so full was it of *objets d'art* of all types, shapes and sizes. The painting we had come to see was hanging in a prominent place to the right of the window. It was a fairly large picture, the overall size including the frame being about two feet wide and two and a half feet tall. Depicted in it, as Holmes's client had described, was a large stone tomb. Around the tomb were a few young trees and beyond it the land dropped away to a broad fertile plain which stretched far into the distance, to where a row of purple hills marked the horizon. On the plain, a few sheep were dotted about and in the far distance was a small fountain of some kind, with a jumble of rocks about it, upon which the water was falling. In the foreground, a rustic figure in leather gaiters and a battered soft hat was leaning on a stout staff as he gazed upon the tomb. About his feet and a little behind him, among the trees, were a few small rabbits, and two or three ducks were waddling past the tomb. Clearly visible on the side of the tomb were the following lines:

> *Death where is thy victory?*
> *Peace doth fill these parks*
> *While water from the fountain*
> *Doth sparkle on the rocks*

'Do you recall the tomb inscription on your own picture?' Holmes asked his client.

'Yes,' answered Dryson. 'I made a note of it in case you asked.' He passed us a sheet of note-paper, upon which I read the following:

> *For thirty years my feet marched*
> *On from east and west*
> *To each corner of the dew-laden far south*
> *Never resting then, now laid down at last.*

'This inscription would certainly not win any poetry prizes,' said Holmes with a chuckle. 'Do you know which of them – if either – is on the tomb in Yorkshire?'

'I'm afraid I have no idea.'

'Are there any other differences between this picture and your own?'

'That little fountain in the distance is not on mine,' replied Dryson. 'Apart from that, the only difference I can see is in the number of ducks and rabbits. There are definitely more of both in this picture.'

Holmes then carefully lifted the picture from the wall and turned it round. 'Hum!' said he. 'The back of this picture has recently been removed and then replaced, using the original tacks. There is a label on the back from the Marchmont Gallery, so this picture is from the same source as your own, Mr Dryson. You had no idea when you purchased your picture that there was another one, almost identical to it?'

'No, I hadn't. I had seen it in Marchmont's window for a few days and looked at it several times, wondering if I should get it. Eventually I went in and enquired about it and the proprietor, a Mr Appleby, informed me that they were selling it as agents for a client of theirs, a widow whose late husband had amassed quite a large collection of works of art which she now wished to trim a little, as she was about to move to a smaller house. He told me the price she was asking for the picture and I went home to consider the matter further. The next day, having made my mind up, I returned and made them an offer – which was a little less than the asking price – and two days later I had a note from them to say that the seller had accepted my offer.'

'Do you know the seller's name?'

'No. I don't think it was ever mentioned.'

'I think we should try to find out a little more about these pictures. Will you come to the Marchmont Gallery with us, Mr Dryson? They are more likely to give us the information we seek if you are present.'

Dryson was quite amenable to accompanying us and fifteen minutes later we were pushing open the door of the gallery, where we were welcomed by a tall, bald-headed man, who introduced himself to us as Mr Appleby.

'My friend, Mr Dryson, recently bought a painting here,' said Holmes.

'Indeed. I remember it well,' returned Appleby. '*The Tomb on the Hill*. Is there some problem with it?'

'No, but he has recently learnt that there is another version of the same painting, also sold by you, I believe, and he is curious as to who owns that one.'

'It is not our policy to divulge the names and addresses of our private clients.'

'Of course, I understand that. But in this case, Mr Dryson simply wishes to examine the two paintings together, out of artistic curiosity. He is sure the other gentleman would be as interested as he is to see them displayed side by side.'

'That might prove somewhat difficult to arrange,' said Appleby.

'Why is that?' asked Dryson. 'Is the owner away?'

Appleby shook his head. 'Have you not heard?' said he in surprise. 'It was in the local paper. The other version of the painting was stolen last week. Two men forced their way into the owner's house while he was out, overpowered his housekeeper and left with the painting. The matter is now in the hands of the police, so I understand.'

'Do you know which police station is dealing with the case?' asked Holmes.

'Chelsea, I believe,' returned Appleby, 'as that is where the owner lives.'

'Thank you,' said Holmes. 'As you will imagine, we are curious to know how you came to be selling two very similar copies of the same painting.'

'They both happened to come on the market at the same time.'

'From different sellers?'

'No, the same seller – the widow to whom I referred in a previous conversation with Mr Dryson.'

'It seems odd that she should have had two copies of the same painting. Might we know her name?'

Appleby hesitated. 'Ordinarily, my client's wish for privacy would preclude my giving you that information. As it happens, however, the lady in question has an appointment to see us this morning.' He glanced at a clock on the wall. 'She is due here in about ten minutes' time. If you wish, you may wait and put your questions to her yourself.'

For a few minutes, we ambled round the gallery, idly examining the various *objets d'art* on display there, then Holmes indicated that we should join him in the street outside.

'There is something odd here,' said he, as we stood on the kerb, a short distance from the shop. 'Did you feel it, Watson?'

'Mr Appleby is very stiff and formal in his manner,' I remarked, unsure what my companion had in mind.

'Yes,' said he; 'but I fancy there is something more than mere formality. It seemed to me that there was a distinct look of apprehension in his eye when I began to question him, as if there were something else, other than simply names and addresses, that he did not wish us to know.'

He broke off as a smartly dressed woman approached the door of the Marchmont Gallery. She was, I suppose, nearer fifty than forty, but her face was an attractive, almost youthful one, and her carriage was erect and graceful. As this appeared likely to be the seller of Mr Dryson's picture, we followed her into the shop, where Appleby introduced us.

'There is not much I can tell you about the paintings,' said she, when Holmes had explained our interest. 'My late husband was the great collector of such things, not I.'

'It seems odd that your husband should have had two paintings of the same scene,' observed Holmes.

The lady smiled and shook her head. 'I quite agree; but for some reason he seemed very keen on it – I don't know why. We had a large house at the time, near Bethnal Green, with a large room on either side of the front door, and my husband hung a copy of *The Tomb on the Hill* in both of them. When I asked him about it, he just said he wished to be able to look at the picture whichever of the rooms he was in. The artist, a charming young man by the name of Andrew Philips, whom I met on several occasions, had originally painted the scene for the Elderslyfamily, who have estates in Yorkshire, I believe. The tomb is apparently that of some ancestor of theirs who soldiered abroad for much of his life. Anyway, they gave Mr Philips permission to enter it for the Royal Academy exhibition, and it was there that my husband saw it and was so taken with it that he asked if he might have a copy. Neither the Elderslyfamily nor Mr Philips raised any objection to this, nor, evidently, to there being two copies, which was what Mr Philips brought to our house in due course. That was about three years ago. Perhaps there was something in the theme of the tomb that appealed to my husband, but it seems a little morbid to me, for it was about that time that my husband first fell ill – a long illness to which he finally succumbed last summer.'

'Might we know your husband's name?' enquired Holmes. 'Then we can look out for any more of his collection which might come on to the market.'

'Why, certainly,' said the lady. 'His name was Henry Cosgrove. You may have heard of him, as he was a prominent lawyer in his day, with a well-known and busy practice in Whitechapel.'

'Thank you. And the artist's address, in case we wish to look him up?'

'He has a cottage to the west of Putney. I can't remember the name of it, but you can't miss it, as it stands all by itself. He says the air there is the clearest in the whole of London, which is why he chose it. The nearest station is the one on Barnes Common.'

'What a very charming woman,' said Dryson when the three of us were out in the street once more.

'Indeed,' I agreed. 'What a delightful voice she has! And what poise!'

'And yet,' said Holmes with a chuckle, 'all the time she was discoursing in so charming a manner, her fingers were clutching the bag she was carrying as a drowning man might clutch at a straw. What, you did not observe it? So tightly was she gripping it that I thought she might rend it in two.'

'What does it mean?'

'I don't know, Watson. Perhaps there was something that Mrs Cosgrove was anxious we might ask her, something she would rather not discuss. But, come! I wish to make a few enquiries at Chelsea police station.'

Dryson asked if he might accompany us, to which Holmes raised no objection, and in twenty minutes we had reached the police station. Our visit there was but a brief one. The officer on duty informed us that a Mr Gerald Tacolstone of Oakley Street had reported the assault upon his housekeeper and the theft of his painting the previous week. 'But,' he said, 'we have had a message from him this very morning, to say that his picture has been returned. It seems that someone rang at his door-bell early this morning and when his housekeeper went to answer it she found there was no one there, but a large packing-case had been left, leaning up against the railings. She and Mr Tacolstone took it into the house and, when they opened it, found it contained his painting.'

'Unharmed?'

'Apparently so. In any case, the matter is out of our hands now. The day after the robbery, we had a message from Scotland Yard to say that one of the detective officers there, Mr G. Lestrade, would be taking over the case. If you wish to know any more about the matter, Mr Lestrade is probably the man to ask.'

'I wonder why Lestrade became involved,' murmured Holmes, as we stood for a moment on the street outside the police station. 'As you now have a different version of the painting, Mr Dryson, it seems very likely that the one you have is Mr Tacolstone's and the one he has is yours. But I think we ought to verify this curious transposition of paintings by paying that gentleman a visit.'

Twenty minutes later, therefore, we presented ourselves at Mr Tacolstone's house in Oakley Street. A stout, rubicund gentleman, with a glint of humour in his eye, he listened with interest as we described to him Mr Dryson's experience and our subsequent enquiries.

'Do you know,' said he at last, 'I am very glad that you have come, for it has quite taken a weight off my mind. I had begun to think I must be going mad. When my picture was returned, so I thought, I rushed to send a note round to the police station, telling them as much. I didn't want them to waste any more time on enquiries now that I had the stolen item back. But I hadn't looked at the picture properly when I sent off my note and, when I did so, I discovered to my astonishment that although the picture was largely the same as before, certain small details in it had been changed. I didn't feel that I could bother the police again over the matter – I thought they would consider me a perfect idiot – and then I began to doubt my own memory of how the picture had been before. I had no reason to suppose, you see, that there was more than one copy of the picture. But now, although the mystery is not cleared up, it is at least a different mystery from what I had at first supposed and does not reflect on my own sanity in any way.'

He took us through to another room, which was as much of an Aladdin's Cave as Mr Dryson's drawing-room. Propped up on a chair was *The Tomb on the Hill* and Dryson at once bent to examine it. 'Yes, this is undoubtedly my version,' he said at length.

'Well, you are welcome to it, I am sure,' said Tacolstone with a merry chuckle. 'The tomb inscription on this one is even poorer than the one on my copy and this one also lacks the odd little fountain in the distance.'

'That is true,' said Dryson, laughing, 'but at least this one is not quite so infested with rabbits as your copy!'

Holmes made a brief examination of the picture, including the back, which he indicated to me had been removed and replaced just as the other one had, then for some time he stood in silent thought, as the two art collectors joked about the relative merits of their pictures. 'I think,' said he at length, interrupting the flow of their humour, 'that there is more to this singular business than any of us can know at present. What I propose is that you bring your pictures round to my chambers at six o'clock this evening and leave them with me for twenty-four hours so that I can examine them together more carefully. After that, each can be returned to its rightful owner.'

Both men readily agreed to this proposal and we left them in a jocular discussion of their hobby, their laughter ringing in our ears as we made our way up to the King's Road.

'Do you intend to go to see Inspector Lestrade?' I asked, as we looked for a cab.

'Later,' returned my companion. 'First I should like to have a word with the creator of these singular pictures, Andrew Philips, who may be able to tell us a little more about how they came to be commissioned. Would you care to come?'

'Most definitely,' I replied. 'I am keen to get to the bottom of the mystery!'

We took a cab across Putney Bridge and along the road towards Richmond, alighting some forty minutes later at Barnes station. It was a surprisingly wild and untamed spot, considering its proximity to London. I could see that in the summer months the heath must have presented a very attractive appearance, but now the bare, leafless trees and marshy ground had a desolate, woebegone look, which was not improved by the wraiths of fog that drifted this way and that with every slight movement of the chilly air. For some time we tramped over muddy tracks from one narrow road to another without seeing any sign of life, until rounding a bend we came upon a small cottage, standing in isolation by the side of the road. Our knock at the door was answered by an unkempt and unshaven young man with a small tumbler in his hand. Bluntly, in a slurred voice, he asked us what we wanted.

'You are Andrew Philips?' asked Holmes.

'What if I am?'

'We wish to discuss your paintings with you.'

'I am not in the discussing vein this morning.'

'It will only take a few moments of your time,' Holmes persisted, 'and you might be able to help us solve a little mystery.'

'Oh, very well,' said the young man in a grudging tone. 'Come in and make yourselves at home.'

We followed him into the cottage and through to a large room at the back, which was clearly his studio. A couple of easels stood in the centre of the room, although there was nothing on them, and paintbrushes, rags and tubes of paint were scattered about everywhere. Along the back wall of the room, a broad row of windows looked out across the common.

'Now,' said Philips, re-filling his glass from a bottle of whisky. 'What do you want? Do you want a tot of this? No? Well, what do you want, then? *The Tomb on the Hill*?' he repeated in a bored tone, as Holmes explained the purpose of our visit. 'I don't remember anything about it – well, perhaps I do: Colonel Sir Spedding Eldersly came home to England about a hundred years ago after a distinguished military career abroad and stipulated that when he died he shouldn't be buried in the church, but at the very edge of the churchyard, overlooking his estates. So he was. Then, a hundred years later, some esteemed descendant of his decided he'd like a painting of the tomb and the view beyond it, and asked me to do it. So I did. It was quite a decent painting, if I say so myself, and it was accepted for the Royal Academy exhibition that year before disappearing off up to Yorkshire, which is where the Eldersly estates are. There. Is that it?'

'Someone saw it at the exhibition and asked if he might have a copy,' Holmes prompted.

'Oh, him! Some solicitor wanted a copy, Eldersly didn't mind and I needed the money, so that was that.'

'But there were two copies made, I believe.'

'So there were. He came to see me when I was halfway through it and said he'd like a second copy. I didn't mind. It was a bit boring for me, but the money was good, so I did it.'

'There were some differences between the two paintings, I think.'

'That's true. All three of them were different, in various little ways. "Can I have more rabbits in this one?" he said, and "Can I have more ducks in that one?" Of course, I didn't care. He could have had six pink elephants in one of them if he'd wanted it. "He who pays the piper calls the tune", as they say.'

'And the inscriptions on the tomb?'

'Yes, he was very particular about those. Load of humbug, really. They didn't make much sense. Think he fancied himself as something of a poet. If he'd asked my opinion, I'd have told him to stick to the law.'

'Have you a record of the inscriptions?'

'I might have,' Philips replied, springing abruptly to his feet. He yanked open a door at the side of the room, revealing a narrow, twisting staircase. Up this his feet clattered, we heard him moving about upstairs for a few moments, then he clattered back down again with a small note-book in his hand. 'I've got the original inscription here somewhere,' he said, turning over the pages. 'Yes, here we are. I copied it off the tomb on the Eldersly estate. I spent a couple of weeks up in Yorkshire and then brought the picture back here to finish it off, which also gave me a better chance of entering it in the Royal Academy exhibition.'

He passed the open book across to us and I read the following:

> *For thirty years I soldiered far*
> *Now here I lie at rest.*
> *Of all the corners of this world*
> *My own land is the best.*

'Do you have a record of the tomb inscriptions for the other two pictures?' asked Holmes.

Philips shook his head. 'The solicitor had written them out for me, along with a lot of other instructions, but he told me to make sure I brought all the papers back with me when I took the finished pictures to his house in Bethnal Green. I don't know why he was so fussy about it. Perhaps he was embarrassed at how miserably poor his attempts at poetry were. I know I would have been!'

We thanked him for the information he had provided and he showed us to the door. 'You're lucky you've found me here,' he said. 'I won't be here much longer. My lease on this old ruin runs out in two weeks and I'm moving somewhere a little more fashionable – Sydney Street in Chelsea, to be precise. I used to think that landscapes were the thing, but they've gone right out of fashion, I'm afraid. Society portraits is the field to be in now, so that's where I'm going – painting flattering pictures of the rich and famous – or those who'd like to be.'

'Best of luck with that, then,' said Holmes with a chuckle.

'We don't yet seem to have discovered anything of significance,' I remarked to my companion as we waited for a train on the platform of Barnes station.

'Perhaps not,' he replied, 'but that in itself is instructive. It suggests that all those little things that we have discovered – that Henry Cosgrove's pictures were not only different from the original painting, but also from each other, and that the backs of both these pictures have been recently removed and replaced – will only reveal their true significance when some fresh fact, as yet unknown, presents itself. These things are like the inner parts of a lock, those pieces of metal of different shapes which are of no significance whatever until one particular key is inserted, when the significance of both their shape and their position at once becomes apparent. I am hopeful that Inspector Lestrade can supply us with that key.'

When we reached Scotland Yard, Lestrade was out, but he was not long in returning and it was with a look of surprise that he showed us into a small cramped office. 'What can I do for you, gentlemen?' he asked as he closed the door.

In a few words, Sherlock Holmes described to him Mr Dryson's odd experience and the trail of enquiry which had taken us from the Marchmont Gallery, *via* Chelsea to Barnes Common. 'And now, Lestrade,' said Holmes, 'you must tell us why you are taking such an interest in the matter.'

'Our interest goes back far beyond the present business, to something else,' the policeman replied after a moment. 'It was somewhat before your time, Mr Holmes, but I know you have studied some of our old records, so I think if I were to say just three words to you, you would understand.'

'And those three words are?' said Holmes, raising his eyebrow as Lestrade paused.

'The Bellecourt diamonds.'

I saw a look of recognition come upon Holmes's features, but Lestrade's words meant nothing to me and I told him so.

'You see, Dr Watson,' said the policeman, who appeared to be enjoying his position of superior knowledge, 'our interest doesn't go back just a few days, or even a few months, but many years. I know that some people enjoy making merry at the police's expense for our not acting quickly enough on occasion, but although we cannot always act as swiftly as a private individual might, our reach, let me tell you, is a very long one. The Metropolitan Police never close a case until it is finally and completely settled. Now, it was, as I say, well before your time, but in the spring of 1871 there was a daring robbery at Bellecourt & Co, the great diamond house in Hatton Garden. The night-watchman was very badly beaten and the thieves got away with a large quantity of stones, valued at the time at nearly twenty thousand pounds. We eventually caught every member of the gang, but we never recovered any of the gems. The ringleader claimed he had passed them to a Dutch confederate, who was supposed to dispose of them in Amsterdam and bring the proceeds back to London, but as the name he gave us was completely unknown to the Dutch police and could not be traced, we concluded that the story was untrue and that the diamonds were still in this country. The newspapers filled their columns with it for some time – "Where are the Bellecourt diamonds?" and so on – and encouraged half the population of London to look for them. But although a large reward was offered for their discovery, the diamonds were never found.

'At their trial, the four members of the gang were sentenced to various prison terms. One died in prison, a second was released four years ago and emigrated to Australia shortly afterwards, a third came out three years ago and seems to be a reformed character. That only leaves the fourth man, the ringleader of the gang and the man we have always suspected had the diamonds. He was released from Dartmoor just two weeks before Christmas.' Lestrade paused and looked at Holmes, a teasing expression on his features. 'No doubt you would like to know the name of this man.'

'It might be helpful, as you seem to think he has some relevance to our case,' returned Holmes placidly.

'His name,' said Lestrade with a chuckle, 'is Albert Cosgrove, brother of the late solicitor whose widow you have met. Something else you won't know, incidentally, as that, too, was before your time, is that Mrs Henry Cosgrove was once better known as Lucy Lambert, the darling of the music halls. I remember going to see her myself – when you two gentlemen were no doubt still schoolboys – and a very fine singer and actress she was, too. But not long after she married Henry Cosgrove she gave up the stage for good, more's the pity.'

'I see,' said Holmes in a thoughtful tone. 'So, to sum up, we have a fortune in diamonds, stolen and never recovered, and the principal villain in the robbery recently released from Dartmoor. What is the official view of the matter?'

'It is believed that Albert Cosgrove gave the diamonds to his brother Henry for safe-keeping shortly before his arrest.'

'This brother was a solicitor, I understand, so he could not have had a criminal record, otherwise he would not have been allowed to practise.'

'That's true. To speak plainly, we were never sure about Henry Cosgrove. He could have been as straight as a die for all we knew, or he could have been crooked. What is certain is that we were never able to pin any wrong-doing upon him, although we often suspected he wasn't quite as upright as he appeared to be. He knew everybody who was anybody in the East End, including some decidedly shady characters for whom he acted as solicitor when they got into difficulties with the law.'

'What makes you think that Cosgrove passed the diamonds to his brother?' I asked. 'Surely there were other ways, safer ways, he could have hidden them?'

Lestrade shook his head. 'We were close on his trail for several days before we caught up with him. He must have known that it was only a matter of time before we got him and that he was likely to get put away for a long time when we did. He couldn't tell what might happen in his absence. If he had hidden them under the floorboards somewhere, the house he hid them in might have been taken over by other people and the diamonds accidentally discovered by some stranger, or, for all he could tell, the house might have been knocked down altogether and something else built in its place. So he had to leave them with someone he could trust and the only person he could really trust was his brother, Henry. Albert Cosgrove knew a lot of people and a lot of people knew him, but he was never very popular. He may have been well connected among his own sort, but the connections were all based on stark fear, rather than any affection, and I don't think he would have trusted anyone with a penny of his money. With his brother, Henry, however, he was on safer ground. It may be, of course, that Henry didn't want anything to do with it, but if Albert had pushed a bag of diamonds into his hand, he may have felt unable to refuse his help. In the first place, blood is thicker than water, as they say, and in the second, Albert Cosgrove is a powerful and violent man, and few have ever dared say "no" to him.'

Sherlock Holmes had listened in silence to Lestrade's account. Now he nodded his head in agreement. 'I imagine you are correct,' said he. 'But now Cosgrove is out of prison only to find that in the meantime his brother has died and his brother's widow has moved house. Where, then, are the Bellecourt diamonds?'

'We have had plain-clothes men watching Cosgrove all the time, to see what he would do,' said Lestrade. 'We have also,' he added in a lower tone, 'got a source of information close to Cosgrove himself. One of his old cronies is keeping us informed as to his movements.'

'With any results?'

'Not so far. Mrs Cosgrove now lives in a new house at Higham's Park, out Chingford way, and Cosgrove went out there to see her soon after his return to London. What passed between them, we don't know, but our information is that he doesn't yet have the diamonds and is talking of going to see her again, so evidently Mrs Cosgrove couldn't – or wouldn't – tell him what he wanted to know.'

'And what is your interest in the painting of the tomb?'

'The day after he visited his sister-in-law, Cosgrove was followed to that picture gallery in Bond Street, where he spent some time. I later questioned the proprietor, a Mr Appleby, who told me that Cosgrove had wanted to know who had bought the two copies of Mrs Cosgrove's painting. He says he didn't tell him, but I don't believe him.'

'Nor me,' interrupted Holmes. 'I can see no other way the thieves could have learnt the addresses of Dryson and Tacolstone. I imagine that Cosgrove offered a bribe which Appleby couldn't resist.'

'Either that or threatened him with violence,' said Lestrade. 'Anyhow, when I heard what Cosgrove had been asking about in the gallery, it rang a bell somewhere in my memory, so I got out all the notes I'd accumulated relating to Cosgrove and the missing diamonds.

I soon found what I was looking for. On one of the last occasions that Henry Cosgrove visited his brother in prison, about a year ago, they had a conversation that was overheard by one of the prison warders. In this, Henry told Albert that he was ill and did not know how long he might live. He then told him he had commissioned two paintings of a scene he thought Albert would like. "One of them is for you," he said. "But if I die before you get out, you might like to have them both, to remember me by. I think you will find them of interest." This conversation must refer to the two copies of *The Tomb on the Hill*, as that would explain Albert Cosgrove's recent interest in them. And yet, when it seems he has finally managed to get his hands on them, he has simply returned them to their owners. It doesn't make sense.'

'I think we may take it,' said Holmes, 'that permanent possession of the paintings is of no interest to Cosgrove. He simply wanted to get hold of the paintings for a short time, in order to examine them. Now, we must assume, he has done so and, having no further use for them, has given them back.'

'Why should he bother?'

'He has probably reasoned that if the paintings are returned, the police will close the matter and he is not likely to be questioned about it. And, in the case of my client's painting, he perhaps hoped that Mr Dryson would not notice the substitution for a while, which would give him the time he needed to examine the painting before the hue and cry went up. Incidentally, if you have men watching Cosgrove, but knew nothing of these thefts until after they had taken place, it must be that Cosgrove took no part in them himself, but got two confederates to do his bidding.'

'That must be so,' Lestrade agreed. 'We must conclude, then, that the diamonds were hidden inside the picture-frames. For the moment at least he has outwitted us.'

'I doubt it is as simple as that,' said Holmes with a shake of the head. 'Cosgrove's brother Henry was a lawyer and no doubt as careful and cautious as such men generally are. He would have realised that hiding the gems inside a painting was scarcely any safer than hiding them under a floorboard. If anyone had chanced to find them there, he could not with any plausibility have pleaded innocence. It would almost certainly have meant a long prison term for him. His life, both private and professional, would have been ruined forever. In addition, he could not be sure what might happen to the paintings after his death. They might, for instance, be sold – as indeed they were. I think, therefore, that the connection between the paintings and the Bellecourt diamonds is an altogether more subtle and less tangible one.'

'What are you suggesting?'

'The tomb inscriptions are different on Cosgrove's two paintings. That is a very curious thing, considering that the two paintings were done at the same time. There must be some good reason for it and it is at least possible that it has something to do with the location of the diamonds.'

'You think the tomb inscriptions could be cryptograms of some sort?' I asked.

'I think it a strong possibility.'

'By George!' cried Lestrade abruptly. 'I think you may well be on to something there, Mr Holmes. During that conversation in prison between the two Cosgrove brothers that I mentioned to you, Henry several times referred to the games they used to play together as boys. "Do you remember how we used to send secret messages to each other in a code that no one else could understand?" he said. Apparently Albert was not very interested in remembering this, but Henry persisted. "We'll have larks again, Albert," he said, "when you get out. Just remember how we worked the secret code, for I might send you such a message again!" I dismissed this conversation as of no importance before, but perhaps I was wrong.'

'It strikes me as highly suggestive,' said Holmes. 'Well done, Lestrade! The thoroughness of your records does you credit. There is some kind of cipher in those pictures – I am sure of it! I have already asked Dryson and Tacolstone to bring their pictures round to Baker

Street this evening, so that I can study them more closely, but now that we have a better idea of what we might be looking for, the results should be all the more interesting! Pray feel free to drop by yourself later in the evening, if it is convenient, and I shall be able to tell you if we have made any progress!'

At six o'clock that evening, there was a ring at our front-door bell, and a moment later Mr Dryson was shown in to our sitting-room with his painting wrapped in a sheet of sacking. Holmes propped it up on a chair and, while he was doing so, the bell sounded again and Mr Tacolstone brought the other painting in, which was promptly propped up on a table at the side of the first one. Holmes poured out four small tots of sherry, and for some time the four of us stood gazing at the pictures and discussing their similarities and differences. Holmes remarked in a gay tone that 221B Baker Street had become quite the bijou art gallery, but I could see that beneath his outward bonhomie he was impatient to be getting on with his examination of the pictures. At length our two visitors departed, Tacolstone having accepted an invitation from Dryson to view his art collection. As soon as they had gone, Holmes brought out an easel and blackboard from his bedroom, set it up in the middle of the room and began to copy on to it the tomb inscriptions of the two paintings.

'I understand your view that the secret is concealed in the inscriptions,' I observed, 'but it is apparent, as you yourself remarked, that the backs of both of these paintings have recently been removed, presumably by Albert Cosgrove.'

'So we must suppose. He was, I take it, unsure at first of the precise meaning of his brother's cryptic reference to these pictures. I very much doubt there was anything concealed there and if there was it won't be there now; but perhaps you had best have a look if you wouldn't mind: there may be something written on the inside of the back-board.'

Carefully, using the blade of a knife, I levered off the backs of the paintings, but there was nothing to be seen there. Meanwhile, my companion was busily copying the inscriptions on to his blackboard.

Then, as I was tapping the tacks back into place, he stood back and surveyed what he had written. From Dryson's painting, the one Tacolstone had brought round, he had copied the following:

> For thirty years my feet marched
> On from east and west
> To each corner of the dew-laden far south.
> Never resting then, now laid down at last.

From the other one, Tacolstone's picture, he had copied the following:

> Death where is thy victory?
> Peace doth fill these parks
> While water from the fountain
> Doth sparkle on the rocks.

'I can make nothing of them,' I remarked after a moment.

'Well, of course, if they are cryptograms of some sort, that is what you would expect,' responded my companion. 'They could hardly be considered very successful as secret messages if their meaning were instantly obvious. There are, however, some observations we can make before we begin. First, to judge from Henry Cosgrove's remarks to his brother, this is a form of cipher the two of them had used as boys, so it should not be too difficult for two grown men to solve. Second, although it must, as I say, appear opaque to a casual observer, otherwise it fails as a cryptogram, it must also be perfectly clear to one who knows the secret, otherwise it would fail on that account. I am therefore confident of getting to the bottom of the matter before I leave this room tonight.'

Holmes fell silent then, and remained staring at his blackboard in perfect immobility for some time, save only when he transferred his gaze for a moment to the paintings. Confident of solving the puzzle he may have been, but when our supper was brought up shortly afterwards, he was still sitting in silence, with no indication that he was making any progress. For myself, I had given up on the inscriptions and was examining all the other differences between the two paintings. In fact, there were not many. The depiction of the tomb, the trees about it and the landscape beyond was identical in both pictures, save only that in the picture which mentioned a fountain in the inscription, a small fountain could be seen far in the distance. In the foreground, however, there were a few more obvious differences between the pictures. The rustic character was the same in both, but the little rabbits about his feet were quite different. In Dryson's picture there were three rabbits, but in Tacolstone's – the one with the fountain – there were five. The ducks, too, were different. In the first picture there were just two of them, but in the second, five. Whether these differences were of any significance, or merely represented a whim on the part of the artist or his patron, I could not imagine, but I was sure that if anyone could work out the meaning of these differences and solve the puzzle, my friend Sherlock Holmes could.

We had been eating our meal in complete silence for some time, my companion's gaze alternating rapidly between the blackboard and the paintings, and hardly ever resting on the plate before him, when he abruptly put down his knife and fork with a clatter.

'I have it!' cried he. 'It was the meaning of the ducks I could not see, Watson, but now I understand it all! Now I know where Henry Cosgrove hid the Bellecourt diamonds!' Then he fell to laughing, as he picked up his cutlery once more and finished off his meal, almost choking as he did so. 'It is often the case with such things,' said my friend in a tone of satisfaction, as he stood up and took his pipe from the mantelpiece. 'You struggle for a while with individual parts of the puzzle, and feel you are making no progress at all, and then, in a moment, like the break of dawn upon the dark sea, light falls upon the whole at once and all is illuminated.'

'I am eager to hear your solution,' I said, joining him beside the fire, as he threw on a few more coals and poked it into a blaze.

'It is soon explained,' he began. 'It is essentially a very simple little cipher, as I was sure it must be. Some of the words in the tomb inscriptions are important, and some are completely unimportant and are present only to disguise the true message. The trick, of course, is to identify those words which are significant. This is where the animals come into the matter. In the picture with three rabbits, every third word in the inscription forms part of the secret message; and in the picture with five rabbits, every fifth word. The function of the ducks – which I confess I could not see at first – is to indicate the word in the inscription at which the secret message begins. Thus, in the one with two ducks, the true message begins at the second word; and in the one with five ducks, it is at the fifth word.

'If we look at the inscription on Mr Dryson's picture first,' he continued, taking a stick of chalk and stepping to the blackboard. 'This, as you see, is "For thirty years my feet marched, On from east and west, To each corner of the dew-laden far south, Never resting then, now laid down at last", and the picture contains three rabbits and two ducks. Therefore we begin at the second word – "thirty" – then pass over the next two words and find the fifth is "feet". The next significant word is the eighth word, "from",' he continued, underlining each of these words in turn, 'and the next "west", then "corner", then "dew", then "south" and, finally, from the last line, "then" and "down". The whole hidden message is thus revealed as "thirty feet from west corner, dew south, then down", in which the word "dew" is obviously meant to stand for its homonym, "due" – a little touch of ingenuity and imagination which I find admirable, I must say. The diamonds are therefore hidden – probably buried – thirty feet due south from the west corner of some building or other structure.'

'Yes, but where?'

'To learn that, we must consult the inscription on the other picture. This, as you see, is "Death where is thy victory? Peace doth fill these parks While water from the fountain Doth sparkle on the rocks", and the picture depicts five rabbits and five ducks. We therefore underline every fifth word, beginning with the fifth word itself,' he continued, suiting the action to the word, 'which gives us "victory, parks, fountain, rocks".'

'What on earth is that supposed to mean?' I asked. 'Does it refer to the Eldersly estates in Yorkshire?'

Holmes shook his head. 'The original painting may have been done upon the Eldersly estate, but I shouldn't imagine that Henry Cosgrove had the slightest interest in that. All he wanted was some way of conveying information to his brother as to where the diamonds were hidden and he hit on the idea of using these pictures to do it. The diamonds themselves will almost certainly be somewhere in London.'

'Where? And what is the point of the word "victory"?'

'Cosgrove would not have wanted to make the location too obvious, and I think he has taken the opportunity to make his cryptic message read a little like a genuine epitaph by adapting those well-known lines from Saint Paul's epistle, "O Death, where is thy sting? O Grave, where is thy victory?". But I strongly suspect that the word "victory" is really standing in for Victoria and that the reference is in fact to Victoria Park in Hackney. He could be confident that his brother would recognise the allusion. The two of them grew up in the East End and probably paid many visits to the park – which, in my experience, incidentally, is often referred to locally as "Vicky Park". Have you ever been there, Watson?'

'Once, at least, when a rather entertaining brass-band competition was taking place there. It's a pleasant spot. But the inscription refers to "parks", in the plural. What does that mean?'

'It certainly appears to be a plural, but that would really make no sense in any context and I suspect, therefore, that although the apostrophe is absent, it is in fact intended to be a possessive. The whole phrase therefore should be read as "Victoria Park's fountain".'

'I don't want to spoil your theory,' I said, 'but I am fairly certain that there is no fountain in Victoria Park.'

'You are quite right, Watson. There is no fountain there, at least, not in the obvious meaning of the word. What there is, though, I seem to recall, is an unusually large and highly ornate drinking fountain, donated by some philanthropist several years ago. That, I think, is what is being referred to. I suspect that Henry Cosgrove instructed the artist to add a distant fountain to that version of the picture with the deliberate intention of obfuscating the issue.'

'What about the word "rocks"? There aren't any rocks in Victoria Park.'

'That, I believe, is mainly there simply to finish the inscription off and make it seem more like a piece of verse, although it is also, of course, common criminal slang for diamonds and other precious stones.'

'You may be right about all this, Holmes,' I remarked after a moment, 'but it seems to me to lead to an absurd conclusion. That Cosgrove's brother would choose to hide an enormously valuable cache of diamonds in a public park seems to me perfectly incredible! Surely that is the very worst place he could choose!'

'Not at all. On the contrary, his choice of hiding-place demonstrates a rare imagination and intelligence. Consider this, Watson: if he buries the diamonds in a private garden, whether his own or someone else's, he runs the same danger as if he had secreted them under a floorboard, which possibility we discussed earlier with Lestrade, if you recall, in that he cannot possibly know what might happen to it after his death, or who might become the owner of the property. In addition there is the possibility that at any time someone might decide to dig over the spot he has chosen, in order to make a new flower-bed. If, on the other hand, he manages to bury the diamonds beneath the turf of one of London's great public parks without being observed, he will know for certain that however many times the grass may be mown and however many thousands of feet may pass over that spot, his diamonds will never be disturbed. But here, I take it, is Lestrade,' he added as there came a sharp ring at the door-bell, 'so we will see what he has to say about it.'

Inspector Lestrade listened with interest to Holmes's analysis of the cryptic inscriptions and the conclusions he had drawn from them. He raised some of the same objections as I had done, but at length was convinced that Holmes was right.

'It does seem very strange, I must say,' he remarked with a shake of the head, 'to try to hide such valuable goods in the middle of a public park, but I have come across stranger things in the course of my work, so I'm not saying it's impossible.'

'Thank you for that ringing endorsement,' said Holmes in a dry tone. 'Now, what I propose is this: it will be getting light shortly before seven o'clock tomorrow morning, so if we meet up at Broad Street station at half past six and take the first train which offers, we shall be able to put our theory to the test at the earliest opportunity. You still have Cosgrove under observation?'

Lestrade nodded. 'He can't do anything without our knowing about it and, although he evidently got some cronies of his to steal those paintings for him, I don't think he would trust anyone but himself to get hold of the diamonds.'

'I agree,' said Holmes. 'We shall turn in early this evening then, so we are fresh for our morning's research. I have a long surveyor's tape-measure and a pocket compass, so if you could provide a sharp-edged spade and a trowel we shall be fully equipped!'

We met in the morning at Broad Street as arranged and Lestrade informed us that he had asked for a couple of men from Hackney Police Station to meet us by the park gates with a van and the necessary equipment, but he also brought some bad news.

'We have lost Cosgrove,' he said, his face grave. 'One of my plain-clothes men followed him to the Bull in Whitechapel last night, but he never came out again, and when my man went in to look for him, he'd vanished. He must have realised he was being followed and climbed out of a back window.'

'Let us hope he has not beaten us to the diamonds,' said Holmes.

'The park would have been locked up at night,' I remarked.

'No doubt, but to a determined man with a ladder, park railings do not present an insuperable obstacle.'

'There is more bad news,' said Lestrade. 'I mentioned to you that we had an informant among Cosgrove's cronies. That was Billy Padgett, but his body was found last night in an alley off Whitechapel High Street. He had been strangled.'

'This is looking bad,' said Holmes in a grave tone. 'Let us be off at once!'

In half an hour we were at Victoria Park. It was a raw, cold morning, with a thick fog in the streets and all across the broad expanse of the park. The park gates were still closed and we waited, shivering at the cold, as the park-keeper emerged from his lodge and unlocked them for us. Then, as a weak grey daylight struggled against the fog, we made our way across the park to the drinking fountain.

'This must be the westernmost corner,' said Holmes, consulting his compass and indicating the edge of a raised slab of stone that surrounded the structure. 'I'll hold one end of the tape-measure, Watson, if you will draw it out that way. We must be as precise as possible. One degree out of true at this end and we will miss the mark by several feet at the other.'

I did as my friend instructed, adjusting my position to right or left as he directed me according to his compass. At length he was satisfied and I stood thirty feet exactly due south of his own position. In a moment he and Lestrade had joined me.

'Now let us see what we can find here,' cried Holmes in a tone of excitement. 'But, wait,' he said abruptly, with a groan of dismay. 'Someone has been here before us!' He bent down and grasped a clump of grass and a six-inch square piece of turf came away in his hand. 'This turf has been carefully cut away and then replaced,' he continued, as piece after piece came away with no resistance and he tossed them to one side. 'I fear we are too late, but push your spade in there, Lestrade, and let us see if there is anything to be found.'

The policeman pressed his spade into the bare earth and levered up a heavy clod. 'You are right,' said he. 'This ground is soft. It has been turned over very recently.' He cast aside the clod and three or four more, then, as he pushed his spade in again, he paused. 'There is something here!' he cried, and leaning back on his spade he levered up a loose clod, which crumbled away to disclose a small tin box with a hinged lid. 'Perhaps we are not too late, after all,' said he, as Holmes took the box from the spade. A moment later, however, our hopes were dashed, as Holmes opened the lid of the box and we could see it was perfectly empty. 'What now?' asked Lestrade, leaning on his spade. 'You were right, Mr Holmes, but too late; and to be right but too late is no better, I'm afraid, than being wrong.'

'Not necessarily,' said Holmes, his brows drawn down in thought. 'We know at least what has happened, even if we were too late to prevent it. At the moment we trail behind the leader in this race, but the game is not yet over.'

'What do you suggest?'

'That we fill in this hole and pay a visit to Mrs Cosgrove at once. You have her address at Higham's Park, I take it? We know that Cosgrove has already been to see her at least once and your information suggests he intends to see her again. I had the impression when we spoke to her at the Marchmont Gallery that she perhaps knows more than she cares to admit.'

Lestrade agreed, and we set off in the police van at a great rate. Through the busy streets of Hackney and Clapton we rattled, along the open, windswept road across the marshes of the Lea valley and into the distant suburbs beyond. Eventually, perhaps forty minutes later, our driver reined in his horses by Higham's Park station. 'This will do,' called Lestrade, springing down. 'It is only a short walk from here.'

He led the way along a side-road and round a corner to where a terrace of substantial houses stood back a little from the road. 'This is the one,' he began as we approached a wooden gate, but even as he spoke, the front door of the house was opened and a tall, thin man in a black frock-coat and top hat emerged, carrying a leather case. He came down the steps from the front door and stood in the gateway, deliberately blocking our way.

'Who might you be?' he asked, making no attempt to get out of our way.

'We are the Metropolitan Police,' answered Lestrade in his best official manner, showing his card to the other man, who took it and examined it closely for a moment. 'And who are you, if I might ask?'

'My name is Sherwood. I'm a doctor. There's a woman in there in a pretty poor state, Inspector. Apparently some roughs broke in during the night or early this morning and beat her very badly. They'd tied her maid up, but she eventually managed to free herself and come for me. I was going to report the matter at the local police station, but seeing as you're here, I'd be obliged if you'd deal with that side of it for me.'

'I certainly will,' said Lestrade. 'Are any bones broken?'

'No, luckily for her; but she's badly bruised. I've done what I can for her and I'll call back later.'

Dr Sherwood went on his way and a few moments later we were admitted to the house and conducted up to Mrs Cosgrove's bed-chamber. She was sitting up in bed, reclining on a mound of cushions. Her face was a mass of bruises, one eye being almost completely closed by the swelling about it, there was a dressing on her neck and one of her arms was heavily bandaged up. Lestrade introduced himself, but her eyes wandered past him to Sherlock Holmes, whom she evidently recognised.

'You were at the Marchmont Gallery yesterday,' she said to him in a weak voice.

'Indeed,' returned Holmes. 'We were endeavouring to solve a little mystery involving two paintings formerly in the possession of your late husband. It is his brother, Albert Cosgrove who has done this to you, I take it.'

Mrs Cosgrove hesitated a moment, then nodded her head in silence.

'I had the impression when we spoke yesterday,' continued Holmes in a soft tone, 'that you were holding something back, something you did not wish us to know.'

'You are correct,' said she. 'But the chief thing I did not wish you to know is what I never wish anyone to know, that my husband's brother is a vicious criminal who has spent some years in Dartmoor Prison. Such information would scarcely be a welcome addition to the genteel conversation of a Bond Street picture gallery.'

'I think there was also something else, more particular to our enquiry.'

'Yes. I was about to tell you. Albert Cosgrove came to see me shortly after his release from prison and asked me specifically about those paintings you were interested in, *The Tomb on the Hill*. I told him I had sold them, at which he cried out angrily.

'"You had no right to sell them," he shouted in a violent rage. "Henry said that they were for me."

'"I did not know that," I said. "Henry never told me."

'Eventually I managed to convince him that I was speaking the truth, but he forced me to tell him where I had sold them and to whom. I told him I did not know the purchasers, that he would have to enquire at the Marchmont Gallery. I assume he did so, but I know no more about that than you.'

'Now,' said Holmes, 'if you would cast your mind back a dozen years: did your brother-in-law call at your house shortly before he was arrested?'

Mrs Cosgrove nodded. 'He came late one night. Henry hadn't seen anything of him for several months. They sat talking for a long time in the study. What passed between them, I don't know. Eventually Albert left by the back way, about midnight. I said to my husband "Whatever you and Albert were talking about, I don't want to know."

'"Good," said he, "because I wasn't going to tell you."

'"Why do you have anything to do with him?" I asked.

'"I don't want to," said Henry, who, I could see, was very agitated about something, "but he's my own flesh and blood and I can't turn him away."

'The very next day, I believe, Albert was arrested, down Limehouse way. Henry never mentioned him again and nor did I. Of course, I read the newspapers, like everyone else, and I heard that the Bellecourt diamonds had never been found and wondered once or twice if my husband knew anything about them. But he never mentioned the matter and I never asked him about it.'

'And the events of this morning?' asked Holmes.

'I was awakened suddenly some time before five, to find a candle lit in my bedroom and a man standing there with a knife in his hand. I opened my mouth to scream, but he clamped his free hand over my mouth and pushed the knife into my neck, and I saw then it was Albert Cosgrove. He said if I let out a sound he would slit my throat. He said he had followed Henry's instructions, to find something that belonged to him, but had found nothing there. I told him if he meant the diamonds, I didn't know anything about them, but he wouldn't believe me and I got a blow for my troubles.

'He asked me if I knew Billy Padgett and I said I didn't. "He's a police spy," he said, "but he won't spy no more. I dealt with him last night good and proper. Now, if you don't tell me where you've hidden the diamonds, I'm going to throttle you like I throttled Billy Padgett and then I'll find them anyway, so you may as well tell me now." His tone was one of evil menace and I knew he meant what he said, but, of course, I couldn't tell him because I simply didn't know.

'I pleaded with him, begged him to spare me, and told him over and over again that I knew nothing about the diamonds, but every response I made to his questions brought only more blows, as he hit me, again and again, more viciously each time. At length he paused and I could see that he was thinking about something. I had the impression that he had had a fresh idea, but he didn't say anything about it to me. He gave me one last blow which knocked me down and I knew no more. When I came to my senses, I was lying on the floor, the room was empty and the house was in complete silence. He had gone.'

'The unspeakable brute,' I said, as we were leaving the house.

'Don't you worry, Dr Watson,' said Lestrade. 'We'll get him and he'll pay for what he's done to that poor woman. But where he might be right now is anyone's guess.'

'I think I know where he might be,' said Holmes, 'and where the diamonds are, too.'

'Where?' cried Lestrade in surprise.

'In Philips's cottage on Barnes Common. We must make all haste to get down there.'

'What makes you think that Philips knows anything about the diamonds?' I asked.

'It's partly a matter of elimination, Watson: Albert Cosgrove clearly hasn't got them, his sister-in-law hasn't got them, the proprietor of the Marchmont Gallery would have had no reason to suspect that there was anything special about the paintings until Albert Cosgrove came enquiring after them, by which time they'd already been sold. That only leaves Philips. He's not stupid and probably realised there was something odd afoot when Henry Cosgrove supplied him with those eccentric tomb inscriptions in place of the original conventional epitaph, and with the specific instructions about the number of animals to be included. And if his suspicions weren't already aroused, they surely would have been when Cosgrove later insisted that all these instructions be returned to him.

'When we spoke to him, Philips claimed that he couldn't remember any details of Cosgrove's instructions, but that doesn't really ring true. Cosgrove would not have simply requested "more rabbits" or "more ducks", but must have specified a precise number, in order for the cipher to work properly, and Philips would surely have remembered Cosgrove's precision on the point, even if he couldn't remember the exact number requested. I was also struck by the way Philips avoided mentioning Henry Cosgrove's name, as if to ensure we made no connection between "the solicitor", as he referred to him, and the notorious jewel thief – which of course suggests that Philips himself was aware of the connection. Then there is the notable fact that Philips appears to be living comfortably enough and is, indeed, about to move from what are probably relatively cheap premises to a much more fashionable and therefore more expensive address in Chelsea, despite appearing to have no work.'

'I noticed there didn't seem to be much going on in his studio at the moment.'

'Not only at the moment, Watson. From the state of his brushes and other equipment, it is clear that no work has been done there for some considerable time, possibly several months. All these things I observed yesterday, but I did not act on my observations for one simple reason.'

'What reason is that?'

'That I am an idiot.'

'But at the time you saw Philips, you knew nothing of the diamonds,'

'That is true. But once we had learnt from Inspector Lestrade of Cosgrove's brother and the Bellecourt robbery, I had ample time to review all I had learnt during the day in the light of that new information. This I did not do. I was so pleased with myself for solving the cryptogram and working out the location of the diamonds that I gave no thought to anything else. That is what makes me an idiot – almost as big an idiot as Philips himself. It is clear to me now that once his suspicions had been aroused, he must have made it his business to find out what lay behind those eccentric tomb-inscriptions. He would soon have discovered the connection between Henry Cosgrove and the Bellecourt diamonds, and then no doubt solved the cryptogram and worked out where the diamonds were hidden. At which point the fool clearly yielded to the temptation of wealth that the diamonds represent. There is nothing that corrupts and destroys a man's life so certainly as sudden wealth, especially if that wealth is unearned. But in this case the danger is yet more serious than usual, for I rather fear that Albert Cosgrove has reached the same conclusion as I have and I doubt that Philips has any conception of the kind of man he is up against. Let us hope we are not too late!'

We had reached Higham's Park station as Holmes had been speaking, where the police van stood waiting for us. 'It will be quicker if we take the train,' said Holmes. He hurried into the station to consult the timetable, but was back again in a moment. 'There is a train to Liverpool Street in five minutes,' said he. Lestrade quickly explained matters to the other policemen, instructing them to notify Scotland Yard at once as to what had happened and where we were going, to arrange for men from the nearest police station to meet us at Philips's cottage and to post a constable in front of Mrs Cosgrove's house in case her brother-in-law returned. A minute later we were in the train.

The traffic in central London was dense and slow-moving, and it took us some time to get across to Waterloo station, Holmes fretting and shaking his head in frustration all the while, but once there we were fortunate enough to find that a suitable train was just about to leave, and soon we were rattling along the viaduct through Lambeth and out to the south-western suburbs. As we alighted at Barnes, the only passengers to do so, the common seemed even colder, foggier and more desolate than on our previous visit. At least on this occasion, as Holmes remarked, we knew how to find Philips's cottage, so could avoid wasting our time tramping hither and thither across the heath, as we had done the previous day.

'I doubt if Cosgrove has been down here before,' remarked Holmes, as he led the way along a rutted track, 'so if he is here it will have taken him some time to find the cottage, and although he still leads and we still follow, we are therefore closer behind him now than we were at Higham's Park. As I told you then, Lestrade, we may still trail behind him, but the game is not yet over!'

We turned from the track into a narrow road, where there was not a soul about. It took us little time to reach the old cottage, where icicles hung from the gutters, and the side wall and the bushes growing by it were covered with frost-whitened cobwebs. We approached cautiously, but saw no movement at any of the windows. At the front door, Lestrade was about to knock, but Holmes put his hand on his arm and indicated the step, where the muddy imprint of a large boot was clearly visible. Without speaking, Holmes then pointed to his own shoe and I at once saw his meaning: our shoes were not muddy; whoever had made the footprint on the step had clearly spent some time tramping about the heath, looking for the cottage. As he put his hand on the door, I saw there was a narrow gap at the edge of it and it was apparent that the door was not closed properly. He pushed gently and the door swung silently inwards. Putting his finger to his lips, he led the way into the house. As we made our way carefully through to the studio at the back, some slight sound from upstairs came to my ears. Then, as we passed through the open doorway of the studio, I stopped in astonishment. If the studio had seemed untidy and disordered upon our previous visit, that was as nothing compared to its appearance now. Every item of furniture that could possibly be upended was lying on the floor, everything that could possibly have been knocked off the shelves and other surfaces was strewn about, smashed and broken, and there on the floor, in the midst of this scene of chaos and destruction, lay Andrew Philips.

I quickly bent down to him, but it took me only a moment to establish that the body was lifeless. Philips was dead. I indicated some severe bruising on the neck which suggested he had been strangled, and as I did so there came a louder crash and clatter from upstairs, as if someone were pulling the drawers out of a tallboy and throwing them on to the floor. The door to the staircase stood open and Lestrade pointed at the stair, but Holmes shook his head and intimated we should wait where we were.

Abruptly, the racket ceased and there came the softer sound of footsteps moving about in the room above us. For a moment, that, too, ceased and all was silence, then there came heavy footsteps on the wooden stair. Holmes stepped back slightly, behind the door to the staircase, and drew his revolver from his pocket, as Lestrade quietly drew out a truncheon from an inside pocket of his coat.

With a heavy, rapid tread, the footsteps clattered down the steep, narrow staircase and in an instant a large, heavily built man appeared before us. He stopped abruptly when he saw us, a look of surprise on his large, coarse face. Then his features twisted into an expression of contempt, vicious and brutal.

'Albert Cosgrove, I am arresting you—' Lestrade began, but he got no further. Cosgrove let out a fearsome roar and started forward. But even as he made to launch his violent attack upon us, Holmes stepped out from behind the door and clapped his pistol to the side of his head.

For a split second Cosgrove stopped, then in a flash he had brought his arm up and knocked Holmes's revolver out of the way, at the same instant drawing a pistol of his own from his pocket and firing it wildly in our direction. There came a sharp cry of pain from Lestrade, but he launched himself forward, striking out with his truncheon and knocking the pistol from Cosgrove's grasp. I flung myself forward and the three of us crashed to the ground in a heap. For a few moments we struggled wildly, then Holmes brought the butt of his revolver down sharply on Cosgrove's head, his whole body went limp and he lay still.

Lestrade quickly snapped a pair of handcuffs on Cosgrove's wrists, then he rose to his feet, grimacing with pain. 'That shot he fired caught me on the left shoulder,' he said. I helped him slip off his coat and jacket, picked up a chair for him to sit on, and examined the wound, which was bleeding profusely.

'You were very lucky,' I said after a moment. 'The bullet has passed clean through your upper arm. It will certainly be painful for a time, but I don't think it has done any lasting damage.' I picked up the cleanest piece of rag I could see on the floor and tied it tightly round his arm. 'You've lost a fair amount of blood,' I added. 'We'll have to get this dressed properly as soon as possible.'

Holmes had been feeling in Cosgrove's pockets while I was examining the policeman and now he held up a small leather pouch, an expression of triumph on his face. 'Here, I think, are your diamonds, Lestrade!' He loosened the top of the pouch and carefully tipped it up, and out on to the palm of his hand tumbled a mass of sparkling gems.

At that moment there came the sound of horses' hooves and a vehicle drawing to a halt outside the front of the house. A moment later a police sergeant entered, followed closely by three constables.

'You're a bit late, Sergeant,' said Lestrade in a tone of bitter humour. 'You've missed all the action. Here's your man, anyhow,' he continued, wincing with pain as he indicated Cosgrove's motionless body on the floor. 'It's Albert Cosgrove. He may look peaceful now, chiefly because he's unconscious, but I'm warning you, when he wakes up, he'll be like a madman in the body of a bull.'

'Inspector Lestrade needs immediate medical attention,' I interrupted, as he rose unsteadily to his feet. 'Is there a doctor's surgery anywhere near here?'

The sergeant informed me that there was one very close, at the west end of Putney, and instructed one of his men to help me get Lestrade there.

'What are we charging Cosgrove with, sir?' asked the sergeant as we made our way out of the house.

'You tell them, Mr Holmes,' said Lestrade in a weary voice. He was now leaning heavily on my arm, and his face had turned an ashen grey.

'You may take your pick,' said Holmes. 'Cosgrove has murdered that man on the floor over there, whose name is Andrew Philips, he almost certainly murdered Billy Padgett in Whitechapel last night, he committed a very serious assault on a woman earlier this morning after breaking into her house, and he has just made a murderous attack on Inspector Lestrade and shot him through the arm. Oh, and while you're reporting all this, you might also mention to your superiors, to lighten the tone a little, that the Bellecourt diamonds, for which half of London has been searching for the last dozen years, are now safely in our hands!'

The Adventure of the Purple Hand

In the year 1890 I saw little of my friend, Sherlock Holmes. From time to time I was able to follow his progress in the columns of the daily press and he appeared from all accounts to be as busy as a man could wish to be, but I missed the close involvement with his cases that I had enjoyed before my marriage, and which a variety of circumstances, both on his side and on mine, now prevented. In one respect at least, however, I was fortunate: that on each of the few occasions I was able to renew our acquaintance, I gained a new story for my records which was the equal in interest of any which I had entered in my note-book in the days when we shared bachelor chambers in Baker Street. Holmes himself observed with amusement on more than one occasion that I was for him the stormy petrel of adventure, and if fate had indeed cast me in that role, I was not one to complain of the fact.

It was a gloriously sunny afternoon towards the end of June. I had had a busy day, but having no further calls upon my time I dismissed my cab in Portman Square and walked the short distance to my friend's lodgings. He was not at home, but the landlady expected him back for tea, so I sat down to wait. I was not the only caller he had had that afternoon, I observed, for a card had been left upon the table, bearing the gilt inscription, 'Star of Kandy Tea Company, 37A Crutched Friars; Mark Pringle, Proprietor.' Across the reverse of the card was printed 'The Company employs only one salesman: His name is Quality' and beneath that, in pencil, 'Vital to consult you. Will call back later', to which the initials 'M.P.' were appended.

Holmes was not long in arriving and it was with evident pleasure that he greeted me. He seemed in high spirits and tossed across to me an old leather-bound volume he had just purchased at a shop in the

Strand. It was a German book, a black-letter edition of Dante's *Divine Comedy*, its binding cracked and faded with age.

'Printed at Mainz, some time in the sixteenth century,' remarked my friend. 'According to the bookseller, there is a curious error on page 348, where "honey" is for some unfathomable reason rendered as "rags"; but I know the man of old and there is no more barefaced rogue in the whole of London. He invents these freaks of printing himself, you see, to excuse his exorbitant prices, and in the hope of attracting the custom of those whose only interest is in such oddities and who are unlikely ever to actually read the books they buy from him. Unfortunately, he himself neither speaks nor reads any language but English and, like the crow in the fable, is evidently incapable of conceiving that anyone else can do what he cannot, so he was somewhat discomfited when I was able to point out to him that neither word occurs on the page in question. But it really is very good to see you, my dear fellow! Indeed, the arrival of a doctor in my consulting-rooms rather completes my cosmopolitan day, for my morning's visitors, if you would believe it, were a Member of Parliament, a lighterman, a coal-heaver and a theologian!'

'There is yet another,' I remarked, indicating the card upon the table by the window.

'Hum! Tea-merchant! Smoked a cigar while he was here. Has helped himself to a drink, too, I see! Why soda water, I wonder? Hum!'

'No doubt a wealthy, comfortable, City type,' I suggested with a chuckle, 'who sells tea from the Orient, but has never been farther east than Ramsgate in his life and would not recognise a tea plant if one were growing in his own garden. It is not difficult to picture him sitting at that table an hour ago, a stout, florid-faced man, with a glass in one hand and a cigar in the other, the very picture of a well-fed, easy life. An impatient and possibly self-important fellow, too,' I added, 'if he could not wait for your return.'

'There *is* such a type,' replied Holmes, smiling, 'but I very much fancy that Mr Pringle is not of it. If you were to dip your finger into this glass of soda water, Watson, you would taste upon your finger-end the unmistakable bitterness of quinine. What would that suggest to you, as a physician, bearing in mind that the man who has been dosing himself with it includes upon his visiting-card the name of Kandy, in Ceylon?'

'Malaria!'

'Precisely. Now, malaria is not contracted west of Ramsgate with any great frequency, as I'm sure you would agree, and nor are its unfortunate victims generally marked for their stoutness or their florid faces. Mr Pringle has evidently spent some time in Ceylon, where he has picked up this most tenacious of diseases, but whether it be his illness or some less tangible worry which disturbs him so today, we cannot tell.'

'What do you mean?'

'You observed the used matches that he left us?'

'I believe I saw one in the dish, with the remains of his cigar.'

'Not one, Watson, but five; five matches for one cigar, mark you. Now, while there is some truth in the popular notion that the pleasure of a good cigar helps one to forget one's troubles, it is also true that one must already be untroubled to some extent, in order to derive any pleasure from the cigar in the first place. Anyone who can let a cigar go out, not once, but four times, is very evidently not in the appropriate state of mind. He has also been pacing the floor and has dropped cigar-ash in several places, as you no doubt observed, which also indicates a mood of distraction.'

'Perhaps he is simply careless,' I suggested.

'I think not, for you can see that where he noticed that he had dropped the ash – just by the corner of the hearth-rug – he has made some attempt to pick it up with his fingers. As to the impatience you ascribed to him, we cannot say; but it seems at least possible that he went out chiefly to get a little fresh air into his lungs, one of the unavoidable effects of quinine being, as you are aware, an unpleasant sensation of nausea.

'You must admit, Watson,' continued my friend, seating himself by the window and gazing down into the street below, as he proceeded to fill his pipe, 'that the balance of probability has swung against your snug, rosy-cheeked City man, and in favour of my perturbed and ague-cheeked tea-planter.'

'No doubt you are correct,' I conceded. 'You almost make me regret that ever I opened my mouth! But, come,' I continued, laughing, 'you have constructed so much of the unknown Mr Pringle; surely you can round out the picture a little now. What age, for instance, would you put upon the fellow and how would you say he is dressed today?'

'He is, I should say, about forty years of age and wearing a tweed suit.'

'Well I never!' I cried in astonishment. 'How in the name of Heaven can you tell that?'

'Quite simply because I see the fellow standing on the front doorstep at this moment,' replied Holmes drily.

The man who was shown in a few moments later accorded in every respect with the inferences my friend had drawn. A tall, handsome, well-built man, he had, nevertheless, an air of weakness and debility about him, as one worn down by a chronic disease. His face was unnaturally lined and leathery for one his age, his cheeks were sunken and of a sickly, yellowish hue and his hair was quite grey. But his grip as he shook my hand was firm and strong, and there was a spark in his blue eyes which showed that the disease had not broken his spirit, at any rate.

'Are you quite recovered?' asked Holmes in a kindly voice; 'or is there perhaps something we can offer you? I observed that you had been dosing yourself with quinine and I know how horribly that can affect the stomach.'

Pringle shook his head. 'It is not the nausea so much with me,' he replied, 'as the infernal ringing in the ears that the stuff gives me. But I've walked about a bit, and looked in a few shop-windows to take my mind from it, and I'll be all right now. Don't ever consider yourselves unlucky,' he added with a flash of his eyes, 'until you've had what I've got. No man ever had a more implacable enemy than malaria, I can tell you: no matter how many battles it may lose against you, it will never give up the war. But I did not come here to discuss pathology with you, gentlemen, and in any case I have learnt recently that there are things which can strike you harder than any disease. I wish your advice, Mr Holmes.'

'I shall be only too pleased to give it, if you will acquaint me with the facts.'

'Well, we'll call them facts for the moment, but what you will make of them, I don't know. A few snatches of conversation here, a trivial incident there – even as I think of these things now, they strike me as amounting to nothing.'

'You had best let me be the judge of that,' said Holmes. 'Pray proceed with your account.'

'I have lived most of my life in Ceylon,' began our visitor after a moment. 'My father had been a successful coffee-planter there, but he lost everything when the crash came – when, in a single season, those infernal spots of mould destroyed both the island's plantations and its prosperity – and, sadly, neither he nor my mother lived to see the success which was later achieved so rapidly with tea. I was fortunate, for I managed to get in on the new business early on and after a couple of successful seasons, with a planter by the name of Widdowson, I decided to strike out on my own. I went in with two other fellows of like mind, Bob Jarvis and Donald Hudson, and by working all the hours in the day, and sometimes, it seemed, more than that, we soon made our plantation one of the finest on the island.

'It was just then, when I was successful – and proud of that success, I don't mind admitting – and more wealthy than I could ever have imagined, that this cursed swamp-fever struck me down. It took poor Jarvis clean away in under a week, so, in a way, I suppose I must count myself fortunate; but I cannot pretend to feel it. For weeks my life was despaired of, until eventually the doctor gave it as his opinion that my only hope lay in quitting the island altogether until the fever was beaten. With great reluctance, then, I returned to England, leaving Hudson in charge of the plantation.

'That was three years ago and things have since gone very well for me in most ways. The attacks of malaria had become so infrequent, until a couple of months ago, that I fondly believed myself fully cured and I have managed to set up a company to sell our own tea – a long-standing ambition of ours – which has been at least moderately successful. I have also during my stay here met and married Laetitia Wadham, the most delightful woman in all the world. We met at Willoughby Hall, near Gloucester, where she was acting as companion to Lady Craxton, and soon discovered that we had much in common. Her father had been for a time a district magistrate in Ceylon and she had thus spent some years there as a child. It was at Gloucester that we were married, a small, quiet affair, for she was almost as without kin as I was myself. She had no brothers or sisters, and her mother and father were both dead. After a brief holiday at Lyme Regis, we took a fine modern villa, known as Low Meadow, which lies beside the Thames between Staines and Laleham. It has splendid gardens, about sixty yards in length, which sweep down from the house almost to the river itself, from which they are separated by a narrow belt of trees. It is a place where flowers bloom and birds sing, and there is all a man could wish for to complete his domestic bliss. Once more my life seemed upon an even keel; once more it seemed that nothing could come to blight my happiness.'

Our visitor paused and, taking a handkerchief from his pocket, mopped his brow, which glistened with beads of perspiration.

'Once more,' he continued after a moment, his voice lower and softer than before, 'once more I have been struck low. And if I had thought malaria to be unseen, insidious, intangible, how much more so is the present evil! Thank you, Dr Watson, a glass of water would be most welcome.

'About seven weeks ago I was, quite suddenly and without warning, laid low with the fever. It came quite out of the blue, for I had not had an attack for nearly a year; but it was as if the disease had been storing its energies for one almighty battle, for I had never been so knocked up by it since I left Colombo and I felt quite at death's door. There I lay, prostrate in my bed, while outside, the sun warmed the garden, and birds sang gaily and a beautiful English spring day took its course. How much worse did it make me feel, to know that just beyond my bedroom window was such peace and tranquillity! It was then that an odd thing happened, from which I now believe I can date the beginning of the trouble which has beset me.

'It was, I believe, early in the afternoon. I had been lying for some time in a fevered sweat, slipping in and out of delirious dreams and barely ever fully conscious. From time to time the warm breeze through my window set the curtains fluttering and I was, I recall, observing this gentle movement when I gradually became aware of voices, speaking softly, in the garden below. I could not tell if they had at that moment begun, or if they had been speaking for some time whilst I had been asleep, but as I listened it seemed to me that one of the voices was that of my wife. Who her companion might be, I did not know, nor, in truth, did I much care. That low, hushed whisper might have been a friend or a stranger, a man or a woman, for all I could tell; for the chief part of my mind was concentrated upon the fiery struggle within my own body and I had little energy left over to eavesdrop upon the conversation of others. By and by, however, I heard a chinking sound, as of a spoon's being stirred in a jug of lemonade, and a few snatches of the low conversation came to my ears.

'"How is he?" came one voice.

'"Bad, very bad," replied the other. "The doctor has practically given him up."

'"How much longer must we endure this torment?" asked the first.

'"A few weeks at the most, so I understand; then all our troubles will be at an end."

'"Good. You do not know how I have prayed for the day it will all be over, and you and I can know happiness once more."

'Whether I drifted back to sleep then, or whether the conversation ceased, I cannot tell, but I heard no more. That night, however, I was sleeping only fitfully, as a result of the fever, when I was rendered suddenly wide awake by a sharp noise outside my bedroom window. The room was in darkness and I was alone, for my wife slept in another room during the course of my illness. For a few moments I lay still and listened, but no further sound came to my ears. Then I heard it, a soft, rustling sound, as of the wind disturbing the shrubs in the garden below; but I could see from the stillness of my curtains that there was no wind blowing. I left my bed, crept to the window and drew the curtain quietly aside. The garden appeared at first to be of a uniform blackness, but gradually I was able to make out the dark shapes of the shrubs and trees. Even as I looked, one shadow seemed to detach itself from the larger shadow of a bush, and flit without a sound across the lawn and into the darkness beside an old stone shed. Almost petrified – for the fever had set my nerves jangling quite enough already, before this unwonted visitation – I watched for fully ten minutes, but saw nothing more.'

'One moment,' interrupted Holmes. 'What was the size of this moving shadow?'

'It seemed at the time somewhat smaller than a man, but it could, of course, have been someone crouching low. It was certainly not an animal I saw, if that is what you have in mind.'

'Do you believe, then, that it was in fact a man?'

'So I should judge,' replied Pringle after a moment, 'especially in the light of subsequent events. But, I must say, it was not a man I should care to meet. There was something so horribly skulking and furtive in the way he scuttled across the lawn.'

'Very well. Pray continue with your most interesting narrative.'

'The next day I was feeling a little better and could not bear the thought of being cooped up in my bedroom again. I dressed, therefore, and took breakfast with my wife downstairs. I described to her the dark apparition I had seen in the night-time, but she was inclined to dismiss it as simply the product of a fevered imagination.

I did not agree with her, but it is true enough that my eyes have in the past been affected both by my illness and by the medicines I have been given to alleviate it, so I did not argue the point. In any case, I had myself devised an explanation which satisfied me at the time: there is a footpath which runs along the bank of the river, at the very foot of our garden, which the locals sometimes use; no doubt the figure I saw was some fellow the worse for drink, who had strayed from the path in the darkness and ended up by trampling through our shrubbery.

'After breakfast I took my stick with the intention of walking to the riverside.'

'Did you not mention to your wife the conversation you had overheard the previous afternoon?' Holmes interrupted.

'Not at that time, no. You will gain some notion of my state of mind if I tell you that the whole incident had quite passed out of my head. When I left the house that morning I had no other thought than that it would be pleasant to sit beside the river for a little while and watch the sunlight catching the ripples on the surface of the water.

'The path to the river runs down the right-hand side of the garden, separated from the boundary fence for the first twenty or thirty yards of its length by a succession of low sheds and storage buildings, in various stages of dilapidation. My way therefore took me past the very spot where I had seen the figure vanish the night before. Imagine my surprise, then, when I saw that upon the whitewashed wall of the shed was the print of a human hand.'

'What sort of print?' said Holmes sharply, sitting forward in his chair with an expression of heightened interest upon his face.

'It had been deliberately done, for it was quite clear and un-smudged. It was of a bright purple colour and showed the whole of the hand. I thought at first that it was a drawing, but saw when I got closer that it was a true print, for all the lines and finger-joints showed up clearly. I also saw then that there was something most peculiar and horrible about it: there, at one side, as one would expect, was the print of the thumb, but directly above the palm were not four fingers, but five.'

'The right or the left hand?' enquired Holmes.

'The right.'

'How high above the ground?'

'I cannot say exactly. About five feet, I suppose.'

'Very good,' said Holmes, refilling his pipe. 'Your case, Mr Pringle, begins to assume the colours of something truly *recherché*! I am most grateful that you have brought it to my attention and I will endeavour to return the favour by bringing a little light into your darkness. Pray continue!'

'Over luncheon that day I mentioned to my wife the mark I had seen upon the wall. "There," I said; "you see, there *was* someone in the garden last night."

'"Perhaps," said she, "although why anyone should do such a silly thing I cannot imagine."

'"Well, it has made a confounded mess of the wall, anyway. I shall have to have it repainted. Incidentally," I added, as something stirred my memory, "did I hear you speaking to someone in the garden yesterday afternoon?"

'"I do not believe so," she answered after a moment, "unless it was the postman. But, wait: you are quite correct dear: a charming woman called, collecting for some good cause or other. She was very tired with the heat, so I offered her a glass of lemonade and we sat chatting for five or ten minutes. That must have been what you heard."

'"I suppose it must," said I. I did not mention to my wife the words which I had thought had passed between them, for I was convinced now that they were entirely of my own invention. I had in the past suffered badly with nightmares when the fever was upon me and had always felt utterly foolish the next day – when my bad dream would strike me as simply absurd and trivial – so I had learnt to keep such things to myself.

'My health picked up rapidly after a few days, thanks to the fine weather and the good clean air I was breathing, and life continued as before. Some time later – about the twenty-seventh of May, if my memory serves me correctly – I returned home, after a week of travelling in the north upon business, to find my wife in high spirits.

"'I hope you do not mind, Mark," said she, "but I have taken the initiative while you were away and employed a gardener."

"'Not at all," I replied. "That is excellent news." We had previously relied on the intermittent services of an old fellow from the nearby village, but he was really past coping with so large a garden as ours now; for although always pretty and full of colour, it has a tendency to run riot if left to its own devices, and for all my wife's enthusiasm and endeavour it had been deteriorating for some time. "Is he a local man?" I asked.

"'No," said she. "He is from Hampshire, a man by the name of Dobson. He had placed an advertisement in the gardening journal and I thought such enterprise should be rewarded. His testimonials were first class and I am sure he will make an excellent gardener. His wife, too, seemed a splendid woman and she will be able to help Mary about the house. I thought they could have the old cottage near the river, and I have arranged for a firm of builders from Staines to come tomorrow to set it to rights for them."

"'You have been busy!" I cried. "And I agree entirely! It would do the old cottage good to have someone living in it again. I was thinking only last week what a pity it was, to have had it standing empty all this time."

'The cottage is an old, low building, which stands just beyond the belt of trees which separates the garden from the river, and has stood upon that spot since long before ever our own house was built. It had become dilapidated over the years, but within a few days, the men my wife had hired had brightened it up considerably: the broken slates upon the roof had been replaced, the guttering mended and the whole of the outside given a fresh, bright coat of white paint. All was finished by the end of the week, when the gardener and his wife arrived to take up residence.

'They struck me as a pleasant enough couple, although oddly matched, I thought, in both appearance and manner. The husband, John Dobson, a thin, angular sort of fellow, with hair as black as his face was white, was taciturn almost to the point of rudeness and had the air about him of one who has suffered much. His wife, Helen, on the other hand, was a small, pink-cheeked and dainty woman, with hair the colour of sand, and quite the most chirrupy and voluble person I had ever met. Still, it was not for their conversation or appearance that they were employed and, in truth, I took little notice of them, leaving it to my wife to issue instructions as to the work they were to do.

'A few days later, rising early, as is my habit, I discovered that I had misplaced my cigar-case. Recalling that I had had it with me the previous evening, when I had sat for a while on the bench by the river, I set out to see if I had left it there. The garden seemed bright and fresh in the morning air, and I smiled as I approached the gardener's little white-washed cottage, nestled so prettily beneath the towering horse-chestnuts, all adorned as they were with their great pink and white candles.

'"What a splendid little house it is!" I said aloud to the morning air. But no sooner were the words past my lips than I saw something which quite stopped me in my tracks and struck the smile from my face. For there, in the very centre of the clean white wall of the cottage, was the print of a human hand. It was in every respect the same as the one I had seen four weeks earlier upon the outhouse wall. It was the print of a right hand, a livid purple in colour, and again with that grotesque and horrible extra finger.'

'It had not been there the previous evening?' interrupted Holmes.

'No. If it had been, I should have seen it.'

'You are certain upon the point?'

'Absolutely.'

'Very well. Pray continue.'

'Anger rose within me that someone had again crept uninvited upon my property in the night and had besmirched this freshly painted wall.

A pail stood nearby with a little water in it and next to it was a piece of rag with which someone had evidently been cleaning the cottage windows. In my fury I plunged the rag into the water, with the intention of expunging the odious mark from the wall. To my surprise and disgust, the rag emerged from the water as purple as the mark it was intended to erase. I tipped the water from the pail and looked with horror at the violet stream which ran out and splashed about my boots. I felt quite unable to comprehend the meaning of this sinister transformation, but I did not loiter to ponder the matter. I quickly located my cigar-case at the nearby bench and hurried in a daze of bewilderment to the house. Just once I glanced back at the cottage to reassure myself that that evil-looking mark was really there upon its wall, and that I had not imagined the whole episode, and as I did so it seemed to me that a curtain quivered at one of the windows, as if someone had hurriedly closed it as I turned.'

'The date of this incident?' enquired Holmes.

Pringle took a small diary from his pocket and leafed through it for a moment in silence. 'I believe it must have been the third of June,' he said at last; 'about three weeks ago.'

Holmes scribbled a note upon a scrap of paper, as his client continued his account.

'The days passed, the wall was cleaned and the incident forgotten; but I began to have serious misgivings about the new gardener. I had soon learnt to tolerate his dark, silent manner – indeed, on the one occasion he had overcome his reserve so far as to actually hold a conversation with me, I had found him both amusing and intelligent, if a little cynical – but what I could not tolerate was the fact that he appeared to do nothing whatsoever to justify the wages he was being paid. Each day I arrived home from town expecting to see some improvement in the appearance of the garden and each day I was disappointed, until eventually I raised the matter with my wife.

'"Dobson does not seem much of a gardener to me," I remarked one evening. "Where are the testimonials he gave you?"

"'I am afraid I have lost them, Mark," she replied in an apologetic tone. "But I do not think you are being entirely fair to the man. He has, after all, only recently begun and there is such a lot to be done in the garden at this time of the year."

'I could see from the expression upon my wife's face that she felt my remarks were impugning her judgement, so I shrugged my shoulders and let the matter drop. When I chanced later to recall the conversation, however, it seemed to me then that she had been just a little too ready with the information that the testimonials were lost. It was almost as if she had been waiting for me to ask; as if, indeed, she had been expecting it.

'A day or two after this, I arrived home in the afternoon and went straight into the garden, intending to sit for five minutes in the sunshine and finish the newspaper I had been reading in the train. After a few moments, however, I became aware of voices in the distance. From where I was sitting, a double row of elms and rhododendron bushes formed a natural corridor, along which I had a perfect view. Even as I looked, two people appeared round the corner at the far end of this corridor, my wife and the gardener. They were walking close together, very slowly, apparently in deep conversation. I was about to call out to them – for they had evidently not seen me – when I realised with a shock that they were entwined in embrace, he with his arm across her shoulder and she with her arm around his waist. My greeting froze upon my lips, and at that very moment my wife looked up and met my gaze. Her mouth fell open and her arms dropped to her side, and for several seconds we stared at each other in silence.

"'What is wrong?" I called, without really knowing why I did so. My wife's face was such a mask of guilt that I could scarcely bring myself to look at it and, to be frank, it was evident to me that the only thing that was wrong was that I had surprised their little *tête-à-tête*. But I called out, nevertheless, and thus presented my wife with an exit from her embarrassment. Why one should wish to assist another to lie to one, I do not know, but my wife took the cue and responded with alacrity.

"'Dobson has sprained his ankle,' she called back. "I am helping him back to his house."

'I threw down my newspaper and hurried over to where they stood. There seemed little wrong with his ankle so far as I could see, but, without comment, I helped him to the cottage and left him in the care of his wife. Lettie had returned to the house, and when I saw her later she made no reference to the incident. As I had decided that I would certainly not be the first to bring the matter up, it remained therefore unaired, although I twice caught her looking at me in an odd fashion that evening, as though wondering what was passing in my mind. Since that time I have never seen the two of them together so intimately, but I cannot of course speak for the times I am away from home.

'If I thought then that I had cause to resent the gardener, I was soon to find out that his wife's behaviour could be equally uncongenial to me. Lettie began to refer to the woman continually, in a way which gradually began to irritate me intensely. It was always "But dear Mrs Dobson says this," or "Helen thinks that we ought to do that".

'One afternoon, I returned home from town earlier than usual and, hearing the sound of female laughter from the garden, I strolled in that direction. As I approached a rose-covered pergola, on the other side of which was a small arbour, I recognised the voices of my wife and Mrs Dobson.

"'I really don't think I can agree with you, Helen," I heard my wife say.

"'But you must, Lettie, you foolish girl. You are simply being stubborn!" retorted the other. There followed a further remark which I did not catch, then peals of laughter. I was surprised to hear my wife indulging in such banter, but I endeavoured not to show it, as I turned into the arbour where they were sitting.

"'Hello!" I cried. "You sound jolly!" But even as I spoke I saw the smiles vanish from their faces.

"'Yes, dear. We were discussing the garden," replied my wife, attempting unconvincingly to force a smile to her lips.

"'Really? And what were you saying about it that was so amusing?"

'My wife gave some response, but it was not very interesting and, in any case, I was not really listening. It was clear that my appearance had as good as thrown a funeral pall over their gaiety.

'Later that evening, when we were alone, I spoke to my wife about the Dobsons.

"'It does not strike me as an altogether good thing for you to encourage Mrs Dobson in such a degree of intimacy," I remarked somewhat stiffly.

"'But we were only talking together!" she retorted hotly. "I suppose you think she is not good enough for me, being only a gardener's wife!"

"'Not at all," I returned. "You know that I do not possess a single ounce of snobbery and you may take what friends you please; but in this case you are the woman's employer and such intimacy can lead to difficulties."

"'I think not," said she simply, "so let us drop the matter."

'I had never heard my wife speak in this way before and I do not mind admitting that I was cut to the quick. I could raise no specific objection to this Dobson woman, other than that she had often struck me as somewhat over-bold in her manner for one in her position, but this, in any case, was not really the point. I felt that I was being excluded in my own house by my own beloved wife and it was this that hurt me so deeply. Lettie perhaps saw this, for after we had remained some time in silence she began to speak to me in a softer tone, but I treated her advances coldly and left the room.

'I could not begin to tell you all the wild thoughts that coursed then through my seething brain, but outside in the night air my head seemed to clear and my resolve to harden. If I had nothing specific against the gardener's wife, I had a veritable catalogue of complaints against the gardener himself. I returned to inform my wife of my decision.

"'It is no good," I began. "The Dobsons will have to go. You should not look so surprised, Laetitia: Dobson has done scarcely a day's work since he came here. I am sure that no one else would have tolerated the fellow as long as I have. Apart from anything else, his gardening skills seem to be non-existent. Why, the man is a perfect imbecile! Only yesterday he pulled up all my sweet williams in the belief that they were weeds!"

'"He has been ill," she protested. "He has had a touch of the sun. He will improve, Mark; you will see."

'"He is certainly sickly-looking: he makes me feel ill every time I see him. But this house is not a charitable institution, Laetitia, and much as I dislike the thought of turning a man out when he has no other post to go to, he will have to go."

'I thought then that the matter was settled and I certainly intended that it should be; but my wife begged and pleaded and cajoled, until once more, much against my better judgement, I relented. I have little doubt that I am a fool, but I could not resist the imploring look in her eyes. There the matter rested and rests still. Do I weary you with my story, Mr Holmes?'

'Not at all,' replied my friend languidly, as he knocked his pipe out upon the hearth. 'But I fail to see in what way I can help you in these matters, Mr Pringle. I make it an invariable rule not to interfere in domestic affairs, for there is generally profit in it for no one.'

'At least hear the end of my story, Mr Holmes, before you make up your mind. On Sunday last I was so weighed down with these problems and, as I now realise, with the beginnings of another bout of the fever, that I found I was quite unable to sleep. About one in the morning I dressed quietly and slipped out into the darkened garden, thinking that a little fresh air would help to soothe my nerves. It had been a very hot, close day, as you no doubt recall, and the night was heavy and black and lowering. As I stepped down the path to the river, a single large drop of rain landed upon my cheek, and before I had gone another thirty yards the skies had opened and the rain was fairly crashing down. I ran for the shelter of an old yew tree which I knew to be just ahead of me, although I could scarcely make out its shape in the darkness. There I was standing, thankful for the dense cover that the tree provided, when there came a series of mighty flashes directly overhead, accompanied by the violent and deafening crack and rumble of the thunder. In an instant the veil of darkness was lifted from the garden and all was illuminated with that strange, ghastly light. With a thrill of horror that set my hair on end, I saw that there was someone upon the path, not thirty feet away and looking straight at me.'

'A man or a woman?' said Holmes sharply.

'A man – so I believe; but I had only a moment in which to judge the matter. For as abruptly as the light had come, the darkness descended once more, just as if a black cloth had been cast across my eyes. I shifted my position and prepared to defend myself, though against whom, or what, I did not know. I must have stood there in that rigid pose for several minutes, but nothing fell upon me but a few drops of the icy rain. Then for a second time the sky was split asunder by the zigzag strokes of the lightning, for a second time the garden was bathed in its eerie white light and I saw that the path was deserted. Whoever I had seen was no longer there. The rain was still teeming down, but I left my shelter and dashed at the top of my speed back to the house. To my surprise I found the garden door wide open, the rain splashing in and forming a puddle upon the parquet floor of the corridor. I was certain that I had closed the door firmly as I went out, and although it was possible that the sudden force of the storm had blown the door open – for in truth the catch is not a very secure one – I was not prepared to take a risk upon the point. I loaded my revolver and made a thorough search of every room in the house, but found nothing amiss.

'My walk had done little for my insomnia, as you will appreciate, and I spent a sleepless night with the loaded pistol at my bedside. In the morning I scoured the garden for any trace of the intruder, but discovered nothing. I had half expected to see another of those infernal hand-prints, but that at least I had been spared. At breakfast my wife announced that she would accompany me up to town, as there was a sale of oriental fabrics at Liberty's which she wished to attend, but I felt too ill and tired to go to work, so she travelled up alone and I returned to my bed, where I slept half the day away. In sleep, at least, I could escape from the troubles which beset me; but it was a false escape, for when I awoke, these troubles seemed to weigh yet more heavily upon my mind and appear yet more insoluble and impenetrable. What power is possessed by this woman, Helen Dobson, that she can gain such an influence over my wife in so short a time? What manner of man is her brooding, taciturn husband? Why does he pretend to be a gardener – which he very evidently is not – and what does he hope to gain by such an imposture? Who is it that creeps about my garden in the night-time and prints his freakish hand upon my wall? Does someone wish me dead? All day long, and late into the night, I cudgelled my brains with these questions and a thousand others, until I began to think that it was all a fevered nightmare, in which no answers or explanations might ever be found, but from which dawn would release me. Alas, this morning I woke up and saw my pistol beside the bed, and knew that some answer must be sought in the world of reality.

'I had heard your name, Mr Holmes, in connection with the Claygate disappearance case, a couple of years ago, and it seemed to me that in you might lie my only means of retaining my sanity. And yet, even as the thought of your reputation brought a flicker of hope to my reeling mind, I still was not sure that consulting you would be the right thing to do. For the matter is so dark and in some ways so delicate and personal—'

'And yet you have come.'

'This arrived by the morning post.'

Our visitor drew from his inside pocket a long blue envelope, from which he extracted a folded sheet of paper. This he passed across to Holmes, who unfolded it carefully and examined it upon his knee. With a quickening of the pulse and a prickling sensation in the hairs upon my neck, I saw that the paper bore but a single mark: the vivid violet print of a human hand.

'Be so good as to pass me the lens, Watson,' said my friend, an expression of intense interest upon his face. 'It is a man's hand,' he remarked after a moment; 'a coarse hand, with short, thick fingers; no stranger to physical work, I should judge, from the general development. Hello! He has a ring upon his second finger. Is this the same as the previous prints you observed?'

'So I believe.'

'There is one point upon which I can set your mind at rest at once, Mr Pringle,' said Holmes with a grim smile. 'Whoever made this print has no more fingers than you or I have: the sixth digit is counterfeit.'

'What do you mean, Mr Holmes?'

'The anatomy is quite wrong. If you will look closely at the fingers you will see that whereas the first three and the last arise from a pad on the palm, the fourth does not, but arises from between the pads of the two adjacent fingers. Do you see, Watson? There is no indication whatever of a metacarpal. He has, it is evident, printed his third finger twice, having previously splayed out his little finger, in order to make room for the addition.'

'Why, so he has!' cried our visitor. 'I can see it clearly now! But why should anyone do such a thing?'

'Ah! That is another question! May I see the envelope which contained this remarkable communication? Hum! Common enough sort of stationery! Posted yesterday afternoon in the West End. Dear me! What a dreadful nib the pen must have – no doubt the address was written in a post office, or the writing-room of an hotel. Well, well! Your name has been curiously misspelt! The remainder of the address is correct, I take it?'

Pringle nodded as Holmes passed the envelope to me and I saw that his client's name had been rendered as 'Mr Pringel'.

'What a most interesting detail!' said Holmes slowly and quietly, apparently addressing himself. With his elbows upon his knees and his chin cupped in his hands, he sat in silence for several minutes, an expression of intense concentration upon his face.

'Do you see some clue, Mr Holmes?' cried his client at last, clearly unable to endure the silence a moment longer.

'Eh? Oh, possibly, Mr Pringle, possibly,' replied Holmes in an abstracted tone. 'The misspelling of your name is certainly a singular thing. It is so grotesque, so un-English, you see, that it argues not simply for the hand of a stranger, who was obliged to enquire your name, but for that of an illiterate or a foreigner, who was then unable to spell correctly the name he was given. The remainder of the address is so neatly and correctly rendered, however, that the first of these alternatives seems unlikely. It also suggests—'

'What?' Pringle enquired eagerly.

'Something I must think about,' Holmes replied at length. 'There is of course a further possibility,' he added more briskly.

'Which is?'

'That the sender of this letter is someone known to you, who wishes to disguise the fact.'

'If so, it is an absurdly crude attempt!' said Pringle with a snort.

'I quite agree. Nevertheless, it is a possibility we must bear in mind. The case is at present a chaotic and confused one, and we cannot afford to dismiss any chance, however remote. Tell me, have you ever travelled in the Balkans?'

'Never!' replied Pringle in some surprise. 'I have not even been near that part of the world, except for a passage through the Mediterranean to the Suez Canal.'

'Your wife?'

'To the best of my knowledge she has only twice been away from England since she returned from Ceylon, and on both occasions it was to stay with a distant cousin who lives on the outskirts of Paris.'

'No matter,' said Holmes, shaking his head; 'you are a finger short, in any case. Is there anyone you would call an enemy – someone who might perhaps feel he had cause to persecute you?'

'None that I know of. I was once called upon to act as a witness to a hanging, during my time in Ceylon, and there was some ill feeling in the area for a while afterwards, stirred up by the man's family; but it was not directed principally at me, for I had no other connection with the matter. In any case the trouble subsided fairly quickly, for the poor wretch had certainly been guilty of the most ghastly murders, as even his own family conceded.'

'You were married at Gloucester, I believe you said,' Holmes remarked after a moment. 'Was that simply because your wife was living in that part of the country at the time?'

'Not entirely. Her family had always lived in the town. Her maternal grandfather, she told me, had at one time been Dean of Gloucester Cathedral.'

'Very well,' said Holmes, leaning back in his chair and tapping the tips of his fingers together. 'The problem you have presented us with, my dear sir, is a most remarkable one, with several features which are not yet clear to me. But if you leave these papers here, I shall give the matter my consideration and let you have my opinion in due course.'

'You have hopes, then, of uncovering a solution?' cried Pringle eagerly. There was something almost pathetic about the beseeching look upon his face, which was terrible to see in so fine a figure of a man.

'There is always hope,' said Holmes shortly. 'Will you be in your office tomorrow? You will? Then I shall call in to see you if I have any news; otherwise please be so good as to call in here on Thursday, if that is convenient.'

'Certainly, Mr Holmes,' responded the other, who was evidently much cheered by Holmes's confident manner. 'But might I ask what steps you propose to take?'

'The only steps I shall take this evening, my dear sir, are to the chair in which you are now sitting, which is somewhat better appointed for prolonged meditation than this one.'

'That is all?' cried Pringle in disappointment. 'You will do nothing more?'

'I shall consume a great quantity of the strongest shag tobacco. It is quite a four-pipe problem and it would be unwise to attempt to come to any premature conclusions.'

Pringle shot a questioning glance at me, then shrugged his shoulders with an air of resignation.

'Did you show this letter to your wife?' asked Holmes, as his visitor rose to leave.

'I saw no point,' the other replied simply, with a shake of the head.

'You are probably correct – at least for the moment – and nor should you mention to anyone that you have consulted me.'

'I should not dream of doing so!'

'Nevertheless, you might let it slip without intending to. Be upon your guard at all times, Mr Pringle! One final thing—'

'Yes?'

'On no account venture into the garden after dark. I cannot pretend to have fathomed yet the mystery which surrounds you, but that you walk amidst great danger I am convinced.'

'Well, Watson,' said my friend when our visitor had left us. 'What do you make of it?'

'Nothing whatever,' I replied with perfect honesty.

'You are a singular fellow, indeed!' cried Holmes with a chuckle. 'I sometimes think that you are quite the most remarkable man in London, Watson; for I have certainly never known another so honest! There are few, I should imagine, who would care to announce their ignorance so candidly; yet, in this case, I should not believe anyone who did not confess himself baffled, for Mr Mark Pringle has brought us quite the most *outré* little problem I have encountered these past twelve months. As he himself remarked, the incidents taken separately could almost all bear an innocent, trivial, even prosaic explanation; but place them together and something more sinister begins to be discernible. The individual incidents are like the flourishes of the piccolo, the flute, the horn; but underlying all of these, barely perceptible save when the piece is regarded in its entirety, is a deep and continuous theme upon the 'cello and the double bass.'

'And yet,' I remarked, 'perhaps these things *are* just coincidences. Perhaps there is not, after all, any connection between them.'

'No, it cannot be,' replied Holmes, his brow furrowed with thought. 'Every nerve of intuition I possess tells me that the events are in some way connected – must be connected; and it is for us to find the connection. The difficulty lies in the fact that the incidents, as reported to us, are not only quite distinct, but, in some cases at least, mutually contradictory. One might, for instance, suspect a mere vulgar affair of some kind between Mrs Pringle and this man, Dobson, were it not for the extremely friendly relations which seem quite genuinely to subsist between Mrs Pringle and Dobson's wife, Helen.'

'There is certainly something suspicious about the Dobsons,' I remarked. 'They have some secret aim in view, of that I am convinced; although what it might be I cannot imagine.'

'And yet,' Holmes replied, shaking his head slowly, 'it does not quite make sense. Consider the matter, Watson: imagine for a moment that you were the one with the secret aim in view. You are not a man remarked for duplicity, nor to any degree a natural schemer, yet surely even you would take great care to conduct yourself with modesty, self-effacement and propriety, and to do all that was required of you, in order to disarm any suspicions that might arise. But the Dobsons, so far from being discreet, seem to have gone out of their way to be conspicuous and irritating to their employer. There seems a want of cunning there!'

'Considered in that light, their behaviour is certainly odd,' I concurred.

'These are deep waters, Watson,' continued my friend after a moment, 'and may yet prove far deeper than we can at present imagine. I cannot help feeling that there is some factor in the case of which we are as yet unaware; some hidden strand, which, if we could but grasp it, might at once pull together all the other strands, unconnected though they now seem.'

'It is certainly a tangled skein at present,' I remarked, 'and I confess that the more I reflect upon it, the more baffling it seems to become. Whatever can be the significance, for instance, of the violet liquid in the pail that Pringle found one morning by the cottage?'

'Ah, there, my dear Watson, you put your finger on what is perhaps the one point in the whole of his narrative to which no mystery attaches,' responded Holmes, breaking into a smile. 'For whoever had printed his hand upon the wall that morning – using perfectly ordinary ink, to judge from this sheet which we have examined – would, in the process, have marked his hand quite as conspicuously as he had marked the wall, as I am sure you would agree. He could of course cover his hand with a glove, but at this time of the year that would excite almost as much comment as an ink-stained hand and, in any case, there may be other circumstances which would render such a device impossible. What does he do, then, to remove the stain and thus preserve his secret, but plunge his hand into the water and rinse off the incriminating ink? It is certainly what I should do in his position. But, come, we are beginning to circle around the problem without ever approaching any closer to it, after the style of our good friend, Inspector Athelney Jones!'

'Very well,' said I, laughing. 'I shall leave you to your solitary meditations.'

'Drop by tomorrow afternoon,' said Holmes, as I took my hat and stick, 'and we can review any progress in the case.'

––––––

At three o'clock the following afternoon I was seated by the window in my friend's rooms, reading the evening paper, when he returned. His face was drawn and tired, but the slight smile which played about his lips told me that his day had not been a fruitless one.

'Tiring weather!' said he by way of greeting, tossing his hat on to the table.

'You have made some progress with the Pringle case?' I ventured.

'More than that,' he replied. 'I have quite cleared up Mr Pringle's little mystery and am now in a position to lay the whole of the facts before him. It was a simple affair after all. You will come with me? If we leave within the half-hour we should be in time to catch him at his office in the Crutched Friars. As to the advice I should give him, however—'

His voice tailed off and an introspective look came into his eyes. It was clear that despite the solution of the mystery, there was something about the case which vexed him still. Without a word he threw off his coat and began slowly to fill his old black pipe with tobacco from the pewter caddy upon the mantelpiece, his eyes all the while far away. A score of questions welled up in my mind at once, but I forbore to voice them, for I knew well enough, from ten years' experience, that he would enlighten me of his own volition when he himself chose to do so and that to question him at any other time was a profitless exercise.

I also knew that he rarely jested when his profession was the subject and I had never once known him exaggerate his achievements, so that if he said he had solved the case, then I knew it must be so, incredible though such a claim seemed. How on earth, I wondered, had he, in less than twenty-four hours, discovered the key that would unlock the mystery which surrounded his unfortunate client? Again my mind turned over the remarkable series of events which Mark Pringle had narrated to us the previous evening, again I pondered the significance of all that he had told us – the disturbing conversation he had overheard upon his sick-bed, the mysterious and grotesque hand-prints, his wife's unfathomable behaviour towards both the Dobsons and her own husband, and the dark, sinister figures that came in the night – but again I was obliged to admit utter and total defeat.

'Your client's part of the country seems to be having more than its share of mysteries at the moment,' I remarked at length.

'What is that?' said Holmes in a vague, abstracted tone, as if so far away in his thoughts that he found it difficult to refocus his mind upon the present time and place. 'What did you say?'

'There is a report in the early editions that the body of a man was found in the river early this morning, just by Chertsey Bridge. There was a knife stuck in his side.'

'What!'

'The police believe that the body had been washed down the river from the Staines area.'

He took the paper from me and ran his eye rapidly down the column, a look of alarm upon his face. '"A short, squat man!"' he cried after a moment, a note almost of relief in his voice; '"with a swarthy complexion and curly black hair, and with a single gold ear-ring." Well, it is no one *we* know, anyhow.'

'So I judged.'

'Nevertheless, Watson, it bears upon the case.'

'You think so?'

'I know so. You remarked the contents of his pockets? "Very little was found in the dead man's pockets by which his identity might be established, although he does not appear to have been robbed: three bank notes in a clip and a small amount of loose change, six whiffs in a pigskin case, a box of wax vestas and a bottle of ink being the sum total; in addition, the cork from a wine-bottle was discovered in the lining of his jacket." Now, why should a man carry a bottle of ink, who does not also carry a pen of any sort?'

'The purple hand!'

'Precisely! Listen: "All labels and marks appear to have been removed from his clothing, as if to prevent any discovery of his antecedents, but inside one pocket of his waistcoat was found a small tag bearing a single word – believed to be the maker's name – in the Cyrillic script in use in parts of Eastern Europe. The possibility that the murdered man was from those parts is given some support by the evidence of the knife that killed him. This is a narrow fixed-blade type, with an elaborately carved bone handle, which is stamped on the blade with the word 'Belgrade'."'

'What does it mean, Holmes?'

'It means that events have moved faster than I expected. If we are to prevent another death we must act at once. Will you come with me?'

'Most certainly. We are going to Crutched Friars?'

'No; to Low Meadow.'

He donned his outer clothes as quickly as he had thrown them off, and in a minute we were in a hansom and driving furiously through the traffic to Waterloo station.

'No doubt you have by now formed an opinion upon the matter,' said Holmes as our railway carriage rattled along the viaduct and through Vauxhall station.

I shook my head. 'I should be very much interested to hear your own conclusions,' I replied.

'You will recall,' said he, after a moment, 'that my client felt confident of only two facts about his nocturnal visitor: that he had a deformed hand and that he was unusually small in his overall figure. But in both these opinions he was mistaken. The hand, as we saw, is in reality quite unexceptional; and it seemed likely, once we had heard that the hand-print was made approximately five feet from the ground, that his figure was unexceptional, too.'

'Why so?'

'Because it would be the natural tendency of anyone making such a print to do it at shoulder height – try it for yourself some time and you will see – and anyone who is five feet to the shoulders is obviously of a fairly normal build. So the intruder ceases to be inhuman and freakish, and becomes instead a perfectly ordinary specimen of humanity.'

'I can see that that would make the matter yet more baffling and difficult of discovery,' I remarked.

'On the contrary, it admits a tiny ray of light into the mystery for the first time.'

'I do not follow you.'

'Consider: if the intruder is not equipped by nature with six digits upon his right hand, then the fact that he prints it in that bizarre fashion is evidently a matter of deliberate choice upon his part. Clearly the print has some very definite significance for him and he must expect that it will have the same significance for others, otherwise there would be little point to the exercise. Thus the print as an unfathomable, purely personal thing quite disappears and in its place we see an item of public communication, which is far more amenable to investigation.'

'And yet I am not convinced,' said I. 'For what possible significance could be possessed by such a grotesque daub?'

'You have not heard anyone speak of the Seven-Fingered Hand?' said Holmes in a quiet voice.

'Never!'

'I must admit that that does not surprise me; there is really no reason why you should; for its activities receive little enough publicity in this country. Indeed, until today my own knowledge of it was exceedingly sketchy and yet it almost comes within my field of speciality. It is a secret society, Watson – that most vile excrescence of civilisation. It sits like a vile beast upon the Balkans, its evil tentacles stretched out to every remote corner, so that there is scarcely a town or village there where it cannot command the allegiance of at least one person; and that allegiance is rarely commanded but for terrorism and murder.'

'It sounds monstrous, Holmes! Whatever is the purpose of such an organisation?'

'Ah! The answer to that question illustrates rather nicely the divergence between theory and practice in human endeavours; for the surprising thing is that the society of which I speak was originally formed of principled, high-minded men, who would never have chosen to meet in secret conclave had they not felt driven to it. Their purposes originally were quite altruistic, their only aim being to petition the authorities on behalf of those of their fellow countrymen whose lot they considered a woeful one. But the society was soon taken over – some would say inevitably so – by those whose very delight it is to be secret, to pass unseen in the night-time with the knife beneath the cloak, to feel a sense of power in the anonymous assassination of the innocent. Soon all pretence of altruism was as good as abandoned and the sole *raison d'être* of the society became its own continued existence, an existence which is sustained and nourished on the terror of the very people in whose name it was originally founded.

'The society's somewhat fanciful name derives partly from the fact that it was constituted originally of groups from seven different provinces, and also from an initiation ceremony in which the new recruit is obliged to make a hand-print upon a document of allegiance to the society. This hand-print, embellished with the addition of two extra fingers, eventually became the symbol of the society. It is used to strike terror into the hearts of its enemies – and this it will surely do, for the society has the deserved reputation of being both implacable and ruthless. I tell you, Watson, a man had rather be in a cage of ravenous tigers than have these gentlemen upon his trail.

'So much I managed to glean this morning, from long hours among the files of old newspapers – steep, steep work, Watson! I also learnt a further fact there, which brings the history of this unholy gang up to date: the Eastern Roumelian section, having evidently transgressed some rule or other, was last year expelled from the society, amid considerable blood-letting. One finger was accordingly removed from the society's symbol, leaving just six – as in the letter my unfortunate client received yesterday morning at his breakfast table.'

'But why?' I cried. 'What possible business can this abominable society have in England? And why do they seek to terrorise Mark Pringle?'

Holmes did not reply at once, but leaned back in his seat and surveyed the tranquil countryside through which our train was now speeding. On either side of the track, a broad expanse of heath-land stretched far away, all dotted over with bright patches of poppies and buttercups. It seemed to me incredible that upon such a day, and in such a spot, these desperate men from across the seas could be pursuing their evil ends.

'Mark Pringle is not their primary quarry,' said my companion at length. 'You will recall that our first surmise upon seeing the envelope with the misspelt name was that Pringle was not personally known to the sender. This suggests as a possibility that it was only because he had been seen in the garden on Sunday night that they had gone to the trouble of learning his name – no doubt from a neighbour – in order to send him a specific warning that he should not interfere in their business. The fact that they were evidently not previously aware of his identity further suggests, of course, that the first two hand-prints were not in fact made for his benefit at all.'

'I do not understand,' I interrupted. 'Does this mean that he is not, then, in danger?'

'I should not go so far as to say that,' replied my friend. 'Indeed, I believe that he is exceedingly fortunate still to be alive. But to answer your questions more fully, it is necessary to go back a dozen years, to when a gentleman by the name of James Green deposited a large sum of money in the vaults of the Anglo-Hellenic Bank in King William Street, in the City. He was, according to his own testimony, the principal in a firm of wine-shippers, who specialised in wines from Greece and the Aegean Islands. At regular intervals after that, further sums were deposited and, from time to time, withdrawals made, either in London or at the branch office in Athens.

'It was only when the bank collapsed, amid a terrific scandal, early in '82, that in the course of attempts to locate all the creditors and settle with them as best they could – which was hardly at all – the authorities discovered that no such person as James Green existed and no more did his supposed firm of wine-importers. The whole elaborate charade had been devised to conceal the fact that the funds were those of the Seven-Fingered Hand – money which had been extorted from the peasants of Eastern Europe, and which was employed in the furtherance of the society's own evil ends and to keep its leaders snug. This emerged at the bankruptcy hearing and the subsequent fraud trial, which created quite a sensation at the time.'

'I believe I recall it,' said I. 'The chief clerk had used his clients' money in a series of wild speculations, each of which had in turn failed. He had thus been driven further and further into desperate measures, and yet wilder schemes, in his attempt to recoup the losses, until in the end the bank had scarcely a penny to its name.'

'You recall it precisely. The chief clerk's name was Arthur Pendleton, who distinguished himself at his trial by showing not the slightest shred of remorse and who was, as I learnt from the court records this morning, sentenced to fifteen years for his troubles. A junior clerk whom he had somehow managed to embroil in his criminal schemes received a shorter sentence, of ten years, in recognition of his lesser culpability and in the certain knowledge that had it not been for the strong and evil influence which the older man had had over him, he would never have become involved at all. The bank was sold off, lock, stock and barrel, but the creditors received scarcely one part in a hundred of what they were owed.'

'You have evidently had a busy day,' said I, impressed by the speed at which my remarkable friend had been able to gather information on such remote matters; 'but I still cannot grasp the pertinence of these matters to the case in hand. Are you convinced that there is a connection?'

'The matter is beyond the realm where it is appropriate to speak of conviction and into that of certainty,' replied Holmes. 'I spent some time this afternoon at Somerset House, which was enlightening, and when I read that the man found in the river at Chertsey had carried an old wine cork in his coat, there remained no doubt what was afoot.'

'A wine cork?'

'He would use it to protect the point of the knife and to prevent the blade from slitting the lining of his jacket, which is where the knife would be concealed.'

'Are you suggesting that the knife which killed him was his own?'

'Precisely. He was an assassin, Watson; that is apparent. But he whom he sought to kill has turned his own weapon upon him. You read that all labels had been removed from his clothes? That is a trade-mark of such men: anonymity is the very essence of their work. No connection must ever be traced between the assassin and the organisation which commands him.'

'Such precautions would appear to suggest,' I remarked after a moment, 'that the man thought it quite likely that he might, indeed, lose his own life.'

'Well, it is an ever-present hazard for the assassin, as you will imagine. But it is not one upon which he may dwell; for he will be aware that failure to carry out his commission will result in the next such commission having his name upon it, not as agent, but as victim. But come! This is Staines and we must make all haste.'

A short journey in the station-trap down a sun-baked country road brought us to the gates of Low Meadow, where we paid off the driver and entered on foot. Up the drive we hurried, round the corner of the house and into the rear gardens. Not a breath of wind disturbed the leaves upon the trees and the air was heavy with the scent of flowers. Ahead of us on the lawn, a handsome young woman in a white dress was sitting on a rug, with a sewing-basket beside her. She started up when she saw us, a look of surprise upon her face.

'Mrs Pringle?' enquired my friend.

'Yes, but—'

'My name is Sherlock Holmes. Pray forgive this abrupt intrusion into your privacy, but our mission is most urgent.'

'You had best explain yourself,' said she with some sharpness, rising to her feet.

'There is no time.'

'I insist upon it.'

'Very well. I have been employed by your husband to make inquiries on his behalf into certain matters which have recently perplexed him. All I have learnt convinces me that there is mortal danger here at Low Meadow.'

'Mortal danger?' she repeated in a tone of disbelief. 'For my husband?'

'No, for your brother.'

At this she paused for a moment and took a sharp breath, then threw her head back with a peal of laughter.

'All you have learnt has evidently been nonsense!' said she. 'I have neither brother nor sister, so whoever has a brother in mortal danger, it is not I!'

Holmes remained quite unmoved by this outburst. 'You cannot afford to play games,' said he gravely, 'when it is your brother's life which may be the forfeit.'

'I tell you I have no—'

'I understand well enough the reasons for your pretence, Mrs Pringle,' Holmes interrupted her, 'but believe me when I tell you that the time for such pretence is past. Perhaps if I tell you all I know, it may convince you that I speak the truth.'

She seemed about to reply, but hesitated, and Holmes hurriedly continued: 'Your brother, John Aloysius Wadham, was born upon the fifteenth of October in the year 1858, at Gloucester. In 1880 he married Helen Montgomery at Guildford. In 1882, whilst employed at the King William Street branch of the Anglo-Hellenic Bank, he became involved in a massive series of embezzlements, as a result of which, when the matter came to light, he was sentenced to ten years' penal servitude.'

'It is false!' she cried out passionately. 'The conviction was false! He only became involved with Arthur Pendleton in an attempt to save that wretched, ungrateful man, but soon found himself ensnared in the other's web of deceit, from which, struggle as he might, he could not extricate himself. No thought of personal gain had ever crossed his mind. One word of the truth from that villain might have saved my brother from an unjust fate; but his heart was stone, his friendship hollow.'

'I do not doubt, madam, that what you say is true; however I come not to accuse your brother but to save him. A few weeks ago, having earned the maximum remission from his sentence and being seriously ill, he was released from prison. Shortly before his release, his wife, who had remained loyal and faithful to him through all the long years of his imprisonment, had been to see you to discuss the matter. Your husband, who for some reason knew nothing whatever of your brother, overheard a part of your conversation, but misconstrued it as referring to himself.'

'Dearly would I have loved to tell Mark the whole truth,' Mrs

Pringle interrupted, a tear forming in her eye, 'but John begged and pleaded with me not to do so. He would not, he said, have his shame and disgrace inflicted upon his sister and her fine husband. I told him many times that Mark would welcome him like a true brother and think none the worse of him for what had happened in the past; but he refused absolutely to presume upon Mark's generosity and I was obliged to keep his existence a secret. I have acted according to his wishes all along.'

'I understand that,' said Holmes. 'It was therefore arranged that he would come here, under an assumed name, in the guise of a gardener, in the hope that he might recover his health in the fresh country air. Am I correct?'

'You are,' said she simply. 'How you have learnt these things, I do not know, but you appear to know all.'

'Unfortunately, that is not all. There are those whose thirst for vengeance is not satisfied by your brother's term of imprisonment.'

'Surely you are not serious, Mr Holmes!' she cried in alarm. 'My brother has more than paid for his foolishness. Can the law not restrain these people?'

'Nothing can restrain them, Mrs Pringle. They recognise no law but their own. You must get your brother away from here. There has already been one attempt upon his life and I fear that the second may not be long delayed. You look disbelieving! Did you not read of the man found in the river this morning?'

'The police believe he came from Eastern Europe.'

'That is from where the danger comes. You recall the strange hand-print which was found upon the shed wall after your sister-in-law's visit? That was the work of these men. They were evidently watching her every movement, aware that her husband would shortly be released from prison, and left their mark to give notice of their presence. Later, when your brother and sister-in-law moved into the old cottage, they came again and again left their mark, to announce that retribution was at hand. Last Sunday night, whilst walking in the garden, your husband surprised one of these men, so I believe, and they subsequently sent him a warning note. In the event, of course, the purple hand meant nothing whatever to him; but these men have the arrogance of all who submerge and hide their own identities in that of an anonymous organisation, and clearly believe that there is no one who will not understand, and know fear, upon seeing their sign. Your husband was fortunate, I should say, to escape with his life. Only the fact that the assassin's work was not completed saved him; for human life is as nothing to these men.'

'But, surely, if the assassin is now dead, we have nothing to fear,' said Mrs Pringle.

'He will not have come alone to England.'

For a minute the three of us stood in silence upon that neat and sunny lawn, and these words of Sherlock Holmes seemed like the evil and insane inventions of a madman. Laetitia Pringle shook her head from side to side, over and over again.

'You cannot simply wish these things away,' said Holmes at length, as if perceiving the poor bewildered woman's innermost thoughts; 'you must act, and act swiftly.'

'What should I do?'

'You must get your brother out of England – yes, and out of Europe, too. You must tell your husband everything—'

His sentence remained unfinished, for with a shrill cry of alarm, a sandy-haired woman burst upon our little gathering from behind a row of laurels.

'Lettie! Lettie!' she cried; 'John has vanished.'

She stopped abruptly as she saw that Mrs Pringle was not alone, swaying from side to side with a wild look in her eye, as if she were upon the verge of fainting. Holmes stepped forward and took her arm gently.

'Do not fear, Mrs Wadham. We come as friends.'

'It is Mr Sherlock Holmes,' said Mrs Pringle to her sister-in-law.

'Indeed?' responded the other. 'Your name is familiar to me, sir, and I have heard that there is no problem you cannot solve; but I fear that in this case your powers are of no avail. My husband seemed so dreadfully ill today that I left him in his bed. Just now I returned from tending the vegetable plot and found him gone, and this note upon the kitchen table.'

With a shaking hand she offered a slip of paper to my friend, which he unfolded and read aloud.

'"My dear Helen,"' he read; '"You will remember how often we strengthened each other with the hope that once I had served my sentence, our troubles would be over and we could put the past behind us. Alas! that hope was futile. I have learnt recently that some who lost money in the Anglo-Hellenic fiasco will not rest until those they regard as responsible are dead. As old Pendleton died in prison three years ago, I am the sole focus for their vengeance, unjust as you know that is. It is a turn of events I had always feared, although I prayed constantly that the threat might be lifted from me. Now hopes and fears alike ill become the moment and I must meet my fate with my own hand. Last night, as I sat beside the river shortly before retiring, the first assassin came; but I am not one who surrenders his life without a struggle, despite the weakness of my limbs. He thrust at me with his knife, but I managed to parry the blow and threw him to the ground. For a time we struggled together on the river-bank, then, without any deliberate intention on my part, his own knife pierced his side, his hand still upon the hilt. I cast his lifeless body into the water and determined to say nothing of the incident to you. I have brought enough trouble upon you and upon my dear sister and her husband: it is time for me to go. It is I alone these devils want; if I am not with you, you will be safe. Please forgive this silent way of leaving, but I know you would not let me go if I spoke these words to your face. Your loving husband, John."'

'What am I to do?' cried Helen Wadham, her voice suffused with anguish.

'When did you last see your husband?' enquired Holmes in an urgent tone, handing back the letter to her.

'About an hour ago; but he cannot be long gone, for I was close by the cottage until this past twenty minutes.'

'He has not passed this way, so he has evidently taken the path beside the river,' cried my friend. 'Come, Watson; there may yet be time to dissuade him from this foolhardy course of action. Alone he does not stand a chance against these men.'

We ran down the path towards the river, the women following close behind. At the cottage Holmes darted in, but was out again in a trice, shaking his head in answer to my query. A little further on, we emerged from the wood and came out upon the river-bank, where the bare earth of the riverside path was baked into hard ruts by the summer sun. To left and right we looked, and a grim sight met our eyes. About fifty feet upstream, the crumpled figure of a man lay athwart the path, his boots trailing in the water. Holmes hurried forward and I followed at his heels.

A swift glance told me that the man was beyond all human help. His shirt-front was dark and horrible with blood, and at the very centre of the stain protruded the carved handle of a knife. A torn sheet of paper had been forced over the knife-handle, upon which was the purple print of a human hand. I knew then that the pale, gentle face which gazed unseeing up at me was that of Mark Pringle's strange gardener and unknown brother-in-law. I pulled the knife from his chest and cast it aside and with Holmes's help lifted the body upon a grassy bank.

'Keep the women back!' said Holmes in an urgent tone, as he bent down on all fours and examined the riverside path intently. But it was too late; they ran forward and would not be restrained. What a horrible thing it was for them to see, and how that horror was marked upon their faces!

I turned as a cry came from somewhere behind us. There, at the foot of the garden path, stood my friend's client. He hurried forwards, a puzzled look upon his face. 'The maid told me she had seen you—Why!

What melancholy business is this!' he cried as he caught sight of the grief-stricken faces of the two women.

Quickly, in a very few sentences, Holmes gave him the gist of all that had passed. I have never in my life seen a man so stricken and mortified in so short a space of time. For a long minute he gazed down at the body of his wife's brother, a deep and unfathomable expression upon his face. 'Had he lived I would have loved him,' he said softly at last. 'Come,' he continued, turning to me. 'Help me bear his body to the house. Though in life he rejected my hospitality, in death shall he have it.'

At the house Holmes secured a map, which he studied intently for a few moments.

'The river twists and turns here,' said he at last. 'If we take the main road we may yet be able to intercept the murderer before he can escape.'

On this occasion, however, my friend's resourcefulness proved insufficient and no trace of the assassin could be found in the area. An abandoned skiff was later discovered upon the opposite bank of the river, and inquiries indicated that the fugitive had crossed over to the Surrey side and made his way down to Chertsey, where he had caught a train to London.

Acting upon certain information provided by Sherlock Holmes, the police later arrested a Serbian who was staying at Green's Hotel in the West End. No effective case could be made out against him, however, and when diplomatic protests threatened to make an international incident of the affair, the police were obliged to let him go. 'There goes a certain murderer!' said Holmes with bitterness, when he read in the paper one morning that the man had been put upon the Calais packet, with the formal warning that he should never again set foot in England.

As for Mark Pringle and his wife, I heard later that he had overcome his illness, and that they had returned to Ceylon and taken with them Helen Wadham, in the hope that a new life amid fresh surroundings might help to erase from their hearts and minds the painful memory of the tragedy which had fallen so heavily upon them at Low Meadow.

The North Walk Mystery

Violent murder will always excite both horror and fascination in the public mind. When the victim of the crime is a well-known public figure, the case becomes a sensation and leaves little space in the newspapers of the day for any other subject. Such was the mysterious death of Sir Gilbert Cheshire Q.C., senior bencher of the Inner Temple and the most eminent criminal lawyer of his day. But the matter never came to trial and those involved were reluctant to discuss it, so that despite the many newspaper columns devoted to it at the time, and the countless number of articles written since, there are some facts in connection with the case which have never been fully reported and I have even seen it described as an 'unsolved mystery'. Having been privileged to be present during the investigation of the crime, I can state categorically that this description is false and it is my hope that the following account will clear the matter up once and for all.

It was a dark evening, late in the year. The morning had provided a brief glimpse of watery sunshine, but the weather had taken a turn for the worse about lunch-time and a dense fog had rolled across the city, filling every street and alley-way with its thick, greasy coils. I was glad on such an evening to be in the warm seclusion of our sitting-room, where a fire blazed merrily in the grate.

Sherlock Holmes had been seated at the table for several hours, occupied in pasting newspaper extracts into his commonplace books and carefully cross-indexing each entry. Eventually, as the clock was striking nine, he put down his pasting-brush with a weary sigh, stood up from the table and stretched himself.

'So,' said he after a moment, turning to me, as he rubbed his hands together before the fire; 'you have seen your friend, Anstruther, and he has told you that he is postponing his holiday until the spring.'

'He hopes for better weather then,' I replied. 'But I do not recall mentioning the matter to you, Holmes.'

'Indeed you did not, Watson, but it is clear, nonetheless.'

'I cannot imagine how that can be, for he only informed me of his decision this afternoon – unless, of course, you heard it from someone else.'

Holmes chuckled. 'I have not left these rooms all day,' said he. 'Fortunately, the materials for a simple little deduction lie conveniently upon the table by your elbow.'

I glanced at the table. An empty glass, a saucer, my pipe and a book I had been reading were all I could see there. My face must have betrayed the puzzlement I felt, for my friend chuckled anew.

'In the saucer is the end of a cigar,' said he, 'and by the side of it lies your old copy of Clarendon's *History of the Great Rebellion*. To anyone familiar with your habits, the inference is plain.'

'I cannot see it.'

'No? You went out at lunch-time and returned a while later, smoking a Havana cigar. You do not generally permit yourself such extravagance, save on your visits to the American Bar at the Criterion, and you do not frequent the Criterion these days, save to meet your friend, Anstruther. I therefore feel on reasonably safe ground in inferring that such was your occupation this lunch-time. You mentioned to me some time ago that he had received an invitation to stay with relations of his near Hastings, either later this month, or in the spring, and you had agreed that, in that event, you would attend to his medical duties for a week, as you did for a few days earlier this year. Today is the twenty-sixth: the last week-end of the month is almost upon us and thus the last likely opportunity for Anstruther to begin his holiday. When you returned today, however, you gave no sign of any impending change in your circumstances, nor of any preparations for imminent medical duties. Unlike the previous occasion when Anstruther called upon your professional assistance, you did not immerse yourself in your old medical text-books, but in your old friend, Clarendon, in whose company you proceeded to fall asleep. I could only conclude, then, that your assistance was not, for the present, required and that Anstruther had postponed his visit to the Sussex coast until the spring.'

'How perfectly obvious!' said I. 'I believe I was still half asleep when you spoke to me, Holmes; otherwise I am sure I should not have found your remark so surprising.'

'No doubt,' said he, sounding a little irritated. 'If so, you are not alone. One might suppose the whole of London to be half asleep, so few have been the calls upon my time in recent days! It is certainly a dull, stale and unprofitable life we lead at present!' He stepped to the window and drew aside the curtain. Filthy brown drops glistened on the outside of the window-pane. 'See, Watson, how the fog creeps about the houses and smothers the street lamps! What opportunity for criminal pursuits such conditions present! What a lack-lustre crew our modern criminals must be if they fail to take advantage of it!'

'I doubt if your professional appreciation of the opportunities would be shared by many of your fellow-citizens!' I had responded with a chuckle, when he held up his hand.

'Here is someone, and in a tearing hurry, too,' said he sharply, as the muffled clatter of hooves came to my ears. 'Perhaps our services will be required at last. Yes, by George!' he cried, as the cab rattled to a halt outside our door. 'But, wait! The cab is empty! Ah, the jarvey himself springs down, with a letter in his hand! Your boots and your heaviest overcoat, Watson! Unless I am much mistaken, villainy has at last shaken off its torpor and walks abroad in the fog!'

There came a sharp ring at the door-bell as he spoke and moments later the landlady brought in a letter addressed to Sherlock Holmes. He tore open the buff envelope, glanced at the single sheet it had contained, then passed it to me and I read the following:

> *Come at once if at all possible. North Walk, Inner Temple. Most savage and puzzling crime.*
> D. STODDARD

'No reply, Mrs Hudson,' said Holmes in response to the landlady's query. 'We shall take the cab which brought the note.'

A moment later we were ready to leave, when my friend abruptly stopped in the open doorway of our room and stepped back quickly to the long shelf which held the reference volumes he had compiled over the years. He took a volume from the shelf, thumbed through it for a few moments, then tossed it aside and took down another. He turned the pages over rapidly, until with a cry of satisfaction he brought the book across to show me.

'Look at this, Watson! It is as I thought!' said he, pointing to a yellowing paragraph cut from the *Standard* and dated ten years previously. It was headed 'EMINENT BENCHER MURDERED IN TEMPLE' and ran as follows:

The murder of Sir John Hawkesworth Q.C., upon the evening before last, at the North Walk Chambers, Inner Temple, seems likely to prove as perplexing as it is shocking. Sir John, one of the most senior benchers of the Inner Temple, and a man as personally popular as he was professionally respected, was bludgeoned to death upon his own doorstep, by an unknown assailant. His door-key was still in his grasp and it is conjectured that he was on the point of entering his chambers when the assault took place, which perhaps indicates that the assailant had been waiting there for him to return. This would increase the likelihood of the criminal's presence having been witnessed, were it not that the recent very foggy conditions have made it difficult for anyone to see even those who wish to be seen. Who the assailant is, and what the motive for such a terrible crime might be, no one can suggest; and we can only hope that some clue to the matter will quickly be discovered.

'In fact, nothing ever was discovered,' Holmes remarked as I finished reading, 'and the case remains open to this day. It was before my own practice was established, but I recall it very well.'

Beneath the extract from the *Standard* was a second item, cut from the *Pall Mall Gazette* of the following evening:

A correspondent, Dr J. Gibbon of South Norwood, writes to inform us that the spot upon which the shocking murder of Sir John Hawkesworth took place has witnessed once before the spilling of blood. Almost six hundred years ago, on a similarly foggy night in 1285, when the property was still in the hands of the Knights Templar from whom the area takes its name, one Edmund of Essex was found fatally stabbed in the North Walk. Officially, the crime remained a mystery and the spot upon which it occurred was said to have been cursed since ancient times; although most modern authorities concur in regarding the Grand Commander of the Order himself as responsible for at least instigating, if not indeed perpetrating the terrible deed, it being common knowledge at the time that the two men had quarrelled. It was the increasing frequency of such scandals which led to a decline in the reputation of the Knights Templar and, eventually, to the suppression of the Order altogether, less than thirty years later.

'The North Walk of the Inner Temple certainly has a sinister history,' said Holmes; 'and now Stoddard reports another "savage and puzzling crime" there! Come! Let us waste no more time!'

In a moment we were in the hansom and rattling through the fog.

'You remember Inspector Stoddard?' queried my friend, as we passed down Regent Street.

I nodded. Stoddard was one of the senior detectives of the City Police.

'I have been able to help him once or twice recently,' continued Holmes, 'and he promised, in return, to keep me informed of any interesting case which came his way. This must be a serious matter indeed, for him to call us out at this hour and on such a night!'

In the Strand, Holmes called instructions to the driver and we drew to a halt opposite the entrance to a narrow lane. Some distance ahead of us, a police-constable stood on duty by a gateway and before him, motionless upon the pavement, was a large group of people, forming a strange tableau in the drifting fog.

'It is murder, by the size of the crowd,' remarked Holmes as we stepped from the cab. 'Come, let us slip in this way.'

I followed him down the dark, dripping lane, where the muffled ring of our feet upon the wet cobbles was the only sound to be heard. Our route took us by narrow alleys, round abrupt and unlit corners, and through small, hidden courtyards. The fog was even denser here than elsewhere and quite a degree colder, as it rolled across the Temple Gardens from the river and brought the chill reek of the Thames to our nostrils. We could see scarcely five paces ahead of us, but Holmes pressed forward without pause through the murk and I hurried after him. Though I knew we were passing among the jumble of old brick buildings which make up this ancient lawyers' quarter, so dense was the fog, that save for the occasional fitful glimmer of a lamp in an upstairs window, I could make out nothing at all of our surroundings.

Abruptly Holmes turned to the left, into a narrow alley-way between two tall buildings. On the right, a door stood open wide, casting a bright rectangle of light across the dark alley.

'The North Walk,' remarked my companion.

Just inside the brightly lit doorway stood a tall, thin man with black hair and moustache, whom I recognised as Inspector Stoddard. He was in conversation with a rough-looking man of medium build, with close-cropped ginger hair and beard. The policeman stepped forward as we approached and greeted us warmly.

'I am very glad you were able to come,' said he, in an agitated voice. 'Sir Gilbert Cheshire has been murdered. This is Mr Thomas Mason, the gate-keeper of the Fleet Street Gate,' he continued, indicating the man by his side, 'who first brought news of the tragedy to the police station. He was also one of the last people to see Sir Gilbert alive in his chambers, when he brought in some coal at about twenty to seven; although Sir Gilbert was seen later by several of his colleagues in the dining-hall, where he dined as usual between seven and eight.'

'The attack occurred on his return from dinner, then?' queried Holmes.

'Exactly. I can give you the essential details in a few sentences, Mr Holmes. That will be all for the present, Mason. I'll call you if we have any further questions. Poor fellow!' Stoddard remarked, when Mason had vanished into the fog. 'He is terribly affected by what has happened.'

'He appears an unlikely character to find in this quarter,' observed Holmes.

'There is a story there,' Stoddard responded as he led us into the building. 'He was once on trial himself, about fifteen years ago, accused of murdering his wife. He might have found himself on the gallows, but Gilbert Cheshire was the defence counsel and got him acquitted. Since then he's been as devoted as a dog to him. It was Sir Gilbert who found him the fairly undemanding post of gate-keeper and general factotum, about eight years ago, when he was down on his luck.'

We followed the policeman into a room on the left of the hallway. All the lamps were lit and revealed a shocking scene. In the centre of the square, book-lined room was a large desk, and behind this, in a chair, was the lifeless body of a large, broad-chested man. His head was tilted back, so that his thick, wiry black beard thrust upwards and his eyes stared blankly at the ceiling. On the left side of his neck was a savage wound, which appeared to have bled profusely, and the front of his garments were thick with blood, which was still wet and glistened in the glare of the lamps. The surface of the desk was strewn with bundles of papers, tied up with red tape. Lying amongst them was a large, brass-bound cash-box, its lid hanging open. Beyond the desk, two uniformed policemen were examining the floor by the fireplace.

Stoddard consulted his note-book. 'As you're probably aware,' he began, 'King's Bench Walk, where many of the barristers of the Inner Temple have their chambers, is just round the corner. This is the only set of chambers with its entrance on this side. Sir Gilbert Cheshire has been head of chambers for ten years, since the death of the previous head. He has two junior colleagues here and two clerks – I have already sent messages to them all. The other two barristers share the office directly across the corridor from this one, the clerks' office is along the corridor to the rear. Upstairs, there are two rooms, Sir Gilbert's private study and his bedroom, for these chambers were also his residence.

'As far as I have been able to learn, the others all left for home at the usual time, after which Sir Gilbert was working here alone. He went over to the dining-hall as usual, at about ten to seven – dinner is at seven – but did not linger over his brandy and cigar, as was his habit, but excused himself on grounds of work as soon as the plates were cleared from the table and was back here by eight o'clock. At around quarter past eight, a barrister by the name of Philip Ormerod, who has chambers in King's Bench Walk, was passing the end of the alley outside – the North Walk – on his way to Fleet Street, to get a cab home, when he saw the door standing open and light streaming out. Moments before that, he had heard the sound of running footsteps in the fog, somewhere ahead of him. Concerned that something might be amiss, he had a look in and saw it as you see it now. In a few moments, he had run to the Fleet Street gatehouse, which is only a short distance, and sent the gate-keeper round to Bridewell Place Police Station to get a constable. They communicated with Snow Hill Station, where I happened to be, and I was here within fifteen minutes.'

'There is no sign of a forced entry at the front door,' remarked Holmes.

The policeman nodded. 'It seems probable that the murderer rang at the bell and was admitted by Sir Gilbert himself. The chambers would, of course, have been locked up while he was away at the dining-hall. The only people with a front-door key, other than Sir Gilbert himself, are the two other barristers, the chief clerk and the gate-keeper, who is responsible for attending to the fires and the like. There is much of value here and, of course, many of these papers are of the most confidential nature.'

'From your information it appears that Sir Gilbert was attacked very soon after his return from the dining-hall,' remarked Holmes. 'It is possible that someone was waiting for him outside these chambers and entered at the same time as he did. Was he quite dead when this man Ormerod found him?'

Stoddard hesitated before replying. 'May I enquire, Mr Holmes, if you recall the Hawkesworth case?' he responded at length, an odd expression on his face.

'Very clearly.'

'Then you will understand,' said Stoddard, 'that Sir John Hawkesworth, who was Sir Gilbert Cheshire's immediate predecessor as head of these chambers, was also murdered. He was bludgeoned to death on just such a night as this, exactly ten years ago. He was attacked as he stood on the front-door step of these very chambers. His assailant was never discovered. I was a young officer at the time and was not directly involved with the case, but of course I knew all about it, for it was the single topic of conversation for some considerable time. There was much talk then, in certain parts of the press, of an ancient curse which was said to lie upon this part of the Inner Temple and of how a man murdered many centuries ago returned from time to time to exact vengeance for his own death. Now, I'm not, as you know, much taken with such stories generally, but it is not the sort of thing you forget. I suppose I have not thought about it now for seven or eight years, but this business tonight has brought it afresh to my mind.'

'I am aware of the story,' said Holmes, a trace of impatience in his voice, 'and was struck by the fact that little had been heard of it before Sir John Hawkesworth's murder. I do not think we should permit our thoughts to become confused by ancient history, Stoddard.'

'Of course not, Mr Holmes,' the policeman returned, 'but I thought I had best mention the matter to you. In most ways this appears a brutal but unremarkable crime and I should not have sent for you were it not that it has a couple of unusual features. The eminence of the victim, for one thing—'

'The victim's station in life is not in itself of any interest to me,' interrupted Holmes. 'What was the other unusual feature?'

'When Mr Ormerod entered these chambers and discovered what had happened,' Stoddard explained, 'he thought at first that Sir Gilbert Cheshire was dead. But as he mastered his horror, he heard a slight murmur escape the poor man's lips. He raised Sir Gilbert's head a little and bent closer to listen. He says that Sir Gilbert coughed and spluttered a little, then murmured "It was he—" followed by more coughing and attempts to speak, then "—Sir John Hawkesworth." A moment later, all life had passed from him.'

Stoddard pursed his lips and regarded Holmes with a querying look, as if wondering what the other would make of this strange information.

'What a very singular pronouncement!' said Holmes at length. 'Is Mr Ormerod absolutely certain on the point?'

'He says he would take his oath on the matter.'

'Where is he now?'

'I sent him home in a cab. He was very badly shaken up, as you can imagine. I have his address – Montpelier Square, in Knightsbridge – if we need to speak to him again.'

Holmes nodded. 'You are not aware of any other Hawkesworth?' he queried. 'No brother or cousin of the late Sir John, who might bear the same name?'

'None but the man murdered ten years ago. His nephew, oddly enough, is a member of these same chambers, but his name is not Hawkesworth, but Lewis. He is the son of Sir John Hawkesworth's sister, who married Sir George Lewis, the well-known society solicitor. He is here now, in the other office.'

Holmes's features expressed surprise.

'He must have answered your summons with great dispatch,' he remarked.

'I had no need to summon him, Mr Holmes. He was here before we were. Just after Sir Gilbert breathed his last, but before Ormerod had left the room to summon help, in walked Mr Lewis through the front door of the chambers.'

'I understood that everyone had left some hours previously,' said Holmes. 'What is his explanation for his reappearance?'

'He left just before six o'clock,' said Stoddard, 'had a bite to eat in a tavern in Fleet Street and set out on foot to pay a call on a friend of his who lives at Brixton. This friend turned out not to be at home, however, so Lewis walked all the way back to town again and was on his way back to his lodgings in Bedford Place, near Bloomsbury Square, when he passed this way and saw the door open.'

'It is a dreary evening on which to undertake such long walks,' remarked Holmes. 'He might have saved himself trouble by taking a train back from Brixton to, say, Ludgate Hill station, and arrived back in town somewhat earlier.'

'He says he felt in need of physical exercise. Do you wish to speak to him now, Mr Holmes?'

'His testimony will keep for a few moments,' returned Holmes. 'I should prefer to have a look round while evidence of the crime is still fresh.'

He took off his overcoat, laid it carefully over the back of a chair and began a methodical examination of the fatal chamber. For some time, he examined closely the dead man, the desk and the chairs, then squatted down to examine the carpet. After a few minutes, he rose to his feet and stood a moment, his chin in his hand.

'The artery has been severed,' he remarked at length. 'There are two chairs behind the desk, the second of which was moved to its present position beside that of the dead man from its usual place at the far side of the room. There is one clear impression of a footprint and traces of several others, not so complete. As they all appear to have been made after a copious amount of blood had flowed, they were probably made by Mr Ormerod. As he has now gone home, however, and taken his shoes with him, we are unable to confirm the matter.'

Stoddard conceded the point in an apologetic tone. 'I had thought we had learnt all we could from Mr Ormerod,' he said. 'It is fairly certain they are his prints, though,' he added. 'As I see it, the assailant was probably on the far side of the desk from Sir Gilbert and leaned across it to stab him. From the position of the wound, it is clear he is right-handed.'

Holmes did not reply at once, but regarded the dead man and his desk in silence for a minute, as if picturing to himself what had occurred earlier. Then he came round to the front of the desk. 'And yet,' said he, 'the desk is a broad one, from front to back. I am not convinced that an average man could reach across it sufficiently to inflict the wound.' He picked up a pencil from a tray on top of the desk, then leaned across the desk-top and attempted to touch the side of the dead man's head with it, but fell short by a good nine inches. 'Unless you are prepared to put out the description of a seven-foot giant, or a man whose arms are four feet long,' he remarked, 'I think we must reject the theory.'

'But the dead man's chair is now pushed back a little from the desk,' Stoddard persisted. 'It is also the sort of chair which turns on its base and he has turned it so that he is sideways on to the desk. If it were tight up to the desk, and facing forwards, you might be able to reach him.'

'The chair may have swivelled round as he was attacked,' Holmes returned, 'but it was not pushed back then, or since, for there is blood all around the foot of the chair legs, but none beneath them. The base of the chair has not moved since before the attack took place.'

'What do you suggest, then?'

'That the assailant was on the same side of the desk as his victim. What is this cash-box, I wonder? Hum! Two or three drops of blood inside, so it was open before the attack took place. Nothing in it now but a few cheques, made out to Sir Gilbert Cheshire.'

'All the money has gone,' said Stoddard. 'That is evidently the motive for the crime. This is the account-book which relates to the cash-box,' he continued, lifting a ledger from the desk. 'I found it in the clerks' office.'

'The last entry in the book indicates a credit balance of eighteen pounds, twelve and seven,' said Holmes, 'so that is the amount which should be in the box. Hum! It does not seem a very large sum for which to commit murder.'

'I have known murder committed for less.'

'That is true. Let us now examine the corridor outside.'

We followed Holmes out into the hallway, where he crouched down and examined the floor closely. A long strip of coconut matting was laid along the length of the corridor. After a moment, he took out his lens and examined a dark smudge more closely.

'It is blood,' said he; 'no doubt left by the passage of Mr Ormerod's shoe. There is little else visible on this coarse matting. Halloa! What is this?' Carefully, he picked up a small object which had lain on the bare floor, just to the left of the matting, almost tucked under the edge. He held it out on the palm of his hand and I saw that it was the charred stump of a match.

Stoddard had bent down with interest as Holmes had spoken, but now he straightened up, an expression of disappointment on his features. 'Someone has used it to light the gas,' said he in a dismissive tone.

'But there is no gas-jet near this spot,' returned Holmes, his eyes darting round the walls of the corridor. 'There is one near the front door and one at the very back, just outside the door to the clerks' office, but not just here.' He turned his attention to the floor once more, his nose scarcely an inch above the matting, as he moved from side to side, like a dog casting about for a scent. In a moment he uttered a low cry of triumph.

'What is it, Holmes?' I queried, leaning forward to see what had aroused his interest.

In answer, he pointed with his long thin forefinger to a small, circular greasy mark on the matting, perhaps three-quarters of an inch across.

'Oh, it's just an old smear of tallow, dropped from a candle,' said Stoddard dismissively.

'On the contrary,' said Holmes in a severe tone; 'it is a very fresh smear. See how it shines in the light!' He took out his lens again and bent very low to the floor. 'There is not the slightest trace of dust upon its surface. In this foul weather and with the fires smoking away all day,' he continued, gently passing his finger over the surface of the tallow, 'this splash could not remain in this state for more than a couple of hours.'

'You may be right,' said Stoddard without interest. 'I think I shall see how my men are getting on.'

Holmes did not reply, but continued his careful examination of the corridor, for all the world like some gaunt bloodhound on the trail. A few feet further on, he stopped once more, his brow furrowed with intense concentration and called me over.

'Look at this, Watson,' said he. 'The candle has dripped again. See how the shape is different.'

'It is more oval than the previous mark,' I observed, crouching down.

'Precisely. What does that tell us?'

'That the candle from which it fell was moving,' I suggested.

'Precisely, the long axis of the splash giving the direction of travel. At the first mark, the candle had just been lit and was stationary. At this point, however, whoever was holding it was moving along the corridor, towards the rear of the chambers.' He crawled a little further along the corridor, to the point at which a carpeted flight of stairs led off to the left. 'See if you can find any tallow on the staircase,' said he; 'I shall carry on to the end of the corridor.'

I did as he asked and examined each step carefully. The stair-carpet was dark, with an intricate pattern upon it, which made my task the more difficult, but in a few moments, I had discovered a very small blob upon the fourth stair, near the right-hand edge of the carpet. I called to my companion.

'There is nothing more to be seen in the corridor,' said he, as he examined with his lens the drip I had found. 'Another oval,' he remarked after a moment, 'but this time, there is also a tiny pin-head of the same substance towards the back of the step. Here, take a look, Watson! The extra drop indicates that the splash occurred when the candle was being carried up the stair rather than down it, and suggests that it was moving at a slightly faster rate than before. Evidently our friend with the candle went upstairs, so let us follow in his footsteps!'

At the top of the staircase was a narrow, dark landing. Holmes struck a match. Immediately ahead of us was a blank wall, on which hung a large painting depicting a full-rigged man-of-war of Nelson's day. To left and right were doors, both closed. Beside the left-hand door was a gas-jet, which Holmes lit and turned up. The door to the right was locked, but that on the left opened easily and, as it did so, I saw that the wood of the door-jamb was splintered. Holmes bent down and examined this and the edge of the door.

'Forced open with a flat metal rod,' he murmured, 'the end of which was about an inch across. Another drop of tallow on the floor,' he continued, pointing to a spot slightly to the right of the doorway. 'Circular this time, indicating that the candle was motionless.'

'No doubt the candle was placed upon the floor while the door was being forced open,' I suggested, but my companion shook his head.

'It is an isolated little gout and perfectly circular,' said he, 'which indicates that it dripped from some height. The candle was still being held.'

We pushed the door wide open and entered.

'This chamber is evidently the private study to which Stoddard referred,' Holmes observed, as he struck another match and lit the gas which was immediately behind the door. It was a large room, perhaps fifteen feet across from the doorway to the wall opposite, but nearer twenty-five feet from right to left. To the right, by the fireplace, stood tall bookcases and, to the left, a number of tables, cupboards and bureaux. Holmes lit a lamp which stood upon a small writing-table and made a circuit of the chamber with the lamp in his hand, eventually stopping before a large, double-fronted cupboard.

'These doors have been forced, too,' said he, 'with the same implement as before; and on the floor to the right is another little gout of tallow.' Carefully, he opened the cupboard-doors. The interior consisted entirely of narrow shelves, all stuffed tight with papers. 'There does not appear to be anything of value in here,' he remarked, 'and yet our intruder has directed all his energies to this one cupboard – none of the other bureaux shows any sign of his attentions.'

'There is no obvious sign that anything has been removed,' I observed. 'Perhaps the damage to the doors was done some time ago.'

Holmes shook his head. 'Where the wood by the lock is splintered, the exposed surfaces are pale and freshly revealed. This cupboard was certainly the focus of the intruder's interest.' He pulled a few papers from the shelves at random and examined them. 'Personal documents,' said he at length; 'old receipts and accounts, private correspondence, letters from Hoare and Co, the bankers in Fleet Street, all jumbled together. It does not appear that the precise habits of mind for which Sir Gilbert Cheshire's professional life was noted were applied with such rigour to his personal affairs. These documents are in a very disordered state!'

In this cold-blooded, detached and business-like manner, my companion sifted carefully through the documents for some time. For my own part, I could not but think of the man so recently and hideously murdered in the room below us, and feel a distinct sense of unease at rifling so freely through his private papers.

'There is nothing of interest here,' said Holmes at length, 'and no obvious reason why anyone should be so keen to gain access to this cupboard.'

He pushed back the last bundle of papers and stood in thoughtful silence for several minutes, until there came the sound of a footstep on the stair and a moment later Inspector Stoddard entered the room.

'Ah! There you are, gentlemen!' said he. 'I thought you would wish to know that Mr Oliver Brown, the deputy head of chambers, has now arrived, as has Elijah Smith, the chief clerk. The junior clerk, Peter Russell, will not be coming. He has been ill all week and has spent the past four days in bed, attended by a doctor.' Stoddard paused a moment, then added in a lower tone: 'I must also tell you that there has been another odd development. Mr Justice Nellington has just called in with some surprising information.'

'Nellington the High Court judge?'

'Indeed, Mr Holmes. He says that he was passing these chambers at about five past eight and heard raised voices. He paused for a moment and as he did so he heard a loud voice say "I have returned!"'

'Nothing else?'

'He says he is a little hard of hearing and, besides, he did not linger, as he was already late for an appointment at Lord Justice Beningfield's lodgings, in Mitre Court. He has been there all evening and heard only a short while ago of the tragedy which has occurred here.'

'How very curious!' said I, as my friend shook his head, his brow furrowed with thought.

'Yes – if one can credit it,' remarked the policeman, in a doubtful tone. 'Might I enquire what has brought you up here, gentlemen?'

Holmes described briefly the trail of tallow, and the forced doors to which it had led us, and Stoddard nodded his head.

'That's one for you, Mr Holmes!' said he. 'I had had a glance up the staircase of course, but did not notice the damaged door, and so did not believe that the intruder had ever been up here. Still, the fact that someone has been rooting around for anything he might find accords with what I had already decided about the matter.'

'Which is?'

'That the assault was made by some low ruffian on the prowl in the fog, who just chanced to pick on these chambers, perhaps because he saw Sir Gilbert entering. No doubt Sir Gilbert offered resistance and received the fatal wound in the struggle. Between you and me, gentlemen, unless we're fortunate enough to light upon some tell-tale clue, which I doubt, or hear something from one of our informers, I don't think we have much chance of ever bringing the crime home. These random burglaries are the very devil to solve!'

'My view of the matter is somewhat different,' Holmes interrupted in a serious tone. 'You say that the evidence of the intruder's presence in this room accords with the view you had already formed. I should have thought it would alter it.'

'A little, perhaps,' Stoddard conceded.

'I should say it alters matters entirely,' Holmes persisted.

'The intruder was obviously a cool hand,' Stoddard began, in a hesitant voice, evidently unsure what the other was driving at, 'to come up here, ransacking the place, when his victim was lying downstairs!'

Holmes shook his head vehemently.

'It will not do, Stoddard!' said he in an emphatic tone. 'How does your theory explain Sir Gilbert's dying words, to which you drew my attention, and the words overheard by Mr Justice Nellington?'

'I mentioned Sir Gilbert's words to you because they were curious, Mr Holmes, but it is obvious that his mind was wandering in delirium and the words are probably of no significance whatever. As to what Mr Justice Nellington says he overheard, I think it very likely that he was simply mistaken. He himself admitted that his hearing is poor. But what, then, may I ask, is your own view of the matter?'

'I should prefer to reserve my opinion for a few more minutes,' replied Holmes. 'It is an interesting case, Stoddard, with some features which may be unique, and I am grateful that you called us in. It is well worth leaving one's fireside for! Let us now go down and hear what the other members of the chambers have to say, and then perhaps we can shed some light upon this most unusual mystery.'

The clerks' office, at the rear of the chambers, contained one large desk in the middle of the room, and a smaller one to the side, with a great number of cupboards and cabinets stacked tightly round the walls. In this room, Holmes and I seated ourselves and a moment later Stoddard entered, accompanied by a tall, portly man, about forty years of age, with thinning hair and a small moustache, whom he introduced as Mr Oliver Brown.

He had left the chambers at about half past six, he informed us, at which time nothing was amiss and there was nothing to indicate that the evening would prove to be at all out of the ordinary. Sir Gilbert Cheshire had been sitting at his desk, reading through a brief, when he bade him good night. No visitors had been expected in the evening, so far as he was aware. After leaving the Temple, he had walked along the Strand to Rule's restaurant, in Maiden Lane, where he had dined alone, leaving shortly before eight o'clock. He had then walked on towards Charing Cross, where he had picked up a cab in the street and driven directly home to his house in Half Moon Street, off Piccadilly.

Holmes then asked him if Sir Gilbert Cheshire had shown any apprehension of danger recently, but he shook his head at this suggestion.

'Not at all,' said he, 'although any such apprehension might not have been apparent, for Sir Gilbert was not one to display emotion at any time. He was a very close man. I have never known him appear either happy or unhappy. He simply pursued his own unswerving course through life.'

'You and he were not on terms of personal friendship?' enquired Holmes after a moment.

'Our relations were purely professional,' the other replied, with a shake of the head. 'I do not believe that Sir Gilbert was ever on terms of personal friendship, as you put it, with anyone. There were a couple of men with whom he would sometimes smoke a cigar after dinner, but that, to the best of my knowledge, was the extent of his social recreation. It was not popularity he desired, but professional success and his desire for that was unbounded. It was for that reason that I was confident, when he assumed the headship of these chambers, ten years ago, that our practice would quickly recover from the tragedy of Sir John Hawkesworth's death. Sir Gilbert was very highly regarded at that time, professionally speaking, and had always had very great ambitions. It had been apparent to me for years that he greatly desired the headship and also to become a bencher of the Temple. He and Sir John had quarrelled frequently, for it was his opinion, often forcibly expressed, that Sir John was deliberately holding him back, by reserving all the most attractive briefs for himself.'

'And your opinion?' queried Holmes.

'I did not agree, but I kept my thoughts to myself, for I was the junior at the time and my opinion would not have been welcomed. Sir John Hawkesworth was a fine man, as highly regarded for his personal qualities as for his professional excellence. He was always extremely kind and encouraging to me and I cannot believe he would ever have acted meanly to a subordinate. His whole character forbade such a thought. Since his death, however, our chambers have acquired a reputation for grim efficiency. "North Walk Chambers will win your case for you", people say, "but do not expect to be much cheered by the experience".'

'Presumably, you will now become leading counsel in these chambers,' observed Holmes.

The barrister hesitated a moment before replying. 'I am not at all sure that I want the position,' said he at length. 'There seems a curse upon the place. No man, surely, would be eager to remain upon the scene of such terrible and inexplicable bloodshed?'

'Did such thoughts ever trouble Sir Gilbert Cheshire?' queried Holmes.

'He never once spoke of Sir John's murder to me,' replied Brown, 'and I cannot therefore say what his thoughts upon the matter may have been. As he was such a cold and unemotional man, it may be that he was quite unmoved by thoughts which would have troubled other men.'

Stoddard accompanied Brown back to his office, to fetch the junior barrister, and we sat in silence for some minutes. My friend's brow was furrowed with thought, and it was clear from the fleeting expressions which chased each other across his features that his swift and agile brain was sifting and re-sifting the evidence, and weighing and re-weighing the facts, to find an arrangement which would balance the scales of probability to his satisfaction.

For myself, I confess that the dark events which had occurred seemed like something from an evil dream and I was still shocked by the horror of the scene in Sir Gilbert Cheshire's chamber. For such a tragedy to have befallen the North Walk chambers once was a most terrible misfortune, but for such a thing to have occurred a second time seemed incomprehensible. My thoughts were interrupted by a remark from my companion.

'You realise, of course,' said he in a quiet voice, 'that Mr Brown could have left his restaurant at, say, ten to eight, walked back here and murdered Sir Gilbert at five past eight, retraced his steps to the other end of the Strand and picked up a cab there, as he says.'

'Holmes!' I cried. 'You surely cannot be serious!'

'I merely point out the possibility, Watson. In this fog, much can happen and be observed by no one.'

'But the empty cash-box? Surely therein lies the motive for this terrible crime?'

'I think not, Watson. These are deeper waters than was at first apparent.'

Stoddard returned before I could question my companion further, accompanied by a young man of about seven and twenty, introduced to us as Stephen Lewis, junior counsel of the chambers. He was a tall, remarkably thin man, with dark hair and a clean-shaven face, which was as white as paper. It was apparent from the nervousness of his manner and the tremor in his voice as he spoke that he was in a state of some considerable agitation. He took a silver cigarette-case from his pocket as he sat down, extracted a cigarette and lit it.

'Such a terrible thing to have happened,' said he after a moment, 'and to such an eminent and highly respected man.'

'Indeed,' responded Holmes in a sympathetic tone. 'I understand, however, that for all his professional eminence, Sir Gilbert was not an especially popular man.'

'That can scarcely be denied,' replied Lewis after a moment's hesitation, in a cautious tone. 'He was known by many people, but intimate with none. I know of no one who considered himself a particular friend of his. He conducted his relations with people at arm's length, so to speak.'

'Was there, then, anyone who might be considered an enemy?'

'None that I am aware of. He had occasionally received abuse from criminals whom he had failed to save, but nothing of the sort recently. For several weeks – almost all the Michaelmas term, in fact – we have been appearing for the defence in the Brockwell Heath Case, which finally reached its conclusion on Tuesday, and in which we were completely successful. One might imagine that that would be a cause for celebration, but Sir Gilbert's mood appeared unaffected. His character was saturnine and dark at the best of times, but recently he had seemed in an even darker mood than usual, and for the past couple of days he had been as limp as a rag and unable to concentrate on the next brief.'

'Do you know anything of the death of your uncle, Sir John Hawkesworth?' queried Holmes after a moment.

'Very little,' Lewis replied, shaking his head. 'I was a mere schoolboy when it occurred, away at Rugby. I know no more of it than anyone might who read his newspaper. The accepted theory, I understand, was that Sir John was assaulted by a thief, who had intended to take his door-key and use it to gain entry to these chambers, but who fled upon realising that his attack, intended to incapacitate his victim, had in fact killed him.'

'And yet, the assault was an exceptionally ferocious one, as I recall,' remarked Holmes, 'Sir John being bludgeoned again and again, in a manner suggesting that the assailant intended more than merely to temporarily incapacitate him.'

'Then it is inexplicable.'

'You have heard, I take it, that Sir Gilbert's last words were "It was he – Sir John Hawkesworth"?'

'Indeed. That, too, is inexplicable.'

'What, if I may ask, brought you back through the Temple this evening, Mr Lewis? I understand that you were walking back from Brixton, to your lodgings in Bedford Place. But surely a more direct route would have taken you across Waterloo Bridge and up Bow Street?'

'That is true,' the other conceded; 'but, as you correctly perceive, I made a detour. I was disappointed at missing my friend and determined to seek out another, a fellow-barrister, who has chambers in King's Bench Walk. Alas, he was absent, too. I therefore resigned myself to a solitary evening and set off, finally, for home. But my way from King's Bench Walk to the Fleet Street gateway brought me past the end of the North Walk, and when I saw the door of our own chambers standing wide open, and the light streaming out of it, I hurried to determine the reason.'

'You suspected something amiss?'

'Very definitely. I knew Sir Gilbert to be a most careful man. He would no more leave his front door open at night than he would leave his purse at the foot of Nelson's Column.'

'And you can shed no light on what has happened?'

'None whatever.'

Elijah Smith, the chief clerk, was next shown in. He was a medium-sized man of about fifty, with a pale, clean-shaven face and a nervous manner. He informed us that there were just two keys to the cash-box, one kept by him and the other on Sir Gilbert Cheshire's watch-chain. He also confirmed that the amount of money missing was as stated in the ledger which Stoddard had shown us.

'Is there any reason why Sir Gilbert should have been looking in the cash-box this evening?' enquired Holmes.

'None whatever, sir. He always left all such matters to me. Every Friday morning I take round to the bank any cheques received during the week and any cash which is surplus to our immediate requirements.'

'At what time did you last speak to your employer?'

'Just as I was leaving, sir; shortly after half past five. His manner was exactly as usual.'

'And you have not seen him since?'

'No, sir. I ate at home with the family, then went round about seven o'clock to see my brother, who lives a short distance away, in Clerkenwell, and was there until the police-constable called.'

After Smith and Stoddard had left us, Holmes sat a while in silent thought. Then he stood up abruptly, as if having reached a decision, and took a few sheets of blank foolscap from the desk.

'Come,' said he. 'Let us see if we cannot make more definite progress.'

'Do you see any likelihood of ever apprehending the criminal?' I asked.

'I have hopes,' said he. 'It rather depends on the statements I shall now take, in the other office.'

In the hallway we met Inspector Stoddard who had just come in through the front door of the chambers.

'I have had another word with Mason, the gate-keeper,' said he. 'He says he remembers now that he saw someone he did not recognise, loitering in King's Bench Walk at about half past four, just as it was getting dark; but as that way through the Temple is used by all manner of people simply as a short-cut from the Strand to Blackfriars Bridge, he did not think it worth mentioning before.'

'That is interesting,' said Holmes. 'Would you be so good as to ask Mason to step across here, Stoddard?'

The junior barristers' office was similar in size to Sir Gilbert Cheshire's, but of a somewhat more cluttered appearance. The fire had been banked up and blazed fiercely in the grate, so that the room was free of the dank, chill atmosphere that pervaded the rest of the chambers. Oliver Brown sat at his desk, a brandy glass in his hand, staring gloomily across the room, and did not look up as we entered. Stephen Lewis was sitting beside the hearth, his head in his hands. The chief clerk, Elijah Smith, was perched on the edge of a chair beside the window, a nervous expression on his face.

'Do you think that we might be permitted to leave soon?' Brown enquired of us. 'It's getting very late and I can't think that there is anything more we can tell you.'

'Very shortly,' returned my companion. 'If you would just be so good as to sign a formal statement, as to when you last saw Sir Gilbert Cheshire alive and your subsequent whereabouts this evening.'

Stoddard had entered as he spoke, accompanied by the ginger-haired gate-keeper.

'There is no need—' began the policeman, but Holmes interrupted him.

'As you say, Inspector, there is no need to wait until tomorrow. We may as well get it over with now and then we shall not need to trouble anyone further. You say you left these chambers at half past six,' he continued, addressing Brown, 'at which time Sir Gilbert was alive and well, walked to Rule's, where you passed an hour, and then took a cab home.'

'That is correct,' the other replied.

'Would you mind signing this paper to that effect, then?' said Holmes, who had scribbled a few lines on one of his sheets of foolscap.

Brown took the sheet from him with a suspicious narrowing of the eyes. 'I do not understand the purpose of this,' said he, glancing at what Holmes had written, and making no move to pick up a pen, 'nor what you suppose its legal status might be.'

'Its legal status,' returned Holmes, 'is simply that it is a statement of the facts, according to you and, as such, you can scarcely object to signing it.'

The other man grunted and, with a show of reluctance, took a pen and signed the paper with a flourish. Holmes then repeated his questions to Lewis, who also signed the paper. He then turned to the chief clerk, scribbled down a couple of lines and passed across the sheet, which Elijah Smith signed slowly and carefully.

'Now, Mr Mason,' Holmes continued, turning to the gate-keeper: 'You last saw Sir Gilbert Cheshire alive at about twenty to seven, I understand.'

'That's right; when I brought in some coal and raked the grates out.'

'And you did not see him again?'

'No, sir, I didn't. I met a friend of mine in the Cock, just afore seven, and was there till twenty to eight, when I came home.'

'Very well. If you will just sign this?'

Mason appended his signature to the few lines which Holmes had written and returned the paper to him. Brown drained his glass, set it down on the desk-top and wiped his moustache.

'Will that be all?' said he in a weary voice.

'We have finished here now,' said Stoddard. 'My men can find no clue, so we may as well lock up, Mr Holmes, and let these gentlemen get off home. We can do no more tonight.'

'I would wish to give you my view of the matter first,' said Holmes, in a tone which commanded attention.

'Very well,' responded the policeman. The others, who had stood up and begun to put on their coats, sat back down again, their expressions a mixture of curiosity and resignation.

'This brutal and shocking crime,' began Holmes, 'appeared at first to be the work of an unknown assailant, someone to whom Sir Gilbert Cheshire had probably opened the door himself and who had then, at the point of his knife, forced Sir Gilbert to open the cash-box, and had, in the course of a struggle, inflicted the wound which killed him.'

'That must be so,' observed Brown, nodding.

'However,' Holmes continued, 'our investigation of the premises has revealed a number of features which cast doubt on such an interpretation. In the first place, there is no evidence of a struggle having taken place. In the second, it is apparent that the intruder lit a candle in the hallway and passed upstairs with it, where he forced entry to Sir Gilbert's private study and broke open a cupboard there, containing personal documents and records.'

There was a murmur of interest at this information and then a silence fell upon the chamber once more, as Holmes continued:

'Once Sir Gilbert had returned from the dining-hall, all the gas would be lit – as indeed was the case when Mr Ormerod passed and saw the open door – and it would therefore have been perfectly pointless for anyone to have lit a candle. Nor, once the downstairs gas was lit, need the intruder have feared that lighting the upstairs gas-jets would increase the chances of his being detected. It seems clear, then, that the intruder lit his candle when there was no other illumination in the chambers, that is to say, before Sir Gilbert returned from dinner. No doubt he lit a candle in order to keep the light to a minimum and hoped to have finished what he was doing before Sir Gilbert returned. But it follows from this, that he was not admitted to the premises by Sir Gilbert, but admitted himself, there being no one else here at the time. It further follows from this that the intruder had his own key, for the door would certainly have been locked.'

There was an odd stillness in the chamber, as those present absorbed this information. Each must have realised, as did I, that the four men who possessed a key to the North Walk Chambers were all together in the room at that moment.

'Now,' continued Holmes, 'we know that Sir Gilbert left the dining-hall a little earlier than was his habit, in order to return here to work. We may suppose, then, that the intruder, believing himself to have time in hand, was surprised when he heard the unlocking of the front door. He must have extinguished his candle, descended to the ground floor and, in his turn, surprised Sir Gilbert in his office. We do not know what Sir Gilbert's reaction was, but it is clear that he knew the intruder, for a second chair was moved behind the desk and placed beside his own: it does not seem likely that a stranger, threatening Sir Gilbert with a knife, would have troubled to procure a chair for himself. The two men evidently sat in discussion for some time. The fact that the cash-box was open before the attack took place suggests that money came into this discussion. What happened next we cannot say for certain, but it seems likely that there was a disagreement, as a result of which the intruder inflicted the fatal wound upon Sir Gilbert.

'The evidence of the wound itself is in my view inconclusive as to whether the assailant was right-handed or left-handed, although I incline to the latter. The evidence of the tallow which dripped from the candle, however, indicates clearly that the man who held it is left-handed. A man may generally carry a candle in the right or left hand with indifference, but if he has work to do – especially work which involves the application of force, such as the bursting open of a door, or a cupboard – he will always pass the candle to his weaker hand. For most people, who are right-handed, this will be the left hand, but tonight's intruder held the candle in his right hand, while forcing the locks with a metal rod held in his left. He is therefore, beyond a shadow of a doubt, left-handed. Having conducted a little handwriting experiment, I am now in a position to state that there is only one man who both possesses a key to these chambers and who is left-handed.'

As Sherlock Holmes spoke these last words, he turned to Thomas Mason, the gate-keeper, whose face had assumed the colour of putty.

'It's a lie!' cried he in a hoarse voice, springing unsteadily to his feet. 'I was never in here!'

'In that case,' said Holmes, 'you can have no objection to a search being made of your quarters.'

'You've no right to do that!' retorted Mason, in a loud, strident voice.

'We'll see about that!' Stoddard interrupted. 'Thomas Mason: I am arresting you on suspicion of having been involved in the death of Sir Gilbert Cheshire. You will accompany me to your lodgings where a search will be undertaken for evidence.'

The inspector and two constables escorted their prisoner from the chambers, leaving the three others in a dazed state, their features displaying the shock and amazement they clearly felt. Sherlock Holmes lit his pipe and sat smoking in silence for several minutes, his brow furrowed with thought.

'It may be that the right man has been arrested,' said Brown at length; 'but the whole affair is still dark to me. I have a feeling that we do not yet know all that there is to know of the matter. Can you enlighten us any further, Mr Holmes? Do you believe there was any meaning in Sir Gilbert's dying words, or was the poor fellow simply raving?'

'Sir Gilbert's words,' Holmes replied, 'as reported by Mr Ormerod, began, if you recall, "It was he", and ended with "Sir John Hawkesworth", with a gap of a few moments in between, during which he struggled for breath. I suspect that in those words Sir Gilbert was attempting to name his murderer.'

'But that is madness!' cried Brown. 'Sir John was himself murdered ten years ago.'

'Quite so. I therefore suggest that a phrase is missing from the sentence, which Sir Gilbert was unable to articulate. The likeliest candidate is something such as "the man that murdered", so that the whole sentence would be "It was he: the man that murdered Sir John Hawkesworth".'

'Good Lord!' cried Lewis.

'However,' continued Holmes, 'if it was Sir Gilbert's intention to identify his assailant in this way, it follows that he himself was aware of who had murdered his predecessor. This raises the question as to how he knew this with such certainty and, if he did, why he had never made public his knowledge.'

'It could be that Mason informed him this very evening that he was the murderer of Sir John,' I suggested.

'Yes, that is possible, Watson, but on the whole I incline to the view that Sir Gilbert already knew the truth behind Sir John's death, had known about it, in fact, for ten years.'

'I find that suggestion quite incredible,' said Brown in a tone of disbelief.

'No doubt,' said Holmes. 'Nevertheless, the indications are there. In the first place,' he continued, in his precise, methodical manner, like a specialist delivering a lecture, 'it is well known that fifteen years ago, Sir Gilbert secured Mason's acquittal on a charge of murder. Presumably Mason felt some gratitude for this. But then we hear that, about eight years ago, Sir Gilbert, actuated by sympathy at Mason's plight, secured him a distinctly undemanding post as gate-keeper here. There seems something wrong with this: Sir Gilbert was not known for any great degree of sympathy; and the favour seems the wrong way about. It is as if there is some link missing from the chain of cause and effect, as we have it at present.'

'Just what are you suggesting?' said Brown sharply.

Before Holmes could reply, the door opened and Inspector Stoddard entered. He informed us that the search of Mason's quarters had revealed a large sharp knife, its blade caked in blood, and a long thin chisel, both wrapped in a blood-stained shirt, and hidden under a sink. An amount of money exactly matching that missing from the cash-box had also been found, in a canvas bag inside a coal-scuttle. Mason had offered no resistance to the search and had shown no surprise when the above articles had been discovered, but had made one surprising request, that he be allowed to make a statement to the gentlemen awaiting his return in the North Walk Chambers.

'I am sure we should have no objection to that proposal, if you do not,' said Holmes.

'Very well, then,' said Stoddard. 'I have already cautioned the prisoner that anything which he chooses to say in his statement may be given against him in court.'

The prisoner was brought in then, his wrists manacled together, and, standing before us, made the following voluntary statement. In the interests of clarity, I have made one or two very slight alterations, but otherwise the statement is exactly as Thomas Mason made it to us that night:

'Yes, I killed Sir Gilbert Cheshire. I see there is no point in denying it now, and I'm not proud of it. But you ought to know that whatever they say about him in the newspapers, and whatever people might think, he weren't so marvellous, neither.

'I first met him when I was accused of murdering my wife and he was assigned to defend me. I was in Newgate when he came to see me. "Don't worry," says he; "I'll get you off." He knew I'd done it, although he never asked me outright. Things was looking black against me and I'd given up thinking about ever getting out; but somehow, in the court, it all came out different. One or two of the witnesses seemed to change their minds about what they were going to say, and Sir Gilbert spoke for such a long time and in such a confusing way, that in the end the jury decided I hadn't done it after all and I could go free.

'I was grateful to Sir Gilbert. I didn't know how he'd done it, but I knew it was him I had to thank for the fact that I wasn't swinging on the end of a rope. But things wasn't so rosy with me even if I was free. I was a slater by trade, but now I couldn't find any work nowhere. The trouble was, a lot of people – all the wife's relations and half the district – knew that I had done it, really, and they wasn't likely to employ me, and I couldn't blame 'em for that. I tried all sorts of different lines, went halfway round the world in a clipper one year, but was still no better off when, about four year on from my trial, I was coming along Carey Street one afternoon, when who should step out of a bookshop in front of me but Sir Gilbert Cheshire.

'"Hallo, Thomas," says he, cool as you like. "How are you keeping yourself?"

'"Not so well as I'd like, sir," said I. "I haven't had more than a tanner in my pocket any time in the past four years."

'"I'm sorry to hear that, Thomas," says he, in a thoughtful voice. "You are still grateful for the little favour I did you the other year?" When I said course I was, he says "Then I have a little favour to ask of you in return, Thomas. Be under the Holborn Viaduct at seven o'clock this evening," says he, "and I'll tell you what I'd like you to do." He slipped two bob into my hand then and walked off.

'When I saw him later, he told me what was in his mind. It seems there was someone standing in his way, professionally speaking, and preventing the light shining on him as he'd like. "If he could be put out of the way for a time," says Sir Gilbert in that slow cunning way of his, "I might find it convenient. And you might find, Thomas, that there was something in it for you, too."

'To make the matter brief: the party's name was Hawkesworth, Sir Gilbert told me exactly what to do and I done it. He'd given me some money beforehand and told me to lie low for a while afterwards, then come back after a year or so and he'd find me a job. Which I did.

'That was all ten year ago. Things have been all right since, but I've never had much money, and when I asked him, the other week, if he could let me have a bit more, he says I couldn't have none. Well, I said this and he said that, and it got so we was almost at each other's throats; and then I said I could stir up plenty of trouble for him if he didn't do right by me. "Oh? How's that?" said he in a cool voice; so I told him: I'd saved a note he'd sent to me in connection with the Hawkesworth job, which he'd told me to burn. I've always found that when someone tells you to burn something, it generally pays to hang on to it.

'"That note won't prove anything," says he; "I didn't commit myself in it."

'"Perhaps not," says I, "but it'll certainly start some rumours off."

'"You'll condemn yourself if you produce that," says he.

'"Oh no I won't, see, 'cause it's not got my name on it and I'll send it anonymously to his Honour, the Head of the Bench."

'I could see that this had worried him. He bit his lip and thought for a while.

'"When I saved you from the gallows," says he in a quiet voice, "some evidence came my way which ended up locked in my private cupboard. If you threaten me, Mason, that evidence will come back out of my cupboard again and you'll swing for it."

'"I know the law," says I. "I've been tried once and found not guilty. I can't be tried again, whatever you come up with."

'At this he laughed. "Dear me!" says he, cackling like a hen. "Dear me, Thomas! You know the law, do you? Well, let me tell you, my man, that I'm the expert, and I tell you that with the evidence I've got hidden away, you could be re-charged, with slightly different words on the indictment, and you'd hang as sure as you're standing here now! If you give me any more trouble, that evidence comes out of my cupboard!"'

'That was a lie,' Brown interrupted. 'You could not be charged again with the same crime.'

'Mebbe it was, but it put the wind up me, anyhow. I didn't say nothing then, but I made my mind up to break into his blessed cupboard one night when he wasn't there and see if I couldn't find his precious evidence. I've had a bit of a wait for the right time, 'cause the gentlemen have all been working late recently, but tonight looked a fair chance, so in I went. I thought I'd have plenty of time, but – curse my luck – he came back early from his supper and heard me moving about, so I had to go down and face him out. He got a surprise when I walked into his office.

'"What the devil are you doing here, Mason!" he cried in a loud, unpleasant tone. "I thought I'd seen the last of you for today!"

'"I have returned," I shouted back at him, "to find that evidence you've got against me."

'"What!" says he in an angry voice. "You've been in my private rooms? This is the last straw, Mason! It's time for you and me to part company altogether."

'"Give me some money and I'll go as fast as you like," says I, as hot as he was.

'"Very well." says he; "and then I never want to see you again as long as I live."

'He fetched the big cash-box and opened it up with the key on his watch-chain, but there was little enough in it.

'"I thought there'd be more than this," says he.

'"Oh, did you?" says I, thinking he was trying to play a game, with me as the fool. I had my knife out and at his throat before he could move. "You find some more," says I, "or you won't leave this room alive."

'"You can't threaten me," says he, and made a grab at the knife. But quick as he moved, so did I and the knife went straight into his throat. I didn't mean to do it, but he brought it on himself, and that's the Gospel truth, if I have to swing for it.'

We all sat in silence as this remarkable and terrible tale ended with these words, and remained in silence after Stoddard had taken his prisoner away. Then Sherlock Holmes stood up, took his hat and coat, and we prepared to leave.

'Can all this be true?' said Brown, in a tone of stupefaction.

'I rather fancy it is,' said Holmes, 'and that Sir Gilbert Cheshire learnt too late that he who conceals a serpent within his bosom will at last feel the serpent's bite himself.'

—————

The following morning's newspapers had been printed too early to include news of Mason's arrest, and it was left to the evening papers to apprise their readers of the latest developments. But by then this remarkable case had produced a further surprise, and I remember vividly the shock with which I read the heading in the *St James's Gazette*: 'TEMPLE MURDER: ESCAPE OF CHIEF SUSPECT'. It appeared from the account given beneath this heading that very soon after he had left us the night before, Mason had suddenly broken from the grasp of the policemen who held him, dashed away, and vanished into the dense, swirling fog.

For twenty-four hours he was sought in vain. But late the following night, a police-constable saw a man crossing London Bridge whom he recognised from the description as Mason and gave chase across the bridge. Summoned by the first man's whistle, a second officer made his way on to the bridge from the Southwark side and Mason, seeing that there was no chance of escape in either direction, threw himself from the parapet of the bridge into the blackness of the river below. The River Police were at once notified and an organised search made, but no trace of the fugitive was discovered.

Three days later, Sherlock Holmes received a letter by the last post which he read and passed to me without comment. It ran as follows:

MY DEAR MR HOLMES,

This is to inform you that a body was washed up by Wapping Old Stairs early this morning, which has now been identified as that of Thomas Mason. The doctor says that his skull is fractured, which was the cause of death, and it is thought likely that he struck his head on one of the stone piers of the bridge when he jumped. I have now made a full report to my superiors of all the facts of which I am aware, and both the Cheshire case and the Hawkesworth case are now officially closed. Thanking you for your great help in the matter, I remain – Yours very sincerely,

DAVID STODDARD

The Secret of Shoreswood Hall

I: The Strange Story of Amelia Davenoke

Of all the many curious cases to which the singular skills of Mr Sherlock Holmes were applied during the time we shared chambers together, there is none I can recall in which the circumstances were of a more dramatic or surprising character than that which concerned the well-known Suffolk family of Davenoke. The sombre and striking events which followed on so rapidly from the marriage of the Davenoke heir and the death of his father were accorded considerable publicity at the time, so that there will be few among my readers who are entirely ignorant of the matter; but the contemporary accounts all suffered from a want of accuracy, and all too often it was sought to remedy a deficiency of fact with a surfeit of imagination, with the result that a cheap and sensational gloss was put on an affair whose macabre details stood in no need of such adornment. It is with the intention, then, of supplying the first full and accurate account of the matter, and of correcting certain prevalent misapprehensions, that the following narrative is set down.

In the latter part of August, 1887, the bright if uncertain glories of an English summer were succeeded by a period of heavy and stifling weather. With each day that passed the air seemed yet more still and close, until I longed for a fresh breeze to blow away the overpowering heat and stickiness. Throughout the day our windows were thrown open to their widest extent, but it did little to relieve the oppressive airlessness of our rooms.

I had descended to breakfast that morning to find Sherlock Holmes in a morose humour. Without comment, he passed across the table a letter he had received by the first post. It was addressed from Phillimore Gardens, Kensington, and dated the previous evening.

'Shall call upon you at ten o'clock, tomorrow morning,' I read. 'The matter is most urgent and important, and will require your undivided attention.' No details were given as to the nature of the problem, but the word 'important' had been underscored three times, the last one ripping the paper clean through. At the foot of the sheet was the signature 'Amelia Davenoke'. I looked up to find Holmes's expressionless grey eyes upon me.

'The lady is perhaps a trifle imperious in her tone,' he remarked, 'but she may be permitted our indulgence, for she is evidently in some distress. The violent underlining has clearly not been done for the reader's benefit, for her pen has run out of ink halfway through it and she has not troubled to re-ink it. We may take it, then, to be more an expression of her own anguish.'

'I seem to remember reading that Sir John Davenoke died not long ago,' I remarked. 'Your correspondent is probably his widow.'

Holmes shook his head. 'He himself had been a widower for some time,' he replied. He took a heavy red-bound volume from his long shelf of reference-books and turned the pages over for a few moments. 'Here we are,' said he, seating himself upon an arm of the fireside chair: '"John Arthur Cavendish Davenoke: Sixth baronet; Member of Parliament for Shoreswood and Soham, '84 to '86. The family has held the manor of Shoreswood in East Suffolk for over five hundred years and was closely allied in the fifteenth century with the Pole family, former Dukes of Suffolk, prior to the downfall of the latter." – a somewhat ancient claim upon our interest, I am afraid – "Arms: argent, gouttée de sang, a lion vorant sable in a bordure of the same."' Holmes shut the book with a bang. 'There is one son who succeeds him, Edward Hurst Geoffrey. Amelia Davenoke is presumably his wife.' He glanced at his watch. 'If her punctuality matches the urgency of her letter, she will be here in ten minutes, Watson, so if you could ring for the maid to clear the breakfast things, I should be most obliged.'

I was seated by the window, reading *The Times*, when our visitor arrived. She was a slight, pretty, almost elfin young woman, with very thick hair of a reddish, copper colour, and seemed as she entered our little room, looking hesitantly this way and that, like an angel from a Renaissance painting. Her appearance would have been striking upon any occasion, but was the more remarkable now for the deadly pallor of her face and the dark, almost black shadows which surrounded her restless, haunted eyes, all of which bespoke some grave anxiety. Beneath the light grey cloak which she handed me, she wore a simple dress of plain moss-green, relieved only by a touch of butter-coloured lace about the neck and wrists. She took the chair which my friend offered her and sat a few moments in silence, her fingers nervously twining and untwining.

'Well, well, Lady Davenoke,' said Holmes at length; 'I understand from your note that you wish to consult me upon a matter of some urgency.'

'That is true,' returned our visitor quickly, raising her watery green eyes to meet my friend's steady gaze. I was surprised to hear that her accent was of the very richest North American. 'Your name was mentioned to me last night by Lady Congrave,' she continued, 'who said she could not speak too highly of you. I gathered that you performed some service for her.'

'A trifling affair, as I recall it, involving a little missing jewellery.'

'I fancy that Lady Congrave herself would not dismiss the matter so lightly,' Lady Davenoke replied with some emphasis. 'I have come to you because I, too, have lost something.'

'Jewellery?'

'My husband.'

Holmes's eyebrows went up in surprise. 'Perhaps you could enlarge upon the matter,' said he.

'Do not misunderstand me, Mr Holmes, if I say that I have come to you as a last resort. My meaning is simply this: that if you fail, then all further hope is useless, for I fear that no one else can help me. Alone I can do nothing. My husband has vanished and left me in dread, surrounded by mysterious forces against which I am powerless to defend myself.'

'My dear madam,' interjected my friend in his most soothing tones; 'it is plain to see that you have been under some great strain lately; but whatever can have occurred to cause you to speak in this fashion?'

She did not reply at once, but passed her hand across her face, as if in an effort to clear her troubled brow. 'Mr Holmes,' said she at length, her voice low and tremulous, 'I have entered the realm of fear and horror, and it seems I may never return. I have, all unwitting, become party to some dark and hidden transaction, some hideous and nameless menace, which surrounds me even now as I speak to you.' She put her hand abruptly to her throat and her eyes darted nervously round the room.

'Lady Davenoke,' began Holmes in a tone of mild reproof. But even as he spoke, her eyes rolled up to the ceiling, a faint gasp escaped her lips and she pitched forward upon the hearth-rug in a dead faint.

We bore her swiftly to the sofa, where I placed a pillow beneath her head. Her pulse was faint, her brow horribly cold and clammy, and for a moment I feared that she would require greater medical attention than could be provided in our small sitting-room. An application of brandy to the lips brought some colour to her cheek, however, and her eyelids flickered and indicated returning consciousness. Then, suddenly, with a startling abruptness, her eyes opened wide and she cried out in a terrible wailing voice.

'The window!' she cried. 'There is something there, outside! Oh, close the window, for the love of God!' Her cries ended in a dreadful, piteous sob and she sank back into unconsciousness.

'Her eyes were not seeing us,' remarked Holmes softly.

I nodded. 'She was undergoing some strange delusion, but it appears to have passed now; her face is relaxed once more.'

We covered her with a blanket and rang for some hot tea. Our landlady was most concerned at the state of the poor young woman, for she had heard her terrible cries and she insisted upon sitting with her until she was fully recovered. Her pulse was steady now and her breathing smooth and regular, and after a short while she opened her eyes again and gazed weakly at us, a look of incomprehension upon her face.

'You've had a faint, my dear,' said Mrs Hudson in a kindly voice, taking the other's hand in hers; 'but you will be all right in a moment, when you've got some hot tea inside you.'

'You are among friends, Lady Davenoke,' said Holmes. 'You have nothing to fear.'

'Oh, if only that were true, Mr Holmes; if only that were true!'

'Perhaps when you are recovered you can give us the details of the matter and then we shall see if we can't set about allaying your anxieties.'

Thus it was that ten minutes later, fortified by strong tea and composed once more, Amelia Davenoke began her strange tale. She was, as my friend had surmised, the wife of Sir Edward Davenoke, who had recently succeeded to the baronetcy upon the death of his father.

'Let us first be clear as to the essential facts,' said Holmes as his client hesitated a moment. He laid out his note-book upon his knee in a brisk and business-like manner. 'Your husband has disappeared. Were you in London at the time?'

Lady Davenoke shook her head. 'No, no; Montpelier, in the south of France.'

'Indeed! And did you report his disappearance to the authorities there?'

Again she shook her head. 'What could they know of it?' she queried in a surprised voice. 'Edward was not in Montpelier, but at Shoreswood.'

Holmes put down his pencil with a sigh.

'My questions seem to create only confusion,' said he, a flicker of a smile upon his lips. 'Perhaps if you tell your story in your own words, the matter will be clearer.'

'Where should I begin?'

'If your troubles began with your husband's disappearance, then begin there; if not, begin at any point that strikes you as appropriate. How you order your account is of less importance than that it is complete.'

'Then I feel I must begin a year ago, when Edward and I first met,' said Lady Davenoke after she had considered the matter in silence for a little while. 'For it seems to me now – but, still, you will understand how it seems to me when you have heard what I have to tell you.'

'By all means,' said Holmes, leaning back in his chair and closing his eyes in an attitude of concentration.

'My maiden name was Adams,' his client continued after a moment. 'My father is Claude Adams, the railroad proprietor. He was in at the beginning of the railroad boom in the States, and the Portland and Vermont made his fortune. He had had little education himself and, now that he was wealthy, was determined that his children should make up for what he himself had lacked. So it was that I came last year to Europe, with my aunt, Juliana Clemens. We were making a grand tour of all that was venerable and historic, and it was while we were in Florence, in July, that I made the acquaintance of Edward Davenoke.

'He seemed to me the most pleasant and engaging young man I had ever met, and we soon struck up a fine friendship. His appearance was thoughtful and studious, especially when he wore his spectacles, but he had a most vivacious sense of fun which was never long repressed. He had with him a Belgian Sheepdog called Bruno, which he had acquired on his travels, and the two of them would sport about the noble streets and squares of Florence in the most incongruous and humorous way imaginable. All too soon after we had become friends, Edward was obliged to return home, to Shoreswood in Suffolk, but before he left he requested that my aunt and I call upon him when we visited England, later in the year. My aunt saw no objection to this suggestion and a date was fixed for our visit, in the fall of last year. For my own part I confess that the remainder of our European tour seemed dull and uninteresting compared to the time we had spent in Edward's company, and were it not for the letters which we exchanged regularly, I do not know that I could have borne the months which were to pass before our boat sailed for England.

'Eventually the day arrived. When I think now—' She paused and gazed for a moment at her clasped hands. 'When I think now of the happiness I felt on that day—' Again she paused and shook her head slightly. 'To have come three thousand miles, for this!'

Sherlock Holmes opened his eyes and, frowning slightly, made a dismissive gesture with his hand.

'Do not distress yourself unnecessarily, Lady Davenoke,' said he in a soft voice. 'Describe each event in the order in which it occurred and, above all, resist the temptation to compare the present with the past; for in any such comparison the past has always the unfair advantage that one's memory of it is both selective and partial.'

Our visitor smiled thinly, but appreciatively, and, after a moment, resumed her narrative.

'Edward met us at Harwich and escorted us to Shoreswood Old Hall, which has been the seat of the family for centuries. It is a curious and not altogether attractive place; a dark and sombre house, built haphazardly of flint, plaster-work and brick, and lying half in ruins. The Davenokes have always been intensely proud of the richness of history which the house represents; but to me there is something chaotic and unpleasant about the place: if it represents history, then it is history as designed by a madman. The interior of the house presents an equally bizarre muddle, where, coming round some dark and dusty corner of a corridor, one will find an ornate Boulle cabinet standing beside a crude, axe-carved stool. There is much of value and interest in the house – the walls are lined with old paintings and tapestries and hung with weapons and curios of every shape and size – but all is dark and faded, and somehow oppressive. I guess I'm not very familiar with your old English houses, gentlemen, but I am sure they cannot all be like Shoreswood. The passages and stairs are shadowy and cramped, the rooms damp, and infested with mice and spiders. A short distance from the house lies what was once the Davenokes' private chapel but is now a mouldering heap of ivy-covered stones. Even in broad daylight an unpleasant air of misery and ruin hangs over this place, but it is at night, when the moonlight falls upon it, that it assumes its most chill and minatory aspect. The locals, I understand, will not approach within a hundred yards of the place after sunset.' Lady Davenoke's voice faltered and an involuntary shudder shook her whole body.

'But at first, although I can scarce believe it now,' she continued after a moment, 'the very oddness and antiquity of Shoreswood intrigued and charmed me. The estate lies in a green and fertile valley, a land of beautiful woodlands and streams, which reminds me very much of my home. My aunt and I took many a pleasant walk with Edward, along the narrow lanes and woodland paths there. His company was a constant and unvarying source of pleasure to me, which is more than I can say for that of his father, I am afraid.' Her voice trembled with emotion and she bit her lip before continuing.

'Sir John could be gay enough at times, when the mood was upon him, but his nature was a precariously balanced one, and a black, bitter side would often show itself for no apparent reason and endure for several days. During these periods it was best to keep out of his way, I found, for he could be harsh and cruel in his speech, and often drank to violent excess. I have since learnt – what is apparently common knowledge in the district – that it was entirely as a result of Sir John's hard and sneering ways that his party lost the parliamentary seat of Shoreswood to their opponents, after it had been held without defeat for very nearly a century. Still, as I disliked and feared the father greatly, so did I love and trust the son to the same degree.

'"You must forgive Father his rough ways," said Edward to me one day, as we sat alone beside a slow, reed-girt stream. "He was not always as you see him now; but Mother's death struck him a grave blow and, to tell the truth, he has never been quite the same man since."

'I was deeply impressed by Edward's concern for my feelings and by his perception of what it was that troubled me; for I had, of course, never voiced my thoughts upon the subject and had striven to conceal my anxieties. In answer to my query, he told me that his mother had died three years previously. She had been on holiday with a cousin in Cornwall and had been stung fatally upon the foot by a weever fish whilst bathing in the sea off St Ives.

"'I am so sorry," said I.

'He shook his head sadly. "She has been greatly missed by everyone," said he. "She was always so generous and considerate. While she lived she had a gentle, uplifting influence upon the whole household; with her death passed away the Shoreswood I had known as a child."

'It was evident that Edward was saddened by the remembrance of these events and I sought to cheer him. I asked him to tell me more of his family. His brow cleared and, with the ready smile which so often illumined his handsome features, he consented.

"'Some say that there has been a streak of insanity in the family all along," he began. My face must have betrayed the surprise I felt at so bald a statement on such a dreadful subject, for Edward took one look at me and let out a roar of laughter. I knew then that he was teasing me, as he had done upon numerous other occasions. I chided him, but could not, I confess, resist a smile myself. There was something so noble and refined about him that the lightest of remarks could sound sublime when it was he who spoke them.

"'I will tell you of the family legend," he continued after a moment, the same smile still playing about his features.

"'Please do," I returned eagerly, for I had heard him allude before to some old legend which concerned his family and their ancestral home at Shoreswood.

"'It is said that the Hall holds a dark secret," he began, "a secret whose origins lie in the distant past. There is, so it is said, a mysterious chamber hidden deep within the bowels of the Hall and it is in this chamber that the secret lies. Of its nature, none can tell. Some say that a terrible monster is kept there, some hideous, unspeakable beast for which the family is in some way responsible; but there are numerous other opinions upon the matter, none of them very pleasant."

'"Surely you do not believe these old legends?"

'"Of course not, dear," Edward replied, smiling warmly and taking my hand in his. "But, really, I can speak with no more authority upon the matter than the local guide-book; for it is only when the heir takes possession of the estate that the secret is vouchsafed to him. It is said, however, that knowledge of the secret turns each happy heir into a sorrowful man."

'"Has your father ever spoken of the legend, or of the secret room?" I asked.

'Edward shook his head. "I used to ask him about it when I was young, but he always brushed aside my questions without answer. Once, however, when I was eighteen, I chanced to raise the subject again, one dark evening after dinner. 'Listen very carefully, Edward,' said my father then, in a grave voice, 'and remember my words. I am going to speak one sentence to you and it will be the only sentence I shall ever speak upon the subject this side of the grave. It is this: The lord of the manor of Shoreswood does not refer to the legend – *never*, you understand – neither of his own volition nor in answer to the question of another.' With that he stood up from the dinner-table and walked from the room in silence. Of course, it all seemed a little exaggerated to me at the time, but I could not help but be deeply impressed by the serious tones in which my father had spoken. Moreover, from that day to this he has been as true as his word."

'"What does it mean, Edward?" I asked, anxious to hear again that laughter which could dispel all my fears and doubts.

'He shook his head, however, and there was a look of perplexity upon his face. "My father is the only one who can answer that question at present," he replied at length, "and he is not disposed to speak upon the matter."

'I did not take any of this very seriously, at the time, Mr Holmes,' said Lady Davenoke in an unsteady voice, 'but now—'

'The old manor-houses of England are full of such legends, Lady Davenoke,' said Holmes briskly. 'They are relics of a bygone age, an age of darkness and superstition, fit material for a history of human folly and wickedness, but of no other value. I have myself often considered writing such a history, but have been deterred by the sheer volume of material available.'

For a second, our client's eyes flashed fire and a look of resolution came over her wan features.

'You would not speak so glibly of old tales had you spent a night at Shoreswood Hall,' said she angrily. 'You would not make merry on human wickedness did you feel it all around you, every waking minute of your life – yes, and in every troubled moment of sleep, too.' She paused for a moment, then continued in an altered tone: 'Oh, but I see it now. I see by your face, Mr Holmes, that you were deliberately provoking me. You hoped to solve my problems for me by ridiculing that which I fear.'

'Nevertheless, Lady Davenoke, what I say is true. There is nothing to be gained by dwelling upon vague and ancient fears.'

'But if the fears become more tangible and immediate?'

'Then they may be justified and I may be able to help you. Pray continue with your story. Despite the various misgivings to which you have alluded, you accepted Edward Davenoke when he asked for your hand, I take it.'

Holmes leaned back in his chair once more, his eyelids drooping, his fingertips together, the very picture of motionless concentration.

'Edward proposed to me on Saturday, November the twenty-seventh, last year,' said our visitor, her eyes shining with evident pleasure at the memory. 'I had never been so happy in my life and, in truth, I believe Aunt Juliana was as thrilled as I was. We at once cabled my parents, who came over as soon as they were able, and we all spent Christmas at Shoreswood, before returning to America in the new year. It had been decided that the wedding would take place here in July, and so it did, just over six weeks ago, on Saturday the eighth. It was then, incidentally, that I first met Lady Congrave, who has recently been so kind to me. She is a distant cousin of Edward's, upon his mother's side.

'We were to have left for the continent immediately afterwards, but Edward's father fell ill on the day of the wedding and our holiday was postponed. Three weeks later, Sir John appeared to be completely recovered and we at length began our foreign travels. Alas! we had been in Paris scarcely two days when news came that he had suffered a relapse and that the doctors feared for his life. Edward at once returned to England, but as arrangements had already been made for us to travel to Montpelier, where friends were expecting us that day, it was decided that I should travel on alone, to explain the circumstances. Edward promised that he would keep me informed by wire as to his father's condition.

'Four days later I received a telegram informing me that Sir John had died in the night. I returned to England as quickly as I could, leaving most of my luggage behind in Montpelier, but it took me a good three days, and by the time I arrived at Harwich I was almost beside myself with tiredness. To my surprise, there was no one there to meet me, nor any message of explanation, although I had sent a wire to Shoreswood, just before I boarded the boat. I wired again from the railroad depot, to say when I should arrive at Wickham Market station, but when the train pulled in there, the only face I recognised was that of Staples, the Shoreswood groom. He is a sour-faced man, certainly not whom I would have chosen to meet me, and I confess I was bitterly disappointed. He informed me, with little effort at civility, that the funeral of his late master had already taken place and that my husband, Sir Edward, as he now was, had left Shoreswood the previous day. This surprised me greatly and I enquired where my husband had gone; but Staples just shrugged his shoulders in a surly fashion and declared that no one had troubled to tell him anything of the matter. If I wished to know more I must enquire of Hardwick, the butler, for he had driven Sir Edward to the railway station.

'When we reached Shoreswood I was further surprised to find that Edward had left no letter of explanation for me. Hardwick seemed most distressed about this and almost came to the point of apologising for it himself, as if he felt he were partly to blame. He is an old and trusted servant, who has been at Shoreswood for many years, and I have no doubt he still regards Edward as the small boy he used to know; but, even allowing for this, his manner struck me as odd and inappropriate, in a way I could not quite define. He informed me that Edward had been obliged to leave for London, to attend to certain urgent matters in connection with his father's estate, but could supply no further details. He had no idea when Edward might return.

'It was scarcely the homecoming I had expected, alone in that unfriendly house, save for a handful of unprepossessing servants, to whom I was a virtual stranger. That night Shoreswood Hall seemed colder and more gloomy than I had ever known it before, but I consoled myself with the thought that Edward and I should no doubt be united once more in a few days' time.'

'One moment,' interrupted Holmes. 'Would you say that your husband's apparently impetuous behaviour was in character, or not?'

'He could he impulsive,' Lady Davenoke replied hesitantly; 'yes, I have known him impulsive in his actions. But he would always keep me informed. I have never known him inconsiderate in that respect before.'

'Perhaps,' suggested Holmes, 'he did not expect to be away very long and thought that he would be back at Shoreswood before you returned from France.'

'It is possible,' returned Lady Davenoke, a note of enthusiasm in her voice. 'Indeed, I think it very possible; I had not looked at the matter in that way before.'

'Well, well, pray proceed with your account.'

'The days passed without any word from Edward and I began to feel that something was very wrong. I felt so isolated and alone in that old dark house. Again I questioned Hardwick, but he could add nothing to what he had already told me.

'"Sir Edward has gone to London," said he. "That is all that I know." And yet, this time I sensed that there was something evasive in his manner, as if perhaps he did know more, after all, but would not admit to it. I felt the same evasiveness when I questioned him as to what Edward had been doing on the days preceding my return. Needless to say, I learnt nothing.

'At night-time my sleep was fitful and light, and I began to fancy that I could hear strange noises somewhere in the still darkness of the old house. Upon the fourth night I was awakened about one o'clock by the distant and muffled barking of a dog. It brought back to my mind Edward's beloved Belgian Sheepdog and I realised that I had not seen the animal since my return. When I enquired of the groom next morning where Bruno might be, I was informed that he was locked up in the stables. I asked for him to be let out, but the man refused in the most surly of tones, saying that he was confined upon his master's own express instructions. Sir Edward had been taking personal charge of the dog's training, Staples informed me, and feared that if he were allowed to roam loose, without his master's control, he would forget all that he had been taught, revert to his former undisciplined state and be forever unmanageable in the future. I argued the point with the groom; but he was adamant that he would not go against what he said my husband had told him and eventually I had to accept it, maddening though it was to yield to his insolent manner. Even the company of animals, I reflected, was denied me.

'I have mentioned that I was having difficulty in sleeping at night, often lying awake for hours at a time, and it was this that took me next day to the family physician, Dr Ruddock. He is a kindly, grey-haired old gentleman, who squinted at me through his old-fashioned gilt pince-nez as I entered his consulting-room. He recommended a herbal infusion for my insomnia and then began to speak to me of the family into which I had so recently married, and to which he had been physician for so many years.

'"They are a highly strung, nervous family," said he. "They find it difficult to approach life calmly, and cannot take rest when they ought. I am hoping," he added with a smile, "that you will have a steadying, calming effect upon young Sir Edward. He is often so serious and intense, and does not feel he can spare the time for leisurely reflection. But he should and you must insist upon it. Matters are rarely so pressing that one cannot lean on a gate-post for five minutes and admire the sunset – yes, and be all the better for it! His father was just the same, you know: always dashing about, as if his life depended upon it. It is my opinion that he might be with us still had he been of a steadier disposition."

"'Of what did he die?" I asked.

'For a moment Dr Ruddock looked surprised. "Did you not know?" said he. "But of course, I was forgetting – you were in France at the time. Sir John had a sudden apoplectic seizure late one night. I was called, but there was nothing that could be done." He shook his head. "To be perfectly frank, it was not entirely unexpected, sad as it was. However, it is Edward's health which has been weighing most heavily upon my mind of late."

'This was news indeed to me, for apart from a slight attack of megrim, to which he is prone, Edward had seemed to me to be in the very best of health when we were last together, in Paris.

"'I suppose the death of his father unseated him a little," replied Dr Ruddock in answer to my query. "The last time I saw him – it would be the day after his father's funeral – he was in a very agitated state. 'Can you give me something to provide me with a little extra energy, Doctor?' said he, gripping my arm nervously as he spoke. 'My dear boy,' I returned at once. 'What you need is a good rest. It is evident that you are overwrought by recent events and by the thought of your new responsibilities. That is understandable, but you must not let things get on top of you. I recommend a week in bed.' 'No, no; I cannot,' said he, shaking his head vigorously. 'I have much to do and no time for lying idly about.' With that he was off, before I could remonstrate with him further."

"'And I suppose you have no idea," I asked, "where it was he was off to with such urgency?"

"'None whatever," replied the kindly old man, with a shake of the head; "nor what it was that he had to do that was so important as to make him ignore his doctor's advice! If it were anything to do with the estate, I imagine his solicitor might know, but I'm afraid that I cannot enlighten you upon the matter."

'I left Dr Ruddock's consulting-room that morning feeling more forlorn than ever. I had the disconcerting sensation that things were afoot of which I knew nothing. Before returning home I visited the church-yard, to pay my last respects to my late father-in-law, and stood long in thought beside his tomb. He at least was now at peace and mundane cares would trouble him no longer; the stewardship of Shoreswood, I reflected with a heavy heart, now lay in Edward's hands and in mine.

'That afternoon I wrote two letters. I had recalled Edward's telling me that, when in London, the family always stayed at the Royal Suffolk Hotel in the City, so I wrote to him there, asking him to get in touch with me and let me know when he would be returning, for I felt in sore need of his company. The second letter was to the family solicitor, Mr Arthur Blackstone of Framlingham, informing him that I should be calling upon him, if it were convenient, in two days' time. I doubted very much that I should learn anything there, but it at least gave me an opportunity to get away for a while from the melancholy loneliness of Shoreswood Hall.

'I took a draught of Dr Ruddock's infusion that night and it seemed to be effective, for I fell asleep more easily than before. Some hours later, however, I was awakened quite abruptly by a noise somewhere in the house. I sat up in bed and listened, my ears straining to catch any sound of the night. For a minute, I heard nothing, then, softly, there came the sound of steps approaching my bedroom door. The flesh upon my face seemed to creep and my heart to stop beating, as those horrible, soft, padded steps came closer. Never in my life had I been so terrified as at that moment. All Edward had told me of the family legend came rushing back to my mind in a confused surge. My throat constricted and I could take no breath. Then, as softly as they had approached, I heard the steps pad away, down the corridor, until I heard them no more.'

'Did the footsteps return the way they had come?' interrupted Holmes, without opening his eyes. 'Did they, that is to say, approach specifically to your door and then recede, or did they merely pass it by as they went from one end of the corridor to the other?'

'I cannot be certain upon the point,' replied our visitor. 'I believe they began at one end of the corridor and ended at the other.'

'Is the situation of your room such that anyone might naturally pass it to reach somewhere else?'

'It is possible. My bedroom is on the ground floor of the west wing – the only part of the house which is inhabited, in fact – and I suppose that one of the servants might have passed my door.'

'You sound doubtful.'

'I cannot imagine what anyone would be doing at that time of night. As far as I knew, everyone had retired to bed long before.'

'Was your door locked?'

'It is impossible to lock it, for there is no key.'

'Very well; pray proceed.'

'On Wednesday I drove over to Framlingham to see Mr Blackstone, from whom I had received a letter that morning confirming the arrangement. He is a large, jovial man and welcomed me into his chambers with effusive cordiality. When I informed him of the purpose of my visit, however, he was quite taken aback.

'"To my certain knowledge," said he, leafing through a sheaf of papers upon his large desk, "there is no outstanding business connected either with the estate or with his late father's affairs which should require Sir Edward's attention at the present. There are a couple of trivial matters, but I am dealing with them myself. Furthermore," he added, a perplexed look upon his features, "that he should need to be in London is a mystery all by itself. For after Sir John retired from Parliament he had nothing to do with London whatever. Indeed, so far as I know, he never went up there once in the eighteen months before his death."

"'Edward gave you no indication at any time, then, of what it was that necessitated his presence in London?'"

"'None whatever and I saw him only a short time ago in this very room, immediately after the death of his father. I am sure that had there been anything upon his mind, he would have informed me.'"

"'What business brought him here?'"

"'I had requested that he come in to see me. There was a minor matter to be dealt with, concerning the tenancy of one of the farms on the estate and also an instruction which his father had given me some time ago.'"

"'Could either of these matters have obliged Edward to leave for London?' I asked."

"'Oh, dear me, no. The first was a very trivial piece of business. The second merely concerned a bundle of old documents pertaining to Shoreswood which Sir John had deposited with me some years ago: upon his death I was to give them to Edward, provided that he had attained his twenty-first birthday at that time.'"

"'He evidently left them with you a long time ago.'"

"'Indeed, yes,' returned the solicitor. He examined his records for a few minutes. "In '68," said he at length; "nineteen years ago. Edward would have been only a small boy of seven or so then. Indeed, it is almost back in the time of old Sir Geoffrey, Edward's grandfather. He was a fine old gentleman. A bit of a madcap, but a grand old fellow nonetheless. What the old documents were to do with, I cannot say, I'm afraid, for the bundle was tied and sealed with Sir John's own ring, bearing the Davenoke crest, and he did not vouchsafe to me the contents. They appeared, so far as I could see, to be a collection of ancient deeds, depositions and so on – papers of such obvious antiquity that they certainly cannot be of any current concern. I am sorry that I cannot assist you further, but do not hesitate to consult me again at any time. I am always here," he added after a moment, with an avuncular smile. "Indeed, I have been here longer than I care to remember. I have handled the affairs of the Davenokes for nigh on thirty years, and seen three generations of them come and go in these chambers."

'I thanked him for his help and left him sighing at the passage of time, and murmuring "dear, dear" over and over to himself. I felt frustrated once more in my efforts to learn what business it was that had obliged my husband to leave for London so abruptly, and it was with great reluctance that I made my way back to Shoreswood. No letter from Edward had arrived in my absence to cheer me and my heart sank yet further.

'That night I placed an upright chair against my bedroom door, with a pair of shoes balanced upon the back, as I had done the night before. Should my door be opened whilst I slept, the noise of the falling shoes would surely awaken me. Against whom or what I sought to protect myself, I could not say; I knew only that I feared the vulnerability of sleep.

'Such precautions began to seem superfluous, however, as I watched the long hours of the night pass without sleep closing my eyes. It was about two o'clock, when a slight noise from the garden caught my attention. It was a hard, clinking noise, as of one stone falling upon another, but distant and faint. I left my bed and pulled aside the curtain. The night was dark and still, and at first I could see nothing, but all at once I descried what appeared to be a faint, yellowish light, moving in silence among the chapel ruins, like a will-o'-the-wisp. For several minutes I followed its movements, round and about the ruins, until it vanished abruptly, as if extinguished. I waited at the window a little while, but it did not reappear. I was turning away, when out of the darkness, from the direction of the ruins, came another faint noise, just the same as the one I had heard before. I pulled the casement shut as best I could, but the wood of the frame is warped and ill-fitting and it is not even possible to close it fully, let alone secure the catch. However, I found a length of ribbon and knotted this around the handles. It was a flimsy safeguard, I knew, but it was better than nothing. As I returned to my bed I realised that I was shaking and trembling in every limb, as if with cold, although the night was a mild one. I hoped with all my heart that the morning's post would bring a letter from my husband.

'Alas! my hopes were in vain; my husband had sent no reply. I passed the day in melancholy solitude, scarcely leaving my room except to take my meals in the gloomy, shadowed dining-room. From the walls above me as I ate, rows of dark and faded portraits of Edward's ancestors gazed down upon me in silence, and seemed to watch me closely with their malicious, staring eyes. The timbers of the floor and the panelling upon the walls creaked and groaned as I sat there. Hardwick informed me that it was the effect of the hot, dry weather upon the old wood, but it seemed to me as if the house itself resented my presence and grumbled with malevolence against me. On a sudden thought, I asked the butler if anyone at Shoreswood had ever seen lights of any kind at night. He shook his head.

'"Do you mean what is termed the 'will-o'-the-wisp', or in some parts 'jack-o'-lantern'?" said he in a thoughtful voice.

'"Yes, that's it, Hardwick. You have seen it then?"

'Again he shook his head.

'"I have heard of the phenomenon, madam, but I regret that I have never been privileged to witness it. I believe it occurs in more marshy areas. I have never heard of its being seen in these parts. Might I enquire the reason for your interest in the subject, madam?"

'"Because I saw a moving light last night, in the ruined chapel."

'As I spoke these words, it seemed to me that a spark of fear sprang up in the man's eyes, but he said nothing. Later in the day I put the same questions to Mrs Pybus, the cook.

'"I don't know nothing of any lights, madam," said she in answer to my questions, "and I am forbidden to gossip about such things."

'"Forbidden?' I queried. "Forbidden by whom?"

'"Why, Mr Hardwick, madam."

'I could get nothing further from her and when I told her she could go, she bustled quickly away, with very evident relief. In truth, I think it very likely that she does, indeed, know nothing; but the butler is a different case altogether and I am convinced that there is much that he could tell me if he would. Unlike the other servants, he is a man of some intelligence and learning, and might, under other circumstances, have made Shoreswood almost bearable for me. But as matters stand, I have come to feel that I cannot trust him.

'When I retired that night, I vowed to myself that if there were no letter from Edward the following morning, I should leave for London in the afternoon. This decision cheered me somewhat, but I still secured the door and window of my bedroom as I had done before. Perhaps these precautions strike you as absurd, gentlemen, as you sit here in the bustling heart of London; but had you spent nights alone in Shoreswood Hall I believe you would understand – yes, and feel as I felt that night. As I was by the window, a sudden slight noise from the garden set my hair on end. What the noise was, I do not know – perhaps an owl disturbing the leaves upon a tree – but my nerves were frayed and the slightest noise was enough to bring my heart to my mouth.

'The moon was shining brightly that night, bathing the lawn outside in its grey light, and I could see quite clearly across to the woods. As I peered out, I saw something which sent my blood cold in my veins. A dark, hunched figure in a long hooded cloak was making its way slowly and deliberately across the lawn towards the house. With a thrill of loathing rising in my breast, I watched, unable to move, as the figure approached slowly in the moonlight. All at once, as on a sudden thought, it turned aside and struck out in another direction, until at length it vanished from my sight round an angle of the building. For twenty minutes I remained by the window, but saw nothing further, and heard nothing but the distant chiming of a church clock.

'I was still awake when the church clock struck the next hour. So disturbed and agitated was I, that I could not think what to do. My dearest wish was to fly from this dreadful house that very minute and yet I feared to leave my little bedroom, not knowing what I might encounter beyond. Even as I debated the matter in my head, a slight noise at the window set me rigid with fear. It was, I suppose, but a very slight noise, as the flutter of a moth's wing against the window-pane, but to me it was like the roar of Niagara. Then it came again, a faint creaking sound this time, and I realised with a feeling of sickness that someone – or something – was endeavouring to open my bedroom window from without.'

Lady Davenoke shuddered convulsively and stared for a long moment at her hands, which she had been clasping and unclasping violently all the while she spoke. Then she raised her head once more.

'Other than a sensation of the blood rushing in my ears, I can remember nothing more,' said she with a deep sigh. 'I evidently passed out. When I awoke it was broad daylight and the birds were singing outside my window. There was no letter from my husband that morning, so I packed my bags and had Staples drive me to the railroad station.'

'This disturbance at your bedroom window,' interjected Holmes: 'were you able to see the cause of it?'

'No. The curtains were drawn.'

'Then it could have been anything – or nothing; the wind, perhaps.'

'But I had seen the hooded figure upon the lawn.'

'Quite so. I do not doubt it for an instant. And you therefore quite naturally drew the conclusion that the two incidents were related.'

'Are you suggesting otherwise?'

'I have no opinion upon the matter, for the data are so far insufficient. There are any number of explanations which might account for what you have seen and heard, and it is much too early to favour any one against the others. It is a capital error to theorise ahead of the data. It biases the judgement. The figure you saw upon the lawn may have been that of a poacher, for example, and may have nothing whatever to do with the other incidents you have mentioned.'

'I understand your point, Mr Holmes,' said Lady Davenoke after a moment. She took a sip from a tumbler of water which I had passed her. 'I am afraid, however,' she continued after a moment, 'that my own conclusions remain unshaken.'

'You may of course be correct. I shall pursue the truth of the matter and then we shall see. What was the butler's reaction when he learnt that you were leaving Shoreswood?'

'He seemed quite disturbed about it, Mr Holmes. Indeed, he attempted rather clumsily to dissuade me from going. So I interpreted his remarks, at least, when he kept repeating that his master would no doubt be back in a day or so. It was almost as if he feared what I might discover in London. When it became evident to him that I was not to be dissuaded from going, he tried to learn my intended destination on the pretext that my husband might return in my absence and wish to know where I was staying. His manner was very agitated, his face the picture of deceit. Needless to say, I did not tell him what he wanted to know. Indeed, the fact that he clearly did not wish me to go merely hardened my resolve to leave at once, and the efforts with which he tried to learn my plans merely hardened my resolve not to satisfy his curiosity. I had been convinced ever since my return to Shoreswood that he was not telling me all he knew, so why should I tell him what was in *my* mind? I could not believe that he wanted the information simply to pass it on to Edward.'

'What happened when you arrived in London?' queried Holmes, as our visitor paused.

'I called upon Lady Congrave, who appeared delighted to see me. She insisted that I stay with her whilst in London and would brook no argument upon the point. She had a friend staying with her – Miss Edith Strensall, a young lady of about my own age – and she, too, was most welcoming. I did not at first tell them what had brought me to London and they did not press me upon the point. The following day – that is, last Friday – I called at the Royal Suffolk Hotel. The manager, Mr Solferino, was most kind to me, but he was unable to help. Edward was not staying there and an examination of the hotel register showed that he had not been there at any time in the past six months. I asked Mr Solferino why the letter I had sent had not, then, been at once returned to me, and he explained that he had assumed that there had been some confusion over dates, and had held on to my letter for a couple of days in case my husband turned up.

'"It has been sent back now, however," said he. "Indeed, I am surprised that you have not already received it. No doubt it will be there by now. Please give your husband my best wishes – when you find him!" he added with a smile, not realising the feeling of utter desperation which gnawed at my soul.

'I spent the next few days endeavouring to be pleasant to Lady Congrave, Miss Strensall and their visitors with increasing difficulty. Finally, yesterday afternoon, when the three of us were alone, Lady Congrave spoke frankly to me and begged me to tell them what it was that weighed so heavily upon my mind. I poured out my heart to them then and was glad afterwards that I had done so. They were most sympathetic and, more than that, they both made a positive suggestion. Miss Strensall declared that she would return with me to Shoreswood – she had no engagements and could leave as soon as I was ready – and Lady Congrave urged most strongly that I put the matter in your hands, Mr Holmes.'

'I am honoured by her recommendation.'

'She said that if anyone could help me, Mr Holmes, it was you; that you had never been known to fail.'

'If only that were true!'

'Mr Holmes, you must not fail this time! You must apply your utmost powers to my case. I am beset by such terrible, terrible troubles. What have I entered into with my marriage? What secret deeds are afoot at Shoreswood Hall? And where, oh where, is Edward? Only my husband can banish my fears and reassure my doubting mind, and only you, Mr Holmes, can tell me what has become of my husband!'

Our visitor's voice had risen with emotion as she spoke, until these last words came in a cry of pleading which was pitiful to hear.

'I shall do all in my power,' said Holmes, in a voice which was at once soft and soothing, and yet contained in it also a note of confidence and authority. 'Your case interests me, madam, and I can understand fully your distress. You have had a number of odd and disconcerting experiences, and have had no one to turn to for comfort. For some of these experiences, singular as they appear, there may of course be a perfectly natural explanation; but there are one or two points in your narrative which do not seem to admit of any very obvious answer.' He sat for a moment in silence. 'I cannot promise complete success, Lady Davenoke, but I think we should be able to make some progress.' He lapsed once more into silence, tapping the ends of his fingers upon his chin. 'Of course,' he continued after a moment, 'your husband may return of his own accord at any time and thus solve your problems at a stroke. Let us hope that that is so.'

A faint smile passed across her features at this remark, but the look of anxiety did not entirely leave her eyes. 'Do you have hopes, Mr Holmes?' said she.

'Certainly, certainly. But first I must ask you an unpleasant but necessary question. Have you reported your husband's disappearance to the authorities here?'

'I went straight to the police after leaving the Royal Suffolk Hotel,' Lady Davenoke replied, nodding her head. 'They could shed no light upon the matter. No body has been found which could possibly be that of my husband, if that is the unpleasant possibility to which you refer. They have also been in touch with the County Constabularies of Suffolk and Essex, in case Edward had met with an accident on his way to London, but both sent a negative reply.'

'Do you know of any relative or friend with whom he might stay?'

'None at all. Edward has not a single close relative and the only friend he retains from his schooldays, Marmaduke Morton of Canterbury, is at present in the West Indies.'

'Very well. When do you intend to return to Shoreswood?'

'Today.'

Holmes's eyebrows shot up in surprise.

'My husband may, as you say, return – indeed, he may have returned already – and, if so, I would wish to be there. I would not go back to that place alone, you understand, but with a good friend beside me, someone with whom I can discuss matters, I believe that I shall be equal to whatever may occur. Besides, telling my troubles to you has fortified my heart and given me new hope. You look doubtful – do you think I do wrong in returning to Shoreswood?'

'It might perhaps be better if you stayed away a few more days.'

'Shall I be in danger there, Mr Holmes?' queried our visitor, with a sharp glance at my friend's impassive features. 'Please answer me frankly!'

'That I cannot say, Lady Davenoke. The matter is not entirely clear to me.'

'Well, I would wish to return if it were possible. Would you wish to forbid me?'

Holmes shook his head with a smile.

'Then I shall go,' said she, returning his smile. 'With Miss Strensall's support I know I shall not be fearful. She is a very sensible woman. I shall await Edward's return at Shoreswood, secure in the knowledge that you are doing all in your power to find him.'

'Very well,' said Holmes. 'I shall be in touch the moment I have any news. And should you require our presence at Shoreswood,' he added after a moment, 'you have only to send a telegram.'

'I shall not forget,' said she.

II: In Which Various Letters are Sent and Received

'What a very singular problem!' said Holmes thoughtfully, as his client's footsteps descended the stair.

'And a singular young woman!' I added. 'One moment she trembles with fear, the next she is so bold as to spurn your advice!'

'Women are a curious mixture of timidity and courage,' remarked my friend, who had risen from his chair and was now gazing from the open window. 'And the advent of either state seems generally to bear no reference to external circumstances.'

Together we watched the slight figure of our visitor, as she made her way slowly along the crowded pavement. Perhaps it was my fancy, but an air of tragedy seemed to hang over her even there, in bustling Baker Street. All at once I had an overpowering sensation of impending doom, an awful conviction that, do what we might, we could not protect Amelia Davenoke from the fate that awaited her. Involuntarily, I shook my head, as if to drive such thoughts from my mind.

'She seems such a vulnerable young lady,' said I.

'It is her youth and inexperience,' replied Holmes. 'What do you make of that fellow over there?'

'The man suffering from toothache?' I queried, glancing across the street to where a man dressed all in black stood by a lamp-post. His dark frock-coat and top hat were both the worse for wear, and about his neck and jaw, making an incongruous contrast with the sobriety of the remainder of his attire, was a red muffler.

Holmes turned his head and stared at me for a moment, his brows drawn into an expression of surprise and puzzlement.

'I was applying your own methods of observation and deduction,' said I in reply to his unspoken question. 'The temperature must be up in the eighties already, so unless he is a madman he must have some very good reason for wearing his muffler. A bad case of toothache seems the most probable answer.'

'Ha! I fancy that on this occasion your explanation is a little over-ingenious,' remarked my friend. There was a trace of a smile about his lips, but his voice was cold and serious. 'Unless I am much mistaken, the purpose of his muffler is not a subtle one, but the simplest imaginable.'

'Which is?'

'To conceal his face. He has shown considerable interest in Lady Davenoke since she left our front doorstep. I should not be surprised if— Yes, by George! There he goes! Your boots and your hat, quickly, Watson !'

In less than thirty seconds we were upon the pavement, but neither our recent visitor nor the man in black was anywhere to be seen.

'She took a cab from the corner,' cried Holmes, hurrying in that direction.

Down King Street as we turned the corner, two hansom cabs were rattling away towards Gloucester Place and were already some distance ahead of us. It was evident that the man in the red muffler had also managed to secure a cab. Holmes groaned aloud and looked about him in desperation. No other cab was on the street. 'Come on, Watson!' said he, and we set off on foot as fast as we could. Ahead of us the two cabs, the one following the other at a short distance, turned left into Gloucester Place and vanished from our sight.

I was quite out of breath by the time we reached the corner and a sudden sharp pain in my left leg served as a savage reminder to me of the wound I bore from the Afghan war. Eagerly, Holmes scanned the busy street ahead of us, his brows drawn down over his piercing grey eyes. The rigidity of his pose, the keen, hawk-like expression upon his face, made him appear for all the world like a bird of prey surveying the field. But on this occasion the hunter's search was fruitless: no cabs were visible which could possibly be the ones we sought.

'They must have turned into George Street,' said he grimly. A few yards ahead of us a cab dropped off a fare and Holmes sprang in. I followed with relief, for the pain in my leg was now severe.

'First right ahead!' called my friend to the driver; 'as fast as you can!'

Along George Street we rattled at a great rate, until we reached the Edgware Road, passing several other vehicles as we did so, but without seeing anything of Lady Davenoke or the man who was following her.

'We have lost them,' said Holmes bitterly, as we faced the crowded, bustling prospect of the Edgware Road. 'They have evidently taken another route. We may still be able to gain an advantage, however!' he cried, his eyes flashing. 'Phillimore Gardens, Cabbie! By the fastest route you know!'

The driver whipped up the horse and we were off at a gallop once more, down to the Park, past houses, shops and gardens, along busy roads and quiet, until we at last turned into Phillimore Gardens, our horse steaming with the effort. The street was almost deserted, save for a workman wheeling a barrow along and a couple of loafers leaning upon a wall talking, one of them clutching a copy of the *Pink 'Un* in his hand. Of one thing we could be certain; at such a pace had we travelled that it was inconceivable that the other cabs could have arrived before us. Now we had only to wait.

For twenty-five minutes we sat there, Holmes with his pocket-watch open upon his knee, but neither Lady Davenoke nor anyone else whom we could recognise arrived.

'It is my fault,' said Holmes at length, in a tone of resignation. 'I had assumed that she would be returning directly to Lady Congrave's house, but she has evidently gone elsewhere. Come! There is little point our waiting here any longer. Let us return to Baker Street!' Though his tone was a philosophical one, there was no disguising the expression of disappointment upon his face.

Holmes went out after lunch, without saying where he was going. I passed the afternoon in an armchair, my aching leg upon a stool, endeavouring to read Colonel Forbes Macallan's *History of the Afghan Campaign*. Certainly the sweltering weather suited the subject of the book, but try as I might to concentrate, I found my mind constantly wandering to our morning's visitor and her recent strange experiences. Lady Davenoke's singular tale, and our hectic dash through the streets, had left a most sinister impression upon my mind.

Why had her new husband, apparently so attentive to her before, now deserted her so abruptly and without a word of explanation? Why, in coming up to London, had he broken with the family tradition of staying at the Royal Suffolk Hotel? What was the explanation for the lights which Amelia Davenoke had seen in the ruined chapel at night-time and for the figure she had seen upon the lawn in the moonlight? Who was the man with the red muffler and why was he following her about London? The more I pondered these matters, the less sense could I make of them. My heart went out to that slight, elfin-like young woman, who walked amidst such mystery, so far from home and family, when she should have been enjoying to the full the first happy months of married life. With all my heart I wished to help her, but felt at an utter loss to know what to do. Fervently I hoped that Sherlock Holmes would conceive some line of inquiry, some course of action which we could follow.

My friend returned at a quarter to six, an expression of fatigue upon his face. He dropped into his old blue armchair and stretched out his legs.

'If Edward Davenoke were staying at one of the many hotels in the West End,' said he after a moment, 'the chances of our finding him would be slight, to say the least. However, we are given to understand that he has come up to town upon business of some kind and it therefore seems likely that he would take a hotel in the City.'

I nodded and he continued:

'This consideration reduces the field of inquiry significantly, for there are far fewer hotels at that end of town than this. Now, I have this afternoon visited every hotel in the City at which our missing baronet might conceivably stay, without finding the slightest trace of him.'

'You must be very disappointed!'

'On the contrary,' said he, 'it is a most pleasing result – for the spirit, at least, if not for the body.'

'I do not understand, Holmes.'

'I mean, Watson, that the result of my inquiries is precisely as I had expected. It is always pleasing to have one's views confirmed. As the chemist tests substance after substance for a certain reaction, hoping all the time in his heart that the reaction will not occur, for it is his theory that it should not do so, so I – the chemist of human complexities – test hotel after hotel for the presence of Edward Davenoke, hoping all the time, in this sense at least, that I do not find him there.'

'Then you do not believe that he is staying in a hotel at all?'

'Precisely, Watson. Pass me a whisky and soda, there's a good fellow – and a cigar, too, if you would be so good; my body could tolerate a little relaxation!'

'But if you are so sure that he is not there, then why look?'

'The spirit of scientific inquiry, my dear fellow. One must test one's theories. What is a theory that is never put to the test? – Nothing but a puff of empty vapour.'

I endeavoured to press my colleague further as to his views upon the matter, but he was unforthcoming. For twenty minutes he lay back in silence in his chair, the blue smoke of the cigar curling lazily up to the ceiling.

'I wrote to Lady Davenoke whilst I was out,' he remarked abruptly, without opening his eyes.

'You sent her a telegram?'

'No, a letter; for I wished to be sure that she was back at Shoreswood when my communication arrived, just in case anyone else there felt an inclination to open it in her absence.'

'You suspect that someone might do such a thing?' I queried, surprised at his remark.

'It is possible and it is not a risk I was prepared to take. I have asked her to confirm that all is in order at Shoreswood and that everyone who should be there was indeed there when she returned. Now,' he continued, rising from his seat, 'I am retiring.' He selected an old brier from a rack of pipes upon the mantelpiece and took up the Persian slipper in which he kept his tobacco. 'Kindly inform Mrs Hudson that I shall not require supper this evening.'

My features must have betrayed the surprise I felt at his retiring at so early an hour, for at the doorway he paused.

'I need to think,' said he, 'and my bedroom, being quieter, suits the purpose better. As for eating, you must be aware that the digestion of food takes oxygen from the brain and is thus inimical to profound thought.' With that explanation he was gone and I saw him no more that night. It was evident, however, that his mind was sorely exercised by Amelia Davenoke's problem, for late into the night I could hear the sound of his footsteps pacing backwards and forwards across the floor of his room.

In the morning, my friend did not show himself until late. His eyes were dark, his face haggard and drawn, and I had no need of my medical training to perceive that he had had little sleep that night. A few letters had arrived for him by the morning's post. These he glanced over mechanically and without interest, his mind clearly elsewhere. Upon opening the last one, however, his expression changed utterly and he sat bolt upright in his chair as if he had been galvanised. It was, I could see, a letter-card, of the type which costs a penny-farthing from post offices, and which can be folded and sealed when the message has been written upon it.

'The matter deepens,' said Holmes in a tone of excitement. 'Take a look!'

I took the letter from his outstretched fingers. The following brief and unsigned message, untidily written in black ink, was all it contained:

> 'Keep out of matters that do not concern you, Mr Holmes. Your intervention in the private affairs of others can do no good and may well bring harm. Drop the matter at once and forget that you ever heard anything of it. I give you this warning for your own good and for that of your client.'

'Whatever does it mean?' I cried.

'Simply that someone does not wish us involved.'

'In the Davenoke case?'

'So we must suppose; I am engaged in no other inquiry at present.'

'But who?'

Holmes shook his head, his brows drawn down into a frown of concentration. 'The letter bears an 'E.C.' postmark,' said he.

'It was posted in the City, then!'

'Precisely, Watson, precisely!'

'The writing is exceedingly untidy,' I remarked, 'which perhaps indicates an ill-educated person.'

'I think not,' returned my friend. 'The letters are strong, firm and regularly formed. They quite lack the artificial and unnecessary flourishes with which the ill-educated feel obliged to decorate their script. In addition, the grammar is impeccable and the choice of words precise. It is apparent that whoever sent this note is no stranger to the art of writing.'

'What then?' I asked in surprise.

'He is a reasonably well educated man – for a man's hand it surely is – who was simply in a very great hurry when he wrote this note.'

'Why should he be in a hurry?'

At this, Sherlock Holmes broke into one of those strange, noiseless bouts of laughing which were peculiar to him. 'Perhaps,' said he at length, 'he had a train to catch.'

For the remainder of the day my friend did not once refer to Lady Davenoke's mystery. In the afternoon he went out for an hour or two, returning with a small brown-paper package, which he placed upon his desk and did not open. All evening he occupied himself with some particularly malodorous chemical experiment, the air of our little room gradually thickening to an unhealthy reek, until I was at length driven to my bedroom by the noxious fumes. As I left the room I bade my friend good night, but he was engrossed over a bubbling retort and did not hear me. It was evident to me that he had deliberately concentrated his mind upon other matters since the morning, in order to drive the Davenoke case completely from his thoughts, that he might return to it afresh and with renewed mental energies at a later date. As I have had occasion to remark elsewhere, Holmes's powers of mental detachment in such circumstances were quite extraordinary. Perhaps, I reflected as I climbed the stairs, he would return to the matter in the morning, if the letter he was expecting from Lady Davenoke arrived then.

We were seated at breakfast the following day when the maid brought up the post. Eagerly my friend sifted through the envelopes with his long thin fingers, selected two and put the rest aside. He tore open the first, glanced briefly inside and tossed it across to me. I was most surprised to see that it contained nothing at all. From the second he extracted a large, folded blue sheet, which he spread out upon his plate and studied closely for several minutes, a frown upon his face, before passing it to me. It was in the neat, rounded hand of Lady Davenoke and ran as follows:

MY DEAR MR SHERLOCK HOLMES,

I was most surprised to receive your letter, which arrived this morning. Your queries are easily answered however: Edward has not returned, but all else at Shoreswood is as it should be, and all the staff were present when Miss Strensall and I returned. I had wired ahead to say when we should arrive and Staples met us at the station with the trap, Mrs Pybus had prepared a meal for us, and I believe I saw everyone else at some time or another soon after our return. As for Hardwick, he was the very first person we met upon our return, for he was at the railway station at the same time as we were. He had just returned on the up train from Yoxford, a village which lies some miles to the north, where he had spent the day visiting his brother, who has been ill lately. He travelled back in the trap with us to Shoreswood. Miss Strensall found that journey a delight. She has now established herself satisfactorily in her bedroom and I have moved upstairs, so that our rooms can be next to each other. I am very much looking forward to enjoying her companionship in the days ahead.

However, to leave all this for the moment, I must tell you my one thoroughly splendid piece of news: When your letter arrived this morning it was not alone, but came accompanied by a letter from my husband! You will appreciate how thrilled I was when I recognised his handwriting upon the envelope. Is not life strange in its odd and unpredictable arrangement of events! It seems that all my worries will soon be at an end. But I will let you judge for yourself and copy down here for you the relevant parts of my husband's letter:

'MY DEAR AMELIA,

How sorry I am not to have written sooner to you. Please forgive me, but I have been ill for some days with megrim and have scarcely left my bed. Prior to that I was so completely occupied in settling certain outstanding matters of my father's that I had energy left for nothing else. I believe now, however, that my task is nearly complete and that I shall soon be returning to Shoreswood – and to you, my sweet.

'You will observe that there is no address at the head of this letter. I decided when I arrived in London that I would not stay at the Royal Suffolk on this occasion but at a smaller hotel. Unfortunately, this has proved less than satisfactory, so I shall be moving this afternoon. I am therefore without an address at present and you will thus not, I am afraid, be able to write to me. Save up all your news until I come home.

EDWARD'

I think you will agree, Mr Holmes, that that is good news indeed! I feel quite foolish to have allowed myself to become so distraught. My heart is so much lighter now. However, I shall certainly do as you requested and keep you informed of all that occurs here from now on.

YOURS SINCERELY, AMELIA DAVENOKE

'Well, Watson, what do you make of it?' enquired Holmes, as he poured himself a cup of coffee.

'It seems the very best news your client could have hoped for,' I replied. 'No doubt the matter will soon resolve itself now. It is good that Lady Davenoke is now so cheerful.'

'Oh? So that is how it strikes you?' said he, passing me the toast-rack. He pushed back his chair in silence and took his coffee cup to the mantelpiece, where he set it down amid a litter of chemical bottles and test-tubes, and took up his black clay pipe.

'I regret that I cannot share your optimism, Watson,' he continued after a moment. 'You will appreciate that I feel professionally responsible for the well-being of my client. From that point of view, this letter she has received is perhaps the most sinister development so far.'

'You amaze me, Holmes! It struck me as extremely cheering!'

'So are fairy-tales, Watson – and they contain as much of the truth as does that letter.'

'Really, Holmes! What possible evidence can you have for such an assertion?'

'The most significant evidence lies in the first envelope I passed you.'

'But that envelope was perfectly empty!'

'Therein lies its significance.'

'Oh, this is absurd!' I cried. 'I can make neither head nor tail of it!'

'You know my methods,' said he laconically. 'Apply them!'

I picked the empty envelope up from the table and examined it. It was very cheap, penny-a-packet commercial stationery, and bore the previous evening's date and the 'E.C.' postmark, indicating that it had been posted in the City area. I remarked as much to my friend and he nodded.

'Your name and address are correctly rendered,' I continued, 'but the writing is very scratchy, indicating perhaps that the writer is careless with his pen, or too mean to fit a fresh nib when one is undoubtedly needed. The writing itself, however, has a certain strength and regularity. It is the hand, I should say, of a man of character and intelligence.'

'Thank you!' cried my friend, choking with laughter and collapsing helplessly into a chair. I looked again at the envelope. 'Holmes!' I cried, 'this hand is your own! You yourself wrote it!'

'Indeed I did,' said he when he had recovered himself. 'I wrote it in a post office and the pen was the best one available, I am afraid.'

'I am glad you find your own jest so amusing,' I remarked with some asperity. 'I was under the impression that we were engaged upon a serious investigation.'

'So we are, my dear fellow, so we are,' said he. His tone was an earnest one, but this served only to irritate me further.

'You go too far, Holmes,' said I coldly. 'You send yourself a letter with nothing in it, open it up and gaze at its emptiness, then pronounce the matter to be of significance. It is significant only of idiocy!'

'There you make a mistake, my dear friend.'

'I think not.'

'But you do, nonetheless. Your mistake is in supposing that I sent the letter to myself. That, I agree, would be idiocy.'

'But you have admitted as much.'

'Not at all. I admitted only that I wrote the address upon the letter, and you leapt to the conclusion that I also sent it. As these actions do go together as a general rule, the conclusion is, I admit, a natural one; but it by no means follows with apodictic certainty. The two actions are really quite distinct, a fact which I feel may be of considerable significance in the Davenoke case. But, come! I have no desire to make further mystery when there is so much already. Do you recall the Baker Street Division of the Detective Force?'

'The Irregulars! Most certainly,' said I, smiling at the thought, despite myself. 'A more dishevelled and disreputable collection of street-Arabs I never saw in my life!'

'Nevertheless, there is much good work to be got from them. You will no doubt recall the assistance they provided in the Jefferson Hope case, and also in that singular business of "The Three Eyes".'

'I am hardly likely to forget either of those cases. You are employing them at present, then?'

'Precisely, Watson. As I informed you the other day, I myself made inquiries for Sir Edward Davenoke at virtually all the conceivable places. The Baker Street Irregulars are therefore trying all the inconceivable places – small hotels, many of them distinctly disreputable, cheap lodging houses, odd rooms that are let in public-houses and so on. I provided their leader, Wiggins, with a ready-stamped envelope, for him to communicate his findings to me – I addressed it myself, as writing is not Wiggins's strong suit – in order that we should not have the house invaded by these boys, as has happened before – much to Mrs Hudson's distress, as you will no doubt recollect. But if, and only if, he was certain that they had looked everywhere, and that there was nowhere remaining where Davenoke might be, he was to seal up the envelope, empty as it was, and send it back to me, to let me know that they had completed their task, and that Davenoke was nowhere to be found. Such a negative message is every bit as interesting and important, you see, as any positive message could be. Knowing the thoroughness with which Wiggins and his friends have always performed the tasks I have set them, I can thus declare with a confidence approaching almost to certainty that the letter which Amelia Davenoke has received is nothing more nor less than a monstrous lie.'

'What, then, do you see as the truth?'

'This is not the time to discuss theories,' replied Holmes after a moment. 'I am not yet entirely clear in my mind about one or two points. One thing that does seem clear to me, however, is that the arrival of this letter is bad – very bad. It rather eliminates the possibility that this whole business is a series of accidents, unfortunate mischances and misapprehensions, and renders it virtually certain that things are as I feared. All that had happened to this point was vague and inconclusive, and susceptible of some innocent explanation or other, however unlikely: thus, the man we saw in the street may indeed have been hurrying to visit his dentist, and the fact that his cab followed Lady Davenoke's so closely may have been sheer chance; the anonymous note we received may have come from some crank or monomaniac who has no connection with the Davenokes whatever – it did not mention any names after all – and the fact that it came when it did may be utter coincidence; the figure Lady Davenoke saw upon the lawn may indeed have been a poacher, the lights some natural phenomenon, the footsteps in the night a servant sneaking to the kitchen for a slice of bread and cheese. But this letter she has received' – he paused to give emphasis to his words – 'this letter, I say, is a concrete, physical lie, which can in no wise be explained away.'

'I see clearly now what you mean,' said I. 'But what can we do?'

'We might do worse than read the book I picked up at Hatchard's, yesterday afternoon,' replied my friend. 'It is always an advantage to understand fully the historical antecedents of a case.'

He took up the brown-paper packet which had lain unopened upon his desk and extracted a red-bound volume. As he turned the pages over, I saw that it was *Robinson's County Guide to East Suffolk*. After a moment, he found what he was looking for.

'"Shoreswood Old Hall, its history and legend", he read aloud. 'I shall give you a *résumé* of the history, Watson, and perhaps when you have finished your work with that egg-spoon you would be so good as to read the section devoted to the legend.'

'Certainly, if it is of interest to you.'

'"The manor of Shoreswood is one of the oldest in the country,"' he began after a moment, '"and has many historical associations. It has been the home of the Davenoke family since the middle of the fourteenth century, for a pipe roll of 1347, in the reign of Edward III, records that one Guy Davernuck was granted the manor of 'Shorriswode' in recognition of the service he had rendered the king at the battle of Crécy, the previous year. In the fifteenth century the Davenokes were closely associated with the Pole family, supporting the claims of the latter to" – this is not very interesting! Let me see – Ah! "At the time of the Reformation, the family remained faithful to the Church of Rome, but although their sympathies were widely known, they appear to have escaped any great penalty upon this account. Later, Roland Davenoke was one of the leading supporters of Mary Tudor's successful claim upon the throne, he being largely responsible for the rallying of English Catholics at nearby Framlingham Castle, from where she marched to London to take the Crown. When Elizabeth became queen, the Davenokes were several times fined for recusancy, and for many years the estate lay under threat of confiscation, but the threat was never enacted. Elizabeth's officers visited Shoreswood on many occasions, acting on persistent rumours that Jesuit priests from France were in hiding there, but none was ever discovered.

'"At the time of the Civil War, Robert Davenoke took the Royalist side and was killed at the Battle of Naseby, fighting alongside Prince Rupert. A tradition in the area has it that the future King Charles II spent a night at Shoreswood after the Battle of Worcester, on his way into exile abroad." – Ha! – If Charles II had indeed stayed a night in every place which lays a claim to harbouring him after the Battle of Worcester, he would never have found time to get abroad at all! What else do we have? Hum! – "In 1738, during the time of Sir Charles, the first baronet, a completely new house was begun three miles away, in the Palladian style then popular. The original house was thence known as 'Shoreswood Old Hall', in contradistinction to the new. So poorly was the new hall constructed, however, that within a dozen years it had become unsafe for habitation and within two dozen the greater part of it was in ruins. Having insufficient capital to effect the necessary repairs, the family moved back to the Old Hall, where they have remained ever since."

'There is little more of interest,' said Holmes, his eye running down the page. 'Ah! Amelia Davenoke is not alone in her dislike of the place. Apparently, David Hume, the philosopher, spent a night there in 1766 and described it afterwards, in a letter to Adam Smith, as "the most repugnant household in which a man was ever required to endure twenty-four hours". Hum! The chapel seems to have had a history almost as chequered as that of the Davenokes themselves. Parts of it are Norman, including one wall which still stands. Listen to this, Watson! – "It was partly destroyed at the Reformation, partly restored under Mary Tudor, forcibly closed during Elizabeth's long reign, and brought to its present state of ruin by Cromwell's myrmidons, since when it has been left to moulder in picturesque decay." What a wealth of history that sentence comprises! But I see that you are ready now to take over!'

My friend passed me the book, settled himself in his chair and put a match to his pipe, as I began the following singular account:

The legend associated with the Manor of Shoreswood, and hence with the family of Davenoke, is among the most remarkable of English folk-tales, containing as it does certain unique features which set it apart from other, similar legends. Yet it has, also, something in common with all such tales, in that it purports to record events which we feel reluctant to credit, but which were apparently well-attested by those present at the time.

Belief in a hidden chamber in Shoreswood Hall, and in a mysterious local creature, unlike any known animal, were both part of the common coin of rural folklore throughout the recorded history of the area. But the two beliefs appear to have been quite distinct and unconnected until the early years of the seventeenth century, during the reign of James I, when there occurred, so it is said, those events which were to forge an inseparable link between them in the popular imagination, and give to the creature the name of the Beast of Shoreswood. It was a dark and superstitious age, between the brash and confident gaiety of the Tudors and the harsh and bitter divisions of the Civil War; a fitting time, one might suppose, for a monster to stalk the shadowed lanes of the Deben valley, striking terror into the hearts of the simple country-folk who dwelt there.

As to the accuracy of the following we can make no claim. It is largely taken from what is probably the best account, that of one Thomas Swefling, a minor tax-official in the area at the time. As he did not set himself to record the events until twenty years after their occurrence, however, his account may contain many errors, which must, of necessity, be repeated here.

In the year 1607, Richard Davenoke was Lord of the Manor of Shoreswood, a man who was, by all accounts, neither better nor worse than his forebears, from which one may conclude that he was known for hard riding, hard fighting and hard drinking, for a general amiability on sunny days and a ferocious, unappeasable temper on dark days. His mother, a woman of

Burgundian extraction, had for many years been a powerful force in the area, but since her death, two years previously, the responsibilities of the district had rested solely, and some said too heavily, upon Richard's shoulders. For he was not by temperament a natural leader of men, and his life had already been touched by sorrow once before. His only brother, Arthur, had been drowned in the moat of Shoreswood Hall twenty years previously when still a small child, and it was often said of Richard Davenoke that this tragedy had so affected his young, impressionable soul that he had ever after borne its mark, and been subject to fits of black melancholy. But greater tragedy was yet to befall him, ensuring that the story of Richard Davenoke's struggle against the Beast of Shoreswood would live forever in the annals of East Suffolk.

In the spring of that year, a series of inexplicable and ghastly attacks were made, under cover of darkness, upon domestic animals as they grazed peacefully in the fields. On each occasion, the ferocity of the attack was marked, but there was no common agreement among the local people as to the nature of the predator. Sentries were appointed and a watch kept, but the killer was never seen. Some argued that a wolf must be responsible, but others, observing with truth that no wolf had been seen in East Suffolk for over a hundred years, whispered darkly of some more unnatural agency.

After this initial onslaught, the attacks ceased for a while, but when they began afresh, as many had feared they would, it was with an even greater ferocity than before. Nothing that lived and breathed was safe from the blood-lust of the mysterious and unseen beast: sheep, cattle, horses and every other kind of harmless animal, all were butchered alike. By this time there was great fear among the local folk as to what the evil creature could be which passed amongst them at dead of night, for in not one instance of this hideous slaughter had an animal been killed for food. Clearly the beast was one which killed only to satisfy its thirst for blood. Then, at last, as all in their hearts had feared, a human victim was taken, a local farmer's son who had been walking home alone, late at night. His body was found by the roadside next morning, almost torn to pieces by the ferocity of the attack.

Armed bands of men were at once formed, under the leadership of Richard Davenoke, to hunt down the beast; but though they scoured the countryside round, searched with hounds, and kept armed watch at night for many weeks, no trace of the mysterious creature could be found. A little later, another man was attacked and killed, then a third, then a fourth and fifth. People spoke now of the Beast of Shoreswood, and dark rumours began to circulate concerning Richard Davenoke's supposedly dead brother. There were some who now recalled a strange deformity of the features which this unfortunate child was said to have possessed, a deformity so terrible that it was said to have given him the appearance of some low animal or rodent. Others remembered tales which had been current in the countryside twenty years previously despite the family's attempts to suppress them, of wild childish tantrums verging almost upon madness.

Perhaps, the rumours now suggested, the story of Arthur's death had been untrue, fabricated deliberately to conceal a truth far worse, that his bestial insanity had obliged his family to hide him away from the eyes of the world, confined for life in some secret and inaccessible chamber in Shoreswood Hall. Perhaps the source of the evil which had thrown such a pall of terror over the countryside was to be found in that dark and sombre building.

As is the way among fanciful and ill-educated people, these rumours soon acquired the status of fact. More and more openly were such thoughts spoken aloud, until they reached the ear of Richard Davenoke himself. Greatly angered, he did all in his power to suppress the rumours, but there were those who said that he did so with a weary reluctance, and without the light of truth in his eye. Certainly, the whole dreadful series of events seemed to have exacted an awful toll from the man. As chief landowner in the area, he had naturally assumed responsibility in the matter, and this responsibility and the worries and cares which came with it had almost destroyed him. Broken in health, his face lined with anxiety and his hair prematurely grey, he went about his daily business with the weariness of one who would welcome the release of the grave. In some, his appearance and manner evoked sympathy, but there were many others who saw in them a confirmation of the very worst of the rumours. A man so racked, they argued, was a man who was torn between two loyalties, who could not bring himself to do what in his heart he knew he must.

The atrocious and bloody deeds of violence continued to occur at irregular intervals, turning the nights of the country-folk to sleepless terror; and as they did so, so did the rumours grow and strengthen themselves by feeding upon the ignorance of the people. There were those who said, although not to his face, that Richard Davenoke should, once and for all, deny upon holy oath, if he could, the stories which were being told against his brother. Some argued for the opening of his brother's tomb, whilst others wished to see a company of local yeomen allowed to enter and search Shoreswood Hall. Where this growing discontent might have ended, no one can say, for all at once, upon a shocking and horrific night in August, the matter reached a final and terrible climax.

In the darkest hours of the night, so it is said, when all had been long asleep, every soul in Shoreswood Hall was on a sudden instant rendered wide awake and struck with terror by the most dreadful and blood-curdling scream. For a long moment, the echo of the scream seemed to hang in the silent air after the sound itself had died, then doors were flung back and the noise of running footsteps filled the stairways and corridors of the Hall. One man cried out that he had seen a crouching figure slip away along a dark corridor, and several hurried that way to give pursuit, but nothing was found. The largest crowd had by now gathered outside the bed-chamber of Elizabeth Davenoke, wife of Richard, for it was from there that the unearthly sound had issued, but none dared enter. Then Richard Davenoke himself stepped to the front of the crowd, and, taking a long-bladed knife from his chief steward, he placed his hand upon the latch. With a resolute and grim expression, he bade all there remain without the door on peril of their lives, then, with a gesture of impulse, wrenched the door open and passed within, bolting it fast behind him.

What took place in that room then, none can tell. Certainly there were cries and groans, and the sounds of a struggle filled the air. Outside the room, the servants of Shoreswood stood listening in impotent and silent horror for what seemed an eternity. Abruptly, the door opened once more, and Richard Davenoke emerged, his clothes torn and his body a mass of cuts and scratches. 'Your mistress is dead,' said he with a face of stone, at which the servants all fell to weeping. 'She is the very last victim that will ever be taken by the monster that has terrorised us for so long. Return to your beds now, and you, Joseph, my good and faithful servant, do you come with me and assist me, in the grim work that must now be done.'

Thus ended the six-month reign of terror of the Beast of Shoreswood, for there were no more killings. The funeral of Elizabeth Davenoke took place a few days later amid scenes of much sorrow, for she had been greatly loved in the district. There were those who said that another ceremony took place also, at dead of night, but if this were so, nothing is known of it, for a veil of secrecy had fallen upon Shoreswood Hall. There was great sympathy for Richard Davenoke in his time of sorrow, and he was never pressed to reveal what he knew of the terrible events of that year. Speculation naturally abounded, but no story was ever either confirmed or denied by the Lord of Shoreswood, who had sworn himself to total silence upon the matter. From that time onward, so it is said, he never once left his estate until the day he died, and scarcely ever ventured outside the Hall itself, spending his days in solitary study and prayer.

Fifteen years later, upon Richard's death, his oldest son, Thomas, promised to make public all he might discover among his father's papers concerning 'The Beast of Shoreswood', but either he found nothing, or chose not to disclose it, for the promise was never fulfilled. The alteration in the young man's character which took place at that time led many to suspect that he had indeed discovered the truth, but thought it better to conceal it. For it is said that from the day upon which he assumed the title of Shoreswood, he was never again seen to smile. Thus arose the tradition that upon learning the secret of the Davenokes, each happy heir becomes a sorrowful man. Fanciful as this must strike the modern reader, it is a curious fact that no Lord of Shoreswood has ever openly disputed the tradition. Indeed, the family's reluctance to speak at all upon the subject of the Beast or the secret chamber is striking, and, moreover, makes it unlikely that any fresh information will be forthcoming in the near future. As to the further manifestations of 'the Beast', an outbreak of sheep-maiming in 1699 was ascribed to it, as were a similar outrage in 1784 and the mysterious disappearance of twenty head of cattle in 1837; but in every case the evidence was scant, and the Shoreswood monster seems to have received the blame only for want of any better theory.

This then is the history of the Beast of Shoreswood, and of

what is known as 'The Curse of the Davenokes'. Is there any substance in these old tales? Is there any dark secret concealed in Shoreswood Hall? Or is the whole story a mere accretion of legends around a mundane and long-forgotten incident? I leave the reader to draw his own conclusions, which will be every bit as valid as the writer's. Those who are interested may read with profit Dr Wilhelm Hertz's monograph *Der Werwolf* (1862) which gives the best general account of such legends.

'What a grim old tale!' said I, as I put down the book.

'Yes, it is charmingly Gothic, is it not?' agreed my friend. 'The author's remark – that later outrages were ascribed to the Beast's activities only in want of a more constructive theory – is a perceptive one. It was ever the case with such legends: once they are established they provide the basis of an explanation – of sorts – for all that would otherwise remain unexplained. This fact is no doubt a great encouragement to would-be malefactors.'

'In the past, perhaps,' said I, smiling; 'but the influence of such tales must now be quite dead and buried – thank goodness!'

'Not necessarily, Watson. Dark deeds have long shadows!'

There was a thoughtful note in his voice, which arrested my attention.

'Surely you cannot think that this old legend has anything to do with Lady Davenoke's case!' I cried in surprise.

'I am very much afraid that it may have,' said Holmes, shaking his head.

'But it is mere fantasy!' I protested. 'We surely cannot give credence to such a farrago of nonsense! Why, you yourself said to Lady Davenoke, only the other day—'

'In this instance,' interjected my friend, 'it scarcely matters at all what you or I believe, Watson. What is important is what may or may not be believed by others. There is something unpleasant about this case; something which smells, like the rot of evil. We shall not cleanse the air and clear the troubled brow of Lady Amelia until we have found the source of the rot and destroyed it – whatever it may be.'

Three days passed and we heard nothing further. Several times I observed Holmes take up the *Suffolk County Guide* and read again the history of Shoreswood and the Davenokes with a frown upon his face. Then he would cast the book aside and close his eyes, and sit an hour in silent thought, his brow furrowed with concentration. At other times he would sit with one of his beloved black-letter editions upon his knee, his fingers picking absent-mindedly at imperfections in the pages, his eyes far away, and the page remaining unturned for hours at a time. Once I heard him speaking aloud to himself in German, and I assumed that he was reading from the book upon his knee until the words 'Davenoke' and 'Hardwick' caught my ear.

'I begin to think that I have erred,' said he upon the evening of the third day, 'in not going down to Shoreswood last week, with Lady Davenoke. I admit to you, Watson, that I believed then that the matter would very likely resolve itself without my intervention. The longer it fails to do so, the greater is the danger to my client's state of mind. It is this that worries me more than any other consideration.'

'More even than any physical danger to which she may be exposed?'

'Decidedly so,' returned my friend. 'You saw the condition she was in, Watson, on the day she paid us a visit: those haunted eyes, those nervous, twitching fingers. I have never seen a woman so near the end of her tether, and what is it now? – five days? six days?'

'She has, at least, her friend, Miss Strensall, to keep her company now,' I remarked. But Holmes shook his head, an expression of misgiving upon his features.

'Perhaps the companionship will be some comfort to her,' said he; 'but a maiden lady, however well-intentioned, is not really what the situation requires.'

'What, then?'

'I think I shall go down tomorrow whether we hear from Lady Davenoke or not,' said he after a moment. 'My presence there can scarcely be less profitable than it is here and it is just possible that I might be able to do some good. I have one or two ideas I should wish to put to the test.'

'Would a companion be of any value to you?'

'My dear fellow! I had quite overlooked your natural diffidence and presumed that on this as on so many occasions you would be my colleague. Will you come?'

'Nothing could prevent it!'

I was awakened abruptly at half past six the following morning by the deafening crack and rumble of thunder, directly overhead. The window in my bedroom rattled violently in its frame, and in an instant I was fully conscious and alert. I leaned from my bed and drew back the curtain, and as I did so a searing white light seemed to split the sky asunder. Scant seconds later the thunder crashed and rolled again, and the house trembled as if struck a blow by a mighty fist. A moment of unnatural silence followed, then the muffled beat of heavy raindrops filled the air and a sudden cold gust blew into the room. How many others, I wondered, of the four millions of souls that surrounded me in this brick-built fastness of civilisation, watched with awe as I did at that moment. For despite his pretensions to independence and aloofness from his fellows, that which unites one man with all others is both stronger and more deep-seated than that which separates them; and there is nothing which unites mankind so readily as the wild and merciless assault of cruel nature.

In twenty minutes the storm had passed away and the sky had lightened a little, but the rain continued to beat down without pause. As I dressed, I observed that it had proved too much for the guttering of the house opposite my window, and sheets of water fell in a dismal and unbroken curtain from the roof. I am not a man much given to fancies, nor one to put faith in portents or premonitions, but I confess that upon that morning the sense of relief which rises with the passing of such a storm was in my case tempered by an odd and troubling sensation of foreboding, as if the overture were finished, and the stage set for a singularly terrible and tragic drama.

There was a knock at my bedroom door as I was shaving and Sherlock Holmes entered.

'The weather appears to have broken at last,' I remarked, gesturing with my razor to the scene outside.

'So has the case,' said he, holding up a sheet of blue notepaper in front of my mirror. I took it from his grasp and turned it to the light. At the head of the sheet was the lion-and-bird crest of the Davenokes, and the date of the previous afternoon. The message was brief and ran as follows:

> MY DEAR MR SHERLOCK HOLMES,
> I beg that you will come down to Shoreswood at once. I have heard no more from my husband. There are lies all about me here and I am being watched constantly. Edith weeps a good deal and is little comfort to me; indeed, I regret that ever I brought her here, poor girl, for I fear that I have only succeeded in luring another victim into this dark web of secrecy and evil. Do not write, for I believe that the incoming mail is tampered with, but come at once and bring your friend Dr Watson.
> YOURS SINCERELY, AMELIA DAVENOKE

'We leave by the ten-twenty train,' said Holmes as I finished reading.

III: The Secret of Shoreswood Hall

The rain was still pouring down when we left our chambers and Baker Street had more the appearance of a river than a road. Fast currents splashed and swashed their way along the gutters, foaming and whirling round obstructions, while heavy raindrops battered the surface ceaselessly, sending fountains of spray high into the air.

Holmes was in a taciturn mood, and spoke scarcely a single word until we had left London far behind and our train was speeding through the rain-drenched Essex countryside. There was a suppressed excitement in his manner which I recognised, and I knew that he was glad to be afoot upon the trail once more and to have left behind the frustrating inactivity of Baker Street. For my own part, however, I could not help feeling that we were bound upon a fool's errand. What could we hope to achieve in Suffolk, aside from giving a little momentary cheer to Lady Davenoke by our presence? Come to that, was it likely that we could achieve even that modest aim? We could not, after all, produce her husband, which was all she really cared about. But I had known my companion well, for six years and more, and had rarely known him be far astray in his reasoning: if he considered it worth our while to travel down to deepest Suffolk, I must suppose that it were so, doubtful as it seemed to me.

Holmes had been staring abstractedly from the window for some time, a frown upon his face, when he abruptly leaned forward and spoke.

'We are running close to the coast,' said he. 'We should be in Ipswich shortly.'

The rain had abated a little now, but still cast its slanted streaks across the carriage-windows and dripped through the crack around the door. The country outside was a dark, waterlogged green, with here and there, a daub of the sad tints of autumn, brown and gold and red.

'How can you tell?' I asked. 'I see nothing that indicates the coast is near.'

'You do see,' said he, 'but you do not observe. Your mind is not trained to read the books in the running brooks, the sermons in stones, as Shakespeare puts it.'

'Pray tell me, then.'

'The trees, my dear fellow. See how they bend towards us as one. There is no surer sign that the coast is near. It is the rude sea-wind that bends and stunts them so, the harsh easterlies and north-easterlies that blow upon this fair coast.'

I saw at once that what he said was true. The isolated trees which dotted the margins of the fields were twisted and deformed, and seemed to reach out to us in silent and grotesque supplication.

'Perhaps there is yet another tree which has felt the blast of these east winds,' added my friend after a moment, in a thoughtful tone.

'Whatever do you mean?'

'I refer to the family-tree of the Davenokes,' said he.

'They are certainly a singular people.'

'More than that,' said he; 'there seems a streak in them that is difficult, stiff and unbending; as if, in learning for so long to resist the winds of these parts, they forgot, in the end, that occasionally everyone must bend a little. You must have been struck, Watson, by their knack of supporting losing causes – the Catholic side at the Reformation, the Royalist side in the Civil War. Depending on one's point of view, they are either very loyal, or simply stubbornly resistant to change of any sort. Well, well, we are nearing our destination,' he continued in a brisker tone; 'let us review the case!'

'That, at any rate, should present no great difficulty.'

'Why so?' said he, an expression of curiosity upon his features.

'Simply because what we know amounts to virtually nothing.'

'Well,' said he amiably. 'State the little we do know, then, and let us see how matters stand.'

'We know,' I began, 'that Edward Davenoke left Shoreswood the day before his wife returned. He has apparently gone to London, although no one can suggest any reason why he should do so. He has written to his wife from there, stating that he is staying in some small hotel or other, but all your resources have failed to find him. Other than that, all we have are on the one hand, the anonymous note you received, telling you in so many words to mind your own business, which may, however, have nothing whatever to do with the case, and, on the other, a young woman who has got herself into an emotional and fearful state over the squeaks and creaks of an ancient house.'

'Capital!' cried my friend, his eyes shining with amusement. 'A very illuminating exposition of the matter, my dear fellow!'

'But if you agree with me,' I protested, 'then what earthly good can be achieved by our running down to Suffolk?'

'None whatever,' said he, shaking his head.

'What!' I ejaculated.

'Fortunately, however, I do not agree with you. When I described your exposition as illuminating, I meant merely that you summarised accurately all the false assumptions which one might make about the matter.'

'Pray, tell me your own views, then,' said I somewhat tartly, for there seemed to be in his voice a tone of superiority which irritated me.

'In the first place,' said Holmes, after a moment, 'you state that we know: a, that Davenoke left Shoreswood the day before his wife returned; b, that he has apparently gone to London; and c, that he wrote to her from there; but in truth we know none of these things. The butler, Hardwick, drove him to the station, but we do not know for certain that he caught a train; and if he did catch a train, we do not know where he went. Lady Davenoke had only the butler's word for it that her husband had gone to London, if you recall her account; no one else knew anything of it.'

'The letter she received came from London,' I remarked. 'The postmark could not have been forged and she recognised her husband's own handwriting.'

'Certainly,' said he; 'I do not doubt that he wrote it. But you had a demonstration the other day that he who writes a letter and he who posts it are not necessarily one and the same.'

'You believe that Davenoke wrote the letter elsewhere and had a confederate post it for him?'

'It is a distinct possibility.'

'Why should he do that?'

'Because he does not wish anyone to know where he is. He would have succeeded in his deception, too, were it not for our intervention.'

'You speak as if you know his true whereabouts,' I remarked in surprise.

'Oh, there is no mystery about that,' said he. 'He is at Shoreswood, of course.'

'What!' I cried. 'You astound me, Holmes! I had no idea—'

'Really? Nevertheless, the indications were there, Watson. Indeed, it has seemed the most likely solution from the very beginning. What business could Sir Edward's father have in London, when, aside from his relatively brief period as a Member of Parliament, he seems to have had nothing to do with the place? Certainly the solicitor knew of none and he has handled the family's affairs for over a quarter of a century. That does not, of course, render it impossible, but it does seem fairly unlikely, to say the least. Then there are the singular circumstances surrounding Davenoke's leaving: why should the butler drive him to the railway station, when a groom is employed at the Hall? Taken along with the butler's subsequent odd and evasive manner, it is a most suggestive point. You will recall also, no doubt, the curious business of the dog. Lady Davenoke was given a singularly unconvincing explanation of his being chained up away from the house; evidently the true reason for his confinement is that if he were left free to roam where he would, he could not have failed to sniff out his master's whereabouts, and so reveal the whole deception for what it is.'

'You have suspected all along, then, that Davenoke had not left Shoreswood?'

Holmes nodded his head. 'But I could not at first be certain,' said he. 'Given the initial data, there were, it seemed to me, seven possible explanations of what was really afoot, some of them, I might mention, taking it as a fact that Davenoke was dead. However, the circumstances surrounding Lady Amelia's visit to us, her return to Shoreswood, and the letters which we both received, served to clarify the matter.'

'How so?'

'In the first place, as you observed a moment ago, Lady Davenoke certainly recognised her husband's handwriting upon the letter she received. This I took as an indication that he was still alive, for it is by no means as easy as it might be supposed to counterfeit someone's hand throughout a letter of some length, especially when it is to be read by one who is very familiar with the true hand. But if the hand were true, the contents of the letter manifestly were not. His explanation of why he had no address at which she could reach him must rank as the feeblest lie I have ever encountered. Indeed, the only rival which springs to mind is the butler's explanation for his presence at Wickham Market station when Lady Davenoke returned there with Miss Strensall. His story of an ailing brother in Yoxford, or wherever it was, was clearly the purest poppycock.'

'How could you be so sure?' I asked.

'Taken with what we already suspected, it was simply too much of a coincidence to swallow. It seemed very evident that Hardwick had travelled down on the same train as the ladies and alighted quickly at Wickham Market before they themselves did so. If this were so, then no doubt it was Hardwick we saw in Baker Street, following Lady Davenoke. Her familiarity with his features accounts, of course, for his anxiety to keep them concealed beneath his unseasonal muffler. No doubt, also, it was Hardwick who posted in London the letter from Edward Davenoke, which his wife received after her return to Shoreswood, and, incidentally, the anonymous note we received at the same time. He probably enquired my name and business of some bystander, while he was waiting outside our rooms in Baker Street, and guessed his mistress's purpose in consulting me. Whatever Edward Davenoke is up to, Hardwick is evidently his trusted lieutenant, fully conversant with the matter and able to act upon his own judgement, for the decision to write the warning note to me – presumably from the post office in the City where he posted his master's letter – must have been his alone.'

'It is certainly plausible, so far as it goes,' I remarked.

'It is the only theory that fits the facts,' returned my colleague. 'Davenoke's presence at Shoreswood – in hiding – will of course go a considerable way to explain all the strange nocturnal comings and goings which have so distressed our client.'

'But how could Sir Edward Davenoke be at Shoreswood and his wife not know of it?' I protested.

'You forget that he has lived there all his life, Watson. He must know of many places where he could remain hidden from view. In fact, however, I believe that he is in the secret chamber which we have heard so much about.'

'But there is no evidence that such a chamber even exists in reality,' I argued; 'it may be mere myth!'

'Possibly,' replied Holmes; 'but there are features about Shoreswood – or its occupants, at least – that make the existence there of a secret chamber rather more likely. The Davenokes were well-known recusants during the religious troubles of the sixteenth century and were often suspected of harbouring Catholic priests. From what we know of the family, I think it more than likely that they did so, and that they had some hidey-hole constructed for the purpose, if one did not exist already. Such priest-holes are a common feature in houses of the period, and the proximity of Shoreswood to the east coast would make it an ideal first staging-post for anyone arriving secretly from the Continent. Then there is the later tradition that Charles II was hidden at Shoreswood for a night: whilst that seems unlikely to be true, it may well be that one of the other Royalist leaders was sheltered there on his way to follow Charles abroad and that it was this which gave rise to the rumour.'

'It is possible,' I conceded. 'What a dark, confusing business it is! What is the purpose of it all? What is happening at Shoreswood? It seems to me that we have learnt nothing that can shed any light upon it at all.'

'There is one thing,' said he. 'But, come! We approach our station! We can continue this interesting discussion later.'

Holmes had sent a wire from London and the Shoreswood trap was waiting for us at the station. We sprang in, the driver whipped up the horse and we rattled off at a great speed. The rain had quite stopped now and the sky was clearing, as the rags and tatters of the storm-rack were hurried on their way by a fresh breeze. We passed at a clatter through the outskirts of a village, then down a series of narrow, sodden lanes, where the arching trees met high overhead in a translucent green canopy and the golden rays of the afternoon sun sparkled upon the damp hedgerows.

After a drive of perhaps five miles, we turned in abruptly at the gates of the Shoreswood estate, where the close ranks of colossal beeches cast a dark and dismal shade. For some time, the drive wound between the trees and passed beside a quiet mere, thick with weeds; then the ground on either hand rose up steeply in banks of crumbling, bare earth, from which gnarled tree-roots protruded forlornly. All at once, we emerged from this gloom, rounded a small hillock and crossed an old stone bridge over a stream, and there before us lay Shoreswood Hall, grey and forbidding, its recesses in deep shadow. But for a curtain flapping from an upstairs window, I should have taken it for an ancient and long-uninhabited ruin.

At the centre of this grim pile, a low flight of crumbling and lichen-blotched steps led up to a dark oak door and, as we approached, this door was opened and a man in the garb of a butler stepped out. He had reached the foot of the steps and was about to speak to us when a second, slighter figure appeared in the doorway and ran with great haste down the steps. To my surprise, I saw that it was Lady Davenoke herself, clearly in a state of great distress.

'That will be all right, Hardwick,' said she, in a breathless voice. 'These gentlemen are guests of mine. You may return to your duties.'

A look of acute surprise came over his features and he made as if to speak, but she paid him no heed and turned to us.

'Please come with me, gentlemen,' said she, her breast heaving violently with emotion. 'I have much to tell you.' She set off at once with short, quick steps, across the lawn, away from the house and towards a dense thicket of trees, one hand clutching her straw bonnet to her head, the other gathering the hem of her light-blue dress above the wet grass. We followed her along a narrow overgrown path which wound about the woods for some twenty or thirty yards, until we reached a small clearing, in which an old and weather-worn stone seat stood in picturesque isolation. All around, and upon the seat itself, the fallen leaves of the previous autumn lay in thick profusion.

'We shall not be overheard here,' said Lady Davenoke breathlessly, casting an anxious glance back the way we had come.

'We are at your disposal,' said Sherlock Holmes in a comforting tone. 'When you have collected yourself, perhaps you could let us have the details of what has occurred.'

'Edith and I returned here full of hope,' responded the other after a moment, 'but we were soon dispossessed of that foolishness. Upon the second night, I was roused from sleep by a tapping at my bedroom door and found Edith there in the darkness, weeping with fright at the strange noises she had heard.'

'What sort of noises?' interrupted Holmes sharply.

'Just as I had heard previously: the soft opening and closing of doors and creeping footsteps upon the stairs. Poor girl! She had come to me for comfort, but that I could not give her, for my blood was as chilled as her own. For twenty minutes we sat together upon my bed, but we heard nothing further. The following day I had her bed moved into my room and since then we have at least had each other's companionship in the night-time. But the evil, secret movements of the night have not abated and our sleep has scarcely been improved. One night we both saw a faint light by the river. I knew then that it was no mere product of my imagination. On another occasion, Edith swore that she saw a stooping figure in the chapel ruins, although I could not myself make it out.

'Even in sleep I am tormented and have had the most terrible nightmares imaginable.' She shook her head quickly as a shudder of revulsion passed through her body. 'Upon the fourth night, Edith was wakened by a noise and saw to her surprise that my bed was empty. Fighting against her fears, she ventured out into the corridor. There, she says, she found me, at the head of the stairs in my nightgown, my eyes staring with horror. Yet believe me, Mr Holmes, when I say that I have no recollection of how I came to be there. It was as if I had been summoned in my sleep by some evil power. Oh, thank God that Edith was there to lead me back gently to the safety of my own room and bed!'

'Has your letter to the Royal Suffolk Hotel been returned to you?' queried Holmes as Lady Davenoke paused.

'About two days after my return from London,' she answered, nodding her head slightly. 'The manager had been obliged to open my letter in order to see who had sent it, that he might return it to the correct address. He had then placed the letter, envelope and all, together with a note from himself, in one of the hotel's own large envelopes, which had been sealed. However, as I came to open this envelope, it was immediately obvious to me that someone had steamed open the flap and attempted, not entirely successfully, to re-secure it. I said nothing, but at once recalled the look of guilt I had seen in Hardwick's eyes as he brought in the mail that morning.

'The following day, to take our minds from the dark conspiracy which seemed to encircle us, we decided to plant a few daffodil bulbs by the edge of the woods. The fresh air, and thoughts of spring flowers, would be a tonic to us both. We found trowels and a small sack of bulbs, and I brought out a couple of old newspapers for us to kneel on. Newspapers and journals which are no longer required are kept in a cupboard near the kitchen, and I had taken a small pile from there at random. As we were engaged in our bulb-planting, Edith chanced upon a humorous item in the newspaper upon which she was kneeling and began to read it aloud.

'"What a preposterous story!" I cried, laughing. "And when did all that nonsense take place, Edith?"

'"Why, just last Monday, believe it or not!" said she gaily, joining her own laughter to my own.

'"One moment," said I, as a sudden thought caused the laughter to die in my throat. "Let me have a look at that paper, Edith." I took it from her and saw that it was the *Globe*, published on the very afternoon of the day I called to see you, Mr Holmes. "Does this newspaper belong to you, Edith?" said I to Miss Strensall. She shook her head. She had not, she said, had any newspaper with her the day we left London, but she remembered that I had purchased one at Liverpool Street railway terminal just before we caught our train.

"'It was not this one," said I, "but the *St James's Gazette* – which is still where I left it, in my bedroom. So how, then, came a London evening newspaper to be in Shoreswood Hall, if we did not bring it?"

'Her face fell grave as she saw my meaning. Instinctively, without thought, we both looked quickly over our shoulders, towards the Hall. Blank, dark windows stared back at us from its drab grey walls, but it seemed to me as I looked that a face had rapidly withdrawn from one of the upper windows even as we had turned.

'The discovery of the newspaper brought home to me afresh the horror of my position, all ignorant of the hidden deeds about me. We had sought to distract our thoughts from such things in the garden, but instead had made a discovery that we could not have imagined. What the significance of it was, I could not see; but I impressed upon Miss Strensall that she must not speak a word on the matter and vowed to communicate with you at the first opportunity.

'I wrote the letter that night and the following day suggested to Miss Strensall that we walk down to the village post office together. As we were descending the steps of the house, Hardwick, who had evidently heard the door, hurried out after us and enquired if he could be of service.

"'I do not think so," said I, and informed him of our errand.

"'If you wish, my lady," said he, "you may give the letter to me and I will have Staples run down with it."

"'No, thank you," I replied firmly. "It is a lovely day and I am sure we shall find the walk beneficial."

'As we crossed the bridge, I glanced back and saw that Hardwick was still standing in the open doorway of the house. I knew that he would dearly have loved to see the address upon my letter, and to read its contents, and I had, I confess, an odd sense of elation to know that for once I was the one with the secret, I was the one causing anxiety in others.'

'Is there anything else?' queried Holmes, raising his head, which had been sunk in contemplation upon his breast.

'That day and the next were mercifully free of event,' replied our companion with feeling. 'But this morning's discovery has quite remedied the deficiency.' She spoke these words with slow emphasis and as she did so the colour passed visibly from her face. It was evident that in speaking to us, the consciousness of recent events had been for a short time banished from her mind, but now, as her narrative was brought up to date, the full horror of them returned to her.

'What is it?' said Holmes in a soft voice, evidently perceiving as well as I the abrupt change in Lady Davenoke's features.

'Oh, it is so horrible! So horrible and pointless!'

Holmes raised his eyebrows questioningly.

'Someone,' she said, with emotion throbbing in her voice; 'someone has killed Bruno, Edward's beloved sheepdog. We found him this morning, Edith and I. He lay just within the woods, near the ruined chapel. He had been struck a heavy blow and the side of his head was a mass of blood—'

Her words ended abruptly and with a terrible wail of grief she began to sob uncontrollably. I gave her my handkerchief and put my hand upon her arm, and she turned to me and wept upon my shoulder.

Somewhere in the distance a woman's voice called. Holmes left us, but returned in a moment accompanied by a small blonde-haired young woman, whom I took to be Edith Strensall.

'Oh, Amelia!' she cried in distress, rushing forward to put her arm round her friend. 'Do not weep so, my dear!'

'What can we do, Mr Holmes?' said the other, her sobs lessening a little. 'Must I live forever in this nightmare?'

'You have been very brave and sensible so far,' returned my friend in an encouraging tone. 'If you can be so for just a little longer, I promise you that I shall have some news for you by tomorrow.'

'Do you mean it?' said she, her reddened eyes opening wide with hope. 'Do you really mean it, Mr Holmes?'

'Most certainly, Lady Davenoke.'

'My husband—?'

'Twenty-four hours, Lady Davenoke, twenty-four hours. For the present you ladies may return to the needlework which our visit has interrupted – there is no mystery, madam; I observed the unmistakable mark of a thimble upon your finger when first you greeted us. Until tomorrow, then!'

The sun broke through the patchy clouds as we left the wood and cast long shadows across the lawn. A warm smell of wet vegetation filled the air and all nature seemed refreshed by the recent rain. Our way to the bridge across the stream took us close by the ruined chapel. Holmes paused there a moment, a thoughtful expression upon his face; then, indicating that I should wait at the edge of the ruins, he stepped over a few loose stones and proceeded to examine the whole area with minute care. Back and forth he went, now standing, now stooping, now down upon his hands and knees, his nose barely an inch above the flagstones. Then he took from his pocket a small, powerful lens, with which he inspected more closely certain marks upon the crumbling walls and floor. From time to time he frowned and muttered to himself, whether in puzzlement or satisfaction I could not tell, until at length, pocketing his lens once more, he rejoined me upon the lawn.

'Come,' said he. 'There is an inn in the last village we passed, about a mile down the road. Perhaps we can get a little sustenance there.'

A pleasant walk of some twenty minutes brought us to the Black Lion, where Mr Jelks, the genial, soft-spoken landlord, produced an excellent meal for us of cold meat and pickles, and a pot of tea.

Afterwards, having booked rooms for the night, we repaired to the private sitting-room upstairs.

'You are no doubt wondering what I intend to do,' said Sherlock

Holmes, when he had lit his pipe and we had smoked in silence for some time.

'I confess that I am quite in the dark, both as to what has gone before and what is to come,' I replied. 'But what puzzles me most is why, if you are so certain that Davenoke is at Shoreswood, you did not apprise his wife of the fact.'

'Our *locus standi* is a delicate one,' replied my friend after a moment. 'Words of explanation were better coming from Davenoke's own lips than from mine.'

'But if such words of explanation are not forthcoming?'

'Then we must act as we see fit. Lady Davenoke certainly deserves an explanation from someone.'

'I cannot imagine what that explanation could be,' I remarked. 'The whole affair is nothing but darkness and confusion!'

'Not entirely,' returned Holmes. 'You must bear in mind that Edward Davenoke's disappearance was abrupt; his wife had had no indication that anything of the sort might occur and such a desertion of his new bride seems out of character for the man. We must suppose, then, that it was as a result of something which took place after his return from abroad. Is there anything we know of which took place then and which might fit the part?'

'All we know,' I suggested, 'is that Davenoke's father died and was buried two or three days later.'

'Anything else?'

'Nothing of significance. He called in to see the solicitor over some trivial matter, just after his father's death.'

'Precisely, Watson! Precisely! There, if you will recall, the solicitor gave him a bundle of old documents, thereby fulfilling the instruction he had been given many years before, by Edward Davenoke's father.'

'The solicitor did not believe the papers to be of any importance.'

'In his eyes, perhaps not. But he was only guessing, from their ancient appearance and from the fact that Sir John had deposited them with him nearly twenty years ago. He had not, as he admitted to

Lady Davenoke, actually read the documents. Let us suppose that they pertain to the family legend.'

'Why should they?'

'Well, what else do you suggest? They are evidently historical and equally evidently of value to the family; otherwise, why deposit them with the solicitor in that way? Moreover, they are sealed personally by Sir John, so that even his trusted solicitor is not privy to their content – a suggestive point, do you not agree?'

I nodded, and he continued.

'Now, we know from tradition that it is only when the heir takes possession of the estate that he learns the family secrets, which are known to no one else: Edward Davenoke said something of the sort himself. But we also know that, according to his father, who seemed to take the matter most seriously, "the Lord of the Manor of Shoreswood never speaks of the legend", or something of the sort – and that prohibition seemed to include his own son. It is therefore apparent that the only way the heir can possibly learn anything of the matter is from documents passed on to him when he comes into his inheritance, documents which are at all other times locked away from human gaze. It seems certain beyond peradventure, then, that the documents which the solicitor passed to young Davenoke, whatever else they may have dealt with, contained details of the legend of the Beast of Shoreswood, the secret chamber and all the rest of it.'

'I see that you must be right,' I remarked. 'Indeed, it seems perfectly obvious, the way you describe it. But if we assume that it is so, where does that get us?'

'It gets us to the point where we must penetrate to the secret chamber tonight,' said Holmes. 'Yes, Watson, we must. For therein lies the source of all that has occurred to so distress our client.'

'But no one knows where it is!'

'It is not the location of the chamber which presents the problem, but its entrance. He who knows the entrance can scarcely fail to find the chamber itself. So our position is not so hopeless as you suppose.'

'You know the entrance, then?' I cried in surprise.

'One of them, at least. There will almost certainly be an entrance to the chamber in the house itself, but we might look for a year and not find it. Fortunately, however, there is also an entrance in the ruined chapel, which has proved somewhat easier of discovery. I had suspected already that there would be an entrance there – Lady Davenoke's account of the noises she had heard there, and the lights and the dark figure she had seen, indicated as much – and my close examination of the chapel this afternoon confirmed all my suspicions. The secret entrance is beneath one of the flagstones. It was simplicity itself to identify, for it was the only one which did not have thick grass growing in the cracks around it. The grass had evidently been cleared away, quite recently, presumably to facilitate the opening of the stone, which must hinge up in some way.

'I was also able to discover,' Holmes continued after a moment, as he refilled his pipe, 'that the man who has been using that entrance and exit is around five foot six inches tall, wears size eight boots with steel tips, smokes a Latakia mixture and wears a very long plaid coat or ulster. So our midnight prowler begins to sound somewhat more like Edward Davenoke and somewhat less like a monster from the deep!'

'How can you tell all these things?'

'His boots had chipped away the stones in no fewer than seven places and left clear impressions in the rain-softened ground at the edge of the ruins. His height I gauge from his stride, a piece of elementary reasoning with which you are no doubt familiar. He had knocked his pipe out against a corner, and some of the unmistakable dark tobacco had remained unburnt. Woollen fibres were caught on the rough edge of a stone, and similar traces where he must have stepped over a raised row of stones at the edge of the ruins indicated clearly that his overcoat must reach almost to the ground. The dog was killed in the chapel, by the way, and dragged to where Lady Davenoke found it. But, come! We must now turn our minds to tonight's enterprise. I have informed the landlord that we shall be out this evening and may be late in returning, and he has agreed to leave a back door open for us. I also took the opportunity when downstairs to locate a stout iron rod in the courtyard. Its usual employment is in the manipulation of refractory cart-wheels, but it should serve us well when we come to lever up the secret door. Incidentally,' he added after a moment; 'I should be obliged if you would fill your brandy flask before we leave. The sky is clear and the night may be a cold one. Now let us rest a little while, and compose our minds in silence, for later we shall need to be alert.'

The sun had already set when we left the inn and, away to the west, where a dark line of trees stood on the horizon, the sky met the land in a band of dull orange. High above us a noisy rabble of crows flew steadily westwards, home to their roost. By the time we reached the Shoreswood gateway, the sky was quite dark and the tree-lined drive ahead of us presented an impenetrable wall of blackness to our view. Down this dark alley we walked, and as we did so there came from time to time slight rustling noises in the undergrowth beside us, as some nocturnal creature scurried away at the sound of our footsteps. Once I was startled as an owl hooted loudly, directly over our heads. It wanted no great imagination to understand the fear and superstition with which primitive man had regarded the long hours of the night, and the unseen creatures which move abroad then. Beside me, my friend walked on steadily in silence. If he were entertaining thoughts like those that filled my own mind he gave no sign of it.

Presently there came to our ears the soft silvery babbling of water, and I knew we were approaching the small river which skirted the house and the chapel. Moments later we reached the bridge. Ahead of us in the darkness lay the yet darker mass of Shoreswood Hall. A single candle shone weakly in an upstairs window.

In silence Holmes motioned me to follow him, as he left the path and crossed the wet turf to the ruined chapel; in silence we sat for perhaps forty minutes, each on our block of stone, like a bizarre pair of statues. The night was indeed a chill one, and when I felt Holmes's hand tap my arm lightly I passed him the brandy flask without query. Shortly afterwards, the candle in the window was extinguished and the blackness of the Hall was complete. Turning, so that his heavy cloak shielded the light from the house, he struck a match and lit a small pocket-lantern, then immediately closed the shutter. 'Come,' said he, rising to his feet.

It was chiefly by the sense of touch that we found the flagstone we sought, and I was able to confirm with my fingers my friend's earlier observation that the grass had been cleared away from its edge. In its place, I felt a narrow space all around, from which a faint whisper of cold, dank air seemed to rise to my finger-ends. He handed me the lantern, and by the tiny slit of light which escaped from it I saw him push the narrower end of his makeshift lever into the crack and press down upon it. There came a scraping noise, as of stone upon stone and the flag lifted an inch or two. I took the weight and, together, with as little noise as possible, we turned the slab right back until it rested upon a block behind it. Lying flat on his stomach, Holmes plunged the lantern into the black hole which had opened before us and from which a foul, mephitic odour now arose. The yellow light of the lantern showed the earth floor below the hole to be some six or seven feet down. An old rotten-looking chest stood immediately beneath us, and had evidently been placed there to provide a step, for its edge was splintered and caked with mud. To one side of this sinister pit, a dark opening indicated where a low-roofed tunnel led away in the direction of the house.

Without a word, Holmes lowered himself into the darkness. 'Be careful of your footing!' he whispered sharply as I made to follow him. 'The lid of this chest has no more strength than a rotten apple!'

In a moment I had joined him and, stooping, we entered the tunnel. Like the pit before it, the walls were clad in crumbling and ancient-looking brickwork, which narrowed to an arch at the top, the whole blotched all over, and covered with slime and the revolting excrescences of mould. In one or two places the brickwork had crumbled to dust and loose earth had fallen in and lay in heaps upon the floor. From these heaps, foul insects scurried and slithered as we passed, like figments of some evil dream. The smell of the damp earth was thick and unpleasant now, and mingled with the more penetrating smell of rot and decay in an almost overpowering stench.

For perhaps thirty yards this vile corridor led us on, now rising slightly, now falling a little, and all the time our backs were bent, for the roof was scarce four foot in height. Glad I was when my companion paused and held out his arm as a warning and I knew that we must be approaching the end. He closed his lantern down to the narrowest of slits and we proceeded then with great caution, our footsteps making no sound upon the earth floor. Presently the tunnel opened out slightly and the roof sloped up to about six feet, and we found ourselves before a stout, ancient-looking oak door. Its hinges were rusted and frail, but appeared from the sheen upon them to have been recently oiled. Through the crack beneath the door came a thin line of light. Holmes motioned me to silence and placed his hand upon the latch.

Quite what I expected to see as the door swung open, I do not know; but it could not have been the strange scene that now met our gaze. Before us was a narrow chamber, its walls formed of large blocks of stone, which glistened green with the damp. There was no window, but immediately opposite stood another identical oak door, and high in the wall to our right was what appeared to be some kind of ventilation-grille. In the centre of the flagged floor stood an old mildewed table upon which were several piles of old documents done up in tape, and a few loose sheets. Beside these stood two bottles of ink, a box of quill pens and a pair of gold-rimmed spectacles, neatly folded. On the floor to the side of the table was a stack of massive old books, bound in wood and leather, atop which stood a low-burning lamp, whose glimmer we had seen beneath the door. To the right of the table stood a simple wooden chair; to its left, against the damp wall, a crude cot bed, upon which lay a man, fully dressed, face down and asleep.

For several minutes we stood there in silence and might have stood there several more; but all at once, as if he sensed our presence – for we made no noise that could have roused him – the figure on the bed stirred, rolled over and sat up, rubbing his eyes as he did so.

He was a slim, pale-faced young man, with a look of studious perplexity upon his features. His dark hair was unkempt, his clothes dishevelled; but, even so, there was something civilised and sensitive about his appearance. No bank-clerk puzzling over an unbalanced ledger, no country parson pondering his next sermon could have seemed less like a denizen of a strange underground lair than this young man we now saw before us. Absent-mindedly, without turning his head, he reached out his hand for his spectacles.

'Sir Edward Davenoke?' said Sherlock Holmes softly. The young man before us started up as if shot, his eyes wide with terror. He sprang unsteadily to his feet, his face as white as a sheet. For a moment I was certain he would faint with the shock of our sudden appearance, but he clutched the edge of the table to steady himself and spoke suddenly and abruptly, in a nervous, breathless manner.

'What! – who are you?' he cried, his eyes roaming wildly from Holmes to me and back again, as if he could not control their movement. 'What are you doing? How came you here? – How dare you!'

'My name is Sherlock Holmes,' said my friend in a calm voice. 'This is my friend, Dr Watson. I have been retained by your wife to find you.'

'But – but she believes I am in London.'

'Fortunately, I did not.'

'But – how came you?' cried the other again, his voice almost hysterical. Then his eyes wandered to the open door behind us and the long dark passage which stretched away. 'You have come through the tunnel!' he cried. 'No, no; that is impossible! No one knows of it! No one can have learnt the secret!'

'There is no secret of man's contrivance that cannot be uncovered,' said Sherlock Holmes softly.

'How dare you!' cried Davenoke, his wild confusion resolving itself into hot anger. 'How dare you intrude upon the privacy of my house!'

'Your wife would have us find you wherever you were,' returned

Holmes; 'that we are here therefore depends only upon the fact that you yourself are here.'

'Why, you impertinent scoundrel! You interfering busybody! You have no right to pry into the affairs of others!'

'Nor have I the desire.'

'What I tell my wife is my own business!'

'But when you tell her nothing but lies, she has a right to learn the truth from someone else. I act only in her interests and at her request. She has been most grievously worried by your unexplained disappearance.'

'I cannot tell her,' said the other after a moment's hesitation. 'I am engaged upon a matter of the utmost privacy, which must remain secret, even from my wife.'

'You are engaged in a study of the family legend, the so-called "Curse of the Davenokes".'

'You seem to know a great deal of my business,' retorted the other, a spark of anger returning to his eye. Then as Holmes did not speak, he nodded his head slowly and when he spoke it was in a more subdued voice: 'Yes,' said he; 'partly that.'

'Richard Davenoke's account, in fact, of the troubles which beset the area during his time, in the early years of the seventeenth century.'

'That indeed forms part of it. You have obviously read something of the matter, Mr Holmes.' There was a note of respect in his voice and also something of caution. 'You will be aware, then, that it is only when a Davenoke succeeds to his inheritance that the secret is vouchsafed to him. I am here because I have sworn to be here. I am acting as I was instructed to act, in a letter which my father left for me with the solicitor. He enjoined upon me that before reading the documents he left for me, I swear an oath upon the Bible that I shall at once study all that my ancestors have written upon the subject, communicating with no one at all whilst I am so engaged, and leaving this chamber only at night-time; and that I shall tell no one of what I have learnt, when I have completed the task. So my father instructed me; so his father had instructed him; so each heir is instructed by the one that has gone before.

'Do not for one moment suppose that I wished to be here when I knew my wife had returned to the house; but there was nothing I could do about it when once I had pledged my word. I had no idea when I began that the task would be so great, and I thought I should have it finished in a couple of days. But there is so much to read, and the script is so ancient and unfamiliar. There are places, too, where it has almost faded from sight altogether, and these passages I am duty bound to copy out afresh, as my forebears have done, that the story be not lost altogether. The history is written in many hands, among which I recognise that of my own father. But, during all the time I have spent here, not five minutes have passed but I have thought of my wife – Heaven knows, I longed to see her again! One night, I even crept to her bedroom window, hoping to catch a sight of her, but the curtains were drawn and the window was closed and secured in some way, so I did not succeed in my plan.'

'You succeeded at least in putting terror into your wife's heart,' said Holmes sternly. 'It was a most foolish thing to do. She had already observed your creeping about the lawn in the moonlight, and believed that you were a phantom from another age.'

Davenoke sat down heavily on his chair and clapped his hand to his head.

'You could at least have sent a message to your wife through your confidant, Hardwick,' continued Holmes, in a tone of remonstrance.

'No, no!' cried the other in a pleading tone. 'You do not understand! The oath forbids me from speaking to anyone, anyone at all. Hardwick brings me food and takes away my empty plates, and that is all.'

'Lady Davenoke heard him, one midnight. That also frightened her.'

'I regret that it did so, but the preservation of secrecy was uppermost in my mind. For it is written that he who breaks his holy oath upon any point shall bring down a curse upon himself and his household.'

Holmes snorted. 'You wrote a letter to your wife,' said he, 'which the butler posted for you, to make it appear that you were in London. If you could communicate to the extent of a lie, you could communicate the truth.'

'Hardwick left a note with my food one night,' replied the other after a moment, 'informing me that Amelia had written to the Royal Suffolk Hotel. At first I intended to do nothing about it, but when he later informed me that she was leaving Shoreswood and would not tell him where she was going, I became desperate. I strongly suspected that she would go to London, and in that moment of desperation I broke my vow of silence, instructed Hardwick to follow her, to ensure that she came to no harm, and hurriedly composed the letter you refer to, telling him to post it while away. I did it for her sake, to reassure her. It seemed the best idea at the time, but I was, as I say, desperate, and not capable of proper judgement upon the matter. I knew I was breaking my oath, but prayed that the curse would not fall upon me. Now, what have I gained? I have succeeded only in invoking the curse while achieving nothing, either for myself or my wife.'

'This talk of curses is pernicious and evil,' said Holmes sharply. 'You must not allow your mind to be prey to such ancient superstitions. The Dark Ages are passed and gone, Sir Edward!'

'Are they?' returned the other. 'Are they indeed? You might speak otherwise had you been confined in this cell as long as I have, Mr Holmes.' He rose to his feet once more, his mouth set in bitter determination, a strange light in his eye. 'Had you lived alone in this hell-hole and spent your every hour in the company of these—' He brought his fist down violently upon the pile of documents which covered the table, sending them flying to the floor. 'Oh, no, Mr Holmes!' cried he, with a horrible, sneering laugh: 'There is more in Heaven and Earth than is dreamt of in *your* philosophy!'

Holmes snorted. 'Let us keep to particulars,' said he sharply. 'What happened to the dog?'

'Bruno? I killed him! Yes, I do not wonder that your features express shock! He had evidently managed to free himself somehow, for as I was climbing out of my rat-hole in the chapel last night he sprang at me without warning, out of the darkness. No doubt he merely wanted to greet his master, but I was unnerved already by what I had been reading and he took me utterly by surprise. Before I knew what I was doing, I had lashed out with the stick I was carrying and caught him heavily upon the side of the head. He fell without a sound and breathed his last at my feet. Already, the curse begins to take effect, you see, Mr Holmes!' A perverse glint of triumph replaced the look of horror in Davenoke's eye as he spoke these last words. 'Deny it if you can!' cried he.

'Tell me then,' said Holmes, answering the vehemence of the other with firmness of his own: 'Who has placed this curse upon you?'

'It is written,' responded the other. 'It is written in the family documents. The Davenokes have been true to their obligations for countless generations.'

'It is written by Richard Davenoke,' retorted Holmes; 'a man as you are a man. What right or power has he to place a curse upon generations unborn? Indeed,' Holmes continued, as Davenoke did not reply, 'if any man has ever forfeited the right to impose obligations upon another it is he.'

'What do you mean?'

'Richard Davenoke was a murderer most foul and bestial.'

Sir Edward sprang back, a look of great fear in his eye. 'You cannot say this!' he cried. 'You cannot know!'

'It is only too obvious. Richard Davenoke himself committed all those ghastly crimes which were ascribed to "the Beast of Shoreswood". He himself was the beast, the only monster who ever dwelt here. To anyone familiar with the ways of evil, the pattern is all too clear. There never had been a Beast of Shoreswood before he invented it. It is the most common feature of all myths: the projection back into the distant and unrecorded past of what belongs rightly only to the present. The invention of history is a great device for those who would hide their own present evil. Richard's younger brother – the one who had drowned in the moat – was rumoured to have had a hideous deformity of the features; but the hideous deformity was in no one's face, but in the mind of Richard.'

'He was totally insane,' said the other simply, clutching his head in his hand. 'The truth was that the brother had indeed drowned in the moat when young, but he had drowned by the hand of Richard.'

'I suspected it,' said Holmes. 'And these papers, I imagine, consist of Richard's personal history of his whole vile, bloody life: a sort of diabolical "Confessions of St Augustine".'

Sir Edward nodded his head slowly, his face haggard and grave. 'How you can know these things, I do not know. The family has kept the secret for three hundred years. The family name has not been stained.'

'It serves no purpose now.'

'I have given my oath to my own father, as every Davenoke has done before me.'

'Indeed, right back to Richard himself, who sought to protect only his own name. It is there the chain begins, in a pool of blood. What one man has begun, another may end. You must break the chain, Sir Edward!'

'I have my duty as a Davenoke.'

'Your first duty is to the living.'

'A solemn oath is a solemn oath.'

'A solemn oath upon an evil issue is no oath at all.'

'Do not fence words with me, Mr Holmes!' cried the other, his voice rising with anger.

'Your wife – Lady Davenoke – has been half out of her mind with worry these last weeks. Does that mean nothing to you?'

Sir Edward did not reply, and it was evident from the tortured twitching of his face that his mind was in a state of terrible turmoil and indecision. Sherlock Holmes's firm manner and clear argument had had some effect, and a battle was now raging in his soul between the forces of light and of dark; between independent reason and the power of tradition. For several minutes a deathly hush fell upon that dank chamber as Sir Edward rocked upon his feet, his head clutched in his hands. At length he opened his mouth as if about to speak, but what he was to say then, we were never to learn. For there came all at once a most startling interruption.

The sound of clattering feet broke suddenly upon the silence and seconds later the heavy door opposite burst open with a crash. In rushed Hardwick, clad only in a dressing-gown and bearing a lantern. His hair was awry, his eyes wild with panic.

'Sir Edward!' cried he in anguish, taking no heed of our presence. 'Come quickly! Lady Amelia has had an accident. Oh, come at once!'

'What!' cried the other.

'She walked in her sleep, Sir Edward. She did not know the stairs. She has fallen and hurt herself. Come quickly!'

We hurried at once from the room, Davenoke leading the way up a steep stone staircase which seemed to be set within the very wall of the building. Under a low arch we passed and emerged through the back of a colossal old fireplace, into a dark and empty room. Through an open doorway we hastened and along an echoing corridor, the madly swinging lanterns casting their wild light upon dark and sombre old portraits, grim suits of armour and heavy medieval weapons which hung upon the walls. Then we were through a doorway and into a wide hall, lit with many lamps and candles.

Three or four people stood in their night-clothes at the foot of the stair, their faces full of fear and apprehension. Before them lay the prostrate figure of Amelia Davenoke.

'I am a doctor,' I cried. 'Stand aside. Do not move her!'

I bent to the still figure at their feet. The luxuriant copper-coloured hair lay loosely upon her shoulders and I moved it gently to one side. There was something horribly unnatural about the angle of her head and neck. Desperately and repeatedly I sought for signs of life, but all in vain. It was clear that she had broken her neck in the fall and would breathe no more. I cannot describe the feelings which coursed then through my soul; I recall only that I rose to my feet and breathed deeply before I could make the terrible pronouncement which had fallen to my lot.

The women present burst forth at once into terrible weeping. I believe, in truth, that they had known the sad fact already, but had hoped against all reason that I could prove their senses to be mistaken. Hardwick began to usher them gently up the stairs and I had turned to say something to Holmes, when we were all struck rigid by a terrible piercing cry.

'The curse is come upon me!' cried the young baronet, in a voice which struck a chill to my soul. 'It has came to pass as it is written!'

'Sir Edward—' began Sherlock Holmes.

'You!' interrupted the other, turning upon my friend with a murderous venom in his eye. 'You dare to speak to me!' he cried. 'Get out! Leave my house this instant! Get out, do you hear !'

After only a moment's hesitation, Holmes made a sign to me and we quickly withdrew.

'It is a terrible thing, to leave him there like that,' said my friend tensely, as we passed through the front doorway into the darkness of the night. 'But, had we stayed, it might have been more terrible yet. You saw the look in his eye, Watson.'

I had to acknowledge the truth of his observation. Dreadful as it seemed to walk away from that tragic scene, there was nothing else we could do. The man had every right to throw us out, innocent though we were of any part in the tragedy which had befallen him.

Not a single word further passed between us that night, but I caught sight of Holmes's ashen face as we mounted the stairs of the inn and saw more clearly there than any words could ever have conveyed, how deeply the death of Amelia Davenoke had moved him. For myself, I confess that I was numb with shock at the events of the evening, and sat long in a chair, smoking my pipe and unable to sleep.

It was scant hours later, and the first grey light of dawn was breaking, when I was roused by a terrific commotion downstairs. At first I endeavoured to ignore it; I needed no further alarms that night. But the tumult increased, until I wearily left my bed, slipped on my dressing-gown and hurried downstairs to see what was the matter.

I found Sherlock Holmes, fully dressed, at the foot of the stairs, in earnest conversation with the landlord.

'There's worse, Watson,' said he, turning to me. 'I am a desperate fool to have left that young man alone last night – a criminal fool!'

'Whatever has happened?' I cried in alarm.

'Shoreswood Hall is ablaze, that's what! They have sent for fire-engines from Framlingham, Woodbridge and goodness knows where else, but I'm damned if it will do any good. Quickly now! Into your clothes and let us see if we can help!'

Two minutes later I was dressed and we were hurrying up the road in the company of three men from the village. It was a chill morning and patches of mist lay in hollows in the fields.

'It seems,' said Holmes to me, 'that not long after you and I had been so unceremoniously ejected from Shoreswood last night, Davenoke decided to make it a general prescription and threw everyone else out, too.'

'What!' I cried. 'Miss Strensall, too?'

'Miss Strensall, Hardwick, the cook, the maids – everyone. Hardwick drove them all down to Wickham, where his sister has a house. However, he found himself unable to sleep for anxiety over his young master; so, like the faithful servant he is, he drove back again to Shoreswood to see if there was anything he could do to help. When he got there the house was going up like a bonfire, from one end to the other, and there was no sign of Sir Edward. He tried to find a way in but the fierce heat drove him back, so he came down and roused the whole village.'

'There'll be no putting it out if it's caught as he says,' said one of the men with us. 'There's too much dry wood in that old place.'

At that moment a great surge of orange flame showed above the treetops ahead of us, like a giant fireball, and the distant noise of roaring and crackling came clearly on the morning air.

'It must be sixty feet in the air!' I cried.

'The roof has fallen in!' said Holmes in dismay.

'Aye!' cried one of the men with us. 'There'll be no saving her now.' We quickened our pace to a run, though each of us knew in his heart that the effort was useless, and when at last we reached the scene, the heat was so intense that we could get no closer than the ruined chapel. Small groups of silent men stood around there in impotent horror as the terrible inferno raged before them with an awesome, deafening roar. From every window the wicked flames blazed and spluttered with the force of a blast-furnace. From the top of the building, dense clouds of smoke and flame surged upwards, and scattered sparks and flaming debris all about us.

'Does anyone know where Sir Edward Davenoke is?' shouted Holmes at the top of his voice to one of the bystanders. In answer, the man raised one finger and pointed it at the dreadful sight before us.

At seven-thirty we finally abandoned our terrible vigil and returned to the inn. The fire-engines had at length arrived but had been unable to approach close enough to have any effect upon the fire. The officers of the County Constabulary were summoned, and Holmes spent a considerable time with them in the parlour of the inn, going over and over the events of the previous night. At length, when our presence could serve no further purpose, we made our way to the railway station, weary and dejected beyond description, and caught the first available train to London.

It was as we were passing Brentwood station that Sherlock Holmes spoke for the first and only time on what was the most melancholy and depressing journey I can ever recall.

'I have failed,' said he. 'I have failed more tragically than I have ever failed before.'

'Nonsense!' I retorted, seeing clearly what was passing in his mind. 'No blame can attach to you. There is nothing you could have done which would have averted this tragedy.'

'I could have told Lady Davenoke all I suspected, when we spoke yesterday afternoon. A positive theory, however disagreeable, is more consoling to the mind than a vague, nameless dread.'

'Perhaps, but the lady was in such a state of nerves that I doubt very much that your confidence would have had any beneficial effect upon her. Besides, you were endeavouring to limit your interference in the matter to the very minimum. Your judgement was sound.'

My friend lapsed into silence for a moment before replying.

'The saddest story I have ever known,' said he then, 'is that of the *Babes in the Wood*.'

My face must have betrayed the surprise I felt at this abrupt and, so it seemed to me, incongruous remark, for he hastened to assure me that he spoke in earnest.

'The whole of world literature contains nothing more pitiful,' he continued. 'There is no tragedy written which is not a mere embellishment upon that theme. What are Oedipus and Hamlet, but helpless babes lost in the thicket of fate, unable either to understand their predicament or to escape from it? In the story of the *Babes in the Wood*, the two infants are banished to the forest by a wicked parent and only spared the axe because the man delegated to do the deed shrinks from it at the last. So they wander together in the forest as the cold night closes in. Without food or shelter, and without either the knowledge or resource to procure them, their tenure of life is a brief and pathetic one. They die unloved and unwanted, forsaken and alone; and when they are dead the trees shed their leaves upon them, as a coverlet, and a robin pipes his song over their grave. And what is so pathetic and moving about their fate? It is that they are so innocent, so helpless. There is no true tragedy in the world's literature which you can name me, Watson, which is not that story retold.'

I was not disposed to argue with him, so I said nothing. Besides, I could see that he felt keenly the sentiments of which he spoke.

'And the profound sad truth,' he continued after a moment, 'which I confess has only come to me as I have advanced a little in years, is that, at bottom, when all the talking is done and the posturing abandoned, we are all lost babes, in the wood we know as life.'

I returned to Suffolk the following week to give evidence at the inquest. No traces had been found of the bodies of Sir Edward Davenoke and his wife, nor ever were. The verdict reached by the coroner's jury was one of accidental death in both cases, it being supposed that the blaze had been started by chance, by one of the many lamps and candles which had been lit that night. Sherlock Holmes, I was aware, was privately of the opinion that, distraught with grief, and driven perhaps beyond the bounds of sanity, Davenoke had fired the Hall himself; but neither Holmes nor I voiced this opinion publicly. Nothing would have been gained thereby, and the matter could in any case never have been proved for certain one way or the other. Of Shoreswood Hall itself nothing remained but a blackened shell upon a blackened field. It had occurred to me in London that the contents of that damp underground chamber in which we had spoken with Sir Edward might have escaped the inferno, but that, too, was empty and black, no doubt overcome by the intense heat of the raging fire above it.

———

This, then, is the true history of the final days of the family of Davenoke, resident in East Suffolk since the days of the Plantagenets, and of how Mr Sherlock Holmes and I came to be involved. It is my hope that this narrative, with all its faults and inadequacies, will go some way towards satisfying the curiosity of those many correspondents who have raised the matter with me, in particular that worthy archivist, Mr Alexander Pargeter of the Suffolk County Records Office at Ipswich. In closing I could do no better than to quote from an article which appeared in the *Daily Telegraph* three days after our return to London, under the heading 'THE LAST OF THE DAVENOKES'. The anonymous correspondent, in a fine essay, demonstrating round good sense and historical perception, comments upon the previous history of the family and laments the death of Sir Edward and that of his young American bride, upon whom so many hopes had rested, and concludes with the following remark:

'With the tragic and untimely death of Sir Edward Davenoke, seventh baronet of that title, and last of his line, there passes away for all time not merely his own family and name, nor yet merely one significant part of the history of the County of Suffolk, but, indeed, a part of the very history of England.'

The Adventure of the Minor Canon

The month of June is a time of long evenings and sunny weather, and a popular choice for weddings and other festivities. Yet, in England at least, the pleasant, balmy days of June are not infrequently punctuated by days of cooler, showery weather. Such days are but a fleeting annoyance to most people, forgotten almost as soon as they have passed; but a rainy day in June never fails to stir up memories for me, for it was on just such a day that the curious case of Martin Zennor was first brought to the attention of my friend, Sherlock Holmes.

Holmes had been busy for several weeks with a singular succession of cases, including the puzzling theft of the Bolingbroke miniature, the strange mystery surrounding 'The Deeping Question', and the sensational murder at the Nonpareil Club, and the unremitting effort he had put into these cases had at last taken its toll upon his strong and resilient constitution. On the morning in question, having finished his breakfast, he stood up from the table, stared out of the window for a moment at the rain-soaked street below, then announced that he was returning to his bed for an hour or two, as was his habit when he was exhausted. Scarcely had these words left his lips, however, when there came a strident peal at the front-door bell.

'Now, who is this,' said he with a weary sigh, 'come to plague us with his problems?'

A moment later, his question was answered. A young man in clerical garb was shown into the room and announced as Mr Martin Zennor. His thin, pale face showed signs of great anxiety and the dark shadows about his eyes suggested that he had slept little the previous night. I hung up his wet hat and coat, as Holmes waved him to a chair by the hearth and took his pipe from the mantelpiece. 'How can we help you,

Mr Zennor?' said he. 'You have, I see, recently arrived in London from the south-east.'

'That is true,' returned the other. 'I caught a train about seven this morning, arrived about ten minutes ago and have come here directly from the station. But how do you know?'

'They have taken up most of the paving stones outside the eastern front of Victoria station in the past few days, exposing the clay beneath. The rain has made this sticky, and it is difficult to avoid getting a little of it on one's instep when passing from the station exit to the cab-stand.' Holmes indicated his visitor's shoes, as he put a match to his pipe and seated himself in the vacant armchair by the hearth. 'Now,' he continued after a moment, puffing gently at his pipe; 'pray give us the details of what has brought you here.'

The young man did not reply at once, but fidgeted with his collar for a moment, then took out a handkerchief and blew his nose loudly. Holmes leaned back in his chair and closed his eyes, his face a placid mask of patience and calmness. Above his head, the blue wraiths of tobacco-smoke twisted and spiralled.

'My situation is a miserable one,' began his visitor at last, passing his hand across his brow, 'almost, one might say, a desperate one. I am accused – and practically condemned already, without a fair hearing – of attempting to steal a sum of money belonging to the cathedral at which I am one of the minor canons.'

'Which is, of course, Canterbury Cathedral.'

'What! You know already? May I ask who told you?'

'You did, Mr Zennor. We know that you have come up from the south-east and you stated that it has taken you about two hours to do so, so clearly the cathedral in question can only be Canterbury. But come, these are mere trifles; let us get down to the matter! You are quite innocent, I take it, of the charge laid against you?'

'Utterly so.'

'Then why are you accused?'

'The money – in the form of a cheque from a wealthy benefactor –

was discovered to be in my possession, shortly after it was found to be missing.'

'A circumstance for which you no doubt have a perfectly good explanation.'

'Unfortunately not.'

'Dear, dear!'

'The cheque was in an envelope in my coat-pocket, but how it came to be there, I have no idea.'

'How very interesting! If you did not put it there, then, presumably, someone else did. Hum! The cheque disappeared, I take it, from the cathedral offices?'

'That is so.'

'And the discovery of it in your possession: did that also take place at the cathedral, or in your lodgings?'

'Neither. It occurred here in London, just yesterday. I had come up to town on a couple of errands, one of which was to convey some papers to Canon Seagrave, one of the Archbishop's clerks at Lambeth Palace. I had also volunteered to bring with me an urgent letter from the Dean of the cathedral to the Archbishop. It was whilst I was there, at Lambeth Palace, that news of the cheque's disappearance reached London and also that the discovery was made that I had it in my possession. The general belief, I imagine, is that I was intending to exchange the cheque for cash at Sir Anthony Ingoldsby's bank, which is at Charing Cross.'

'He being the benefactor you referred to?'

'Precisely. He had made out the cheque for a hundred pounds, and had signed and dated it, but had been unsure to whom the cheque should be addressed, so had left that part of it blank.'

'Tut tut! A most inadvisable procedure! What a temptation such an unfinished cheque left lying about must present to the unscrupulous!'

'Well, the office in which it was left "lying about", as you put it, was, after all, in the cathedral precincts. One might perhaps be forgiven for believing that in such a place, the temptation to which you refer would be negligible.'

'Perhaps one might; but it is still unwise to leave such a temptation unguarded. It is generally a mistake to rely too heavily upon the innate virtue of those with whom you have dealings. It is always more agreeable to be pleasantly surprised by the appearance of virtue than to be disappointed by its absence. However, leaving such general considerations aside, the fact remains that the cheque vanished from the cathedral precincts in Canterbury and reappeared in your coat pocket in London. Could this not have been simply a mistake of some kind? Could the cheque not simply have been put in the wrong coat pocket?'

'That would, I agree, be the obvious conclusion; but it does not seem possible in this instance. It is not simply that the cheque should not have been in my pocket, it should not have been in anyone's pocket. It was in a tray on a shelf in the office, awaiting the arrival of the Dean's secretary, who would deal with it.'

'Who has access to this office you refer to?'

'Anyone, really. The door is never closed.'

'Is there always someone present in the office?'

'No, not always. It is the centre of activities for the minor canons, and people are coming in and out of it all day; but quite often, when we are all busy elsewhere in the cathedral, it is left unoccupied.'

'I see. And is it anywhere near where you hang your coat up?'

'Yes. There is a short corridor just outside the office, leading to the cathedral yard, in which there is a row of coat-hooks. All the minor canons hang their coats up there.'

'I suppose the coats all appear very similar,' remarked Holmes after a moment. 'Do they ever get muddled up?'

'It does happen occasionally. Of course, the coats are all marked somewhere with their owners' names or initials, but these marks are not all in the same place and sometimes, when people are in a hurry, they don't trouble to look for the mark, but just guess which coat is which.'

'I see. So, if, as you say, there was no legitimate reason for the cheque to be in anyone's pocket, it could not have been a simple accident, but must have been put there deliberately, for some reason. Do you consider you have any enemies, Mr Zennor, anyone who might wish to incriminate you?'

Our visitor shook his head. 'I am absolutely sure I do not. Of course, there is sometimes a certain degree of mild rivalry among the minor canons, but on the whole, I believe, we rub along very well together. No one could possibly gain anything by trying to besmirch my reputation.'

Holmes frowned and sat in silence for several minutes. Then he put down his pipe and took out his note-book. 'Perhaps,' said he, 'you could give me a list of all the minor canons at the cathedral. I think I shall have to speak to them, for it may be that, although innocent of any direct involvement in this puzzling matter, one or more of them may have seen or heard something which could cast a little light on it.'

'Certainly,' replied our visitor. 'There are six of us altogether. Apart from myself, these are Stafford Nugent, Wallace Wakefield, Hubert Bebington, Michael Earley and Henry Jeavons. We are all under the supervision of Dr Glimper, who is in overall charge of most day-to-day matters at the cathedral and who answers directly to the Dean himself.'

'Is there any seniority among the minor canons?'

'No. Except, of course, for Dr Glimper, we are all on a level footing.'

'What sort of a rule does Dr Glimper exercise over you?'

'When I was first there,' replied Zennor after a moment, 'I heard how ferocious and harsh he was to those under him; but in fact I have not really found him so. He is certainly strict, with regard to adherence to rules and regulations, and an absolute stickler for the observance of all formalities, both great and small, but behind his rather forbidding exterior, I believe he is quite kind and understanding of one's occasional failings.'

'What is his view of the present business?'

'He is convinced that it must be some kind of bizarre accident or mischance, although he can suggest no convincing explanation for it.'

'He believes in your innocence?'

Our visitor hesitated. 'I think so,' he replied after a moment, 'but I am not certain of it. I was interviewed on the matter late last night by the Dean's private secretary, Dr Wallis, with Dr Glimper in attendance. Dr Wallis was very sharp in his questioning, I must say. "This is a very serious matter, Zennor," said he, "and if you do not tell the truth, the consequences may be disastrous for you." I insisted that I *was* telling the truth and knew no more about the matter than anyone else; but he did not appear satisfied. Dr Glimper suggested that one of the cleaners might have accidentally knocked the envelope containing the cheque off the shelf and into a dustpan, and then, not noticing it until in the corridor outside the room, might have believed it had just fallen from one of the coats and thus – erroneously – replaced it in a random overcoat pocket.'

'How did Dr Wallis respond to that suggestion?'

'He described it as the least convincing explanation he had ever heard for anything in his life. Later, Dr Glimper told me that he could not protect me unless I told the absolute unvarnished truth. I do not wish to do my superior an injustice,' Zennor added after a moment, 'but there was an expression on his face that suggested to me that he is more concerned with protecting his own office, and the good name of the minor canons in general, than with my own personal fate. I saw a similar expression on the features of my colleagues, yesterday evening. No one will say to my face that they think I am guilty, but it is clear that most of them feel that I have brought shame on them all, unjust though that is. I thus find myself, through no fault of my own, utterly friendless in my hour of greatest need.'

'That is unfortunate,' responded Holmes. 'It is certainly one of the most desolate of experiences, to be accused – or even suspected – of something of which one is perfectly innocent. But, why does anyone suppose you would commit such a crime, Mr Zennor? What do they believe you intended to do with the money?'

'Unfortunately for my case, I have spoken once or twice recently of the somewhat straitened circumstances in which my mother and sister find themselves since my father died, and it is believed by some, I think, that I intended to give the money to them. Of course, it is absurd to suppose that I should steal money belonging to the cathedral to give to my relatives, and just as absurd to suppose that, were I to do so, my relatives would accept it.'

Holmes nodded. 'But if people are determined to find an innocent man guilty, they will always manage to find some plausible motive to ascribe to him. Now,' he continued, with a glance at the clock, 'there are other questions I wish to ask you, but I also wish to interview your colleagues while the events of yesterday are still fresh in their minds. Do you think I will be able to see them today?'

'Yes, that should be possible. Almost everyone was out on some business or other yesterday, but – apart from Jeavons, who is away all week – everyone should be there today.'

'Excellent!' cried Holmes, whose energy and enthusiasm appeared to have returned in full measure at the prospect of an interesting case. 'What I suggest, then, is that we catch the next train down to Kent and continue this discussion as we travel.'

Thus it was, that, forty minutes later, the three of us were seated in a fast train, as it made its way down through the damp-looking Kent countryside.

'If you would tell us everything that happened to you yesterday,' said Holmes, 'and everything of which you are aware that happened to your colleagues, then we might be able to form a mental picture of how Sir Anthony Ingoldsby's cheque came to be in your pocket. Omit nothing, however trivial, which might conceivably have a bearing on the matter.'

'Very well,' said Zennor. 'Probably the first notable thing that happened was that Jeavons left for the railway station very early – about seven o'clock – as he was travelling up to Grantham in Lincolnshire, where his parents live. His father has been ill recently and he was given special permission to take a week's leave of absence to visit him. You have asked me about the overcoats and whether they ever get muddled up, and, oddly enough, such a mistake did occur yesterday morning, for, about an hour after Jeavons left, I heard Earley saying that he thought Jeavons must have taken his coat, as he couldn't find it anywhere.

'At about half past eight, Earley and Wakefield left together for the railway station. The former was going to see someone in Ramsgate, the latter was travelling to Rochester, where he was to be interviewed for a vacant position.'

'One moment,' interrupted Holmes. 'If Jeavons had taken Earley's coat, then whose coat was Earley wearing?'

Zennor shook his head. 'I don't know for certain,' said he. 'I didn't hear him make any further remark on the matter, so I suppose I just assumed he had found Jeavons's coat and gone off in that.'

'Are their coats of a similar size?'

'Yes, they are. As a matter of fact, all the coats are practically identical, except for Wakefield's, which is a size larger. Shortly after Wakefield and Earley left, I saw Bebington going off into town. I believe he was going to the stationer's shop, to purchase ink or nibs, or something of the sort, and didn't intend to be out for very long. A few minutes later, I went to get my own hat and coat, before leaving for the railway station.'

'Did you verify that the coat you took was your own?'

' Not then, although I did later, as I shall explain in a moment. At the time, I was in too much of a hurry and I can't remember giving the matter any thought. I just assumed the coat was mine. There were only two coats still hanging in the corridor then – it was raining quite heavily yesterday morning and everyone who had gone out had put a coat on – and the other one had a frayed lapel and didn't look like mine.

Anyway, I put my coat on and set off. A couple of minutes later, I was caught up in the street by Stafford Nugent, who informed me he was intending to catch the same train. We walked on together for a few minutes, then he stopped and said he'd just realised that he'd forgotten the book he had intended to take back to the library at Lambeth Palace. "You go on to the station, Zennor," he said, "and I'll catch you up later." With that, he turned and hurried back to the cathedral. I continued to the station, where I caught the 9.05 to London. At that time, Nugent had not reappeared, and I assumed he had been delayed for some reason and would catch the next train.

'At eleven o'clock, my train reached Victoria. I knew that the person I had to see at Lambeth Palace would not be there until the afternoon, so I went down to Brixton to see my mother and sister, and took lunch with them there. I eventually reached Lambeth Palace at about two o'clock, hung up my hat and coat, and went in to see Canon Seagrave at the appointed time.'

'Where did you leave your coat?' interrupted Holmes.

'I don't imagine you are familiar with Lambeth Palace,' responded Zennor, 'so I will describe the relevant part to you. There is a side-door from the garden, which is the one we always use. On the outside of it, against the wall of the building, is a glass-enclosed verandah, in which there is a row of coat-hooks, hat-stand and so on, and a large bench – like a settle, but with a lower back – on which visitors can sit and wait if they have arrived early for their appointment. I hung my coat up there and proceeded in through the door, to where Canon Seagrave's secretary has a desk.'

'One moment,' said Holmes. 'Were there any coats already there, when you hung up your own coat?'

'No, the coat-hooks were empty.'

'And when you came out?'

'When I came out,' responded Zennor, 'which was at about ten past three, there at first appeared to be no coats there at all and for a moment I was nonplussed as to what had become of my own coat.

Then I leaned over and looked behind the bench, and saw that my coat was there, in a heap on the ground. It had obviously slipped from its peg. I picked it up, dusted it off with my hand and put it on. Outside, in the garden, I paused a moment, to neaten myself up a bit, when I felt something in the inside pocket of the coat. I unbuttoned my coat, put my hand in the pocket and pulled out a long envelope. It wasn't sealed and I was just opening it to see what was in it when someone spoke, just behind me. I turned, to see that it was Canon Seagrave and his secretary.

'"What is that you have there, Mr Zennor?" asked Canon Seagrave.

'"I don't know," I replied. "I have just found it in my pocket."

'"You had better let me have a look at it, then," said the canon, holding out his hand.

'I handed him the envelope, he opened it, and the two of them said, almost together, "It is Sir Anthony Ingoldsby's cheque!" Apparently, news had reached them just moments earlier that the cheque had disappeared from the cathedral office at Canterbury. "How do you come to have this cheque in your pocket, Zennor?" asked the canon in a grave tone. I told them I had no idea, that I had not even been aware that the envelope was in my pocket until a moment before. This was the gospel truth, but I realise it must have sounded highly improbable. "I think," said Canon Seagrave, "that we will hold on to this now. It can be deposited in the bank in London just as well as in Canterbury. As for you, Zennor," he continued, "I think you had best return at once to the cathedral and explain all the circumstances to your superiors there." In other words, as was obvious, he didn't believe a word of what I had told him, but he was washing his hands of the matter and consigning me to the mercies of the cathedral authorities.

'It was as I was walking from Lambeth Palace to the railway station that it suddenly occurred to me that the coat I was wearing was perhaps not my own. With an uprush of hope at the thought that I might have found the explanation for this baffling puzzle, I stopped in the street and pulled out the lining of this right-hand pocket. Alas! my hopes were dashed. The coat was undeniably my own.' As he spoke, he had suited the action to the word and had pulled out the lining of the pocket to show us. There, written quite clearly in indelible pencil, were the initials 'M.Z.'.

'I therefore returned to Kent,' continued our companion, 'in a state of complete gloom and mystification. I have since been quizzed repeatedly on the matter, but have been unable to throw any light on it. I think they find the whole business astounding, and cannot entirely bring themselves to believe that one of the canons could be guilty of such a deceitful act, but can see no other explanation. Nor, I admit, can I. But for the fact that I know for certain that I did not take that envelope, and had never even seen it before that moment in the garden of Lambeth Palace, I, too, should be inclined to think I must be guilty! And if that admission sounds slightly insane, then it is no more than a true reflection of my mental state!'

Sherlock Holmes sat in silence for some time, his brow furrowed with thought. 'It is always a curious thing,' said he at last, 'when all the evidence in a case points to one specific conclusion and yet, at the same time, you know for certain that that conclusion is false. It is enough to make anyone feel unhinged, Mr Zennor. However, my dear sir, you must not despair. Let us forget about conclusions for a moment and consider some of the details. It is interesting, for instance, that you did not notice that there was anything in your pocket until that moment in the garden of Lambeth Palace.'

'I think,' said Zennor, 'that when my coat slipped from the peg and fell to the floor, the envelope must have become slightly twisted in the pocket and that that is why I noticed it. It was, after all, only a very slim envelope and if lying flat was probably undetectable.'

'That is possible,' said Holmes. 'What of the other papers and letters you had brought up to London? How had you carried them?'

'In a small leather case. I don't generally use the coat pockets for anything, except sometimes for my gloves.'

'I see. Before you proceed with your account, can you remember the last time you, or any of the others, saw Sir Anthony Ingoldsby's cheque before it disappeared?'

Zennor thought for a moment. 'It was certainly on the shelf in the office at twenty past eight in the morning, when the office and the corridor outside it were busy with people coming and going, for Wakefield made some little joke about its being left lying about. A couple of the others laughed and Dr Glimper ticked them all off for what he described as "inappropriate and unseemly levity". After that, I have no further knowledge of it.'

'Very well. Let us return once more to Lambeth Palace, then. I am interested in the hat-stand in the verandah. You said that when you arrived, there were no coats hanging on the pegs there; but can you recall if there were any hats on the hat-stand?'

Our companion closed his eyes and frowned, and remained in silent concentration for several minutes. 'Yes,' said he at last, 'there *was* another hat there. I remember now that I nearly knocked it off as I was hanging up my own.'

Holmes nodded and scribbled something in his note-book. Then, for several minutes, he sat in silence studying his notes and I saw that he had drawn a complex-looking diagram, consisting of dots, arrows, connecting lines and, here and there, little stick-men. For some time he stared at what he had drawn, then he looked up.

'That looks very complicated,' I ventured.

'It may appear so at present,' he responded; 'but it will no doubt become clearer when we have spoken to some of those involved. Tell me,' he continued, turning to Zennor, 'were you able to see if there was anything beside the cheque in the envelope you found in your pocket – a letter, for instance?'

'No, there was nothing in it but the cheque itself.'

'Was anything written on the envelope?'

'No, it was perfectly blank. I did later find a scrap of paper with a note on it in my pocket,' added Zennor after a moment. 'I'd never seen it before and only noticed it when I was travelling back to Canterbury on the train.'

'Why did you not mention it before?' asked Holmes in surprise.

'It did not seem of any importance,' replied the other. 'The issue was whether I had stolen Sir Anthony Ingoldsby's cheque or not. My head was in a whirl from that, so the fact that there was a scrap of paper in my pocket seemed of little consequence. As I mentioned to you earlier, the minor canons are in the habit of borrowing each other's coats and one does sometimes find odd things left in one's pocket.'

'Do you have it with you?' asked Holmes.

'Yes, it is here,' said Zennor. He put his hand in his inside pocket and produced a small square piece of paper, which had clearly been torn from a larger sheet, and passed it over to us. Upon this little sheet was written the following brief message:

London, Thursday, 22nd
St Mark's, Ham. X.
Four o'clock

'It appears to be an appointment of some kind,' said Holmes. 'Does it mean anything to you, Mr Zennor?'

'Nothing whatever. Off-hand, I don't think I even know any church dedicated to St Mark. Nor have I ever been to Ham.'

'Do you know Ham, Watson?' Holmes asked me.

I shook my head. 'As far as I'm aware it lies somewhere on the Thames between Richmond and Kingston, but I don't think I've ever been there.'

'Of course, this note may not be connected to the disappearance of the cheque,' said Holmes, 'but, if not, its appearance in your pocket at the same time as the cheque is something of an odd coincidence. The Thursday it refers to is tomorrow, so if we don't succeed in getting to the bottom of the matter while we're in Kent, it may provide us with another line of inquiry.'

The rain was falling in a fine drizzle as we left the station at Canterbury and made our way to the cathedral through the narrow streets of the old town. As we turned a corner, we almost bumped into a stout young man in clerical garb, hurrying in the opposite direction.

'Hello, Wakefield!' said Zennor.

'Hello,' returned the other, but seemed disinclined to stop.

'This is Mr Sherlock Holmes,' said Zennor. 'He is looking into the matter of Sir Anthony Ingoldsby's cheque.'

'Oh, is he?' said Wakefield in a sarcastic tone. 'Best of luck with that!' he continued, turning to Holmes. 'As I understand it, there's not much to look into about it! Now,' he said, pushing past us, 'I really must be off!'

'I am sorry he was rude to you,' said Zennor, as we continued on our way. 'He can sometimes be a little short in his manner.'

'No matter,' said Holmes. 'I could see all that I wished to know.'

We reached the cathedral precincts in a few minutes, and our guide conducted us through an ancient gateway, round a corner and through a low-arched doorway into a short corridor, along the side of which hung three black raincoats.

'This is where we generally leave our coats,' said Zennor.

'Can you tell to whom these coats belong?' asked Holmes.

'They will all be marked somewhere,' replied Zennor, turning back the cuffs and looking in the pockets. 'Yes, this one is Nugent's,' said he at length, 'this next one is Bebington's and this third one is Dr Glimper's.'

'You are wearing yours at the moment, as is Wakefield,' said Holmes in a thoughtful voice. 'Jeavons has gone off to Grantham wearing Earley's coat, according to the account you gave us earlier, so where is Jeavons's own coat?'

Zennor shook his head. 'Perhaps Earley is wearing it,' he suggested.

'No, he isn't,' came a voice from an open doorway, a little further along the corridor, and a moment later, a bespectacled young man thrust his head out of the doorway and regarded us for a moment.

'Hello, Earley,' said our companion.

'Hello, Zennor. What's all this about?'

Zennor introduced us. 'These gentlemen are trying to help me solve the riddle of how Sir Anthony's cheque ended up in my pocket. I think Mr Holmes feels that the muddle over the raincoats may have contributed to it.'

'I never thought of that,' said Earley in a thoughtful tone, stepping out into the corridor. 'I don't know if it could really have affected anything, but the coats certainly got in a muddle yesterday, there's no denying that!'

'You went to Ramsgate, I believe,' said Holmes.

'That's right,' returned the other. 'I left about half past eight in the morning. I was going to walk to the station with Wakefield, but I couldn't find my coat. Wakefield got a little impatient and said he couldn't wait, so he set off without me. I realised at length that Jeavons must have mistakenly taken my coat – he's done that before – so I took what I thought was his and dashed off to catch Wakefield up. I didn't come back until about four o'clock in the afternoon and heard then what had happened. Don't worry, Zennor,' he added. 'I'm sure it will all get sorted out. It must just be some silly sort of mix-up.'

'When you returned,' said Holmes, 'you presumably hung your coat up here?'

'Yes.'

'But Jeavons's coat is certainly not here now, so I think you must have been wearing someone else's coat yesterday.'

'Yes, I think perhaps I was,' agreed Earley, looking a little embarrassed. 'It fitted me well enough, anyway,' he added with a chuckle.

'Is there anywhere else that Jeavons might have left his coat?' Holmes asked.

'It might be in his room.'

'Might we see?'

'Yes; I will show you,' said Earley. 'He has the room immediately above my own. It will not be locked and I don't think he would mind us looking in.'

He turned, led the way further along the corridor and up two flights of a steep stone staircase, until we found ourselves in a narrow corridor with a steeply sloping ceiling.

'This is Jeavons's room,' said Earley, opening one of several doors in the corridor, and we followed him into a small bedroom. In a moment there came a murmur of satisfaction from Holmes, as he found a black raincoat thrown over the back of a chair, and almost hidden under a dressing-gown. For a moment, he searched the coat for some sign of ownership, then pointed to a clear 'H.J.' printed on the inside of the left cuff. Again he took out his note-book and made a brief note in it.

We were just leaving Jeavons's bedroom when we heard rapid footsteps on the stairs, and a moment later a pleasant-faced, dark-haired young man appeared on the landing.

'Ah, Zennor,' said he. 'There you are! Dr Glimper has been looking for you! But who are these gentlemen?'

Zennor introduced the newcomer to us as Stafford Nugent and explained to him our purpose in being there, at which Nugent nodded his head. 'I'm sure if you wish to ask me any questions about yesterday, I will do my best to answer them,' he said, addressing us.

'If you could just give us a brief account of your day,' said Holmes, 'from about half past eight in the morning until you arrived back here in the afternoon.'

'It is soon told,' said Nugent. 'I left here about a quarter to nine and got back about five o'clock in the afternoon, and nothing of any significance happened all day.'

'That's not quite right, Nugent,' said Zennor. 'You walked halfway to the railway station with me, but then came back here for that book and I didn't see you again.'

'Oh, of course,' said the other. 'I was forgetting that. Besides, I didn't realise you wanted every little detail. Very well, then. I left here in a hurry, just after quarter to nine, caught Zennor up in the street and we walked on together for a few minutes. Then I remembered that I'd forgotten a book I'd borrowed from the library at Lambeth Palace, which I had intended to take back, so I came back here to get it.'

'What time was that?' asked Holmes.

'About nine o'clock. I got the book from my room, which only took a few moments, and was leaving once more, when I noticed as I passed the coat-pegs downstairs that there was a raincoat hanging there which looked somewhat more like mine than the one I was wearing, which didn't seem to fit me properly, so I took that one off and put the other on, and dashed off to the station. I was too late to catch the train, however, which had gone at five past nine, so I spent about forty minutes drinking tea and reading, until the next London train came in, at about ten to ten.

'I reached London shortly before twelve, stood talking for a while to a friend I met in the street outside the station and got to Lambeth Palace just after one o'clock. I concluded my business there quite quickly, but then spent a long time in the library, talking to the chief librarian. I borrowed another book and left about quarter past two. I then got a fast train from Charing Cross and was back here by five.'

'When you were hanging your coat back up downstairs,' said Holmes, 'did you notice whose coat it was?'

Nugent shook his head. 'I've no idea,' he said; 'but I'm not going to apologise for it: if someone hadn't already taken mine I shouldn't have had to take someone else's. That's the only thing I know for certain about it, that it wasn't my own.'

'How can you be so sure?' asked Holmes.

'Because one of the buttons on my coat is very loose – hanging by a thread, in fact – and the buttons on the coat I'd been wearing were all firmly attached.'

'Well, that is very interesting,' said Holmes.

Nugent looked surprised. 'I shouldn't have thought the state of the buttons would be of any great interest,' said he.

Holmes smiled. 'Something can be interesting,' he returned, 'not because of its own intrinsic qualities, but because of its relation to something else.'

There had come the sound of heavy footsteps on the stairs as they had been speaking. Now we all turned, as an older, dignified figure appeared at the head of the staircase. The young men fell silent and still, waiting for the newcomer to speak.

'What is all this noise up here?' he asked at length, in a deep, grave voice. 'And who are these gentlemen?'

'Dr Glimper,' said Zennor, taking half a step forward and addressing the older man: 'this is Mr Sherlock Holmes and Dr Watson. They are looking into the mystery of Sir Anthony's cheque on my behalf.'

'What!' cried Dr Glimper, in a voice like thunder. 'Do you mean to say that you have gone behind our backs and hired some sort of detective? You add the insult of contempt for the Dean and myself to the shame and disgrace of what has already happened? You two,' he continued, addressing Nugent and Earley, 'be about your business at once! I am surprised at you, permitting yourselves to be embroiled in such behaviour! As for you, Zennor: be in my office in three minutes' time! These men have no business here. Visitors are strictly forbidden without express permission, as you are fully aware, and they must leave the premises at once! At once, do you hear?'

'Yes, Dr Glimper,' said Zennor in a subdued tone, as the older man turned and descended the stair. Nugent and Earley quickly followed him, and, for a moment, Zennor, Holmes and I were left alone. 'You had better go at once,' said Zennor. 'I seem to have only made everything worse. All this talk of buttons and raincoats has got us nowhere at all. I am still the one in whose pocket the stolen cheque was found. I am still the one condemned, though I am perfectly innocent.'

'On the contrary,' said Holmes in a reassuring tone, 'I now believe I know what happened yesterday, although I cannot yet prove it. Do not permit yourself to become down-hearted or disconsolate, Mr Zennor, for it will achieve nothing. Believe me when I tell you that all will be well! Now, I have three quick points to make to you. First, how can I speak to Hubert Bebington? It is important that I see him. It will complete my investigation here.'

'He will be in the library. It is part of his duties. You had better not go along there yourself, but I can ask him to meet you outside the main gate, before I go in to see Dr Glimper.'

'Very good. Second, do not, under any circumstances, mention to anyone at all that little scrap of paper that you found in your pocket and which is now in my own pocket-book. Not a word, you understand, not a syllable!'

'I will do as you wish. What is your third point?'

'That you come to our chambers tomorrow, by lunch-time at the very latest.'

'That may prove difficult.'

'But you must, Mr Zennor! The whole future course of your life may depend upon it!'

'Very well. I will do all I can to be there. Now you must leave and I must face Dr Glimper.'

For several minutes we waited in the street outside the main gateway and were almost on the point of giving it up, thinking that either Zennor had not been able to communicate with Bebington, or Bebington had declined to see us, when, abruptly, a freckled face surmounted by a mop of sandy hair appeared round the corner of the archway and a young clergyman stepped into view.

'Ah, there you are!' said he. 'You are Mr Holmes, I take it. Zennor says you wish to ask me about yesterday. There's not much to tell,' he continued, as Holmes nodded. 'I was in the library most of the day. It was very quiet. Everyone else had gone off somewhere for the day, so I was all by myself.'

'But I understand you went out to the stationer's shop,' said Holmes.

'Yes, that is so. I went there first thing in the morning, but was out less than fifteen minutes, and after that I never left the cathedral all day.'

'What time was it that you went to the stationer's?'

'A few minutes after half past eight, which is when the shop opens. I was back again by ten to nine.'

'Do you know whose coat you were wearing when you went out?'

Bebington frowned. 'What a strange question!' said he. 'As a matter of fact, I assumed it was my own when I put it on, but later realised it wasn't.'

'Why are you so sure?'

'It had an ink-mark on the sleeve, which mine certainly does not. When I came down into the corridor where the outdoor coats are hung up, there were two or three of them hanging there and I just took the one I thought was mine. I didn't think it really mattered whose coat it was, anyway, as I knew I was only going to be out for a few minutes.'

'And when you returned?'

'The clothes-pegs were all empty. I remember noticing that. So I just hung up my own hat and coat, and took my stationery supplies off to the library.'

'Thank you,' said Holmes. 'You have been most helpful.'

'Have I?' returned the other, a look of curiosity on his features. 'I'm sure I don't know how!'

On the train back to London, Holmes was in a state of barely suppressed excitement, and it was clear that he considered that he had made some definite progress in the case. He opened his note-book at the page on which he had drawn numerous lines, arrows and little stick-men, laid it on the seat beside him and pored over it in silence for some time.

'I don't know how you can make sense of all those squiggles,' I said, leaning across and studying it with him. 'It looks too complex for the human brain to take in!'

'On the contrary,' said he; 'it is, essentially, very simple.'

'I suppose those little stick-men represent the minor canons.'

My friend shook his head. 'No,' said he. 'The little circles with the initials in them are the minor canons. The stick-men, as you call them, represent their raincoats, which generally followed a different course during the day from that taken by their owners. It would perhaps be clearer if I had had a coloured pencil with which to draw the lines relating to the raincoats. You would then be able to see more clearly the contrast between where the men went and where their coats went. I must remember to carry a red pencil with me in future, to allow for such eventualities!'

After a while, Holmes put away his note-book and replaced it on the seat with the little scrap of paper that Zennor had found in his pocket. For some time he stared at this with a frown of concentration, then with a sigh, he took his watch out.

'It would be helpful if this train would go a little faster,' said he in a tone of impatience. 'I can do nothing more until we return to Baker Street. There, the last but one piece of the puzzle should fall rapidly into place!'

My friend's progress was destined to be somewhat less rapid than he had hoped, however. By the time we reached London, the rain had stopped, the clouds had begun to break up and the sun was peeping through, but it was evident from his manner that Holmes was perfectly oblivious to this improvement in the weather. Not a word did he speak until we were back in our lodgings, where he placed the scrap of paper on the table, got out a pile of maps and volumes of reference, and for several minutes turned the pages in silence. Then at length, with a groan, he looked up, a crestfallen expression on his face.

'What is it?' I asked.

'Check number one,' said he. 'There *is* a church at Ham, Watson. Unfortunately, it is not St Mark's, but St Andrew's.'

'Perhaps there are two churches there,' I suggested, but my friend shook his head.

'The information in this volume is very detailed, but there is no mention of a St Mark's. Of course, the word "Ham" on this note is followed by a full stop, so it may be an abbreviation of a longer name.'

'Hampton,' I suggested, 'or Hampton Wick.'

'Let us see,' said Holmes, turning the pages rapidly. 'Hum! No good, I'm afraid. The church at Hampton is St Mary's. That at Hampton Wick is St John's. There is also somewhere called New Hampton, but the church there is St James's. The large "X" on this note puzzles me,' he continued, looking again at the scrap of paper. 'Of course, people often write "X" as an abbreviation for "Cross" in place-names such as Charing Cross, but I can't recall anywhere called "Ham Cross" or anything similar.'

'What about Hammersmith?' I suggested. 'I have never heard anyone speak of "Hammersmith Cross", but there is certainly a cross-roads there.'

Again Holmes turned the pages over rapidly.

'No good,' said he at length. 'The church at Hammersmith is St Paul's. Let us see what Hampstead has to offer! No, that is St John's.'

'West Ham or East Ham, in the East End,' I suggested.

'I'm afraid not, Watson,' said my friend after a moment. 'The church at East Ham is another St Mary's, and that at West Ham – in the district of Upton, it says here – is St Peter's.' He sighed. 'This is proving more difficult than I had expected!'

'Do you not have an alphabetical list of London churches anywhere?' I asked, but he shook his head.

'It's probably too late now to get hold of such a list,' said he with a glance at the clock. 'I can make inquiries first thing in the morning, but, as you know, I dislike leaving things to the last minute and had hoped to get the matter settled this evening. Of course, I know of a couple of churches dedicated to St Mark: there is one scarcely a stone's throw from here, in the Marylebone Road, for instance, and another south of the river – in Kennington, if I recall correctly – but none is in a district which might be known as "Ham". And then there is this capital "X". What is the significance of that?'

'Perhaps it is simply a symbol for a church,' I suggested, 'as you sometimes see on maps.'

'Yes,' returned my friend, 'but if so its presence in the note seems completely superfluous; and, in any case, if it were simply an abbreviation for "church", one would expect to see it after the word "Mark's" and before the word "Ham". Let us see if we can find anything on any of these maps,' he continued, handing one to me, and opening another one out for himself.

'What am I looking for?' I asked, as I spread the map out on the hearth-rug.

'I cannot precisely say,' returned Holmes: 'some likely-looking church, some reference to St Mark's among the street-names, somewhere that might be known as "Ham".'

'There are a few streets in Fulham which bear that name,' I remarked, after several minutes had passed in silence, 'but I cannot see if there is a church there and, in any case, I can't imagine that anyone would abbreviate "Fulham" as "Ham".'

'There is also a small hospital known as St Mark's,' responded my companion, 'but it is in the City, near Aldersgate station, so I don't think that that is of any use to us.'

Holmes fell silent again then and when I glanced up I saw that he was studying the little note once more, with the aid of his magnifying lens. Abruptly, he let out a little cry, as of surprise or enlightenment.

'Watson!' said he in an urgent tone. 'I have something of great importance to tell you!'

'What is it?' I asked, rising to my feet.

'That you have, all this time, been sharing rooms with a complete idiot! I deserve to be kicked from here to London Bridge for not seeing the truth earlier! Come and take a look! Do you see?' he continued, as I bent over the little note. 'What appeared to be a capital "X" is not that at all! It is in fact a lower-case "t"! It has been written in a great hurry and the vertical stroke is falling over backwards, while the horizontal stroke is rising from left to right. Of course that explains why there is a full stop after it!'

'What does it mean?'

'It means I must take a short walk on this beautiful evening,' said he in a cheery tone, looking out of the window at the cloudless blue sky. 'Would you care to accompany me?'

'With pleasure!' I said, laughing aloud at the sudden improvement in his mood.

'Good man! Your hat and coat, then, old fellow, and let us be off before the daylight fades! I will explain where we are going as we walk!'

A few moments later, we set off up Baker Street, crossed the Marylebone Road and headed north towards St John's Wood. At St John's Wood Church we turned westwards and along past the cricket ground. Now that the rain had passed away and the sky had cleared, it was a warm and pleasant evening.

'You see,' said Holmes, 'as soon as I realised that the letter in the note was not an "X" – which had made no sense to me at all – but a "t", it at once struck me that it might well be an abbreviation for "terrace", which supposition was strengthened by the fact that the "t" had a full stop after it. And as soon as that had occurred to me, I at once thought of Hamilton Terrace, which, as you have probably surmised, is our present destination. There are dozens of other street-names in London which begin with the syllable "Ham", but very few suitable candidates for "Ham-something Terrace". Now, I know for certain that there is a fairly large church on Hamilton Terrace – a handsome edifice, as I recall. It is not very old, but has a certain solidity and quiet dignity. I have passed it several times in a cab, but have not had reason to stop there and cannot recall what name it bears. If it is St Mark's, Watson, then I am sure we have solved the riddle of that little note!'

We had turned northwards again as he had been speaking, into Hamilton Terrace itself, and now proceeded in the soft evening sunlight up this very broad road, lined on either side by handsome villas. After a few moments, we could see a church in the distance, on the right, and as we approached it I could sense an increasing tension in my companion's manner. In a few minutes, we had reached a cross-roads, where Hamilton Terrace is crossed by Abercorn Place, and on the north-east corner of this cross-roads stood the church. Behind the low wall round the churchyard, a large sign proclaimed that this was St Mark's.

All my friend's tension seemed in an instant to evaporate and he clapped his hands together in delight. 'Q.E.D.!' cried he in triumph. 'Now, my dear fellow, I suggest we continue our walk down that hill over there to the Edgware Road, where we can probably pick up a cab to take us to a decent restaurant. I think that our efforts today have merited a good supper!'

Our involvement with the case was not yet finished for the day, however, for when we returned to Baker Street, we found a letter from Zennor awaiting us, which had been delivered earlier in the evening by special messenger. With an expression of surprise, Holmes tore open the envelope. The letter within ran as follows:

MY DEAR MR HOLMES,

I had thought that it might prove difficult for me to keep our appointment tomorrow. However, a fresh development has rendered that somewhat easier, although the development itself is an unwelcome one. In short, I have now been suspended from all my duties at the cathedral and placed on indefinite leave, until the Dean and Chapter have had an opportunity to consider the whole matter in detail. I am therefore writing this note to you from my mother's house at Brixton and will call at your chambers tomorrow lunchtime, as you requested. Do not take it amiss if I say that I have little confidence that I shall ever be cleared of the false charges against me. The matter seems so dark and inexplicable, and I have almost given up all hope.

YOURS VERY SINCERELY, MARTIN ZENNOR

'Poor fellow!' I said, as I finished reading. 'He must feel that his whole world has collapsed about him.'

'Let us hope, then,' said Holmes, 'that we shall be able to lift his spirits a little tomorrow!'

———

In the morning, a fresh band of rain had blown in across London and I awoke to the patter of raindrops against my bedroom window. It was clear that it had rained heavily in the night, for the plane tree behind our house had a drenched and bedraggled appearance. By the time we had taken breakfast, however, the rain had stopped, although the sky remained grey and overcast. After breakfast, Holmes's attempt to return to his bedroom for further rest was this time successful and I did not see him again for two hours. I passed my own morning in writing up the case as I saw it so far, although, in truth, I could make little sense of it. It was clear from what I had seen of the hieroglyphics in Holmes's own note-book that he regarded the muddle over the minor canons' overcoats as an important part of the case, but I could not really see how that helped us. The envelope with the cheque in it had undoubtedly been found in Martin Zennor's own coat, and he had undoubtedly been wearing it at the time, so the fact that some of the other young men had taken the wrong coats did not seem to make any difference. Zennor stated that he had not put the envelope in his pocket, and I saw no reason to doubt that, so therefore someone else had done so, but who, when and why?

When Holmes eventually re-emerged from his bedroom, he appeared refreshed and was clearly in good spirits. He ordered a four-wheeler for three o'clock, remarking that although it would mean a long wait for us at St Mark's, he wanted to make sure that we arrived there well before anyone else did.

Zennor arrived promptly at lunchtime, and shared our simple meal of cold meats, bread and cheese. He appeared very pale and nervous in his manner, although he cheered up a little as Holmes plied him with questions, about his various duties at the cathedral, about his family and about the families of his colleagues. Whether any of the information Holmes elicited by these questions was of any relevance to his view of the case, or whether he was simply trying to distract, and thus cheer, his client, I could not say, but so lively and enthusiastic was his conversation that the time flew by, until, at five to three, a ring at the front-door bell announced the arrival of our cab.

'Your hats and coats, gentlemen!' cried Holmes, springing to his feet. 'Courage, my dear sir!' he said to Zennor, clapping him lightly on the shoulder. 'Your ordeal is almost at an end!'

'I wish I knew what was going to happen,' returned his client, as he took his hat and coat from the peg.

'We none of us know precisely what is going to happen, even two minutes in the future,' said Holmes; 'but I think I can promise you this, at least, Mr Zennor, that by the end of this week you will have returned to your duties at the cathedral without the slightest stain on your character!'

It took us less than ten minutes to reach our destination. As we approached the cross-roads, Holmes instructed the cabbie to drive slowly past the front of St Mark's and continue on towards the north end of the road, where it meets Carlton Hill.

'No sign of anyone at present,' said Holmes, as we passed the churchyard, 'but let me know at once if you see anyone loitering about.'

Zennor looked out of one side and I looked out of the other, but there seemed to be no one at all about in the whole of that broad, quiet thoroughfare. When we reached the end of the road, Holmes told the cabbie to turn his cab round, take us halfway back to the church and let us down there. 'We'll walk the rest of the way,' said he, as we alighted and he paid off the cab. 'It seems to me that the north corner of the building, where there is some projecting masonry and a large laurel bush, will be the best place for us to wait. It is impossible to say from which direction anyone will come, but whichever it is, we should be well-enough hidden there.'

We did as Holmes suggested, positioning ourselves behind a large buttress and, as we did so, a fine drizzle began to fall. This was not very pleasant, but it did not appear to trouble my friend, who kept his eyes fixed on the churchyard before us and the road beyond. In truth, there was little enough to be seen there, for very few people passed by, and I rapidly formed the conclusion that Hamilton Terrace must be one of the quietest large roads in the whole of London. Because of this, our vigil seemed an inordinately long one, although, in reality, it was little more than forty minutes.

All at once, when my thoughts had drifted far away, a man – a dirty, rough-looking individual – appeared from the right, from the north end of the road. I felt Holmes's hand on my shoulder, pulling me in a little more behind the laurel bush. We watched as this man glanced furtively this way and that, as he approached the gateway into the churchyard. Then, in one swift movement, he had opened the gate and slipped in; but instead of walking up the short path to the church door, he quickly crouched down behind the low wall, just to the side of the gateway, so that he could not be seen from the road. Moments later, a large delivery van clattered by, and as it did so he raised his head slightly, to see over the wall and watch its progress. Again he looked furtively to left and right, and then bobbed his head down again to hide. Whether this man had anything to do with our reason for being there, I had no idea, but it seemed clear that he was fearful of being discovered by someone. Holmes touched Zennor on the arm and, with a raise of his eyebrow and a nod in the direction of the newcomer, made a silent enquiry; but Zennor shook his head, his features expressing complete ignorance as to who the man might be. Holmes frowned and a variety of emotions passed quickly across his face; but before I had time to consider the matter further, we heard the rapid approach of a cab from along Abercorn Place. It slowed down at the cross-roads, then swung round sharply into Hamilton Terrace and pulled up at the gate of the churchyard.

A moment later, a man stepped down from the cab who was

instantly recognisable as Dr Glimper, the supervisor of the minor canons at Canterbury Cathedral. What he might be doing here, I could not imagine, and I wondered if he had followed someone – possibly Holmes's client – to London. Whatever his purpose in being at St Mark's, it looked as if he was about to receive an unpleasant surprise, for as soon as he opened the gate, he would see the man hiding behind the wall. He put his hand on the gate and pushed it open, and at that moment the man behind the wall sprang up. Dr Glimper took a step backwards in alarm and I thought for a moment that the other man was about to attack him, but then the two of them began to talk animatedly, walking slowly up the short path towards the church door.

Abruptly, they stopped, evidently as a result of something that Dr Glimper had said, for the other man began to remonstrate with him violently, waving his arms wildly in the air. For several moments they stood there, speaking in raised voices, although I could not catch what they were saying. Then, abruptly, they stopped again, and looked hurriedly this way and that, as if they had heard something.

'Come on!' said Holmes. 'This has gone on long enough!' He stepped briskly forward, into the open, at which the two men looked round in alarm.

'You traitor!' cried the rough-looking man to Glimper. 'You have betrayed me!'

'No, no!' returned Dr Glimper. 'I assure you, I have no idea who these men are!' But even as he spoke, he evidently caught sight of Zennor, behind us. 'Zennor!' he cried. 'What on earth are you doing here?'

'So,' said the other man, raising his arm aggressively, 'you *do* know these people! So you're a liar as well as a traitor! You stinking, slimy scug!' He then concluded his remarks with a string of foul oaths.

'We have come,' said Holmes, addressing Dr Glimper, and ignoring the other man's outburst, 'to learn why you attempted to steal the cathedral's cheque.'

Dr Glimper's mouth fell open, his eyes were wide and wild, and his whole expression was one of the utmost terror. Before he could respond, however, there came the most surprising interruption. The rapid clatter of hooves and the jingle of harness came from somewhere to our right, from the north end of Hamilton Terrace, and an instant later, a large police van came into view travelling at tremendous speed. It drew to an abrupt halt at the church gate and three policemen sprang down.

'You swine!' cried Dr Glimper's companion, and, launching himself forward, struck the clergyman full in the face with his fist. Then, as Glimper fell to the ground with a pitiful cry, the other man bolted and sprang over the side-wall of the churchyard into Abercorn Place. Two of the policemen at once gave chase, while the third, in the braided uniform of an inspector, approached us and introduced himself as Inspector Jackett.

'Are you the vicar of this church, reverend?' he asked Glimper, as he helped him to his feet.

'No,' replied Glimper, touching his cut and bruised face gingerly with his hand. 'I am the brother of that poor wretch you are chasing.'

'What!' cried the policeman in astonishment: 'the brother of Jake Sligo, the most notorious burglar in north London!'

'I didn't know he was using that name. His real name is Jacob Glimper.'

'Well, well,' said Inspector Jackett. 'I know he's used several aliases, but I've never heard that one before! You do know,' he continued, 'that we have been on his trail for weeks? No? Well, I can tell you he is wanted for questioning for at least eight burglaries, five violent assaults and two counts of attempted murder. We finally tracked him down to an address in Kilburn, but when we went there this morning, he'd already left. We've been hunting for him all day and finally got a tip from a carter that he had seen a suspicious-looking individual hiding in this churchyard.'

'I swear I knew none of this,' said Dr Glimper in a tone of utter dejection. 'I do not live in London, but in Canterbury, where I am connected with the cathedral. I have neither seen nor heard from my brother in many years. But I recently got a letter from him, from an address in Kilburn, telling me that he was in serious trouble and begging me to bring some money to him here today, so that he could get away and start a new life elsewhere. I assumed that he owed money to someone, that is all.'

'And did you bring him any money?' asked Inspector Jackett.

'No,' said Glimper. 'I was just telling him that I had been unable to get any, when you arrived.'

'Who are these gentlemen?' the inspector asked, turning to us.

'They have nothing to do with the matter,' replied Glimper; 'at least, not directly. I suppose it must all come out,' he continued after a moment, in a tone of resignation. 'I attempted – unsuccessfully – to take some money from the cathedral office to give to my brother. He sounded so desperate, and I thought if I didn't give him something he might come down to Canterbury and ruin my life as he has ruined his own. These men must have been following me, and witnessed what happened here.'

'Are they inquiry agents?'

'One is, I believe.'

'Do you agree with what he says?' the policeman asked, turning to us.

'Not exactly,' said Holmes. 'This young man here,' he continued, indicating Zennor, 'has been falsely accused of trying to steal the money that Dr Glimper mentioned. He asked me to look into the matter, and when I did so, my enquiries led me to suspect that the true culprit was Dr Glimper himself. We also found a note, naming this place and time for a meeting of some kind, so we made sure we arrived here first, so we could see for ourselves what the meeting was about.

'As for you, sir,' Holmes continued, turning to Dr Glimper, 'your behaviour has been disgraceful. Your loyalty to your brother is understandable, even if your chief motive seems to have been to preserve your own position at the cathedral; your succumbing to the temptation to steal the cheque is also understandable, if highly reprehensible in a man of your position and learning; but your treatment of Mr Zennor: that, sir, is unforgivable. To allow a young man you knew to be perfectly innocent to suffer the shame of baseless suspicion, and the scorn and distrust of his companions and superiors, when all the time you had it within your power to free him in an instant from these chains of disgrace: that, sir, is despicable!'

At that moment the two policemen reappeared from the direction of Abercorn Place and between them they held Dr Glimper's brother. As they approached us, he let out a stream of foul abuse, directed particularly at his brother, who hung his head in shame.

'Put him in the van,' said Inspector Jackett.

'You see a gulf between us,' said Dr Glimper, looking up abruptly, 'but it was not always so. It is not I who have risen, but he who has fallen. We are from a good family and I am sure the Glimpers of Newbury are still well spoken of. My brother was educated at one of the finest schools in England, and had all that a good education and a loving family could provide. But his course was set on dishonesty, deceit, debauchery and depravity, and this is where that course has led him. You are right, sir,' he continued, addressing Holmes, 'to call me despicable in my treatment of Zennor. It is the lowest, meanest act of my life and I despise myself for it. But I shall make amends at once and tender my resignation this very day. I shall make a full statement of the facts to the Dean this evening, totally exonerating Zennor and confessing my own guilt.'

'Before you do any of that,' said Inspector Jackett in a dry tone, 'I shall need your full name and address, and those of these other gentlemen, too. You may be called as a witness in the criminal proceedings against your brother.'

———

I asked Holmes that evening, as we discussed the case over supper, whether he had already suspected the truth before Dr Glimper had arrived at St Mark's.

'I was tolerably certain of it,' said he, nodding his head.

'I don't see how you could be,' I responded. 'When I saw the notes you had made, they appeared to consist chiefly of a series of zigzag lines, interspersed with hieroglyphics! How that could possibly indicate Dr Glimper's guilt, I cannot imagine!'

Holmes chuckled. He reached for his note-book and opened it at the relevant page. For a moment, he studied it in silence, then he passed it to me. 'I suppose it does look a confused muddle if you don't understand what it represents,' he conceded; 'but it's not really quite so complex as you suppose, Watson.

'To begin with, we were presented with the problem of how the envelope containing the cheque had found its way into Zennor's coat pocket. He had not placed it there himself and therefore someone else had done so. He also said that it was practically inconceivable that anyone should dislike him so much as to place it there deliberately in order to incriminate him. This I accepted, not simply because it was Zennor's opinion, but also because such an underhand scheme was very unlikely to be successful. If, for instance, he had noticed the envelope when he first put on his coat at the cathedral, possibly in the company of others, he would never have been suspected of trying to steal it. Suspicions were only aroused because of the somewhat odd circumstances in which the envelope came to light: the hue and cry had already gone up over the theft in Zennor's absence, and he was then seen, when alone in the garden of Lambeth Palace, to be doing something with an envelope he had just taken from his pocket. This is what roused suspicions against him.

'So, if the envelope had not been placed in Zennor's pocket deliberately, either by himself or by someone else, then it had been placed there in error. But what could that mean? Zennor told us that there was no legitimate reason for the envelope to be in anyone's pocket – the Dean's secretary was to deal with the cheque later – so the reason was clearly an illegitimate one. In other words, it must be that someone had intended to steal the cheque and had meant to place it in his own pocket, but had made a mistake and put it into Zennor's pocket instead. How could such a mistake have occurred? Only, surely, if the raincoats had got muddled up. Thus you see, Watson, that even on the most preliminary analysis of the matter, I was drawn to the conclusion that the whereabouts of each of the coats on the day in question was likely to be crucial to the solution of the case.

'This is where we come to that diagram you see before you. Now, altogether, there are seven overcoats to consider, the six belonging to the minor canons and that of Dr Glimper, which are all customarily hung in the corridor outside the cathedral office. But we can immediately eliminate several of them from our inquiry, which helps us enormously. That is the significance of those little stick figures you see at the top of the page, which have a line through them. Henry Jeavons had left about seven o'clock in the morning, wearing Michael Earley's coat, so that coat can be removed from the equation. But Jeavons's own coat was left, not in the corridor, where anyone might use it, but in his bedroom. So that coat, too, can be eliminated. Then there is the coat belonging to Wallace Wakefield: he is a somewhat larger size than anyone else and would very quickly have realised his mistake had he put anyone else's coat on, so he was undoubtedly wearing his own, which can, therefore, also be eliminated. This leaves us with the coats belonging to Martin Zennor, Stafford Nugent and Hubert Bebington, which are all the same, and that of Dr Glimper, which is slightly larger.

'Now we know, from the testimony we heard, that Zennor arrived back at Canterbury wearing his own coat, a fact he verified by examining the initials in the pocket, and that Nugent, who had also been up to London, was wearing a coat that fitted him, but which was not his own as it did not have the loose button which he mentioned to us. This coat could only therefore have been Bebington's. Hence, the coat that Earley was wearing, when he left to go to Ramsgate, which he admitted was not his own, but which he said fitted him perfectly well, must have been that of Nugent. As Earley was away in Ramsgate all day, only arriving back in the late afternoon, Nugent's coat can therefore also be eliminated from the equation. The only coats which are relevant to our little problem, then, are those of Zennor, Bebington and Glimper.

'When Nugent was first leaving the cathedral precincts, there was only one coat remaining in the corridor, so he took it and hurried off to catch Zennor up. He had got only halfway to the railway station, however, when he remembered the book he had intended to take back to Lambeth Palace. He therefore returned to the cathedral to get the book, but saw when he did so that there was now another coat hanging in the corridor which looked more like his own, so he took off the one he was wearing and put on the other. It seems certain, then, that the first coat he took was that of Dr Glimper, which is why it didn't fit him so well, and the second coat either Bebington's or Zennor's. Where had this second coat come from? Clearly it had been used by Bebington when he went to the stationer's. He had gone out five or ten minutes before Zennor and Nugent left, and had returned a few minutes after they had gone, and perhaps seven or eight minutes before Nugent came back to get his book. You will see I have marked all the timings down the edge of the page. But Bebington told us that the coat he was wearing during his brief visit to the stationer's was not his own. It was, therefore, Zennor's, and Zennor himself must have gone off to London wearing Bebington's coat.

'It was, I believe, during this period of just under ten minutes, when Zennor's coat was the only one hanging in the corridor outside the cathedral office, after Bebington had brought it back, but before Nugent returned and took it, that Glimper put the envelope, cheque and note in the pocket. He would, under the circumstances, have been in a highly nervous and hurried state, for someone might have come by at any moment and seen what he was doing, so no doubt when he saw a single coat hanging there he assumed it was his own. This is the only explanation that covers all the facts. No doubt Glimper intended to travel up to London later in the day and cash the cheque there, but, shortly afterwards, Nugent came back and, exchanging Glimper's coat for Zennor's, therefore went off to London with the stolen cheque in his pocket.'

'But if Nugent inadvertently brought the cheque up to London,' I asked, 'how was it that Zennor ended up with it?'

'That occurred at Lambeth Palace,' replied Holmes. 'You will recall that when Zennor arrived there, he saw a hat on the hat-stand, but no coat on the coat-hooks. But it was a wet day, and anyone arriving there would surely have been wearing a raincoat and would have hung it up with his hat. What must have happened, then, is this: that the earlier visitor – which must have been Nugent – hung his coat up hurriedly and carelessly and as he proceeded into the building it slipped from its peg and fell in a heap on the floor behind the settle. When Zennor arrived, he saw no coat there, hung his own hat and coat up and went into Lambeth Palace to keep his appointment. Some time later, while he was still engaged in there, Nugent came out, took the only coat that was hanging there, which he assumed to be the one he had arrived in and left. When Zennor emerged, he at first saw no coat, then found the one behind the settle and he, likewise, assumed that it was the one he had arrived in. Oddly enough, it was actually his own coat, but that was the first time all day that he had worn it. The remainder of the events you know. Is that all clear, old man? Do you understand now the point of that diagram you are studying?'

'I believe so,' I said, with some hesitation. 'I am sure your analysis is correct, Holmes and, in any case, the arrival of Dr Glimper at St Mark's confirmed it beyond doubt.'

Holmes nodded. 'There was one other possibility I considered, which was that Stafford Nugent had stolen the cheque, when he returned to collect his library book. But if he had done so, I argued, he would surely have taken a little more care to ensure he took the correct coat when he left Lambeth Palace and that he still had the cheque with him.

'Therefore, although it was always possible that no one would turn up today for the meeting at St Mark's, especially as the stolen cheque had been recovered, it seemed to me that if anyone did so, it would undoubtedly be Dr Glimper.'

'Amazing!' I cried.

'Elementary,' said Sherlock Holmes.

The East Thrigby Mystery

It may be imagined that the long and intimate acquaintance I had with Mr Sherlock Holmes should have sharpened my interest in crimes and mysteries, and in those special methods which he used to solve them. I found myself sometimes, as a result, considering unsolved mysteries from earlier in the century and wondering whether, had my friend's unique skills been at the disposal of those who had investigated them, they would have remained unsolved. Occasionally, I was able to persuade Holmes to discuss such matters and never failed to be impressed by his insights, but more often he would decline to enter into such speculations, remarking that the solution of any mystery, criminal or otherwise, invariably lay among the tiny details of the matter, and it was just those details that were most often lacking in the accounts of such cases as I read to him from time to time.

On one notable occasion, however, I did succeed in drawing my friend into a more detailed discussion of an unsolved case, when he was able to shed light on the matter in a remarkable and surprising fashion.

It was a dark winter's evening and we had been reading in silence on either side of the fire for some time, I with a volume of unsolved mysteries, he with a recent treatise on the poisonous properties of vegetable alkaloids.

'It is a singular thing to consider,' said I, looking up from my book, 'that of all the many millions of people in England, some of whom may be reading this book tonight as I am, there is not one who knows the solution to this mystery. One might have supposed that the application of so much collective brain-power to the problem would inevitably have produced a solution by now.'

My companion put down his own book and took up his old brier pipe and a handful of tobacco from the Persian slipper which was hanging on a hook beside the fireplace.

'But as I have remarked before,' said he, 'the authors of such works generally set out to entertain rather than enlighten, and to that end present the facts in a sensational rather than an analytical fashion, which tends to obfuscate and cloud the issues involved, rather than clarifying them.'

'Sometimes, perhaps, that may be true,' I returned, 'but not, I think, in every instance. Take the case I have just been reading, for example. The author describes the events with great clarity, yet the matter remains utterly mystifying. The events take place in a quiet country district, in which nothing of sensation has occurred in a century, the local inhabitants going about their business in the most regular, peaceful way imaginable, until one summer, twenty years ago. Then, like a bolt of lightning from a clear sky, there are a series of mysterious burglaries, and a well-known local man is found murdered one morning in a country lane. No one can suggest why these things have happened, nor who might be responsible. No strangers have been seen in the area, except for a highly respectable family with children who have rented a house there for the summer. Immediately following this brief period of dramatic incident, the entire district settles back once more into its customary state of somnolence, from which it has never emerged since.'

'Where did these incidents take place?' queried Holmes, a note of interest in his voice.

'Somewhere called East Thrigby. It is a village in the Lincolnshire Wolds, a few miles from the sea.'

My friend nodded his head in a thoughtful fashion. 'I thought your description of the case sounded familiar,' said he. 'As it happens, your example is an unfortunate one for your thesis: there is one person at least who knows the truth of what happened at East Thrigby.'

'Of course, the criminal himself must know the truth.'

'That was not my meaning.'

'Who then?'

'I was referring to myself, Watson.'

'You?' I cried in surprise.

Again Holmes nodded. 'I was present, a young lad, when the events you describe took place.'

'And you believe you know the truth?'

'I am certain of it.'

This was a surprise indeed, for I had never heard Holmes refer to the matter before. I asked him why, if the truth were known, it had never been revealed. He did not reply directly, but sat in silent thought for several minutes.

'The case supports my contention that it is in the details that the truth is to be found,' said he at length, 'for I can trace my own understanding of the matter to the moment I recalled how someone had polished his boots. I imagine you would be interested to hear an account of the case from my point of view.'

'I should be fascinated,' I returned; 'for it interests me greatly.'

Abruptly, he stood up from his chair and disappeared into his bedroom, returning a few minutes later with a flat wooden box, about eight inches square and two inches deep, tied up with red tape, such as might have contained a small painting or a precious china dish.

'This,' said he, setting the little box upon the floor and unfastening the tape, 'is all I have left to remind me of my stay at "The Highlands" in the Lincolnshire Wolds and of what became known as "The East Thrigby Mystery".'

He lifted the lid and I saw that the box contained a small, wooden-framed mirror which exactly fitted the box. The frame was painted light blue, and stuck all over with sea-shells and little pebbles. Holmes lifted it carefully from the box, laid it upon his knee and gazed for several minutes at this pretty little object, gently running his fingers over the patterns on the shells, as if the past might be conjured up for him as much by touch as by sight.

'It was a particularly fine, warm summer, in the mid-sixties,' said he at length. 'I was a mere lad, in my twelfth year. A distant relation of mine – I addressed him as "Uncle Moreton", although the relationship between us was not in fact as close as that – had taken a house for the summer on the edge of the Lincolnshire Wolds, not many miles distant from the sea. He and his wife, known to me as "Aunt Phyllis", had a child of about my own age, a daughter by the name of Sylvia – although she was always known as "Sylvie" – and I was to spend the summer with them. The household was completed by Matthew Hemming, his wife, Ursula, and their son, Percival, who was a year or two younger than me. The Hemmings were distant relations of Aunt Phyllis's, but not related to me.

'It was interesting and varied country where we were staying, Watson. To the east, the land lies as flat as a sheet of paper all the way to the sea; to the west, towards the river Trent, it is much the same; but running up the middle of Lincolnshire, like a knobbly spine, are the rolling hills of the Wolds. If the lowlands have little but flatness to them, in the Wolds there is scarcely ever more than a hundred yards of level ground. This elevation leads to some varied and unpredictable weather. The heavy rain clouds that on occasion blow across England without shedding their load are forced upwards when they encounter the Wolds, and the result is very often a heavy downpour just a short time after the sky had appeared a clear and empty blue. The weather was generally fine throughout our stay there and such cloudbursts were not frequent, but there was a memorable one on the evening that Uncle Moreton and Mr Hemming decided to walk the few miles over to Tetford. Uncle Moreton was a great admirer of Dr Johnson, and had heard that that venerable sage had visited the White Hart at Tetford in the middle of the last century when speaking to the local literary society, which was one of the chief reasons Uncle Moreton had wished to spend a holiday in the Wolds. He and Mr Hemming received a thorough soaking for their enterprise, but their spirits remained undampened, and they regaled us at breakfast the following morning with an account of how they had enjoyed a glass of beer while sitting on the very settle from which Dr Johnson had held forth to the local worthies a hundred years before.

'As for East Thrigby itself, it was one of those places that scarcely merit the title of "village" at all. It was a very broadly spread parish, but save for a row of cottages and an old decrepit-looking inn near the church, there was no natural centre to it, the other houses and cottages being scattered far and wide, often hidden away down the narrow lanes that criss-crossed the rolling countryside. Not a very likely spot for dramatic events and mystery, you might imagine. But those intent upon wrongdoing will generally find a way to achieve their ends wherever they are, and the scattered nature of rural homesteads can make the uncovering of their crimes all the more difficult.'

'You sound somewhat cynical,' I interrupted, laughing at the serious tones in which my companion spoke. 'East Thrigby sounds a perfectly idyllic spot to me.'

'Perhaps I am,' my friend conceded. 'But my professional experience has taught me that human nature is much the same everywhere. Besides, East Thrigby was not such an unblemished paradise as you perhaps suppose. There was a troublesome family in the village, by the name of Shaxby. It sometimes seems there is a mysterious law of nature that ordains that there is one such family in practically every parish in England, whose entire *raison d'être* seems to be simply to create nuisance and annoyance for their neighbours. To judge from what I heard subsequently, the Shaxbys were responsible for almost everything discordant and unpleasant that ever occurred in East Thrigby. Drunkenness, fighting, general disorder, wanton damage and petty pilfering: all these had been either proved or suspected against the Shaxbys. One of them in particular, Michael Shaxby, a rough, burly young man of nineteen or twenty, who was known to be the ringleader of all the most rowdy youths in the district, was regarded as a bad lot, and it was generally felt that he might well rise up by degrees in his criminality until he ended up on the scaffold. He was pointed out to us one day, I remember, as he walked past our house with a swagger, tapping a stout stick upon the ground as he went, for all the world as if he were strolling along one of the most fashionable streets in London. He struck me at the time, I admit, as a rather dashing figure, something like a brigand chief or pirate captain; but, of course, an eleven-year-old boy is not generally the best judge of someone's true merits.

'Now, to pass from the general to the particular: two nights before we arrived in East Thrigby there had been a break-in at the rectory and a valuable pair of silver candlesticks had been stolen. This was, in a sense, the start of the trouble that was to befall the village, although no one then could possibly have predicted what would later occur. It was widely believed that Michael Shaxby was responsible for the theft, but as his family were prepared to swear that he had never left their house on the night in question, there was not much that the local constable or anyone else could do about it, save for repeatedly questioning them all in a vaguely menacing manner which of course achieved nothing. Does the account in your book mention the Shaxbys at all, Watson?'

'It certainly mentions a troublesome local family, but it gives them a different name. The author explains in a general preface to the book that he has been obliged to change many of the names of the people in his narratives to allow himself to speak freely and honestly about them without risking a legal suit for defamation.'

Holmes chuckled. 'That is always a danger for such authors, unless their material is centuries old. Oddly enough, it is often the worst of people, those least deserving of respect, who are the quickest to resort to the law-courts in such circumstances. However, I am under no such restrictions, so you can be assured that the account you receive from me is the precise truth in every respect, names included. At first, of course, I was not aware of anything amiss in East Thrigby, but, like everyone else, saw only the attractive appearance of the fields and hedgerows, and the quaint and pretty cottages nestling among them.

'The house that was to be our home that summer was a solid, handsome brick structure which had been built for a wealthy eccentric about fifty years previously and, as it occupied the highest point for some distance round, given the somewhat whimsical name of "The Highlands". He had apparently wished to have fine views from his new residence and these there certainly were. From the sky-light of one of the attics, it was possible to see far across the flatlands to the east, towards where the German Ocean ceaselessly pounds the low sandy shore. Surrounding the house on all sides was a large garden. To the rear of the house much of this was taken up with a smooth and well-kept croquet lawn, where the adults often played. We children, too, were introduced to the game, but found it difficult. Once we had mastered the rudiments, therefore, we tended to wait until the adults had finished and then play a game of our own devising, with somewhat more relaxed rules. At the edges of the croquet lawn were two or three small flower-beds with rose-bushes in them, but most of the rest of the garden was given over to specimen trees and large, spreading shrubs.

'Close by a side-gate in the garden wall was an enormous laurustinus bush which had spread so much, in an arching fashion, as to form a sort of hidden cavern beneath it, the floor of which was covered with a carpet of old leaves. We children quickly discovered this and at once established a camp in there which we termed our "den". There we would meet in the morning, consume ginger beer and biscuits and plan our activities for the day. Sylvie was keeping a sort of holiday diary, in which she recorded all our plans and their outcomes. Her mother was of an artistic turn, and as well as making numerous sketches and watercolours of the countryside, showed us how to press leaves and flowers. This inspired us to attempt to make a complete record of every plant in the garden, from the largest tree to the humblest wild flower. This activity of course consumed a great deal of paper, paint and crayons, but Aunt Phyllis had come well furnished with these articles and encouraged us to use as much as we needed.

'During the first few weeks we made brief acquaintance with many of the local folk, including Mr Giles Stainforth, a wealthy man and keen art-collector, whose house was about a quarter of a mile away and who was thus our nearest neighbour. He was hardly ever at home during the week, but spent much of his time in London, and although he kept a pony and trap, used it only to go to and from the railway station at Alford, the pony being fed and watered by one of the local youths who acted as his groom when required. Uncle Moreton made an arrangement with Stainforth that we might borrow the pony and trap whenever we wished, which was a great convenience. One particularly fine day, Uncle Moreton, Mr Hemming, Percival and I made the journey in the trap all the way to the sea near Mablethorpe. It is a wild and desolate coast there, Watson, with mile after mile of sand dunes and very little else, where the wind blows constantly, whipping the tough grass on the dunes this way and that with a relentless fury, and although the sun was shining, our bathe was a decidedly bracing one.

'In those early days, we also met Mr Cecil Crompton, a very learned-looking man with a high domed forehead, who would often pause as he passed our gate and stand in amicable conversation for some time. He was, I gathered, some kind of historian, with an enormous fund of facts and figures relating to the history of the Wolds. On one occasion, when Crompton had gone on his way and tea was being served, one of the adults remarked that he appeared to have devoted an enormous amount of study to his subject and was evidently a man of independent means. Mrs Hemming agreed that he appeared to be fairly wealthy and, without thinking, I offered the opinion that he was not quite so wealthy as she supposed, at which all the adults turned to me in surprise. Although Sylvie and I were not actively discouraged from joining in the tea-table conversation, it was only rarely that either of us spoke and then generally only when directly addressed, so that my abrupt and uninvited intrusion into the adults' conversation may have appeared a little ill-mannered to them, but in those days I had not learnt that it was sometimes better to keep my observations to myself. Now, as everyone looked at me, I felt distinctly uncomfortable to be the centre of attention.

"'What makes you say that, Sherlock?" asked Uncle Moreton, an expression of both curiosity and amusement upon his face.

"'He cleans his own boots," I replied, wishing I had never opened my mouth.

'Uncle Moreton laughed. "Now, how on earth can you know that?" he asked.

"'He had a thin line of boot-polish along the outer edge of his right thumb," I explained. "It's very distinctive. When you're using a cloth to polish your boots, you nearly always get such a mark in that exact place."

"'What an oddly observant boy you are!" exclaimed Aunt Phyllis, somewhat ambiguously, leaving me unsure as to whether I should feel complimented for being observant, or hurt at being thought "odd".

"'You may be right about the boot-polish," said Uncle Moreton, "but there may of course be reasons other than lack of means why Mr Crompton does the polishing himself. He may, for instance, enjoy doing it – other people's tastes are often very different from one's own – or he may think that no one else would do it so well. Most likely, I would guess, is that he doesn't want to over-work his housekeeper and thinks she already has enough to do without having that particular chore on her list. People tend to keep fewer domestic servants in rural parts such as this and are often afraid of losing them as they can be so difficult to replace. The problem is often not so much a lack of means as a lack of suitable candidates."

'I remember this conversation vividly for two reasons, Watson. First, because of the part that the smear of boot-polish was to play in my reasoning later and, second, because Uncle Moreton's willingness to enter into discussion with me about it was something I had never experienced before. Usually, any observations I made were simply ignored and on the rare occasions they were not, they would be dismissed out of hand, or I would be rebuked for speaking out of turn. That Uncle Moreton had exposed the weakness in my deduction did not trouble me at all. I could see that he was right: my observation was sound enough, but in making my deduction I had over-reached myself; there were, as he said, other possible explanations. But the fact that he had at least recognised the essential point of my observation and considered it worthwhile to engage me in debate on the matter was for me a moment of great significance, and emboldened me to express another and more important opinion to him later in the summer.

'About that time, we also got to know Constable Pilley, the local policeman, a large, smiling man who never seemed to have much to do, but who, to my young eyes, cut a most impressive figure in his dark uniform and brass buttons. The first of all these acquaintances who stayed to take tea with us in the garden, however, was the rector of the parish, the Reverend Amos Beardsley. I cannot pretend that I could follow all his conversation, which ranged over many subjects, from the geology of the Wolds to what was then the highly topical issue of Church governance, but the Reverend Beardsley evidently found it a stimulating experience, for he very soon became a frequent visitor. He was a widower, I understood, his wife having died some years previously, and he struck me, I recall, as a nervous and possibly lonely man, who was glad to find some new and agreeable company.

'One sunny afternoon, he brought with him one of the local farmers, a very large, broad-shouldered and ruddy-cheeked man, who gloried in the name of Mr Pigge. His manner of speech was quite different from that of Mr Beardsley, being slow and somewhat ponderous, but he seemed to amuse Uncle Moreton and the other adults. He mentioned Mr Crompton several times, generally in a distinctly disparaging tone, and although it of course meant little to me, I gathered from Pigge's remarks that Crompton regarded himself as the local scholar *par excellence* and was keen that everyone in the parish should acknowledge the fact.

'When Mr Pigge had left us, the Reverend Beardsley explained that Pigge and Crompton had had a disagreement three years previously, which had become rancorous, and the two men had scarcely spoken to each other since. Crompton, it seemed, had become convinced that there were important Roman remains under the corner of one of Pigge's fields and had wished to conduct an excavation there. This proposal the farmer had rejected out of hand, insisting that he needed to use every square foot of his land for his crops. Crompton had pressed the claims of archaeological discovery and the advancement of historical knowledge, but Pigge had just as vehemently pressed the claim of his own livelihood and, as the land in question belonged to him, his view had of course prevailed. This disagreement might have faded into the past and been forgotten, but a more recent incident had apparently rekindled the embers of dispute between the two men. Just two months previously, Crompton had unearthed a Roman coin of some kind, which discovery he had announced triumphantly to the world, whereupon Pigge had accused him of digging in his field without permission and had said that anything found there rightfully belonged to him. Crompton had retorted that he had not set foot in Pigge's field, but had, rather, found the coin upon his own property. Pigge had insisted that someone had certainly been digging in the corner of his field, Crompton had denied vehemently that it was he, and there, somewhat unsatisfactorily, the matter had rested.

'What else Mr Beardsley had to say, I did not hear, for Sylvie and I were then excused from the tea-table, and went off to find something more interesting to do than sitting there listening to the adults' conversation. I had recently discovered the delights of tree-climbing and there was a particularly large, spreading tree at the bottom of the garden that I wished to attempt. Sylvie came with me, for although Aunt Phyllis had forbidden her to climb trees, as being both dangerous and unladylike, she always took a keen interest in my attempts, calling up to me and quizzing me as to what I could see from my elevated perch, and recording in her diary anything that seemed to her of particular interest, such as the discovery of a bird's nest. Percival did not accompany us. He, too, had been forbidden to climb the trees. In fact, he had been forbidden to do almost everything that seemed to me of interest. Mrs Hemming had for some reason conceived the idea that Percival was a delicate child, who had to be protected from the rough and tumble of life. There never seemed to me to be much wrong with him that an increase in exercise and a decrease in cake-consumption would not have remedied; but on this occasion I was glad he was not with us: the tree in question presented a formidable challenge and I considered that his presence would only have hindered me. As it turned out, however, it would have made no difference. The trunk of the tree was so perfectly smooth and branchless at the bottom that it defeated all my attempts to climb it, and, reluctantly, I was obliged to admit defeat. Casting around for something else to do, Sylvie and I decided to leave the garden altogether, and push our way through the hedge into a neighbouring field which was lying fallow that year and had nothing in it but tall grass and weeds. There we lay down and crawled along on our fronts like native trackers. There were always lots of rabbits bobbing about in that field and we wanted to see how close we could approach to them before they noticed us.

'We were doing reasonably well, although the rabbits had begun wrinkling their noses and glancing suspiciously in our direction, when the whole lot of them abruptly turned tail and bolted for cover under a dense tangle of brambles at the edge of the field. Sylvie turned her head my way and was about to speak, but I put my finger to my lips. Some distance ahead of us, a man had entered the field from a lane at the side. He had a black beard and a dark hat pulled down low on his brow. We lay still in the long grass and watched him, and it was evident that he had not seen us. Slowly, in what struck me as a highly furtive manner, he made his way towards the garden hedge of The Highlands, until he was right up against it. For some time he stayed in that position, peering through the foliage, and it was clear that he was watching Uncle Moreton and the other adults in the garden, for I could hear their voices quite clearly. Eventually he turned away, made his way back across the field the way he had come and vanished from our sight once more.

'"I wonder who that was," I remarked.

'Sylvie pulled a face of mystification and shook her head. "A stranger," she whispered at last, and added that there seemed to be something sinister about him. I agreed, and from that moment on the gentleman in question was always known to us as "the sinister stranger". Who he was, and why he should be spying through the hedge at our relatives, we could not imagine, but it certainly seemed odd. We debated whether we should inform the adults, but in the end decided against it. As we were discussing the matter, we heard Percival calling to us from the garden, so we returned that way, and as the croquet lawn was free, occupied ourselves in our own unique version of that game for the next hour or so.

'The following day Mr Cecil Crompton himself called by and was invited to stay for tea. He was, I must say, the very image of a scholarly gentleman, with his shining bald head and wisps of white hair about his temples. He was undoubtedly a very erudite man. He had written a pamphlet on the history of East Thrigby, a copy of which he had brought with him and presented to Uncle Moreton, as he had promised on a previous occasion. This history apparently encompassed more than two thousand years, for there were, he said, clear indications that the Wolds had been settled by Ancient Britons when the lowlands to the east and west had been uninhabitable marshes. His own particular interest, however, was the period of the Roman occupation. Uncle Moreton mentioned as tactfully as possible that we had heard about his disagreement with Mr Pigge, at which he shook his head in a gesture of dismissal.

'"That doesn't matter now," said he. "I certainly believe that there may be the remains of a small fort or barracks under part of Pigge's field, but it's not so important now. I have made far more important discoveries during the past eighteen months. I have managed to trace the line of an ancient road southwards from Pigge's field, and have discovered that there are Roman remains under my very own house and garden."

"'How exciting!" cried Aunt Phyllis. "Was that where you found the Roman coin?"

'Crompton nodded. "Yes. It has been thrilling, I must say, to learn that I was living on top of such historic remains. I had always known that my house, High Grove, was built upon the site of a small Tudor dwelling which itself had replaced a mediaeval structure, but the discoveries of the past eighteen months suggest that the site has been continuously occupied for almost two thousand years. Last summer I communicated my discoveries to a correspondent of mine at St Stephen's College in Cambridge and he arranged for a couple of very keen undergraduates to spend half their summer vacation up here, helping me with the excavations. By the time they left, we had dug up half the garden in our efforts to establish the outline of the buildings that had once stood there and were convinced it was the villa of a fairly high-ranking Roman official – possibly a district governor of some kind. You must come over some time and have a look!"

"'We should be delighted to," said Uncle Moreton. "When would be convenient?"

"'There's no time like the present," returned Crompton with a chuckle. "If you've finished your tea, I'd be pleased to show you over the diggings this evening."

'This suggestion met with general agreement and in a few minutes we had set off to walk the mile or so to High Grove.

"'Do you know anything of Tacitus?" Crompton asked Uncle Moreton as we walked along.

"'Not a great deal," replied Uncle Moreton. "I read some of his shorter works when I was at school and a lot more when I was up at Oxford, but I regret to say that I've forgotten most of it now. How about you, Hemming?"

"'Pretty much the same, I'm afraid," Mr Hemming replied. "I do remember enjoying some of his biography of Agricola."

"'Ah!' said Crompton. "That is interesting, for it was of Tacitus's account of Agricola that I wished to speak. As you will no doubt be aware," he continued, "Agricola was not only a military commander and governor of the province the Romans called Britannia, but was also, of course, Tacitus's own father-in-law. It was no doubt this personal acquaintance with his subject that enabled Tacitus to recognise in Agricola a man of high principle and unimpeachable moral standing. But although Tacitus clearly knew Agricola well, it has never been established whether he had a similar personal acquaintance with Britain, or whether his account of the people here was based entirely on secondary sources, including of course Agricola's own records of his time here."

"'I seem to remember a suggestion that Tacitus might have served as tribune for the soldiers and spent some time in Britain in that capacity," said Uncle Moreton.

"'That is true," responded Crompton, nodding his head, "but no one knows for certain. It would therefore be of great interest if it could be established that Tacitus did indeed visit Britannia, either before he wrote his book on Agricola or afterwards."

'Uncle Moreton nodded his head in agreement. "I don't suppose we're ever likely to know that now, though."

"'You mustn't be so pessimistic!" said Crompton with a chuckle. "One can never tell when new historical evidence may come to light, even after two thousand years."

'There was a note in Crompton's voice that suggested he had something specific in mind. Uncle Moreton evidently noticed it, too, for he turned to Crompton with a look of surprise on his face. "Don't say you have found something relating to Tacitus in your own excavations!" said he.

"'Nothing absolutely conclusive," returned Crompton, "but something which is highly suggestive. I don't know if you're aware of it, but there is some evidence that a cousin of Tacitus's wife held a minor administrative post in the province of Britannia, possibly in this very part of the country. It is therefore perfectly conceivable that Tacitus himself stayed in these parts before or after he had composed his *Agricola*. I was aware of this before I began my own digging, but had never really given it much thought, as it seemed somewhat unlikely. However, my excavations at High Grove have cast the whole business in a new light and have made the possibility seem a much more likely one. Part of the floor of the villa that has been revealed by the digging is covered with tiles and one of these, which I only uncovered two months ago, has an inscription on it which mentions Tacitus by name."

"'How thrilling!" cried Uncle Moreton. "What does it say?"

"'Unfortunately, the tile is broken. Part of it has crumbled to dust and part of it is missing altogether, so all I have been able to make out is *Tacitus in pomario*."

"'What does *pomario* mean?" asked Mrs Hemming.

"'An orchard' I think," suggested Uncle Moreton. "Is that right, Mr Crompton?"

"'Yes," agreed Crompton, "or possibly simply a garden with fruit trees in it. There is probably a verb missing and perhaps also an adjective qualifying *pomario*. So we cannot say what Tacitus was doing in the orchard, nor where the orchard referred to was situated. It may be he is described as walking or sitting in the orchard – who knows? Similarly, whether the orchard in question was one attached to the villa the remains of which lie under High Grove, or was somewhere else entirely, we cannot say. However," he continued, "I am always optimistic that further excavations will turn up more evidence."

"'What you have found so far is amazing enough!" said Mr Hemming with enthusiasm. "Have you publicised it yet?"

"'Well, I have notified the British Museum, if that is what you mean; but the wheels of the British Museum grind very slowly, I'm afraid. They informed me that they receive news of several such discoveries every year and are not able to investigate them all immediately. So when they will put in an appearance in our humble parish I don't know. I have also written to the people I dealt with before at Cambridge University and they are sending someone down in a week or two."

"'Does the coin you found date from the same period as Tacitus?" asked Uncle Moreton.

'Crompton shook his head. "Not exactly," said he, "but it's not much later. It's a denarius of the reign of Hadrian, from about twenty years or so after Tacitus might have been here. As you're no doubt aware, the Roman occupation of Britain lasted almost four hundred years and one might, of course, expect to find artefacts, coins and so on from any time during that very long period, so to find a coin from so close to Tacitus's time was rather exciting. To be honest, I am not much of a coin expert, and when I found it, I was not really sure what it was. It is quite scratched and battered, and some of the lettering on the edge is missing. I thought at first it was from the reign of Titus, then wondered if the face on it might be Hadrian. In the end, to decide the matter, I sent off for an authenticated denarius of Hadrian from an antiquarian coin-dealer in London, and from that I could see at once that mine was one of Hadrian's, too."

"'And you definitely haven't been digging in Mr Pigge's field?" asked Mr Hemming in a mischievous tone.

"'Certainly not," said Crompton in a tone of humorous indignation. "If anyone has really been digging there as Pigge claims, I think it must have been one or two of the local boys. No doubt when they heard I had found something interesting they thought they would like to find something, too. I might mention, incidentally, that my discoveries have caused a certain amount of envy locally, largely among the ignorant, who have no idea how much time and effort I have put into the excavations. The last time I dined with Mr Stainforth, two or three weeks ago, we discussed this very point.

"'Depend upon it, Crompton,' said he: 'any good fortune you have is sure to be resented by someone, who will not appreciate the effort you must always put in to persuade fortune to occasionally smile upon you. I shouldn't trouble yourself about Pigge, who is as ignorant a man as I have ever met. You can always rely on me to support you in any dispute with that oaf!' But here we are, ladies and gentlemen! Come in and inspect my discoveries!"

'We had turned down a narrow lane off the main road as Crompton had been speaking and come to a wicket gate in a tall hedge, which he pushed open. The front garden of his property was modest in size, with a small lawn and rose-bed. He did not pause there, however, but conducted us directly round the side of the house to the rear garden. This was much larger – perhaps a quarter of an acre – and, save for a strip of grass by the house, was in a state of great upheaval, with numerous shallow trenches and mounds of freshly dug earth. In the bottom of some of the trenches I could make out half-buried rows of brickwork. "As you see," said Crompton, waving his hand at these diggings, "this area has been the focus of most of the activity. The enthusiastic young students from Cambridge were an enormous help to me last summer. You will appreciate by the extent of it that I couldn't possibly have achieved so much by myself. Since they left, I have carried on alone, but at a much slower rate." He led us on a path of wooden boards across the soft earth, towards the far corner of the garden, where an area of about fifteen feet square was covered with tarpaulins, their corners weighted down with small stones. Some of these Crompton picked up and tossed to one side, then he rolled back one of the tarpaulins to reveal the ground beneath. There were more rows of ancient-looking brickwork there and, between them, about two feet down, what appeared to be a tiled floor. The tiles were about six or seven inches square and of a dull reddish colour. Most were perfectly plain, but one to which Crompton drew our attention had some very neat writing inscribed upon it, although the lower half of the tile was broken off and missing. I leaned closer to get a better look and read *Tacitus in pomario*, as Crompton had described to us.

'"Oh, this is wonderful!" cried Aunt Phyllis, craning forward to get a closer look. "It is so interesting to see how the craftsman has incised the letters so neatly. Do you mind if I sketch it?"

'"Why, not at all," returned Crompton, looking pleased at Aunt Phyllis's enthusiasm.

'She took a small sketch-pad and a pencil from a little bag she was carrying, and began to sketch the tiles before us. "The tiles are a good rich red colour," she remarked without looking up from her drawing. "It really needs a bit of paint on this picture to do them justice. Were Roman tiles always this colour?"

'"Broadly speaking, yes," returned Crompton, "although they vary slightly from place to place, depending on the nature of the local clay deposits. As a matter of fact, this was a question that interested me, as there was some difference of opinion about it: whether the tiles and bricks had been produced locally, or had been carted in from further afield, from Lincoln, say, or from somewhere in the Trent valley. I therefore dug up some reasonable-looking clay from that field over the hedge – the farmer, Mr Thoresby, is a somewhat more obliging gentleman than old Pigge – and made a series of experiments, using the oven in my kitchen to fire the clay. The results were fairly conclusive, as far as I was concerned: my efforts, amateurish though they were, ended up precisely the same shade as these skilfully crafted Roman bricks and tiles, thus suggesting that they, too, had been made locally. Incidentally, the Romans sometimes used a method of heating their houses in cold weather by constructing channels under such tiles as these for hot air from a furnace to pass along, but there is no such arrangement in this case, which lends support to my theory that this was purely a summer residence for a wealthy individual who spent most of the year somewhere else, probably in Lincoln – or *Lindum* as the Romans called it."

'For some time we ambled round the excavations, while Crompton pointed out features of interest to us. Then he fetched from the house the two Roman coins, and we were able to see that the emperor's face on both was the same, although the one he had found in his excavations was quite badly damaged, with some of the edge broken off. Finally, as the sun was declining in the west, casting a golden glow over the countryside, we thanked our host for showing us round and made our way home. It was clear that everyone had enjoyed the visit immensely, and the adults chatted enthusiastically about the surprising wealth of history to be found in this obscure corner of the country. "I had thought it was thrilling enough to sit on the bench that Dr Johnson had occupied a hundred years ago," said Uncle Moreton, "but to walk on the floor where Tacitus may have trod nearly two thousand years ago is even more amazing."

'The following day was dull and overcast, and we spent most of it in Louth, the nearest town of any size, where Aunt Phyllis found a small mirror in a battered frame in what she described as an "old curiosity shop". This is the mirror you see before you, Watson. She made us promise that the next time we went to the sea we would take a basket with us and collect as many pretty little shells and pebbles as we could find. "And then," said she, "I will show you how we can decorate this mirror to make a keepsake of our holiday."

'On the way home I gave fresh consideration to the big spreading tree at the bottom of the garden and thought of a way of overcoming the difficulty of the first few feet. As soon as we got back, therefore, I found an old cask and, with Sylvie's help, manoeuvred it into position at the foot of the tree. Standing on that, I was able to stretch my hand up to a small clump of twigs and thus pull myself up into the main branches of the tree. After that, progress was not too difficult, although I did not manage to get anywhere near the top. At the place I had stopped, about two-thirds of the way up the tree, there was a comfortable place to sit, and from that vantage point I was able to survey the rolling countryside which surrounded The Highlands. In a narrow lane in the distance I saw a man I recognised as Mr Crompton, clad in a linen jacket and straw hat. Further away, round a bend in the same lane and thus out of sight of Mr Crompton, another man was approaching. He was clad in a dark suit and hat, and I recognised him as "the sinister stranger" that Sylvie and I had seen in the field next to The Highlands. On this occasion he had a child with him, a boy of about my own age, as far as I could make out.

'As I watched, the two men came in sight of each other and, as they did so, Crompton stopped abruptly. A moment later he had resumed his leisurely walk and the two men gradually approached each other. When they met, they paused for a moment and engaged in conversation, but it was not for long, and they soon went their separate ways. All the while, I was conscious that Sylvie was still standing at the foot of the tree, waiting to hear from me, and I felt sorry and a little guilty that I was enjoying being up the tree and she could not. I was therefore about to descend when something surprising occurred which arrested my attention. Mr Crompton had stopped and turned to look at the retreating back of the other man. For a long moment he just stood there staring, as if he had perhaps remembered something he had meant to say, but then, abruptly, he raised his hand and shook his fist at the other man. A moment later he had turned away once more and resumed his course down the lane. Startled by what I had seen, I quickly climbed down and described it in detail to Sylvie, but neither of us could think what to make of it. Again we debated whether we should mention what we had seen to the adults, but again we decided against it.

'The next day dawned bright and clear, and over breakfast Uncle Moreton and Mr Hemming decided that we should make another trip to the coast. "We don't know how long this fine weather will last," remarked Uncle Moreton, "and we might not feel much like bathing if the air turns colder."

'As we left, the wind seemed to be getting stronger and by the time we reached the coast it was blowing very sharply off the sea, piling up the waves and sending them crashing on to the shore in a cascade of foam. We had our bathe, but it was a very boisterous one, and I think we all had to grit our teeth a little to enter into that wild maelstrom of chilly water. Afterwards, with chattering teeth, we collected as many attractive shells and pebbles as we could fit in the basket we had brought with us and set off for home, cold and exhausted but feeling pleased with ourselves for our hardiness.

'When we reached The Highlands, we found that Sylvie and the two women had already cleaned and smoothed the frame of the mirror, and had just finished applying a second coat of blue paint to it, making it look very smart. Sylvie and I then set about washing all the shells and pebbles in a bowl of water in the garden and laying them out in rows on an old towel so that we could choose our favourites. We were busily employed in this way when Mr Crompton came in through the garden gate. He came over to see what we were doing, and when I explained about the mirror, he clapped his hands together in delight. "How very artistic," said he. "I'm sure it will look splendid!" At that moment, the adults emerged from the house to take tea in the garden and invited him to join them.

"'This is not purely a social call," said Crompton as he sat down at the table. "The fact is, I wondered if I could ask a small favour of you. I am going to see my sister, Ethel, in Nottingham tomorrow and shall be away for a couple of nights. My housekeeper will also be away, as I have given her a few days off to visit some relatives of hers in Boston. It's annoying these two things coming together, but they were both arranged some weeks ago. At the time, it seemed the most sensible and convenient way of proceeding, but now all I can think of is that the house will be left completely unoccupied, and after the recent burglary at the rectory I am worried that someone will take the opportunity to break into High Grove. Of course, I've notified Constable Pilley that I shall be away and he will no doubt keep an eye on the house during the evening, but I thought that if you could perhaps walk over there once or twice and just sit in the garden for five minutes, that might be enough to put potential burglars off."

"'I'm sure we'd be delighted to," said Mr Hemming.

'By the time we had finished tea, the paint on the mirror-frame had dried, and Sylvie, Aunt Phyllis and I began to position the shells and pebbles to best effect, fixing each in position with a blob of glue. Percival took no part in this. He had developed a persistent cough since our return from the coast, which got worse during the course of the evening, and by bedtime he really seemed quite ill. I was moved out of the bedroom he and I had previously shared into the spare bed in Sylvie's room, but all night I could hear him coughing and wheezing, and the sound of his mother's footsteps going back and forth on the landing outside the room. In the morning it was clear that neither Percival nor his parents had slept much during the night, and after a heated discussion in which Mrs Hemming berated her husband for subjecting Percival to the cold winds at the seaside, she decided that she would take him up to London without delay, to consult the specialist who had treated him for some similar ailment the year before. Aunt Phyllis said she would go with her for company and, after a hurried breakfast, the pony and trap were brought round and we all set off for the station at Alford, with poor Percival wrapped up in a blanket.

'When the London train had left, Uncle Moreton, Mr Hemming, Sylvie and I sat for a few moments in silence in the trap. Everything seemed to have happened in such a rush, including catching the train, which had been achieved with only a minute or two to spare, that I think we all needed a little while to catch our breath and order our thoughts. "I think," said Uncle Moreton at length, "that we perhaps won't go straight back to The Highlands, but will first make a little trip to Louth and take lunch there. I have been observing you playing in the garden, Sylvie, and it seems to me that – whatever anyone else may think – you would really like nothing better than to climb up that big tree with young Sherlock here. I thought as much," he continued with a chuckle as she nodded her head. "In that case we must provide you with a proper tree-climbing outfit!" Once we reached Louth it did not take long to find a suitable outfitters and Sylvie was soon "fully equipped", as Uncle Moreton described it, with corduroy breeches and a linen shirt.

'Upon our return to The Highlands, she and I at once set about climbing up the big tree from which I had watched Mr Crompton and "the sinister stranger". To begin with, I had to help her, but, to tell the truth, she soon proved herself every bit as accomplished at climbing as I considered myself to be. By leaning out in what seemed to me a very daring way, past a clump of little branches, she succeeded in climbing even higher than I had previously managed. I followed her example and we found ourselves a very comfortable perch from which we could survey the countryside for miles around. As we sat there, commenting on the different colours of the many fields we could see and the little cottages far in the distance, a horse and cart came into view, trundling at an easy pace along a nearby lane. On the seat was Mr Pigge and another man, whom I recognised after a moment as Michael Shaxby. To see a highly respected local farmer consorting with the young man I had been told was the local ne'er-do-well was certainly a surprise.

'"Perhaps old Pigge has offered him a job, to keep him out of mischief," suggested Sylvie. "Mama is always saying 'the devil finds work for idle hands'."

'At that moment we heard Uncle Moreton calling to us from somewhere in the garden, to tell us that tea was ready, so we descended quickly from our lofty perch, which gave him something of a surprise. "I had no idea you were up there," said he. "I hope you don't end up in the clouds!"

'After tea, Uncle Moreton applied a coat of varnish to the frame of the mirror, shells and all, to seal it and give it a glossy shine, as Aunt Phyllis had instructed him that morning. While he was doing that, Mr Hemming said he would stroll over to Crompton's house, to look it over, as he had promised we would. When he returned, some fifty minutes later, Sylvie and I were in our den by the gate, bringing our note-books up to date, and Uncle Moreton was sitting nearby, smoking his pipe.

'"You will never guess who I met, prying about in Crompton's garden and peering through his windows," said Mr Hemming to Uncle Moreton, as he came in at the gate: "just about the last person in the world I should have expected to see in such a rural backwater as this: John Clashbury Staunton. I'm sure I must have mentioned his name to you at some time. He and I were up at Cambridge together, and everyone knew him as one of the most brilliant undergraduates that the old university had ever seen. Unfortunately, his character was not quite as elevated as his intellect."

"'What do you mean?" asked Uncle Moreton.

"'He was always very off-hand and rude in his manner, and had a knack of falling out with almost everyone he met. On top of that, he had an obsessive belief that people were spying on him all the time, trying to steal both his belongings and his ideas. He and I had been great friends during our early days at college, but fell out badly later."

"'Why was that?"

"'He accused me of stealing something from his room. Absurd, of course, but I wasn't the only one he accused in that way. It was ironic, then, that the only person who was ever actually caught prying in other people's rooms was Staunton himself, for which he came close to being sent down. However, he managed to talk his way out of that particular difficulty, did brilliantly in his examinations and went on to become a successful classical scholar, in demand not only at Cambridge but everywhere that scholarship was valued. You might imagine from this that his future life was set fair, but trouble seems to have followed him around wherever he went. From what I've heard, he has managed to quarrel with practically every other scholar in his field, accusing more than one of them of stealing his ideas. Then there was the business with his wife and the dark rumours that were circulating when she abruptly disappeared. But wait a moment," said Mr Hemming, breaking off, stepping to the gate and leaning out into the lane. "Staunton said that he would call on us later. Yes, he's coming now. Look," he continued, turning once more to Uncle Moreton, "I haven't got time to explain, but whatever you do, don't mention his wife. Do you understand?"

"'Why, certainly," replied Uncle Moreton in a tone of surprise.

'A few moments later, Mr Clashbury Staunton arrived at the gate, and to my great surprise I saw it was the man that Sylvie and I had called "the sinister stranger". With him was the boy I had seen previously. Uncle Moreton called to us and as we emerged from under the laurustinus, he looked, I thought, a little uncomfortable, as if he had not realised that we were so close and would probably have overheard his conversation with Mr Hemming. We were introduced to the newcomers, and Uncle Moreton asked if the boy – whose name was Adrian – would like to be shown round the garden.

"'I'm sure he would," replied Staunton, answering for the boy in a deep, sepulchral voice. "Go and play with Sherlock and Sylvie, Adrian." Sylvie and I conducted this boy to what we considered the most interesting corners of the grounds, including our den beneath the laurustinus, but nothing seemed to fire his enthusiasm and throughout the whole time he spoke scarcely a single audible word. Presently we were summoned back to where the men were sitting, and shortly afterwards Staunton and his son left. Now, Watson, I must confess to a shameful secret. I have not very often been an eavesdropper, but on that particular occasion I was consumed with curiosity to learn what it was about Staunton's wife that had caused Mr Hemming to warn Uncle Moreton against mentioning her, and I therefore went out of my way to listen in upon some of their conversation later in the evening. Much of it was irrelevant, some of it I could not understand, but the gist, as far as I could make it out, was that it was general knowledge that Staunton had treated his wife very badly, and when she disappeared one day without any explanation, rumours had soon arisen that he had murdered her and hidden her body somewhere. These rumours grew – as rumours tend to – until the police began to take an interest and interviewed Staunton on the matter. Eventually, several weeks later, the truth came out: deciding that she could no longer live under the same roof as her husband, Mrs Staunton had simply packed a bag one day when he and the boy were out of the house, and, with the assistance of an old friend in London, had taken herself off somewhere. When this became generally known, it caused an enormous scandal in the society in which they moved, and Staunton himself suffered a complete nervous collapse over the matter and spent several weeks in a sanatorium. Upon his partial recovery, he had been granted a prolonged leave of absence from his duties in Cambridge, whereupon he had taken a remote house in the Lincolnshire Wolds and lived there in solitude with his son. They had been there about eighteen months at the time of our visit.

'The next day was fine, if a little breezy, and after Uncle Moreton had applied a second coat of varnish to the frame of the mirror, the four of us went for a long walk to a picturesque little babbling brook where we had a picnic and Sylvie and I did a little paddling and fishing with our nets. On our way back to The Highlands, Mr Hemming made a *detour* to Crompton's house to see that everything was still all right there. When he rejoined us later, he reported that there had been no one about and everything had seemed to be in good order. It therefore came as a great surprise when, the following day, Mr Crompton himself arrived at our house early in the afternoon in a state of great agitation. Breathlessly, he told us what had happened. He had arrived back that morning with his sister, who was to stay with him for a few days, and had found that his house had been broken into while he had been away.

'"But when I looked it over yesterday," said Mr Hemming, "everything seemed all right. There was no sign of any of the windows having been forced, or anything of the sort."

'"They appear to have gained entry through a small pantry window," said Crompton, "then wedged it shut again with a sliver of wood, no doubt to hide the fact that it had been forced open. My Roman coins have been stolen and, worse than that, they have dug up and stolen several of the tiles in the garden that were covered by the tarpaulin, including the one inscribed with the name of Tacitus."

'"Oh, no!" cried Uncle Moreton in dismay. "That is terrible! Have you informed Constable Pilley?"

'"Of course. But I doubt it will do much good. I told him it is his job to prevent such things happening, but the useless, idle lie-abed just says he can't be everywhere at once, as if that entirely exonerates him from any responsibility. He has sent for some kind of detective officer from Lincoln to look into the matter, but who knows when he will get here? In the old days, all the respectable people in a parish would band together to make sure that this sort of thing did not happen. Nowadays, we are so modern that we have our very own constable, so of course people just leave everything to him and don't take any responsibility themselves. Well, I for one have had enough of this modern, irresponsible world. I'm going to do something about it!"

'Crompton was not entirely specific about what he intended to do, but the general impression was that he hoped to persuade his neighbours to join him in patrolling the country lanes after dark. This seemed to me at first a wonderful idea, but that is because eleven-year-old boys rarely appreciate the practical difficulties inherent in such plans. In any case, it would only have been of any use if the lanes had been full of marauding bands of robbers every night, which even I could see was unlikely to be the case. Not long after Crompton had left, Constable Pilley called by to ask if we had observed anything the previous night which might cast light on what had happened, but we were unable to help him.

'"Was anything else stolen, apart from the coins and the tiles?" Uncle Moreton asked.

'The constable shook his head. "It's clear the thieves knew what they were after. The two coins are more or less identical, I understand,' he continued, consulting his note-book, "except that one is in better condition than the other. I am informed that each of them is a denarius from the reign of Hadrian, if that means anything to you gentlemen. Mr Crompton tells me that they are not especially valuable, as such things go, but even so, I reckon they would fetch a few bob somewhere, which would be enough to make it worth someone's while to steal them. It's the tiles that puzzle me more. I can't see where they could be sold without it being obvious where they had come from."

'"I suppose some unscrupulous collector of such things might buy them and ask no questions as to their provenance," Mr Hemming suggested.

'"Or perhaps someone simply took them out of spite," added Uncle Moreton; "someone who envied Mr Crompton's good fortune in having them on his property."

'"Perhaps," said Constable Pilley, closing up his note-book. "We shall have to wait and see what Inspector Tubby makes of it when he gets here. He should be here tomorrow morning."

'That evening was a very windy one, and I went to sleep to the sound of the trees in the garden creaking and groaning, as the gusting wind blew them this way and that. Some time in the night I awoke abruptly and lay there listening, as a variety of different nocturnal noises came to my ears. They might have been anything – a small animal scurrying about, perhaps, or a branch being blown down – but to one whose head was full of thoughts of burglars they sounded like nothing so much as the latch of the garden gate being lifted, followed by footsteps on the path. I leaned from my bed, pulled back the curtain and looked out, but the night was very dark and I could not see anything. For some time I lay awake, my senses straining to catch the slightest sound, but heard nothing more.

'In the morning, as we were taking breakfast, the road outside seemed uncommonly busy and Uncle Moreton left the table to see what was happening. There had been the sound of vehicles passing and numerous voices. He did not return for nearly twenty minutes and when he did his face was grave.

'"It's a bad business," he said in answer to Mr Hemming's enquiring look. He glanced in our direction, then beckoned to Mr Hemming to join him in the hallway, which he did, closing the door behind him. Of course, Sylvie and I at once got down from the table and went to listen at the closed door. "It's Mr Crompton," we heard Uncle Moreton say in a low voice. "He's been found dead in the road, not far from here. It seems he was clubbed to death, some time during the night."

'The next few days were strange ones. Crompton may have been only a slight acquaintance, but his death, and the dreadful circumstances surrounding it, cast a pall over our stay at The Highlands. Although Uncle Moreton and Mr Hemming did not discuss the matter openly in front of us, one way or another Sylvie and I learnt whatever there was to know about it, in the way children do. The facts of the matter, which were soon established, were as follows: after he had left our house, following his tirade against Constable Pilley and his declaration that he would take a personal stand against what he saw as the local lawlessness, Crompton had called upon those of his neighbours he considered might be agreeable to his ideas. Each had listened to his proposals, but had declined to participate, regarding Crompton's scheme as, in the Reverend Beardsley's words, "unlikely to achieve anything". Undeterred by his neighbours' lack of enthusiasm, however, Crompton had determined to press on alone with some kind of night-time patrol.

'At half past ten that evening, just after his housekeeper had retired for the night, and as his sister was about to do so, Crompton had announced that he was going out on patrol. A brief altercation with his sister had ensued. She told him that it would not do any good, that he would only make himself appear ridiculous, but, undeterred, he left the house at about eleven o'clock, equipped with a small pocket lantern and with a life-preserver attached to his wrist by a loop of cord. That was the last time anyone saw him alive. His body was found the following morning by the boy who attended to Mr Stainforth's pony, stretched out face down in the road near Stainforth's house, his life-preserver still attached to his wrist. The back of his head had been crushed in by what appeared to have been a fearsome blow from a cudgel or some similar blunt and heavy weapon.

'As the body was found scarcely twenty feet from Stainforth's gate, on the road between his house and ours, Constable Pilley – and Detective Inspector Tubby, when he arrived – gave particular attention to Stainforth's house, to see if anyone had tried to break in there during the night. The house had been completely unoccupied, for Stainforth himself was away in London as usual, and the only domestic servant he employed was a local woman who came in to see to his cooking and laundry when he was at home, but returned to her own house when he was away. The policemen soon found evidence to confirm their suspicions. A few feet to the right of the front door was a sturdy wooden trellis, for the support of climbing plants, which went all the way up to the sill of a first-floor bedroom window. This window stood slightly ajar, and it appeared from marks visible on the window-sill and on the trellis immediately below it that someone had recently climbed up there.

'A wire was at once sent to Stainforth's address in London and he returned that evening. In the company of the policemen, he then made a thorough examination of the inside of the house, but declared in the end that as far as he could see, nothing had been taken or disturbed. The open bedroom window had certainly been forced, however, for a close examination of the frame revealed that the paintwork at the edge was scratched and chipped, as if someone had inserted a blade there to force up the catch. A subsequent search of the garden turned up an open clasp-knife of a common type, on the ground under a bush by the gate. The conclusion of the policemen, then, was that Crompton had surprised someone in the act of breaking into Stainforth's house. This person had jumped down to confront him on the garden path and probably threatened him with the knife. That the assailant had made at least one slashing attack on Crompton was suggested by a long shallow cut across the palm of his right hand, as if he had tried to ward off an attack. It was supposed that Crompton had then struck the knife from the other man's grasp with his life-preserver and sent it flying to where it was subsequently found.

'A bruise and cut on the bridge of the dead man's nose suggested to the policemen – who had seen similar wounds among the roughs of Lincoln – that Crompton had been punched in the face. Then, it was supposed, realising that he could not hope to overcome his opponent, who was no doubt younger and stronger than he was, Crompton had turned and fled out of the gate, but his assailant, catching up with him in a few strides, had struck at him with a bludgeon of his own and delivered the fatal blow to the back of his head.

'So much seemed clear, but did not help at all in establishing the identity of Crompton's assailant. The only real clue was the clasp-knife, but that was of little help, for it was, as I mentioned, a very common type. There were no initials or other distinctive markings upon it and there was probably one such knife in every household in the district. Indeed, when Michael Shaxby was questioned on the matter, he was able to show the policemen what he claimed was his own knife, which was still in his possession. Shaxby had been one of the first people questioned by the police, but they subsequently questioned everyone in the district as to what they might have heard or seen on the night of the murder, without advancing their knowledge in any way.

'Uncle Moreton and Mr Hemming discussed whether we should stay on in East Thrigby or leave straight away, and Hemming said he would write to his wife and see how matters were progressing in London. Her reply was not long in coming. This informed him that although Percival was now much better than he had been, he was still not fully recovered, and she and Aunt Phyllis had decided not to return to Lincolnshire, but to stay with a relative in London until the end of the summer. Mr Hemming and Uncle Moreton then reconsidered what we should do in the light of this and decided that we would stay just one more week. Meanwhile, Sylvie and I still played in the house and garden, but in a subdued sort of way. The Highlands seemed now a much quieter and less lively place, few visitors called by and sometimes, so it seemed, no one spoke for hours on end.

'Two days after Crompton's murder came a surprising development. Michael Shaxby's younger brother, David, came forward with the information that he had found one of the stolen coins in the field next to Crompton's garden which belonged to the farmer, Thoresby. He admitted that he had found it the day before Crompton had been killed and had been slow to announce his discovery, but said he had been shocked when he heard about the murder, unsure what to do and frightened that he would be suspected of having something to do with Crompton's death. Of course, the policemen didn't entirely believe him at first, although a point in his favour was that he had volunteered the information, rather than simply throwing the coin away. Despite repeated questioning he did not change his story and the police were obliged in the end to conclude that it might well be true. If so, it probably meant that whoever it was that had broken into Crompton's house had made his escape through a gap in the hedge into Thoresby's field, where he had accidentally dropped the coin.

'Sylvie and I continued to climb as high as we could in the big tree at the bottom of the garden, where, in our lofty perch, we would sometimes sit together in silence as the wind blew in our faces, and survey the quiet, peaceful countryside spread out all around us. It still bothered me that we had been unable to reach the very top of the tree, and one day it occurred to me that if a thick clump of small branches which blocked the way to the summit might be removed, we should probably be able to ascend the final few feet. I therefore asked Uncle Moreton if I might cut these branches off with a small saw I had seen in the garden shed. He was at first somewhat dubious about this proposal, on the grounds both of my safety and the question of disfiguring a tree which did not belong to us. However, I eventually persuaded him to allow it by promising to take no risks in the matter, and assuring him that the change I hoped to effect would not be visible from the ground. With the saw tied with a length of cord round my neck, I therefore clambered up the tree and set about my task, with Sylvie just below me, ready to receive the sawn branches, repeatedly urging me to "be careful". It did not take long to complete, for the branches in question were relatively thin ones, and then, with the saw and the branches disposed of, Sylvie and I squeezed ourselves between the remaining branches and ascended in happy triumph to the very summit of the old tree. The wind was strong and blustery that day, and as it buffeted our faces and hair, we could feel the tree moving beneath us, like a ship rocking gently on the billows of the ocean.

'That night in bed, however, the triumph of our achievement was driven from my mind by another thought, vague and nebulous, which, in some odd way, linked our tree-climbing achievements to the death of Mr Crompton. There was some parallel there, I felt, some analogy that my brain could not quite grasp, as if the thought were nudging me from behind a thick veil: I could feel its pressure on my mind, but could not make out its shape.

'When I awoke the following morning, the same thought was still running through my head, but I now saw things more clearly: just as I had removed an obstacle in order to reach the summit of the tree, so I must remove an obstacle in order to solve the mystery of Mr Crompton's death, and the obstacle I had to remove was the primary assumption that everyone had made about it. Immediately after breakfast, Sylvie and I repaired to our den beneath the laurustinus. There, in the seclusion of our secret meeting-place, I told her my theory about Mr Crompton's death. She was a quick, intelligent girl, and at once understood my reasoning and the significance of the facts on which I had founded it. For some time we discussed what we might do to confirm or refute the hypothesis and decided at length that we would make an expedition to look for evidence. We had been forbidden to leave the garden of The Highlands since the death of Mr Crompton and so were obliged to do so in a furtive manner. When we were sure that Uncle Moreton and Mr Hemming were occupied in the house, we made our way through a gap in the hedge near the bottom of the garden, which was hidden from view by a large bush, and so passed through the field where we had stalked rabbits and seen Mr Clashbury Staunton, and into the lane beyond, which was sufficiently far from the house that we could not be seen there. We were gone for less than an hour and returned before our absence had been noticed, feeling pleased with ourselves.'

My friend paused at that point in his account and sat staring thoughtfully into the fire for some time. Then he took up his pipe again and lit it.

'And that,' said he, when he had been puffing away contentedly for a moment or two, 'concludes the story up to the point when I made my views known. Does the account in your book include any facts I haven't mentioned, Watson?'

'Only one thing that might be important,' I replied after a moment, as I turned the pages over to refresh my memory. 'Of course, the author gives a little more detail about some things, and a little less about others, but save only your personal recollections of your holiday, your account and his are very similar. He does mention that Clashbury Staunton had had a very public quarrel with Pigge some time before, accusing the latter's sixteen-year-old son of throwing stones at his windows. But that is probably not of any relevance, as Staunton seems to have fallen out with almost everyone at some time or another, including, surprisingly, Mr Stainforth, with whom he had an acrimonious disagreement over some question in the history of art. The one possibly significant fact that the author mentions and you have not is that four weeks after the murder of Crompton, Michael Shaxby was arrested in Lincoln while attempting to sell the antique candlesticks that had been stolen from the rectory. He claimed he had found them in a field somewhere and did not realise they were the stolen ones.'

Holmes nodded. 'I heard about that later,' said he. 'Of course, no one believed his unlikely story about the candlesticks, and he was charged with the burglary at the rectory and sent for trial at the Assizes. While in custody he was questioned repeatedly on the other matters – the burglary at Crompton's house, the attempted burglary at Stainforth's, and the murder of Crompton – but denied all knowledge of those crimes, and as the police were unable to find any evidence against him, no charges were brought. At the Assizes he was found guilty of the burglary at the rectory, and sentenced to three years in prison, but the other crimes were never solved, and the cases remained open, as, indeed, they do to this day. Does your author reach any conclusions?'

'He considers the likeliest suspect, despite his denials, to be Michael Shaxby, or possibly one of his brothers. The fact that the burglar resorted to such extreme violence against Crompton suggests, he argues, someone of a brutal character, and the Shaxby family seems to have had more than its fair share of those. But he also considers the farmer, Pigge, a possible suspect, bearing in mind the enmity that existed between him and Crompton. He was, the author says, a big strong man, and could easily have inflicted the savage blow that struck Crompton down.'

'That is true, and there had certainly been a very public dispute between the two men over the finding of the Roman coin. But why does your author think that Pigge might have been attempting to break into Stainforth's house?'

'He gives some detail on the economic circumstances of the period, and explains that many of the farmers in those parts had made practically no profit at all for several years and were in severe financial difficulties. He thinks this may well have been the case with Pigge, and that he might have been driven in desperation to find something of value in Stainforth's house that he could sell, no doubt inspired to do so by the burglary at the rectory – which, incidentally, he believes was almost certainly committed by Shaxby, as the police alleged. One point against Pigge's involvement in these crimes, however, is that entry to Crompton's house was effected through a small pantry window, and the author thinks it doubtful that Pigge could have squeezed his massive frame through such a narrow space.'

Holmes nodded. 'Any more possible suspects?'

'The author mentions also the animosity between Crompton and Clashbury Staunton, and is aware of the latter's quarrelsome nature, and of his antecedents in general – although not, I think, of his slight connection with the household at The Highlands *via* Mr Hemming. How maddening it must have been, he suggests, for a man of such learning and scholarship, so jealous of his own qualifications and his standing at Cambridge, to have to put up with a rural figure such as Crompton crowing about his discoveries and being so highly esteemed in the district. His annoyance at this, and the general bitterness of his disposition, the author suggests, might have led him, in a moment of anger, to resort to violence against the other man.'

'Does your author suggest what Staunton might have been doing at Stainforth's house?'

'Not really, except that Stainforth was to some extent a friend and ally of Crompton's. But Stainforth was also, of course, a collector of works of art, some of them very valuable, a fact of which Staunton was aware, as he had visited Stainforth's house once or twice, before the two of them fell out. The author speculates that there was perhaps something in Stainforth's house that Staunton wished to get his hands on, but he cannot suggest what that might have been.'

'Anything else?'

'Nothing much. The author remarks that the household at The Highlands decamped fairly quickly after the terrible events that had so disturbed the district, but, as he himself observes, that was not, under the circumstances, so very surprising.'

'Very well,' said Holmes after a moment. 'I shall tell you now what happened next. I have mentioned that Sylvie and I had made an expedition in the morning to look for evidence. That same day, just after lunch, I asked Uncle Moreton if I might have a private word with him. He was naturally surprised at this request, but acceded to it and the two of us withdrew to the study.

'"Now," said he, as he closed the door. "What is all this about, Sherlock?"

'"I was wondering," I replied, "what you should do if you know something about a crime that's been committed: if, for instance, everybody is puzzled about it and you think you know the truth."

'"Strictly speaking," said Uncle Moreton, "I think the correct procedure is to inform the local Justice of the Peace, but in practice the easiest thing is to tell the police. They will look into what you have told them and decide whether to bring the matter before the J.P. or not. What is it that's on your mind?"

'"The recent burglaries and the death of Mr Crompton."

'"I don't think anyone has the slightest idea about those things," said Uncle Moreton, shaking his head.

'"I do," I said.

'Uncle Moreton's eyebrows went up in surprise. "You?" he asked in a tone of disbelief. "What can you possibly know?" He sat down in the chair by the desk and pulled another chair forward for me. "These are very serious matters, Sherlock. Someone has been killed. Someone else could be hanged for it. It is not something that can be treated as a game, or as an exciting opportunity for amateur detective-work."

'I assured him that I appreciated the gravity of the circumstances. "Sylvie has seen what I have seen," I continued, "and she agrees with me."

'Again he looked astounded and shook his head dubiously. But he could see I was in earnest. "Very well," said he after a moment. "Tell me what you know."

'"First of all," I began, "you remember that Mr Crompton was right-handed?"

'"I don't think I ever noticed whether he was or wasn't," responded Uncle Moreton in surprise.

'"He polished his boots with his right hand, if you recall," I said: "the smear of boot-polish was along the side of his right thumb. Also, on one of the occasions he took tea with us, he made a note about something in his pocket-book and wrote with his right hand."

'Uncle Moreton closed his eyes and concentrated, as if picturing to himself the scene I had described. "Yes," said he at length, opening his eyes. "I believe you are right. As to the boot-polish," he added, "I will have to take your word for that, as I didn't notice it. But what does it matter whether he was right-handed or left-handed?"

'"The cut from the knife was across his right palm."

'"Yes, as you would expect. If someone was attacking you with a knife, it would naturally be your stronger hand you would use to defend yourself."

'"But he had a life-preserver attached by a loop of cord to his wrist. As he was right-handed, that would be his right wrist. The point of having something attached to your wrist is so that you can grip it quickly and easily. If, as people suppose, Mr Crompton came upon someone at Mr Stainforth's upstairs window, trying to force it open, he would have seized his life-preserver and held it at the ready, as he confronted this person. Then, if this person – the burglar – had sprung down and attacked him with the knife he had been using to force the window open, Mr Crompton would have defended himself with the life-preserver and although he might have been cut on the back of the hand, he could not possibly have been cut on the palm."

"'Perhaps the other man wrenched the life-preserver from his grasp and he was obliged to use his open hand to defend himself," suggested Uncle Moreton.

"'But they say the life-preserver was still attached to Mr Crompton's wrist when his body was found. So if the other man had seized hold of it, that would, in a sense, have tied Mr Crompton's right hand down, attached as it was to the life-preserver by the cord. He would have been more likely to have used his left hand to defend himself against the knife. Besides, if the cut had been made that way, I think it would have been quite a savage one, but from what I heard it was only a shallow cut."

"'That is true," said Uncle Moreton. "I saw it. It was certainly a long cut, all across the hand near the base of the fingers, but it was very shallow and had not bled very much. But if you doubt the official opinion of what happened, Sherlock, what is your alternative?"

"'That Mr Crompton himself caused the cut on his hand by gripping the blade of the knife."

"'What! But I thought your whole argument was that he would not have used his right hand to defend himself against the knife."

"'He was not defending himself. The knife was already in his possession. I believe he felt it slipping from his grasp and instinctively tightened his grip on it, but in doing so he gripped the blade rather than the handle."

"'How could the knife already be in his possession?"

"'Because it always had been. The knife was not that of some other person, but was Mr Crompton's own."

"'I see. That is possible, I suppose. You think, then, that in the struggle, the knife was knocked from his grasp and, despite still having the life-preserver, he turned and fled?"

"'No," I said. "There was no struggle."

"'What! How could that be possible?'

"'Because there was no one else there to struggle with. Mr Crompton was all alone. It was he who was trying to break into Mr Stainforth's house, using his knife in his right hand as you would expect, the same hand from which the life-preserver was hanging. I believe it had been his aim all along to break into Mr Stainforth's house, and his talk of patrolling the country lanes was a mere blind, to conceal his real intentions.'

"'I must say I find that suggestion utterly incredible. Who, then, struck the blow that killed him?'

"'No one did. I think that when he eventually managed to force open Mr Stainforth's bedroom window, it probably swung outwards rather suddenly – it was a very windy night and it is a casement window, as you no doubt observed – struck him hard in the face and knocked him from his precarious perch. He would have fallen backwards head first – it is quite a long drop – and in landing struck his head very hard on one of the stones used to edge the flower-bed by the house wall. It must have been then that he instinctively gripped the knife which he felt was slipping from his grasp. I think he then struggled to his feet and made his way to the gate, where, no doubt dazed and in great pain, he tossed the knife away and stepped out into the lane. But he had not gone twenty feet when the effects of his terrible wound overcame him and he dropped down stone dead.'

'Uncle Moreton sat for some time in silence, considering what I had said.

"'It is certainly an interesting theory, if a highly improbable one,' he said at length, "and I will treat it with the respect it deserves. But it raises two major questions, Sherlock. First, why on earth should Crompton be trying to break into Stainforth's house? Second, what proof could there possibly be that you are right? You cannot make such wild claims without good solid evidence.'

"'I can answer the second question first,' I replied. "I already have the evidence.'

"'What!'"

"'Sylvie and I went over to Mr Stainforth's house this morning and found the stone on which Mr Crompton had struck his head. It has a very sharp edge and is covered in blood.'"

"'How is it that the police did not see it, then?'"

"'Because they did not think to look for it and because it is almost completely covered by some thick, low-growing herb – thyme, I believe. It is not thick enough to have softened the blow, but thick enough to conceal the stone from a casual glance.'"

'Uncle Moreton again sat in silence for several minutes, then, abruptly, he sprang to his feet. "I must see this for myself," said he. "Come along!"

'In the garden of Stainforth's house, I showed him the stone, which was almost completely hidden beneath a mat of thyme. For several minutes he examined it with great care, moistening his finger and rubbing it on the top and side of the stone, then he stood up and nodded his head. "I believe you are right," said he simply. "It is smeared with blood and I can think of no way that that could have happened except as you describe."

'As we left Stainforth's garden, Uncle Moreton suggested we walk a little further along the road and consider the matter further. Presently, we came to a grassy bank, where we sat down. It was a quiet, somewhat dull day and there was no one about.

"'Now," said Uncle Moreton, "I think, Sherlock, as your Aunt Phyllis remarked, that you are a very observant boy. But if you are right, as I now feel sure you are, we are still left with several unfathomable mysteries. First, why was Crompton attempting to break into Stainforth's house? What on earth did he hope to find there? Second, who was it that burgled Crompton's own house, and took the coins and tiles? And, for that matter, who stole the candlesticks from the rectory?"

"'I have no idea who took the candlesticks," I replied. "Perhaps it was Michael Shaxby, as the police suspect. I don't think that the burglary at the rectory is relevant to any of the other things, except that it was probably the inspiration for them."

"'What do you mean?'"

"'I think that the burglary at the rectory gave someone else the idea of doing something similar at Mr Crompton's house.'"

"'Another member of the Shaxby family?'"

"'No.'"

"'Who, then?'"

"'Mr Crompton himself.'"

"'What! But that is ridiculous! Why should Crompton burgle his own house? And in any case, how could he do it? He was away in Nottingham at the time, on a visit to his sister.'"

"'I think he did it the evening before he left for Nottingham. He could be fairly sure that no one would bother unfastening the tarpaulin to inspect the Roman tiles while he was away, or would notice that the pantry window was unfastened and wedged shut with a small piece of wood. He could then pretend to discover the 'burglary' on his return.'"

"'But why should he stage a pretend burglary? What could he possibly hope to achieve by it?'"

"'The removal of things that were a danger to him.'"

"'What 'things'?'"

"'The tile that had the name of Tacitus on it and the Roman coin he claimed to have found in his garden.' I told Uncle Moreton then of the occasion when I had observed Crompton and Staunton meeting in a nearby lane, and of how angry Crompton had appeared at the other man. "We had heard that the expert on Roman remains was coming soon from Cambridge," I said. "Perhaps Mr Staunton, who is also something of an expert on the classical period, knew that Mr Crompton's 'discoveries' were fraudulent and had warned him that he would expose him if he persisted in making his claims. There certainly appeared to be great ill-feeling between the two men." I then described to Uncle Moreton the occasion when Sylvie and I had seen Clashbury Staunton peering through the garden hedge at our relatives. "Mr Staunton seems to have an odd taste for spying on people and prying into other people's business," I said. "Perhaps he had observed Mr Crompton making the 'Tacitus' tile himself, in the course of those experiments with the local clay deposits that he described to us."

"'It is possible, I suppose,' conceded Uncle Moreton in a reluctant tone. "But what, then, of the attempted burglary at Mr Stainforth's house? What could be the point of that?"

"'I doubt there was anything there that Mr Crompton wanted. I think that by forcing a window open there, he was just trying to add support to his claim that there were burglars active in the district, and thus make the break-in at his own house seem simply part of a general pattern and not a special case in any way."

'Uncle Moreton considered the matter in silence for several minutes. "What you say is certainly plausible, Sherlock, but there seems rather a lot of extravagant speculation in it. Is it not equally possible, considering the ill-feeling between them, that it was Staunton that stole Mr Crompton's tiles and coins?"

'I shook my head. "My theory is the only one that can properly account for all the facts. If Mr Staunton – or Mr Pigge, for that matter – had taken the tiles and coins, there would have been no reason for Mr Crompton to have staged the break-in at Mr Stainforth's, as I'm sure he did. He could not possibly have supposed that his friend, Mr Stainforth, had had anything to do with the theft of his possessions. In any case," I added, "there is another very good reason to suppose that Mr Crompton took the tile himself."

"'Oh? What might that be?"

"'If anyone else had stolen it, either for gain or simply out of spite, he would only have taken the tile with Tacitus's name on it. All the other tiles were plain and of no particular interest or value. Yet Mr Crompton said that several tiles had been taken, including, of course, the one bearing the name of Tacitus. There would seem no point to that, unless there was also something special about the other, plain tiles that were taken. I think that, like the 'Tacitus' tile, they had been made by Mr Crompton himself, probably to surround the 'Tacitus' tile, so that the inscribed tile didn't stand out as obviously different from the tiles next to it. If so, he wouldn't have wanted the expert from Cambridge to see them."

"'You seem to have thought of everything," remarked Uncle Moreton after a moment. "You have observed things closely that no one else has even noticed at all. But what makes you think that there was anything fraudulent about the coin that Crompton said he had found?"

"'Chiefly because it was 'stolen' along with the tile," I returned. "If it had been a genuine discovery, Mr Crompton would not have needed to have it disappear."

"'I see. That certainly makes sense. But if so, Crompton must have bought not one but two coins from the coin-dealer in London."

"'That is what I believe," I said. "I think it likely he himself damaged and disfigured the coin he claimed to have found, for the same reason, I imagine, that he damaged the 'Tacitus' tile: to give it an air of verisimilitude which a 'perfect' discovery might not have had. Of course, both of the coins had to be 'stolen' together, as a real burglar would not have taken one and left the other. But Mr Crompton was probably reluctant to lose everything, and no doubt it was he himself who threw the 'purchased' coin over the hedge into the field, where he could, so he hoped, pretend to find it later."

'Uncle Moreton rose to his feet. "Come along, then," said he. "Let us see if we can decide the matter one way or the other."

'The door of High Grove was opened by Crompton's housekeeper, a melancholy expression on her face. She showed us into the study, a large room at the back of the house, where we were joined a moment later by Crompton's sister, Ethel. Her face, too, was marked by sorrow and it was clear she felt the loss of her brother very keenly.

"'I am sorry to intrude upon you at such a time," Uncle Moreton began, "but I wondered if I might see the Roman coin – a denarius, I believe – which your brother bought from the dealer in London – the one that was found in the field. I wanted to familiarise myself with it in case I chanced across the other one, which I know was fairly similar."

'"So I understand," returned Miss Crompton. "Yes, I should be pleased to show it to you, and you need not apologise for the intrusion. I am sure my brother would have been delighted at your interest."

'She took a small silver coin from the corner of the mantelpiece and handed it to Uncle Moreton. "My brother was a very fine man," she continued as we examined the coin, "a fine scholar and a great intellect. One of his deepest regrets was that, living where he did, he had so little opportunity for intellectual conversation, and he told me how much he had enjoyed his discussions with you and your family."

'"Rest assured, madam, that the pleasure was entirely ours," responded Uncle Moreton. "His death is a great loss, not only to his family and friends, but to the parish in general. I wonder," he continued after a moment, "if you have the invoice from the dealer that came with this coin. I am no expert on such things and should like to know as much as possible about it."

'"I think my brother kept such documents in here," said Miss Crompton, opening the lid of a large bureau that stood by the wall. For a few moments she sifted through a pile of papers, then extracted a sheet. "I think this may be it," said she, passing it to Uncle Moreton.

'He took it to the window and held it so that I could see it, too, as he read the coin's description aloud. '"A silver denarius of the reign of Hadrian, minted in Rome about AD 120,"' he read, followed by some technical details regarding the silver content and so on, but as he did so his right index finger indicated to me the "quantity" column. To my very great dismay, this stated, not "two", as I had hoped it would, but just "one". It seemed that my theory was false. A moment later, however, and my disappointment had vanished. I leaned over and pointed with my own finger at the date of the invoice, which was May the fifth, more than a month before Crompton had claimed to have found a coin on his property, and more than two months before he said he had bought a coin from a dealer. As he continued to read, Uncle Moreton put his free hand on my finger and moved it away from the date. "Thank you very much for showing us these things," he said to Miss Crompton as he finished reading. "It is very kind of you."

'We had walked some way back along the road before Uncle Moreton spoke. "It seems pretty clear, then," he said at length, "that Crompton did purchase two coins, although not both at the same time, and that the one he claimed to have found was as much a purchase as the other one. No doubt the excitement and interest generated last year by his discovery of the remains of the villa had abated, and, disappointed by his failure to make any further significant discoveries, he succumbed to the temptation to fabricate a couple for himself."

'We walked on in silence for some time, until we came again to the grassy bank and sat down once more.

'"There are two thoughts uppermost in my mind," said Uncle Moreton. "First, with regard to Mr Crompton's sad progress from local celebrity to violent death, I am reminded of an observation of Dr Johnson's, in his commentary on one of Shakespeare's plays, to the effect that 'villainy has no natural stop; crimes generally lead on to other crimes, until, at last, they terminate in ruin'. Second, I am very sorry that we had to practise such a deceit upon Miss Crompton in that way. We had to know the truth, but I still feel ashamed of myself. It is clear she thought the world of her brother and I am sure she was right to do so. He was, in his own way, a fine and worthy man, for all that we have discovered about his dishonesty in this instance. Can you understand that, Sherlock?"

'"I think so," I replied; but young people are harsher judges of ethical questions than their elders, and I did not at that moment fully share my relative's estimate of Crompton's worthiness.

'"I therefore think that we – and Sylvie – should keep what we know to ourselves. The man is dead now and no purpose can be served by sullying his memory."

'"But it may be," I argued, "that Michael Shaxby or someone else will be charged with his murder."

'"If that were to happen, we would of course tell all that we have discovered. I will keep a close eye on the matter, but if no one else is accused of the crimes, I will say nothing and you must do the same." Uncle Moreton glanced at me, as if to read my thoughts from my features. "We would not wish to inflict further pain upon his sister unnecessarily, Sherlock. The pursuit of truth may be the highest intellectual aim that man can aspire to, but sometimes knowledge of the truth must be sufficient reward in and of itself, and nothing further is to be gained by publishing one's knowledge."

'The weather began to deteriorate as our holiday drew to a close, and for two days the rain was so heavy that we were scarcely able to leave the house. Then, at the end of the week, with all our trunks and bags packed, we caught the London train at Alford. We were met at King's Cross station, where the crowds, the bustle and the noise seemed a world away from the emptiness and quiet of the Wolds. We had said our goodbyes – for we were all going off in different directions – when I saw Sylvie say something to Aunt Phyllis and a moment later she ran over to me with a small brown-paper parcel in her hand. She partly unwrapped it and I saw that it was this mirror.

'"This is for you," said she in an abrupt, embarrassed tone, pushing the mirror into my hands. I protested that I could not possibly accept it – she, after all, had been much more responsible both for its design and for its execution – but she insisted. Then she leaned very close to me and whispered something in my ear, but at that moment a nearby locomotive let out a piercing blast on its whistle and I did not catch what she said. Whether it was something about herself or about me, about the mirror or even about Mr Crompton, I could not tell, and before I could ask her to repeat it, she had dashed back to her parents and they had left the station. Later, I discovered she had written her name on the back of the mirror.'

My friend turned the mirror over and I saw the name 'Sylvie' written in large letters, in pencil, across the back.

'Unlike the inscription on Crompton's tile, this one at least is authentic,' said Holmes in a dry tone, 'and this mirror is all that remains of that holiday long ago. And now, Watson,' he continued, 'as we sit here discussing these ancient events, we must presume that East Thrigby continues much the same as ever it did. No doubt the winds still whip the grass upon the sand dunes by the sea and bring heavy downpours to the villages of the Wolds. No doubt, too, the country folk go about their business in their old, unhurried way, the rabbits still play in the meadows, the brooks still babble on and the drama of what happened all those years ago is all but forgotten. And you and I, my dear fellow, are now the only people alive who know the true facts of the East Thrigby Mystery.'

The Adventure of Juniper Cottage

'Democritus or Heraclitus?' said Sherlock Holmes in a thoughtful tone. 'For which of them should we cast our vote?'

It was a fine day in the early spring. My companion having no urgent call upon his time, I had managed to prevail upon him to rise from the couch upon which he had spent most of the previous day, and take a walk with me about the bustling streets. For several hours we had ambled, from the West End, by way of the Strand to the City, with many a *detour* into curious old alleyways and odd, hidden courtyards, all of which yielded points of interest to my friend's keen powers of observation and inference. At length we found ourselves upon the steps of the Royal Exchange, at the very hub of the City, and stood there for some time, watching in fascination the ceaseless and ever-changing flow of humanity passing back and forth along the streets that radiate like the spokes of a wheel from the Bank of England.

'It was a point of dispute among the ancient Greeks, as you no doubt recall,' continued my friend, a note of humour in his voice, 'whether the world we see about us is composed of many quite separate atoms, as was argued by Democritus, or is in reality, despite appearances to the contrary, all one, as Heraclitus urged. Now, you and I may have a strong predisposition to regard these people who are passing before us now as perfectly distinct individuals, but, you must admit that, in the mass, they bear more than a passing resemblance to mere waves, like the waves of the sea, which come and go upon the shore!'

'That can scarcely be denied; although I doubt if they themselves would thank you for the observation.'

My friend laughed, in that odd, noiseless way which was peculiar to him.

'Perhaps not,' he conceded. 'We stand now,' he continued after a moment, 'at the very centre of the greatest city since Byzantium was in its pomp, perhaps the greatest city there has ever been upon the face of the earth. Millions jostle past us, each pursuing his own ends, and yet each, too, playing his part in the whole. Every one of them is connected in a thousand hidden ways with the others, making unseen and unimaginable patterns of action and influence all about us. And yet, were we to rise up from where we now stand, float above this scene of tremendous activity, and observe it from on high, it would resemble nothing so much as a bee's nest. The thousands of comings and goings, which appear so random to us now, would be seen from afar to form the sort of intricate, rational patterns which one may observe in a hive of bees.'

'It is certainly a busy scene,' I remarked, smiling.

'Indeed; save for two gentlemen standing idly upon the steps of the Royal Exchange!' said he, consulting his watch. 'This walk has been splendid exercise for the body,' he continued in a brisk tone; 'but my brain cries out for stimulation, Watson! Let us return now to Baker Street, and see if any of these busy bees has called to seek our services. It is possible, for we have been out for three hours. As I have frequently observed, there is nothing more likely to stimulate a client to call than to leave the house for a while!'

I laughed. 'I am surprised at your embracing such an irrational and illogical precept, Holmes! In another, I should term it superstition!'

'I cannot wonder at your regarding it in that light, Watson,' said he with a chuckle. 'But before you convict me of a woeful lapse from that strictly scientific mode of thought which I hold so dear, I would point out: a) that there is no logically valid method by which I can prompt a client to call, and thus any method, however illogical, is as good as any other; and b) that, in any case, as the old adage has it, life is greater than logic!'

When we reached Baker Street, a commissionaire from one of the nearby premises ran up to us.

'Excuse me, gentlemen,' said he. 'You have a visitor, and a rum, fidgety cove, if ever I saw one. For twenty minutes he was a-walking forwards and backwards, backwards and forwards, on the pavement here. 'Is this where Mr Holmes, the consulting detective, lives?' says he to me. 'It is,' said I. 'Would you like me to introduce you?' But he shook his head. 'No, thank you,' says he. 'I'll just consider the matter a little longer.' Then he was back to walking up and down as if his life depended on it, for another ten minutes afore he went in!'

'Excellent!' cried Holmes, rubbing his hands together. 'A man with a problem, evidently! Let us hope it is a stimulating one!'

A young man stood up from the fireside chair as we entered our sitting-room. A clean-shaven, slightly built man of about thirty years of age, he was neatly dressed in a dark grey City suit. He introduced himself as Sidney Potter, and was, he said, a clerk at Lloyd's.

'Pray be seated,' said Holmes, 'and tell us what brings you here. You evidently regard the matter as important, to have taken the afternoon off, and come here direct from Lloyd's. The ink upon your finger-ends tells me that you have been hard at work this morning.'

'Indeed,' said our visitor, looking in surprise at his ink-stained fingers. 'I don't know whether my little problem will be something in your line or not,' he continued, 'and, to be frank, I hesitated considerably before deciding to consult you; but I will give you the details of the matter and see if you can make anything of it.'

'You have my full attention,' said Holmes, leaning back in his chair, closing his eyes and placing his fingertips together.

'I am a married man,' Mr Potter began. 'I have had a good berth in the City for twelve years now, and have lived in Lewisham since my marriage, seven years ago. My parents are both dead, I have no brothers or sisters, and my only close relative in recent years, other than my wife and small son, Horatio, has been my mother's brother, Major Ullathorne, my uncle Henry. He was warned by his doctor some years ago that his heart was not strong, and he died, alas, eight weeks ago today, of a sudden heart seizure.

'He had spent his entire career with the Royal Medway Regiment, and, after his retirement, lived in quiet seclusion near Woolwich, which is where the regiment has been stationed for many years. His house, a pretty little place known as "Juniper Cottage", lies within easy walking distance of Woolwich, but is in a very rural situation, at the end of a long muddy track. He had only one near neighbour, an old friend of his, Major Loxley, a retired fellow-officer from the Medway Regiment, who writes cookery books under the name of "Major L.". I had visited my uncle many times, with my parents when I was younger, and, since my marriage, with my wife, and had always enjoyed the rural charm of the place. When his will was published, a few weeks after his death, I learnt that his entire estate had been left to me. There is a sum of money – not a great amount, but a pleasant surprise, nonetheless – a few little items of moderate value, and, principally, Juniper Cottage.

'Now, my wife and I had been considering for some time whether we ought to move house. Lewisham has become much smokier since we first took up residence there, and Horatio suffers occasionally from croup. When I inherited Juniper Cottage, it therefore seemed a wonderful opportunity. It is a much healthier spot in which to bring up a child, and as all the trains from Woolwich pass through London Bridge station, my daily journey to work would be a very easy one. Mrs Potter and I discussed the matter fully, examining all the arguments for and against such a move, and, in the end, decided that we would do it. We therefore moved ourselves out there two weeks ago.

'It is certainly a very pretty spot. The cottage is built on high ground, looking down from a distance upon Woolwich and the river, and at the back is a large garden, which faces south and has the sun upon it from dawn to dusk. The garden is beautifully kept, for Major Ullathorne was a very keen gardener. From the study, a pair of French windows leads directly on to this garden, and in the summer months he would generally leave these French windows standing open all day, so that the scents of the garden drifted into the house. We looked forward to following his example.

'The house is at present still full of my uncle's furniture and possessions, and it will be some time before we have sorted it all out. He was a very neat and methodical man, but he had acquired an enormous number of curios and trophies from his travels about the world, and parts of the cottage resemble a museum. For the moment, therefore, we have left most of our own furniture in our house in Lewisham, on which the rent is paid up for another two months.

'I have described the cottage to you in some detail so that you will appreciate what an idyllic spot it is. However, from the moment we arrived there, there has seemed, also, something odd and mysterious about the place. On the day we moved in, we found that a pane of glass in the kitchen window had been broken, and it was clear that someone had forced an entry and had been in the house. The papers in my uncle's study had been rifled, and were in a state of considerable disarray. Daisy, my wife, is of a nervous disposition, and was very anxious at the thought that the intruder might return, but the local policeman, whom we sent for, thought it unlikely. "A house standing unoccupied for several weeks is too tempting a target for some roughs to ignore," said he, "but now that you are in residence, I should not think they will trouble you again." Daisy was reassured by this, and we put the matter behind us, and set about making the cottage feel like home.

'Three days later, the evening brought high winds and a very heavy rainstorm, and we were sitting cosily by the fire, listening to the racket as the wind hurled sheets of rain against the window, and hoping that the tiles upon the roof were all sound, when, to our very great surprise, there came a sudden violent jangling at the front-door bell.

'I hurried to open the door, and found a man of about my own age standing upon the step, dripping wet. He nodded his head to me, and as he did so a stream of water fell from the brim of his hat like a waterfall.

'"Come in, come in!" I cried, hauling him into the house and closing the door against the driving rain. "Whatever are you doing out in this weather, and at this time of night!"

'My wife hurried to fetch a towel, and as he was rubbing his face with it, he introduced himself as Jonathan Pleasant. He was a tall, strongly built man, with close-cropped ginger hair.

"'Come to the sitting-room fire,' said I. "I am glad we are able to offer you shelter from the storm," I added, thinking that he had lost his way in the dark, and had simply chanced upon our house. His response, however, quickly disabused me of that notion.

"'Are you,' said he, "Mr Sidney Potter, nephew of the late Major Henry Ullathorne?"

"'I am,' I returned in surprise.

"'Very good,' said he, as he warmed his hands before the blazing fire. "Then you are just the man I am looking for; and I, I may tell you, am just the man that *you* are looking for!" So saying, he took my hand in his and wrung it vigorously.

"'Your meaning is not clear to me, Mr Pleasant,' said I, puzzled by his manner.

"'No?' he returned, flinging himself down in an armchair, crossing his legs, and, I must say, making himself very much at home. "You, Mr Potter, desire to sell this house. I am correct, am I not? And I, Mr Potter, desire to purchase it. What could be simpler!" He leaned back in his chair, winked at my wife in a conspiratorial manner, as if I were a half-wit, and chuckled heartily.

"'Pardon me,' said I, "but I regret that you have been misinformed. I have no wish to sell this house. On the contrary, my wife and I have recently resolved to make it our permanent abode."

"'What!' cried he, springing up as if galvanised. "Can this be true? Do you mean to tell me that I have come all this way, in this foul weather, and have turned my ankle over in the lane, simply to have my offer thrown back in my face, and be dismissed without a minute's consideration!"

"'I regret the weather,' said I, feeling a little uncomfortable, "although it is scarcely my fault. Nor is it my fault that you have been misinformed. Might I enquire the name of the agent who told you that Juniper Cottage might be up for sale?"

'He ran his fingers through his damp hair, and sat back down, a look of the most utter disappointment upon his features.

'"It was not an agent," said he at length. "It was a very knowledgeable man I met at the inn down the road, the Rose and Crown."

'Mr Pleasant explained that he was a commercial traveller for a stationery company, and having been a frequent visitor to the Woolwich area, considered that it would be an agreeable spot in which to live. He had mentioned this fact to a chance acquaintance at the Rose and Crown, who had informed him that Juniper Cottage was about to be put up for sale.

'"He is a large, loud man, with a grey beard down to here," said Pleasant, holding his hand halfway down his waistcoat front. "I dare say you know him well, Mr Potter."

'"I have never seen such a man," I responded.

'"That is odd, for he certainly knows all about you, or about your house, at any rate," insisted our visitor, in a tone which seemed to imply that I was lying to him. "He informed me that you were desperate to sell, as you wished to move immediately." He paused. "I could make you a very handsome offer," he added after a moment.

'"The house is not for sale, and that is final," said I, in an emphatic tone.

'"Very well," said Pleasant, nodding his head. "I shall not mention it again, Mr Potter."

'It was still pouring with rain, and the wind sounded even more violent than ever, so I threw more wood on to the fire, my wife made a pot of tea, and we sat for a long time in conversation. Our visitor was amiable enough, once he had dropped the subject of the cottage, and our talk rambled hither and thither in an agreeable fashion. He had been to the theatre the previous evening, he informed us, to hear Jenny Beach sing her latest song, "A Teardrop on a Rose", and he entertained us for some time with an account of this, and other similar anecdotes.

'The evening wore on, but the storm did not abate. Eventually, it was time for bed, but the storm was as loud and violent as ever. It appeared, as our visitor observed, to have set in for the night. I could not possibly turn him out in such weather, stranger though he was, especially as he had mentioned that his sprained ankle was beginning to ache badly. I therefore offered him a shakedown on the couch, which he accepted gratefully, apologising profusely for putting us to trouble. My wife found a couple of blankets for him, and there, in the little sitting-room, we left him for the night.

'Some time later, I was awakened from sleep by what I thought was distant thunder. But as I lay awake in the dark, I heard the same low, rumbling noise again, and I realised that it came from downstairs. For a moment I felt in a panic, and thought we must have burglars, then I recollected our visitor, and sighed with relief. Evidently he had moved a chair, or some other piece of furniture, to make himself more comfortable. I was just dropping off to sleep again, however, when I heard more quiet noises from below, the scraping of a table leg upon the floor, the opening and closing of a cupboard-door, and so on. I could not conceive what he was doing, but as the noises presently ceased, I did not think the matter worth getting out of bed for.

'In the morning I tapped on the door of the sitting-room and pushed it open. There appeared to be no one there, and for a moment I thought that Mr Pleasant had already left us. Then I saw that he was crouching down on the floor, peering under a bureau. He sprang up when I addressed him, and explained that he had dropped a coin, which had rolled under the bureau. "It doesn't matter," said he: "it's only a halfpenny." He accompanied me to the dining-room for a little breakfast, but as we left the sitting-room I observed that some of the pictures on the walls were hanging crookedly, and I could not help but wonder again what our strange visitor had been doing during the night. Whatever it was, it had evidently not affected the recuperation of his sprained ankle, which appeared to have mended completely overnight.

'I was a little late – as a result, no doubt, of my disturbed night – and had to hurry off to the railway station, leaving Mr Pleasant to linger over his boiled egg. On the way down the lane, however, I chanced to meet our neighbour, Major Loxley, who had been out early to buy a newspaper. I explained to him about our visitor, and asked him if he would look in at Juniper Cottage, in case my wife was concerned about the presence of a stranger there. This he agreed to do.

'When I arrived home that evening, my wife informed me that Major Loxley had called, as I had requested, but that while she was speaking to him at the front door, Mr Pleasant had disappeared from the dining-room. They had found him in the study, looking through the volumes in the bookshelves. My wife says he appeared a little discomfited at being discovered there. Several of the books were out of the shelves and stacked upon the floor, and, as they entered, he was rapidly turning over the pages of an antique copy of the Old Testament.

'"Pardon my boldness," said he; "but having put my head into this room by mistake, I could not resist having a look through this fine collection of books."

'"You might have asked permission," said Loxley, in a tone of censure; but as the other was profuse in his apologies he did not press the matter further. Shortly afterwards, Mr Pleasant left.'

'Do you know if Major Loxley knows of the man with the beard that your visitor claimed to have met at the local inn?' queried Holmes.

'I put that very question to him when I called round to see him, on the evening of the following day. He said he knew of no one in the district who could be described as "large and loud" and with a long grey beard, and we could only conclude that Mr Pleasant had lied to me. Bearing that in mind, and also the forced entry which had occurred before we moved into Juniper Cottage, I began to speculate as to whether my late uncle might have had objects of value in the house of which I was unaware. Loxley, however, thought not.

'"Major Ullathorne picked up many odd curios in the course of his travels," said he, "but none, so far as I am aware, of any great value." He did think, however, that some of the books might fetch a few pounds. "The Old Testament that was interesting your visitor, for instance," he continued. "I happened to notice that it was once the property of J. Hardiman Smallbone, and was signed by him, which probably makes it of some value."

'My features must have betrayed my puzzlement, for he quickly explained that this man Smallbone had been a local parson in the latter half of the last century, whose fiery and impassioned sermons had brought him celebrity throughout north-west Kent. Any volume which had been part of his own private library would have great value for his admirers and possibly also for the County Archive. Major Loxley considered that it might be worth my while to have some of the older books valued, and recommended a book-dealer in Woolwich, by the name of Vidler. As I was keen to dispose of some of my uncle's possessions, in order to make a little more space in the cottage for our own belongings, I took up his suggestion, and we arranged to take a box of books down to Vidler's shop the following afternoon, which was Saturday.

'Mr Vidler was interested in the selection I took to show him, and appeared about to make me an offer for the lot. But as he was deliberating, I began to have the odd and disconcerting feeling that someone was watching me. Once or twice, out of the corner of my eye, I had had the impression of a face peering round a doorway at the back of the shop. I looked up sharply, and as I did so a face withdrew behind the door-frame. It was only a momentary glimpse I had, but in that fraction of a second, I had the distinct impression that the man watching me was none other than Jonathan Pleasant, the man I had put up at Juniper Cottage on the night of the storm.

'"There is something very odd afoot here," I said softly to Major Loxley. "That man, Pleasant, is following me about!" To the surprise of the old shop-keeper, I made a sudden dash towards his back room, with Loxley at my heels. But as we reached the doorway and looked into the room, a door in the opposite wall banged shut. We could not get it open for a moment, and when we did we found ourselves in the narrow lane which runs behind the shops. We could hear hurried footsteps ringing upon the pavement round the corner, and ran in that direction, but when we reached the corner, there was no one to be seen.

'"Whoever it was, he has vanished," said Loxley, scratching his head, and we returned to the bookshop. Mr Vidler made me an offer for the box of books, but I felt put out by what had happened, and not in the mood for concluding a bargain, so I told him I would consider his offer, but, for the moment, take my box of books back home again. As I was gathering them together, I asked the shop-keeper if he knew Jonathan Pleasant, and described him. He said he did not, but said that there had been a customer of that description in the shop shortly before we arrived, and that he might have slipped unnoticed into the back room as we entered. I was about to leave then, when it struck me that there were fewer books in the box than before. At first Mr Vidler disputed the matter, but when I insisted upon it, he let out a little cry.

'"Oh, of course!" said he, as if in sudden recollection. "Do excuse my carelessness, Mr Potter! I carried a volume to the window, to study it in a better light, and forgot to replace it. Here it is!" he continued, picking up a volume from a shelf behind where he was standing. It was old Hardiman Smallbone's copy of the Old Testament.'

Sherlock Holmes rubbed his hands together and chuckled. 'Excellent!' cried he, with the enthusiasm of a wine-connoisseur who has taken his first sip of a particularly rare and fine vintage.

'My story interests you, then?' queried Potter, a note of relief in his voice. 'I had feared that you might think it too trivial a matter to concern yourself with. It is, of course, of the first importance to me, for I am determined to get to the bottom of why I am being persecuted by this man, Pleasant; but I can see that it might strike an outsider as a somewhat inconsequential business.'

Holmes shook his head emphatically. 'One must never prejudge such a matter,' said he. 'One of the most terrible cases I was ever involved with began with the arrival of a packet of children's wooden bricks in the post one morning. Besides, the great big crimes, which feature so frequently in the newspapers, and in connection with which you may have seen my name, are all too often banal and uninteresting, for all their sensation. The connoisseur of such things, Mr Potter, when presented with a choice between a pint-pot of weak and mediocre beer and a thimbleful of an exquisite and refined liqueur, will always choose the latter. Your case interests me greatly, and I should be pleased to look into the matter for you. Are we now up to date?' he continued, glancing up at the clock. 'I should like to see Juniper Cottage for myself, this afternoon if possible, and if we leave now we should be able to catch the three o'clock train from Charing Cross.'

'I believe I have told you most of it,' returned Potter. 'I can give you the remaining details as we travel.'

'Capital!' cried Holmes, springing from his chair. 'Let us be off to Woolwich at once, then. You will accompany us, Doctor?'

'With great pleasure!' said I. Mr Potter's curious little puzzle had fired my imagination, and I was keen to see the scene of the mystery for myself. What Holmes might hope to learn there, I could not imagine, but knowing his profound mental resources, I could not doubt that we should leave Juniper Cottage knowing more than when we arrived.

Once we were aboard the train, Holmes's client resumed his account.

'Following the incident at the bookshop,' said he, 'I gave the matter a lot of thought, and discussed it exhaustively with Major Loxley, who was tolerably familiar with my late uncle's affairs, but we could make nothing of it. It seemed to me, on reflection, that the man calling himself Pleasant – I put it that way for I have come to feel that it is not his real name – had the cut of a soldier. He was tall and upright, clean-shaven, and with close-cropped hair. This made me wonder if he was from the local barracks, and if the whole matter were not perhaps connected in some way with my uncle's old regiment. For although he had been retired from active service for some years, most of his friends and acquaintances were men from the regiment, and he was a frequent visitor to the barracks.

'I therefore called in a few days later, and asked to speak to the commanding officer, Colonel Headley, whom my uncle had known well. I was informed that he was absent that afternoon, at Rochester, but his adjutant, Major Felgate, was most obliging. He is a very smart-looking man, with a black moustache, and very sharp, inquisitive features. He expressed concern when I described to him the odd visitor we had had at Juniper Cottage, and the other incidents.

"'I cannot recall offhand that any of our men exactly matches the description you have given me,' said he, stroking his moustache in a thoughtful way, "but I shall make thorough inquiries. If it turns out that any of our men are concerned in the matter, I shall get to the bottom of it, Mr Potter, you may be assured of that. Major Ullathorne, your uncle, was a very well-respected figure here, and the Royal Medway Regiment would certainly feel it its duty to do all it could to clear up any little mystery connected with one of its finest former servants."

'He said that he would communicate with me when he had any further information, but I have heard nothing so far, so it seems he has not yet managed to discover anything.'

Sherlock Holmes nodded. 'Your uncle's death was sudden, you say,' he remarked after a moment. 'Was he at home when he died?'

'No, his body was found on the Plumstead marshes. Apparently he had taken himself off for a walk there.'

'Indeed? That is a fair step for a retired gentleman,' observed Holmes. 'Was it his habit to take such long walks?'

'Not that I am aware. His heart being weak, he was inclined to become breathless if he walked too far.'

'Well, that is curious. There was an inquest, presumably.'

'Yes. No one could shed any light upon why he should have been out on the marshes on a damp afternoon in February, but as the cause of death was established beyond question as heart failure, the matter was not pursued. The County Medical Officer said that the strain of the walk, perhaps exacerbated by the cold weather, had undoubtedly contributed to the heart failure, but that my uncle's heart having been weak for years, he might have gone at any time.'

'That is true,' I remarked. 'With conditions of that type, any stress or strain, physical or mental, is liable to hasten the end.'

'I see,' said Holmes, nodding his head in a thoughtful way. 'Is there anything else you can tell us, Mr Potter?'

'There is one more thing. It may have absolutely nothing to do with the present business, but I think I ought to tell you, for it was certainly odd and unusual. I had quite forgotten about it until these recent events. It was on a Sunday, during the hot weather last summer. I had gone down with my family to visit Major Ullathorne and take tea with him at Juniper Cottage. After tea, we sat for some time in the garden, talking and watching little Horatio play, but our conversation was interrupted by the door-bell. "Now, who on earth can that be, on a Sunday evening?" said Uncle Henry, and it was clear that he was not expecting any other visitors. He hurried off to answer it, for his maid had gone home for the week-end, and we heard him admit someone to the house. The garden in which we were sitting being at the back of the cottage, we could not, of course, see who had entered at the front door, but we could hear the sound of low voices through the open French windows of the study. Presently my uncle reappeared through these French windows, his features very serious, and, I thought, a little agitated.

'"Do excuse my rudeness," said he in an apologetic tone, "but I am afraid I must ask you to leave, Sidney. Something extremely important has cropped up, and I must devote my full attention to it. I do apologise."

'"Do not concern yourself, Uncle," said I. "Daisy and I were just thinking of making our way home, anyway. The light will be going soon, and we don't want to be walking down to the railway station in the dark." As I informed him, it was quite unnecessary for him to apologise. My uncle was one of the most polite and considerate men that I have ever met. Besides, it was clear that whatever the information was that his caller had brought, it was of a very serious nature, for I had never before seen him appear so anxious.'

'That is interesting, and suggestive,' said Holmes, as Potter paused.

'Of course, it is impossible at present to say whether the incident has a bearing on recent matters or not, but you were right to tell me of it.'

'Do you see any chink of light in the mystery?' asked Potter. 'I confess I see none at all. Why I am being plagued by this man, Pleasant, and why he and others should be so determined to get their hands on Hardiman Smallbone's Old Testament, I simply cannot imagine.'

'The matter is not yet entirely clear to me,' answered Holmes, 'but a pattern is certainly discernible. The case contains one or two suggestive features, the chief one being, perhaps, the business of the crooked pictures on the sitting-room wall after Mr Pleasant's visit. There are several different lines of inquiry open to us, so it should not be too long before we hit upon the truth. But here, unless I am mistaken, is our station, so let us make haste. I confess I am keen to see Juniper Cottage for myself!'

We had left the railway station and were walking through the bustling town, when Potter drew our attention to two military men some distance ahead of us, on the other side of the road.

'That is Colonel Headley and his adjutant, Major Felgate,' said our companion. 'I wonder if they have any news.'

We crossed the road and soon caught up to the two soldiers. Potter introduced us, and Major Felgate, in turn, explained matters to the senior officer.

'This is the nephew of the late Major Ullathorne,' said he.

The Colonel shook Potter warmly by the hand. 'Ullathorne was a good friend of mine,' said he. 'I was very shocked and saddened by his sudden death.'

'Mr Potter consulted us a week or two ago,' Felgate continued, 'over some odd occurrences at his house, Ullathorne's old quarters. It seems possible that one of our men has been making a nuisance of himself, and I said I would look into the matter.'

'It was concerning that business that I wished to speak to you,' said Potter.

'I am afraid I cannot linger,' interrupted Colonel Headley. 'I have an appointment to see Colonel Shacklewell of the Artillery in ten minutes, so I shall have to leave you in the capable hands of Major Felgate.'

'Should I order the carriage?' enquired the major.

'No, I only have the one appointment, so I'll walk,' returned the other. 'It's not far, and the exercise will do me good. I'll be back later this afternoon. Major Felgate can give me the details of this business later,' he continued, turning to Potter. Then, with a little bow, he hurried off, and turned up a side-street.

'I have a little office at the Arsenal, gentlemen,' said the major. 'If you would come along there now, I can tell you what I have been able to discover so far.'

Five minutes later, we were seated in Major Felgate's private room. For several minutes, he leafed through papers on his desk.

'To be frank, Mr Potter,' said he at length, 'I have not been very successful so far. I have been extremely busy lately, and have not been able to devote as much time to the matter as I would have wished. I delegated two of my men to look into the matter of your Mr Pleasant, but they have not so far managed to identify him, and I am beginning to doubt that he is a Royal Medway man. It may be that he is a civilian employee, here at the Arsenal, for I believe that Major Ullathorne was on friendly terms with some of them.

'One possibility which has arisen in the course of our researches, however, is that your late uncle may have been indebted to someone, either in the regiment, or at the Arsenal.'

'That would surprise me greatly if it were true,' responded Potter. 'I never heard that Major Ullathorne was ever in debt in his life. He conducted both his business and his personal affairs in a most careful and correct manner.'

'Quite so. I do not doubt it for a moment. Nevertheless, the suggestion is that in return for some favour, at some time in the past, Ullathorne had promised some possession of his to his creditor. It was probably not anything of great value, but simply something which had caught the fancy of the man he was obligated to. In which case, it may be that his sudden and untimely death occurred before the debt had been discharged, and his creditor has therefore decided to lay his hands on what he feels he is owed.'

'Do you have any evidence that my uncle was involved in such a transaction?' asked Potter in a tone of disbelief.

'There is a rumour to that effect.'

'But if someone feels he is owed something, why has he not simply approached me on the matter?'

'Perhaps because the nature of the agreement between the two men was a strictly informal one. If he has no evidence of the debt, he may think it unlikely that you would believe him.'

'Well,' said Potter, as we walked up the hill after leaving the Arsenal, 'I was not particularly impressed with Major Felgate's theory, I must say.'

'It does seem a trifle unlikely,' Holmes agreed, 'and somewhat inadequate as an explanation of recent events. I sense that there may be a little more involved in the matter than the major's theory allows.'

A walk of about twenty minutes brought us to the lane which led up to Juniper Cottage, and a further five minutes up the steep, rutted track brought us to the garden gate. Two large, dark juniper bushes flanked the gateway, meeting above it to form an arch. Beyond the gate, a short paved path led up to the front door of the pretty little cottage. On either side of the porch stood currant bushes, covered with vivid red blooms, and in beds to the side of them, bright yellow daffodils nodded their heads in the breeze.

Mrs Potter had evidently heard our approach, for she opened the door as we reached it. Her husband introduced us, then gave us a little tour of the curious old building. In the room which had been Major Ullathorne's study, a pair of French windows stood open, and we passed through them to a large and level rear garden. Beyond the neatly trimmed lawn was an area of fruit-trees and bushes, and, beyond that, a small wood separated the garden from open country. Away to the right, over a tall hedge, the chimneys of another cottage were visible, which Potter informed us belonged to Major Ullathorne's old friend, Major Loxley.

After a glance round the garden, Sherlock Holmes returned to the study, and began a systematic examination of the room. Carefully, he lifted up every picture on the wall and peered behind it.

'Are you looking for something in particular?' queried Potter, a note of puzzlement in his voice.

'A concealed safe or cupboard,' returned Holmes as he continued his examination. 'The pictures were askew after Mr Pleasant's stay here, and it is possible that he had been looking for something behind them. It is a not uncommon ruse to conceal a small safe behind a picture. Another favourite hiding-place,' he continued, moving to the bookshelves to the left of the French windows, 'is behind a row of books. Your visitor may have thought that a possibility, too, for your wife remarked on the fact that he had taken a number of books from the shelves and had stacked them in a pile on the floor.'

Methodically, Holmes removed groups of four or five books, and felt carefully in the recess behind them, until he had examined the whole bookcase in this way. 'There is no sign of anything there,' said he, as he put the last of them back. 'Of course, if there is such a hiding-place, it could be anywhere in the house, but the study seems the likeliest spot. Let us now try the floor!'

A couple of small Indian rugs were laid across the dark, varnished wooden floor, and these Holmes rolled up and placed to one side. Then, down on his hands and knees, he felt carefully with his finger-tips all over the floor. 'This may be something,' said he at length, pausing near the corner of the hearth. 'Ah! There we are!' he cried in triumph, lifting a small, square section of wooden flooring, which was hinged at one end.

Potter and I bent forward to see. In the recess below the floor, a few inches down, was a small metal door, about a foot square. From the centre of this door protruded a large horizontal handle, and around the handle were three concentric enamelled rings, each of which was marked with the letters of the alphabet.

'I had no notion that such a safe existed,' said Potter in surprise. 'I was not aware that my uncle possessed anything of sufficient value to warrant such a thing.'

'Mr Pleasant, I suspect, was aware of it,' said Holmes, 'and perhaps other people, too. I very much fancy, Mr Potter, that this little safe is the source of your recent troubles! Now, let me see! The handle will not move, so the safe is locked, as one would expect. Now, the lock, as you will observe, is an unusual one. There is no keyhole, so it is apparent that the locking and unlocking of the safe door is achieved by positioning these rings in a certain way. It is not a new idea – such locks were in use in the sixteenth century, and possibly earlier – but there have been great improvements in the design in recent years. One advantage of this type of lock is that there is no key to be lost or stolen, but a disadvantage is that one must ensure that the combination of letters required to operate it is not forgotten. The chief flaw of the design, however, is that if there is any play, any freedom of movement between the rings, then it is sometimes possible, by the application of gentle pressure, to feel when each of them is in the correct position, and thus to open the safe without ever having been made privy to its secret combination.

'Let us have a look at it,' he continued, lying full-length upon the floor, with his face close to the recess which held the safe. Slowly and gently, he began to turn the lettered dials. He was still so engaged, his face a mask of concentration, when Mrs Potter brought in a tray piled high with tea things.

'Goodness!' cried she, as she saw the hole in the floor, and Holmes lying full-length next to it. 'Whatever is this!'

'Mr Holmes has found a safe which belonged to Uncle Henry,' replied Potter, a note of excitement in his voice.

'Indeed I have,' said Holmes, looking up with a wry expression upon his face. 'I have found a safe, but I am unable to open it. It is evidently a very superior model, with closely machined locking parts, for there is no play whatever between the rings. Your arrival with tea is most opportune, madam, for a cup and a pipe, and five minutes' quiet reflection is what is now required!'

For some time we sat sipping tea and smoking our pipes in silence, then Holmes rose from his chair with a sigh.

'Well, well,' said he. 'We may as well try some of the more obvious combinations. I can see no other strategy at present. Your uncle's full name, Mr Potter?'

'Henry Alfred Ullathorne.'

'Initials H.A.U., then. Let us try those letters and see if they produce any result!'

For a moment he twisted the dials on the safe door, then attempted to turn the handle, but it remained as immovable as before.

'Now the same letters in the reverse order,' said he, twisting the dials once more. 'No! That is no better!' he announced as he tried the handle again. 'Your mother's maiden name, Mr Potter?'

'Frances Mabel Ullathorne.'

'F.M.U., then. No! That is not it, either! Married initials F.M.P.: No! No good!'

Thus we worked our way through two dozen or more combinations without success. The initials of almost everyone Potter or his wife could think of were tried, together with such miscellaneous items as R.M.R., for the Royal Medway Regiment, and P.I.P., which was the name of a cat once owned by Major Ullathorne, but all suggestions were equally in vain.

'It is possible that there is a note of the combination somewhere among your late uncle's papers,' remarked Holmes at length, 'although I rather doubt it. As it is only a matter of three letters, he would be unlikely to forget it, and thus would probably have felt no need to write it down anywhere.'

'I wonder if Major Loxley would know?' said Mrs Potter. 'He and your uncle were old friends, Sidney. He may have some idea of the letters your uncle would choose.'

'What an excellent suggestion!' returned Potter. 'I shall fetch him at once. I shall not be a minute,' he added as he stepped out of the French window and crossed the lawn to the hedge near the back of the garden.

In a moment he had returned, accompanied by a bluff-looking, elderly gentleman, with snow-white hair and moustache. We shook hands, then he bent his mind to the task.

'I do recall Ullathorne mentioning something about a safe, a year or so ago,' said he, 'but I did not know where it was. I'm afraid I have no idea what the combination might be.'

'We are open to any suggestions,' said Holmes in a dry tone.

'Let me see now,' said the major. 'My own initials are P.Q.L. I don't imagine he'd have used those, but it is possible, I suppose.'

Holmes turned the dials and tried the major's initials both backwards and forwards, but with no result. A few further suggestions were tried, but the handle of the safe remained resolutely immovable.

'Could the lock not be drilled out in some way?' queried Potter, scratching his head.

'It may well come to that,' returned Holmes, 'but it will not be easy. These modern safes are specifically designed to resist drilling. You had best apply to the manufacturers for advice. They may have some suggestion to make.'

'That sounds the best idea,' Major Loxley concurred. 'Might they not have a record of this safe's combination?'

Holmes shook his head. 'That is unlikely,' said he. 'Most safes of this type have adjustable cogs on the inside of the door, so that the owner can set the combination to whatever he pleases, before closing the door. I have little doubt that, whatever the combination is, it was known only to Major Ullathorne.'

'It is quite a problem, then,' said Loxley with a sigh, rising to his feet. 'I shall leave you to it, gentlemen. I am sorry I was unable to be more help, Potter. Do let me know if you have any success with it, won't you!'

'We appear to have reached a dead end,' said Potter, in a tone of disappointment, when the major had left us.

'We have met with a temporary check,' corrected Holmes. He leaned back in his chair and lit his pipe. 'It is clear,' he continued after a moment, 'that someone wants something that is within this house. There was a burglary shortly before you moved here. Whether anything was taken on that occasion we cannot say, but we must suppose that the enterprise was not entirely successful, for the attention devoted to the cottage has not ceased. It seems certain that the visit you had a couple of weeks ago from the man calling himself Jonathan Pleasant was devised solely to give him an opportunity to search the house for something. That something, to judge by his mode of search – moving pictures on the wall, peering under the furniture, and so on – was this safe. Clearly, he knew of the safe's existence, but not its whereabouts. Now, it would appear, from your account of the matter, that the safe remained on that occasion undiscovered. We cannot, therefore, expect all this mysterious activity to come to a halt, and must prepare ourselves for further attempts upon the premises. Our chief problem is that our opponent – or opponents, perhaps, for we do not know how many of them may be involved – may decide to lie low for a while, and wait for a suitable opportunity. This might suit them, but it does not suit us. I think we must try to force the pace a little, to flush our quarry out into the open, and the only way we can do this is to oblige our opponents to burgle the house at a time not of their choosing, but of ours.'

'How on earth can we do that?' asked Potter in a tone of puzzlement.

'What I propose,' responded Holmes, 'is that you send a note to Lloyd's, informing them that you will be unable to be present tomorrow to attend to your duties. You must then spend tomorrow disseminating as widely as possible the following information:

'One, that you and your family will be away tomorrow night, staying at your old house in Lewisham. Two, that upon the following day, workmen will be arriving to render Juniper Cottage more proof against burglary. Three, that an expert locksmith from the safe company will also be coming that day to open your uncle's safe. You must then take your family to Lewisham at five o'clock tomorrow afternoon, and meet us upon the down platform of Lewisham station at seven o'clock prompt. Is that all clear?'

Potter nodded his head, but there was an expression of bewilderment upon his face.

'It must be made perfectly clear to any aspiring burglar,' explained Holmes, 'that tomorrow night represents the best, perhaps the only opportunity to break into Juniper Cottage. We must force him to come – and we must then be here to meet him!'

'I understand,' said Potter; 'but how do you propose that I should disseminate the information you mention?'

'Oh, there are many ways. You must sow the information broad-cast across the district – at the village shop, at the post office, at the railway station, and so on. You might also call in at the Rose and Crown for a glass of beer and inform the landlord of your plans. That alone should guarantee that everyone in the parish is privy to your arrangements before the day is out.'

'Very well,' said Potter. 'I will do my best.'

'What of the business of the books?' I queried. 'Why did Pleasant follow Mr Potter to the bookshop? I presume that it was he that instructed the bookseller to attempt to appropriate one of the volumes, although I cannot think why. What bearing, if any, do these incidents have upon the case?'

'We cannot yet say for certain,' returned Holmes. 'Their significance may be central to the matter, or only peripheral. I have examined the book which appears to be the particular focus of interest – Hardiman Smallbone's copy of the Old Testament – without discovering anything especially remarkable about it. I could essay at least seven possible explanations for Pleasant's interest in it, but until we have more data, such speculation is both futile and dangerous. It is a capital error to theorise in advance of the data, for it biases the judgement, and one finds oneself unconsciously attempting to twist the facts to fit one's theory. However, I have hopes that tomorrow night will furnish us with the data we require!'

We waited for some time at Woolwich Arsenal station for a train to take us back to town, and for much of this time Holmes sat in silence, as if lost in thought. A fast train from London had just pulled in, and I was idly watching the crowd of passengers who had alighted on the opposite platform, when my companion abruptly spoke.

'I have my suspicions,' said he.

'Of what?' I queried as he paused.

'I suspect,' he continued after a moment, 'that in some profound way, which our limited intellects cannot fully grasp, Democritus and Heraclitus are *both* correct.'

'Oh?' said I, surprised by this digression in his thoughts from the business that had brought us out to Woolwich.

'Yes,' said he. 'Watson!' he added abruptly, in a more urgent tone, nodding his head in the direction of the down platform.

The train there was drawing out of the station, and we could now see the passengers clearly, making their way along the platform. I followed my companion's gaze, and descried a tall man, wearing a heavy overcoat with the collar turned up, and with a soft hat pulled down over his brow. His shoulders were hunched, and he hurried along the platform, as if anxious not to be observed or recognised. At the last moment, however, as he was leaving the platform, he turned his head slightly, and I saw, to my very great surprise, that it was the commanding officer of the Royal Medway Regiment, Colonel Headley.

'Now, what do you suppose that Colonel Headley has been doing up in London?' said Holmes. 'And why is he trying so hard to avoid being seen?'

'I seem to recall,' I remarked, 'that when we saw him earlier, he said that he was paying a call on some local officer.'

'So he did,' agreed Holmes, nodding his head in a thoughtful way.

The following day was cloudy and dull, and darkness was falling by the time we reached Lewisham station. After a short wait, we were joined by Mr Potter, and caught the next train out to Woolwich, by which time the night was pitch black. We walked briskly up from the town, meeting no one on our way, until we reached the long, quiet lane which led up to Juniper Cottage. Some distance along a road to our right a light indicated the position of the Rose and Crown, but all else was utter blackness.

'There are no lamps up here,' remarked Holmes, 'which suits our purposes admirably; for it is vital that we are not seen. Come! We must not speak again until we are safely in the cottage garden!'

A long, slow walk up the deeply rutted track brought us at length to the garden gate, where Holmes paused a moment, listening intently for the sound of any movement, before passing through and following the path round the side of the house to the rear garden. In a few moments we were in position, crouching among a clump of laurel bushes at the side of the garden, close by the orchard.

'From here we should be able to see anyone who comes,' whispered Holmes. 'Now we have only to wait.'

And a long, cold wait it was, too. Faintly, I could hear a distant church clock strike the half-hours, and each time it struck, the temperature in the garden seemed to have dropped another degree. Holmes had brought with him a small flask of brandy, which he passed to us, and its warmth has never felt so welcome to me as on that icy night. From the hiding-place in which we crouched, like hunters of heavy game awaiting the arrival of some mighty and ferocious beast, we had the whole of the back of the house in view. Holmes's opinion was that the French windows of the study presented the most likely point of entry for a burglar; but had an attempt been made to break in at any other part of the house, there is no doubt we should have heard it clearly, for, save the occasional hoot of an owl, the night was utterly silent and still.

The church clock had struck ten, and I was straining my ears to catch any sound from the lane, when I was startled as Holmes plucked suddenly at my sleeve. I stiffened, all my senses alert. His keen hearing had evidently detected a sound I had missed, and I waited tensely to see what would happen next.

What happened was so utterly unforeseen that I almost cried aloud in surprise. I was leaning forward slightly, to detect any sign of movement along the path at the side of the house, when there came all at once a rustling noise from the bushes behind me. I bit my lip to stifle a gasp. So concentrated had my thoughts been upon listening for sounds from the lane, that it had never occurred to me that an intruder might take a more circuitous route to the cottage, by the open land to the south. I held myself perfectly still, scarcely daring even to breathe, lest that slight movement give away our presence. After a moment, the sound came again, a little closer. It crossed my mind that it might be a fox, then, before I knew it, I could feel the movement as well as hear it, and could hear also heavy breathing. I was standing slightly to the right of my two companions, and someone, or something, was approaching immediately behind my right shoulder. Then, so close that his coat brushed my sleeve as he passed, a dark, burly figure in a long coat pushed through the bushes, stepped on to the lawn and made his way to the back of the house.

There he bent to the lock of the French windows, and a slight, metallic, scraping noise came to my ears. Clearly, he was trying to force the lock with a knife or similar implement. After a moment, Holmes plucked my sleeve once more and stepped out upon the lawn. Silently, and with great caution, the three of us approached the stooping, intent figure, then, at a signal from Holmes we made a sudden dash and flung ourselves upon him. With a desperate wail of fear, he fell to the ground in a heap, and the knife tumbled from his hand and clattered on to the flagstones below.

Quickly Holmes lit a lantern, as Potter and I held our quarry in a firm grip. Then he held the lantern up to the intruder's face, and I gasped in surprise. For the mysterious nocturnal visitor was none other than Mr Potter's neighbour, Major Loxley.

'I think you had best explain yourself,' said Holmes in a severe tone. 'Have you the key to these windows, Mr Potter?'

Potter found the key, and in a minute we were in the study of the cottage, with all the lamps lit. Major Loxley sat slumped in a chair, his head in his hands, moaning softly to himself, like a man in the last reaches of despair.

'Well, Major,' said Potter at length. 'We await your explanation! What is the meaning of this?'

'The meaning,' returned Loxley in a broken voice, 'is that I am ruined!'

'Come, come,' said Holmes. 'You were a good friend and neighbour of Major Ullathorne's. Though your present behaviour is astounding, I am sure there must be some explanation for it, and perhaps, if that explanation is good enough, Mr Potter can be persuaded not to press charges.'

'You do not understand,' said Loxley, looking up. 'Any charges that Potter might bring against me are as nothing, and I would face them without concern. But to explain my actions I must reveal my shame.'

'We must have an explanation,' insisted Holmes.

'Very well,' said Loxley after a moment. 'It can make little difference now. You perhaps know something of the history of the Royal Medway Regiment? Few regiments have had a more honoured history. We were represented with distinction in the Peninsular Campaign, at Waterloo, in the Crimea, India and elsewhere. In recent years, however, the regiment has been on home duties, at Chatham and Dover, and here at Woolwich, to where the regimental headquarters was moved some years ago. During this time, a terrible change has come over the regiment. It may not be apparent to outside observers, but it is clear enough to those who know it from within, and who knew it in its better days. It is as if a corruption has entered into the body of the regiment, and once in, can neither be driven out nor destroyed, but must inevitably spread, in the end, to all parts. My opinion as to the origins and cause of this has varied over the years. There have been times when I have felt that the blame lay entirely with one man, or one small group of men, the few rotten apples in the barrel, which inevitably corrupt the rest; at other times it has seemed to me as if a general malaise has swept over the whole regiment, like the visitation of a plague.

'I will not trouble you with the details. It is enough to tell you that colossal amounts of public money have found their way into private pockets, and that the regiment's guard duties at the Royal Arsenal and the Royal Dockyards have provided ample opportunities for personal enrichment for those who sought it, from petty pilfering and the unauthorised sale of public property, to frauds on a scale so massive and audacious that you would scarcely believe them possible.

'A few years ago I was offered something by someone I knew. It was only a trifle, and seemed unimportant. In my own defence I will say that I did not fully understand at the time that I was accepting stolen property, although I think I knew in my heart that the transaction was not an entirely honest one. But having thus accepted a part of this corrupt bounty, I subsequently found it much more difficult to resist the persuasive pressures which were put upon me to play a part in various fraudulent schemes. Thus, little by little, I slipped into the mire of dishonesty.

'At length, the few remaining honest men in the regiment began to see what was taking place about them, although it had been concealed with diabolical cunning. Your uncle and I had both been retired some years by this time, Mr Potter. Late last year, he was secretly approached, as a man of outstanding character, and asked to conduct a discreet investigation into the matter, as he subsequently confided to me in the strictest confidence. No one could be certain who, among the present strength of the regiment, could be trusted and who could not, which is why they had turned, in desperation, to Major Ullathorne. As an honoured former officer of the regiment he was welcome wherever the Royal Medway was represented, and could freely go anywhere, and see anything. His brief was, by conversations and discreet enquiries, to discover, if he could, the heart of the corruption which had infected the regiment. All this, I say, he confided to me, never suspecting for a minute that I myself had been touched by the tainted finger of corruption.

'I was prepared for the worst. Had Ullathorne lit upon any fact which implicated me in any way I should have accepted whatever fate had in store for me. In the meantime I kept my shameful secret locked in my breast, and feigned ignorance whenever he spoke to me of the corruption he was uncovering.

'Unfortunately, discreet as Ullathorne was in his enquiries, his enemies got wind of what was afoot. The first I knew of it was when they approached me, and asked me to find out what he had discovered. I told them I knew nothing, but they were not satisfied, and told me that, unless I helped them, my own part in the shameful business would be exposed to public view. I knew that this was no idle threat, and gave them a small amount of the information which I had gleaned from my conversations with Ullathorne. One thing I did know – which I told them, as I did not believe it would be of any use to them – was that Major Ullathorne had had a safe fitted, late last year, in order to keep secure the documents relating to his investigation. Until you showed it to me yesterday, I had absolutely no idea where the safe was situated and had made no attempt whatever to discover it, deeming it better for me, under the circumstances, to remain in ignorance. What I did not know, I could not be forced to reveal to another. I did have one other piece of information concerning the safe, however. Ullathorne had informed me one evening that the lock was of the combination type, and that the key to the combination was hidden in a book.'

'J. Hardiman Smallbone's copy of the Old Testament,' interjected Holmes.

'Precisely, Mr Holmes. I told Ullathorne that it didn't sound a very secure hiding-place. "Why, anyone might find it there!" I said. He laughed at this, and pointed out that the book was a big one. "As you may be aware, Loxley," said he, "the Old Testament contains thirty-nine books, nine hundred and twenty-nine chapters, and nearly six hundred thousand words. They made me learn that at school! My enemies wouldn't know where to begin their search! Patience – a great deal of it – would be the chief requirement, and that is something they do not possess!" The thought of this appeared to amuse him greatly, and he laughed for several minutes.'

'You gave this information to your villainous colleagues, presumably,' said Holmes.

'I did,' replied Loxley, hanging his head. 'I thought it would be of no use to them, as neither they nor I knew the whereabouts of the safe.'

'So they sent Jonathan Pleasant here to try to find the safe and its secret combination. When he was unsuccessful, in both respects, they told you to persuade Mr Potter to sell Smallbone's book to the dealer, Vidler, whom they had presumably bribed to make him do as they wished.'

Loxley nodded his head in silent acknowledgement of these charges.

'Who is this man, Pleasant?' asked Holmes.

'A member of the conspiracy,' Loxley replied, 'no doubt chosen for the task on account of his persuasive manner of speech. In himself, he is unimportant, merely one of the small fry that are always to be found swimming alongside the great sharks.'

'Hum!' said Holmes. 'Let us take another look at the book.' He took the old volume from the shelf, and turned the pages over for several minutes. 'I can find no marks upon the pages,' said he at length. 'Did Major Ullathorne have a favourite chapter, or verse, Major Loxley?'

'Not that I can recall,' returned the other.

'Nor I,' said Potter.

'We could try the letters "J.H.S.", the initials of the original owner,' I suggested.

'What a good idea!' cried Potter. 'That may indeed be the answer!'

'Let us try it, then,' said Holmes. In a moment he had rolled back the rug and lifted up the hinged floorboard. Then, lying full length upon the floor, he carefully turned the dials on the safe door. I watched with keen anticipation as he gripped the handle and applied pressure, but there came at once an expression of disappointment upon his features, which dashed my hopes. He then tried the same letters in the reverse order, but fared no better. For some time, then, he lay upon the floor in silent thought, until, all at once, with a little cry, he raised himself up on his elbow, and turned his attention once more to the lettered dials.

'What is it?' I queried.

'An odd little idea that has occurred to me,' replied he. 'It may be as useless as the others. Let us see!'

In perfect silence, we watched as he applied pressure once more to the handle of the safe. Without a sound, and with no apparent resistance, it turned smoothly through ninety degrees. Then he pulled it gently upwards, and the safe door opened smoothly and noiselessly until it stood upright from the floor. With a little cry of triumph, he reached his hand into the recess and withdrew two long, bulky-looking manila envelopes.

'Hurrah!' cried Potter. 'Well done, Mr Holmes!'

'What was the combination, and how on earth did you discover it?' I asked.

'The letters are "J.O.B.",' replied Holmes. 'The Book of Job is the only one of the books in the Old Testament whose title consists of just three letters; and Job, if you recall, was noted for his patience, a quality to which Major Ullathorne had drawn particular attention.'

'Of course!' I cried. 'How obvious!'

'Everything is obvious when once it has been explained to you,' returned Holmes, a trace of asperity in his voice. 'There is nothing else in the safe,' he continued, 'so we must take it that these two envelopes contain all the information and evidence that Major Ullathorne had managed to gather on the regimental corruption before his untimely death.'

'We must place them in the hands of the authorities without delay,' said Potter.

'You will do no such thing,' said a voice behind us, in a harsh, icy tone. 'Hand me those envelopes at once.'

A cold, creeping sensation seemed to pass up the back of my neck, as I turned my head. There in the open French window stood a tall, strongly built man. He wore a long, heavy brown coat, the collar of which was turned up high, and a soft, broad-brimmed brown hat, pulled low over his brow. But his face was what drew my attention, or, rather, his lack of face, for it was completely covered by an oblong of black silk, in which slits had been cut for his eyes. In his black-gloved hand was a revolver, pointed directly at Sherlock Holmes. How long he had been standing there, I had no idea, but it was clear that he had witnessed the opening of the safe. For a long moment no one moved or spoke.

'Hand over the envelopes,' he repeated, 'or I fire the gun.'

'I know who you are!' cried Major Loxley suddenly, in a loud, angry voice. 'The fountain-head from which all abominations flow! That mask doesn't hide you from me!'

'I'd have thought you'd have enough sense to keep your mouth shut!' returned the other in a menacing tone.

'I've kept my mouth shut for too long already!' cried Loxley. 'I should have exposed you years ago! You poisoned my life, as you poisoned the lives of everyone you came in contact with.'

'Be quiet, you old fool,' cried the intruder in an angry tone, 'or you'll end up like your interfering friend, Ullathorne!'

'What! You killed him!'

'No, I didn't. How was I to know the feeble old fool would have a seizure as my men were asking him a few questions. You!' the intruder continued in a louder tone, turning to Holmes: 'Mr Busybody Holmes! Hand over those envelopes now, or you're a dead man! I'll give you five seconds!'

'You villain!' cried Major Loxley, rising to his feet.

'Get back, you fool!' cried the intruder, turning the pistol upon the major. 'Get back!'

For a split second, Loxley hesitated, then, with an inarticulate cry, he flung himself at the intruder. The pistol cracked, and a spurt of blood showed near the major's collar, as he reeled round with a groan and fell heavily to the floor. In that same instant, and before the intruder could recover from the major's assault, Holmes had sprung across the room like a cat, and seized hold of him. In a second, the two of them had crashed and tumbled out of the French window and into the garden. Potter and I sprang up at once and raced after them.

It was evident that Holmes's adversary was an immensely powerful man. Over and over they tumbled across the muddy lawn, their struggle illuminated by the weak yellow lamp-light from the study. Potter dived in to lend his assistance, but the outcome of the struggle was still not clear. But I had seen as I dashed from the study that the intruder's pistol had fallen from his grasp and lay in the flower-bed by the window. Quickly I snatched it up, and, with a shout, clapped it hard to his temple, and he lay still.

In a moment we had lashed our prisoner's arms and legs with a curtain-cord. Then Holmes bent down to the still, silent figure. 'Let us see this villain's face,' said he. He grasped the black silk mask and pulled it away, to reveal the snarling, twisted features of Major Felgate.

———

The evidence which Major Ullathorne had gathered before his death, together with certain information which Colonel Headley had lately managed to acquire, proved sufficient to break the power of Felgate's criminal organisation, and to send everyone connected with it to trial. It was, we learnt, Colonel Headley himself who had visited Major Ullathorne's cottage so mysteriously the previous summer to request his help, and we also learnt later that on the day we had seen the colonel at Woolwich station, he had been returning from Westminster where he had had a secret interview with the Prime Minister and the Secretary of State for War, to brief them on the state of affairs at the Royal Medway's headquarters. He had harboured strong suspicions of Major Felgate and one or two other officers for some time, and was determined that they did not learn of the steps he was taking to bring about their downfall, and cleanse the Royal Medway Regiment.

Alas for that famous old regiment, despite the trial and conviction of Felgate – whom Holmes declared to be one of the most plausible villains he had ever encountered – and Colonel Headley's Herculean efforts to root out the wide-spread corruption, it survived little more than ten years as an independent regiment, being merged during the 'nineties into one of the larger Kent regiments. Major Loxley, I am glad to say, recovered fully from his wound, which was not so serious as at first appeared. In the court proceedings which followed the arrests, a lenient view was taken of his involvement in the matter, in consequence of numerous mitigating circumstances, and he was able at last to enjoy a peaceful and untroubled retirement as neighbour to the Potters, who, to the best of my knowledge, live still, to this day, at Juniper Cottage.

The Mammoth Book of the Adventures of Moriarty

Ed. Maxim Jakubowski

Available to buy in ebook and paperback

The devil has all the best tunes . . .

From Hannibal Lecter to The Joker, from Captain Hook to Lord Voldemort, it is often the anti-hero who truly captures our imagination.

Even that inimitable and seemingly immortal fictional detective Sherlock Holmes would be a lesser figure without his nemesis, Professor James Moriarty, with whose life Holmes's own is inextricably linked. But, while Moriarty may be evoked in passing in a few stories, the master criminal - Holmes's 'Napoleon of Crime' - actually appeared in only two of the original Holmes stories.

This imaginative collection of short stories, not all of them featuring Holmes or Watson, redresses that balance, bringing Moriarty to vivid new life, and not simply as an incarnation of pure evil.

The Mammoth Book of New Sherlock Holmes Adventures

Ed. Mike Ashley

Available to buy in ebook and paperback

The biggest collection of new Sherlock Holmes stories since Sir Arthur Conan Doyle laid down his pen - nearly 200,000 words of superb fiction featuring the Great Detective by masters of historical crime, including Stephen Baxter, H. R. F. Keating, Michael Moorcock and Amy Myers.

Almost all the stories here are specially written; the cases presented in the order in which Holmes solved them. The result is a new life of Sherlock Holmes, with a continuous narrative alongside the stories that identifies the 'gaps' in the canon and places the new and hitherto unrecorded cases in sequence. Plus an invaluable complete Holmes chronology.

The Mammoth Book of Sherlock Holmes Abroad

Simon Clark

Available to buy in ebook and paperback

Sherlock Holmes at his most ingenious in 15 exotic new mysteries

In this wonderful anthology of 'hitherto lost' tales, the Great Detective travels to the far ends of the earth in pursuit of truth and justice.

A host of singularly talented writers present a thrilling new dimension to Holmes's career whilst superbly capturing the spirit, style, suspense and atmosphere of Conan Doyle's best work.

With stories from Simon Clark, Andrew Darlington, Nev Fountain, Paul Kane, Johnny Mains, William Meikle, David Moody, Mark Morris, Cavan Scott, Stephen Volk and many more.

How To Write Crime Fiction

Sarah Williams

Available to buy in ebook and paperback

Using examples from contemporary crime writers, this book provides practical pointers, clear explanations and inspiring exercises to develop your skills

It will equip you with a comprehensive overview of all the different kinds of crime fiction to help you identify the sort of novel or short story you're best suited to write. You'll learn about the tricks and techniques used by bestselling authors to make their stories work, with explanations and exercises so that you can hone your own craft and find your own voice – and tell your story in a way that will captivate readers.

From the darkest noir to the most comfortable cosy, from the courtroom to the morgue, crime writers' secrets are laid bare for you to explore, learn from, apply and make your own.